TRIALS
OF THE
SERPENT

· BOOK I: THE FINAL TRIAL ·

TRIALS
OF THE
SERPENT

K MANSFIELD

VISCERA
EQUINØX

ISBN 979-8-9894731-0-6 (paperback)
ISBN 979-8-9894731-2-0 (hardcover)
ISBN 979-8-9894731-1-3 (ebook)

First Edition: January 2024

This paperback edition first published in 2024

CONTENTS

ACT I

BLACK SUN

WARM MONTHS AND THE CRY OF WAR

The Island was peaceful this time of the year. Summer, they called it, was long and prosperous, here lasting several weeks longer than miles north where the colder temperatures already began to take hold. Soon the frost will begin to appear, lingering long after night leaves us. The orchards will begin to die and in retiring from their long season of offering, will finally feel rest as the last orange falls. The seas will soon turn cold, changing the air surrounding us. Yet not here, not at least for another few weeks. I could hear the rolling waves from the sea where I stood, on hot bright stone, almost blinded by its propensity to reflect the fire of the Day Star. Its power was one I would not test, could not afford to test. I closed my eyes for a moment, smelling the salt in the air as each wave crashed upon a shore miles from here. I allowed my vision to return to me, watching the surrounding walls with focus. Amplified in my head was the cacophony of sounds surrounding. The songs of birds, cries of the insects in the grass. My hand gripped cold steel, my arms covered to protect my skin from the piercing rays above.

I took a large breath in, feeling the warmth coil inside my lungs before pushing it outward in a heavy exhale. The light scent of orange blossoms growing where land met water was pungent, strong in the air that was warmed from months of sun on the sea. They came with such force that you could catch their scent while standing in the towers of the fortress, overlooking the grounds where I stood this very moment. The stonework shimmered in the midday sun, as rich as gold in its appearance. It looked majestic, almost making me forget why I was here, why I lived here. Surrounding me was a rich world of viridian, come to prime by enduring the rains from the mainland. It was darkened only by the fortress' shadow, which despite its striking face, stood over us in an obscurity of servitude. It was only this time of year that shadow poured into the labyrinthian pathways, yet another message from the earth regarding Summer's end.

The old walls of the labyrinth stood the test of time, and like all monoliths, the fables of their creation and use had as well. Presently it was used to place man against man, the one with superior skill surviving the event. I slowly walked between the old stones, taking a deep breath and listening closely. The wind overhead was quieted where the walls were highest, making footsteps easier to hear, breathing, the gripping of weapons. Yet presently, all that was accompanying me were my own thoughts.

I knew the labyrinth well by now, being chosen for this same event year after year. The purpose of which was to either sharpen the skills of his existing assassins, or to invite prospects into his ranks. This knowledge of the maze was an advantage over whatever soul was brave enough, or foolish enough to wander here, The Island ruler's love of thrill was at work. Yet I could not help but feel as if I was chosen for a reason above his mere thrill seeking. It was seven years past I had been led here, my own wandering bringing me to the edge of the marsh where curiosity vanquished instinct.

My thoughts silenced and I closed my eyes, moving them back and forth beneath their lids. Within this sightless void I began to hear the faintest sound of a heart beating. West. I turned in that direction, placing a hand on the wall closest me.

My opponent was walking slowly, his heartbeat rapid. Fear and hesitation overcame him, leaving focus and drive to dwindle. We approached one another, the sound of his heavy breathing now audible. The man let fear control him, anxiety. The beats of his heart increased in number as he turned each corner, heavy exhales accompanying them. I let him wander for a few moments until he reached the center of the maze, a large statue of a snake coiled between the four pathways.

Hesitation ensued as he measured his options, taking an equal amount of time to stare at each opening created by the thick walls of old stone. He started to drag his sword along the wall, an invitation for his opponent to face him, or find him. Naturally, I opted for the latter, appearing from the shadows behind him. I covered his mouth as I stabbed him through the center, twisting my sword before I pulled it out. Emerging from the maze before my master's tower, I dropped the corpse on the ground in front of me.

The sound of a horn came from his balcony, a sign of his approval, and a sign of his demand to continue. I bowed my head once and walked back into the labyrinth, ending my journey where only a small statuette of a woman could see my face. Weeping. I had often wondered if this was something master had placed here himself, or if she had been here for long years, waiting. I stood with her for a few moments, immersed in the mystery of stones depicting human emotions such as joy or sadness, and awaited my next adversaries.

It was a while before I heard them, different tones and sounds coming from different places within the maze. Two, in total. I wished to end this quickly but knew doing so would be considered disrespectful to both my master and the sanctity of this event. It was not my place to question why they were of such importance to him, yet every time I was placed inside the maze, or upon the courtyard I could not let the thought wander from me. I remained stagnant for a while, debating whether or not I'd let them find me or hunt them as I had the last. I supposed it did not matter, in speculation. They were only here for me to kill them. I quickly turned the corner nearest me, walking down the narrow corridor to my left. In one motion, I drew my weapon and stabbed forward, feeling a familiar warm fluid cover my sword hand. In leaving him, I turned my attention to the pulse that remained with me. Staggering, not from anything relative to feeling. Following the sound, I discovered who it belonged to. A young boy, who had not yet seen his sixteenth year, his heart dampened by illness. He had a large gash on his chest, the scent emitted from it pointing to the onset of infection. His arm was shaking as he felt a patch of vines along the wall, pulling to determine their strength. He grasped them, climbing so that he was above the wall. A vantage point. He had a strong will to live about him, the creativity of a child overcoming the instincts of humanness.

I found myself watching his actions, fascinated in his outward thinking. However, as unfortunate as it was, he was here for only one reason. In haste, I climbed the wall behind him, lowering my head slightly before I quickly took his life. The only solace of the act was sparing him a painful, slow decay from his prior wounds. There was no honor in taking the life of a child, yet to master all humans were alike, and if he bade it so, their deaths were too. And so, I collected the corpses of both, dragging their arms behind me. I reached the opening to the outside world. The sun had reached its intensity, burning the sky in rage. I pulled the cowl further over my eyes, my head down, against all customs. I quickly dropped my dead as offerings, silently anticipating the sounding of the horn from the tower. After a few thankless moments it came to pass, and before I could enter the maze the sound of a different horn reached my ears. The horn of summoning. He wished for my audience.

The tower was a long walk from where I stood, the others waiting on the field below for their part in the event. As I made my way toward them, the Serpents avoided my gaze, ensuring to congratulate my victories by only nodding their heads in my direction. It wasn't customary, yet they were afraid to approach in formality. The ones yet to be judged however did not turn from my eyes, resulting in cowering, and the signs of a developing madness. I broke eye contact, hearing their hearts return to a pace of normalcy. Whispers, and a voice from one of my brethren in arms. I did not turn from my path until I felt a hand on my shoulder, the one man who was not afraid to speak to me.

"Yet another success for you my friend, I hope one day to acquire your skill."

"Your words honor me, Dacian. I hope your matches fare well," I answered.

"They shall. I will see you again in the compound."

"On the side of the Serpent." I answered and placed my hand on his forearm. Climbing the hill I thought about the rarity of a mission during the plain of judgment. It concerned me greatly, because of its infrequency, yet the decision to raise me to the rank of high assassin made me realize my roles in master's urgent and immediate needs. I moved through the echelon quickly when I first arrived here, surviving all three of my judgment tests with ease. From there I succeeded in every mission and altercation placed before me with no great injury.

I reached the thick golden doors, pushing them open. The guards on either side watched me closely but kept quiet. Their distrust didn't dishearten me as their eyes would never dare meet my own. I listened not to the whispers, but paid attention to the last sets of stairs I would need to cross before gaining entrance to the tower. A tower that was well guarded. An aspect I grew to question. He thought them weak, this I knew. He trained them well, yes, in the circumstance the Serpents were gone, and a second line of defense was needed. However, our entirety away at once was almost as scarce as my being called to the tower at this time.

My master stood at the windowsill, continuing to watch the fights below us. He signaled for his servant to sound the horn, calling the next of us to begin. His advisor watched me near him, his eyes not moving from me even as I bowed my head and moved my right fist over my heart. The way we were taught to greet him.

His gaze left only as I removed my hand from my cloak, pulling it back to my side as my master spoke to me.

"Cethin, There's no mistake you are the best assassin on the continent, yet everyday you astound me. It seems as if in judgment you resort to stealth, to watching your opponents."

I said nothing, only looked upon the back of my master until he did not speak. He wished for my voice. "It is as you taught us. In the world, you wish for us to be shadows. The name of who committed the act is nothing in comparison to the act itself."

"Yes, it seems that you are well in never forgetting that," he said and turned from the window, ordering a Serpent-past of the name Eshkan to watch the event taking place below. He nodded and walked toward the window, unmoving.

"Thank you, Master," I said quietly, yet pronounced.

"Tell me then," he said, turning to face me, "Your abilities given to you from birth far exceed the things you have been taught here. The methods. I am sure you use them to your advantage, yet it is not what you entirely rely upon."

"I do, yes, it is natural for me, instinct. But you did not choose this because of what I am."

"You survived your test. You showed us that day that it did not matter how many I placed against you, that your will to live overcame it all. Your instinct."

"Yes. And since then, because of my survival I was forgiven my trespasses and exalted your ranks. It is only respectful that I honor the events by your teachings."

"You have succeeded and remained victorious throughout every test that I have given you. Every event I've held. For years you have avoided injury. I believe it is time for the greatest honor I can give," he said and walked toward the large etagere that lined the wall in the back of the room.

"Vortain, if I may," Jadoq began, "placing a man against this beast produces an impossible outcome for anyone to survive. He can hear their hearts beating as he passes them, the ultimate hunter. If you continue this way, you will have no new men that will be judged in success."

"I do not wish to test new men in success when I place them against him, Jadoq. I wish to measure his," he answered in haste and continued.

"You know that he will always be successful," Jadoq answered. "At this rate there will be nothing that can be thought of that would see him fail."

"It is not my wish to see him fail," Vortain answered and looked toward his advisor with sincere eyes. "You question my gesture?"

"No," Jadoq said simply, averting his eyes. "But you grant an honor that has thus far been reserved for humans."

"It is reserved for whomever I wish to bestow it upon. Do not forget that."

"He has proven that he is a dangerous creature. You should have killed him the moment he defied you," Jadoq answered, vindictively.

The scars on my back were from the blades of the whip, to match the scar I had given my master when I believed my strength to be best used against him.

"He is my best assassin. No one dares rise against him once they've discovered what he is, Jadoq. A creature that has complete control of fear."

I no longer moved, only listened to the words that I knew but wished to avoid. I didn't want them to speak of me this way, and I had tried my best to distance myself from what everyone knew my race to be.

"I will award him for his service and his loyalty to me by doing whatever I can to make things right. He was not raised by his race. Does not have knowledge of things they are taught while young. I do not believe he should be robbed of those things because he is here in service to me."

"Sire that is madness. He has struck out at you before; he is already controlled by the darkness inside him. He…"

"He is controlled by me and me alone. I will give him what is written in his blood. It will do well for the contract that is coming. You know well of what I speak."

I remained quiet, knowing this conversation was meant for being carried on without my audience. Jadoq's dislike for me was evident in every act I committed, and in return, my contempt of him was as well known among the ranks. Everyone knew I would execute him given the chance, and yet he seemed to think himself safe. His raucous words proved that. I knew that one day Vortain would tire of protecting him.

"Cethin, the mission I have for you is one of great importance. In the city of Arriksmad there is a man by the name of Gendair Valkurdi. The taking of his life is instrumental," he answered.

"His faults?" I asked. I knew it wasn't my place to question, but it is something I ask every time I am sent away. I would not allow myself to be used as a tool for genocide.

"He is making a weapon that will change warfare, powerful. No man should have it. This weapon will test the mind. I want you to relinquish the weapon from him and kill him."

"Yes, Master," I answered and bowed my head, placing a fist over my chest and returning it to my side.

"Now, return to your chamber, a meal awaits you there. I want you ready by dawn."

I relieved myself from the position of acknowledgment and respect, turning from the balcony to make the climb down the stairs.

"Cethin, one more thing."

I stopped, tilting my head slightly to hear my last order.

"We will decide what happens with the weapon once you return here to me," he said.

"Master," I said quietly, and began to descend the stairs. His confidence in me was astounding. Every right for my abilities of course, but his confidence in me to retrieve something he knew to be dangerous was what resonated. However, he knew well that he had something I wanted, which probably stood for his trust within me. As I exited the palace, I realized how dark it became, the courtyard already empty except for the few guards that were on watch. They walked their residual patrol, eyes darting across all corners of the gardens, the terraces. I was careful in my steps, giving them no reason to deem me suspicious. Though I was of the highest order, the fact that I was a nonhuman caused them more alarm than a man would, walking the courtyard at night. The discovery happened only five years ago, in this very place...

◆ ◆ ◆

I stood in the field before the large stone maze, my hands bound and at the mercy of two guards who had spears pointed into my back. I had just been pulled from the marsh that hid this place in entirety, entering the isle with hungry, blood-spattered eyes. I had murdered two guards before being captured by five Serpents, their advantage over me at that point being my starvation. I looked ahead, the sun setting at my back. The forefront of the old stone walls were decorated lavishly, tapestries hung from the pillars bearing the mark of a red serpent, coiled around a golden ring. I felt the tips of spears press lightly in my back as a horn sounded in the background. Measuring my options of escape as I was pushed inside with no weapon and bound hands, I entered.

I was certain that the guards were those of the person who was sending me to my death. I had not seen them. A thick musty cloth obscured my sight as I was knocked from the conscious realm upon my arrival here, a boot to the back of my head. When I came to, I was already in the dungeons, the scent of water from the leaking ceiling serving only to pull me from slumber. Yet these thoughts began to deviate me from the matter at hand, and I quickly ended them. I continued inward, scanning the walls with my eyes and making note of all the passageways and possible avenues of ambush. The sun was setting rapidly, and there would be a moment's window between that and the rise of the moon. Therein rested my advantage. I took a deep breath and chose my path before hearing three different pursuers. Their hearts spoke different stories as they entered, breaths hushed. One was afraid, pulse elevating as what I could only assume was his turning of corners. The next was slower, yet irregular. His time on this earth was numbered. The last intrigued me. Steady, even. The man was not gripped by fear, but by focus. He would be first.

I neared him, knowing that I'd somehow have to relinquish his weapon to cut my binds. I turned the corner adjacent to him just as he had, catching him by surprise briefly before he reached forward with his weapon, catching me in the chest. I moved my hands toward the top of his blade, using the rope on my wrists to twist it from his hands, severing them in the process. Quickly grabbing his fist, I squeezed my hand around his fingers, using the extent of my strength. He cried out and I grasped his neck, slamming his head into the wall until it turned red with what gave him life. I reclaimed his sword from the floor, moving from his corpse, but not far. The others would have heard him by now and would be on their way to investigate. It was only moments before one turned a corner in front of me, calling for the other to flank from behind. I was limited on time. I began to assault him with heavy blows, the steel of the fallen clashing against my assailant's blade. I had almost backed him toward the opening when I heard the other from behind me. I landed a blow, cutting his arm and quickly scaled the wall, jumping over two of them before hitting the ground and finding a place to fight to my advantage.

I heard them scurrying, climbing the wall after me. The only thing I could do was bide my time until the sun set. I continued to turn corners, hearing them shout from above me, jumping from wall to wall in order to cover ground. Pressing my back against a wall in shadow, I listened to the footsteps of the guards cease. They lost me. I climbed quickly, cutting one down at the ankles. As he fell, I threw my arm in front of him, stabbing him in the center before regaining my position in the dark. It was then I heard the last drop to the ground, treading very lightly. Taking one deep breath, I vaulted the wall and jumped on top of him, attempting to knock the weapon from his hands. He slashed at my chest, eyes coming across the first laceration I incurred. Avoiding the pain as best as I could, I took my sword and stabbed downward, pinning the man to the ground through his shoulder. He screamed, and I tore his throat from him to heal my wounds. I left the labyrinth that night, walking back out toward the field in blood drenched satisfaction, looking up toward the tower in the light of the moon.

◆ ◆ ◆

The vision had ended as I reached my door, a small chamber farthest from the others, yet the most equipped. I took a deep breath before entering, allowing the day's tidings to become stagnant so I could relax. Turning inward I noticed a large stone pitcher in the middle of the only table in the room. One of my only requests. I strode across the room, pouring half into a small wide bowl, washing my hands and face. When I bent slightly, I could feel the scar stretch across my back from a memory, that day.

The water felt cool against my skin, and I was almost too caught up in a small feeling of serenity that I couldn't hear the voice from behind me. I suddenly felt a hand upon my back and with one movement I turned, grabbing a wrist and shoving a small body into a wall. I looked, only to see that it was a woman, clad only in a tiny red dress. I could now smell her as she began to speak.

"So, you are the one who they speak of."

I ignored her, returning to my water and took my cloak off, tossing it aside. She could now see my skin, the various scars across my arms and shoulders, symbols along every one of them. "You wish to rush something you will not enjoy," I answered, now rubbing my hands across my arms.

"There are many things I enjoy," she said taking a step forward.

"Whatever they told you is a lie," I said, cleansing my neck and chest. They were the same as my arms in appearance, each fragment of words meaning something different, something unknown.

"So, I am not here for your pleasure?" she asked, crossing her arms curiously. I turned, stretching my neck and shoulders before looking upon her.

"That depends on what you mean by the word," I said, taking steps toward her. She did not move; did not understand why she was here. She jumped at the chance to meet a brave soldier, for stories of glory in the shedding of blood, or whatever other lie she was told. A commoner taken from the corners of a nearby mainland city trying to stay afloat in a world so geared against her. For a moment, I felt bad for her. Master always assumed that I enjoyed more of the women than what took place, and occasionally when I performed well in what he asked me to do, he would bring me someone easily deceived. It made no difference, though.

"Likely you were approached by guards who promised a different encounter than your usual engagement or meeting. But you don't want to be here. This is the last place on earth you'd want to be," I said and grabbed her arm, laying her down on the ground. "If you have any gods to ask things of, now would be the time," I answered and revealed my eyes to her. Before she could scream, I silenced her and continued with my ritual.

Night continued its claim on the world, darkness coveting skies, creatures nocturnal and full of life. The silence on the Isle was thick, almost impossible to bear. Its weight on the ears was not unlike gravity. I remained in my chamber until dawn, resting before the carvings etched into the stone floor, now filled with blood. They had told me I made them one night when I was fevered, speaking in a tongue no one here knew of. Most here feared me, and for their sanity would not venture past the compound. Even though I was bound to the wills of my master, I was distrusted in the den by all but one, Dacian.

I continued to rest, wondering what lay in wait ahead. This assignment was one of great importance it seemed. A powerful weapon in the hands of a human. I was reluctant to believe it, though I knew that a report such as this could not have been made in error. Suddenly, I was disturbed by the opening of the door to my chamber by two guards. I kept my position, head bowed. It was usually guards who did not follow orders who were sent here for punishment for what they had done. I found it comical, as I should have found it offensive. They were sent here as punishment, to rid of what I left behind.

"You are summoned," a guard answered, looking in at the remains of the woman who had been convinced to stay the night with me. Her legs and torso were devoured. Her throat barely resembled that of which it was before, and her face was covered in blood. I felt the sudden disgust of one at the sight, and he held the hilt of his weapon tightly.

"Am I to go to the tower?" I asked sternly.

"Yes, Master Vortain wishes for your presence in the court-yard." The other answered, his words soft, showing he obviously had avoided looking into my quarters.

I rose and grabbed my cowl, an item I was commanded to wear, and placed it over my shoulders. As I approached the door, one of the guards remained.

"I am summoned," I said.

"You're sick. I don't know why he keeps you here. Feeds you. You've no place among humans. You should be removed," he answered.

"No, just not human. It is no different from when you prepare an animal. Is it not why only people from the mainland are chosen for me?"

"We are not beasts like you," he said defensively.

"I tried to be civil, as I was told to be. Do not make me become different."

"Are you threatening me?"

"No more than you were me just now," I answered, grabbing a sword from the table. The one weapon I was allowed when not on duty in case an invasion should occur. The man pulled for his sword when the second guard grabbed his forearm, interrupting him.

"We are not here to settle differences," he answered.

I pushed past, quickly turning back around. "You," I said, pointing to the man who had remained mostly quiet until just a moment ago. "Will you escort me to the courtyard?" I asked, placing my sword on my side and walking to the pathway leading uphill. I turned again when I realized he was not behind me. "Guard," I said, pulling him from his hesitation. It took a moment before he moved, walking only a few feet behind me.

"You ask for me to escort you… why?" he asked, striding to my side.

"Not many interject for those with such extreme differences. It shows pure of heart," I answered.

"Pure of heart?" The guard asked.

"It's a story I was told by a fisherman in the eastern Baeld before I was brought here to be judged. There is a temple, in the Aubergrun hills with a wall entirely made of pearl. It symbolizes the purity within. Those with pure hearts are rewarded. To live among the monastery in peace, to learn their ways."

"A temple? I have never heard the story."

"It is a journey to get there from what I've heard. But at what cost to live in peace?"

"And is that what you wish? To live in peace?"

"A fine thought yes, but not for me. I am a Sardon. We feed among the living, so we must kill. But you still have hope. I suggest you finish your service and go find it. If you have never slain, you will be met with success in your travels."

"To live in peace." The guard repeated, this time a statement.

Upon reaching the courtyard I was met by master and his personal guard. He was quick to speak to me, his curiosity stronger than his will to send me off, for the moment.

"Ah, Cethin. You arrive with escort?" he asked, curiously.

"A wish, my lord." The guard answered.

"A wish? Strange as it may seem, I question it no longer. Now that you are here, see to it that you visit the armory. You will need your sword; Valkurdi will be heavily armed to protect his experiments."

I acknowledged him in custom. "It shall be done." I looked up again, my cowl still shielding my eyes.

"Declan, go to the armory and escort Cethin to the south watch. It is from there he will begin his journey," Vortain said and handed the guard a small decorative object. "Keep this key someplace safe. Not a word to the others."

Declan nodded, and took the key, placing it in his armor.

"I grant you both leave."

I began walking before Declan, heading to a place I knew well. I was often on missions far from the isle without any of the other serpents knowing I was gone. Most of them went off in pairs, completing tasks together, all except I. Dacian long wished to be my aid on a quest, yet master would not allow it. Why he wouldn't was only something I could speculate. I heard Declan's footsteps behind me, drawing close but then falling back. Hesitation.

"Have you something to say?" I asked, calmly.

"The temple in the hills, how long is the journey?"

"From here, weeks. But do not fear, you will find it once you've reached Aubergrun. It lies between Cilevdan and Septentria."

"Why do you give such tidings to men who fear and ridicule you?"

"Like a flower, the hearts of men have a distinction. Some nectar is sweet and others foul. You cannot judge one for the misdeeds of another, though not easily so."

"You are wise... but the others call you a beast."

"They do not see what I am outside of the courtyard, outside of my chamber."

"So, you are not what they say, a beast?"

"I agree with you, though again, the others will not accept this. They refuse to take the time to get to know me."

"There is something more within you." Declan answered, confidently.

"I honor your opinion. Do tell no one of what we've spoken. Master won't appreciate switching a life of violence for peace, though servitude for servitude." I've often thought of escaping the isle, only coming to the realization that the world out there wasn't any better than the world here.

"Yes, of course. We are all here for some purpose," he answered and strode ahead to open the door to the armory. He attempted to fit the key into the lock, but pulled it back toward him, inspecting it. "He must have given me the wrong key." Declan said and placed it into his armor. "We will have to wait for the patrol to return."

I nodded, the only purpose of the gesture being to garner silence. There was something more to this contract than Vortain was letting on. Only a few moments passed before one of the guards returned, Declan greeting him as customary.

"We must gain entry." He stated and looked toward me. "Master Vortain wishes for him to prepare for his task."

The sentry nodded, placing his key into the lock and propping it open with one confident turn. Declan nodded at me once to establish that I was entering without him and stood by the door next to the sentry, unspeaking. A few moments passed before it was only Declan's breathing I heard beyond the door.

I looked around, my eyes coming across all the weapons that were stored here. It was not as magnificent as master's armory in the tower, yet it still held treasures that belonged to lands distant from here. Objects picked up during assassinations, raids, events that masked our efforts. It has been a long time since I walked into this room, and even longer still since I had held the object of my current desire. It had been longer still since I last held the blade, the memory taking me back to the summer rains of Adenza. The mission was a complex one, the objective being to dethrone a rising figure that would lead the small country to tyranny. At first it seemed strange that Vortain would have me meddle in political affairs, that was until I realized that the man was intent on forcing the Adenzian princess to wed him. Vortain mentioned some time later that she was an important figure to the Genisian oracles, and that not interfering with the matter would provide an outcome far worse than the contrary. The weapon proved useful in silencing the tyrant, Vortain's creed of silent killings remaining an enforced priority.

The sword was called Seligsara in the tongue of my people. Though I didn't know if it translated to anything. Master told me it was brought here years before I had been found, by a Sardon who said he was from the Coven of Shadow, The Coven of Tarporen. He spoke in common tongue and said that it was only to be used by one. After which point, he spoke what could only be a name, handed Vortain the sword and died before him. He was intrigued by it and told me only after I had completed the last trial. His verdict was that I had to earn its place in my hands. He swore that I knew the Sardon, but it was impossible. I could not speak the language of my people. I did not know of my inheritance, or that another like me even existed prior to coming to the isle.

I ceased the thoughts that evolved from its mystery as I moved forward and took Seligsara in my hands. The blade was miraculous. A dark black, shimmering a deep red against the light of the candles in each corner of the room. I had forgotten the pleasure of having it in hand. I thought about leaving it here, taking another weapon in its place. It wasn't likely I'd fail, but I always seemed to ponder its accompanying me, and what would happen to it if I perished. Perhaps one of the blades from Verassen would do, or a dagger from the isles of Caraima. Despite my hesitation, I took the sword in hand. If I were to retrieve a highly sought after weapon from a highly fortified city, I would need to be nothing more than a shadow.

Turning to retrieve my final weapon, I felt a breath at my back. I moved my sword backward, feeling a spot of flesh at its mercy.

"Hold, brother." A voice I did not recognize, but it was not unlike mine. "Did you think that I would never find you?"

I turned, my eyes coming across a Sardon that resembled me. "Who are you? Why do you claim to be my brother?"

"I am no claimant, Morcant. I am your flesh and blood, your kin. But you don't remember that do you?"

"You call me by the wrong name."

"I do not." The man answered. "You and I belong to the same family, and though you may have forgotten who you are, we surely have not."

"I have been in the same place for five years, undisturbed. Why do you come to me now?" I said, second guessing my decision to pull my blade from his skin.

"I must say, it took me a while to find you. Your aura, though strong, is hidden. I am impressed."

"State your intentions," I demanded, studying his demeanor.

"You've not even given me time for a proper introduction. I am Vihren, your brother." The Sardon said and laughed. "It is interesting how introductions go based upon upbringing. You're suspicious, observant. I can tell you wish you'd have turned in such a manner to keep your blade in a position to easily strike, but your curiosity won over your instinct."

"And you're keeping your own aura suppressed. Also deceiving those around you about the true nature of your power. You're either running from something, or you only reveal it when necessary."

"Not bad, though you've one error. I'm running from no one. I want no one to fear me, it is already our disposition. I've learned to control the power of my gaze for quite some time now. It makes it easier to blend in a crowd, and suppressing ensures no one can feel my presence."

"I thought it impossible."

"Come with me, and I'll teach you."

"I cannot. I am needed here, a purpose I must see through to the end."

"I understand, perhaps I should explain why this is important. This is about Seligsara. Though I cannot say much here. I don't know who may be listening. There are creatures out there, either more powerful, stealthier than you or I. But you and Seligsara are important to our race."

"I hear your words, but we are at an impasse."

"I was told not to intervene, but there is something in motion that needs your attention. You are placed in a difficult situation. You are either to continue the cause you've been pledged to for the last several years, or finally ascend to what you were chosen for." He answered.

"The only thing that requires my attention is the task at hand," I answered. I could see my stubbornness was irritating him, though patience was the only trait that rested in his eyes. He was powerful, this Sardon.

"It will all be revealed to you in time, we have enemies you and I."

"Because of our blood?"

"Yes," he answered and took to shadow, disappearing. He appeared in the light of the torch on the other side of the room. "You must come to Morrenvahl. Our lord informed us that you would, but something has catalyzed. We are running out of time. The blood of Zerian runs through us."

"I already told you. My attention is focused on the task at hand."

He sighed and moved forward. "Raise your weapon," he said.

"I've no wish to fight you. You've done nothing to offend me."

"We will not fight. Raise your weapon." He repeated, sternly. I was reluctant, but slowly held Seligsara in front of me, my wrist turned toward him to show a posture of peace. He took a deep breath and wrapped his palm around the blade, his eyes closed as if trying to fight through the pain. I stiffened, immediately feeling the effects of his blood. My vision suddenly turned to shades of red as I heard his voice and saw the front of a sanctuary hidden in the cliffs of Morrenvahl. "You'll know where, now." He said, again disappearing in the shadow of the room.

"What happens here?" A guard asked from the door. Declan was silent, his eyes showing shame at the other guard's intrusion.

"Nothing. I tend to my business of late," I answered.

"I heard voices, whispers. Who is there with you?"

"None tread here but me, what ails you that you question me in such a way?"

"I brought him here directly from the order of Master Vortain. No one was inside. I unlocked the door just moments ago." Declan answered.

The guard held his stance, his hand on his weapon. "Silence!"

"Do not be a fool; to offend one of Vortain's highest is to offend Vortain himself. Do you wish to live to see the change of seasons?" Declan answered. The guard calmed and huffed in my direction. "He's not right this one. Something sinister lies here."

"Mere superstition will not grant you the answers you wish."

"What transpires here?" a louder voice from outside. Cahya, commander of the guard.

"Nothing Siress, I only look after the Sardon as he gathers equipment…"

"If only such words were true…" Declan muttered.

"Hold your tongue!" the guard barked.

"So, you lie. And what are you doing so far from the citadel? Declan's absence is answered for. I demand an answer from you," she said.

"I heard voices from within the arms chamber… I … I was checking on suspicion of intrusion."

"Are you not intruding on the affairs of this Serpent here?"

"I was acting on my duty," he answered.

"Your duty is to respond to the citadel when there is a discussion of our matters. A lamb who strays from the pasture is bound to be ravaged by wolves. Especially when his bleating is heard for nothing more than sounds of falsehood. I will tolerate this no longer. You know the punishment for disobedience."

"Siress, I can assure you…"

"Do you take me for a fool?"

"No, I only…"

"Wish to attempt to use your words to work out of this. Perhaps if you'd have taken responsibility the punishment dispensed would be less severe. Yet you mock me." She looked to the man on her left and spoke. "Morard, take him to the dungeons."

Morard nodded and acted in haste. Cahya was stern; her rule over the guards was led by respect but at most, fear.

"Cahya!" a voice from the hall. "There is a small boat, seen in the waters, several feet from the isle on the east side."

"Does it bear any mark of significance? Have you seen anyone?"

"Neither," the guard replied.

"Take to the shore and take as many as seems necessary. Report to me once you've returned."

"Yes Siress. Declan, assist me." I recognized him, a man that was often seen in the yards, working closely with the person who trained the guards in combat.

Once we were alone, Cahya walked into the armory, looking into my eyes briefly as she passed. An invitation to follow. "Cethin, a word," she said softly.

I nodded my head slowly, acknowledging her request.

"You're leaving."

"I am."

"Where do you go?"

"Arriksmad. I leave this day, a few hours from now," I answered. "But you must…"

"Discretion, as always."

"I meant to say something else."

"I apologize," she answered, her eyes lit with curiosity.

"It is not of importance. What can I do for you?"

"You ride for Arriksmad. I need you to bring me a vial of Avandia."

"You feel the need for purity?" I asked, trying to keep the sounds of distress low.

"I assure you it is not what you think. I was cursed as a child. This is all that keeps them away."

"Your request is accepted, Cahya."

"Take this, it will buy three," she answered softly.

"How did you get this onto the Isle?"

"I've an outside contact. It is no small trouble for her to arrive here, but she manages. I'd send her for Avandia herself, but if she was caught placing coin at our exchange..."

"She risks this?"

"I saved her as a child. She believes she is indebted to me, though I tell her otherwise."

"Consider it done," I answered, bowing my head and heading back towards the courtyard.

"And Cethin..." I turned my head slightly to the left. "Be careful."

I continued, hearing the wind through the trees. A soft and gentle whisper, the leaves timid. Without the power of the wind to muster their voices they were dormant. I heard nothing beside them, not even my footsteps upon the ground. The silence would change when I entered the city, a place that held no room for a nonhuman. Though the people would never know one walked amongst them. The only feature that would give me away were my eyes, which I kept hidden at all times except during a fight. I was confident in my abilities to emerge victorious, yet hypnosis was a better option for someone wishing to remain unseen.

My thoughts shifted back to what the Sardon said to me. There was something in motion that needed my attention. I knew I should only be focusing on my mission at hand, but being confronted directly by another Sardon, let alone my own blood after a life of silence, could not keep question from mind.

Upon reaching the courtyard I was greeted by Vortain and Jadoq, who the reins of a large horse. It neighed upon my approach.

"Cethin, you remember your mission?"

"Completely."

"Only murder those who get in the way of your success. If you must feed, do so where the remains will not be found."

"Naturally, Master."

"Ah... I see I forget your instincts. Apologies. Do you need more from me?" he asked.

"No, Master, I will ride now for Arriksmad."

"You have three days to complete the task, and a fourth to return here. I suggest you do not stay in town long after it has been done."

"Yes, Master."

"Did you give offering at the tomb?"

"My apologies, I did not. Morard was given the task to handle a boat offshore and took Declan as assistance."

"You must. I shall open it for you. Walk with me," Vortain said and motioned for Jadoq to take the horse back to the stable.

"You must never forget to give offering to the fallen, Cethin," Vortain answered, his eyes on the path ahead. "Do you know why?"

"Each contract honors the dead, and the dead honor them."

"I understand things have always been difficult for you, being here. The men do not look to you as one of them."

"I've tried my best to remain so."

"They will never see you that way, Cethin. Why do you try to appease them?"

I sighed. "I do not, I try to make things simpler for you."

"My meaning in saying this is I know you do not see the customs as a way of life. You were born a different being. I need only remind you as an advisor, not to scold. I wish you to accompany me, so that we may give offering to the dead together."

"You do this, why?"

"I've an amiable amount of respect for you. Respect I thought I could never have for a nonhuman," he answered, moving his head to look at the sky. "This discovery and experience are most honored."

I nodded my head, looking at the path before me. The structure was in sight, the first of us lay entombed there. It was separate from the tower, where those who had since passed were placed in individual graves within the wall. We approached the doors, Vortain placing the key within lock. The sound that was made showcased how antiquated the passage was, its origin never being disclosed to us. We entered the antechamber, the scent of a previous offering still lingered behind. Black currants and dried teakwood sat in a bowl at the end of the room, prepared for me by one of the few priests that still lived here to tend the halls. Vortain took it in his hands as we entered the next chamber. He strode to the center of the room, placing the bowl on the floor and knelt at it, waiting for me to do the same. As I knelt next to him, he took a deep breath and lit the contents aflame, the scent filling the chamber as the smoke rose.

"Grant your kinsman by bond the honor of blood, that he may be hidden beneath your shadow, your silence a shroud," he said and bowed his head. My eyes scanned the room, watching the tops of the coffins. Vortain stood, a sign for me to follow.

"Safe travels, Cethin. Remember, return once you've completed the mission."

I nodded my head and placed my fist over my heart, walking through the hall and exited, heading to the stable. The horse chosen for me seemed unsettled, as they all do at first. I approached slowly, reaching my hand in kind toward his muzzle to calm him before attempting to climb on. Once he accepted my presence, we made haste toward the bridge, his hooves heard thundering the ground. Riding through the forest would see me to Arriksmad faster, the major advantage being avoidance of the main road. Entrance to the city could prove difficult. It would be well spent in thoughts of the morning's events.

The morning around here was peaceful, deceiving. The marsh made no noise as we rode through it, being careful to travel over the portions of land I knew weren't weak and collapsible. The horse I rode, the one they called Dornus, would have a difficult time treading through the thick and deep waters. The ride became quicker once we had made it from that point, traveling then into the Glendoryn forest. It would be safe to pass through here given the time of day; yet passing south of the Lake of Knights led to the road. I stopped two or three times along it to give my horse water from the leather pouch that had been placed in my provisions by one of master's servants before I left. I drifted from here, letting my mind bend around the appearance of the man who claimed to be my brother today, the armory. From there, I listened to the sounds of the forest on this warm summer morning. I sat against a tree, pulling the map that was given to me by Vortain. The point of entry was heavily guarded, yet there was a portion of wall broken, a testament to its age. Sufficient enough to place my weapons in so that I may enter the city in disguise. The city was vast, with many places for my target to hide. I would have to plan my approach carefully. The only information given to me was that he visits the market for supplies, and then returns to where he resides. It would have to be enough. Master's spy reported that he was unable to follow him closely, events in the city caused his gathering reconnaissance there risky. I studied the map for a time and proceeded.

The forest was vast, easily traversable. As I neared the edge of it, the road came into sight. I stopped, climbing from my horse only to take my weapons from within his saddle. I stroked his muzzle, whispering a word to him that he knew meant to stay. I rushed through the forest, jumping over roots raised in the ground, heading toward the city walls at a point where I would not be seen from the gate. There was one guard walking the wall atop, and another at the bottom. I'd have to watch them awhile, study their habits and patrol. The crack in the wall wasn't entirely noticeable, the guard below walking by it without inspection. My eyes shifted to the one above, who looked to either side of him. He then disappeared from view, and after waiting a moment to see if he'd emerge, I waited for the other to pass by before moving forward to place an arm around his neck, pulling him into the woods and sticking a dart into his neck. It was enough to paralyze him for the time being, sending him into sleep for a few days.

The poison from a Saitza snake wasn't necessarily fatal, but its effects were undeniably useful to our craft. Vortain stressed that he wanted no deaths unless necessary. I laid his body amid a soft patch of moss, the trees enough to provide ample cover from the eyes of any passersby or the wall above. I waited for a few moments, listening carefully to what surrounded me. Heartbeats, the shift in the winds, footsteps from those on the other side of the walls. The guard was returning to his post.

Quickly, I ran toward the opening, careful not to kick up any dust in my haste. Looking into the crack revealed the back of an old house in what appeared to be a less traveled part of town. I slid my weapons inside of it so that the pack fit snug without possibility of being seen and walked quickly left, pressing my back against the nearest tree as the guard's head appeared over the wall. It was time to return to my mount.

He remained where I had left him. Standing amid the wood with careful eyes. He was anxious, the feeling coming off him was powerful. I approached him, the steed watching me from the corners of his eyes. It was clear something was bothering him, though I felt no threat in the immediate area. I closed my eyes and took a deep breath, reaching for the saddle. I climbed it, guiding him to the tree line of the forest. The road was desolate, not a sound to be heard aside from the birds above me in the canopy. We emerged onto the road, heading toward the stables that lined the front most portion of the wall near the entrance to the city. A lone stable hand waited outside them, taking a large gray mount from a man in dark clothing. They exchanged hands quickly, the man walking to the city gates. The guards inspected him for weapons, asking what his business in town was.

I didn't realize Arriksmad would be occupied by seemingly militant guards. The city was only known to me as the religious capital of Terrenveil, its name coming from the final battle Araele fought in the old age. The stable hand watched as I dismounted, and I handed the reins to him along with a gold coin Vortain had given me with my provisions. I made my way toward the guards, smelling the smoldering coals of the day's fire pits that had only hours before cooked the savory meats of bear or pig, palatable for all who could pay the price. There were few torches that lit the walls of the city, a sign the visibility of guards would be poor. The one on the left let a long slow yawn leave his mouth before standing upright, focusing upon my approach.

"Stop. What brings you to Arriksmad?" The guard on the right asked, just as the other tensed.

"I come for Avandia, and to go to the white temple to secure a few blessings."

"So, an Araelian. Why mask yourself the way you do?"

"I was disfigured as a child. Hot coals thrown in my face. I come from a faraway land. Customs are different there. Upon visiting this land for trade, I was shown the hope of the Lady of Light."

"I see. You may enter traveler, but let it be known that any laws broken are not taken lightly."

"Araele's blessing be upon you," I added convincingly, and strode through the gates. The city was preparing for sleep. Few patrons fixed things outside their homes, one tending a bucket on their shoddy front porch. A torch emitted the sounds of a weak fire, yearning for rest. I would have to wait until morning to begin to scout for where this man resided. I doubted that he would place himself somewhere easily seen. I also needed to find a place to rest. All of the cities' important structures were listed on the map I studied. The barracks, the dungeon, the temple. I could study the layout and remain disguised. Listening to conversations to gain possible leads would be my first order of business.

I headed toward the side of town behind the merchant district in order to retrieve my weapons from the wall. Dusk created desolation. The sounds from the town quieted. A laugh from a small child in the house behind me was the only sign of life as I reached into the crack and pulled the satchel from it. I unwrapped it only slightly, looking at Seligsara. I couldn't easily conceal the sword. I'd need to find a safe place to store it during my visits to the market. Climbing the nearest roof, I overlooked the merchant's district. The torches were beginning to burn out, leaving the city dimly illuminated by the light of stars. Behind me was a terrace covered in vines, partially rusted and bent due to their force. A start, though it would not keep out the cold of the night. I needed to find an empty cellar, perhaps even an abandoned house in the poor district and make use of the contents within. I turned my gaze to the east, my eyes coming across the temple of Araele. Perhaps finding shelter would be easier than I thought.

I ducked slowly, making sure no guard would see me coming, and made my way down the side of the building, making use of its many windows. I was a pilgrim, making his way to secure blessings for those he had promised. It was one of my many hopes that the priests weren't as curious as the guards were. The white stone steps leading to the sanctuary were bright, even on this dark evening. They said it was a sign of the goddess's everlasting love and hope, so that all who are lost may find her. I was about to discover whether or not revealing myself to them would be unwise.

The architecture on the rooftop was intricate, an old-world style that revealed the age of the building itself. I jumped onto the building's side, grasping onto the ledge above one of the arched windows. From there I climbed upward, each movement quicker than the last. I risked being seen by the guards on the wall if I continued toward the north end of the temple. I would have to set up beneath the base of the dome where beneath it, inside, Araele's statue rested. My contract ritual was to spend one night in the city, taking in the sounds and scents within its walls. In becoming my surroundings, I could easily detect nuances and shifts in its mood. Nestling in between two mounds surrounding the dome, I looked up into the starless night sky. The moon, large, was in the distance favoring a populace elsewhere. I closed my eyes and took a breath, meditating heavily on the world around me.

Morning. As I set foot on the first stair, I drew a breath, looking upon the structure before me. I knew my tongue to be smooth in situations such as this but felt there was a risk that my eyes could give me away. Leaving hesitation behind me, I strode to the large door, opening it with its wooden handle. The inside was neat, and only a few priests were attentive at this hour. Early as it was, I could only pick up a few more that were sleeping. I knew Araele's was a strong and prevalent religion in Terrenveil, strictly followed by the queen. Because of this, I wouldn't have guessed that there would only be a small number of disciples here in her own city. I walked through, seeing the carvings on the walls and the paintings near the small altars used for conversation. I reached the center of the temple before I was noticed.

A priest approached me, his demeanor warm yet hesitant. "Welcome to the temple of Araele, traveler. What brings you to her walls?"

"I am here to secure blessings for children along the roads, and to fill a need for a particular struggling with a hex."

"The altar is for your use." The priest said, his attention shifting to my sword.

"A more pressing matter first," I said, showing him a small pouch. "I'll need Avandia."

"An antiquated method," he answered. "However, I do have vials on hand."

I offered my thanks, and the man was off, into a storeroom past the prayer benches. In order to keep my disguise to a man who was already suspicious, I walked inward toward the altar. Several priestesses were seen inside the sanctum, one of them old. She was anointing a child, her pointer and middle fingers moving across the arch of his brow bones, myrrh and lavender. The youngest priestess looked at me with bright playful eyes. She had unwillingly come here, perhaps as a punishment from her father for committing acts that secured her humanness.

I crouched slowly at the feet of the statue that adorned the back wall, using what I could of my vision to determine if the area was as scarcely traveled as I believed it to be. I would wait until the cover of darkness to make my retreat to the roof, dusk quickly approaching. It was no more than a moment later that the priest returned, his hands cradling the object of Cahya's desire. I passed him the pouch when he was within reach, and the exchange was made. "Will you be needing anything else?"

"No, this will be all. Though you may see me back here in time."

"You're not planning on leaving this night, are you?" the priest asked. The question was perplexing and unexpected.

"I was, though your question makes me believe I should do otherwise."

"I don't know from where you come, though I can tell it is not from these lands. The king's men are in the city. The unrest and war preparations has made them vigilant."

War. So, this is why I am to retrieve the weapon; to hinder a side of a war that I would not understand. However, it was deemed necessary by my master. I questioned it no further. "You urge caution."

"Yes," he answered. "They would not hesitate in questioning a traveler, especially if they believed him to be involved. Their methods are less than humane."

"I thank you for the admonition."

"There are rooms available for your use beneath her holy light."

"Thank you for your hospitality," I said, bowing my head slightly, hoping it would be seen as a gesture of gratitude. I didn't quite know the religious customs of the land, aside from what Cahya would tell me when she visited me, but a guess was just as good as anything else. The priest led me to a doorway beyond the sanctum and pointed to the room immediately left. I hoped the priest would begin a prayer as I had suggested, but he pointed out something I wished he had not.

"The willing concealment of your eyes speaks for your heart."

"Walk with me," I said and moved my head toward one of the rooms on the left, a thick cream and gold colored curtain covering the entrance. The man nodded, but with some hesitation. I moved the curtain, waiting for him to make entry before me and closed my eyes to isolate sound from sight. The priestesses were still attending the others, no chance they would overhear our conversation.

"You have knowledge of there being a Sardon within your temple. But it is as you've remarked, I wish no harm to your people, nor harm to them by my being here. The Avandia, I thank you for it. But feigned ignorance that I'm in the city is as important for me as it is for you. Despite how curious I am as to why you've helped me; I shall question it no further.

"A warning? You believe that my knowledge will cause harm."

"Inadvertently, yes," I answered.

"I see," the man said, nodding. "Then I will not ask... But..."

"By dawn, you will find this room empty. Once I am done here our paths will not cross again," I answered.

The man nodded, silent as he entered a room across from me, where a priestess began to speak to him. I heard their voices, soft murmurations. The guards in the city posed more of a concern to me than anything else. They would be more alert in their passing with the kingdom being under threat of war. I could only imagine the number of civilians who had already fallen victim to their unrest.

If I wasn't cautious, I could be added to that number. If I were to reveal myself, the city would be subjected to panic and hysteria. Or far worse, the mission would be completely compromised, the weapon gone, and Cahya's life at stake. Vortain would discover I was at the Araelian temple for her. She would confess to it.

I pulled the map from my belongings, looking it over carefully. The market district wasn't far from here and would be a good place to start. Eshkan had mentioned a contact in the city. Someone was supplying my target, or else he was that skilled in remaining unseen, traveling place to place without eyes upon him. I doubted the latter to be true. There were a few places of interest Eshkan had marked. A bathhouse to the district west, and the villa of the town's patroness. A compound due east, one that was rumored to house those who took goods to Defaltor. And at last, the market.

I ultimately decided the bathhouse would be the place I investigated first. The place was for the wealthy, it would be foolish to be seen nearby. A religious city had limits in commerce, though the temples were not harrowed for coin by the monarchy. The bathhouse. I would travel to it quickly.

◆ ◆ ◆

Petrichor. It had been a while since the isle last saw rain, the mists rolling toward us from the sea warned of its coming a day prior, Vortain giving out orders to prepare for the storm. I was given watch on the night it came, posted at my usual place beyond the sight of the tower, west of the Den. She came to me that night amid the darkness, and we remained tangled until dawn forced us from one another's arms...

◆ ◆ ◆

The door to the bathhouse was ornate, architecture of the elden. The traits gave it away. Depictions of Ulane the sea goddess bordered the top of each pillar. Although she was disguised as an aquatic dragon, I was surprised the small sculptures hadn't been defaced by Araele's chosen. Something to investigate for the curious anthropologist. I waited for the guards in the street to pass before I scaled the wall leading toward one of the windows toward the roof. The scent of salt was prominent as a woman dressed in loose red robes walked from the room, carrying a large pot in her left hand, pressed against her hip. Once she made her exit, I nestled in between the pillars in the corner overlooking one of the baths, closing my eyes. Some time had passed before I heard voices at the bottom of the room, five men walking inward. They took the towels from their bodies and lowered themselves into the bath. I studied their faces, their expressions, the sounds of their hearts. Their speaking at first was of no importance, and I believed Eshkan's contact to be either mistaken or foolish until one of the men took lead of the conversation and spoke of the mountain.

"Everything seems fine in this part of the land, Raem," the taller of the group submitted, watching as the addressed crossed his arms in disdain.

"That doesn't mean there isn't a problem elsewhere. You ignore infection at the source, ultimately it spreads." A man from the Baeld. Thick, with red hair and a beard to match.

"And you think the war an infection?" the man with his back to me laughed. As he shook his head, his flaxen hair jostled freely. "If anything, it will boast the strength of Terrenveil's army."

"You mean give the Reaper control," the man across from him replied. "Really convenient for a war to be happening after his appointment, yes?" Fearful.

"Come now, Scahl. You're too stupid to put that thought together yourself. Who you been speaking to?" the Baeld asked. "Statements like that might make people think you a traitor."

"Hold, Kalmus," the tall man answered. "Scahl is a boy yet."

"And you think that makes him less capable of speaking ill against the monarchy, its legion?"

"I knew his father. He didn't give him much direction before he passed. That's exactly why I'm looking after him."

"The boy, or whoever he spoke to, may not be wrong." An old man. As the four quieted, I drew a breath, focusing. "The king may be doing as he should, rallying his army in response to the threat from Mauros. But that soldier is not of this world."

"You believe those who say he's a monster?"

"Rumors don't invent themselves, Ahnd," the old man replied.

"Have you ever seen the man?" Ahnd asked, waving his hands upward. "Do you believe them too?" he laughed. "Goddess above.

So, you're suggesting that the commander of the king's army is working with Mauros?"

"Absolute madness to put a statement like that into words." Kalmus answered. "Monster or not, I never want to meet the man."

"So. Your fear lies not with speaking ill against the king, but."

"Do not sit in my company and tell me what I fear, old man." Kalmus stated, taking an aggressive stance.

"Enough." Ahnd answered angrily. "I did not invite you all here to quarrel over rumors and speculations like a pack of rabid dogs." One exhale. "Raem began to say something about the problem existing in the northern reaches, near the walls. Perhaps the threat will be quelled at the source and won't even reach us."

"We can hope." Scahl answered and nervously wrung his hands.

"Why so frightened?" Raem answered. "Your province is farther south than most."

"I've seen what ignoring a rumor does to a family. It destroys it. One by one until it's dead. Twisting it, bleeding it. Using it to strengthen itself until there's nothing left," he said, staring off into space, his eyes unmoving. "And if he is what they say he is, what of our fates?"

"You've been to the witch again, haven't you? I see it in your eyes boy." Kalmus said and leaned forward.

"Leave it." Anhd stated.

"She the one been putting these ideas in your head?"

"I said leave it." Anhd repeated himself, enunciating the last word with a bite.

"She said." Scahl started, blinking several times before continuing. "That when you call upon the old magics, the ones scorned by this temple, this city, this kingdom… She mentioned the Reaper. Mentioned that he'd come here for something."

"The holy city?" Raem asked. "Did she say why?"

"Please don't tell me you're buying into the words of some hag. Clearly…"

"Tst." Anhd hissed.

"She said there was something very old here. Very powerful. But that is all she said." Scahl answered. "And we went back to erasing the haunts. Her scent is all I truly remember when I leave her. Peonies and Jasmine."

Old. Powerful. The weapon was here. A loose fabrication from a witch. But where was she? Learning all that I needed, I made haste toward my next destination. A compound toward what was known as the poor district, resting in the shadow of the Villa. Eshkan said that they may know something, but that it would be wise to uncover that as truth without mentioning the weapon at all.

I made it to the compound quickly, thinking on a basis in which to enter when opportunity presented itself. A man was tossed from one of the shoddy huts, two others following him into the streets. The larger of the two grabbed a hold of his shirt collar and stood him upright, pushing him against the wall of another house. The other strode forward, quickly checking the man's pockets before speaking. "If I find out you're working with them…"

"I'm not, I swear on it. It's exactly as I say it is, send one of your men to Thurlowe. He will tell you the same."

"Drop him." An order. "We will accept your word if you accept my apology. But first." In one motion he pulled a knife from his pocket and severed the man's finger, barely waiting for the screams to cease before he turned with one parting statement. "Lie to me again, and I'll take your hand. I can assure you that's less of a punishment than what Thurlowe would dispense. But, if it's exactly as you say it is, you know that."

He was dropped on the ground when his assailant made signals with his hand, and I noticed that everyone else who'd seen the event unfold quickly made themselves absent. The men walked inside the largest of the nearby houses, their voices muffled as they closed the door behind them. I moved to the back of the house, taking advantage of a nearby open window. I wouldn't enter this time, but it proved a beneficial place to listen.

"Do you really think that man is working with Thurlowe?"

"If I didn't, I wouldn't have let him go. I tire of his sending me fools," the leader announced to no one in particular, looking down at a map on an old wooden table.

"He mustn't believe we're serious, then."

"He knows we're serious, Van. No one contacts the criminal overlord of a fortified city with something such as this and isn't serious."

"So why does he send fools?"

"Because he thinks we won't be able to pay him," the leader sighed and looked up. "We need the provinces to make good on their pledge. The last meeting proved fruitful, but Thurlowe doesn't supply for free."

"What do you propose we do? Some of them are too frightened to join, and we can't yet trust the others."

"They'll be forced to decide soon enough. The situation in Mauros will make clear to them that a change in leadership is necessary. By whatever means."

"Mauros... you mean if it escalates to war? Ahten, what are we going to do if they invade?"

"The war will be handled. You know that the only reason our pathetic king stands a chance is because of his commander's army."

"You mean the commander of his army?"

Ahten laughed, shaking his head. "My resources in Rustanzen say that the king has stalled on an offer of aid. Do you think that was his decision alone?" He stood back, walking toward the wall behind him, lighting a torch. "If we can somehow dethrone the king, we'll have the Reaper to deal with. That will be the real task. So far, we've no idea how to do that. He has the entire army standing with him. Even if we were to have our own, the numbers wouldn't compare. And that's not even what is most concerning."

"You can't believe the rumors, Ahten."

"And why not? If they are only rumors he keeps appearances well." Ahten answered. "Some of the province leaders are so convinced that they've taken up sourcing protection trinkets from the witches on Wolfskile."

"Heresy?" Van said and took a breath. "They'd risk being burned themselves because of a rumor?"

"Repeat that to yourself. Think about it." Ahten said and grabbed dried weeds from a cloth. "The state of this kingdom is madness. Some of the leaders are actively planning rebellion. That is why we need Thurlowe's resources. But until we can get the others to agree we've nothing to bargain with."

Rebellion. Another facet to the jewel. I quickly left the window, heading back toward the temple when I caught a faint scent of Peonies and Jasmine. I followed it, making haste through the streets. I stopped, pressing myself against the wall to a building as a guard passed on the wall above. Once I was sure he was out of earshot, I continued, the scent becoming stronger as I approached the Patroness' villa. She was sitting in the courtyard, tending to orchids, singing to herself. Midday.

I looked up to the wall, watching the portion that was partially covered by a large tree. A maiden appeared from the front steps of the villa, distracting the Patroness for a moment. I took the opportunity to make it to the tree, and toward the back of the courtyard. Not here. The back wall of the villa revealed an open door on the second level. I made it inside, following where the scent was strongest. Past the handmaiden's quarters. I quickly removed myself from the sight of a woman who was sweeping, waiting until she exited the hallway to continue toward the room of the scent's source. The largest bedroom in the entire villa. The Patroness. She would be here before long. I walked past curtains that separated her washroom from where the bed rested and closed my eyes.

Hushed voices. She was wishing her handmaidens goodnight. I waited a moment before walking into the room, watching as she stared out her window into the night. She turned toward her vanity and looked at me, fright in her eyes. "If you're here to hurt me…"

"I am not," I said and placed my hands forward. "Normally I wouldn't be confronting a mark like this, but I am in need of the information you have."

"A mark?" she asked, her eyes softening with water. She was empathetic, emotional, afraid.

"Someone of interest. As I said, I've no intention of hurting you."

"Then why do I interest you, stranger?" she asked and pulled her shawl closer to her shoulders.

"A boy, a witch. Peonies and Jasmine."

Her eyes widened after the statement left me. "Please. You must tell no one," she said and moved to her vanity, placing a small bowl on top of it, the flowers inside.

"I will not ask you to explain your practices to me, nor ask you for ritual," I said. Normally I'd have removed the hood from my head at this point, but the woman seemed so delicate that such a thing could harm her. "You spoke of a weapon to him. I'm not sure why, nor will I ask. But I need to know where it is."

"I see," she said and took a deep breath, placing the bowl back from whence it came. Have I your word that you will not harm her?"

I remained silent, watching the witch carefully.

"A woman. She does not have the weapon, but she tends the house of he who does. I need your word that no harm will come upon her."

"You have it," I answered. "She is innocent."

"Oh, but you don't understand. So is he," she answered and sat at the window. "I've a feeling you aren't here to use it for ill will. I sense a purpose in you that is not tied to gain, but to shadow."

"You are not wrong about that," I said.

"I know it is not safe here. It is only a matter of time…" she stopped, looking out toward the moons. "Where will you take it?"

"Somewhere it won't be found. But I will not say much else. If you were interrogated…"

"If someone was coming for me, I'd spell temporary amnesia. Your secrets are safe with me, as are all who seek my council."

"A Magar," I said, difficulty hiding the intrigue in my voice. "I thought Cilevdan mostly free from magic, let alone Terrenveil."

"You are very wrong about that. I was sent here to protect it and the occupation of patroness fell into my lap. Some people have taken to calling me a witch," she said and moved her chestnut-colored hair from her smooth face, freckles across her cheeks. "Though I suppose any earthen remedies not mentioned in the tomes of Araele are heretical."

"Yes, but Patroness?"

"It was a risk. But there was no other place for me to enter without suspicion. You see, the Patron of this town had a beautiful daughter named Amalie. Twenty-seven years ago, when the family was traveling to the Mountain, as they call it, their carriage was ambushed by heretics. Her parents were killed. Her father, quickly. Her mother left to scream while they sacrificed her. Her brother tried to run but was gutted by more of them, waiting in the woods. I came across the massacre and dispelled them. Quite risky for me to do so, I know. But I've never been one to play it safe, and the others disapprove of it," she said and let out a breath. "I saved Amalie from them. Brought her back here. She was young when it happened, and she did not want me to leave her side. I protected her, ensured that no one would contest her rightful title to the house. It was two summers past that she died of a fever. I've been here ever since. So, while I'm less watchful of the weapon than I'd like to be, the woman in the marketplace is my eyes."

"I'm sure finding someone you trusted was difficult."

"It would have been, if not for Amalie and the bond with her handmaidens."

"It seems chance favored you."

"That it has. But I suppose with the weapon gone I can return to Stirae."

"The others won't hunt it?"

"That I cannot say for certain. I told them that under no circumstance was it to be touched by any of them while I was here. But, if you're taking it to where it won't be found, you should have no trouble," she answered. "The marketplace. Tomorrow. You'll want to be there just after dawn. You'll recognize her by this scent." The Magar said and removed a vial from her vanity, walking over toward me and moving it beneath my nose. She withdrew after a moment, placing it away.

I nodded my head toward her, lowering it significantly to display my gratitude. I'd rest another night in the temple, and at dawn, I'd find my target.

After arriving there, the priest seemed open to my staying. Though he couldn't well deny a weary pilgrim shelter. I entered the same room I had previously, and laid on the bed, which smelled of straw and leather. Rest. I had a few hours before morning. I allowed my mind to empty, which led ultimately to the closing of my eyes. Through unconsciousness I felt the dark begin to recede, and the stars fade out one by one. The air began to warm as the winds reflected the shift of the tides upon the rising of the sun. I rose, grabbing my sword quickly. There were footsteps nearing, heavy and armored. I made sure to leave nothing behind and unlatched the back door to the outside world, closing it quietly and quickly climbed up onto the roof. Guards... seven of them, one speaking to the head priest. The look of surprise on his face showed he was just as alarmed as I was to see soldiers of the legion here. The tidings of war seemed more relevant now.

"C...Commander... what brings you to the small town of Arriksmad?" he asked, fear in his voice.

"You're a smart man, priest. Or at least I'd like to think so. Do you think so?" the commander asked, removing his helmet.

"Well. I..."

"I asked you a question," the man said, looking downward quickly before crossing his arms and taking a breath.

"Araele says not to exalt ourselves above others, but yes. I'd say that I am."

"Save your goddess. We're searching the city. There is unrest in the provinces, and Ozrach wants it answered."

"I can assure you there is no unrest here... The rule of Terrenveil is strong over the people of Arriksmad."

"Is it?" the commander asked, looking around at the houses just south of the temple. He moved his hungered gaze back to the priest, speaking. "Then that means you won't have any problem with the temple being searched?"

"I do not see why that is necessary, Commander. I have only been tending to the sick and dying inside, the ones that were given no relief from the plague."

"Your incessant worry about the plague is bothersome. It no longer exists, Hadrach. We're searching the city. Which means that anything you have seen of suspicion should be given voice. If I find that you are keeping secrets... well it just means that I will return here a less patient man."

"There is nothing in my temple that would interest you or the legion."

"Then you won't mind us having a look inside then? Especially with your mention of the legion's interests?" the man known to me only as the commander asked, the delivery perfect. Hadrach had to think for a few seconds before he spoke.

"Absolutely not. But I won't allow it. The last thing anyone needs is a group of the king's soldiers ransacking the temple because of mere suspicion. I don't let anyone in here other than for guidance, service or prayer."

"It just so happens that Ohric is Araelian." the commander said. A young soldier stepped forward and nodded toward his commander. Hadrach stepped aside reluctantly as Ohric failed to meet his gaze, pushing past him gently to enter the temple.

"Queen Neraea is too, and she will be hearing about this."

"A statement that needed no voice. She is also a reason we were sent here, for Ohric to check the temples. Strange of you to think we'd ransack your temple when your queen holds the precious Lady of Light so close to her." The commander said, the last part mockingly. He moved his head, revealing a wide dark scar along his jawbone stretching to his left eye.

"I do not fear you like everyone else does." Hadrach answered. "Araele is my protector."

"Fear has nothing to do with this, as I've not issued a threat." He sighed, beginning to laugh. "Araele. Do you think Araele will save you when Mauros invades? Or if a rebellion causes the city you love to burn to the ground over the course of a night? Do you think she will save your priests and priestesses from brigands who will carve a path of blood through whatever remains? Or do you think she will just watch while all these tragedies happen around you?" he continued. "You'd endure all of this and praise the sun that rises the morning it ends. You'd thank her for your life. Yours. While most everyone you love perished in a razing that no goddess should ever see unto her people."

"Stay your tongue of heresy in my presence." Hadrach gasped.

"That's what I thought."

Ohric stepped out from the door, looking around the street before addressing his commander, which caused him to shift his gaze. "Savantin. There's nothing inside. Nothing out of place."

Savantin let out a sigh that showcased irritation and pointed an equal number of men in two directions. "You had better pray it isn't the war that brings me back here," he said and turned off toward the other buildings in the city, Ohric following him. My discretion would have to increase. I wasn't sure how long they would stay here. My only hope was that they would clear out before morning. Avoiding the city guards was something I could easily handle, but the patrol of legionnaires would be more vigilant. Beyond that, the appearance of the legion's commander was troubling. Enough was spoken about him to urge caution, which brought my mind to the aforementioned rumors concerning him. What were they?

Leaving the rooftop, I waited in an alcove and listened for the sounds of the market. It was beginning to liven, blacksmiths and artisans opening their shops. The fire pits smelled heavily of charcoal which gave off a tremendous amount of heat. I scanned the area, knowing that I'd have to stay hidden in the crowd to avoid being seen by guards on the wall. I took the time spent watching for the woman to appreciate the things I didn't often get to see. The tapestries hanging from the central stall were long and rich in color, textiles that were enough to befit a queen. I often wondered why merchants of this sort would set up their goods for sale in a city like this. The roads were well traveled, yes, but mostly by pilgrims who owned nothing but the cloth on their flesh and the few belongings stashed away in a bag made of old leather. It wouldn't be a bad life, experiencing new places, going where you wanted to go without bound. However, living at the mercy of human kindness when in need of shelter was a large deterrent, other than that of my life's debt.

I watched a few women come and go from the stalls, a few priestesses carrying food toward the poorer looking part of the city. I watched as a mother led her children through the district. Many women were seen, but not the one carrying the scent the Magar revealed to me, not until past midday. She was holding a basket of food in one hand and using her other to fasten her cloak to her chest. The scent from the vial was strong, lending to my thoughts of it being worn for the sole purpose of locating her. I waited until she passed by the main stalls, moving from my place behind the large stall holding trinkets that boasted travels to Adenza. It was out of the sight of beggars, the true eyes of the market.

She continued along, hurrying as the crowd started to thicken. I had no issue in keeping up with her. The woman finally made it past the market, turning left toward the back section of the wall that bordered Arriksmad from the Glendoryn. She looked around to make sure no one was following her, and slowed her pace as we approached an old portion of the wall, appearing to be in semblance of age to the temple itself. She looked around once more, moving something from her cloak and placing it inside one of the hollow bricks. I made my way to her back, quickly following inward. The stones closed the passage behind us, my hand over her mouth. She began to struggle, and I removed my arm from her body, only for her to turn around and face me.

"You cannot yell, or the city guards will know you're here. Now I know of this place, and the duty to protect its secret rests upon your shoulders," I said.

"What do you want from me?" she asked, her eyes narrowed in what could only be rage or defense.

"From you? Not much. The Magar told me where I'd find you. You needn't fear for your life."

She took a breath outward and closed her eyes. "If she told you about this then I'm sure that means she'll be relieving me of my position."

"The arrangement that exists between you two, I am unaware of. I've come here for one purpose only."

"The archivist."

"Archivist?" I asked.

"Come with me," she answered and picked the basket up from the ground, wiping the sides from dirt it'd acquired in the struggle. I accompanied her on a walk toward the back of the wall, where a large stone dais sat. She placed her hand on top of it until the topmost stone emitted a blue light. Magic of the Magar less than a mile from the temple. The ground beneath us began to shift, a part of the floor rolling open. Once stone had finished moving upon stone, an unbearable silence greeted us, the nothingness unlike anything I'd ever witnessed. No voices, no sounds suggesting what might wait below. Nothing. She pulled a torch from her cloak, taking a clear stone and next striking the top of it to create a burst of white fire. It revealed a staircase spiraling into an abysmal dark, a magical barrier of incredible strength and talent.

Once we made it down a few of the steps, Seligsara began to shake in its scabbard, something I had never known it to do. The woman looked toward me, and then forward, the fire losing heat as its light became more intense. I pulled my hood so that it covered my eyes more as we continued, finally reaching the bottom. Seligsara continued to shake, quicker now as we traveled down the hallway. The air was stagnant, the area completely arid. The woman stopped me, the light exaggerating her eyes and taking most other features from her face. "He does not know you are here. Please take care in how you speak."

I nodded, not knowing whether or not the woman knew I was here to kill him. The Magar seemed to, though, yet still led me on this path. As the woman strode forward with the basket of bread and cheese in front of her, we came into a circular room. Directly in its center was a black crystal the size of a fist in a glass jar. I neared it, Silegsara ceasing to shake. I was intrigued by the connection between the two, and why it caused her to tremble. My questions were answered as I moved my hand to touch the glass.

"I knew you would come. They told me you would." The voice of an elderly man. I turned, looking at what I had heard. He could be no younger than seventy, and held a cane in his old, feeble hand. As he walked in toward me, I saw now that he was blind, his eyes two milky spheres set back within his head. He was kindred, and weary, the traits written behind his voice. The woman raised an eyebrow in question, placing the basket near where a bed was made. She raised her torch toward another in the room, and its light dispersed, lending to the others that were posted upon each pillar. He remained unmoved by the sudden brightness, where I raised my arm to block my eyes to adjust.

"I have prepared it for you, made sure everything is precise, but we are running out of time," he answered, reaching the table and feeling across the surface. "Ah, you see it. It isn't stable there, son. It must enter your flesh, bond with your blood, or else it'll release its energy within this very place. It's too old to hold it inside."

"What is it?" I asked.

"You mean they haven't told you? I figured your sword would have told you why to come here." The old man answered, nearing its containment.

"I was told to come here... but never was I told why," I said. A lie. I would not kill this man. Vortain could decide my fate upon my return.

"You look upon the Black Sun of Zerian, as old as your race itself," he answered.

The weapon. It could not be used by man after all. The dark multi-faceted stone shimmered as Seligsara would after a bloodletting, and as I looked on, I wondered how this plain, yet remarkable looking stone could even be considered a weapon. "How did you come to keep it?"

"Something we agreed upon a long time ago. One of yours saved my life during an Archegal raid. While I'd love to share with you, I fear we don't have much time. The Oracles predicted this day, young Sardon. The Magar doing all she could to protect it. But sometimes fate cannot be stopped, only changed."

"You are certain this was meant for me?" I asked.

"I know you are the one, Morcant. You must not be afraid of what happens next," he said and finally found the glass vase on the table. "Sit in the chair and strap your right arm tightly to it. There should be no problem with the bond," he said. I listened, not knowing what else to do. As I sat in the chair, feeding my arm through two leather straps and pulling them tightly, I looked at him. He instructed the handmaiden to retrieve a pair of tongs, and she carefully pulled the Black Sun from its resting place. She grabbed his hands, placing the tongs in them.

"I don't understand. Who told you that I would come here?"

"There are things you will not understand now, but once you find them, you will know what it is you were meant to do."

"Them... my people?" I asked. I suddenly looked for the woman. She was watching silently, her hands on her offering.

"I assume you have fed recently?"

"Yes," I answered and placed Silegsara in the chair next to me with my free arm.

"I am at the mercy of your self-control. If you feel as if you cannot last it, restrain your other arm. There can be no disturbance now, there is no time."

I nodded, sitting back in the chair. The man handed me the tongs and told me to make sure not to drop the stone. It was captivating in color, so black that it would disappear in shadow, but almost shimmered purple in the light of the room. There were gold swirls of color in certain facets, and I kept turning it to watch them in motion. He took a large knife off the table, its blade scarlet from being rested in fire. I braced for the pain as he cut into my forearm, beginning at where my elbow bends and traveling down to the wrist. My arm began to bleed as he pulled the knife away and recovered the tongs from me. "The pain will only last shortly," he said as he placed the top of the crystal close to my skin.

The man exhaled and placed the pointed top of the stone into the wound he had just made, letting the other point fall toward my wrist. Within a moment the wound turned black and began to fuse together. I heard it speaking immediately, and my arm shook as I felt the stone's energy run throughout my body. I felt pain increase within seconds, feeling as if something was eroding the muscle in my forearm. Throbbing, reminding me how I had felt in Ophidian after my limbs were bleeding and raw from training. My arm felt heavy, as if I couldn't lift it even if I mustered all of my strength. I felt my heartbeat quicken to console my body to what it was enduring, and suddenly it was over. It was then I heard footsteps and angry rushed yelling from upstairs.

"As foretold." Gendair said. I pulled the straps off my arm and grabbed Silegsara, standing quickly. I was surprised at my ability to swiftly move the limb that was just victim of operation. I looked around, trying to anticipate an exit.

"There is only one other way out." Gendair answered. "But I cannot travel it. I fear I am far too old. I will only be a hindrance to your escape."

"I'll not leave you here to die by their hands," I answered.

"I have lived to serve my purpose, and my debt to your people has been paid. I can now be with my family."

"I know it is your wish," I answered. "But I will not abandon you to them."

"Morcant."

"There is no debating this. We will leave this place together."

"And then what? Where do you expect me to go?" the man asked.

"We will go to the Magar," the woman answered and looked toward me. "I will take him and go first. I trust you to protect us."

"You have my word," I said. The woman grabbed her torch and walked toward a large stone wall; it began to fade, revealing an opening. "You must keep up. Once we reach the exit, I can seal all the doors."

I nodded, listening to the shouting above the staircase, indicating a search. She and Gendair made it through the door, walking down a narrow pathway. The farther away her torch got from the room, the darker it became, until it was pitch black behind us. More shouting was heard, and a dim light was seen from where Gendair resided.

"Who are they?" I asked, the path narrower in some areas over others.

"Soldiers of the royal guard. The Oracles told the Magar that they would arrive. A Sardon artifact in Cilevdan. One of the covens is here, yes, but the artifacts were thought lost to the world. All aside from Seligsara."

"The king is looking for the Sun?"

"We have not yet discovered why."

"You must go to your people, Cethin. It is what they told me you must do."

"I'm not at liberty to choose."

"You must." Gendair said and stopped walking, the woman urging him to continue. The shouting became louder, an indication they found the path out. "It is the only way to end what has already begun."

I placed my hand on his shoulder and helped the woman in moving him to the exit, the corridor behind us becoming brighter. We made it into a chamber where the air was lighter, rushing in from a door that appeared to be of the physical world. The woman turned to the end of the path behind us, taking her torch and tracing the opening. It suddenly closed, all sounds from behind us ceasing.

"We shouldn't tarry," the woman stated. "I will get him to the Magar, but we will first hide to wait for the streets to empty."

I nodded to her and looked out toward the forest. "Safe travels to you both. Thank the Magar for me."

The woman smirked. "She will not want your thanks. But I will let her know that the Sun has been recovered by you. She will be pleased when the old man and I arrive at her doorstep."

"Of course," I said and began for the stables.

"Morcant." Gendair said gravely. "Remember what I said."

I left them both, running quickly around the wall toward the front of the city. The commander and his men were looking for the Sun. A weapon, but not an ordinary one. The entire mission had become unordinary. I needed to return to Ophidian as soon as possible and alert Vortain of what transpired.

The stable was in ruin. All the horses had been slain, arrows to their necks, or throats slit. Their blood painted the hay in different shades of red; their eyes stained the same colors. They were desperate in making sure no one left the city. I bent down to my horse, moving my hands across his chest. The blood was cold now, a sign that they had done this upon entering this morning. Feeling his cold bristle like hairs, I untied the reins around his face, cutting the straps. Taking a few steps, I threw them as well as the saddle into the woods behind the stable's cabin. If they came back here, they would certainly discover that the reins were made of materials not native to the mainland, as I'm sure in haste, the horses were not searched before.

Bowing my head to the horse, I apologized for the way he had been mercilessly killed and began for the forest. I would have to keep to the trees, covering my tracks as I went along. I used the growing dark to my advantage, entering the forest between a bush and a large tree. As the night went on the sounds of the forest shifted. The frogs and crickets made a jubilant chorus among the otherwise silent night; their incessant chirps conducting a melody. An owl joined in on occasion, searching the forest floor for its next meal. I heard dogs howling far off in the distance, at least three miles. The scent of blood was heavy on me.

I stopped, bending down to the edge of the Lake of Knights. I reached into it, surprised by its warmth. My hand almost disappeared beneath the surface of its dark waters, currently dedicated to reflecting the gloomy canopy above. I returned my arm above the water's surface, inspecting it. The blood became part of the vast dark pool before me. Swallowed, consumed. As I backed away, I looked down at the ground where I had just knelt, seeing that there were no impressions of my feet upon the soft edge of the water. Satisfied, I moved on, hoping my trail would be cut off here.

Dogs barked loudly in the distance, and I could not yet determine whether they were in pursuit or not. I was unsure if they were chasing at the behest of the soldiers, or if they made the forest their home. Either would be dangerous, the first however, with added threat. I couldn't risk soldiers finding Ophidian, and decided to wait for my pursuers, sitting upon a large rock in the middle of the clearing I ventured to. I closed my eyes, listening to the sounds around me. Within moments, I rose quickly, pulling my sword and slicing a wolf across its chest. Three came from the trees, snarling and snapping their jaws. I made quick work of them, taking a glance around before rushing toward my destination. While I should have spent more time ensuring I had no shadows, I knew that when I made it to the marshlands it would be impossible for anyone to pursue. It was vast, dark and eerie, impossible to navigate. The ground was not solid, and merely stepping upon it could have a man drowning beneath the murky waters thickened by mucous covered plants. Dogs would have the same problem, and horses even more so. I knew I was at least a day away from the isle, and expelling this much energy would have me needing to feed sooner than expected. I knew what I could afford to do and what I could not. I looked down to my side, seeing the pouch I had secured. It reminded me instantly of Cahya, and my thoughts moved to her...

◆ ◆ ◆

It was a cold night, wind ravaging the outside world, making thunderous shrills as it passed the windows of my shelter. I rose from my cot at the sound of aggressive knocks on my door. My task of patrol was next, and I would soon be subjected to the harshness of Ophidian's winter. I often wondered why the guards weren't exclusively sentry, but Vortain's word wasn't mine to question. I remained silent, taking the wooden sword that was left at the door.

"A serpent knows how to dismember his victim when given nothing but his own body to strike with," Vortain said at the beginning of the day. We were to fight with nothing but our limbs, sore and bleeding. We were not yet allowed to hold blades, for his trust in us had not yet been given.

I was led to the hill where the compound was, joining two other Serpents. It was then the guards left us, heading back to their quarters where a warm meal and fire likely awaited them. The Serpents walked behind me, as all did when they accompanied me on watch. The the fury of the wind was powerful, so if the men were speaking ill of me, it would go unheard. I remained silent for most of my time on watch, eventually taking to the south wall where the others would not venture. It overlooked the cemetery and was unusually quiet no matter the time of day.

The guards conjured up some kind of folk tale about a woman singing from the old grass covered headstones. The song would abruptly end, and soon after she appeared to them at the bottom of the wall.

I waited, looking at the grove of trees surrounding the south side of the compound, separating the guard citadels and den from the village. I wondered what life was like there, but a Serpent was not permitted to travel beyond the trees. The boneyard was our constraint. I had gone against the wills of my master too many times to further test his patience; the multiple wounds on my back were still sore from several days ago. I was made to ignore the pain, to continue with constant reminder that my defiance would be met with punishment. I remembered every moment of it, the blades cascading toward me, ripping indignantly into the skin of my back. My curiosity concerning the village was not worth another round of Vortain's choice of discipline.

Suddenly, from below me I heard a voice. I looked down, seeing not a ghost, not a spectre, but the shine of a helmet from the lone torch gripping the stone wall. I looked around me, moving to the wall's edge. Jumping off, I landed where I noticed the light and stood silently. I heard the voice a second time, however this time, I heard my name. I followed the sound into the Gravekeeper's quarters, finally coming upon who it belonged to. She stood quietly, her green eyes shining in the light of the torch, dark skin flawless and full of beauty.

"Why have you brought me here?" I asked, looking behind me and closing the door.

"Your fight today was impressive," she answered, taking her helmet off and placing it on the old wooden table.

I said nothing and watched her eyes scour my form. I looked around, smelling no aroma of cooked food from hours past. The keeper hadn't been here since morning, which was unusual.

"When I was a girl, I was cursed by an old woman, hateful she was. She said there would be no way to break it, so I am forced to live through these night terrors and visions. She said if

I was brave enough to conquer fear then they would cease. You asked why I've brought you here. Will you help me?"

"I can tell you what you fear," I answered, not knowing whether to offer her my assistance or to leave. Either way a transaction of risk would be made. She, as Commander of Vortain's guard and citadel, was a dangerous person to cross. However, if I remained here and was spotted, I was subject to death at the hands of my master. She too would suffer the same fate. The curse was causing her great suffering.

"So I've heard. Show me then, what it is I fear," she said at last, approaching me.

"Stay distanced from me," I answered and removed my hood, her eyes meeting mine for the first time. She stared into them, and I read her instantly. She began to quiver slightly, the light leaving her. I broke contact and she returned from hypnotism to a normal relaxed state.

"What is it?" she asked softly, trying hard not to show she was overwhelmed.

I exhaled quickly, replacing the cloak over my head. "You fear this place. Dying here without ever being able to explore the country, never again tasting the fruits of your homeland. You fear being killed in the theater of war, your blood pouring on the soil of a foreign place because of a man who holds your fate in his hand," I said.

She was quiet for a moment, taking a breath. "It is this place I must be free of," she said finally.

"You cannot," I answered.

She looked at me harshly and I ignored the glance, continuing my train of thought. "I have seen what comes of defying him. It is no small punishment. You have risked much to get to your position, I know. If you defy him now, he won't just give you scars as he's given me. He will carve you as a bird for feast and leave you in the forest to be devoured by wolves. Or worse," I said.

"I have survived my scars from him," she answered and pulled her sleeve back, revealing several large cuts on her shoulder.

I removed my cloak, giving her a first look at my arms. They too had incisions on them. I pulled the shirt off my skin, turning so that my back was exposed. The marks of the daggers that had entered my skin were revealed to her, now. At times I wasn't sure which caused more pain, the initial contact of the blades, or their withdrawal from my flesh.

"I see you have survived them too," she answered.

"Next time I won't be so lucky. He has already threatened to kill me once. Scars won't be punishment if I cross him again," I answered.

"No one will ever know we were here," she said and reached for her helmet. I went to grab my cloak, and she stopped me, asking me to join her on a walk up the stairs. When we reached the top, she pushed a hatch open that led to the roof and looked around before climbing upward. I followed, looking toward the patrol walls. Though I didn't believe anyone could see us due to the lack of visibility with there being no moon overhead, we could not be too careful. I joined her in sitting on an old rug, and we looked up at the stars. Although I could sense content within her, I also sensed sadness. She was alone here in this place. Every person she interacted with was to listen to her orders, the only people who did not were Vortain and Jadoq. Jadoq. I'm sure he belittled her as he did me. She was the only woman to have a position of power; Vortain's own wife dying of the plague long years past. We waited there, for hours, quietly speaking to one another under the cover of howling wind. It was near dawn before we parted ways, reluctantly. I was back in my chambers before daylight, giving into sleep.

CHAPTER 2

THE FIRES OF Λ DARKER STORM

I made it past the marsh mid-morning. Security, peace, rest. Words couldn't describe the feeling I obtained as I set foot on the solid ground of Ophidian, and as I made my way to the heart of the isle toward the flagstone ground, I was greeted by Eshkan.

"Was the information useful?" he asked suddenly, not sparing a moment to let me speak.

I nodded and pulled the map from my cloak, handing it to him. "I learned very many interesting things during my time there. Did you know the Patroness is a Magar?" I asked.

"A Magar? I didn't know any magic wielders still traveled Cilevdan," Eshkan answered.

"That was exactly my thought," I said. "In the bathhouse I gained information about a healer that lived in the area, her scent described by the boy who spoke of her. I followed traces of it back to the Patroness' villa."

"Impressive," Eshkan said. "I'm assuming she was there because of the weapon?"

"Yes, but, interestingly enough, she led me right to it." This caused Eshkan to raise an eyebrow and cross his arms. Amusement. "She wasn't there to take it but to protect it."

"A strange stance for a Magar to take. Did she mention others?" he asked.

"No. But, she wasn't the only surprise that waited in the city," I answered.

"Master has requested your presence in the tower. He said no matter the hour, I am to watch for you and give you those words."

"Tell him, if he is awake, that I mean no disrespect, but I have had quite a time trying to return here. I wish nothing more than to rest, and as soon as my eyes open, I will report to him immediately," I answered.

Eshkan looked at me strangely, but then took his normal stance. "It shall be done," he answered and nodded his head slightly, heading off toward the tower. I sighed in relief. My chamber was close to here, and the only place I had to venture through now was the courtyard. I heard the voices of the stone whispering inside my head, but I didn't understand any of its words. It was angry; I could perceive this from its tone. The longer I ignored it, the louder it became, which really began to disrupt my concept of rest. What I needed was to feed. Dangerously so. The pain that I experienced was not like any I've felt in ages. I prioritized sleep above it and laid on my cot, trying to drain out the whispers by filling my mind with my own thoughts. Exhaustion finally gave way, and I fell out of consciousness, leaving the day's gatherings behind me.

I heard a bird outside of my lone window, singing upon a thin mahogany branch. He was taking pride in his plumage, vividly displaying himself in front of the lush summer leaves. His chorus was diverse, low and high tones gracing his voice. Suddenly, as soon as he came, he flew off, spooked by the footsteps outside of my door. I rose, seeing two of Vortain's personal guards at the entrance.

"Come with us. He wants to see you immediately."

I nodded and rose, grabbing Seligsara. The guards put their hands on their weapons and I sheathed it, holding my hands in front of me to show peace. "It's important for what I must tell master, I mean no harm or disrespect," I answered knowing that if I made a move considered unjust in their eyes I would be attacked. They let me walk in front of them, not binding my arms back like they would anyone else who had prolonged debriefing. I was surprised they were treating me this way, but perhaps Eshkan had told them I was weary and needed to feed. In ignorance, the isle thought that if I didn't feed, I would become hostile or irascible. I was, before I had learned to control it of course. It didn't mean I'd never again become enthralled by my instincts; it had been a long time since that had come to pass.

When we reached the tower, the guards stopped at the doors to master's sanctuary, and turned to face the hall. I pushed the doors open, and instantly upon entering, Jadoq jumped up, pointing at me.

"There he is now. You ought to give him a few days in the dungeon for going against your orders to report to you! And he brought that vile weapon! He suggests assault with its presence!"

"Calm Jadoq. I am sure he means nothing by it," Vortain said and turned from the balcony toward me. It was a place he often stood when he was pensive or troubled. "Cethin. Why did you not report to me last night when you returned?"

"My sincere apologies master, but there was trouble in Arriksmad. My horse had been slain; I ran here through the marsh without as much as stopping to breathe," I answered.

"Eshkan had said you were weary. What kind of trouble waited for you? When he scoped the city, he said it seemed quiet."

"It was quiet, but just before I found the weapon things changed," I answered.

"Go on," Vortain said, removing his folded hands from behind his back, placing them at his sides.

"I found cover in the Araelian temple. From there I planned on visiting every location of interest Eshkan marked."

"You went into an Araelian temple?!" Jadoq shouted. "That was a risk he should not have taken."

"Jadoq, we must let him finish his report," Vortain said, which caused him to sit, crossing his arms in rage.

"I figured that the temple would be the best place to listen for secrets. The priestesses are young. They travel the entire village each day. They tell one another what they've seen. That did not prove as fruitful as I'd have liked, but I did learn that the kingdom is preparing for war."

"War?" Vortain asked and looked toward Jadoq, turning his eyes back to me. "Did you find out anything else?"

"Concerning the war, no. But some of the provinces are planning to dethrone the current king."

"Things are more complicated than I thought."

"There's more," I said. "At one point I heard men speaking to the priest outside. They were the king's soldiers. One of them was looked to as a leader. He seemed interested in searching the city, which caught my attention. They called him Savantin," I answered. Jadoq's eyebrows curved desperately over his eyes. "The Commander of Ozrach's guard? In Arriksmad?

"It seems sound enough that the army would be present due to rumors of war... but why was *he* there?" Vortain said, stroking his beard in thought. "Go on, Cethin. What else?"

"It seems he was there for a purpose. When I went to retrieve the weapon, they somehow found where it was being held. I recovered it, but I was chased. I left the city, only to discover that they had killed all the horses in the stable. I hid the saddle in the forest and covered my tracks at the Lake of Knights. But that's not the only part that's troubling," I said.

"I think you've said enough," Jadoq answered quickly.

"Jadoq! Keep your tongue within and let him speak!" Vortain growled.

"The weapon... Valkurdi didn't develop it... What was in the old man's keep was the Black Sun of Zerian. And even more strange, is when I entered his domain, he knew me... he knew who I was and said that he had been waiting for me," I answered.

"Where is it now?" Vortain said suddenly. I looked at him, not knowing how to give him an answer. "Cethin, where is it now? Does he have it? Do they have it?!"

"I have it. But he wouldn't let me leave until he..."

"Until he what?" Vortain asked sternly, causing my silence. "What are you talking about?"

"This crystal, this Black Sun, it speaks. It wants to be used and cause destruction. If the wrong being gets their hands on it then..."

"What have you done with it?" Jadoq asked.

"Jadoq if you interrupt him one more time, I will cut out your tongue!" Vortain shouted angrily. Jadoq's face turned to one of outrage but calmed quickly. I had to hide a smirk. Though I knew how frazzled Vortain must be to verbally assail his own advisor.

"If this crystal reaches the hands of a human it will kill in a continuous chain until it reaches the hands of someone that can use its power. I had no other choice but to comply. He sliced open my forearm, and placed the crystal there," I answered.

"I can see why you precaution it so... I myself did not know that it was the Black Sun... I do not appreciate your defiance, although in your best judgment. We will have to discuss what happens next."

I nodded. "I was told that it was meant for me to have."

"So, it's harmless," Jadoq said.

"It is far from harmless. It robs minds, steals souls. It is an evil stone," Vortain said.

"The only reason I complied with the words of the archivist is that he said I was the one they were waiting for. And..." I stopped, knowing that bringing up the altercation with my brother would not make things any better for me.

"And what?" Vortain asked.

"And... I didn't want to bring it to destroy what you've made here." My thoughts on Cahya.

This statement caused Jadoq to laugh, which immediately turned my every feeling toward anger.

"You dare laugh at me when it is my duty to protect you? You are spineless. You know nothing of honor, nor the sacrifice I just made," I said. The voices from the souls trapped within the Sun were angry, hungered and vicious. It had its eyes on Jadoq in this moment, and in my anger, abhorred him.

"Don't expect me to believe you did this out of the kindness of your heart." Jadoq laughed. "You wanted this to happen. You wanted that weapon for yourself."

"Continue to speak to me that way and I will make you wish you never belittled me when you knew me to be as calm as I am now."

"Cethin, I know you've had quite some trouble on your last mission, but threats are still forbidden," Vortain answered. Jadoq's face again turned to one of outrage as he looked to Vortain indignantly. "When a Serpent meets you with respect, you meet him the same."

"Well, it's quite clear he's not to be trusted. The weapon is..."

"Is a Sardon artifact. If he'd have brought it here in its raw form, we'd have all been hunted. We're their prey, Jadoq. But it would have likely turned the entire Isle to madness before they arrived."

"So, you agree that it's dangerous? Jadoq asked.

"I know how dangerous it is. We are not here for a history lesson; we are here to discuss what happens next."

"What happens next is he uses that weapon against us. This is what he wanted this entire time. You cannot expect me to believe otherwise."

"You fail to see how fortunate we are," Vortain said and crossed his arms. "Imagine the damage it could have done. Not only here, but somewhere else. You heard him. Savantin and his men were in Arriksmad. They nearly found it. Imagine it in their hands!"

"We've an even bigger problem now. It's here and in the hands of a Sardon. Won't the others be searching for him now?"

"Leave us," Vortain said suddenly, looking toward the door. I bowed and placed my hand over my heart when Vortain shook his head. "Not you, Cethin."

"What?"

"I did not whisper." His voice stern, angered.

Jadoq stood, his eyebrows furrowed in outrage and confusion. He looked at Vortain who didn't speak another word, his eyes focused upon the door. He walked out furiously, heading toward his quarters.

"Thank you, Master," I answered, graciously.

"Think of it as a sign of respect. I admire one who thinks for himself in the best interests of others. It is what I've always liked about you. You are not afraid to bend the laws if it means more lives will be spared."

"I had a good teacher," I said, thinking back to the old mariner. "Perhaps there is a reason I was led here when my human caretaker died," I answered.

"Everyone who exhibits change deserves a chance. No matter where or how they were born, what paths they have crossed or who they've angered," Vortain said and sighed. "Relaxation will be permitted until I say otherwise. I imagine what transpired with the weapon was very painful."

"It had to be done," I answered, looking down at my forearm. Swollen. Thick black veins.

"Valkurdi. What became of him?"

"I could not kill him. He was innocent," I stated. "There was a Magar in Arriksmad. She was sending a woman with food and water. I followed her in. The three of us escaped together and parted soon after.

"This becomes more interesting by the moment," Vortain said. "We will discuss things in detail tomorrow. There is something I am planning that I want you to be present for." I nodded, trying to show gratitude for the honor he had just given me. I turned away, leaving for my chamber. Before I had made it to the door, I was interrupted.

"Cethin... I feel something is at play beyond our knowledge. Keep the sword in your possession for now."

I bowed my head, and left the tower, thinking only now of rest, but as I continued down the long staircase, my thoughts became of Cahya. I felt the pocket on the side of my body, still feeling the vials wrapped in their thick burlap covering. I was thankful I hadn't dropped them in the forest while making my escape. It would have been my conviction. Cahya's conviction.

Vortain. That was another manner altogether. I wondered what his meaning was for including me during his next plot. It was an honor that only Eshkan currently held. If my presence was any inclination to how serious this upcoming mission would be, I had a lot of preparation to do. I couldn't help but wonder if it was the tidings of war or the news of a rebellion that sparked his sudden urgency.

Caught in my thoughts, I ran into Arven, who was about to find his place in waiting for the judgment to begin. I moved my hands in front of me offering my apology. "Sorry, my brother," I answered and began to move among the others. I was then stopped by two others.

"Cethin, a word," Ledgus said, motioning his head sideways. I looked at them both very briefly in suspicion but followed them past the crowd when I saw the look of concern in Arven's eyes. Once we made it behind the building closest the Den, Ledgus looked around the other side before speaking to me.

"Word is you've found what master had sent you after."

I crossed my arms but offered a nod, still wondering why we were in conference.

"Is it as they say it is? It is a weapon that bends the souls of man?" Arven asked, worriedly. As youngest of the Serpents he was still very poignant and concerned. Not many thought he would last the trials, but he lasted them as strongly as any other.

"None will suffer the madness it brings," I answered. "I will not allow it."

"You still have it? He let you keep it?" Ledgus said, in shock.

· 72 ·

"Master and I both knew the risks of its allowance to be exposed. What is your concern?" I asked.

"With a reputation such as that, we didn't know what to expect. We weren't so worried about master... but of Jadoq."

"Your concerns are shared," I answered, though my contempt of him was known.

"Arven overheard something he wasn't supposed to when you were gone. He wouldn't tell anyone but me. But seeing as how it sounds grim, we've decided to pass these words onto you. Arven was to watch the marsh the evening of your departure. On his way back to the den, he saw lights in the study at hours where it would normally be in complete darkness. He went to investigate and found Jadoq. He was looking through things, gathering things, talking to someone."

"The behavior of a man up to no good. Did you see who he was speaking to?" I asked.

Arven shook his head. "But I heard her voice. She was hidden in the shadows; I could not make sight of her. I didn't recognize it at all. It sounded quiet and enthralling. Like no woman I've heard before," he said. "I hid myself well, Jadoq did not know I was there."

"That sounds like information best shared with master?" I answered.

"Arven fears that if he tells master, then he will be punished for wandering from the wall," Ledgus said.

"I see. We should investigate this further."

"You're suggesting we spy on him?" Arven, full of questions.

"It is the only way that you will not receive punishment or retaliation. If Jadoq overhears one of us speak to Vortain he may cover his tracks. My presence has been requested tomorrow morning in the tower. Jadoq should be present. Then will be a good time to search his quarters."

"And now?" Ledgus asked.

"Vortain is in his tower, but Jadoq is not with him. He was dismissed."

"We will begin tomorrow, then."

I nodded. "Afterward we will meet where the grove meets the cliff's edge."

After confirmation, we exchanged farewells, and I began to head to where I knew I'd find solitude. I made it unnoticed and traveled upon the dirt path away from the chambers. The wind drew strength, and I closed my eyes, inhaling. I took in the generous sounds it created as small blossoms were torn from the cherry trees with its every amiable gust. I was alone until I made it to the backside of the grove's path, hearing a voice call my name. I turned, seeing a decorated guard waiting.

"Morard," I answered, surprised by his appearance. Typically now he would be in the courtyard, but I didn't see him at his usual post.

"We must make this short; I don't have long before I am missed," he answered. He didn't have a hostile mannerism about him, but I was suspicious of everyone now. A result of my decision in Arriskmad. "What is it we must do?" I asked.

"Cahya cannot meet you. She has fallen ill, nothing too serious. She has just been nauseous since this morning."

"She shows no symptoms of the plague?" I asked. Even though its onslaught had come and gone, there were still scares of it on the mainland.

"No, she said that she feels fine now. But she has sent me to collect what she has asked of you," Morard answered.

"Make sure it reaches her. I know how important it is," I answered and looked around before pulling the burlap pouch from my cloak. I made a fist lightly, making sure the vials were intact before I gave them to Morard. He peeled the flap back partially, looking upon the white vials that were stored inside. "Avandia," he answered and folded it back over placing it in his chest plate. "Then I too know how important this is. How were you able to slip it onto the isle past Vortain?" he asked.

"There is an excuse for being late to report when you're a Sardon. I simply made it seem as if I was incapable of meeting with him the night I returned and needed to hunt. He won't argue with me," I answered.

"So, you would lie to protect her?"

"More bend the truth," I answered.

"I shall take it to her now. She is in the infirmary with the doctor," Morard answered.

The infirmary. I was not allowed there unless ill or wounded. No Serpents were. "Make sure no one else sees this. All three of our lives would be at stake," I answered.

"I am aware," Morard answered and began to walk away. He stopped for a moment and turned, seeing that I hadn't left yet. "She told me to tell you not to go tonight, and that she would come to you."

I nodded and turned to leave, knowing even more suspicions would arise from being dormant. I supposed that Cahya had to tell someone about her meetings with me, though I was unsure if it was this day, when she felt ill, or for a time before that. I could tell Morard was protective over her, in his mannerisms of speaking to me. I thought nothing of it, and only hoped he would remain silent on the subject. She would remain on her side of the isle, and I mine, only meeting in public when circumstances allowed. I took a breath. I needed to feed, desperately. Typically, a criminal needing executed would be fair for me to take. The guards at the prison enjoyed my coming, and often wanted me to perform the killing before them. I would call them sick, but their fascination with me was better than what I was usually met with. I didn't have the energy to leave the isle and hunt near the marshland, and now with my recent return, I wasn't sure I would be given clearance to leave. I knew my direction now and followed the road to the dungeon with no hesitation.

I reached the building within minutes, looking at its shoddy exterior. The stone was crumbling, and large cracks appeared to be incisions on its once fortified facade. Vines had overtaken one side of the wall, their roots taking hold of the old porous stone. Despite what the outside looked like, the inside still held criminals, murderers and thieves, keeping them there with little effort. I myself had been on the inside several times, waiting out my fate behind large rusting iron bars. The scars on my back were a reminder of many things. As I reached the door, I knocked, waiting to hear voices inside.

I was met by a loud one, who walked with heavy slow feet. He staggered as he approached the old door, sliding the lookout bar back and looking upon me with his bloodshot earth-colored eyes. He wheezed as he looked back to his patrol partner and let out a laugh.

"Cethin, good to see you back, lad," he answered in his rich accent, undoubtedly of the Baeld. His breath smelled of ale, something forbidden on duty, but went unnoticed in this part of the isle. It was forgotten.

As he opened the door the ale was more apparent, and he backed away from the entrance, his chain mail hanging from his torso. He was a portly man, sent here to guard the prisons after he was injured in battle. The scar on his left arm was proof of the incident. Large portions of it were missing and several fingers were also claimed victim. He smiled at me, his red beard hiding the creases of skin near his mouth that were very evident next to his eyes.

"Have you come to take another one of 'em away?" he asked, turning his back and sitting his tankard on the table. He looked at his partner, who I had never seen before.

"Where's Jalen?" I asked softly, moving my face away from the man sitting in the corner. The prisoners had already begun to be silent, knowing what was at hand.

"Jalen. Ah... His child is sick. A fever. He was to stay home until it passed. You know how Vortain is about the children," he said, moving several empty bottles off of the small table behind him. "I haven't heard from him since. This lad won't give 'ya any trouble though. Will ya Jorgren?"

The new guard, Jorgren only looked at me, as if uninterested. I looked back to Haldis, who was grabbing the keys to the cells, thumbing through them. "There are new ones here. Just arrived last sun. They were interferin' with the last Serpents' mission. Can't remember who it was now," Haldis said, unlocking the door to the cell chamber.

"Wait. This man, he's a Serpent?" Jorgren asked, standing from his quiet table in the back.

"Well, who'd ye think he was? The faerie that takes your teeth at night when you put 'em under the pillow?" he answered, jamming the key beneath the door handle.

"What's a Serpent doing here?" he asked.

"Don't ask questions you don't want to learn the answer to," I answered, turning toward the door.

"But aren't you supposed to stay at your compound?" he asked.

"Cethin comes every now and again to clean out the cells."

"Haldis with all respect..."

"Ah Jorgren wouldn't want to know anyway. Too weak a stomach this one... Ah!" he said, finally unlocking the door. He pushed it open and walked in, chuckling softly. The only bit of excitement he got to see anymore was when I visited.

"I have not!" Jorgren said, coming toward me and looking in. "I'm just curious. I've never seen a Serpent short of when I was accepted into the guard."

"And that's why you're here wit' me," Haldis said from inside the cell block, his laugh still heard from my position.

"Everyone has heard the stories. There is no discretion unless you wish it so," I answered and pulled the hood off my head. He glanced at me, and I remained careful. Although this was a place where my presence was welcomed, any action not seen as customary would be punished. He was intrigued by the symbols on my head coming over my ears and to the sides of my eyes. They were visible through my hair, which I shaved close to my scalp. Though I kept my eyes from him, I could tell he was looking at their vibrant yellow color, and their reptilian irises.

"You're..."

I nodded, cutting him off before he could finish. I felt the stone in my arm beginning to heat from my thoughts of finally gaining sustenance. It was whispering, and the sounds were easier to ignore now that I was among my peers and not Vortain, Jadoq.

"I've heard stories from the West, about a whole race of you. I never believed them until now."

"There would have been no reason for it," I answered and turned away, walking into the door of the chamber. As I entered, I could smell them, the prisoners, their fear escalating. Heartbeats quickened as I walked past a few cells and sweat began to accumulate in their glands. I walked past one cell, containing a young woman with light brown hair. She sat in the corner holding her hands against her knees. Her bonds were worn thin, and rope burns around her wrists, jewelry from the past few days of attempted escape.

"Why is she here?" I asked. Her tan eyes flashed up at the sound of my voice and I looked at her for a moment, the anger and hostility dying down. I moved my gaze from her eyes, looking at her hairline to avoid a further collapse of her character.

"Theft. She was in town, a wanderer. She was caught trying to steal from your Den brother on his last mission."

I turned away from her, walking towards the next cell. She remained quiet until I reached the door and suddenly got up, moving toward the bars keeping her inside.

"I didn't steal from him," she answered.

I turned my head slightly, listening to her breathing. It was normal, quite relaxed. "He had dropped something in the market square. Something important. I didn't want to make a scene. I knew he was there for a reason other than to buy trinkets or silk scarves. I picked it up and followed him... wanted to put it back in his pocket before anyone could notice. If I had approached him, he would have killed me, accused me of stealing it. But I didn't, wouldn't dare to," she answered.

"The girl speaks the truth," I answered. Haldis looked at me strangely before answering. "If she is, it doesn't matter anymore. She can't leave here."

"But she doesn't have to die here in this cell. Send word to Vortain. He will transfer her to the village if he believes it to be true."

"He didn't believe her the first time. That's why she's here," Haldis said, laughing.

"He didn't have my word the first time," I answered looking toward her. Her eyes were beseeching, helpless. I looked away after a minute, turning toward another cell in the corner I had not seen when I had walked in.

"That one..." I answered. "...And the cell next to it." I said, looking upon the men in their cells. One avoided looking at me, and the other held an expression of rage and anger. I would let him hear the screams of the first to change his mind.

"I've made my decision." I said and turned to Haldis, taking my cloak off and hanging it on a low support beam. The woman looked at my skin, the scars, the words. I ignored her change of emotion as I looked to Haldis for the opening of the cell. He tossed me the keys and pointed at them.

"They come right back to me when you're done here," he answered and removed himself, his heavy footsteps becoming softer and softer until the door closed. I looked at the keys for a moment and turned to the girl holding my hand out in front of me, a warning to keep distance.

"You'll want to close your eyes for this. The screaming will be loud; you'll hear blood in their voices. Tell yourself it isn't real," I answered and turned away, opening the door to the cell of the first man. I grabbed his head, bashing it into the wall, pulling him backward by his shoulder. He was silent until I began to tear his skin, flaying it back with my thumbnail. I pushed him against the wall, digging my fingers into his collarbones and pulling them apart, ignoring the blood that splashed on my face. My arm became warm as I pulled bone from flesh, pushing it back toward his shoulder. He screamed loudly now, his voice beginning to become muffled by the amount of blood accumulating in his chest. I pushed his head back, biting into the cavern I had just made in him, ignoring his futile blows to my arms. The Sun was satisfied now, whispering softly in its several different voices. I made quick work of the man, my energy exhaustion in Arriksmad more drastic than I had thought.

I began to get near his ribs, leaving his organs intact, trying to keep him alive just a while longer before I would move on. He continued to yell in pain, but his voice became quieter as the voices of the Sun became louder. He finally had no more to offer me and I pushed him against the wall, going into the hallway to grab Seligsara. I looked down at the corpse, the head untouched as well as his lower body. The organs were loose upon the ground in delicate red detail, showing prominently through the bones I had left behind. Most of his torso had been devoured along with his neck, and the meat in his upper arms. His hands and forearms were still attached to his bones, covered in bright red blood from deep within his body. I closed his eyes to remove him at last from the world and left the corpse among the straw.

When I exited the cell, I caught a glance of the girl who had opened her eyes when the man had stopped screaming and began whimpering. My eyes met hers for a second as I took my sword in hand, looking at the blood on my chest and arms. I turned now to the man who once held eyes of anger, now widened in disbelief. I grasped the correct key from the ring and held it vertically, placing it into the lock on the cell door. I heard his sounds of protest, his fear rising as I began to turn it. It was stuck for a moment, and I pulled it to the right, the lock coming undone.

"No... no no!" the man yelled, backing away into the corner. I smiled, tossing the lock and swinging the cage door behind me roughly. It wasn't long after that I was finished with him, though I took my time in nourishing myself. I left him in the same condition as the other, satisfied that it would be some time before I would have to feed again. The Sun finally became quiet, its whispers dying down to nothing.

I left the cell, grabbing my cloak from the beam. I moved to the cell with the girl, who, now frightened, backed into the farthest corner. "I can make the sounds disappear."

"And why would you do that for me?" she asked, her voice shaking.

"Because you were never supposed to be here," I stated. After a moment she moved forward, slowly.

"And if you do, what would it mean?" she said, her voice more confident now. She moved forward to the door, looking at me. "Why are you helping me?"

"It's as I said."

"I'm your prey. All of these people are your prey."

"I'm not a mindless predator," I said quickly. "Or else I'd not be here seeing murderers to their deaths." She continued to hesitate, and I exhaled, turning to leave when she stopped me. "How would you make them disappear?"

"You were a beggar. While you were bereft of a place to live you were loyal to your gods. Gods that would not approve of the willing magic from a nonhuman." She said nothing to my reply, the sounds of dripping water heard from the cell where I was kept ages ago. "If you wish to forsake your Gods, I can remove the sounds from mind."

"I will keep them. My Gods will not abandon me, nor I them," she said.

I rose and returned to where Haldis was, sitting in the chair talking to Jorgren who was left without response. I placed the keys on the table in front of the door, blood causing them to shine red amid the candles in each corner of the room. Haldis' smile was loud from behind me. I didn't have to even look upon his face to acknowledge it. I ignored the look of disgust and shock from Jorgren, and went off into the midday sun, heading to where I could wash the blood from my body.

I reached a small pond, taking my cloak and hanging it on a branch, resting Seligsara against the tree. I caught a glance of my own reflection, my face covered in blood. My eyes were satisfied, a hollow golden, well rested and focused. As I moved my arm in to grasp a fistful of the river to cleanse my chest, the stone began to burn, so much that it felt like my arm was being encased in ice. It began to speak one word, over and over in its several voices. I looked at it, my arm shaking as it continued to speak to itself, the sensation heightening. I sat backward, still watching it, expecting the ice to become visible.

I spoke the word aloud. The stone stopped speaking suddenly, ice crystals forming in the air wherever I moved my hand. I pulled it up toward me, turning my hand over and over. Placing my hand on the water's surface, I repeated, letting my voice become loud. The water around my hand began to freeze, the ice creating swirls as it began to spread toward the other bank. I removed it, and again stared at my fingers. So, this is what Sardons were born into. The ability to harness matter.

I sighed and dropped my hand to my side, lying back on the grass. I felt dizzy, the sensation stopping momentarily. I rose and again dipped my arms inward, moving them across my chest and then my face. This was most important. I watched my reflection disperse as I reached into the water another time, rubbing my face vigilantly. As I finally made myself presentable, I walked back up to the compounds following the scent of orange blossoms as the grass turned to road. The walk was time I needed to process what I learned. Before today I never knew about the quarrels of the king and his legion, or its commander. The events would be a mystery until Vortain decided to investigate them, as I knew he would. He would be immediately sending his spies out for more reconnaissance, Eshkan among them. This had to be what the meeting tomorrow would envelope. A distraction for Ledgus and Arven to investigate Jadoq's involvement with an unknown woman in Vortain's tower.

The sun climbed directly above the earth. The shadows of the buildings weren't sure where they were supposed to be, now small and only peeking out from corners. It was hot now, the water I had just used to clean myself no longer upon my body. It dried as I was halfway up the road. I began to hear the clashing of metal and shouts as I was nearing the tower, the world continuing as I slipped away. I walked into the arch of the Tower quadrant, watching as two of my brothers were sparring, throwing their swords at one another without relent. I quietly moved through the crowd, standing in the stands among the others who were not chosen for training this day. Though they were merely training, they did not fight in reticence. They were drenched in sweat, heat cascading off stone, sending fumes to join the sky. I took a breath in, feeling just how humid the air was in my lungs. Suddenly, the fight was over, and one man pushed the other to the ground, disarming him. Vortain stood, giving his order for it to end.

"Again!" he said and signaled for the next pairing to enter the ring. I approached, taking the empty seat next to him, the one where Jadoq usually sat. Suspicions further rose. Vortain watched the Serpents, speaking only after they had met one another with the signs of brotherhood and respect. A custom that preceded each match.

"Cethin. I wanted to speak further with you regarding your recent securing of the Black Sun," he said, turning from the match to look at me. "Its appearance at this time is a topic worth discussing, but beyond that, the appearance of the men you mentioned troubles me deeply."

"As it does me," I replied. "It doesn't seem like it was mere chance that they'd not only arrive when they did, but to share interest in what we were trying to secure."

"We share the same concern. But let us start with the Sun," he said. I nodded, waiting for him to continue. "In all my life, I had never met a Sardon, not until the day the blade ended up in my possession. Years later, you appeared here, and now this. Part of me wonders if the isle somehow was born into a revelation regarding the return of Zerian."

"Return?" I asked. Being ignorant of my own culture was bothersome. The only books Vortain had that were written in a tongue familiar to me did not delve into history, but mythologies, speculations.

"Yes. You see he was trapped in what your people call "the endless" a time after he formed the Sun. Though, it isn't very much known to me how, or why. The only books I was able to recover on the subject without gaining too much attention were brought here by Eshkan when he was in Ascaria."

I looked at him briefly, averting my eyes as to not assail. "I did not know it was more than Valkurdi's wish to have it ripped from the hands of those who would use it for harm."

"It is much more than that. You were right when you discussed its potential to cause untold chaos. Which is what leads me to the men that were trying to take it from you. They are agents of the king, the ruler of the lands just outside of the isle. He is a greedy man, consuming whatever he can from his people. These men could only be seeking the Sun to bring it to him. I do not expect I need to elaborate that thought," Vortain answered.

"No. They seemed pretty intent on securing it."

"Herein lies our predicament. It is our duty to stop him, Cethin. As I uphold my duty to keep peace within the realm. A man such as him planning something this bold troubles me. We do not know how the Reaper got the resources to find Valkurdi, which is something I am investigating. If he has spies as good as ours, it is worth confronting. I do not believe he will stop. It isn't over. If he cannot secure this artifact, he will try to locate another."

"I understand. What would you have me do?" I asked.

"I have begun to fabricate a plan. I will send Eshkan to travel the area, see if he's heard anything within the neighboring villages. I fear a return to Arriksmad too soon may end badly. I will also be choosing a few of you to aid him in whatever he needs. We must handle this delicately. Our efforts have not uncovered the locations of any other artifacts, but that does not mean that Savantin knows something we do not. If Eshkan can send word to our contact, we may be able to discover more than what is on the surface. More of this will be discussed tomorrow. At the moment I am trying to discover who can and cannot be trusted."

The man continually surprised me. Vortain looked at me and placed a hand on my shoulder, squeezing it gently. "I want to commend you for your service, but there are no amount of words I could give that would express my gratitude. The task ahead will not be easy. It will be far from easy. It will require a lot of sacrifice, and good people will die. But I need you to remember that no matter the cost, he mustn't find anything else. Meet me in the tower at dawn."

He trusted me. The man who for years kept me isolated from the men I was supposed to call brother, the man whose men belittled and mocked me, the man who at first imprisoned me here trusted me. I nodded, taking those last words as my invitation to leave. I made distance from the center of the isle, heading toward the compound. Now that the hour was late, I could reach it with ease. The patrols were predictable now, my meetings with Cahya being often enough to know them. They were always in formation of a pair, one trailed by another, with a guard watching from the rooftops. I often thought about the meaning of this, aside from the usual curfew for ourselves and noncombatants. Avoiding them was easy enough, and the infirmary was not too far from here.

There were candles lit inside, seen clearly from the window. The nurse brought a cup to the bedside, leaving several small items as well. Upon a breath, I caught the scent of honey and tea. She left in the same manner she entered, closing the door behind her. It was then I made my entrance, watching as Cahya's chest rose and fell with each breath she took. I had to wake her although I did not want to, she looked peaceful in her resting. I sat beside her, gently taking my hand toward her face and moving it against her cheek. She opened her eyes slowly, smiling when she came across my face.

"Cethin," she said and sat up, using her hands as a brace. "I wasn't expecting you."

"Isn't that the best surprise?" I laughed. "Morard said I could find you here."

"And I trust Morard also said that you were to wait for me to come to you," she smiled, looking downward and shaking her head in a lighthearted laugh.

"Did you get what I brought for you?"

"Yes, he brought it to me this afternoon. How fared your mission?" she asked softly.

"Not as planned. There were complications, many of them. Vortain sent me to Arriksmad to retrieve a seemingly dangerous weapon from a man who was crafting it."

"And so, you did…"

"Yes, but when I got there, I discovered that the weapon he was describing was The Black Sun of Zerian. The man who held it wasn't a danger, so I did not kill him. He was blind, waiting for me. He said it was foretold but he didn't mention by whom."

"A religious man?"

"No, something different."

"So, you didn't kill him. How did Vortain react?"

"He did not give it a second thought. As soon as I let him know what was in the old man's care, he understood. I helped the man escape with the help of a servant of the Magar."

"Escape?" she asked, alarmingly. I should have used a more careful word.

"When I arrived in the city, it was quiet. I gathered information and investigated every place that Eshkan marked. When I woke on the morning that I would find the servant, the Commander of Ozrach's guard was there. At first, I believed him to be no threat. He mentioned war, and said they were searching the cities. But shortly after I arrived where the Sun was being held, they found me. I was not followed. I thought of it only after I had left that…"

"Someone told him of your being there," Cahya answered.

"Yes. I noted that as a possibility," I said, raising my head. "A few of the others, they've come to me with strange news, things they've seen, heard."

"I have my suspicions. Morard said he's seen strange things in the waters, heard strange noises from the marsh."

"Have you not told Vortain?"

"I have. But he says that with the change of season the wilderness is doing things on its own accord to prepare for the snow. You don't think he has something to do with it?" she asked.

"No. He was completely surprised when I told him what was happening, what had happened. When I returned, he pressed the subject more than once. Sharing interesting words with me. I have new concerns. The kingsmen were looking for this, for reasons unknown to us all. I am confident I lost them, covered my trail. I do not think our arrival in Arriksmad at the same time was a coincidence, but beyond that, does it also mean that they are searching for means to rid the world of dark artifacts? I doubt that. They would use it for destruction, for power."

"It does seem strange that something hidden from the world for so long comes into the plans of two separate parties."

"Vortain suspects that because of this, the king will be seeking out other means of power. I do not disagree with him, but with that thought on forefront, I believe he will misappropriate attention that should be used to watch whoever planned this mission with him."

"I do imagine that would be difficult. I can't conceive of anyone having connections such as those, or how one could even establish that. You don't think it was his spy?"

"I thought of that at first. But Eshkan is cunning. He'd have covered his tracks more carefully." The statement caused Cahya to nod, taking a deep breath in.

"I had second thoughts, on who had discovered the sanctum and entered it so soon after I did. There was no indication that it was the kingsmen, though I don't know who else it could have been. I heard them, could see their torches."

"It could have been no one else, Cethin. You think the town guard would have done it?"

"You're right. I am thankful that I reached the Sun before they did. Unspeakable things could have happened if it was taken by anyone else."

Cahya was silent for a moment, and then nodded softly, looking up at me. "The weapon… the Black Sun. Where is it now?" she asked.

I drew a breath in and raised my arm, folding my cloak's sleeve back around it. When I freed my skin, she saw the long dark scar that ran from wrist to elbow on the inside of my forearm. "It's here."

"Inside your arm? Does it hurt?"

"No, but I can feel it… hear it. It speaks."

"What does it say?"

"I don't know. I catch words here and there, from when I met my brother in the armory, from when I would be caught in those trances, but those words are only few. I don't know what else it says, and when I ignore it, it becomes louder… angry."

"This plan of Vortain's… what does it entail?"

"I do not yet know. We are to meet at dawn. He did not disclose to us how long I would be with him."

"I see. Do all you can to seek answers, Cethin. Not just for what is happening, but for yourself."

"Myself?"

"Yes. You've lived a strange life, one that I hope has been fulfilling, but you have not been able to visit where you came from. Know the language of your people. You have inherited the weapon of a Sardon warrior. It has fused to you. Surely this must mean something," she answered.

Her words were truth. A man had come here claiming to be my brother, claiming us to be Bloodheir a day before I left to seek the Sun. I had no knowledge on how to command it, only that words released the power of the souls inside. If I was to protect it from falling into the wrong hands, from consuming lives, I would need to know how to speak to it.

"Perhaps I should discuss this with him," I stated. "I assume he has other plans for me, but this cannot be ignored. I don't believe this will be the last effort of the king in trying to retrieve the Sun. But I want you to promise me something."

"Anything."

"If something happens here, while I am gone, I want you to run. Do not fight them."

"Cethin I..."

"Promise me."

"I promise."

"I know I lost them in the woods. But if someone on the inside is contacting them, and if they come here searching for this the result will be the same."

"Do you anticipate it?" she asked, her eyes twinkling against the flame of the candles.

"I do not know. I will return as soon as it is possible, as soon as I accomplish whatever it is he asks of me. If I come back and you are not here, I will meet you in Sanhai, and from there we will head to Varrus."

"The Baeld?"

"No one will search for us there. Sanhai is a day's travel north, if you reach the road that separates Septentria from the Pass you will have gone too far. There is an inn, closest to the port. The tender will not turn away a woman on the run. Offer her help until I arrive. She was a friend of my mentor. Mention Braeg, she will remember."

"You've put a lot of thought into this."

"Things have turned quickly in the past few days."

"Do you think you will leave at dawn?"

"I suspect he will want us to start immediately after he's spoken. I fear I will have little chance to see you once he's made his decision on where I will go," I answered. She looked down for a moment, looking at me and placing a hand on my cheek. "I've made you a promise, but I want you to make one for me. Whatever you find out there, whatever you must face, return to me."

"You needn't worry about that," I said, suddenly wincing.

"What's wrong?" she asked, moving forward from her position on the bed.

I raised my hand up to signal for her to stay relaxed. "I don't know what it wants, but it wants something."

"Does this happen often?"

"Yes. When I do not react to it. There is only one way to see this end," I answered and looked toward the door where footsteps were heard outside.

"We've little time before she returns to check on me."

"I can hear her. Do not fret," I said.

"These are frightening times. Your plan. Varrus. Is that what where we will go?"

"If not now, then soon," I answered and stood. I kissed her on the forehead, and she pulled me back down to her, initiating one last long kiss before I exited the window, climbing onto the roof. I headed back to my quarters, taking little time to enjoy the night on my venture back. Opening my door, I listened to the familiar creaking as I shut it behind me, placing Seligsara beneath the cot on which I slept. I laid back, taking a few breaths before closing my eyes. I removed thoughts of anything else but what dawn would bring and drifted into sleep.

◆ ◆ ◆

I was caught amidst a memory of a mission I had taken part in years ago, when I was ripped from slumber by the sound of an explosion. I rose quickly, grabbing my sword and pulling a shirt over my body. I moved to the window, seeing nothing but smoke and flames on the other side of the island. Portions of the sky began to glow a bright orange, the smoke billowing from the source like a monstrous black cloud. The ashes were enough to burn the eyes, and I could hear screaming in the distance. I looked around my room for a second, thinking of anything I would need to take with me, and grabbed the amulet that was given to me by the mariner. I pushed my door open hastily running from my chamber to the den. Kicking the door open, I saw the horrors that lay before my feet.

Slain, tens of them. Blood took hold of the floor as my brothers were laying in death, blood from their mouths. In their chests was carved a symbol, two lines down either side of their rib cages, and what looked like an upside-down sickle in the center. Lines and shapes carved on each side. I looked on, seeing the faces of men I had lived with for years, except for one. I did not see Dacian anywhere. My eyes moved to the table; I noticed a considerable amount of powder around one of the water goblets. I pulled a pouch off the wall and used my hand to slide the substance inside. Leaving, I headed to the one place I thought he would go. The smell of blood was strong as I neared the armory and I took a breath before turning the corner, knowing I would most likely be in for a fight.

I pressed my back to the wall and looked around, seeing that Dacian and Declan were fighting together against several men. Suddenly the shared thoughts of a traitor on the isle seemed more than likely. My thoughts momentarily jumped to Cahya. If she was still in the infirmary, she would be an easy target. I moved, cutting the head off a guard who had just attacked Declan. I fell into formation with them, and after exchanging a few swings of Seligsara with another man's steel, I disarmed him, stabbing him through the center and sliding my sword out of his side. I kicked his corpse away and after he landed on the ground, Dacian made it through his last adversary.

"These men, have you seen them before?" he asked, cleaning the blade of his sword on the back of his arm.

"They're King Ozrach's men."

"The king?" Dacian asked in surprise.

"Yes. I have suspicions of why they are here, but we cannot be certain until we get one to speak," I answered.

"I left as soon as I saw the first fire. I didn't think anything of it... our Den brothers... who survives?" he asked.

I shook my head. "It is only us now. All were killed, symbols carved in their chests."

Dacian looked down for a moment as if to pay respects, but looked back up suddenly, speaking. "We need to keep moving. If Vortain is still alive we need to protect him. Undoubtedly whatever they are here for lies with him if they have not yet found you."

A good point. I nodded and turned to where the fires burned, stepping forward. Declan followed, speaking. "I have not yet seen any of the battalion. When I saw the fires, I came out to the armory immediately, to try and seal it off or move the weapons so these men could not find them. I was beaten here by those guards we had just killed, Dacian saved me."

"Where were you before the attack?"

"On my way to the citadel. Morard said that he was holding an important meeting."

"They will pay in blood for what they've done." Dacian cursed.

"It is a great offense, but we must keep our heads. If we begin to fight from our rage, they will overpower us." Just as I had finished speaking, we heard screaming from past the dungeon, toward the infirmary. I turned suddenly, heading off in that direction. My life here was over, and I needed to protect the one person I was taking with me.

"Cethin, where do you go?!"

"We need to protect those who cannot protect themselves. Vortain has his guards, his soldiers. Those in the village and the infirmary have no one," I answered and ran off. I didn't even look to see if Dacian or Declan had followed me. The infirmary was in sight, and more horrors awaited us there. There were guards, laid out on the ground in pieces. A pile of their limbs was lying just next to them, stacked about a foot high. They were on fire, the stench coming from the burning flesh enough to make one sick. As the fire ravaged the muscle and skin the smell wafted through the air in the form of a large smoke cloud. Few of the men were still breathing, coughing as their own blood filled their throats. They were drowning slowly. I moved to one, lifting him up by his shoulders. His legs were limp in front of him, and his skin was pale, losing pigment as he lost blood. They must have just been here.

"What did you see?" I asked.

He coughed, blood splashing from his mouth. "You must hurry. They're going to burn them all; they're locking them in the citadel," he said and coughed one more time before becoming lifeless. I moved my fingers over his eyes before setting him down upon the soaked ground. I stood and turned toward the infirmary.

"You heard him; we have to head to the citadel!" Dacian said.

"You go ahead, I have to make sure there is no one inside that lives," I answered, looking at the building that was smoldering. I didn't have the strength to see her dead, and if she was, I knew I would have to force myself to keep my composure.

"Splitting up would be a bad idea. We will wait here while you go inside but make haste. The villagers have only us," Dacian answered.

I nodded and walked forward, pushing the door back onto the wall as I entered. It was off its top hinge, severely battered and broken in. As I moved toward the room that I saw her last, I noticed that things had been rummaged through and knocked over. The bed had been stabbed in certain places, but there were signs of a scuffle on the floor where blood made a trail out of the window. I busted through the other door and saw that even the nurse was not spared. She was half lying on a bed, her legs on the floor, blood coming from the top of her head. I began to feel rage as I left the building, rejoining Declan and Dacian.

"Anyone?" Declan asked.

I shook my head, seeing Eshkan come over the hill. He was holding his upper arm and rubbed it, his eyes coming upon us. He suddenly moved his hand urgently toward the building signaling us to hide ourselves. Dacian grabbed the arm of Declan, who wasn't familiar with the Serpents' code and pulled him behind the infirmary. I climbed the roof quickly, ducking behind its decorative arches. Eshkan moved close to the door of the infirmary, stopping and catching his breath. As he turned, seven men came over the hill. "There he is! He's one of them! He's the archer!" a man shouted.

"He wants one of them alive. This one might know where it is."

"I don't care about that. I want to find the bitch that cut out my eye!" another growled from the back.

Cahya. She was alive.

"Grab his arms!" the man in lead shouted. When they reached Eshkan, I jumped down from the roof, cutting one in two at his shoulders. I spun my sword, taking another man's head off. When the others armed themselves, Dacian came from behind them, stabbing one through the center. He turned for another and grabbed him, kicking him down and sending him to his death.

"Leave that one!" I said and pointed to the one who had a large gash where his eye once was.

Dacian nodded and Declan came out from behind the building, looking at the ground before him in shock.

"Put them in the pile. I don't want their leader to even distinguish which dead are his," I answered and faced the last standing. He held his sword out to me, and I closed my eyes, opening them again and staring into his. As I began the hypnotism the Sun began to speak. It was enjoying this, and it wanted more. As the man began to quiver, I kept hold, seeing his fears in my head. He suddenly dropped his sword and dropped to his knees. I kicked his sword from reach and released my hold on him, pulling his helmet off of his head. I was unable to read his eyes. Darker magic was at work, here.

"What... what are you?" he asked.

"Why are you here?" I asked.

When I was met with silence, I moved in to punch him and he flinched, begging me to wait. "A weapon!"

"A weapon. Do you know what they speak of?"

"No. We were only supposed to make sure that there would be no problem in retrieving it."

"So unarmed innocents, they pose a threat to you? Killing them is eliminating a problem?"

"He said to find it by any means."

"Who?" I asked, softly at first. Upon no answer from the man, I raised Seligsara to his throat, this time shouting.

"You think I'm afraid of dying by the sword? It is a death entirely less painful than what would happen if I talked. I would rather you kill me," he said.

"Then let's change that," I answered and cracked the bones in my neck and shoulders. "If you tell me what's happening, I'll decapitate you. Quick, mostly painless. If you don't, I'll devour you while you still live," I answered and opened my mouth, my jawbone softly cracking as I revealed two rows of teeth.

"Alright alright!" he shouted. "We are here because he's searching for something. He's mad. Insane. He will stop at nothing until he has it. He doesn't care who he must kill, what he must do. His madness grows stronger as he does."

"Savantin," I answered.

"Now you understand. I would rather you kill me."

"Who led him here?"

"I don't get told the details. I am only an instrument," the man stated.

"The woman who cut out your eye, where did she run?" I asked.

"Back to the village, but I didn't find her while I was there. Filthy..."

I moved Seligsara across my body, cutting the man's head off.

"Searching for something..." Declan stated.

"The Sun, it must be," I answered.

"Who is this man? Who leads these savages?" Declan asked, dropping his spear in disbelief.

"When the time comes that we confront him, I will be the one to do so," I answered and looked toward the village. "We need to move. You heard the man. Madness."

"He's likely already found Vortain," Dacian answered.

I looked toward the village, knowing that if Cahya had indeed run there then she may be in danger of being corralled with the others. She could protect herself, I knew, but she would need help if there was any hope of saving the others.

"No. Vortain has guards for his protection. We should go to the citadel, and save whoever remains," I answered.

"My blade follows yours," Dacian answered.

I turned to Eshkan and looked at his arm, realizing that he had already tied the wound closed with a piece of cloth he had torn from a fallen soldier. He nodded at me as he picked his bow up off of the ground and we headed off toward the citadel, hoping the ash would not yet stain our faces.

◆ ◆ ◆

Vortain paced the balcony of his tower angrily, spinning harshly as he looked at Jadoq. "I cannot believe that this day has come! After years of careful planning and hiding my land away someone lays siege!" he shouted.

"It must be the Sardon, Vortain. Why else would this happen directly after he had completed the last mission? Retrieved for you one of their artifacts. Perhaps they know it is here and are coming for it."

"That is impossible! Do you see what happens just below us? These are mortal instruments of war!" Vortain continued, his voice still loud, still angry.

"We will find a way out of this... Whoever has done this will pay their price, I'm sure."

"Jadoq, everything burns. Look at my island! It crumbles as we speak here like cowards in this decorated tower. They will come for us next, once everyone else dies."

"Close, very close," spoke a dark voice from the hallway.

Vortain looked wide-eyed to the door as a man stepped in, his armor bloodstained and ashen. His eyes were dark and held a chasm he had never seen in his life. He was a large man, not very tall but indeed very thick. His armor, due to his size, had to have been crafted just to fit him, which meant he was of importance somewhere. He took care of himself, as he appeared to have only muscle upon his body, which indicated he took his life as a warlord very seriously. Vortain was unsure of what to think until the man looked at Jadoq and laughed quietly. "So, this is where you think it lies. I'll have to admit, I would have eventually looked past the marshes, but this has saved a lot of time."

"Who... Who are you?"

"You want to know who I am?" the man asked. "I don't see why it is a need, since you will not live much longer."

"I want to know the man who has placed my land in peril so that when I am sent to my gods, I will forever curse his name."

"Bring me their fury, upon the name Savantin. But do not forget the man who betrayed you."

Jadoq opened his mouth in outrage, stepping forward. "You were not to say!"

"You! You are the one who did this?! Who led this monster and his men here to destroy our home?!" Vortain cried, an inhospitable rage taking his voice, turning toward him.

Savantin continued to look at them with his darkened eyes, a smirk taking his face. He had seen his share of betrayals, lived through them himself, but he never tired of watching a friend turn on another for the illusion of exalting himself.

"Vortain don't act so surprised, when you took him in you should have known that with him would come things we don't understand," Jadoq answered.

"You don't know what you've done Jadoq! Do you really think there will be a place for you once this land dies?! I have been your friend, your protector, have offered you a new life for all these years, only for you to throw it all away while you watch innocents drown in the blood of this mad man!" he said.

Savantin laughed, placing his helmet on Vortain's table. He looked at the maps that were strewn about it, rubbing his hand all over them, causing them to smear in blood. "I think now is the time to tell me where it is," he said and moved forward and pulled one of his swords from his side, ordering Vortain to kneel.

He shook his head slowly. "I will not."

"Then it seems as if we will do this my way," Savantin answered and grasped his sword, his large hand making its hilt seem small. "There is a box rumored to be on your land. Tell me if it is."

"I know not of what you speak," Vortain said, his voice shaking.

"Do not lie to me. Its last known location was Morakesh during the raid seven years ago. I've been to every cavern, hold, fort, and village that houses thieves. It must be here."

"Even if I knew, I would not tell you where it is just so you can bring darkness and shadow upon the world. My oath, the oath I swore to uphold means more to me than anything you could do," Vortain answered. Savantin moved forward, his free hand open to grasp Vortain's neck when Jadoq intervened.

"Tell him where it is Vortain! If you do not, he will kill you. Is hiding it worth your life?" he said.

"I have other means of persuasion. If you won't comply with threats on your life, then this might make you do otherwise," Savantin answered. He turned, grasping a torch from the pillar near Vortain's study. He hesitated for a moment and in a breath, placed it on a sconce outside of the balcony's ledge. Trails of flames traveled from the bottoms of the citadel up onto the roof and within minutes, a large glow of orange took over the sky. From the balcony, Vortain watched as the citadel began to burn; sounds of people screaming filled the air and traveled to his ears on clouds of ashes. Vortain struggled to move, sadness covering all other emotions on his slightly wrinkled face.

"I will stop the fires; I do not wish them to die. But if you know anything, now would be the time to reveal that."

"Burning buildings and killing innocents will not grant you your wishes. Though you promise to spare them, they would be blessed to die now rather than live to see what you would become with that power in your hands. I would rather die, would rather them die than tell you anything," Vortain said. "You do not frighten me, Seraphice."

Savantin looked up and smiled, offering a laugh. "Then I shall make those words your last," he answered and grabbed him by the neck of his shirt, throwing him into the marble pillar that overlooked the balcony. His body was flung quickly through the air, and Savantin moved with it, grabbing Vortain's head before he could fall off. He took his sword and shoved it through his skull from beneath his chin, pinning it to the pillar. Jadoq looked on in horror as Savantin placed his hand on Vortain's cheeks, and opened his mouth with his thumbs, letting blood pour all over his hands as he looked at his sword shining in red from the back of his throat. He smirked and pulled the sword out of his head, his body falling upon the ground. He looked to Jadoq who began to panic, searching through his robes quickly.

"You think whatever you have to offer me will save your life?" Savantin asked, a curious tone to his sadistic voice. "I have no pity for people like you. You're a louse, feeding upon the collapsing empire around you. You didn't anticipate how this would go; I can see it in your eyes. You now regret the decision to even contact me. Don't fret. You'll not be alive to see what comes of it," he continued, raising his blade toward the darkness of the adjacent room.

"You've killed the only one who would know where it rested. Killing this man will do nothing to aid you," the voice of a woman warned.

"Killing him will be for a promise unanswered. I always provide my end of a bargain. But their lives depend on whether or not they provide theirs," Savantin answered.

"It was out of my control. I could not make him talk! I... I can still find the Sardon for you. Let me go out, I will approach him and lead him here... to his master."

"If I wanted the Sardon, I would have killed him in Arriksmad."

"But he has something of value, something you could use. He has the Sun of Zerian," Jadoq answered in a rush.

"This I know. But it is not the Sun that interests me," he answered and ran his hand down the blade of his sword.

"It doesn't change the fact that I still don't know where it is!" Jadoq said.

"What if it is not here at all? And the man was really telling the truth?" the woman said.

Savantin closed his eyes and exhaled angrily, looking toward Vortain's workshop.

"Think of it. We could not find it on his maps, his records. He kept lists of everything his Serpents brought to him, did for him in the book on his desk. I could not find any notice of it anywhere, not even mentions of it."

"Don't tell me it isn't here, Sindara," he answered darkly.

"Perhaps one of the thieves you've visited lied to you. One of the fortresses."

"They know lying to me is followed by reprisal."

"Not everyone is afraid to cross you, Savantin," she answered.

"They should be," he answered and grabbed his helmet, moving his hand over the top of it, painting a stripe across the front in Vortain's blood. He began to walk toward the workshop when Jadoq stopped him. "You know, you haven't left me with such a kingdom to rule," he said, sneering.

"You think that because I've decided to turn away that you can bark and demand more from me when you have provided me with nothing?" Savantin asked, wheeling toward him. "You'd best silence that forked tongue of yours."

"You told me that when you were done here that I would be the new ruler of this place, you would keep it away from the eyes of your king! You've left it in shambles!"

"But up until now I've let you keep your pathetic life without begging for it."

A look of confusion crossed Jadoq's face just before Savantin approached him, pulling another sword from a sheath on his side.

"No, don't! I'll look for it myself! I'll search over every inch of this place!" Jadoq cried.

"Do you see how weak you sound? You should have just remained in silence," he said and stabbed the sword from his left hand into Jadoq's right side. "You shouldn't have let Sindara's words give you courage. Look at where it's brought you," he answered and plunged his other sword into Jadoq's left side.

"You sick... bastard..." Jadoq said as his voice began to fade. Savantin released the hilt of his left sword and pushed Jadoq's head back with his palm, forcing eye contact. After a few seconds, he replaced his hand on his sword and crossed the blades through Jadoq's torso, cutting him into two pieces. Blood squirted on his face from the incisions he made in Jadoq's flesh. When he was done, he put his swords away, moving his tongue to remove the blood from the corner of his mouth. He looked upward, speaking. "Sindara, reveal yourself," he said, his voice sounding more beast than man.

The silence that answered enraged him, and he walked towards Vortain's workshop, disappearing into the dark of the room. He remained there for several moments, tearing the room apart, looking for any clue of his longing.

◆ ◆ ◆

The road was painted in the color of the night, the air polluted by ash and smoke. The buildings were now smoldering, and the dirt path was lined with carrion, all in the same condition as those we encountered before. I felt the ground reverberate under my feet as I ran toward the village, hearing nothing now but the crackling of fire and collapsing of houses. The village itself was abandoned, whoever remained was dead, lying along the road or charred, now giving smoke from their heated bodies. The same symbol that was carved into the chests of our fallen was painted on several doors. I could only imagine the atrocities that had been committed while we were elsewhere. We moved past it, coming into the vicinity of the citadel just as the burning began. I then heard the pleas of the people inside as the roof caught fire, followed by banging on the door. As we rushed to its position, we began to fight off the men that threw the torches on the building, making it a pyre. As we continued to fight, I noticed Cahya and Morard just on the other side of the field, fighting off more of the intruders.

I cut down two soldiers, Dacian by my side. Eshkan had stayed with Declan, teaching him the battle stance of a Serpent as the enemy drew near. I turned, shouting to Dacian amongst the sounds of horror. "Help me reach the door. If I can unbar it, then we can release the villagers!" I said. He nodded, killing another man as he ran towards us in rage. I stabbed my sword into the chest of one, ripping straight through his armor. Dacian and I cut our way to the door of the citadel. A large wooden square bar was propped against the door; two hook-like fixtures holding it up. It seems they had brought their own tools of destruction to our home.

"The fires, they have already begun to consume the door. I cannot touch the bar without burning my hands," Dacian shouted, pulling his second sword from the sheath on his back. Eshkan and Declan had climbed to a building to make use of Eshkan's bow. As it seemed I had an opening, I turned to the citadel door, looking down at my arm.

"I will remove it! Cover me!" I hoped that the Sun would save my skin and placed both hands on the bar, pushing up against it. It moved slightly and I pushed again, ignoring the pain it caused in my right arm. When I could no longer avoid the stimulation of pain, I backed up, taking one deep breath before I lifted my left arm to grasp it again. The bar began to rise, and I threw my arm aside, the bar following it. The few who survived were burned badly, their skin charred beyond recognition. They coughed and cried in pain, mourning over dead family members. I felt their sorrows flood out as I opened the door, black smoke pouring from the opening. Suddenly, the roof made a large creaking noise, and I backed away shouting, "It's coming down! Hurry!"

The victims began to move, their pained and raw limbs carrying them away from the site. A mother holding her baby against her skin had lines of pale flesh down her face from where her tears had carried the ashes down her chest. The horror of the sight we were all witnessing was becoming graver as the victims helped those who could not walk. I looked again to the citadel before heading up the hill, Dacian grabbing a small child whose legs were completely stripped. I now knew my enemy; he was relentless, mad. Just as his man said.

"What do we do now?" Dacian asked me, placing the child in the grass. The child looked up at him, thanking him before he collapsed against the ground, breathing heavily.

I continued to look at the damage around me, still thinking of what was yet to be done. I was instantly pulled from this thought when I felt a strong slap across my face. Keeping my composure, I watched as Morard pulled Cahya back, holding her arms behind her.

"You brought them here! They killed all those people!"

"Cahya, calm. I don't believe he brought them here. The marsh was empty upon his return," Morard answered.

"Don't let your grief take advantage of you. You know the suspicions we share. None followed me here. I made sure to cover my tracks and remove my scent in the Lake. Whoever told them to come here set it up to look like I am the enemy," I answered and took a breath, calming my sudden spike of rage. "The man whose eye you tore from his face. We found him. He told us his commander was insane. Searching for something that he would do anything to find," I answered.

Cahya finally calmed herself and pulled her arms from Morard's hold, angrily. She shook her head looking at the small boy lying in the meadow. Looking up at me, I could see the regret in her eyes. As she began to speak, I held my hands out before me to let her know that I understood her striking out, but it wasn't good enough for her.

"I'm sorry I assaulted you. It was not right of me. Seeing these innocent people burned and sent to death weighs heavily on my soul. I should have known better than to think anyone could have followed you," she answered and looked down again.

"Mend this later. We must keep moving. If we remain here too long, then they will likely find us. We should see if Vortain is still alive," Dacian said.

"You haven't attended to Lord Vortain?" Morard asked in a curious outrage.

"No. These people needed our help. Vortain has men to protect him in an attack like this. These people have us," Dacian answered.

Morard nodded and looked at the tower. "What do you suggest we do?" he asked.

"I suggest one thing," I answered. "We kill whoever remains there. Leave Savantin to me, but I want Jadoq alive," I answered.

"You're going to take your hatred out on him now that there is an opportunity?" Morard asked.

"No. I think he knows exactly how they've come to arrive," I answered and turned away, walking down the battered and shamed road toward the tower. The isle was eerie now, and it felt as if everyone was finally dead. I had no way of knowing if any of the burn victims lived through their injuries, or what they would do now that their homes, their lives, were in ruin. They had no one to look to for guidance now, the man that had promised them safety for their entire lives was now invisible amongst a land of peril and death. We continued to smell burning flesh, tearing through smoke and ash as we made it to the stones that symbolized the Trials of the Serpent. The courtyard looked the same as the rest of the island. It was painted in blood, ashes of what once were human beings spread among it. Upon the white stone of the stairwell leading to the tower, one of Vortain's guards rested, holding the gaping wound where his heart had been severed from his chest. He was motionless, his last breath of life was taken where he lay.

"He's there now," I answered and drew my sword.

"Don't charge, my brother. As of now we have the advantage of surprise," Dacian said, holding my arm back.

"We may be too late," I said and ran up the stairs, passing through the hallway. The tapestries had been torn down, Vortain's bodyguards laying in pieces about the corridor. I was beginning to become entranced by the heavy scent of blood all around me, and I could tell that my eyes were becoming darkened by my sudden wants. He was trying to weaken my mind by luring me through endless masses of blood. He knew his enemy well it seemed, and yet I knew next to nothing about him. Nearing Vortain's door, I raised my hand to push it open and found myself hesitating for a moment before proceeding.

It was like the rest of the isle, dark, destroyed, covered in blood. My master's corpse was lying on the ground, his face torn apart, covered in blood and yellowed juices from a wound that went through his skull. Even more confusing was that Jadoq lay a few feet from him, also torn apart and covered in his own liquids. His heart was also missing, just like the man at the base of the tower.

"Nothing remains," Declan said. "How do we know what happened?"

I walked toward Jadoq's body, looking through his stained robes and pockets. I finally found a small black book and tossed it to Cahya. "Let's see if our suspicions were correct," I answered.

Cahya nodded and opened it, looking at the words on the pages. "It was him," she answered after long as her eyes moved across the pages. "He was corresponding with him. There are letters here, from that monster... and someone else. It's a woman's handwriting, must be, only signed with the letter S. But even more troubling... there is word of a contract here. One for the entire force of Serpents… you were going to be sent to kill the King of Terrenveil," she answered.

Dacian spit upon Jadoq's corpse, and though I wish I had the satisfaction of killing him myself, I felt no need to do the same.

"There's something about you here… but there's something else, in a letter from the man… Savantin."

"What does it say?" I asked.

"It says that he had traveled through the different places where thieves are known to be residing, and he has not found it yet. Thing is, I don't know what *it* is," she answered.

"Keep reading. If we were supposed to be sent to kill the king, maybe his presence here is reason. But who is the woman?" Eshkan asked.

"Perhaps we can find something in Vortain's record room," I answered and moved my head aside in one jerk, signaling Dacian and Declan to come along with me. Eshkan nodded and waited silently with Cahya.

The room we entered had been ransacked, shelves thrown about, papers everywhere. Vortain's books hardly resembled themselves anymore, and bloody handprints covered multiple surfaces. Dacian moved to one of them and placed his hand over top of it, looking at me.

"How big is this man?" he asked, surprised at how large the handprint was. The print did not look like it belonged to any mortal.

"We will have to be careful when gauging him. I don't think we are dealing with just a man," I answered.

"What then?" he asked.

"I don't know. For a long time, the world believed all nonhumans to be exterminated. Perhaps we are dealing with a survivor," I answered.

"Halbane's curse. What have we gotten ourselves into?" Dacian asked, rhetorically. Whenever he brought up the religion of his people, I knew to remain silent. He was in a state of great thought and dismay at this moment, and the utterance of his religious customs marked it.

I looked at the table and noticed that beneath the chair, where the rug had been moved, there was the corner of something reflective. I pushed the chair aside and bent down, pulling it out from beneath the table, revealing a mosaic on the floor, and in the center of it, a small handle.

"Declan, get the others," I said, turning to him. As he obeyed, pointing to my position, I pulled on the handle. After a few tugs it became loose. They joined me shortly and I looked at the pattern of the crimson snake on the floor, surrounded by a ring of gold. A very intricate design. In all my time here, I had never seen anything as decorated.

"Let's see where this leads," I said and pulled the handle with force, up out of the floor, turning it around. The reflective stones began to turn outward from the pattern, the crimson of the snake and the black encircling it began to turn out and layer the golden ring. They suddenly receded until they left a large hole surrounding a set of stairs.

"What is this?" Morard asked suddenly.

"I'm not entirely sure yet. But I intend on finding out," I answered and pulled one of the torches off the wall, tossing it to Dacian.

"Cethin, do we follow?" he asked.

"I may need your assistance," I answered and began my descent.

Dacian nodded and looked at Eshkan, who readied his bow. Cahya readied her ax and Dacian looked at her instantly.

"Don't think that because I am not a Serpent that I cannot aid your cause," she said.

"Those weren't my thoughts at all Siress. My thoughts were of your lack of hesitation," Dacian answered.

Morard looked at him and slowly pulled his sword from its sheath. "We all go," he answered and walked to the edge of the steps, taking a breath before heading down them.

When they finally reached me, I held my hand up, stopping them before they stepped in front of me. "His men are here," I answered and pulled my sword slowly.

"What?!" Morard asked. "How could they have gained access to such a place?"

"It seems Jadoq's treachery was deeper in vein than we realized. Perhaps it is best we go ahead," I answered. "I'll scout ahead."

"Where should we await you?" Cahya asked. "Do you think it safe to wait here?"

"I don't think there are many of them left on the isle. Perhaps here is best," Morard answered.

I nodded, looking at Declan. "If more approach, make it to the tower," I said and signaled for the others to follow me. We walked in silence, crouching beneath a half wall.

"They're looking for something," Dacian said, watching them as they moved their torches toward the walls.

"But what?" I asked and moved forward, taking cover in the shadows they created. As one walked past, I lunged forward, grabbing his mouth and stabbing him in the chest, turning my sword so that it carved through his heart. I pulled him backward into the darkness, obscuring him from sight. As the next turned, drawing his weapon, an arrow sailed through the room, piercing his throat. Dacian vaulted the wall, checking the man's pockets.

"Nothing," he answered.

"This one has something," I said and stood, pulling a small trinket carved from bone. "There's a symbol. Vortain was right. They're looking for artifacts of power."

"Voices, down the hall," Eshkan answered and strung his bow. I nodded and turned toward the shadows, Dacian creeping forward.

"Do you think anything is really down there?" one of the men asked as they neared, the light of their flames illuminating the entryway of the room.

"Savantin wants every corner checked. He does not care how long it takes us."

"It would be a lot easier if he told us what he was looking for."

"He wants anything relative to the culture here. He himself will decide what is important and what is not," his counterpart fired back. Dacian looked to Eshkan who nodded, and he sprung forward, cutting the closest to him down at the knees and cutting his head from his body. Eshkan landed another shot, dropping the other. I moved forward then, approaching the entrance, carefully listening for movement. Upon hearing none, I waved the others forward, entering the next chamber. More of them, a few sets this time, examining the coffins that lined the room. Two had already been opened, the corpses inside looted of belongings. Eshkan strung his bow with two arrows, aiming toward the back of the room. He nodded toward us, and we rushed forward as he let them go, taking out two guards. I chose three men on the left, side stepping carefully as I watched their movements. As one attacked, I parried him, avoiding the strike of another. He overstepped his position, and I plunged my blade into his back, pulling it out and forward to block the next assault. Kicking him in the stomach, I moved my blade behind my head, listening to the sound of steel on steel. Moving my body but not my sword, I slid my blade downward to become unlocked. I pushed him forward and flipped my blade to my other hand, to sever his arm from his body. I turned to my other opponent, an arrow hitting him in the head just as he had reached me. Looking toward Eshkan, I bowed my head in gratitude and turned toward the downed man who was cursing as he held his injury. Blood leaked from him quickly, covering his remaining hand.

"That is for desecrating our ancestors," I stated and pushed his sword across the room. "And this is for what you've done to those people." I slashed him across the throat, leaving him as he fell to the floor in a quick death, the gurgling sounds ceasing. Dacian had dispatched the remaining two, placing his fist over his heart as his eyes came across the burials.

"Despicable," he said, and reached into the armor of his dead, recovering the medallions of Serpents and placing them on each coffin.

"We should hurry," Eshkan stated and moved forward, an arrow ready for launch. "There's no telling what else they are doing down here. Looting is a dishonor they ignore. If there is anything else here, they will find it."

We moved to the next chamber with haste. Torches had been left in the sconces on the walls, the scent of smoke heavy in the air. "They've moved from here, very recently. It smells as if these had just been lit," I said and looked toward my forearm where the Sun was speaking wildly in my head.

"How far does this lead?" Dacian asked, looking around the room.

"Be sure we've made no mistake in coming here. I don't mean to sound rash, but if we perish, then who will save the others from their fates?" Eshkan said.

I nodded. "Our fates are all the same now, to die by his hand or to destroy it. There is no running, no hiding in the shadow. He will either find what he is looking for or die when he has it in his hands. We've seen his determination."

"But sheer determination cannot win him his desires," Dacian answered.

"Did you see what he did to our home? With just twenty men and a skulking rat? It is not his determination that will win him his desire but his command," I answered. "It is best we do not underestimate our enemy. This time, we are not the most powerful force about," I answered. I had suddenly realized how harsh I sounded, but Dacian did not take it to heart.

Eshkan had already moved ahead, slowly reaching the hall to the north of us. He had his bow still strung, looking at the sconces of the room and up into the roof. "This place is older than the tower itself. Look at the stonework on the walls. It's Brisleng and Moonstone. They stopped using Brisleng in the second age. The tower is made of Winestone," Eshkan said and began to scratch a part of the wall with his nail. "The outer coating is soft. This place must be hundreds of years old. Maybe even a thousand."

"How is it so preserved?" Dacian asked.

"Is the origin of the Serpents that old?" I asked, looking at the carvings in the wall.

"Vortain said seven hundred. At the beginning of his family. His ancestor was a serpent himself, but they branched away from the practice and began to show interest in the slave trade. That is why it is the way it is now. The master teaches, and his serpents are students," Eshkan answered.

"Do you think any of us ever made it here before?" I said, almost captivated by the glory of just how old the room was. Before now I hadn't given much thought to how long our legacy had been, or where we were on its timeline.

"No, especially since it was hidden beneath Vortain's records room. A room that only he is allowed to see. Not even Jadoq was allowed passage inside," Eshkan answered. I was surprised he of all was still using the traitor's name. I'd never asked him what his relationship with Vortain was like, knowing it was a very close one. I knew he was hurting, though he held the pain of loss well.

"More of them, just ahead," Dacian answered.

"Leave them to me," Eshkan said and descended the stairs in silence, raising his bow and firing. He quickly strung another arrow and took down the second guard before he realized his comrade had fallen. Their torches fell, Dacian moving forward to grab them. As he had, part of the floor fell in front of him, and he propelled himself backward. I began to breathe deeply, trying to silence the Sun, which had not stopped chanting since we had entered the tomb. It was eager for use. I closed my eyes, moving my hand outward and toward the fallen flame. It had quickly jumped into my grasp, and I curved my palm, wincing slightly at the feeling of sudden heat. It extinguished suddenly, my hand still feeling warmth. Dacian looked on in bewilderment, and Eshkan only allowed himself to look but for a moment, using the light to scan the path ahead.

"There is a sconce on the wall, just there," he said and pointed. "The floor doesn't seem to have given way too much. We can still cross in safety," he said, sparking my curiosity on what was beneath us. I lit the sconce, my brothers careful in their steps to reach me.

"The path ahead seems quiet," Dacian said and peered onward.

"There is something about this room... it's emptiness that interests me," Eshkan answered.

"Should we press on?" I asked.

"A moment. I would like to make note of what is on the walls." I stopped, allowing Eshkan to continue with his investigation. This place was strange, old and undoubtedly full of secrets. My eyes wandered to Seligsara and I found myself staring at the hilt, the beautiful reddish black stone that made up most of the handle, surrounded by a piece of black metal that was said to be forged by Zerian himself. Beyond the beauty of the sword was the Sun itself, lodged in my arm by an old man. I recently acquired two very important pieces of Sardon history, yet I did not know our language. I should be ashamed, should feel weak, yet I could not. I would not allow myself. It still held a heavy weight in my mind, after all, how was I supposed to be the last Bloodheir if I did not know how to fight and be as our ancestor himself? That was hard to grasp. Bloodheir. I was not raised among my family, my race, was not even given the rites of passage as a Sardon warrior. How could I be one of the last remaining Bloodheirs of Zerian if I was cast away from my home and made to grow up with a human in the fishing villages far from Morrenvahl?

I continued to mull over the thoughts in my mind, looking absentmindedly toward the ground as Eshkan grasped one of the fallen torches, walking the walls in silence. I could tell Dacian's eyes came across me, staring at me. I could almost hear his thoughts, wondering why I was standing here in a seemingly thoughtless or even pensive stare. He continued on, however, leaving me to the demands of my mind. I closed my eyes now, focusing on what my brother had said to me earlier. That even, was a concept that I believed a delusion. This man had claimed himself to be my brother, my kin, someone of the same blood. This meant another Sardon who was Bloodheir. This could either be an opportunity or a trap. Perhaps this man who made such claims was not a friend at all, but an enemy, after what had just been given to me. It seemed relevant; people were after the Black Sun of Zerian.

Eshkan hurriedly called us over to a portion of the wall where he discovered a pressure plate behind an empty torch sconce. He motioned for Dacian to find something to fit inside and walked toward the other side of the room where a table and several tools sat. He returned shortly with what appeared to be the leg of a chair. Eshkan examined it, looking it once over quickly before shrugging and sliding it into the sconce. It seemed he had pleased it, as a portion of the wall slid back, creating a deep scraping sound as it retreated permanently.

"Shall we close it back up behind us? Prevent anyone entry?"

"We should see if there is another way out before we do so. We could end up sealing ourselves in. We would die down here without anyone knowing where we were. You and I would probably end up Cethin's meal before he met his own death. That does not sound like the kind of fate I would enjoy," Eshkan answered.

Dacian looked at me and then at Eshkan, moving forward in silence. Dacian had a great amount of trust and respect for me, but at the same, once I am pushed to my limits, I am no more civilized than a starved animal. This he knew, but often forgot. As we walked into the hallway leading from the ceremonial room, I watched grimly as the light began to dissipate. Would it follow us here as it had before? Or was our blessing at its end? I braced myself for what lay ahead, hoping that my speculation of the placement of the corpses was correct. If the men that rested here were only bones, then our worries were none.

The path was desolate, eerie and quiet, as the hall to a tomb should be. No one had been down this far in hundreds of years, and the condition reflected that entirely. I wondered what this place looked like years ago, the fade on the walls indicated that they once held a paint of probably a light blue color, adorned in gold etchings as shown by the interesting façade where wall meets ceiling. Perhaps it smelled once of musk and spices as the tower did, wreaths of burning flowers and herbs presented at the foot of every coffin bed for the safe passage into Basilin's realm of glory. I could imagine the priests carrying them softly down this hallway, treading lightly in their thin shoes made of animal hide. But that was a very long time ago, before the people of these lands settled past the marsh and all that belonged were the tribes of the tundra. As we walked farther and farther down the hall, it became dark, until the silence of the hall became larger, deeper. We entered a chamber at that moment, and I quickly moved my hand to my sword. I held my breath listening to nothing but the countless beats of my heart.

"What is it do you think they stored here?" Dacian asked, looking at the scrolls on small ledges of the wall.

"Records of some sort?" Eshkan guessed, moving the torch with care toward them. He looked at me with quiet anticipation. "This is no records chamber. It's a burial hall," I answered, looking down a dark corridor, seeing what looked to be coffins and decorative jars. I could hear something within the next chamber, and I carefully pressed my back to the wall, looking around the corner of it. My sight had not failed me. There were large stone slabs that looked like coffins, with large jars atop them. Adorning the jars were Scalestone and pearl, both expensive and hard to come across in this region. I was beginning to wonder what bond was held on this place, and as soon as I had thought it, my question was met.

We entered and a breeze tore through the corridor behind us, causing the lids to fall off the jars. Black ashes swirled from them, forming soldiers before us, adorned with armor of the Serpents put to rest. "Who trespasses in the tomb of the Serpents?" one asked, his voice grim and dark.

"We do not trespass here," Dacian answered.

The soldiers instantly turned to Dacian, one of them walking toward him slowly. "This one's a Serpent, and the one with the bow," the soldier said, walking past Eshkan. I could now smell their armor, tarnished from hundreds of years of rot.

"Then what are they doing here?" another asked. "We can surely kill them for their trespasses."

"Wait," I answered, holding my hand up in front of my heart. If we had all had the same training through time, they would know it was a sign of peace. "We do not mean to intrude on your grave, ancestor. We are here because someone has betrayed the Master family, and we must find note of whatever the man was looking for."

"Someone betrayed the Master family, and the Serpents were not his aid? Hmph. No honor left."

"We could not aid him, because we are the three who remain. Our den brothers were killed in their sleep. This was found near their water supply. I think they were poisoned," I answered and tossed a pouch to one of them.

The soldier looked inside and dipped his finger in it, tasting it. He made a face instantly and tossed the pouch back to me. "A variation of Rythran, though I'm not sure which. An apothecary could tell you where it came from."

"How could someone have poisoned the water supply without one of us taking notice?" Eshkan asked.

"Jadoq likely had opportunity when he oversaw the amount of food our brothers were being given," I answered.

"You," the lead soldier asked, pointing to me. "Lower your cloak. I wish to see your face," he continued.

I placed my hand over my heart and did as I was commanded, hearing cries from the other soldiers. "What has he done? A Sardon? Blasphemy."

"I know I am not of tradition. Until today I thought I was leaving this place behind to be free, to travel where I want and on my own volition. But with what happened to this place, once my home, I decided I will do whatever it takes to find out why and punish the one responsible. They stand with me," I answered.

"You say one man did all of this?"

"The one who led the murderers here is dead, fell by something he summoned but couldn't control. We fought most of those the summoned left behind, but he was not among those dead," I answered.

"You have a fire within you; I see it behind your eyes, even as you speak to us in peace. It is troubling, but then it brings much hope."

"This fire was extinguished by years of discipline and higher thought but has been reset by the hatred and lies that have recently befallen us," I answered.

"You may pass within our halls, but once you've reached the inner chamber, you will discover if you are worthy enough to retrieve the most sacred of our honors," he answered.

"Wait," Eshkan said.

The soldiers looked at him and complied in silence.

"There were letters, correspondence between the traitor and the murdered. In these letters, a box is described. You wouldn't happen to know anything about that would you? Is it here?" he asked.

"I can tell no one the secrets of this tomb. Those who have already passed the trials may enter, and find out for themselves," he answered. With those last words, the five soldiers became ash again, clouds flying to their respective jars. Their lids clasped on tightly, one of the jars shaking slightly as it leveled itself out.

"They cannot reveal the secrets, but we may search," Eshkan stated. "Vague, but straightforward."

"Perhaps they are best left," I answered. "If all of this was to find a box, it must be something formidable."

"Then shouldn't we find it? To make certain that no one else does?" Dacian asked.

"He left without it, which makes me think that it isn't here," I stated and took a deep breath. "The inner chamber, they mentioned the most sacred of their honors. Does this seem something worth gaining amid this?"

"We have already made it this far," Eshkan stated.

"And without answers. There is much to be done," I stated.

"I agree with Eshkan. We are the last remaining Serpents. The very last. We do not know whether or not we will be successful in putting down this menace. I know I would regret never seeing what rested here if I were to fall in battle."

I nodded, understanding his sentiment. "Then we enter."

At the end of the chamber was a large door, the gold patternings that were once vibrant in color were dulled, missing in some portions. I wondered why it hadn't been tended to, and what the reason was for what seemed to be hundreds of years of abandon. Eshkan placed his hands on the rings of the door and pulled them open, different air rushing to our lungs. This room held amber light within it, one that seemed to be its own entity, sustained by nothing but itself. As we walked toward where the light was strongest, we heard a breath and suddenly the stones that composed the back part of the wall turned, revealing a coffin with a decorative sword sitting on top. The door slowly closed behind us, the sound of stone scraping on stone.

"Vortain's ancestor... the first of the serpents..." Eshkan said slowly, falling to his knees. I couldn't tell if it was in relief, or to pay respect to the first of us. I slowly made my way to my own, bowing my head in the direction of the coffin, and standing only after I placed my hand over my heart.

"This is the ancestral sword. The one that the First himself used as he created and brought glory to our lineage." Eshkan said.

"You should take it," I said suddenly, looking toward him. He looked at it with wide, peaceful eyes, as if he had just met his creator.

"I dare not. Though it was revealed to us I feel it too sacred a weapon for me. It was said to have been crafted from pieces of the Lord Basilin himself... How could any of us wield such a thing?"

"Because we are all that is left. If not us, then who? Who will ever hold it again?" I said.

"No one. It will rest here," he answered, still not removing his eyes from it.

"For undying centuries. This tower will crumble of dormancy, become overtaken by the native plants of this land until some other finds it. Someone unworthy," I remarked.

"It should go with us," Dacian said out of silence.

"Then you should take it Dacian. You were the one to first seal a bond of companionship with Cethin, a companionship that holds the remaining of us together to this day. While the rest of us mistrusted, feared, avoided, you were the one to uphold the true honors of brotherhood and never look past him for anything other than being a Serpent," Eshkan answered.

Dacian nodded. He took the sword, staring at it in his hands. The blade was beautifully crafted, a silver blade housed by a green hilt of stone carved to resemble a snake, blue gems within the eyes. There was a sense of wonder in Dacian's, humbled that he was holding a piece of something that meant so much.

Eshkan looked at me suddenly, speaking in a deep and recently unburied emotion. "Cethin, I am sorry that I was not more like Dacian when we lived for all those years in peace on this isle. Please forgive me, and may we live to fight together in friendship and courage, or may we die at each other's sides as true kin," he said.

I looked at him and he held out his hand. We grabbed each other's forearms and gave a strong nod before removing touch and looking over to Dacian. "I am honored to wield such a weapon."

"Then this choice was the right one," Eshkan answered.

Dacian placed his sword beside the coffin, resting a hand against it in thanks, and turned to us in silence.

"Now, let us find a way out," I answered.

"Happily," Eshkan said and looked around. "There are so many doors. We could be down here for a very long time."

"This door isn't moving," I said and looked to where we entered. There was nothing on the walls that suggested it was operable.

Dacian looked at each door leading elsewhere, examining their frames. "There are symbols on each. Though I've no idea what they mean."

Eshkan moved a torch to them, stopping at the door farthest left. "This one," he answered. "This one leads to the grave of Syamet."

"Syamet?"

"She was... one of the first. But the legends say that she was buried alive."

"Buried alive?" I asked, walking toward the door and looking at the top of it.

"When trying to familiarize myself with the history, master took everything he had about her and burned it. We will need to be strong if we are to leave this place."

"There is no other way?"

"The other doors will all likely lead nowhere. Tespet. Merren. Aeyesh. Gerut. Sce. Syamet. Yeshten," Eshkan said, moving his torch to each door until he stopped in the center of the room. "Master seemed very serious about this. The others were at rest before they were placed into their chambers."

"At rest?" Dacian asked. "You mean to tell me that we're about to enter a tomb of a wight?"

"As I said, all that is known to me is that she was buried alive, the records were burned. He warned me that no good would come of investigating it further, only concluding our meeting by saying that if Ophidian were to ever fall, he hoped this would fall with it."

"Perfect," I answered and sheathed Seligsara. "So, we've no idea what awaits us on the other side."

"One final trial," Dacian said, his sword still in hand. Eshkan closed his eyes and took a breath, resting his hand over the lever for a second before pulling it. Air rushed outward as the stone door slid into the roof. The symbols scrawled on the door with chalk disappearing with it.

"The binds are severed. Let us do this quickly," Eshkan answered.

The old torches that lined the walls took a weary flame, revealing a hallway of skeletons. Eshkan placed his own torch to the wall, shaking his head and standing upright.

Fingernail marks. They were trying to escape."

"What happened here?" Dacian asked.

"Only two ever entered a chamber prepared for one of the newly fallen," Eshkan stated. "Or so was reported. The bodies were wrapped in oiled cloth, set inside their coffins by a chosen two who burned incense to line the halls before leaving. This... something terrible happened here."

"Keep focused," I answered. "I don't think we're alone."

The room opened into a circular shape, half-written symbols on the floor covered in the bones of seven men. The walls were covered in burn marks, a few of them leading to a small hallway beyond it.

"What is this place?" Dacian asked, moving toward the center of the room where a small black stone pillar stood, a bangle sitting on top of it. It was made from gold and appeared large enough to sit around an upper arm. Another gold band in the form of a snake was wrapped around it in different directions, its head pointing downward, when if worn, would point toward the elbow. It had two shining gems in it that were yellow in color.

"Her belonging," Eshkan said. "Each Serpent was entombed with a belonging. Yeshten and his sword. This must be hers. There is no coffin... no diffusers of incense..." Eshkan began. "She was being punished... but for what?"

Dacian looked toward him, and I looked around the room. Claw marks on the walls from the fingernails of the dead. Skeletons were in piles, weapons old and dusty by their hands.

"This isn't a burial chamber. They brought her here to die, to kill her," Eshkan said.

"Kill her?"

"Think about it. Every Serpent sent into the afterlife, to Basilin, had a very specific burial ritual. Even those for centuries after this tomb, up in the tower. Each had a belonging to take with them, set inside the coffin. Incense to mask the scent of death as they passed through to the other side. There is no coffin, so one of these sets of bones belongs to her. She was being punished… but for what?"

"They didn't kill her," I said and crouched down to a set of bones. "But it doesn't look like any of these bones have been fractured."

"It's obvious they wanted to escape, look at the walls," Dacian said. He moved his torch toward the back of the door, more scratch marks along it.

"And it's obvious master wanted this place to be forgotten," Eshkan returned, walking toward the pillar. "Whatever happened here… we should look for an exit, and quickly."

Dacian moved to the bangle now, moving his torch close to it. The light radiated caused me to turn my head aggressively toward the wall on my left. I closed my eyes tight, holding to darkness for a few moments. Opening them slowly, I blinked several times to try and regain sight. The room had brightened significantly, perfectly revealing the scars on the walls. There were marks from a blade in the back of the door, a set of bones beneath it.

"Look," Dacian uttered as he moved to the far wall, pointing to where something was written on the wall with the tip of a blade. "There will be no light enough to stop the will of his kin."

"That is not of our world," Eshkan said quietly.

"Why would the way out be in this room?" I asked and walked along the far wall. "These men were sealed inside this room; they couldn't get out. The plan was that she wouldn't either, must be, or else these men wouldn't have been sent here to kill her. To be forgotten among the ancient bones of the dead."

"Which is precisely why Vortain would place something like that here," Dacian said. To that I offered a nod. It sounded painfully characteristic.

"So, it's here, but it won't be located without labor. But if she knew Vortain as well as we do, or as well as he's allowed us to know him, he wouldn't risk it."

"Sent to a chamber to be slain by those closest to her doesn't sound like the fate of someone he'd want escaping," I said.

"Those closest?" Dacian asked.

"Serpents. Look at the pendants on the floor," I said and reached over, pulling one up from the ash. It glistened against the light from the torch, from the slowly dimming bangle. "Cruel, if you think about it. Sealing them all in here to kill one another. Why not execute her like he did with Renma?"

"Because Renma was a traitor. This isn't a traitor's death, it's… something else."

"We'll never know," Dacian said. "It's not our mystery to solve." He received nothing but a raised eyebrow glance from Eshkan and silence from me, which caused him to look up and shake his head. "Knowing you, it's ours now," he muttered. "And you?" he asked, turning to me.

"This will likely be the last time any of us will be here. Might as well," I said.

"This place was supposed to be forgotten."

"I'm not planning on ever bringing it to conversation," I answered simply and walked toward the far wall. "Her bones are here somewhere. We should find them and put them to rest."

"A noble gesture."

"A cautious one." Drawing back to the story of the ghosts on the cliff in Harbortow. They could find no bones to bury or consecrate. "You know Basilin's prayer for the fallen better than any."

"That would not help. I don't think she remained to this world any longer," Eshkan said. "I've found them."

I joined him in crouching down toward the floor, Dacian approaching with his torch. "Her teeth. Pointed all around from the fourth and back. Before you there were no non-human Serpents. Vortain's family did not trust them. Most people didn't."

"What then?"

"The only non-humans with the power to transfigure to this degree, that I'm aware of anyway, are Viscera. Would make sense why she was brought here. But something doesn't feel right about that. A Viscera cannot be trapped," Eshkan said. "They are fearsome, being able to project their soul into another form, causing its death as their bodies follow. When master left the tower at times, times I was not ordered to be his shadow, I read some of the tomes. Interesting really, I could go back and procure some."

"In all your travels you have not heard of this? There will be no light enough to stop the will of his kin?" I asked.

"Not that I can remember, and that's not something one forgets," Eshkan said. I sighed, and headed back into Yeshten's tomb, grabbing a bundle of tied up herbs.

"What are you doing?" Dacian asked.

"Giving her peace," I said as I entered, and crouched down, accessing the pile of bones. After a few moments I placed them on top of her. "She might have died as something else but in life she was the same." I stood from the bones, looking up at the back wall to the rightmost corner. "That stone is different."

The others turned their heads as well, Dacian moving his torch to reveal a patch of gray among the dusty brown room.

"Search the corners," Eshkan said and walked beneath the gray stone. "That must be a different part of the tower completely."

"It may be the only way out," Dacian said and led his torch along the wall, stopping at a crack in it. "Looks like it could give way."

I looked up at the wall, the crack stopping after eight feet. "It's not touching the roof. Let us break it."

"It's weak, already crumbling. I see wood on the other side," Dacian replied, grabbing a small wooden beam off the ground. He hit the wall several times, the stone beginning to chip and crumble away. After the next few hits, I moved to the wall, pulling loose chunks of stone away as he continued to hit them.

"Is it... is it a bookshelf?" Eshkan asked and moved forward, helping to pull the stone away. Once an opening large enough to pass through was clear, we kicked in the wooden barrier, revealing itself to be just as Eshkan suspected.

"A punishment shack... It makes sense, but why on this side of the caves?" he asked, looking around at the tools.

"Perhaps this was a punishment itself. Cursed to torture but being tortured as well."

"Either way, we're free," I said. "Let us go."

Eshkan nodded and moved inward, lending me his strength. The old iron door gave way, placing us in the shallowing caves on the far side of the compound nearest the prison.

"I always knew there was something more to this place," Dacian answered and looked toward the ceiling, water dripping from the jagged rock formations above.

"Other than punishment and pain? I suppose it was the best place to hide a secret such as this," I stated and stepped across the long planks of rock, bolts attached every few feet. They were still wet from the river, which retreated for unspecified amounts of time. "No one would enter this place willingly." As the last word left my tongue, I could taste the water in my lungs from being chained to the stone, being helpless for days. My brothers said nothing to me as we returned to the tower. Morard had not moved from his position, and the others sitting upon the stairs.

"So... what did you find?" Morard asked.

"Nothing short of a sword. We have more important matters to attend to," I answered.

"Indeed," he returned, taking time to observe each one of us.

"Are there any of your guard left alive?"

Morard shook his head. "No. Whoever escaped the fires were nailed to the doors of the barracks. We are all that is left. Not even the prisons were left unscathed. They either killed or drowned anyone inside.

"The prisoners?"

"Every last one of them. I had been there before I found Cahya. She said the infirmary suffered the same fate."

"As did our den brothers," I answered. "There are too many of them to carry to where the lifeless sleep."

"It would be dishonorable to leave them," Dacian said.

"We're not left with much choice," I stated.

"Let's have a look," Eshkan said and began toward the Den. My thoughts shifted to my enemy. The mystery accomplice was who I wanted to pursue. Though it seemed impossible now. Planning an assassination was pushed to the forefront of my mind as we reached the Den.

Dacian opened the door and moved his face downward, as if trying to overcome his sudden sadness. Everything was in its place, the goblets on the table, and the knives on the wall. The powder that the ancient Serpent had called Rythran was only vaguely on the table's surface now. It had to have been what caused their sleep through the entrance of the intruders. Damn Jadoq's very soul. I wish I could raise his corpse so he could suffer death a second time, but I felt as if what he went through initially was worse than anything I could dispense. An image of his corpse flashed back into my mind, four pieces of clothed meat lying on the ground, heart missing. Eshkan bent down to one of our brothers, turning him over to clearly see his chest. He placed his hands on either side of it, moving his head to either side.

"This was cut in by a molten blade. It was almost cauterized after it was cut, but they were stabbed in their throats. They bled out in seconds, probably felt the beginning of these scars." Eshkan cursed and stood from the corpse, pushing the chair in angrily at the table. "This was a strong poison if it rendered them helpless."

"Eshkan, the symbol... have you seen it before?" I asked.

"No. I have not. But I know where we can go to discover what it means," he answered and turned to me, moving his arm outward toward the door. We reached the edge of the compound, Cahya striding up to my side.

"Earlier," she said, her voice soft.

"It still tears at you," I answered, a nod in reply. I took a deep breath in and looked toward the trees. "Don't let it. It's behind you, behind us."

"I still can't believe they're all gone." She looked toward the grove, petals taking the skies to join with the embers. I knew she hoped the trees would survive the flames. They were what she enjoyed most about the Isle.

"It'll be answered in due time."

"That doesn't make it hurt less," she stated and shook her head, tears coming from her eyes.

"Nothing will," I answered and moved my hand to them, wiping her tears.

Eshkan led us to the stables, looking around it in frustration. The large stable was destroyed, its foundation now merely pieces of charred wood in the ground surrounded by ash. Despite this, there were no signs of horses. Perhaps they had taken them for use as their own supply.

"What do you suggest we do now?" Dacian asked.

"I've not figured it out yet. We cannot walk to Defaltor."

The City of Thieves. A place where everyone was suspicious, yet upheld honor to a code that no one dared to break. Their leader was said to be vengeful and would hire blades to track and kill whoever had crossed him during their stay in his city. An idea I was against, but the possible lead on Savantin's accomplice was in the hands of Eshkan, now.

We made it to the southern part of the island, where the water was shallow enough to cross back onto the mainland. Declan found several horses corralled together and set off to retrieve them. They must have run when they saw the first of the fires.

The instinct for survival in animals was astounding, to know and feel the presence of death. Declan returned, holding the reins of several of them. As he neared me, they began to stir, neighing and snorting softly.

"They seem frightened, but other than that, fit for travel," he answered and handed reins to Cahya and Morard. "There is another horse farther in the marsh, she will not respond to commands."

"How many horses are there? Enough?" Eshkan asked.

"If we retrieve the frightened mare then yes, if not, one of us will have to share a horse," he answered.

"I will get her," Dacian answered, and moved forward.

"Maybe I should," I said, putting my hand on his chest. "Not all animals react to me well. Perhaps if I can convince her, she will come." As I walked out toward the marsh, I held my hand out in front of me, moving slowly to see if she would let me grab her reins without trying to protect herself. She began to whinny and huff as the others had, moving her feet in a nervous shuffle. I spoke to her calmly, making my voice seem as soft as possible. When I reached her, she became progressively louder, but when I continued to speak, she began to calm. I finally grabbed her reins and used the saddle to climb on her back, giving her a soft stroke or two down her mane. She was nervous, I would have to be gentle with this one. I didn't want to make a wrong move and have her attempting to throw me from her back. When I met with the others, they had already chosen their mounts, and were eager to travel ahead.

"Do any of you want to turn away now?" I asked, looking upon their faces which met me with surprise. "Vortain is dead. There are no expectations. No tasks to carry out. Nothing to plan. You're free, now. We don't have to stay here."

"I will aid as much as I can to see this monster slain," Morard answered, and looked toward Cahya who did not move her eyes from the woods ahead. I knew she would not turn from this path.

Not now. I now looked to Declan, who was hesitantly rolling the reins of his horse in his hands.

"Declan?" I asked.

He waited a moment before speaking and finally looked up at me. "I will travel with you as long as the road remains favorable to my direction. But when our paths diverge, I will go to Aubergrun, and make a life there," he answered.

"Among the priests?" Dacian asked.

"Mine is not a life of war. I was born into life on this isle, and while I've never resented it, I've never enjoyed watching the killing either. I have never ended a man's life, and am not fit to do so," Declan answered.

"Did your family perish in the fires?"

"My family died long ago. My father died trying to escape. My mother passed away while giving birth to my sister. She also did not live to see past that day."

Dacian nodded and quieted. "My apologies. It was not my intention to bring to mind memories so foul."

"It was long ago. I was raised in the orphanage, outside the grove nearest the village," he said, becoming occupied in a thought. His face created a small smile, and straightened to showcase sudden pain, as if feeling the emptiness of death once more.

"Where do we head from here?" Cahya asked, pulling the reins of her horse tightly as if to calm the steed.

"We go north. Once we reach the Talimas road, we will go east. Defaltor should be reached by next sundown," Eshkan answered, and turned his horse in that direction to ride off. The mounts were a strike of luck I was not anticipating. It would have taken days to reach the City of Thieves on foot. Acquiring horses there would have been a hindrance, as performing tasks enough to gather six would take long months. Time we did not have. Ever more troubling was the thought of being assailed on the roads. My thoughts moved to my race back to Ophidian from Arriksmad, and to the priest who had interjected on my behalf. I had hoped he wouldn't be the next to fall.

"How is it you know of this place?" Cahya asked.

"I spent most of my time away from the isle. I would visit cities, some far from Cilevdan. Cethin can tell us of the time he spent in Adenza. It was very different from mine; I can assure you." Eshkan laughed. "I was the cartographer, the informant, the eyes of Vortain away from his land."

"I can only imagine the wonders you've seen," she replied.

"We will be spending much time on the roads together. I see no better way to pass the time than to speak of them."

"You did all of this for him willingly? You never ran?" Cahya asked.

"I arrived at the island a boy. Fifteen years old. One night was calmer than most, though very cold. It was the middle of winter, but we were able to build fires long into the night without the winds rushing to defeat them. My mother was cooking dinner when we heard the first of the screams. Monsters. Descending on us from the ridge ahead. We didn't know where the guards had gone, we assumed they were somehow killed. We grabbed our weapons, used only to hunt and to protect ourselves from the other tribes if need be. I grabbed my sister and was told to stay inside while my mother put out the fire. She opened the flaps to the shelter, and smiled at us before she was torn away by one of the beasts. My sister screamed. I tried to cut the back of the shelter open before they made it inside, but it was useless. One of them made off with her, and in seeing the bloodbath that became of my village, I started running. I made it past the edge of the mountains, to the lake of ice. I almost made it to where it had melted, and at this point could see the isle. I twisted my ankle severely while trying to jump into the water, one of them grabbing onto my leg. When I thought, I was going to die, arrows came from the trees, killing the monsters. A man came down from the branches and picked me up, carrying me across the courtyard and up into the tower. Jadoq, he was the one who said I should be killed, that I was useless and that my injury would only put the rest of the village at risk. It was Vortain who had decided to spare my life and train me. If I had decided to run, no one would ever find me. He taught me to not only be a serpent, to strike from the shadow, but he taught me to be the shadow itself. That was twenty years ago. My life will be spent to avenge him," Eshkan answered.

"It seems as if we all have a story that ties us here," Cahya answered.

Morard nodded, but said nothing.

"He was a good man," Dacian answered and took a breath, petting along the neck of his horse. "The story of how I came to be here would be unbelievable, had Eshkan not seen it with his own eyes."

"Ah, Tzukari. One of my more interesting summers."

"I was born son to a house servant of one of the land barons in Tzukari. No one knew who my father was. But at five years old, my mother was killed, and with no father, the baron decided he was going to sell me at the market stall in Asan. I didn't know why Eshkan was there, but he was in the market the day I was to be shown to potential clients. He ended up tricking the baron into selling me to him for a steed he didn't have, and we left the city six days later. I learned from him, as we had to avoid any of the baron's men on the streets." Dacian laughed. "I remember the look on Vortain's face when Eshkan arrived with a small child in the tower."

"'I asked for a staff and you brought me a boy,'" Eshkan said. "His exact words. I was scouting the city for rumors about the Staff of Mieranza. After finding a fruitless few, I saw Dacian while passing the market. After our return, he showed Vortain all he learned from me in that week we spent together."

"Even taught me the native tongue of Terrenveil, Cilevdan," Dacian said and smiled, closing his eyes. "I remember being in the study for hours of the day. I taught him phrases in Tzukarian that we would use when Jadoq was around. He would get so angry. They were nothing of importance. What capacity of language did a young boy have? I would train with Eshkan in stealth and with blade until I was old enough to train with the Serpents. I owe my life not to Vortain, but to Eshkan. It's true, Vortain was like a father to me. But it is because of Eshkan that I still breathe."

"I did not know this side of him," Morard stated. "I rarely saw the man. I'd see Jadoq most. Angrily storming about the mess halls in search of Cahya or Czejane."

"Czejane," Cahya gasped. Morard shook his head and Cahya inhaled, her eyes closed to acknowledge the loss.

"Honorably, Cahya."

"Eshkan. What is our plan once we make it to Defaltor?" I asked, looking toward Cahya in sympathy.

"I have contacts there. There will be food and water provided to us. While this sounds benevolent, I advise you to stay within walls. The city itself is dangerous. Its keeper does not like violence within the walls, but we will be among those who make their own way in the world and survive by any means necessary. I suggest we take care to hide anything of value from sight."

"So, we are to stay concealed while you look for answers?" Cahya asked and rode ahead to flank Eshkan. "It is my will and wish to assist."

"Trust me, you do not want to wander about the city with us. Relax. Take some time to rest. We have all survived something truly terrible."

Even though she nodded, I knew she did not like his suggestion. She hardly rested. The nights she did not sleep, she suffered nightmares. Cruel visions, inability to escape. I hoped the road ahead would offer her peace. Though peace seemed an unachievable concept.

We began to travel through what became the Forest of Glendoryn. Much different now, as the season began its steady change. As we passed the Lake of Knights, we began to hear the growls and voices of the Vix, which were rumored to crawl up from beneath the mirrored waters of the lake to hunt. So long as we kept the fire tended, our horses would not become targets. They were restless, pawing at the ground and watching the trees. I looked toward Cahya, who was sitting close to the flame, staring into it with sadness in her eyes. I stood to go to her, Morard sitting at her side. I was hesitant in approaching. I wanted to console her, but I knew the guard's general dislike of me. I pushed the thought away, joining them alongside the blaze. Morard quieted, Cahya looked toward me and managed a smile.

"I was just telling Morard that beyond this canopy there is a cover of stars. The passage of time is unchanged by the events that take place," she said and sighed.

"Do you wish to see them?" I asked.

"The edge of the forest is far from here," Cahya answered. I stood and held my hand outward, offering it to her. "We needn't reach the edge."

She smiled, placing her hand in mine. I pulled her upward, leading her past the horses and into the night where my senses took lead. There was a clearing close by, one I used to lead my own horse to when I passed through here. The thick trees gave way, the clearing lit with the light of the moon. Fireflies performed their dance above the grass, searching for their ladies in waiting.

"The moon," Cahya stated and pointed upward. "It's a different color tonight."

I looked upward, the light it emitted was soft, though its surface was a deep red in color. The moon seemed to do this every few weeks, though it was for a reason unbeknownst to us. It was then Cahya looked at me, moving the hood from my face. "Is this a place you'd visit often?"

"Whenever my destination was best reached through travel here, it was where I would rest. I'd watch the stars and wonder if you were looking at them from the Isle. The rest of the journey would be long and dark until I reached the roads. From there, time was spent constantly keeping watch of what surrounded me."

"We used to lead lonely lives. I always wondered what the purpose of that was. Why we were not allowed to love. All of us. The women in the village were always carrying children. Wombs full and homes abundant. That is not a life I would choose, but they were surrounded by family."

"Perhaps Vortain thought it would somehow impede what we were meant for."

"What we were told to do," Cahya answered and looked down briefly before turning her gaze back toward the sky. "I suppose none of it matters now."

"We'll go where we choose when this is over. Mordestai, Rustanzen. We could even go beyond. There are beaches in the Baeld that are made entirely of colored stone. You've made mention many times that you wish to see Stirae. Just you and me. No objective, no mission, no order."

"That is the day I look forward to most," she answered and placed her head on my shoulder. We stood there for a time, watching the sky. A few hours passed, and we made our way back to the camp. I walked over to Dacian, relieving him of his watch and sat against the base of a large oak tree. The others would rest, now.

My thoughts returned to the men who razed Ophidian. The affairs of humans were only made my business by a man who was now dead. I should feel free of it, traveling now to gain the knowledge of my people, or taking Cahya away from this place. She was always in awe of the stories I'd tell her when I returned from time away, when Vortain was asleep in his tower. But I couldn't abandon this. Not now. The mystery that surrounded the attack needed to be solved: Why so many people lay dead. Why something was being searched for in a place that was secluded from the rest of the world?

Somehow, I felt the king had no knowledge of what came to pass, unless Savantin had convinced him somehow that we were a threat to his kingdom with the information provided by Jadoq. I immediately cast the thought aside. I knew nothing about this king, and if Savantin was any representation of him, the attack could have been planned and the lives at stake overlooked without care. My mind would not be free of these thoughts for a time, and they continued to weigh on me as we began to ready our horses for travel. Hours passed before we came to a point in the forest I did not recognize. Eshkan held his hand up, signaling us all to stop. He climbed down from his horse and walked over to a large, felled tree, looking over the side of it.

"Come. There is something here," he told us.

"I'll stay with the horses, Declan, stay with me," Dacian answered. "We can't have them running off."

I climbed off my horse, Cahya and Morard following me. When I made it to where Eshkan was, I saw the blonde prisoner girl, her hands unbound finally, and her dirty garb further soiled with blood. Her face had a large scratch over the front of it, and she had a large hole in the center of her chest, filled with only a small amount of blood.

"Nightwolves?" Morard asked.

"It is possible, but the wounds... they do not suggest a Nightwolf attack," Eshkan answered.

"She escaped somehow. I saw her in the prison just before the attack. But how she managed to make it out when everyone else perished is a mystery," I answered.

"Do you think she was let out?" Morard questioned.

"Maybe so, by Haldis. We had just proven her innocence. He probably let her free when the attack started so that she would have a chance," I answered.

"The poor woman," Cahya said. "She was likely running home."

"These wounds are only a few hours old," I answered, placing my hand on her arm, feeling her skin. "And her body temperature is only now chilling. Whatever killed her may be lingering. Perhaps it was interrupted. But the animals around here do not leave carrion behind," I answered.

"Maybe interrupted by Savantin and his men when they rode back through here," Eshkan said and placed his fingers on the inside of a deep hoof mark. "The only road to get to Terrenveil through here is the Northern Pass," he answered.

"We may yet run into those bastards again," Cahya answered.

"It's a possibility, but they must pass through the smaller winter towns before they reach the roads that lead back to the Mountain. We will be heading east, through the plains and the forests," Eshkan said.

"I do not wish to see them," she answered. "Not yet. I am afraid rage will overtake me. I will not fight as I should."

"If we continue in this direction, we will not have to worry about that. This print was made about the same time as the death of this girl," Eshkan continued.

"How many of them do you think survived?" Morard asked.

"That I cannot say for sure," Eshkan answered. "We fought many of them before joining you and Cahya."

Morard took a moment to nod before continuing. "He will undoubtedly fetch more of them when he returns."

"When I was in Arriksmad a priest was beginning to tell me about rumors. Savantin arrived and after some exchanges, he said *you had better hope it's not war that brings me back here*. A war could complicate things. We should find out more," I answered.

"A war may work in our favor," Morard said quickly. "They will be distracted. It will slow Savantin and his plotting."

"Perhaps. Eshkan, your contacts. What kind of answers do you hope they'll provide?"

"They might not know what this symbol means. But they'll know someone who does. Come, it's not much farther now," he responded.

As we continued along the road, I could hear the exchange of words between Cahya and Morard. They were careless in their means of speaking, louder at times, at times quiet. They laughed and told each other things of which I did not understand the lighthearted, joyous connotation. I often wondered if Sardons spoke to each other as humans did. Laughed, joked, smiled. I wondered how it was they spoke to one another. I had never laughed a day in my life. Smirked, maybe, but never a full out laugh. I couldn't imagine my kind doing the same. I tried to drown out their sounds and listen to the environment as much as I could. The birds softly calling to each other in the treetops, the wind gently rustling the leaves. Farther off I could make out the sounds of an owl, hooting just loud enough that his voice could be carried. He was on his nightly hunt, preying on whatever small bird or field rodent was unfortunate enough to come within grasp of his talons. That, I understood.

I knew we were reaching farther east when I heard the sounds of bats. They liked the cold and darkness of the Eastern forests. I remembered always seeing them when I had lived with the fisherman, and upon coming to Ophidian, I missed the sounds they made as they sailed the night skies in search of small, winged insects. Living with the fisherman was perhaps the most shaping part of my life, being raised by him even more so. As often as I wondered what my life would be like if I was raised by my own kin, it was more often that I wondered what it would be like if the mariner hadn't passed away. I was left to the world, an infant, swaddled and hidden beneath an old tree. But he found me one night, his hound leading him to my location.

He dealt with the fact that I fed upon humans fine, although he didn't find out until I was about five, when I began to show signs of hypnotism in my eyes. He didn't know what to believe at first, thought maybe I had been possessed, even tried to cure me with prayers from Taranost, the sea god to which he preferred to pray. He took me outside to his stable, to see if I was just going through a phase or a fever. I ran that night, killing a lost man upon a trail. Braeg found me the next morning, passed out by the half-eaten corpse. Instead of killing me, like any other man would have, he took me back to his home, cleaned me up, and sat down next to me at the fire with his glass of alcohol.

He began to tell me stories of his early seafaring days. He spoke of large sea serpents, mermaids, and the merchant's cove that rested on the other side of the sound. I listened intently, I had never been on a ship, and wondered if I would ever have the chance. I was enthralled, being as young as I was, the world was still filled with wonder and mystery. He told me of the woman he loved, a fair beauty named Elesette. He always returned to the village of Harbortow, bringing back sea glass and other trinkets for her. When he finally found the courage to ask her to be his bride, he returned from a fishing excursion to find that she left their small town to live with a soldier of the king's legion. Of course, he was heartbroken. He blamed himself for never formally expressing his love for her.

I asked him why he never went in search of her, why he chose to remain here in this place. He only answered with the words, *A man who knows one life cannot hope to trade for another after being in one place for so long.* After that he set his glass down, pet his dog on the head and left us there by the fire. I fell asleep after that, only briefly remembering my feeding. It took a few more times until I fully developed control over myself, my inheritance, but the man was patient with me. Perhaps I made him think of the son he could have had, if he had pursued Elesette. I thought nothing of her until now. Maybe she was still alive, still in Terrenveil.

It wasn't long before Eshkan had us stop; we reached the end of the forest, the dark purple leaves of the Zanto bushes bearing great significance. They only grew in this part of the world, sustained by the humidity and the black waters of the Lake of Knights. It was said that when the rain fell from the sky here that it was the color of wolves. The mariner paid great attention to the rain. The shifts of the winds and the tides. It was his calling, it seemed, to be married to the sea.

Eshkan stopped us again before long, looking up and down the long dark road to make sure that we were alone. Enemies were abundant the further one strayed from the Isle. Soldiers, animals. Brigands, Eshkan mentioned. I doubted the possibility of brigands greatly, we were still far south enough to be close to the rule of Terrenveil. I spoke nothing of it, for the argument would lead nowhere, and kept my eyes open across the road.

Cahya stopped, taking a moment to stretch her legs. Declan did the same as I climbed off my horse and met with Eshkan.

"How far are we from Defaltor?" I asked when I had approached him.

"Perhaps another day. If we keep pace we should be there by the rise of the next sun," he answered.

"Will you be able to travel the rest of the way; your wound is ..."

"I will be fine. Once we get into town, I will see about stitching it. I wasn't able to recover anything from the isle to tend to it. Everything was damaged."

I nodded. "I don't think there will be any protest from the others if we stop."

"We cannot. The open road is not a good place to be when a war starts," Eshkan answered.

"We need to find out what Savantin is planning. If we don't, then we are left with nothing. War or not," I said. I took a breath before I looked back to my horse and nodded. "I will tell the others you lead the way."

Eshkan shook his head once and climbed back upon his horse, stroking it down the mane. "We will also need to see to it our horses are watered and fed. We will stop at the next lake and get some grain when we enter town."

I walked back to where the others were standing, and Dacian, still on horseback, strode ahead.

"What's going on?" Cahya asked.

"Nothing. The road is nearby. We will stop at the next water source so that our horses may drink, and then we continue," I said.

"How long will we be in the city?" she asked.

"I don't know. I don't want to be there for very long, but if we hope to discover what our enemy seeks, we will need resources," I answered. I knew I didn't have to tell her that the town would be dangerous. Eshkan's admonition was enough.

We reached the Talimas road within a few hours of our last interruption. It would be about a day of travel from here. I was highly anticipating discovering what this symbol meant, and if it would give us a place to begin in planning our attack. Yet beyond this, I was seeing the world with new eyes. I was free. Despite it, there was one last assassination that needed to be performed. I thought of what it was I would do once my enemy breathed no more, but I was continually unsure. I was a trained killer. I couldn't yet fathom what life would be like in abandoning that path. Would the fishing towns of the Baeld be the best place for me to go? Beyond this thought, the coven of my people came to mind. My appearance there would be inevitable.

I remained quiet for the remainder of our journey to town, gently cradling the reins of my horse. Another hour passed before Eshkan ultimately decided it was best we found a place off the road to retire for the evening. I nodded, offering to take the first shift of watch over camp. As Dacian started to look for wood with which to build a fire, I picked the base of an old oak tree and rested against it, holding Seligsara in my hands. We were lucky in finding horses that still had packs on them. Though Jadoq probably packed what he could in the event he too had to leave the Isle. I took a breath in and listened to the others as they unraveled the small, rolled blankets off the horses' sides, laying them strategically on the ground. Most of them were in good condition, but appeared to be from the village, which led me to think that perhaps others must have known something was amiss and plotted escape. However, the horrific truth remained. I silenced my mind and looked off into the distance, listening to the echoes of the night. Not far from here I could hear a fox, rummaging through nearby bushes. Closer still was the breaking of branches from what sounded like a raccoon. I listened harder however, for other never-mentioned creatures of the night.

Whatever killed the prisoner girl was still out here. I would be able to keep most creatures away, at least as long as my last meal would hold me over. The lack of blood meant a lack of power to influence other creatures around me. After about an hour or so of continued menial sounds and echoes, I heard footsteps from the camp up to my position. It was Cahya, revealed to me by the sound of her heart. She sat next to me, pulling a blanket around her shoulders. She was chilled from the night air that had come with the drowning of the sun behind the mountains, but only expressed it now, as everyone was sleeping. She looked up into the starless night sky and sighed, crossing her legs beneath her.

"It's strange, isn't it? I thought I would never see you again, not after the night you left the infirmary. Now here we sit, side by side, listening to night creatures and fighting for ourselves in a world I thought I would never again see either," she said, her eyes unmoving. "We could never be while we were in his kingdom. And now there are bittersweet thoughts that come from its demise."

I remained silent for a while. She finally leaned against the tree also, looking out into the night. "I cannot sleep. Not after what happened," she said.

"It is not coming so easily to me, either," I answered.

"I can't believe Jadoq betrayed him like that. The letters... It was terrible," Cahya answered. She sighed, leaning her head upon my shoulder and closing her eyes. "I suppose we should rest," she said, and drifted off into the dark of the night. I remained awake for some time after, watching the forest and the skies above.

CHAPTER 3

INEXORABLE DARKNESS

The snow began to pick up as they reached the old horse trail only known to the land as the Northern Pass. The breath of their horses was visible in the air, signifying the drastic drop in temperature. It didn't stop them, as they rode quickly up the beaten dirt trail carved between two large rock formations not big enough to be called mountains, yet larger than the hills in the east. It was made by hundreds of years of travel, the books said, and was even one day long ago used by the native tribes to trade and bargain with other, farther-off camps. The stories didn't matter anymore, for the division of the kingdoms ensured all trade across borders ceased. It was foolish, Savantin thought. No harm came from trading with the Septens. Food, furs, trinkets. But he supposed that was why he was not involved with the politics of the kingdom. They passed a marker several miles ago stating which way to travel to reach their destination, the Great Mountain of Terrenveil.

It was a place Savantin did not yet wish to return to. Much awaited him. A report on his findings, informants to meet with. Beyond all of this he knew that he would need to begin to plan his next venture. What had just happened was chaos—something that, despite his position, he did not enjoy. Chaos meant too many factors that could result in failure, and in ending what had just transpired, he tried not to mark it as such. Most of his men had deserted, left to their own devices. If they weren't murdered by the survivors, they'd be robbing the dead. A large gust of wind returned his thoughts to the present.

They left their warmer clothing in one of the trading outposts outside of Arriksmad, others purchasing their fur for coin. Ohric didn't know why it was necessary but trusted in the actions of his commander. He still worried about the deserters, though Savantin assured him that they would pose no threat. It was true, though. Before they reached the Isle, the men were told that the only way out was to die, or to be as death itself. Still, it would not erase the thought from his mind. Ohric looked over to his commander as he rode forward on his horse, his helmet still stained in blood. Most of his armor was, though he took part in so little of the killing himself. Ohric took no lives on the Isle, as Savantin had honored his expressed opposition to it. Though, in arriving there, he realized that the heathens that inhabited the villages were not a part of Araele's light, and in turn, were not a part of the world he should be saving. He shivered as a gust of wind carried legions of small snowflakes up the hill, rushing about as if they had just been given orders. He took a minute to unravel the pack behind him as they kept moving, almost not noticing that Savantin had stopped. His commander didn't move his head as he looked around, his eyes scanning their surroundings like an animal searching for prey.

"There are brigands, watching us from behind on either side of the road," Savantin said, his voice low.

"I didn't see them," Ohric whispered back, careful not to move his head.

"You will," Savantin answered and rode forward, slowly.

Ohric didn't understand how anyone with intelligence would ambush them, their border beginning just after they had passed that sign. Everyone knew the penalty for killing travelers along the roads in the rule of Terrenveil. He had no doubt it happened often, though. The king dissolved the guards he had once placed along the borders to protect citizens because it cost too much to keep them there. Savantin attributed it to Ozrach's carelessness and greed. Ohric thought it was because the king had lost his way. His wife however, Neraea, the queen—she was a woman to be admired. Graceful. Her belief in the Lady of Light was what would restore the kingdom to its former state. He was sure of it. Savantin didn't believe that, though. Ohric tried to concern himself little with what his commander believed and stuck to his resolve.

As the pair reached the top of the road, two men walked out from behind the rocks, three more behind them.

"You should have remained in hiding. At least then I could have continued to pretend that I didn't know you were there," Savantin answered.

"Get off your horses and give us your goods. We'll let you live if you do," the man in the front said. He was a small skinny man, a large beard covering the stretch of his face. You needed one out here to protect your skin from the lashing winds and the ice storms.

"It'd be best you listen now, 'fore we kill you and take it anyway. You're running out of time," he continued, forcing his voice out of his cold lungs.

"I'll take the remainder of that time and propose something in opposition. Take your ragged horde and head east, back toward the tundra. You know you are not permitted on this part of the road."

"You know you are outnumbered. Just climb off your horse and this won't get messy."

Ohric looked to his commander, not knowing what their next move would be. He didn't want to surrender his horse, which he knew wouldn't be the issue at hand, but he didn't want the horse to be harmed. Only Araele knew when they would find another village to purchase a pair. She was silent now.

"If you want to do it this way, why don't we fight for it?" Savantin answered.

"Fight for it?"

"If you are bold enough to try and rob two soldiers upon a road belonging to Terrenveil then why not fight? It's the only way you will have a chance at acquiring anything of mine," Savantin answered.

The men stood, looking at each other for a few moments before their leader rushed, raising his sword up to knock Savantin from his horse. Savantin grabbed the blade, pulling his own and cutting the man in half. He tossed the man's blade aside and turned his horse, looking at the three men behind him. Their leader's legs had slid down the ice-covered road in a trail of blood. Savantin ignored the blood coming from his palm, the cut large and deep. He only watched the eyes of the men who were standing in front of him. A few looked on in horror, the others averting their gaze.

"I see no one else wants to follow in his footsteps," Savantin answered, waiting a moment before turning to Ohric.

"I wait for your word," he asked, looking at the one closest him. "Shall we kill them for preying upon innocents? You know that is what they were doing before we passed."

One of the bigger men spoke up, his brown beard moving as he spoke. "It wasn't our idea to come here."

"Oh?" Savantin asked.

The man nodded and swallowed before he spoke again. "It was his. He is the one who has the map. We are from the tundra. We don't know what exists outside of it."

Savantin looked at the man, and then over to Ohric, offering a laugh. "Do you think that matters to me? You followed him out here."

"Honestly, we did not know where we were," the man said, looking away.

"I do not wish to expend the energy it would take to kill all of you. But if I hear of you on this road again, I will have you dragged to Terrenveil behind horses. If you survive once you enter the gates I will kill you myself. Are these terms acceptable?"

The man with the brown beard nodded and thanked him, turning away and heading east. Savantin turned his horse and began to ride up the hill, Ohric grabbing his horse's reins and following. Savantin took a deep breath, exhaling and turning to Ohric.

"You question my actions?"

"You... let them live..." Ohric answered.

"I see it's been a long time. I don't kill everyone, Ohric."

"I know you are weary; I am too. But your hand..."

"Speak nothing of it. I feel fine," Savantin answered.

"I can tell when it is about to happen. That is why I am still here, isn't it, why you haven't killed me yet," Ohric said.

Savantin shot a glaring eye at Ohric, and then began to laugh. "There are plenty of reasons I haven't killed you. You are trustworthy. Do you know how many men I had to kill until I found you?"

"I've heard the stories."

"Okay, then."

Ohric took a breath and watched as the gust of cold air left his mouth. "You missed this moon. You don't want anything to happen when we are in town. If word of it reaches Ozrach then you know what will happen."

"I have Ozrach in the palm of my hands. He won't dare to speak out against my wants, my judgment. All the better reason to display it to him. He already suspects it. It is no secret where I was born."

"I am only voicing my opinion. It is also no secret that he has ordered many of the priests of your home killed for fear of the practices."

"He fears my home because he is weak."

"It doesn't offend you that he kills priests from Seraphician because of their heritage, their religious beliefs?"

"What a man does in fear weighs not on the mind of a man who lives without it. He's a pawn, Ohric. We'll see our wishes granted soon enough," Savantin answered.

They rode on from the Northern Pass in silence, their horses moving slowly among the more frozen roads of their expedition. It would be hours, maybe even the rest of the day before they would reach the small town of Glacier Ridge. He hoped it would come to his sights soon. He desperately wanted a warm room, and a bed to match. He let his thoughts wander to just days present, knowing the patience he must embody upon his return home…

◆ ◆ ◆

Savantin closed his eyes and took breath to regain control of his mind. It had been a long day thus far, the menial tasks that awaited him served only to drag out the hours. King Ozrach ordered him to go over maps of the surrounding areas. The queen wanted the roads secured at all times, so that her priests could better spread the word of Araele throughout Terrenveil, and so her zealots could punish heresy wherever it was found. His thoughts immediately moved to whom he would relinquish the task to. Minutes passed before there was a loud knocking at the door to his quarters, one of his guards entering sight.

"Commander you're needed in the throne room with no delay," he said, the urgency in his voice monumental. Savantin nodded in response and waited only for the door to close before he began to dress himself for the occasion. He wondered if this would be something of importance, or if the royal family would further cause aggravation by designating tasks to him in which he had no professional interest. He quickly left, making his way to the room in the center of the castle. Opening the doors, he saw what seemed to be a usual visage of the ordinary. Ozrach was sitting anxiously upon his throne, Neraea next to him, scorn lacing her green eyes, red hair tumbling from her small crown. Haemad was pacing next to them while a bloodied soldier was kneeling on the ground before them, two guards standing on either side. Ohric was quietly watching from a post on the right side of the room, his face obtaining some vigor from its previously lazy expression.

"Thank the goddess," Ozrach answered, his frame sliding against the sides of the chair as he stood. "This man… he has returned from the group of men you sent to the Northern border just this morning. He said that…"

"Let him speak to me," Savantin stated. "I've no interest in hearing words second-hand."

"Very well then," Ozrach answered and sat again, taking to silence.

"The battalion still remains, Commander. I was able to warn them of what I saw before I made it back here," he said, his words shaking as much as his body was. "It was my morning to check the border. I woke my partner and we set off. My partner, Giules, he saw a deer just over the other side and thought if he could kill it, we'd have enough for the cook to make a decent stew. We crept along the wall until we reached a ditch, and I waited in the cover of bushes for him to signal me through. He killed the deer, and started to drag it back when he was killed in kind. Several arrows piercing his armor," the soldier said, and swallowed.

"A just death. Invasion and poaching. This is not alarming to me. Surely there is something else to this story that would justify having me pulled from my quarters at this hour."

"Yes. This was not alarming to me either, sir. After hearing his scream, I waited in that ditch, listening as rushed, angered voices approached me, the sound of his body being dragged along with them. They cast his body in next to me, standing there for several moments as if to ensure there were no more of us. I didn't move, hardly took breath as his lifeless face stared into mine, blood running from the wound on his head. It was only when they turned to go back from where they came that I rose, but before I left, I looked out over the field and noticed tents, tens of tents each holding a considerable number of soldiers."

"Mauros's army is populating near our borders?" Savantin asked hastily.

"Well, we don't know..."

"I'm sending troops there at once. If their king thinks that occupying the borders sits well with me then he is a fool."

"Don't you think that would just provoke..."

"He has already initiated provocation, Haemad. I won't be audience to his threats without answering them."

"What if it is just an exercise?"

"As idiotic as that sounds I have an answer for you. If they decide to invade us, we will have ample defense. If we are finished here, and this man has nothing else of note, I have preparations to make," Savantin answered and turned to leave the room, listening to the bickering between king and advisor in his exit. The two frustrated him. They'd ask for his appearance yet question his solutions on a matter they had no mind for. He supposed he should have waited for Ohric before he made his exit. The task regarding the maps would have been handled by him without question. He sighed and continued his path toward the barracks, knowing that his coadjutant would look for him as soon as possible.

Once at the barracks he pushed the door open angrily, looking around for the first captain that came across his eyes. He didn't care much for who he sent to the border, just that bodies occupied it. The soldiers within immediately adjusted themselves to appear orderly as his eyes searched the room, hungrily. It wasn't until he made it past the front part of the barracks that he was spoken to by the man he'd be sending away.

"Commander... a surprise visit. How can I be of service to you?"

"I need you to take your troops to the Northern border and report to me if you see any activity regarding Maurosce soldiers. You depart immediately. Tell your men to gather their belongings and begin travel."

"Yes sir," the captain answered and wheeled around to heed orders, the tone of the response evident that he had questions he did not give voice. He was a younger captain, only a few years older than Savantin himself. It occurred to him that he didn't remember his name and searched his brain for it until he lost the desire to pursue. He hoped that the tension at the border would escalate so that he could traverse Terrenveil instead of being trapped in the castle to brood and plot. He longed to be free of it, more than anything he lusted after his entire life.

Savantin took the long way back to the castle, walking through the poorer districts where he witnessed people turning into their homes with hushed voices. A few watched him pass by; others continued on with their work. Farmers, mostly. A few soldiers who had survived battles but could no longer fight. The poverty disgusted him. Yet he could not give up his role in the kingdom that generated it, not yet.

The castle was eerily quiet as he entered. Handmaidens were tucked away in side rooms, preparing for a task deemed important by the queen. It was no secret Neraea was trying to conceive, however the focus of her husband was more directed to the near nightly parties and feasts he held to gain favor from the leaders of the provinces.

Haemad approached him suddenly, as if in tradition, at a time he had no will to be bothered or stopped. It was almost as if his thoughts of the royal family bore a horror he had been lucky enough to avoid until now.

"Savantin?" Haemad squeaked. The sound of his voice added to the irritation. Savantin turned to where he heard his name being called and said nothing, waiting for whatever infuriating or trivial comment would be uttered. "Your presence is requested this evening in the Great Hall. And as much as you don't want to go, it too pains me to have to say that it is mandatory. Two hours, don't be late."

Savantin said nothing and watched as Haemad scurried off to prepare himself for what was the most arduous task of his day. He would probably change his attire, spending one of those hours deciding upon which would best suit the event. He had probably had another tailored in town recently. His coin earned from advising the king, and Savantin couldn't help but laugh at the concept, was spent on additional garb for the lavish feasts Ozrach held continuously. He couldn't fathom a reason, though the court made little sense to him. Their sole purpose was to make decisions for people and extort them, taking their coin to line their own pockets. Even his legionnaires saw little of it, the promise of being fed and housed was expected to be enough for them to stay. Hypocrisies were many here. The royal family and its affiliates were held to the same standards once. This was only one of the many reasons he detested being a participant at the Great Hall.

Two hours. He could find Ohric in that amount of time, tell him about the maps and ensure Neraea's crusaders were kept safe. He often wondered if Ohric wanted to be out there on the roads with them. He didn't yet know if Ohric would be too afraid to approach him and ask his service be returned with the freedom to lead Araele's people. The last place Savantin had seen him was the throne room. He knew he'd no longer be there now. The man was strangely elusive. Ohric had few places he frequented, among those being the temple or patrolling the southern walls to watch the river. Much like himself, he thought. He'd start at the place he less detested, and headed toward the southern wall in hopes he needn't search further.

The scent of the water reached him long before his destination was in sight. It was once a source of water for the purpose of drinking and cleansing before the Verain was discovered. He climbed the steps that had been forged into the wall, watching as two guards walked past him after nodding their heads in his direction. Savantin returned in kind, taking a breath as he strode forward. It always took months to stop new recruits from saluting him as they hurried past. He didn't much care for the nature of rank. A breath of relief left his lungs as he came across Ohric, staring out into the field before them as the sky darkened. His coadjutant had not heard him approaching and shook a little as he said his name.

"I know I should be more attentive than that," Ohric admitted.

"Yet I am not going to give you admonitions of enemies using stealth. I'm not your mentor, Ohric. I'm your friend."

Ohric nodded and cast his gaze back out over the river. "It's just mesmerizing to me. Of all the beauty and grace there is upon the earth... there is a small piece of it right here."

Savantin let him continue, staring at him blankly for the observation he himself could not make. Rivers were rivers. Walls, walls. There was no symbolism in night becoming day and the contrary. Everything just existed to him and either aided or hindered his cause.

"What brings you out here? I so rarely see you at this place."

"You, actually. I've been asked by our ever so gracious to mark new paths for patrol so that Neraea's priests can travel without harm."

"Do you think in light of recent events..."

"I don't. This was asked of me before the man returned from the front. I thought you should know about it regardless."

"A kindness. My gratitude. Did they stress any urgency?"

"They did not. I see it as a preventative measure. This should have gone to you and the temple," Savantin answered and took a moment to look over the river before turning to leave.

"Where do you go?"

"I've been summoned to discuss Mauros over dinner. There isn't anything to discuss. They are ignorant in handling war. If Ozrach was left to the decision we'd be submerged in chaos, and I'd be left to pick up the pieces for him yet again." A reference to the first war Savantin had fought in, the war where he became Commander.

"Inform me of the outcome when you see fit. I'll take my leave now, look over those maps."

"Don't give it too much thought. I'll need you in the times that come ahead," Savantin answered and headed back toward the castle. He arrived early, of course watching as servants began preparation. Elaborate tablecloths and silver off of which to eat. It was before he could exit that he was approached by the head servant, an older woman that had served the former queen. Her husband was killed in the war that preceded Ozrach's marriage to Neraea and she never forgave the world for what had happened. It was her cold-heartedness that had many avoid her, and the women whose lives dictated that they work under her watch were nary expressive.

"What gives us the pleasure of your audience this evening?" she asked, her dark narrow eyes attempting to stare into something past his frame.

"You should know how this works by now. Royalty eats here, the servants eat in a room, separate this, and the dogs eat outside the walls until life throws them a bone. It seems I've found one."

"They focus too much on flesh and blood but not enough on bone. I've seen many things, Commander. I've seen people lie to those they love to gain wealth and favor and I've seen love so strong that it's held when two are torn apart. Two different types of people embody these events. One, flesh and blood. The other, bone." It was that statement she left with, off toward the room where the servants would have their dinner. A more degrading version of what he unwillingly would be subjected to in half an hour's time.

He waited along the outsides of the room until the candles were lit, the catalyst to its beginning. Savantin sat five chairs down from Ozrach's place, Neraea would be to his left, and Haemad his right. He was uncertain of how many people would be in attendance but wanted as much room between himself and the rest of them as possible. It was Haemad who entered first, which caused Savantin to inhale and close his eyes to mentally prepare himself for the conversation he'd be involved in. The man's face brightened when he saw him, approaching with haste.

"I didn't expect you to be here before royalty, Savantin."

He said nothing and watched Haemad sit, being careful not to show anything in his eyes. It was once Haemad got comfortable that he continued to speak, taking the silence as a sign to continue. "Nice, isn't it? Tonight, the menu is very palatable. Getting used to it could be tragic, though. Enjoying it."

"Rest assured that I will not enjoy it," Savantin answered and looked toward the goblets, already filled with wine and water. Haemad scowled, taking a gulp of wine into his throat, nearly finishing the amount in his glass. "Well. Events as of late are quite alarming. Mauros to wage war here. Have you thought about the domestic effects of this?"

"Repeating myself is something I've no interest in doing. You'll hear what I have to say soon enough," Savantin answered and crossed his arms, sitting so that the back of the chair rested against his own. Haemad continued to drink, likely thinking of a reply when Ozrach entered, Neraea a few steps behind. Her face of disdain spoke volumes, perhaps an argument, or perhaps the fairy tale of being carried away by her prince from life on a farm had lost its luster and reality finally set in.

"Perfect!" Ozrach exclaimed before sitting in his chair. "I'll have the servants bring the first course. Let us talk about Mauros." Haemad had livened, Neraea's distaste for her required presence was shown even further by her silence. She grabbed a goblet from in front of her, taking a swallow of drink in the same manner Haemad did. Ozrach cleared his throat and looked toward Savantin who had not taken his eyes off him since he entered the room.

"Have you something to say?" the king asked, finally.

Savantin moved a hand outward to hurry the king's speaking before returning it back to his chest in his prior crossed gesture.

"That soldiers report has come as a surprise to all of us I'm certain. The peace my father made with Mauros years ago was never broken, at least not to my knowledge."

"Perhaps the king has passed," Haemad offered, fueling Savantin's impatience.

"If the king passed then word of it would have spread by now," Ozrach countered.

"We don't know that. It could be recent. Perhaps this is the result. A king passes and successor motions for war to expand their kingdom."

"Declaring war so soon after taking the throne isn't wise," Savantin stated. He hoped to remain quiet for most of his time here, but it seemed the conversation would remain pointless speculation if he failed to interject.

"So, you're saying perhaps the king didn't pass?" Ozrach asked and grasped a turkey's leg off a plate as a servant passed, setting it down in the center of the table.

"The only aspect that concerns me being here is the soldiers that were seen beyond the wall," Savantin answered. His response caught an irritated look from Neraea, and one of surprise from her husband.

"Don't you care why?" Haemad asked. "Knowing someone's motive would help careful planning."

"I've planned carefully. I've sent a battalion to the North in the event Mauros scales the wall to raid and have instructed the captain to send word if it occurs. Waiting to discover motive will only give them more of an advantage over us. The only thing we have is time."

"Time? How can you say we have time? We don't even know what they're planning."

Savantin heavily exhaled after Haemad finished, his incessant questioning becoming too much for him to withstand. "Now that we know Mauros is fortifying their borders, we have time to act. Or do I need to stress that in simpler terms?"

"Enough," Ozrach said and reached for another leg of turkey. "It seems I cannot even hold a dinner without tension."

"I'll put this as respectfully as I can. The frivolity of politics disinterests me. I'm here to ensure that Terrenveil remains fortified. The decisions I make are based upon calculation, logic, reason. Mauros deploys its soldiers along our borders, logic speaks plans to raid. Whether or not this happens, we need to be prepared. I'll be taking several battalions with me to quarter in each one of the provinces. The ones along the borders will suffice for now. Town guards do not stand a chance against the Maurosce."

"Don't you think we should let the provincials know about this?" Ozrach asked.

"You'd warn them of my coming when there are rumors of rebellion?" Savantin asked, trying to keep the intonation of disbelief hidden.

"I think it best to let them know about Mauros and about your men."

"You only care about your image in their eyes now that it's probable they're plotting to dethrone you. Why warn them at all? They won't have time to hide anything they may be planning, and I fortify the provinces. All of your concerns are dealt with. Or tell them. It makes no difference to me."

"What would your first move be?" Haemad asked.

"I send additional battalions to the eastern and western walls. I will take a small group of men to the south and see if there are any signs of entry by sea. I'll stop by the holy city on my way there. I haven't forgotten about that," Savantin said and looked to Neraea. "Ohric will accompany me. He will make sure the city is in order and the priests are still taken care of. Once I've done those things, I will return."

"And the provinces?"

"I will take men there myself once I return from the South. The borders are priority."

"What do you think of all of this?" Haemad asked and turned to Ozrach who was working on the plate before him.

"Don't waste your breath. My terms weren't up for discussion," Savantin said and stood. "I've work to do." He only partially listened to Haemad's sounds of outrage as he left the room. He entered the hallway to his chamber, nodding to the two guards posted at the top of the stairs. As much as he knew he needed rest, he'd receive none. The day before travel was always restless.

Everything would have to wait until his return, but he wasn't leaving the castle for the reason he implied. There was something in the south that had gained his undivided attention. As soon as he entered, he moved to his table and pulled the first map off the top of it, looking closely at the one that lay just beneath. An island. He hadn't known it existed before, not until his confidant returned to him one day with a map and compass that charted her travels. It was something that instilled new hope in him where anger and frustration had taken residence.

He moved to the window to look out over the city beneath a darkened sky. It was short lived, as his heart began to beat heavily in his chest the moment his eyes came across the largest star. He quickly drew the shutters and heard a noise behind him as the door closed. He laughed softly and looked down, his hands resting on the windowsill. "I'm surprised you're here while dinner is happening just a few floors below us. Surely, you'll be sought after," Savantin said and turned around, watching as the queen strode inward, sitting on the chair closest to his charting table.

"I told them I was feeling ill. They won't seek me, at least not until after the courses are gone and there is nothing left to speak about."

"You're certain that was the smartest excuse? You know how your husband is stricken with paranoia over the plague."

"As I said. There is too much focus on the event at hand. What would be most surprising is if he actually heard the words I said when I dismissed myself," Neraea answered and picked up the bottle of wine that was sitting on the edge of the table. "Have you been to Castana?" she asked and set the bottle down, shaking her head. "You and I both know how incredibly boring it is to be in their company. Not to mention how horribly painful. If Haemad so much as breathes in my direction some days, I seek out ways to exile."

"So why don't you?" Savantin asked. "You used to be able to get him to do anything."

"That was before he discovered things that he enjoys more than sex. He's a simple man, pleasure to him dictates the decisions he makes."

"That I'll agree with. Though to some degree it's the same for all of us," Savantin answered and moved to his armoire, closing its doors. It was hard to enjoy speaking to Neraea. She had grown to be a heartless woman. He assumed it was because she discovered that all of the riches in the world could not give her happiness, and in discovering how morbidly wrong she was, having trapped herself in a life of lovelessness, it froze her heart. "Why not run?"

"Leave the castle? You know I can't do that. They'd hunt me until the end of my days."

"Yes. But it's an excuse."

"You wouldn't understand," Neraea answered defensively, crossing her arms and crossing one leg over top of the other.

"More than you know. You don't want to make the change because you've grown accustomed to your life here. The pleasure of royalty dictates your decision to stay. If you planned it well enough you could go anywhere. You could be a merchant, traveling to Rustanzen to trade spices. Board a boat from Harbortow and be free of this place."

"If only it were just that," she answered softly, averting her eyes.

"You want to love and feel loved. All of the hate you feel, pain, sadness. It could be erased by that simple feeling of your heart beating quickly at the sound of someone's voice. The thought."

"Is that what you want, Savantin?"

"My life is spent in seeking purpose. It is a dangerous place to become lost."

"In this search, certainly you've found something," Neraea answered.

"Not yet," Savantin said and sat in the chair across from her. Her being here could only mean a few things. She often sought companionship from others but didn't know how to relate to them. In ways he felt bad for her. She was a product of her environment, trying to survive in a world that was against her. He tried to help her, once.

"Sometimes I feel it will never end." Neraea sighed and moved her head aside, her long red hair falling from where it had been pinned up and into her crown. She shook her head a second time, taking it off and setting it on the table. "This was a gift as much as a curse. Sometimes I feel an inkling of the girl I was before I came here. And yet it seems so far away, so intangible."

"Chase it," Savantin answered. "There is a difference between chasing things that make you feel alive and seeking purpose. Sometimes we fall in line with both."

"Do you find yourself to be the person you just described?" Neraea asked and uncrossed her leg, moving to stand. She let her dress fall over her skin, moving her hair to one side of her body. Savantin rose from his seat, moving her toward the wall closest them. "I was describing you," he answered and moved his lips to hers. He felt her tongue, warm inside his mouth. Her heartbeat steadily rose as they continued. He pulled his face away from her and looked into her deep green eyes. "I can't give you your sense of purpose, Neraea. I can merely be what makes you feel alive."

CHAPTER 4

Λ MΛRK ΛMONG THIEVES

Defaltor came into sight as we crossed the bridge giving us passage over the Frost's Kiss River. The horses' hooves were heard in unison over its old surface, the wood announcing our combined weight with creaks of disdain. The river traveled all the way from the North where it was frozen solid, melting only after it reached the climate of our region. Its source untouched by humanity, legend stating a large cavern full of glaciers even farther away from Terrenveil was its mother. It was chill to the touch on even the hottest summer day. Anskirre, Eshkan stated, created the river herself.

We reached the gates after a few moments upon the bridge and dismounted our horses, walking next to them with reins in our hands. Eshkan raised his fist, knocking on the large wooden door a total of three times. A man opened a small door at our eye height, not reaching below our chests. His face was lightly dusted in dirt, and his voice was deep and strong. He had deep brown eyes that were set back in his head, surrounded by a full head of hair and a short beard. He had a deep red scar that crossed his throat and appeared to curve over his shoulder and into his clothing. "State your business," he said gruffly and looked across our faces, chewing on something tough and smoky smelling.

"Mercenary work. We've come to see the market, and have contribution," Eshkan answered.

He seemed satisfied enough with his answer and closed the door, opening the gate using a large pulley contraption. He looked at us haughtily, his suspicions still around him, but ceased to watch our movement after we made it to where houses began to line the street. He closed the gate, saying something to the man next to him under his breath. I briefly made eye contact with Dacian, signing to him the symbol for shadow. He nodded and walked ahead towards Eshkan. Cahya was looking around at the buildings across the street, knowing very well almost everything here once belonged to someone who didn't know they would be parting with it. Every shopkeeper was a fence for a thief who networked a certain area. She was suspicious of every being that took breath, I could hear her words without her giving them voice.

Those who traveled paths less favorable came here to purchase what goods were available at the market, or to propose contracts to thieves or mercenaries. Those who affiliated themselves with darker professions also passed through, cultists, magick users. There was rumor of the Viscera Osculate passing through here to deal in human harvesting. Most tried desperately to keep the name from their tongues. The cult was secretive, which made any rumor about their appearance here surprising.

Alongside this, anyone who opposed the lord of Defaltor was tossed in Frost's Kiss River to be carried to the hot and steaming jungles past the marshes. They would decompose within days there, species of ant and other insects removing whatever was left upon bone. I wondered if anyone ever witnessed the bodies as they traveled down the currents, and simply looked away from them as they passed through. Declan suddenly spoke, stopping us in our tracks.

"Where should we tie our horses?" he asked, looking around.

"Anywhere will be fine. Inside the walls no one takes from one another, for fear that they and their entire family or namesake will be destroyed. People who live and travel here are to respect the laws of the city's lord. It's been that way since the city was built," Eshkan answered.

"That's a strange concept," Cahya said.

"But it's accurate." Eshkan led us to where other horses were hitched, using the reins of his own to tether it to one of the posts. "Tonight, we can keep them in a stable for a small fee."

"But we have nothing," Cahya said.

"Don't worry about that." Eshkan smiled, looking down at his shoulder. He pulled the cloth from it with two fingers, making a face of disappointment. "I'm going to see about this wound. You wait here and make sure there's no trouble. I'll be back within a few minutes," he said.

I nodded and looked at Morard, speaking to him. "Go with him, in case there's a problem." He looked perplexed at first, but nodded, catching up to Eshkan.

"Why not send me?" Dacian asked.

"I need you in case we are attacked. This is unfamiliar territory," I answered, looking around at the people moving about. This was the closest town to Ophidian. It seemed unlikely that Savantin or any of his men would come here. Even if they had left their armor in the forest, they would not be able to hide that their weapons belonged to the Kingdom of Terrenveil. They would not rid of those. I rested with that fact, but let my suspicions remain.

"Do you think this is wise?" Cahya asked.

"It is not clear. But the people here have been all over the world, have seen things, experienced things. Have knowledge of symbols and cults. It shouldn't be long before we find information. Or at least a lead," I said.

"But at what cost?"

"This may be the safest place for us. We do not know if we were reported to be enemies of the kingdom."

"You're right." She sighed. "I will keep my eyes watchful."

"I'll be able to join you once I'm done scouting. I don't think anyone else should be on the streets tonight. We've only just arrived here."

Cahya nodded. "And until you know what the area is like..."

"I understand the lord of the city has his laws but that does not mean that they're being strictly followed. He may have eyes everywhere but you and I both know that isn't enough."

Eshkan was back out into the street within moments as he had promised, Morard walking next to him. He looked at us and moved his head toward a bigger building across from the stable, walking towards it without a word. The house we were led to didn't look customary for a town such as this. Lavish looking stairs announced a large door that was deep in color, torches on either side of it. When he opened the door, we were greeted by a woman who was holding a large glass of wine in her hand. She set it on a small table by the door and swallowed what was in her mouth before she spoke.

"Ah. Visitors," she said and glanced at us. She raised an eyebrow and continued to speak, picking up her glass once more. "Though not the usual type. Who are you, and what brings you here?" she asked.

"My name is Eshkan. Varsenius sent me here, said you owe him a favor, and this is how you could repay."

"Did he now?" the woman asked, bending toward him slightly. Narrowed brown eyes and smiling red lips showcased her intrigue. "Usually, it isn't me who owes favors."

"He told me to let you know that he will forget about your debt if you do this for him."

"Debt? Is that what he called it? I see you know some valuable information. He always likes to have his favors repaid in likeness." She laughed. "Tell me what you need."

"I was stabbed when our home was attacked. The blade was tipped with some kind of Rythran. I don't know how I am still breathing, perhaps it wasn't enough to kill me," he answered.

"I see. And your friends? Will they need to be patched up too, Eshkan?" she asked, rolling the sleeves of her short burgundy dress up to her elbows.

"That will not be necessary, Madame Karstentia. But we will need a place to stay, if you would be ever so gracious," Eshkan answered. She looked at him, amused, and then looked into a room to the right of us. She looked toward a woman that was standing at the end of a large staircase, instructing her, "Parsena, entertain my guests while I take care of our friend here." She grabbed Eshkan's hand, pulling him into a room behind a curtain.

Once they disappeared from sight I began to look around, watching as women occasionally exited rooms and traversed the staircase upward. Moments later, men would emerge—in one instance a woman—and leave the house quietly. A brothel. The eyes and ears of the area. Secret keepers, and sources of knowledge undisputed. Eshkan continued to impress me. We sat among the plush, lined benches, Morard releasing a sound as he stretched his legs out in front of him.

"I've never seen anything like this," he said. "The tower was the nicest place on the Isle, but it never felt this welcoming."

"It does certainly feel welcoming," Cahya answered as her eyes moved quickly around the room, suspicion cradled within them.

"Can I get you anything to drink, to eat perhaps?" Parsena asked politely, smiling.

Everyone exchanged glances in silence until Cahya spoke, moving the dark hair that had become stuck to her forehead in the night's travel.

"We are hungry, thirsty, tired, but we don't want to impose. If you do not have sufficient supplies to feed us, we can go elsewhere. We don't have much to give, our home was burned to the ground," she said.

"Oh Miss, you are not imposing at all. Friends of Varsenius are welcome to anything here," she answered.

Cahya's expression became one of intrigue and it was only seconds later she agreed. "Then yes, we would love to have a meal and some water." Parsena nodded and made her exit, walking into the room to our left. Her form disappeared behind large, dark curtains, which again became stagnant sentry moments after she passed.

"It seems Eshkan knows quite a good contact here," Declan said.

I nodded in agreement and sat down next to Morard, resting my aching, tired body. The Sun was speaking now, quickly, in dark chants. It was restless, I was restless. Cahya must have noticed my fatigue because she began to lean over to me when Parsena returned with a man pushing in a cart full of plates of food. I wondered how Eshkan's contact was involved with this place, and what debt a Madame could owe to someone. Questions for another time.

"Aelus, these go to our guests," Parsena said. "If they require anything else, we are to see it met."

The man nodded and began with Dacian who graciously thanked him. Once he got to me, I held my hand out and spoke.

"Though I appreciate the kindness you are extending to my friends, I must decline," I said, hoping the statement would not bring about further questions. He skipped me, after nodding silently and moving along to Morard. I closed my eyes trying to focus on the sounds beyond the door to the streets.

"You said that you'll be scouting the city?" Cahya whispered. She noticed my hesitation and continued. "Do you wish for me to tell Eshkan anything?" she asked.

"No, only that I've stepped out and I'll be back soon enough," I answered. "You're in good hands here. These people have seen and heard things that could dethrone kings."

"That is what worries me."

"These people have no allegiance to Terrenveil. They've no reason to help him."

Moments after the statement left me, Cahya nodded, looking over at me. "Be careful."

I rose, quietly making my way back out into the streets. I wasn't sure where to begin. I was merely making observations, strolling, listening. But I found myself searching for an objective.

I wondered how Eshkan did it all these years. Sought out things he didn't know he was seeking. I looked at the world around me, people walking through the streets with their eyes occupied in watching everyone surrounding. It was difficult, near impossible to remain inconspicuous in a city where every person that passed by on the streets studied your appearance, and formulated thoughts on what you might be doing within the walls.

I took a breath of midday air into my lungs. It was beginning to become warm due to the sun just overhead, climbing to where it would be most intense. I rolled my sleeves back and looked at my arms, watching as small black scales began to follow the trails of my veins. A direct result of the sun upon skin, though it was occurring at a very slow rate. The Sun had something to do with this. Typically, the transformation would occur within minutes, the natural armor of a Sardon creating a shell around the vessel which housed blood and soul. I rolled my sleeves back over my forearms, heading toward the entrails of the city, past the market and a large inn. I didn't hear much that was worth investigating. A heist being planned within the walls of the royal city. A bunch of mercenaries being hired to hunt down a hoard of bandits near the Southern Pass. Not one mention of the king or his men.

I continued into what appeared to be markets that the city's many denizens necessitated. An armorer stood near his shop, looking toward a woman who swept the outside of a building that housed bows and arrows, made aware to me by the sign that hung outside. She turned to enter the shop and her pendant caught my eye, causing me to follow. After opening the door, I noticed that she had climbed a ladder, tending to something above shelves that lined the back wall.

"You come to buy something, Kesl? Or is it to ask me again about what I keep in my safe?" she laughed and turned, looking down at me. "Oh, I'm sorry, I thought you were..."

"The man outside the armorer's shop," I answered.

"Ah, you saw him too?"

"If he thought he was being discreet he's sorely mistaken."

"He's grown somewhat fond of me in the past few weeks," the woman stated and grabbed a bow from the top of the cabinets and gave it a once over before she descended the ladder quickly, not turning her back to me.

"A skilled archer, but no faction," I said and walked inward, looking at the arrows she had on display. "Did they give you that pendant after you left the Mountain?"

The woman's eyes widened as she pushed the pendant behind the cloth of her shirt, tying the front of it tighter. "This pendant has not come into my possession through service."

"I see. But any trinket from the legion, and worn, is either earned or gifted. So," I said and placed my hands on the counter. "When did you leave the Mountain?"

The woman closed her eyes and let out a heavy sigh. "Listen, I've not seen you before, and I remember every face that I see. Trying to peg me as a sympathizer or spy? I can assure you I am neither. You're asking questions that wouldn't be taken so kindly in other parts of the city."

"Other parts of the city don't house the shop of a woman who hides a legionnaire's pendant beneath her tunic."

"What is it that you want?" the woman asked, her sharp blue eyes focused.

"As you can see, I do not come from the Mountain. So however that pendant came into your possession is not the reason I ask about it."

"So why do you ask about it, then?"

"I need information," I said and paused for a moment to listen for any sound that would give away people within earshot. When I was satisfied, I continued, watching her expression change. "What do you know about the legion's commander?"

"I know to stay away from him," she answered and placed the bow on the glass case directly in front of her. "There's not much else to say. Aside from rumors there's not much anyone knows about him."

"Who would?"

"You're asking after a very dangerous man..." she stopped and tried to look at my face from beneath my hood. "Ah. Nonhuman. I won't bother asking for your name, then. I know I shan't receive it."

"Nor will I ask yours. So let us have a conversation about rumors," I said and leaned against the pillar in the center of the room.

"Well, for starters, the princess was to be wed this week. But she ran away a few months ago. Word, is they sent the commander and his men to track her down and it was reported that she was seen dragged off by nightwolves."

"The princess is dead?"

"People say he did it. Though it won't be investigated or tried. Princess Zerae was the only heir to the throne. It was forbidden to speak of after the vigils."

"Forbidden to speak of her?"

"All of it. She ran away. Said to have fallen in love with a man in town. When they were discovered together, his death was ordered. Because of it, she took a few things with her and left in the middle of the night," the woman answered. "I imagine they told the Prince of Lederes that she was killed during a trip. With having no other heir to the throne, Queen Neraea is most likely trying to give birth to as many children as she can until they produce a boy," the woman said and sighed. "Honestly I wish the bloody castle would just collapse, and the royal family with it."

"You harbor resentment."

"What gave it away?" she asked. "If you really must know about the pendant, it was my brother's. Family died when we were children. He died in battle and his pendant was sent to me as condolences."

I stood from the pillar and nodded my head toward her once, turning to leave when she spoke.

"I'm not sure how long you're staying in Defaltor, but you're welcome to stop by here when you aren't on business." She winked and opened the display case she was standing nearest, continuing her tasks. I offered a smirk and opened the door, returning once again to the streets. Unsatisfied given the lack of anything credible to relay to the others, I continued, coming across a large city square. A large house sat in the background, assumed to belong to the Lord of the city. There was a smaller stable due east of the house's courtyard. I wondered if Eshkan had plans to get inside. I headed off toward the house, to get a good look at how difficult it may be to gain entry when I noticed a man near the blacksmith's, watching me from his place near the smelter. At the moment I thought it better to continue moving, but was waved over, the man extending his left hand. The pointer and middle fingers were directed toward me, thumb relaxed to the side as his other fingers curled beneath his palm. There was no avoiding him now.

I was careful in approaching, watching the man's eyes as I neared. He was dressed in a dark gray robe with a heavy hood that covered most of his face. The arabesque pattern that lined the hood was golden, filled with black satin. This was no merchant.

"I see the man at the gate was not mistaken," he said.

"Now I have a face to dispel the mystery of why we were followed."

"Not followed. Marked," the man answered. "But it makes no difference now. The man was right, and his service will continue."

"What is the purpose of this?" I asked.

He laughed and shook his head. "This meeting is not of purpose, but of chance. Follow," he stated and led me toward the back of the forge, where two buildings formed a passage. The scent trailed through it, the sound of clinking metal becoming softer as we wandered until we reached a wall with no door. I focused on the man's movements for a moment, hand flat at my side near the hilt of Seligsara. He raised his arms, speaking words in a language unlike any I'd ever heard in Cilevdan, and a reddish mist covered the walls until they grew black in color. He turned toward me and moved his right hand out in front of him, turning it so that his palm was toward the sky. "You lead the way, now. Don't hesitate. There is only one path."

Reluctantly, I followed his instructions. The scent of the forge was replaced with one of burning spices used to cover blood. As we traveled past the corridor, there was a large sanctum with several rooms lining the curve of the walls. The man walked forward, urging me to follow. We passed others dressed in a similar fashion to him, watching me carefully, their voices inaudible whispers. Beyond the sanctum rested an alleyway that opened up into what looked like a row of endless rooms, a large one in the center. I followed the man into it, a large table greeting us, a few others sitting. A darkened bronze candelabra rested upon it, a smaller one on each side near the table's edge. Two people in similar robes walked into the room from stairs that rose behind the table. Someone of a shorter stature followed. The others in the room bowed their heads as they approached the table. Everyone sat, with the exception of the one who had entered last, the man urging me to do the same.

They removed their hoods, a sigil on their foreheads. Viscera. The one who was revered as their leader removed her hood last, long black hair surrounded her face. Her eyes were the color of steel, and as piercing as the color suggested. Around her markings were short horns that surrounded her forehead as if they were a crown, disappearing beneath her hair.

"Why so tense, Sardon? You act as if we've invited you to your death." She laughed, a small smile taking her lips.

"Invited?" I asked. There would be no way to trick or outsmart her. I could only leave now on her terms.

"Unless I'm mistaken, you are sitting at a gathering in which I have called everyone present to attend."

"And why call me here?"

"To enjoy one another's company, mostly. We'd be meeting under very different terms if I wished it so."

"I am aware."

"How very perceptive of you," she answered and narrowed her eyes, which in turn darkened in color. Powerful. I averted my gaze. I could not afford to upset her.

"I only meant to say that there must be a purpose for calling another nonhuman into your world that exceeds pleasantries. I mean no disrespect." As much as I wished to leave, I knew when it was better to bury longing.

"I see. You wish to get to the point. Time is not on your side, is it Sardon?" she asked and ordered a man to a room beyond this with one point of her finger. "How disappointing."

I waited for her to continue, attempting to relax.

"You are correct, it is not often I invite other nonhumans to my table. I prefer to interrogate them, to ensure they will not unleash chaos in my city. But I sensed something very different from you upon your arrival here. The very second you passed through the gate, you were eager to leave the walls."

"Now it is you that is correct. I do not wish to cause you any trouble."

"That is why we are sitting here, and you are not in one of my cells."

"Forgive me for not understanding," I answered.

"Perhaps we can help one another."

"In what way?"

"In time, you will realize when you need us most," she stated. "That is why you are sitting here. Think of it as..." She moved a hand to her lips and clicked her tongue once, returning to the conversation. "A pleasantry that precedes an alliance."

An alliance with the Viscera was something I would only agree to upon my dying breath. But they were powerful, diminutive, secretive.

"What do they call you, Sardon?" I was not given the time to answer before she closed her eyes and raised her fingers to call for a cease in motion from everyone in the room. "You do not go by your given name," she said, a smirk taking her face.

"As I am sure you do not."

"Ylth," she answered. "Crown of the Viscera, and Lord Deventer's fifth in command.

"Cethin," I said.

"Allow me to send you off with a proper meal. The humans here do not take kindly to those who are not like them, if you have not discovered that already."

"Would that have anything to do with your presence?" I asked. "Or has the hatred for nonhumans always existed?"

"The reason it exists is not of importance, Sardon, and I suggest you not ask about it further before I deem you as pestilent as they," she answered, her eyes changing with her tone. "You will need me more than I need you. Do not let your arrogance and pride stand in the way of that."

"You mentioned needing me."

"It is as I said, in time all will be revealed. Let us enjoy this time together. The others in your party... they do not join you on your stroll. Why is that?"

"They seek rest. It is something humans need far more than we," I stated.

"Ah a Sardon among humans. I noted one woman among you and thought maybe she too was like you, as you are known to travel in pairs."

"She is human," I answered, raising my eyes to meet hers.

"Hm. Protective... interesting."

"Leave her out of our discussion." My voice took a tone of warning. We searched one another's eyes for a moment, hers becoming as black as the void.

"Your transcendence," one of the men said. He stopped as he realized her eyes turned toward him, refusing to return to the color that indicated her relaxed state.

"Do your best to no longer question me, or I will devour you," she stated. "I grow hungrier with each moment that passes."

The man she had ordered out suddenly returned, a worried look on his face. "Your transcendence. There is something you must see." She acknowledged him with a nod and looked toward a man and woman sitting at the end of the table.

"You. See to it that the Sardon and she both are accommodated. The rest of you, with me." She looked toward me. "Forgive me for leaving so abruptly, but remember my words, Sardon. Until we meet again."

The others rose and left the hall, the woman remaining seated with me. I had wondered why a Viscera crown was so adamant about providing me with a meal but would not question further. This would save me from having to hunt, and I could better serve my company. I wondered what they were doing in the absence of my presence there and wondered even further about Cahya. I looked toward the woman who sat a few chairs down from me, silent. The question of why she was not called to follow the others came to my head but was answered when she shifted in her chair and it was revealed that her womb was very ripe. It was later discussed over the large amount of meat she was given that she was chosen to carry four future cultists, and that the discovery was only made a few short months ago. The cult was growing, despite the lack of knowledge about it in most of the world. I made quick work of the sustenance provided and stood to leave when the two cultists followed my actions.

"We were asked to see you back to Defaltor, Sardon," the woman answered.

I nodded in silence and began to follow them through their city, taking in every sight that I could. I supposed it was very rare to be called here and live to speak about it. That was worth remembering, though, I wished to never return. The couple opened the wall as before, and after a few moments I saw myself again standing in the corridor that stretched beyond the market. I quietly made it past the blacksmith and his crowd without attracting attention, making my way back toward the brothel when I was approached by two men.

"'Ey. Outsider."

I ignored them until one placed his hand upon my arm, forcefully. "He's talking to you."

"I heard him," I stated. "I've no business with you."

"That's where you're wrong."

"Do enlighten me," I said and pulled my arm from his grasp.

"One of you shows up into town, and people start going missing," the second man stated and moved part of his coat aside, revealing a blade.

"And so, you resort to threatening me in the streets. Didn't think murder was accepted by the city's lord."

"And what do you know about the city's lord?" the other asked mockingly, the alcohol heavy on his breath.

"How do you think he would react to trouble in his city, to murder in the streets? As much as I wish to avoid it, you wouldn't touch me again before I severed the head from your shoulders."

The drinker lurched forward but the other held him back. "Don't be a fool."

"I can smell the blood on his breath," he said and pushed his cohort backward. "He's killed recently."

"I've not killed anyone."

"And what makes you think either of us will trust you?"

"You might not trust him, but trust me," a man answered and pushed himself off the stairwell he was sitting on, walking over. "The man was with me beyond the walls before we came here together. He was finishing his business in the market, and I awaited him here."

"And just how do you know this... beast?"

"We worked together once. The rest is no business of yours. Now go, before I alert the rest of the watch of your meddling."

The two men looked at us before they walked off, the person who had intervened on my behalf shaking his head. "There are louts all over the city, pay them no mind."

"Have we met?" I asked.

"Not officially," he laughed and extended his hand toward me. "The name's Averail."

I looked at it a moment before shaking it, reading over his body language and carefully watching his friend, who had chosen to remain behind. "Cethin. Will he not join us?"

"No, pay him no mind either. He does not speak, has never spoken. I've not seen you around here before," Averail said and fixed his hat. "When did you arrive?"

"Just this morning.... It seems you've been here a while."

"I've more or less called Defaltor my home for the better part of a decade. I'm an unofficial watchman. The uniform doesn't suit me, but I also don't like trouble. It disturbs peace."

"I see."

"Cowardice is a trait of most prejudice. They weren't going to attempt to murder you out in the open. But I'd still watch for them. Alone they pose no threat, but the hive mind is a dangerous thing. Luckily, they fear the wrath of their lord more than the occasional nonhuman. They believe the babble of the goddess Araele concerning the purge, though I know not one of these people believe in her." He sighed. "They're just looking for something to destroy."

"Rest assured; I do not care to be here long. Once I have completed my business here, I will be on my way," I said. His stepping in was revealed to be nothing more than procedure, and I wished to end the conversation abruptly. I bid him farewell and began to make it back toward the brothel, eager to discover what was next.

I returned, hearing laughter the moment I stepped inside. A woman, the Madame, followed by the laughs of Dacian, Eshkan, and Morard. I quietly made my appearance at the door, seeing that the Madame was entertaining them with story and drink.

"Ah... I see your friend has returned... And a handsome one at that," she said flirtatiously. She winked at me, though I could barely see her eye behind her bangs, her long brown hair. Previously pinned to the top of it, she must have wanted to become comfortable after she began to drink. "So now I suppose you are all off on the business you have come to our lovely city for?" she asked.

"Yes, unfortunately we must leave your hospitality for a few hours. Pressing matters cause our appearance here," Eshkan answered.

"Hm. I see. Well, do come back tonight. You must have somewhere to rest. Surely you don't have anywhere else in mind."

"Nowhere at all," Eshkan said and removed his gaze from her eyes to mine. "Are you ready?" he asked.

"Where is Cahya?" I asked.

"Ah he asks after the lady," Madame Karstentia said, and laughed. "She waits in her chambers, just beyond those pillars and to the right."

I garnered a look from Eshkan, Morard letting out a quiet sigh. "She will perhaps want to accompany us," I stated. "I dare not argue with her."

"Wise," Morard said.

I nodded and followed the Madame's instruction, coming across the room and pulling the curtain aside, startling Cahya. She pulled the flowing, lilac-colored robe she was given around her torso as if she was made cold by the outside air.

"We have to leave this city as soon as possible," I said. "I don't like it out there."

"I can't imagine why," she said, her tone of sarcasm evident.

"I was witness to something that made me feel uneasy."

"You, uneasy?" she asked. "Cethin what is going on? What happened?"

"I wish not to discuss it while we are still here. It may frighten you."

"I will be the judge of that," she said and crossed her arms.

"My apologies. There are Viscera."

"In the city?!"

"They operate here. Their leader mentioned that we would be meeting again in the future, and she mentioned you as well."

"What do they want with me?" she asked quickly.

"It was not revealed."

"Cethin the Viscera are dangerous."

"I needn't a reminder." As soon as the words left my mouth, I noticed that she averted her gaze, light leaving the expression on her face. "Forgive me," I said and grabbed her hand. "I don't think it is safe for us to remain here any longer than we must. Will you be joining us?" I asked.

"No. It is better if I do not go with you. With the mention of the Viscera, and further mention of their knowledge of me, I do not feel comfortable." I looked at her in question but did not pursue. "Do not worry, Cethin. I will wait here with the others and rest. If I must protect myself, the others, I will."

"I will return soon," I said and picked her hand up off her lap, kissing it. After returning to the others, I watched as the eyes of Eshkan moved from the Madame toward me.

"I take it you are ready now?" Eshkan said. I nodded and made sure my weapons were intact. "Cethin, you and I will travel to what's referred to as *the bottom*. Dacian, I want you to go around the west side where the bets are usually made. We are looking for a man with red hair and a scar across his eye that looks like an arrow. If spotted, we are going to tail him to where he is staying so we can confront him. Dacian, if you find him, you make sure to return to us before approaching him. He looks harmless but he is not. Getting him to talk will not be easy."

"What shall I do?" Morard asked and crossed his arms. "You know damn well I will not wait here."

"Go with Dacian. An extra pair of eyes will not hurt."

Dacian nodded and patted Morard on his shoulder before turning toward the door.

Eshkan and I split from the others, walking silently along the streets. We caught the eyes of a few people when I strode forward, walking alongside him. "Perhaps it best we make conversation so that we don't seem..."

"Suspicious?"

"For lack of words, yes," I answered. "We can still be observant."

"What is it you wish to talk about?" Eshkan asked. I had never been asked this question before, my loss of words returned to me. "Very well then," Eshkan returned. "I'll start. Surely you have plans for when this is all over. Granted we don't die pursuing our mark," he amended.

"I want to see more of the world. Aside from when I would be sent out to kill, I was behind walls. Cells. I want to see the world with fresh new eyes. It has been a very long time since I've placed foot upon shore with anything other than blood on my mind, the stress that comes with it. Imagine seeing Stirae for… well for nothing more than just to see it. Surely the magic will be even more captivating."

"You and I want the opposite," he laughed.

"No more adventures?"

"Not for a very long time. I'll settle somewhere. Though not in my homeland. I fear I could not withstand the temperatures anymore, despite it being in my bones. There is a place for me, out there."

"I hope you find it," I stated.

"In due time, Cethin. Come, our destination is not much farther." I nodded, taking to silence once again. Despite the aggression and hatred the townspeople displayed toward non-humans and the arcane, the fences in the market beyond the smithy and city square were filled with items that previously belonged to both, or so the sellers claimed. One shop had large red gems displayed in a small basket. Five, to be precise, said to have come from the hearts of slain Viscera. I imagined them to be rubies stolen or found in a cave nearby. All the documented tales of Viscera labeled them difficult to kill. Though, I had heard the gem myth before. I had no access to the books that emerged from the purge killings, however.

There was a collection of fangs that belonged to several species of nonhuman sitting in an ivory box on one of the smaller stands operated by a woman dressed in a dark leather. Among these items were artifacts used by the same creatures for ritual and sacrifice, as well as other related antiquities. I ignored it the best I could, averting my gaze as to keep sights unwanted, unseen. I decided eventually not to allow myself any thoughts and to just continue toward wherever Eshkan was leading us. It was short lived. I couldn't help but wonder how often Eshkan came here. With a contact of his bestowing a gift as gracious as a safe place to rest, I assumed it was more than once or twice. I wondered if he had affiliation with any of the nonhumans that passed through here, or any of the cults. I doubted it, for he had not spoken of it since we arrived, nor had gone to see anyone else to my knowledge. If it was in my absence that this occurred, Cahya would have spoken of it. Her commitment was to aid whoever survived Ophidian, but her loyalty was to our relationship. If anything seemed awry, suspicious, dangerous, she would give it voice. I admired her guidance, her observations. I longed for more time to share with her. Part of me wished I could abandon this, could begin a life with her elsewhere, but shook thought from mind as it seemed we reached our destination.

I followed Eshkan into a tavern just on the other side of town, the smell of alcohol becoming thick in the hot air, tainted with the breath of its many denizens. A few of them turned from their glasses to get a glance at the door. They turned back to their tables as quickly as they had looked, continuing conversation with their peers. There were many coins on the table for the tenders to collect; a sign that they had been here for a while, slowly greeting intoxication. Two people stood behind the bar, a woman ignoring the taunts and provocation from the heavily drunken guests just before her and wiped the counter with a dampened rag. The man continued to serve drink from a large pitcher, taking in several coins for each one he poured.

I have never seen a place such as this in my travels, a place where men willingly pay to become inhospitable, and with lack of self-control. I didn't understand the custom of it, but I watched as Eshkan strode to the front, looking around at the people inside. He didn't seem satisfied as he quietly looked at their faces, passing the several old men in the corner who were practically sleeping at their table. As he continued, the man from the front gate came in the door, looking around the room. He did not notice me standing to the left of the door frame, hidden partially by the shadows made by the lack of windows on this immediate level of the building. Eshkan noticed him too, and moved quickly, cloaking himself behind a crowd of men singing and dancing as he made his way to me.

"He's not here," Eshkan said softly. I looked around once more and watched the gatekeeper hastily remove himself from the bar. We waited a few moments before leaving the establishment, re-entering the streets with caution. In glancing around the streets, I saw no trace of the man, but immediately wondered if he found a spot from which to watch us. I could not smell him, however, it seemed he was gone.

"We shouldn't stay in the open too much longer. Do you think that man was looking for us?" I asked.

"If it comes to a confrontation, we will deal with him. I was told that we can be led to a meeting with the criminal overlord," Eshkan said. "I'll admit, I did not want to come face to face with the man, but we will need weapons and armor if we are to survive on the roads."

"Nothing's free, Eshkan."

"I have a plan," he said, and began to walk past me.

I grabbed his forearm and pulled him aside, pointing to a small symbol carved into one of the buildings. "Have you seen these around?"

"Yes. What of it?"

"There are rumors that the Viscera has sources inside many cities and strongholds that provide them with objects of their trade. That glyph means that this household is either protected or a supplier. We will want to be careful. If we start any kind of trouble, we will be guests of their prisons. You could end up as worse," I answered.

"We can't stop now just because of that obstacle. If these men begin trouble with us then surely the difference will be known, unless you know otherwise," Eshkan answered suspiciously.

"We should just be as quiet as we can in our methods of retrieving knowledge," I said.

"That we shall. There is a butcher just up the road from here. If we don't find him here, then perhaps Dacian and the guard have had more luck." Eshkan took a step forward but stopped and held his hand back to me. He nodded his head toward a man that had just stepped out from one of the homes close to the tavern, adjusting his shirt beneath his belt. He seemed to be preoccupied with his attire, pulling his dagger closer to his side as he stumbled out of the house. We heard the shouting of a woman from inside and she suddenly appeared in the door, throwing a glass vase at the man. She missed him by several feet, swinging her blonde hair around and shouting a few more curses at him before slamming the door. He sleepily ignored her outrage and continued along the street, careful not to step on the several glass shards as he made his way toward the shops.

"That's who we've been seeking?" I asked, watching him in disbelief. After the event that had unfolded, he appeared not to know much of anything.

"Trust me on this. My source isn't wrong. We will tail him, and as soon as he evades the sight of the common folk, we will confront him." I nodded and Eshkan turned his face toward me as the man walked by. He ignored us, continuing to the tavern. Eshkan shrugged and offered a small laugh. "Well, we won't be as suspicious as we were the first time."

When we opened the door, a man was thrown past us, crashing into the barrels in the corner. Another patron of the city followed him, jumping on him, and began beating him with his fists, an act of violence from his stupor. We moved quickly to the other side of the room as the attention was diverted to the fight. Our mark watched as the two men wounded one another, a smug smile on his face for a moment as he went behind the bar and opened a door next to the wall of bottles. Eshkan turned to me and looked at the two men fighting. The one on the ground landed a good punch in his assailant's jaw, causing him to fall backwards towards a group of men in dark leather clothing. Without saying a word Eshkan quickly kicked out the legs of their table; timing it so that the brawlers appeared to be the reason for its collapse and subsequent ruination of their drink. They stood angrily, beginning to fight with the two who had originally begun their skirmish. It was then the barkeep fled from behind his counter, brandishing a sword to get the men to calm down. We didn't remain long enough to see what happened and moved toward the bar when the rest of the faces in the room turned toward the table of mercenaries.

I opened the door quietly, looking inside to see an old storage room filled with hay and barrels, the stone walls lined with shelves that held some of the same bottles in the tavern room. We entered it, and Eshkan shut the door quietly behind us as we searched the room for another passageway. Our mark did not very well conceal his entrance to a room beyond, a bale of hay was left pushed aside which revealed a small, wooden door on the ground. Eshkan bent to it and lifted the handle partially, waiting for any kind of noise within. After hearing nothing he confirmed no one was listening and pulled it up fully, gently resting the door against the wall next to us. I entered first and began to hear their frantic voices.

"Did you tell him anything else that I need to cover up?" a man asked, his voice full of anger.

"No. No. I told him nothing. But it's not like words mean anything. If he wants to know something he will figure it out another way. He's resourceful. We both knew the risk."

"What you need to do is get rid of that woman. If you spent half as much time with our preparations as you did screwing around with her we wouldn't be in this situation. She's a liability.

If he realizes that we're onto him then she'll undoubtedly be captured and used as bait to get you."

Eshkan nodded to me, and I jumped from the ledge, moving forward and waiting behind the wall. There were two men in addition to the one we had followed. One of the men was leaning against a post in the back of the room. His skin was dark, close in color to Cahya's. The other was pale, his dark hair curled and cut at a length just above his shoulders. I raised three fingers to Eshkan and he signed the symbol for silence. He did not wish to engage them at this point.

"How will they know about her?"

"Don't be a fool," the Mordestan said and moved forward. I turned to obscure myself. I knew what their voices sounded like, now. "Don't you think he has men watching you, just as you're watching him? You worked your way inside. But that doesn't mean he trusts you."

"Do you think we were followed?" our mark asked, turning toward the door.

"Why do you think we chose this place?" the pale one asked mockingly. "You're not exactly known for sobriety."

"You dreadful…"

I heard a crossbow being raised, and a hurried demand from the Mordestan followed. "Thurlowe stand down. We cannot hope to defeat him and his men if we do not work together."

"Do not insult me again," Thurlowe said gravely.

"What is the next step in our plan?" the Mordestan asked. "Kinsey, speak."

"After an excursion with one of his at the narrow, I learned that he's receiving a shipment tonight. I didn't catch what it was, but with the way his appointed was talking about it, it must be important."

"Which means that something is being smuggled into the city," the Mordestan stated. "What do you think?"

"We know too little. But we shouldn't leave this to chance," Thurlowe answered. "We should intercept."

"Who do you suggest?"

"I volunteer," Thurlowe said as he moved something across the room. "I need to make sure that this is done the right way."

"I don't feel comfortable risking you," the Mordestan returned. "But I also don't trust anyone else to be able to handle it. Fine."

Eshkan suddenly reached for his dagger seconds before a golden one was poised to strike his throat. A woman suddenly came into view from the shadows. She tightened her hold, causing Eshkan to shake his head. "Both of you, inside." I complied with her demand, turning from the wall and walking forward, my hands very visible at my sides.

"Zheki, what have you brought us?" the Mordestan asked, looking at Eshkan's face and toward me.

"They were already here when I arrived. The hatch wasn't very well hidden it seems," Zheki stated, her voice almost monotone in delivery. A seasoned mercenary, this one.

"Kinsey I could kill you for your negligence and we'd be better off," Thurlowe stated.

"Speak."

"This is an interesting arrangement," Eshkan answered. I looked over to him, my expression twisted in confusion, but decided to remain quiet and let him handle things. "A Mordestan, a reject from the Baeld, and a man from Kathai, all who have found themselves in the gracing presence of an Abissian."

"Very perceptive, Septen," the woman stated and removed her cowl. It revealed long silver hair, shining against her bone-white skin. It was then I noticed that her eyes were fully white in color.

"Is it true what they say about you? That you mostly rely on hearing to see?"

"It is," she answered. "It is why your Sardon over there could not hypnotize me if he tried."

"Since you've made it clear," I said and moved the hood from my head.

"You have an interesting arrangement yourself," Thurlowe said, and held his hand out toward Eshkan. "We can stand here swapping stories all day or you can explain why the both of you were listening in on our meeting before I decide to kill you for your espionage."

"A smart man never reveals his sources, but I was told, from someone who is not involved with your enemies that you may be able to tell us what a certain symbol means."

"I'm not an anthropologist. But you've interested me. How do you know this person is not involved with my enemies when you've no idea who my enemies are?" Thurlowe asked.

"He's since retired from the trade. But he told me that if anyone knew what this was, it would be you."

"I find it hard to believe that a symbol is the only reason you sought me out."

"I was also told that you may be in the position to let go of some weapons and armor if we helped you."

"It just so happens that we were planning something, and since I'm sure you heard every word of it, you'll be perfect."

"Thurlowe," Zheki stated and removed the dagger from Eshkan's neck. "How do you know we can trust them?"

"Someone who is brave enough to seek me out asking for arms knows well enough already not to cross me. And if that isn't enough, his friend Varsenius wouldn't appreciate it very much if we killed him in the stead of his betrayal."

Eshkan sighed, nodding. "Perceptive."

The vagary of the situation was becoming troublesome. It was clear now that Thurlowe oversaw the operation, as the Mordestan assumed silence again. I wondered what his part in this was, and why he was so far from home.

"I'll identify your symbol as an establishment of good faith. You help us with our endeavor this evening, and I'll consider your request for arms," Thurlowe answered.

"Accepted."

"You don't have much of a choice," Zheki hissed and walked forward.

"Play nice with our new associates. You're going to be accompanying the Sardon while he scouts."

"Do I get a say in any of this?" I asked. Everyone's eyes were on me at that moment, including Eshkan's. I managed a small shrug before returning to silence, watching as the Mordestan began to look over the notes that were on the wall to his left.

"The symbol. Show me," Thurlowe said and rolled his hand twice.

I pulled a piece of cloth from my cloak and placed it on the table before him. On it I had drawn the symbol that was left on our dead. Thurlowe looked at it and moved his head downward in a sigh, laughing softly, raising his crossbow. This caused the Abissian to draw her weapon, as well as the Mordestan.

"Where... where did you see that?!" Kinsey asked suddenly, becoming frantic.

"Explain yourselves now, before I decide where I'm leaving your corpses," Thurlowe said.

"It was carved on the chests of our people the night our city was destroyed, burned to the ground. Only six of us are known to have survived. Maybe a few civilians. If they lived after the burning it wasn't long," Eshkan answered.

"It doesn't sound unlike them. The question you should be asking is why they were in your city in the first place," Thurlowe said and looked at it again, sitting back, and placing his crossbow down. "That there is the Sigil of Bloods, carved by members of the Mask of Death."

"Forgive me but we aren't familiar," I answered.

"I didn't expect you to be. It was an order started by several guards of King Telmanos almost a hundred years ago. They were mostly interested in gathering riches when they went on war raids, but it evolved into something different, something darker probably eighty years back when its original creator died in a battle and one of his followers took the reins. After that it was rumored that they began to look for artifacts that belonged to nonhumans. The Viscera, nightwolves, revenants, Abissians, Sardons." I looked at him and averted my gaze quickly. "The king never approved this savagery, such intimacy with the nonhumans, and when he came close to finding out who was leading them, he was poisoned in his sleep. His eldest son, Axen became the king until he too met an unfortunate fate. Now we have Ozrach, who has been in the business of pretending it doesn't exist for about thirty years now. I guess he's never really had to face it since there has been no war," Thurlowe answered.

"Until his commander returns from what he's done to our people and somehow convinces him otherwise," I answered.

Thurlowe looked up at me, curiosity in his voice. "You mean to tell me the commander of his guard was there?" I nodded and crossed my arms in frustration. It seemed he had a reputation everywhere.

"I'm surprised so many of you survived. If he's somehow involved with the Mask that means that something... terrible is being planned."

"What do you know about him?" Eshkan asked.

"I had the misfortune, yet pleasure of being in his presence once. He too, came to me looking for information. He was looking for some kind of box. He wouldn't tell me what was in it, or why he sought it. Only that it was very old, and it was created a very long time ago."

"It must be what he came to our land looking for," I answered.

"I'm under the assumption that he did not find it."

"Yes. He went home with nothing but blood on his hands."

"I cannot help you with the commander. But do this task for me and I will give you the arms you need. Anything," Thurlowe answered.

"When do we begin?" Eshkan asked.

"At nightfall." Thurlowe moved pieces of paper that were on the table and revealed a map of the city. "The only way to get anything inside is through the main gate. You, and Undai will...

oversee things as they enter the city. We'll just have to acquire city watch uniforms. I will handle that."

"Thurlowe how do you expect…"

"You know better than to question my methods," he answered and shot a glance toward Kinsey who immediately silenced. "Kinsey, I'm assuming since you were invited to the narrow that you will also be present for this shipment?"

"Yes, I am to meet his appointed there once the sun has vanished behind the clouds, not a moment sooner."

"Which means that dusk is when it will enter the city. There will be a shift change. I will try to acquire those uniforms as quickly as I can and will be back here in a hurry. Zheki, I want you and the Sardon to get to the narrow and scout. If there are any of his men present, we need to know about it. We also need to know where the guards are positioned. Their shift changes may be predictable, but their positions are not."

"It will be done," Zheki answered and motioned for me to move ahead. I looked toward Eshkan and he gave one nod. We emerged back into the bar, Zheki fixing her cowl before moving forward. "I will take us to the narrow. Follow my lead and don't stray. You don't want to be caught there. I cannot save you."

"I can handle myself," I answered.

"If you were aware of the situation, you would know that I am fully capable of dispatching a few human guards. I mean that if you are spotted then I cannot step in. It would risk the mission."

"I see. Forgive my arrogance. These are trying times."

"Indeed," she answered. "Let us hope this plan goes off without a hitch. Thurlowe is rarely wrong."

"What is his cause?" I asked. "I am only asking out of curiosity. A trait I picked up from humans, I admit."

Zheki laughed and looked toward me. "They do tend to transfer feelings. I will make it quick. There are three gangs in Defaltor. One is a petty group of louts who only target the nonhuman. Racists. Believers in the purge. What they are unaware of is that there are nonhuman species in existence that do not prey on humans for sustenance."

"Eahie, Abissians," I stated.

"To name a few," Zheki said. "The other gang is a criminal one, gaining followers under their leader, who is only known to us by the name Kavir. He has rivaled Thurlowe for a long time. Thurlowe's operation began here long ago. Kavir moved in a few years after."

"So, he's trying to rid of his rivals?"

"Thurlowe is involved in the black market. He provides things to nonhumans. Most find that distasteful, but, as you can imagine, that is why I have chosen my alignment with him. Kavir's men are known for their aggression toward us, and there have been many killings on his hands. That has attracted the attention of city watch. While we knew this was the shape things would take, it has also made things difficult for us. Black Market work is tricky. The city lord does not take kindly to it. He does not like things to be out of his control," the woman sighed and placed a hand on my shoulder. "Forgive me for being so abrasive upon first meeting. I only wanted to make sure they were in no danger. They are like family to me. The red-haired one... can be an annoyance at times. But he means no harm. Thurlowe found me outside the walls one day. I was on the run. I am lucky he found me. He took me back to his hideout, past the markets and into the old lofts. We've been together ever since."

"I understand. I am protective over my friends as well."

"Here," Zheki said, crouched down as she strode over to where two houses came together. "These are the narrows." I looked around, understanding now why the sector was given the name. The rowhomes were close together, about four windows up. "We must take to the top of that tower and scope the roofs."

"I'll go."

Zheki immediately pushed past me and looked up toward the tower. "We go together. We both may see very different things." I nodded at her response, looking at the tower that watched over the city. I walked closely to the walls, ensuring no one from the watch would see me begin my ascension and grabbed hold of a door frame, following each window and old straying stone. I did not wait for the Abissian, looking upward to see where I could safely scout the area without risk of falling, or being spotted. Three watchmen in total, one toward the back end of the narrows, two on either side. There were humans, dressed in brown leather and hoods on their heads on the top floor in the second, fifth and ninth set of row homes. Toward the one in the very back that faced the tower, indicative of a split in the street, another was on the third floor, their eyes focused. As she turned her head I turned to the side of the tower quickly, pressing my back against the wall above a window frame.

I looked around for the Abissian, and after not being able to spot her, climbed downward, moving back to where we had waited before. Two people passed by, speaking about a mark they recently emptied. A woman followed—swords on her back held in scabbards of shimmering green reptile skin placed her from the Barapha empire to the east. Once the street had quieted, I saw gold shimmers of light appear before me until they shaped a woman, Zheki arriving from it. "Three guards, people stationed along the houses heading straight through the narrows."

"Another on the house at the end of the street," I stated. "But as the road bends I can see nothing."

"Good eye. We will take to the roofs then. Three guards will be easier to evade," she answered and jumped up to a ledge, springing to another immediately and pressing herself against a raise in the roof's architecture. I followed, balancing myself to regain footing and stood behind her, peering around the other side. "I know you can hear heartbeats... as they are mostly my way of seeing humans. Changing form is too risky, at least until the sun leaves us. We must make note of the shift change before we return to Thurlowe with our report."

"The guards look tired. Hopefully an indication that it is soon."

"Anxious?"

"No, eager." I answered and watched the patrol patterns. Zheki nodded in response.

The Abissian sat, closing her eyes and focusing her hearing. Time passed, at least an hour due to the position of the sun in the sky. Zheki opened her eyes suddenly and looked at the guard closest to us on the left. "Footsteps on a ladder nearby. Now may be the time."

She pointed downward and immediately descended. I followed, catching a peek at a watchman relieving his brother in arms. Zheki began to take a swift pace, and I moved through the crowd to keep up with her. We walked past the tavern and headed right, following a passageway through an old courtyard. Old gravestones lay beyond an old and forgotten chapel. She climbed down into a hole in the chapel's foundation, and I followed, looking at the massive space that was covered by an old wooden floor. Eshkan and the Mordestan were in their disguises, Kinsey speaking to Thurlowe who stood forward and walked toward us.

"Well?"

"His men are very present, even more so than the guards. They're hiding in the rows along the streets, top-floor windows."

"It sounds like they'll be keeping an eye on you two," Thurlowe laughed.

"Why not confiscate the shipment at the gate?" Eshkan asked. "Won't he think the watchmen would have taken it?"

"The point is not that the shipment goes missing. The point is that he realizes that it was taken from him by me," he answered sternly. "Now that we're all here, I'll go over the plan. You two will take place of watchmen at the gate. The owners of those uniforms won't be awake until sometime tomorrow."

"You'll identify the cart being driven by a Rustanzi," Kinsey answered. "They will be wearing a large pendant with the symbol of an eagle on it."

"No doubt they'll try to distract you so that they are not investigated. Mark every notable detail about the cart and the company of the driver that you can. Fall for whatever tricks they may have. I want that cart to enter the city," Thurlowe said.

"I'll already be with Kavir's men waiting to receive the shipment. This is why I need you and the Sardon to follow me on the best route you see possible. I have no idea how many men will be there. And... I'll also need you to save my skin if something goes wrong," Kinsey instructed.

"If everything proceeds according to plan, I will arrive to intercept the shipment, and you two will descend from the rooftops to provide muscle. I don't think he'll let it get away without a fight."

"We shall see you at the narrows," Zheki answered and motioned for me to follow her out.

"No, stay hidden," Thurlowe said. "I'm sure there he will have men waiting for the arrival of the cart. When I enter, descend only if I'm surrounded."

"Descend?" Zheki asked. "The guards."

"If you make your way onto the rooftops from the district of silence, it should give you enough time to hide yourselves in the niches of the older buildings," Kinsey suggested. "It's about time for me to go, if I don't arrive at the designated time, they will start to wonder what's happened."

"Go. Both of you know what to do," Thurlowe said, turning to the Mordestan. "Go around the back of the cemetery, head up the canal and into the streets. You know the way." The man nodded and Eshkan followed.

"We're off too, then," Zheki answered.

"Be careful," Thurlowe said, looking directly into her eyes. She nodded in response, and I followed her back out into the streets through the chapel.

"The district of silence is a strange place," she started, looking through the streets to ensure that there were no eyes upon us. "Tens of years ago one of the Viscera was slain there. She was overrun, eight men continually stabbed her in the street until she no longer breathed. The men died over the course of a week, lesions appearing on their skin. They vomited their organs, their eyes turned yellow. It was said that one of them tried to take his own life but couldn't. He tried to hang himself, but he wouldn't hang. Tried to slit his throat, but he didn't bleed. He was meant to endure that sickness until it slowly killed him, as it did the others."

"A curse?" I asked.

"No one knows. But her murderers were not the only ones it claimed. The survivors of the area moved out of their homes. The entire street is empty and has remained that way since her death. The gangs won't target the Viscera now, but everyone else is still target to their hatred."

"I suppose that makes it easier for us to sneak through undetected."

"Yes," Zheki said. "Most people are superstitious, so they won't remain there for fear of it still being cursed. Though we should still be careful. It'd be the perfect place for those hiding from people on the outside. Or those who wish to remain forgotten. I doubt they'll give us trouble, though."

"Noted," I answered.

We began to travel the streets until the number of people that traversed them became scarce. Zheki stopped, standing in front of a street full of buildings that looked to be the very first of the town, possibly built before the walls. But what was even more remarkable was the sound. Silence. Absolute. No voices from people, nor creaking of floorboards. I wondered how well Zheki was able to see, though she seemed to make confident progress as she walked along the street. I kept pace with her, ensuring to be exceedingly vigilant in watching the buildings around us. She proved to be right, though, I could pick up on nothing aside from small animals that made their homes in the buildings' walls.

"Here," she answered as we approached the end of the street. I could hear a myriad of voices from the other side of a low wall, life in the city beyond this hollow. I saw a stone out of place, and moved toward her, offering her a step up onto the roof overhead. I used the stone to follow, grabbing the edge of the roof. Zheki grabbed onto my hand and pulled me upward, signaling to me so I didn't stand. She, of course, was unaware of my past life. I didn't spend any time correcting her. Beyond our stay in Defaltor, I doubted we'd ever cross paths again.

"There seems to be some sort of structure on the roof just ahead, though I cannot see it very well. There is not enough noise from the street for me to utilize."

"I'll go ahead. Stay close to me."

The structure she pointed out was a stone terrace, nothing but empty nests once belonging to birds inside. "Can you see the courtyard below us?" I asked.

"It should be surrounded by homes. A dead end of sorts, unless you use the entry beyond that last house to the right that leads to the canals as an escape. Thurlowe has been here for a long time, he knows a lot about the city. I've accompanied him on his walks after dark. Look. There's Kinsey with one of Kavir's men," Zheki said, moving forward. The two were conversing with pace, Kinsey completely relaxed. His heart rate was that of a human at rest, his smile and laugh proving naturality. I could see now why he was chosen to work within the inside of enemy ranks. Calm, focus, deceit.

"No sign of the cart yet," I stated and attempted to isolate the sounds surrounding me.

"It will come," the Abissian stated and looked downward. "Perhaps we should get closer?"

"No. Thurlowe said he wanted us to wait to descend. I'm sure he has reason for it." I looked toward the opening in the streets, the cart was rolling into view, the Rustanzi driver climbing down from atop it. He walked toward Kinsey and the other, speaking in his native tongue. Kinsey began to speak to him in return, translating between the two. Indispensable. A smart man. The man began to point toward his cart in haste, demanding what could only be payment. Two Rustanzi women were on the back of the cart, swords on their backs. There was a lack of trust that fueled tension.

The man Kinsey accompanied pulled a generously sized coin purse from his tunic, and the Rustanzi ordered his counterparts to retrieve the item of desire. They passed the leather pouch toward him. He smiled, saying one word to Kinsey who returned a phrase. The Rustanzi's handed the cart over to Kavir's men, and it was taken to a courtyard nearby, Zheki and I quickly following. Kavir's men began to leave the courtyard, leading the cart along when Thurlowe stepped out from a building beneath us, laughing.

"You!" Kavir's trusted exclaimed. "Shouldn't have come here alone, you're outnumbered."

"Tsk tsk. How presumptuous. It may appear that way now, but you should know better than that."

"Way I see it is we could beat you within an inch of your life before anyone even knew you were 'ere."

"You don't have the stones," Thurlowe stated. "It's a shame Kavir isn't here himself. He could have made such an outlandish remark to me that I'd half believe. Send him my regards?"

"All of you!" a voice from the street. "Comply or meet your fate!"

"City watch," Zheki gasped. "Time to go."

"What about the others?"

"They'll know where to meet us," she answered and grabbed my wrist, leading me back toward whence we came. We weren't the first ones back to the chapel. Eshkan and the Mordestan were there first, laughing about something until we arrived in the room. "Where are the others?" Eshkan asked.

"Thurlowe will be arriving shortly. City watch ambushed the courtyard. I've no doubts he made it to the canal," Zheki answered.

"City watch?" There was alarm in the Mordestan's voice. "I wonder if they followed the cart after it passed through the gate. We did not notice anyone watching, but the way it was guarded is enough to provoke suspicion."

"I wonder if they confiscated whatever was left on the cart, too," I answered. "Are you certain he'll be back here? Or do you think we'll have to break him out of their prisons."

"He'll come back," Zheki said sternly and sat at the chair in the far corner of the room. "It's likely that the Watch went after Kavir's men first. They are idiotic enough to organize exchanges like that despite being wanted men. It most likely gave him time to slip away. Can't say the same for Kinsey, sadly. But he's been known to serve sentences before. The man can talk his way out of anything. If he got caught, he'll be out within a few days' time after he convinces the warden that he had nothing to do with it."

"Hope you all didn't miss me too much," Thurlowe announced, walking into the room, the bottoms of his boots wet. "A bit of excitement. Procuring the package would have been a bonus, but Kavir will soon know that I'm one step ahead of him. And his men didn't see either of you. You keep your anonymity," he removed his hood and leaned against the table in the room, crossing his arms so his hands were across his biceps. "The watch should be a bit busy with the apprehension of Kavir's men in the narrows. Zheki, I want you to lead the Sardon and his faction to the Lofts tomorrow at midday. He and I have a matter to discuss." Zheki nodded and stood, smiling at us as she vanished, small white lights glistening brightly before they followed suit.

I made my way out into the streets, following Thurlowe for several moments before I spoke. "The matter to discuss?"

"Not here. Follow."

"Understood."

Thurlowe sighed and looked up into the sky. "I assure you that I do not wish to continue the secrecy any longer. I know a good man when I see one. I know you can be trusted."

"My intention of the following isn't meant to disparage your observation, but how do you know that?" I asked.

"Curious sort, aren't you? I suppose that's what Zheki liked about you. I can tell her demeanor changed when the both of you arrived back at the chapel."

"She mentioned you."

"You needn't speak of it; I jump to no conclusions. She and I have a strong foundation. This much I'm sure she revealed to you."

"Yes," I answered. The way she spoke of him was the same way I'd speak of Cahya. Admiration, adoration with a strength of nature in opposition to the amount it was given voice. We passed the inn and continued into a section of lower streets. After traveling through several avenues, Thurlowe looked around before opening a hatch that led outside the walls. I followed, only to watch him open a second that led back into the city. Defaltor became an interesting place, our new contacts equal to that trait. We stood in some kind of cellar, Thurlowe continuing forward to make quick work of a Kathairan lock affixed to the door that separated us from our destination. Once on the other side, he pushed a brick into the wall and it moved, revealing the inside of a small, yet decadent house.

"I trust you will keep this a secret," Thurlowe said and placed his cowl on a golden coat rack.

"What is this?" I asked, looking around.

"You look upon the home of the city's lord." I watched him for a moment, uncertain if he had just elected me to go on a daring heist with him. In my silence, Thurlowe closed his eyes briefly to sport a smile, and laughed. "Don't look so anxious. He's only just recently arrived home," he said as he walked up a set of stairs toward the upper level of the house. I took to following him, jogging to catch up.

"You mean to say that you…"

"I've only been playing double for a few years now, there's a reason for knowing Defaltor so well. My father died ten years past."

"So why the charade?"

"A question I knew would come. I don't like things going on without knowing about them. So, to be able to infiltrate the criminals that entertain the idea of forming an underworld in my city, I had to. As lord, I must train and instruct my guard on how and where to strike. I have a reputation to uphold to anyone that resides or travels here. I must be harsh and strict with judgment. But I must also keep peace between the people that have chosen to make this place home. When needed, that means I execute those who have made themselves problems, whether they're human or not. As a boss of the underworld, I'm able to learn what most would keep secret from the city's authority. This way I'm in control of both," he answered.

"Care to elaborate," I answered.

"Now you see why I am in such a position to compensate you and your friends. My reason for bringing you back here was to confirm trust. And to also demonstrate why I am not to be crossed."

"Does Zheki know about this?" I asked.

"She does not." Thurlowe sighed. "I have my reasons for keeping it a secret from her, for now. Our coterie runs smoothly. One day I will have to resign, and I'd like for her to be at my side. As for her taking you to the lofts, meet her at the chapel. You don't have to go out the way we came in. I'll escort you to the front door."

I nodded, walking alongside the man, thinking about the events that took place as I made my way down the large stone steps that led to his home. I began to like the city more than I expected to, surprising given my original opposition to spending even a night here. They seemed like good people, and in a time where so many horrors befell my own coterie, were warming to find. As I made my way back to the brothel, there were a few other night travelers in my midst, and I avoided looking toward anyone in order to conceal my face. It wasn't long before I opened the doors to the brothel and was suddenly greeted by Parsena, who curtsied.

"The others have already returned and were shown to their chambers. May I show you to yours as well?" she asked softly.

"When did they get back?" I asked.

"Eshkan arrived recently. The young one said for me to tell you that they uncovered nothing, and he was weary," she answered.

I nodded softly. "You can show me to my quarters." I wanted to go to Cahya, but she was probably already sleeping. I wasn't sure how many restful nights we would have from this day forward, and this may be the only night for a long time that we wouldn't be upon road.

"I can come and wake you at any time necessary. It is my duty to accommodate my Madame's guests," Parsena offered.

"When the sun is beginning to rise," I answered.

"That is when you shall be awoken." She turned abruptly, but then turned back, pointing to two rooms by large pillars. "You may choose either one to stay in," she answered, moving her yellow hair from her eyes.

"Thank you. It is late, you should gain rest too," I answered, dismissing her. When I moved the dark purple curtain from the doorway of the room to the left, I noticed there was nothing inside except for a thick bed of furs and candles with the aroma of lavender and vanilla. It was soothing, calming. I wrapped the curtain into the door frame behind me and moved the outermost layer of fur over, placing Seligsara beneath it. I didn't know how much rest I would attain this night. We gained powerful enemies within two days' time, though it seemed we gained powerful friends as well. I mentioned the Viscera to only Cahya, the person I trusted over anyone else. The words of their leader reverberated in my head. There would come a time when I needed them. I hoped that day was far off.

I drew a breath and closed my eyes. It was not long after this that I had drifted into sleep, waiting for the sunrise…

◆ ◆ ◆

"*This is when you'll need the light.*" A voice, feminine, one I could not yet recognize. I wandered along the trees, which became stronger, the roots above ground, entangled in one another. I could smell the sea less and less now, having left it behind. I continued forward, moving through the forest as fast as I could, following the voice and the scent that its bearer embodied. It became farther away, too, and I was suddenly left in a copse of trees, a hollow center, darkness...

◆ ◆ ◆

I awoke to the sound of a breath. I saw the silhouette of a woman in the dark and reached slowly for the handle of Seligsara. It wasn't Parsena, for this woman had no scent to her. Her heartbeat was so quiet that it could very well be that there was none. Perhaps she was only a shadow; that I was wearier than I realized. I felt as if my distrust for the security of the house in addition to the dream I just had was affecting my mind. Eventually the silhouette, what I thought to be a woman, dissipated. The darkness of the room was potent, now still and quiet. There was no sound to be heard, not even a breath or whisper. I remained, with eyes open for another hour before Parsena pushed the curtain from the door frame, speaking softly. I rose, signaling to her that she need not come any closer. When she withdrew back into the sanctum, I pulled my shirt off the dresser, pulling it over my head. I heard something heavy fall to the floor, and I watched it roll. The light from the candles produced a gleam across its surface. I picked the object up, looking into it. It was dark, shining. Perhaps a piece of stone, or a gem. On the back of it, a symbol was carved, as well as what appeared to be characters that I could not make out. I was suddenly interrupted by Eshkan, who folded the curtain back abruptly. "Are you ready to go?" he asked.

"Someone was in my room last night," I answered, abruptly, without thinking.

"What?"

"Someone was in my room last night. I can't find my cloak, and there was something in my clothes... there was..."

Suddenly, the Madame walked into the doorway. Her hair was pinned back by two amethyst picks, matching the color of her dress. It was low cut and ended above her knees. The pieces were separated by a slit that went up toward her waist, covered in a layered black lace that ruffled beneath it. She smelled of night flowers belonging to the dark wood, just east of the region. An expensive scent.

"I'm certain you all slept well last night. I told my girls not to disturb you while seeking stories. It was a challenge for them. It isn't often they get to see such handsome and beautiful warriors. Usually, the company we get around here is more..." Karstentia sighed, bringing her left hand down to her side. "Well, not as easy on the eyes. And dreadfully boring," she decided.

"Thank you again for your hospitality," Eshkan answered.

"The pleasure is mine. Will you be staying this evening?" she asked, looking below Eshkan's belt, then up toward his eyes, adopting a smirk on her face.

"We wouldn't want to overstay our welcome."

"Nonsense. Perhaps tonight your friends shall wish to indulge in a little fun." The Madame winked, heading outward.

"What kind of favor did she owe your contact?" I asked, suddenly.

"I don't know, and it is usually better not to ask. Basilin must not have left us completely."

"Basilin." I laughed. "I think this has more to do with your charm."

"So, it may seem," he answered. "Our new contact. Do you trust him?"

"Yes. In our excursion he revealed something to me that he claimed to have told no one. I believe him. Though I still do not understand why I was chosen."

"You have a friendly face." Eshkan laughed and quickly patted me on the shoulder, turning away. His sense of humor was amusing. I was beginning to see more of the people I was in the company of. Friendships I never would have gained if not for the Isle, yet personalities I never would have seen if we remained there. I took one quick look around the room, shaking my head and joining the others. I had odd feelings about what I saw in the dark hours of the morning. Suspicions.

"It is best we be on our way," I stated. "The sooner we meet with Thurlowe, the sooner we can leave town." I was met with silence, nods. I didn't think much of it as we made our way into the streets, Cahya moving forward to walk alongside me.

"What happened yesterday? Eshkan didn't seem too keen on releasing details."

I looked back toward him. He was entertaining the others with a story. Morard laughed, trying to invite Declan to lighten his spirits. The man seemed deeply disturbed by the events that took place, his face often unchanged. A blank expression taking residence among his features.

"We gained allies. We did something for them and were promised weapons. Whatever we needed."

"Resourceful allies, it seems," she said softly. "The symbol, what of it?"

"It belongs to a faction called the Mask of Death. The commander seems to be a part of it. They siege lands looking for lost artifacts belonging to nonhumans. It is conclusive."

"Very. I'm sure the both of you have a plan?"

"We'll formulate one soon enough. We know what the symbol is, now. Though I'm not sure where to go from here."

"We will discover it yet. To where are we going?" she asked, looking at the sights that the streets had to offer.

"There is a chapel a few streets away, buried by buildings that surrounded it as the city grew, I suppose. We are meeting one of our contacts there and are being led to a place they call the Loft." She nodded in response and was silent for the remainder of the journey. After we entered, we reached the basement, Zheki rising from her seat upon one of the tables.

"I was beginning to wonder if you would arrive on schedule," she smiled. "Your friends are not what I was expecting. I suppose your arrangement is as strange as mine. Come. Thurlowe is waiting for us. We'll take the canal. There are too many eyes in the streets this morning."

Morard and Declan seemed captivated by the Abissian, and in assuming they had never seen one before, I supposed it was natural. She was wearing a sort of leather armor, revealing to us intricate markings in small, lined patterns across her arms and neck equal to her eyes in color. Their abilities still had them pegged as evil among many religious factions and those who hated anyone that was not humankind. Abissians were peaceful people, living in cities that could only be reached by searching forests, and discovering how to cross worlds. Few of them traveled to this plane of existence, and fewer stayed.

The canal was not as long as I expected it to be. Old shoddy scaffolding that scaled the walls led up toward an opening in them, its half-wooden interior displaying age. There was a door at the end of the room we had just entered, Thurlowe leaning against the wall in front of it. He came forward once we approached, looking everyone over.

"They're chasing the commander with you?" he asked, his tone one of astonishment, he abandoned it as he ordered us inside, Zheki closing the door behind us. "I'll show you to my armory in just a moment. But I thought it best we reveal what we know about the current state of Terrenveil and its army so that way may aid your cause."

"Our gratitude," I answered. "From where we come... we are out of touch with the affairs in most parts of Cilevdan."

"I assumed as much, forgive me. With a statement as bold as your vow to stop him I believe it best we aid one another."

"It seems he is not well liked in most places," Cahya stated, moving forward from her position behind me. Thurlowe's eyes lightened. "Ahh you are in company of a Mordestan as well." Cahya was not sure how to react to his response until he furthered it. "I call upon Undai often. He keeps my temper controlled."

"We are known best for soothing," she laughed. "I'm sure Undai has told you the story of Makai and the fire."

"Yes, yes. He's taken to mentioning that when I am letting my rage think for me. He is Makai."

"We are also known for recalling our folklore," she laughed.

"Defaltor is a place where many stories are heard. But his are always the most important," Thurlowe answered. "If he were here right now, he'd reference Ahoni and the season of rain."

Cahya smiled, "A favorite of mine. To our topic of discussion."

"Do you have a plan for dealing with the commander?" Thurlowe asked.

"Not as of yet," Eshkan stated. "But there are a few options."

"Discuss."

"We know what you know, sadly. Though, I wonder how often he is able to leave the castle, hunting for this box," I said.

"Yes. We established this. He hasn't had much time to leave, of late. It seems that even with the rumors of provinces rebelling that he is not being granted his wishes."

"There are rumors of a rebellion?" Cahya asked.

"I don't know how truthful they are, though I was contacted by a man named Alaies in Sathenne. When the commander came here, he left his men at the gate aside from his most trusted. Of course, they did not bear the armor that bore the coat of arms of Terrenveil." Thurlowe sighed. "He sought me out immediately. He found Undai first, and I'll admit, I did open conversation with asking how he found him. That's honestly the only reason I agreed to an audience. He's a mysterious man. Intimidating. His presence is... unnerving but he is also interesting. It was after a few minutes of terse exchange that he asked about the box. I regretted my decision to speak to him immediately. He seeks the Box of Barroqas."

"Min alnaeam argia askatu," Zheki said and held her hand up toward her neck, her symbols emitting a soft, timid light. "You're certain?"

"Yes," Thurlowe stated. "It is an evil that was lost to the world a very long time ago. Its origins date back to the remaining cults of shadow-dwelling entities that were slain in the purge of Araele. It is said to hold the last of their power. I didn't know much about it until after he left. I managed to find whatever I could in the texts I've... acquired... since I've arrived here."

"It was meant to recreate their race in the future. A man would become a monster. A woman would bear a full-blooded child. It is said that because it holds the essence of their people, whoever opens it will become as powerful as their most ancient. This man must be stopped," Zheki continued, moving her hand from her neck.

"The Ones Who Came Before," Declan said, suddenly. The focus of the room shifted toward him. Zheki nodded. Declan took a deep breath, and continued, slowly. "My mother, before she died, would tell me stories during nights where I could not sleep. The entire Isle was to leave behind their faiths for devotion to Basilin. But she could not abandon her own. Their name was lost to time, only known as The Ones Who Came Before. They were said to have been the first. Born from them came the other nonhumans."

"So, we find him before he finds the box," I answered. "It seems to be the only option we have."

"What if we took a different approach," Morard stated. "We could travel to Terrenveil, seek audience with the king."

Thurlowe began to laugh and resumed his position of leaning against the wall. "What evidence do you have that would condemn him? While what happened to your home was truly tragic, there is nothing that links his being there. Listen to my admonitions well, he is his own authority in that kingdom. Any accusations made against him will be met by his hand. The king will do nothing. It's been that way ever since he was made commander."

"You know much of Terrenveil's affairs?" Morard asked.

"More than I care to. Some of the patrons of the provinces have taken to contacting me for arms. I've unfortunately had to decline most of them. I simply don't trust them to keep Defaltor's name from their mouths if captured. I feel for their cause, don't mistake me, but if the legion is led here, I do not think the city would survive even a night."

"You're afraid," Dacian spouted. "Those people are being oppressed."

"Watch your tongue," Thurlowe said quickly and looked toward Eshkan and I. "You are lucky your aid to me was as important as it was. And luckier still that I hold as much interest in preventing the box from being found," he shifted his gaze to Dacian in continuing his speech. "I hold no tolerance for assumptions nor insults. Those people are being oppressed by their king because they have failed to dethrone him. Their failure is because of their fear. They cannot be blamed for it, but they also cannot be helped by being given arms. They are not soldiers. They would be killed within hours. Their best chance at survival as it stands is not arming themselves."

"He's right," Eshkan answered. "Arming a few hundred rebels will be worthless bloodshed."

"I'm happy we agree. I have met with Alaies of Sathenne a few times. In secret, of course. He keeps me updated on the affairs of the Mountain, with my word that I will aid him when I can. And it seems like I've just found a way."

"We should go and meet with your contact, then?" Eshkan asked.

"As soon as possible. The rumor of rebellion is no secret, but it's the threat of war with Mauros that is most alarming. That alone is enough cause for Savantin to spread his armies across Terrenveil."

"And in turn hunt for the box," Zheki stated.

"Meet with Alaies. From there you can plan your attack as you see fit. I know that both of you are skilled, which leads me to assume that your company is also. In some respects," Thurlowe continued and looked toward Declan. "You. You carry no weapon."

"Nor will I."

"You see this war as not yours to fight." Thurlowe shifted his eyes toward me, then. "Wise. Come, the armory awaits."

When he opened the door, I was in awe of how much was stored in such an inconspicuous place. There were rows of swords, axes, maces. A few shields were stacked in the corner, pieces of armor in an opened chest that sat alongside full sets. "I told both the Sardon and the one who accompanied him that you could help yourselves to whatever was desirable. I understand that the armor may need to be fitted but there is a blacksmith in town should you need his services. Speak to me before you make your way out and I will pay the blacksmith preceding your visit."

"Generous," Dacian said.

"We've an interest in the same cause, now. Sardon, follow me."

I looked back toward Eshkan and Dacian, suggesting my departure. "Shall I meet you back at the brothel, then?" I asked.

"Ahh the renowned and resourceful Madame Karstentia," Thurlowe remarked. "A very smart woman. Information from her always comes at a price, and her business keeps her house the most visited by travelers from across Cilevdan, even Rustanzen. I'm assuming Varsenius has something to do with that, too," Thurlowe stated and offered a two-finger salute toward Eshkan. "Zheki, I'll meet you back here very shortly. There is something I must show the Sardon."

"I'll be waiting." She smiled.

Thurlowe led me toward the back of the building, and then to a door that led out into the street. The two of us traversed the rooftops quickly, covering ourselves from the sight of any guards. "I must take you back to the manor once more. There is something within its walls that will be of use to you. Now tell me. What occupation did you take before your home was taken from you?" he asked.

"We were assassins. Implements to keep evil men from carrying out nefarious deeds. There was once a time I couldn't care less for that cause. The world of men is ever changing. But after what happened, and knowing what we know now, it is something I cannot ignore."

"I could have guessed. The footsteps of both you and your counterpart were silent. Your weapons announce you as killers. No blade that intricate falls into the hands of someone or is protected by the hands of someone that does not kill," he said, as we entered the manor the same as one night past. He led me to a large library, a sundial sitting in its center. It seemed suspicious to be in an enclosed room, but the man presented himself to be eclectic, and most who knew him probably would not give it a second thought. Thurlowe reached it, pushing its large arm inward, moving it across the floor only slightly. "Down there. I will follow."

I climbed inward, grasping onto the ladder that appeared to have been built ages ago, reinforced in certain areas by large iron nails. Once my feet reached the bottom, I heard a torch being lit behind me. Thurlowe took the lead, and I followed him into a room that was filled with coin. Alongside it were gemstones, ledgers, artifacts. Toward the back was a large case, covered by a large old cloth. Its color had faded over the years it seemed; a light and faded brownish purple. Thurlowe grabbed its edge and pulled it off, revealing a set of armor that was dark and alluring. It was made of thick black leather and different metals. Remarkable. My eyes came across the hood, moving quickly to the metal pauldrons, which were attached to the bodice from beneath the metal inner shell.

"It was a Sardon's..." I said, nearing the glass to look upon it further. It was striking, the deep gray metal was shining just dimly against the torches of the room, giving off what appeared to be every color in the spectrum.

"It was. A man came here trying to sell it on the market. No one would buy it, understandably. But of course, word spread quickly. My father took interest and bought it off the man for a large sum of money. He questioned the merchant and asked how he came into possessing something such as this, thinking that maybe someone had replicated it from similar materials. But the man insisted that he found it in Morrenvahl."

"Found it?" I asked, looking at Thurlowe for only a few seconds before returning my gaze back to the armor. It was captivating.

"Yes. Which he thought was a lie until he was shown this piece of it," Thurlowe said and opened the case, pulling the arm forward. On the left vambrace there was a circular hole. "This here. He said that it was to hold the stone that symbolized the life of a Sardon. When it is missing it means that whoever owned this armor is no longer alive. My father tried to get him to part with the stone as well, but he wouldn't."

"Do you think the man killed its owner?" I asked, my eyes upon the vambrace.

"Doubtful. He said that he wanted to give the stone back to the family. I don't know how Sardons live, but we never saw the man again, though not unusual in a city like this. I thought he was a fool. A kind sentiment, yes, but I was certain they'd believe him to be the murderer. Or a thief. Why only return the stone?" Thurlowe said and stood back. "I was only eleven years old when this arrived here. I was wondering if it was going to be a part of my treasury for all of time."

I reached into my pocket, suddenly, remembering what I had found on the floor in my room at the brothel. In my hand was a black gem that resembled a diamond. I moved it around in my fingers, looking at the symbol steadily before pushing it into the hole in the armor.

"It's... yours?" Thurlowe asked in confusion.

"It can't be. When did it arrive here?"

"Almost seventeen years ago."

"I was but a year older than you, and in the care of a mariner in Harbortow. This stone was with my things this morning."

"Your people are calling you back to them. This proves it," Thurlowe said, looking at the armor. After a few moments of silence, he looked back at me and placed his hand on my shoulder.

"I've one other thing for you," he answered and walked over toward a different case on the wall, opening the door and reaching inward. He removed his hand, holding a small cylindrical vessel. "When Savantin came to Defaltor, he met with me at the Spindel. Unfortunately, when a city such as this exists, it is a destination for people who wish to deal in unconventional business. I'm certain he paid a generous sum to Madame Karstentia in order to get Undai's name. After all, her only real allegiance is to her girls and to the city lord." Thurlowe laughed. "She couldn't have lied to him; he would have known."

"Understandable," I answered. "May I see it?"

He placed the vessel in my hands, and I turned it over, looking at the intricate sigils carved into its sides. Thurlowe withdrew his hand, and I noticed a marking on his wrist, disappearing beneath the sleeve of his tunic. "What is this?" I asked, deciding not to speak of it.

"It's a part of the legend of the box. Rumored to be one of the keys. There is a key to open this, and once opened, this will open the box. I couldn't part with it. This, this creation, it's beyond me. No amount of coin was worth the risk of it falling into the wrong hands. The only thing I can do now is entrust it to you."

"You're... giving it to me?" I asked.

"I can think of no safer place for it. Its seeker was already here. If he decides to return, he will not find it. I'm mildly surprised he did not first come to the manor. Though I'm happy he did not. He likely would have discovered my secret."

"He misjudged your resourcefulness."

"Yes, at an advantage to us. I will not ask what you plan to do with it. It may be very well that he returns here and attempts to use different means of gathering information. There is no way to destroy it. I have tried. It's a beautiful object, yes, but if the legend is true... it is a danger to all of us."

"Zheki seems very adamant in stopping this."

"Adamant?" Thurlowe offered a chuckle and moved his hands outward. "When she's adamant it turns into devotion. She's well-intentioned but fearful. Brave when she has to be. She may even work up the courage to help you."

"I could say the same of Cahya. I'm the only nonhuman she's ever been close to. Most of them frighten her. But with humans, she's a powerful leader. Fearless. Confident. She's the most remarkable woman I've ever met."

"I am surprised Zheki took to me, though timid at first. The bonds we form are powerful. Shall we go?" he asked.

"Yes, I should get some rest before we set off. It seems we will be staying another night after all."

"I meant to bring it to mention. The quiet one, he doesn't seem to want to follow."

"I don't believe he will. But I understand, as what we are attempting may very well end our lives," I answered.

"Where do you think he will go?"

"I'm not certain, though I am sure he will leave that information with me. He could have gone anywhere after we left the ruins. He trusts us."

"Although he may not follow, he still plays an important role," Thurlowe said and headed toward the ladder. Once we made it back into his manor, we made our exit and headed into the city. I was surprised he was accompanying me, though we were mostly silent. Before we parted ways, he stopped, taking a breath and looking at the brothel. "When you reach Sathenne, give Alaies my regards. Let him know that you're planning to strike the kingdom, but do not reveal Savantin's intentions. That would cause him to panic. From there you will be able to help one another."

"My gratitude, Thurlowe. If we are to fail..."

"If you are to fail, know that we will also attempt to see this to its end. If you succeed, return to Defaltor. You'll find that these walls have much to offer."

Our last words to one another. I made haste toward the brothel, our departure nearing as the sun changed position overhead.

CHAPTER 5

BLOOD BENEATH THE VEIL

Savantin and Ohric climbed off their horses once they arrived at the Great Mountain of Terrenveil. Ohric instantly grabbed the fur coat that was hanging in his horse's part of the stable and quickly put it on. Savantin ignored the growing cold as he burst the door open and marched off toward the castle. Ohric silently followed, waiting for his leader to speak. He hadn't since they killed the bandits on the road. The guards at the door of the castle moved aside quickly, disregarding their commander's wishes in not acknowledging him in a salute. Savantin seemed to ignore that as well, pushing the large doors open and walking past the several people that hurriedly removed themselves from his path. Haemad was there to greet them, his sight invoking an added rage.

"Ah I see you've finally returned," he snapped. "Hopefully your absence brings back some news worth hearing."

"Stay your tongue before I cut it from your mouth," he said and pushed his shoulder into him as he walked past. The man crumpled beneath his force, obviously not expecting the reaction that was given. Savantin didn't look back at him, and Ohric followed, listening to his commander's heavy footsteps. Just before they had reached the doors to the throne room, Savantin turned to Ohric and spoke.

"Do not speak until Ozrach addresses you, and even then, nothing of where we have just been. The Southern border will be his only concern."

"Of course. You know he will ask about your men."

"I will handle that," he answered. Ohric nodded and Savantin turned, opening the doors abruptly.

"Savantin! What is the reason you interrupt at such an hour?" Ozrach answered, sitting up in his seat, his eyes moving away from his court. His face turned from outrage to concern in an instant, his eyes widening as he thought of their condition. They were covered in blood, gashes across various parts of the coadjutant's body. He would have to make this work to their advantage, as opposed to it seeming like a weakness.

"I was under the impression that any word I bear from my travels is more important than entertainment and frivolity. I have urgent news from the southern border that we are to discuss with no audience," he answered.

The king waved his hand, dismissing the council, Neraea watching Savantin's every move. He felt her lusting eyes on him yet ignored them as he dealt with her husband. When the court funneled out of the room, Ozrach spoke.

"What happened to you? Why are you covered in blood?"

"My men were killed upon the road by a group of bandits. It seems as if they are more in number than we thought."

"On my roads? Near my provinces?" Ozrach asked, his voice raising several octaves. It was customary for his outbursts, though not intimidating in the slightest.

"So, it seems. Ohric and I managed to kill off most of them. Whoever remained escaped," Savantin answered. Ozrach looked to Ohric who nodded slowly.

"There were so many of them, your majesty." Ohric was skilled at keeping his words to a minimum. He did not wish to draw attention to himself. His hatred of being audience to the royal family was known to his commander, so he was only involved if necessary.

"Where did this happen?"

"We finished our investigation of the south. It seems the Maurosce have no presence there. We were heading back toward the provinces when they attacked," Savantin answered.

"These groups cannot continue to raid my lands! I've ignored their proximity to the border, and this is the thanks I'm given? And to assail my guard..."

"I warned you that allowing that was foolish. This needs to end. Mauros is threatening war, your provinces are looking to dethrone you, and bandits stalk the borders and kill unsuspecting travelers. Yet you would have me here, looking over maps to protect priests and zealots?" Savantin asked. He was flawless in his art of deceiving them.

Ohric continued to remain silent as commanded, and the king was sitting in his chair, completely irate. After a moment he looked up from his pensive glare and spoke. "I will send more men to the border to deter bandits or any tribes from hunting on our side. I will decide how to..."

"They killed my men!" Savantin shouted angrily, his voice echoing throughout the empty room. As if the king did not know how to respond, Savantin continued, "You cannot tell me that the provinces knew nothing of their intrusion. Their defiance is based upon resentment, or else this would have been reported to you. The town guard would have taken the liberty to remove the bandits themselves."

"You said you had already punished the ones responsible, Savantin. I will send men to deal with whoever commits these crimes again."

"As always, you do not understand what I am trying to convey," Savantin answered, his patience on the brink of nonexistence. "Not only do we have to worry about the Maurosce, if bandits were in the Southern reaches, the provinces know. For whatever reason they are neglecting to report it. This cost me good men."

"We cannot possibly exhaust resources on both fronts. We need all of the soldiers we can expend at the borders," King Ozrach answered.

"You cannot think of them as separate fronts, Ozrach," Savantin said angrily. His disrespect went ignored as he continued to speak. "If Mauros invades, we must have men to hold the borders, but we also need to remind your people that their treason will not be unanswered, especially as war draws near. A Mauroscan invasion could be what these provincials are looking for in order to make a pact with a stronger force. If they aid the invaders, then your rule will come to an end before they reach the Mountain. The only hope you have at combating this is if I send my men to fortify both the borders and the provinces," Savantin answered.

Ozrach moved his hand to his chin, moving his fingers through his beard. It was an anxious tick, something he did often when speaking to his commander.

"My men think that you no longer care about the possibility of rebellion, and if that is the case then why not join them?" Savantin added, the last line for persuasion.

"The city of Arriksmad... what did you find there?" Savantin took a deep, heavy breath. The king's ability to shift topics was one of his most irritating characteristics, especially in this aspect. This was at most a facade. The king was religious, or claimed to be, but the sole reason he so adamantly entertained the protection and fortification of Araele's temples was to please his disloyal wife.

"Nothing to report. Ohric checked the temple to ensure there was no threat," he answered and looked at Neraea, knowing she would have protested if he had entered the walls himself. She averted her gaze for a moment, a small smile on her face. When Ozrach finally answered, it was nothing of importance, as expected. He would need to invent a way to dismiss himself.

"So that leaves the provinces, and the borders."

Savantin nodded, uncrossing his arms and dropping them to his sides. "Much needs to be done. I will start at dawn."

"So, you will come up with a plan in order to both fortify the borders and inspect the provinces?"

"I have one," Savantin answered and turned to leave when Ozrach stood.

"You will share it now."

"I didn't think my means interested you as much as knowing you did not have to become involved. Since you have made it abundantly clear that you detest it," he answered. "I will leave the castle guard and enough men to protect the Mountain in the event Mauros does become bold enough to invade, but I will be sending battalions to each border under the watch and command of my most trusted captains. I will be in command of the provincial operation."

"Don't you think you should send someone who can better relate to people?" Neraea suddenly said, looking him in the eyes. After a darkened glare from him she returned her gaze to her husband.

"My presence there will ensure that they will not carry out any plans they may have laid. Try to deny it," Savantin said and kept gaze on Ozrach.

"You are right. There is no better deterrent," he said, his tone one of defeat. "But by the goddess do not kill them, Savantin. If you are trying to deter a rebellion, you will have to act in the best interest of the people."

"Something you have been avoiding for years," Savantin answered. "I don't have much to work with so I will do whatever I see necessary. Either I fortify your hold over this land, or it ends. I'd like to think your interests rest in the former," Savantin stated.

"Get the job done, I do not care how," Ozrach said flatly, Neraea's face of outrage ignored.

"Consider it done," Savantin answered and bowed his head, turning. He spun his hand to signal Ohric to leave too when the king interjected.

"Savantin... Is there anything else you wish to tell me?" he asked.

Savantin moved his head to the side, not moving from his position facing the doorway. "No, that is all," he answered.

"Wash yourself of that blood. Tomorrow morning, before you leave, I am holding a meeting of the provinces, and I want you to be present. It is past time I act. And with your troubling report there couldn't be a better time," Ozrach answered.

Savantin continued without acknowledging his request, Ohric following close behind. The king's insistence on having a gathering of the provincials was as foolish as it was futile. His sudden care of their interests was a mocking and would clearly be seen as such. The greedy would hold no opposition to his rule, and the courageous would be willing to fight for their citizens. He hoped he would have to interfere as minimally as possible with the patrons, though he knew that he would have to be invested. It didn't leave him with much time to continue his search for the artifact of his desire, but it would have to do. They left the castle and walked toward the barracks on the outer walls, climbing a set of stairs before reaching a large room. When he made it to his quarters at the end of the hall, Savantin bid the guards relief for the evening. Another detestable order by the king. He did not know why Ozrach insisted they be stationed there, but he was too angry at the moment to be able to give it further thought.

"Savantin, wait," Ohric called. In his rage he did not realize his coadjutant had followed him. He turned, calming for only a moment.

"Are you sure he will never find out about the isle?"

"What? Do you fear the wrath he may incur? He would not face it. Everyone who knew is dead. Anyone that would tell him is dead."

"Yes. You are right. But what are we to do now?" he answered.

"It appears we will just work with what we have," Savantin said and opened the door to his quarters, placing his bloodstained helmet on the table nearest the door. "I told that fool to keep the patrons out of this. This will only make it more difficult for me to find it." Savantin continued, his voice raising. "I could have sworn upon it being on that island. I would have faced Norahn himself."

"It was hidden well from history, Savantin. That is no fault of yours."

"I won't rest until it is in my hands," he answered and took a breath, resting his head against the wall for a moment.

"Have you taken care of the letters?" Ohric asked.

"They've all been burned. Don't be paranoid. He will never know. However, we do have another pressing matter to deal with, everyone entrusted to the circle is dead. We can't worry about that now, but we will need a group of men to take with us. Men that won't question my whereabouts. Men that will listen to you as you act in my stead in the event something happens while I'm away," Savantin answered.

"I will approach them tonight."

"I will not have time to look them over until after this meeting that Ozrach is hosting tomorrow. Now that he's called the patrons to council, I have no choice but to appear before them. This severely hinders my progress. They will be looking for me, expecting me."

"And if he'd just let us go, we would have had more freedom to continue the search," Ohric finished.

"This is only an inconvenience. I will have to revisit my research. We're finished here," Savantin said.

Ohric nodded and looked at the floor. "I think I am going to retire for the evening shortly after. I am still feeling those restless nights upon the road." Ohric hadn't told him the reason. He didn't dare to. It wasn't like Savantin to be that consumed in anger.

"Rest. When morning comes, we will speak then," Savantin replied. When Ohric left, Savantin closed the doors to his chamber, taking the steel armor off his chest. He went into the next room where he knew hot water was waiting. Ozrach had forgotten what it meant to care for his forces, the women of the castle entering the barracks to aid the legion's cooks as quietly as they could. He sighed and picked up the cloth sitting on the edge of the water tub, and dipped it in the bucket, washing the blood off his arms.

He began to think of the Isle, second-guessing the possibility of having overlooked it. His spy had assured him that it was not there, having examined every inch of the island over the course of a few months. The traitor insisted that someone knew of its whereabouts, and only proved to be a monumental waste of time. His method of murder was a testament to that. Savantin sighed and removed his tunic, tossing it onto the table with the remainder of his armor. Frustrated and exhausted, he felt that no amount of rest would return him to the state of mind he wished for. The stars overhead played part in that; his increasing animosity was a feeling he couldn't fend off. Not yet.

He exhaled deeply as the water ran over his skin, the blood running off it. Its warmth was becoming scarce as the season turned. Autumn was always colder here and approached faster than any of the provinces south. Septentria played a direct part in that, the winds blowing across the tundra and through the mountains. He was interrupted suddenly by the lock of the door handle clicking, and the opening of the door itself. He turned around, seeing that his visitor was none other than Neraea, her long red hair loose and flowing. She removed the cloak she wore to slip past the guards, dropping it onto the floor.

"Tell me," she said, her eyes focused on him. "Do you enjoy your hold over him?"

Savantin offered a laugh, continuing to cleanse himself of blood before he turned to her. "We both know that is not the reason you are here," he answered. She watched the bloodied water run off his chest but kept her composure long enough to circle back to her previous concern.

"I wish to know what I have asked you. I demand an answer," she said sternly.

Savantin smiled and walked toward her, looking down into her face. "Is that why you've come to me with your hair down?" he asked, not breaking his eyes from hers. He smirked and turned away, walking back over to where the tub of water sat, placing the cloth on the edge of it.

"It is not for my enjoyment that I speak to him that way," he answered finally. "It is that I will not allow myself to be commanded by someone so dense."

"I have heard different things," she answered.

"There exists one person that I share my words with when it comes to discussing the king, and unless you heard these words from him then you should know them well to be lies," he answered. The queen was silent again, looking at the walls. "If it bothers you, then why do you continue to come here most nights asking me to give you what your husband will not?" he asked seriously, turning back around to her. It seemed she didn't have an answer for that either, and spun around, heading toward the door.

"This will stop whenever I want it to be so. Because what I say happens. Because you must listen to me," she answered.

"Until I kill your pitiable husband," Savantin answered. "Make no mistake, Neraea. I answer to no one."

"And what if I no longer want that? Your depravity and bloodlust make me turn my head. Instead of answering to a lazy and idiotic mule it would be to an unnerving tyrant. I would be better off killing him myself, and taking this kingdom for my own," she answered, turning back and taking a step forward.

"Except you didn't plan out the details. Who is to say you wouldn't be the first suspect. You would be subjected to the rigorous torture of treason that would be done unto you by my hands. You forget who unites traitors and enemies with their ends. Of course, if you were to do it, I wouldn't tell a soul. That doesn't interest me. But don't believe yourself to be untouchable. People know how miserable you are, Neraea."

The queen remained silent a moment, before answering. "I have often thought about the details. You are only in your position because of Ozrach. If I appoint someone else in your position, the people will certainly see that as more than acceptable. I have my own secrets."

"I won't waste time entertaining that remark. It is impossible for you to threaten me. But, if you do kill him and I let you get away with it, then you'd have only made it easier for me."

"Do you honestly think that if I became the ruler of this kingdom, I would display any sympathy for you after all the things you've done away from the castle? What you are? I would sooner have you killed..." She stopped at that last word, regret.

"Careful, Neraea."

"You aren't as powerful as you think Savantin."

"Prove me wrong. No matter what you think you can do, I promise that I am more resilient. You're lucky that I am amused by you."

"You would speak threats... to your queen?" she asked in outrage.

"If you kill him and take the throne, then there is nothing to hold me back from taking it. Not my men, not your council. Those men are mine; they listen to me. Not you, not your weak, useless husband. Your eight guards wouldn't survive me let alone the entire legion. This kingdom is already mine," Savantin answered. "Where did your sudden hatred come from, Neraea? That is the only aspect of our exchange that interests me. I was once the only person who didn't make you feel alone, your words. But now you've decided to sever that by attempting to belittle me with words and ideas that you know would fail."

"The way you speak of the provincials. Why do you so boldly state that you will go there with the intention of murder?"

"Murder?" Savantin laughed. "Those words never left my lips. I merely stated that I would do whatever had to be done. Your husband determined what amount of bloodshed he'd accept."

The queen said nothing, caught up in an outrage she did not recognize. To this, she watched Savantin go on about cleansing himself. She was hesitant in saying much else.

"Why are you still here?" As if to irritate him, Neraea sat, sighing heavily and moving her head downward. "You must understand what position this places me in." she continued, looking up at him as if to garner sympathy.

"There is nothing to understand, Neraea. You've done nothing to help the people of your kingdom. Only those who have pledged themselves to your goddess have received any help from you. In their eyes you are just as guilty as he is. You are too consumed by your faith to aid other people who believe differently. Need I remind you of your solution to banish non-believers from Terrenveil?"

"No, you needn't remind me," Neraea countered, her words sharp and quick. He remembered the day that a lone crusader stumbled into the city's gate, a sigil carved into his chest. The rest had been killed, their heads on pikes along the Tepenes Pass. The crusaders mistook Viscera for unarmed heathens, and after exhaustive torment with black magic, they killed each other with their bare hands. It was what they deserved.

"You've overlooked your people for so long that they will never forgive you. Continue to place faith before humanity. We'll see the result of that soon enough."

"I assume an apology would mean nothing?"

"It would, had been something forgivable," Savantin answered and finished the task at hand, moving toward an old armoire. "You've lost control of everything around you. Yet the only person who you've ever found solace in, you've just scorned. You shouldn't be here," he stated and turned his eyes from her gaze. It was impossible to find sympathy for her any longer. After a moment she left, shutting the door and moving down the hallway.

Savantin closed his eyes, letting a gust of air from his lungs. He didn't have a lot of time before his presence was required at the meeting that Ozrach threw together. The island proved to be nothing more than a dead end. He was frustrated, mostly so by his trust in Jadoq, and the woman, Sindara. He still hadn't found her; his only lead now was to discover where she had gone. Months of planning resulted in nothing.

When he took leave to inspect the provinces, he could return to Winds Hollow. He could begin there, where he met her in an ale house. It was a strange arrangement, and in truth, Savantin thought he may have been walking into a trap when she asked them to meet there. Fearlessly, however. Winds Hollow was large, houses were spread out and mostly surrounded by ruins that were covered in ice and snow most months of the year. He often questioned why people took residency there, but with it being a town less traveled, understood. Despite there being no temple, priests and priestesses chose to land there as well. He smirked suddenly at the thought of Neraea. She was angry with him, over fallacies and rumors created by the council about his character. Ozrach's mentioning of murdering provincials on his campaign was as unsurprising as it was insulting. It seemed the fallacies were easily believed, of course showcasing that the royal family truly did not know him at all. He had an idea who put the thoughts in the monarchy's head to take seed. There were reasons of course, why Haemad would do something like that. They had never seen eye to eye, not since it was exposed where he was from.

The court was caught up in a pathetic number of superstitions. It was amusing, to say the least. When the lead of the king's court discovered him to be from Seraphician, they were instantly enthralled with the stories of the dark priests who took male children to the dark, crystal-covered caves in the North turning them into monsters when the night took the sky. He laughed at this thought often, had people studied the cultures of his homeland, they'd know that not all children were taken. He supposed it did in some way work to his advantage but ignored further thought, gathering a pair of pants from the armoire across the room. Rest was in order. Those nights on the road were indeed restless, as Ohric described.

Savantin wondered why Ohric hadn't told him the real reason he wasn't sleeping. The reason no one slept easy in Terrenveil. The rumors of a Seraphice among them had them paranoid. But why should he let them think more of it? It was much more beneficial to have them fear him for his reputation alone. He moved to the bed past the tub of water, the smell of blood now heavy in the room. Lying backward, he exhaled deeply before closing his eyes, not even bothering to lock the door to his chamber before sleep carried him away.

Savantin awoke to the sounds of knocking upon his door, and looked out the window suddenly, seeing that the light of the sun had already come up over the edge of the mountain. Within a minute, one of the guards had opened the door slowly, peeking his head in. Haemad suddenly burst past him, walking toward the bed in a huff. Savantin sighed and rose, towering above Haemad once he was on his feet.

"You know your presence is mandatory at this council today do you not?" he exhaled, stepping back suddenly. "The king questioned your whereabouts, and I volunteered to find you. Me. Out here past the castle walls. You must wonder what the reason for that is?"

"Do you know how much it pains me that you're still alive?" Savantin asked, walking past him to the armoire.

Haemad said nothing, for he knew there was nothing to say. It was their king's fault it was this way. Ozrach would take no action against him, out of fear, or loss of reputation. The lands knew that Terrenveil was not a beast to be messed with, but that was only because of its legion. If the bond between commander and king was broken, surely the militia's allegiance would follow.

"It is about to begin you know; you should make haste to the throne room. Our king will want you to speak about whatever it is you did out there."

"Then it is to the king I will speak. Leave now; you have served your purpose of pestering me. I will be there when it begins," he answered hastily, pulling pieces of armor from a chest and setting them on the table next to him. He covered up what looked like a map, and suddenly removed his gaze from the deep black wooden chest and to Haemad's eyes.

"Do you not understand what I have just asked of you?" Savantin asked, darkly.

"Yes, but he told me to make sure you were going to be in attendance, and at the exact time he has specified."

"I do not need an escort. Now go, before you're the reason we're both late. I won't bother explaining the details of why that would be," he answered coldly. Haemad nodded and walked out, passing the guard in the hall. He could hear his footsteps become quieter until they no longer resonated against the cold stone floor. The guard appeared at the doorway in this instant, adding a cough before speaking. "I'm sorry Commander, I tried to keep him out, but he told me that if I didn't let him in…"

"Pestilence has no boundaries," he answered. "While I am out, I want you to stay here and make sure he does not come back. Do not let anyone in unless it is Ohric. I trust I do not have to plan for your failure."

The guard nodded and turned his back to the room, watching the hallway and moved his head only once as Savantin exited and shut the doors. He was mostly grateful that he was given this task, the rate of pay was something his family relied upon, but the possibility of failure was always a terrifying thought. There was only one person he answered to, and while most days he rarely saw Savantin, there was still a possibility.

Savantin sighed, attempting to mentally prepare himself for the hours ahead. This wouldn't take long if he limited the questions from the patrons. To some, that would be eliminated if he was very detailed about his venture. However, it wouldn't stop certain members from talking until their mouths became dry. He knew which ones were notorious for trying to gain blood from a stone. Reaching the throne room, the guards posted there uncrossed their weapons, bowing their heads down, a salute they could not decline to perform. Savantin nodded to them and continued, Ozrach sitting next to Neraea, who looked away childishly as he entered the room. He ignored her eyes, taking note of the two trusted guards of the king, standing on either side of the thrones. Surrounding them were council members, and socially respected members of families who lived in the immediate rule of Terrenveil, under the shadow of the mountain. There were also financiers, and other men whom he recognized the faces of, but did not care to recall their names. The room became silent as he walked toward the thrones and stood off to the side, the elaborate wine-colored tapestries of the kingdom behind him. It was at this time the king began to address them. He stood, making his voice as loud as he could.

"Citizens of Terrenveil and patrons of the provinces, there is no reason to delay the meaning of this council, so I will relay words in short. The past few weeks have been very troubling for our kingdom. We have tried to seek out means to avoid your direct involvement, but it seems that we have run out of options. We must prepare to defend ourselves against an attack."

"An attack?" one of the older men of shorter stature gasped. There were several voices from the crowd, whispers and louder, speaking amongst themselves. It was normal. They would gossip or come up with a unified answer before offering their own concerns. None spoke for themselves in this court.

"Reports from the Northern border indicate that Maurosce soldiers have been seen in numbers. We must work together to defend our land should they decide to invade," Ozrach answered.

"You said this report came from the northern border?" a man asked from the back of the room, one of the wealthy from a province south, given his accent. Savantin hadn't paid attention to the man before, hadn't cared to even acknowledge him as a person.

"Yes. Just on the other side of the wall. It was reported that tents were seen. We have not yet discovered what they are planning, but we are working diligently to discover this."

A truth Ozrach had no knowledge of. He'd say anything to these people to pull them from rebellion. Savantin sent a spy with the coalition north. Whether or not he'd discover anything was another matter entirely.

"This is troubling," a woman dressed in a heavy fur coat, covering a long, elegant dress spoke, lifting her voice so that it would be heard over the room of men. "Opskaven, as I'm sure you know, has no walls. It is an open city, newer. It would be the first to burn if we are invaded."

Opskaven. He heard the name before and began to think of where it was located. Of course, it was a town known for logging the tall timber trees that grew near the tundra line. She must have inherited the manor recently, as he had never seen her before this day. She looked perhaps ten years older than he was, give or take. Women were often unheard in the court due to the kingdom's dated views, so if he would side with her, she would remain loyal.

"I can't let my people fear for their lives so much that they leave. They should feel safe, yes, but the trade would suffer severely," she continued. "A loss that the kingdom cannot afford to have."

"I will ensure your province is protected." Savantin said. It wouldn't be difficult. He would leave additional soldiers there for her peace of mind. He didn't care to stay long but knew he would have to do something to secure a place for his men to stay. The area was of interest to him.

"Opskaven thanks you." She responded, evoking a response from a man nearby.

"You do not have walls, but many of us do. We live in older cities, where people used stone to keep the creatures out. So, what is it you must say that causes us to be here?"

"When the king asks your presence, you do not question its meaning. You come, listen to what must be said, serve your purpose and leave," Gideon, one of the younger patrons said suddenly. Savantin liked the aggression in him but wondered about his allegiance to Ozrach. He could either be an asset or a pest.

"We will need to work together in order to ensure the safety of the kingdom," Ozrach repeated.

"I find it touching that you care so much about our wellbeing now that the kingdom is in danger," another answered, his lax posture showing his general disinterest in being present. Savantin shared that sentiment.

Ozrach looked over to Savantin, and back to the representatives. "It is only now I call you here because of the changes that must follow. With the provinces being so sparsely spread across my kingdom, I have given complete jurisdiction of the fortification of the provinces to the commander of the legion," Ozrach answered.

"You give control to your commander as if this is a time of war?" a man asked, a confused tone in his voice.

"I give control to my commander to make sure that war does not begin. He will not fail me. I will not look weak in the eyes of the world and take no action when a kingdom threatens war."

"Your majesty, I must say this is a brash decision. We have heard nothing but the dark rumors spawning from this Mountain of Terrenveil itself about how your commander is..."

"Is what?" Savantin asked suddenly, looking to where the voice came from in the crowd. He stepped forward, making his presence known among them. He stopped at the top of the middle stair leading to the thrones.

"Well, I have no doubt that he will do what is in our best interests in fortification of the provinces," the woman from Opskaven answered. "His reputation only means that my people will stand a chance against the Morosce if they do plan to invade."

"His reputation is frightening among the people," a provincial answered, somewhere along the side wall.

"Do not speak as if I am not in the room," Savantin stated. "Would you rather your guards defend your province if the Morosce invade? Men and women who have not formally trained in years? I'll not let that happen when there are so many lives at stake."

"I can't believe there is even protest to this," Gideon muttered. "Do you all value your people so little?" This gained an angry response among some of the older patrons, who had taken to shouting. The others, speaking quietly among themselves. There was only one man who wasn't speaking. Savantin tried to bring forth his name in memory but could only identify him as the leader of Sathenne.

"Gain control of yourselves!" Ozrach shouted. The crowd began to quiet, their attention turning once again toward their king.

"You," Savantin said suddenly, causing the man from Sathenne to raise his head in his direction, speaking. "Yes, Commander?"

"How do Sathenne's guards fare?"

"Lazy and demoralized. I can't imagine the guards of any province to be different. You are correct in saying that if Mauros invades, we will stand no chance. Their armies have a reputation for being ruthless in battle. Their form, impressive."

"You are familiar with their combat?" Savantin asked, crossing his arms. This interested him. It had seemed to interest Ozrach too, as he stroked his beard. It meant nothing, though. He was easily amused and for meaningless reasons.

"I am. I visited Mauros a long time ago, as a boy. When my father was ill, my uncle decided we would venture there. He was killed in Sidoa, a raid on the city during their civil war. The soldiers made quick work of the rebels. I ran for days to make it back here. Though I won't take any more of your time with stories from the past, I know we are not here for my nostalgia."

A respectable man. That made one province. His appearance was noteworthy, something Haemad would scoff at. He hadn't seen him since the meeting began. Ironic. The patron held a cane, though he could not be past his mid sixtieth year. His clothes were ordinary, a dark-blue tunic, dark pants and shoes made of leather. Before seeing this, he doubted that any province was free of the greed that ran uncontrolled through the kingdom.

"The impending war will frighten our people enough," the man from the wall answered.

"That is why you keep the tidings of war from your tongue," Savantin answered. The man silenced, molding back into the crowd. The whispers began to quiet until there was nothing left.

"I will be disembarking shortly after our meeting has concluded here. As for rumors, your concern matters little. It should be directed toward the safekeeping of your holds and of your people," Savantin answered. "Mass panic does not do well for trying to maintain strength. When you return to your provinces you are to act as if this meeting was routine. Inciting fear in your people will only make it more difficult to secure the area. Once my men and I have arrived, we can discuss the reason with them."

"I don't know how I feel about that," an older man stated, moving his cane in front of him. "Shouldn't it be known that there is a threat of invasion on the rise? So that people may decide whether or not they should remain here or move to safer cities?"

"While we are trying to prevent the cities without walls from being overrun, we are also trying to prevent people from leaving. A last resort should be retreat," Savantin answered and moved toward the crowd, Ozrach at his back. "We are not abandoning your people, and neither should you. This is where their homes are, their livelihoods. We needn't incite panic at a mere threat. This is why we are taking precautions. Perhaps our presence will make them feel safe, and they will think twice about leaving their lives behind."

"I think they should be able to decide for themselves regardless of whether the legion is promising presence or not," one of the quieter patrons answered.

This caused Savantin to sigh. His patience was lost. "Do what you will. I am only acting in the best interest of the people. Whether or not you decide to act in their best interests remains with you," Savantin answered and turned to leave when Ozrach stood. "Certainly, we can come to some kind of agreement here," the king stated.

"Agreement? On intentionally misleading our people regarding Mauros?" a patron asked.

"If you've a problem with my course of action then save me the trouble and express it while I am in your presence, I have no time for games. Do these terms at least sound simple enough to you?" Savantin asked, listening to the silence slowly escalate to jumbled whispers.

"Perhaps you should have explained to us more prominently why we are all being spoken to as if we have no choice?" said the same man as before. Savantin was tired of hearing this man speak. His impudence and bold questioning were becoming intolerable.

"I am not a part of the court, not here to represent a province, nor am I expected to act like it. I am the commander of the king's legion, doing whatever I feel is necessary to fortify and strengthen your cities. I will ask once more. Do these terms sound simple enough to you, or do I need to dilute it further?" Savantin asked.

"Yes, and highly anticipated. The sooner my residents feel secure in their own homes, the better off we will all be," the Opskavenian woman answered. "I implore you all think about what your provinces offer regarding trade. If Opskaven is overrun, there will be no timber. Timber that could be used to defend yourselves. To repair walls that are damaged."

"When I have made it to your town, I will see to it that your concerns are taken care of," Savantin answered, shifting back toward the rest of the room.

Gideon spoke again, his voice cutting through the room. "A smart woman. I will not see Egelle be seized." Egelle was the province that bordered the Baeld, and the richest of them all. Savantin knew well why he eagerly awaited the presence of the legion. Others began to speak among themselves, Ozrach waiting to see if anyone else spoke before concluding the meeting. The moments of silence proved themselves a tease, as a portly man, the noble representative from Marchent, lifted his voice.

"What are we to do when you are in our towns?"

"After we conclude our meeting, nothing. You are to merely resume life. Continue as you would if I were not there and we will stay without sight of one another," Savantin answered.

"We have no say in what is to happen to our towns?"

"My terms are not up for negotiation," Savantin answered and closed his eyes for a moment, turning to move back to where he was earlier positioned. Once he had done this, king Ozrach stood.

"We have an understanding, then?" he asked, looking into the faces of his reluctantly gathered crowd. He took the silence for a unanimous agreement and then spoke the words to conclude the council. "My commander will disembark, and he will follow whatever path he sees fit to fortify every city within our reach. As for the borders, he will have battalions sent this day to ensure that any problems that may arise there end swiftly," Ozrach answered and then dismissed his guests. They left slowly, speaking in whispers as they exited through the large, throne room door. Savantin remained only to see if his king needed to speak to him. Fate had favored him, for the moment it seemed.

He was appreciative of this time he could spend away from the kingdom. He would be able to move forward with his plan and use this time to gather information. However, locating and dealing with the defying provinces would be a conflict of interest in following whatever fragments of history he had left to search for the box. It was not something he could simply entrust to Ohric. If he wasn't present, things would seem suspicious, and word of his absence would likely reach Terrenveil before he had the time to travel back from his hunting. He could always feed the people's obsession of him being a Seraphice and let them believe that he went hunting for a different reason. As this thought crossed his mind, he realized that that too would be another thing he would have to make time for. He should have ended both Jadoq and his master's lives similarly when he was on that isle. That would have been a sacrifice to hold him over for nights to come.

"Savantin, a word," Ozrach answered once the remaining noblemen, and Queen Neraea too, had left.

Savantin said nothing and looked at his king, nodding once. He should have anticipated this.

"I know this is a lot to ask, but I want you to take care when investigating Aluard of Larient. He may have dodged some of the rulings here and there, but he is an old friend of my family. Unless he is engaging in serious offenses such as harboring enemies of the kingdom, I want you to give him gentle guidance back into our ways."

"I am not an advisor. I am a soldier. I've no interest in this."

"Yes, but I cannot risk sending anyone from the court with you. I know how much you dislike the court, how they will get in the way, and it may risk the entire campaign. Just do as best you can so I do not have to resort to that."

"It shall be done," Savantin answered, and turned away, taking several steps to the doors.

"Savantin, one more thing."

Savantin stopped walking but did not turn to see his king. He remained tense, impatience slowly rising.

"These rumors you mentioned before I dismissed the council..." Ozrach began. Savantin took a breath in, still not turning from his position toward the door.

"Frustrating how they continue to return to the tongues of the subjects, the people. They know nothing of my homeland and have made assumptions based on their ignorance."

"Perhaps..." the king answered. "You may go. I know how much work you have ahead of you."

He disliked speaking of it. Disliked how often it was brought forth in discussion. He knew that Ozrach would do all he could to avoid discovering the truth. If others discovered it, they would want the king to act and when he failed to do so, the people would further deem him unfit to rule. This would be more difficult than his current arrangement, though not by much. They would likely appoint one of the council or a patron, people who knew how valuable he was in his current role. For now, he would have to remain silent in it, as he had things to take care of while he was out in the world for Ozrach's campaign.

He left the room then, making his way out of the castle. Ohric would be awaiting him with the small number of men that would accompany them. He had it planned already. Battalions would be sent to the borders, and smaller ones to each province. In honesty, he did not care much about those who were planning the rebellion. He and his men could easily kill those who decided to uprise, and afterward he could slip away while deeming his absence as tracking down anyone who ran. He had methodically planned for every possible outcome, all except one. A Morosce invasion. They were stealthy and would attempt to make their way into the cities by killing whomever they could silently. The man from Sathenne was correct about their form being impressive. They would be fighting at the gates of the cities, hoping that enemies did not make it over the walls undetected to flank them from behind. He hoped it would not come to that.

When he made it to the barracks, he noticed a group of men readying their horses as well as more, fighting across the yard with one of the training officers. Past the housing area, Ohric was speaking to roughly fifteen men, very quietly. There were two standing at the entrance to the gazebo and courtyard, who watched closely as Savantin walked inside. They saluted him immediately, which he ignored and the change in their position instantly grasped Ohric's attention.

"Here he is now," Ohric said and stood immediately, brushing his armor down over his leggings. "Sir, these are men I have selected."

"I recognize none of them," Savantin answered.

"You are Commander? The one people speak so timidly of?" a boy, of about nineteen years of age asked from the back. Savantin raised an eyebrow as the boy continued, his voice adopting a tone of interest. "I have heard the stories about the battle over Ispranzi."

"Ohric, who is he?" Savantin asked, narrowing his eyes to see the boy better. He was behind two large men, instantly identified by their traits. One was from the Baeld and another from Mordestai, both sitting in silence.

"He will be perfect for this, I can assure you that," Ohric stated.

"You haven't let me down before," Savantin answered and strode forward, looking at the men Ohric had picked for him. "I trust Ohric has let you know why you are here," Savantin stated. "In the event your Captains have not relayed information regarding the state of the kingdom, it is dilapidating. Mauros is only the first of our concerns. Amid the possible invasion, there are provinces suspected of plotting to overthrow the king. We are traveling to each province in order to secure them, as well as investigating each to see if there is any evidence of treason."

"I'm assuming that you have called us here for something exceeding usual protocol?" a man in the front asked, his accent placing him from Esperanus.

"Your assumption is correct, but do not speak out of turn. I wasn't finished," Savantin stated, watching as the man very slightly shrugged his shoulders and took to crossing his arms. "There are only two coteries that will be heading investigations. One led by me, and a second led by Captain Brevil. We will be traveling through Terrenveil undecorated, while the battalions ride a day behind us until we've concluded our search. Ohric has chosen you to ride with us."

"May we speak?" the man from the Baeld asked. Savantin held his hand forward a sign for the man to continue. The man cleared his throat and wiped his large forehead. "So, we're to search provinces for any signs of plots?"

"Under my guidance. We will be quietly searching homes and buildings. I'm expecting the patrons to be alerting their people of our coming although I've advised them not to. If they are committing treason, they will be hiding it well. If they are found to be traitors, that will be handled differently."

"Who will transport them back to Terrenveil?" another man from the front asked, deep voice, dark haired.

"I have appointed a few men with each captain leading the battalions with a carriage for transport. You needn't worry about that. What you have been chosen for is important. I trust Ohric's judgment in that what I have before me is a group of capable men, and not just a group of regular legionnaires. Of course, I can only tell you what is expected from you at this moment. The expectations will be changing as we progress."

"When do we leave?" the boy from the back asked.

"You. Come forward, what is your name?" Savantin asked. It had been a while since he had seen someone so eager, though he was very young. Most his age were devoted; they lacked the feeling of importance in their lives, so they joined in hopes to find it. As time progressed, they lost that hope, and fell in line with the others. Days became weeks. Weeks, years.

"My name is Blacwin, Commander."

"Blacwin. You seem anxious. How long is it you've been with the legion?"

"Three months, sir. Though that does not mean that I will disappoint you. I will do whatever is asked of me without hesitation or failure," Blacwin answered, and stood in the front of the tables, looking directly into the eyes of his commander.

"Let us hope your words don't betray you." Savantin shifted his gaze across the men before him, noting that the only two men to have come from areas outside Terrenveil's rule was the man from the Baeld and the Mordestan. He had almost asked what brought them to the legion, but didn't, as he assumed it would be some story about needing the income or losing their homes and joining as a last resort. That could be true for the Baeld, anyway. The four major cities were formed by their ancestors, who were mostly pirates and raiders that decided to settle and earn their coin by bringing back whatever they *found while at sea*. He wondered now, how Ohric knew these men. There was a silent arrangement between him and his coadjutant to leave religion out of shared affairs. However, Ohric was someone he commended highly despite his faith. He supposed that he could be less apt to point it out if the topic arose, the man had never let him down before.

"You are to rest in the barracks closest to the castle wall this evening, we will leave at dawn. When we are finished here you will be training under Captain Brevil's eye while Ohric and I arrange our agenda for the coming weeks. We do not yet know how long we are expected to be away from the Mountain. Be back to the barracks by dusk. You will be fed and are expected to rest. I believe I do not have to relay the consequences if you do not arrive here at dawn."

The men shook their heads, which was enough for him. He dismissed them, hoping that he wouldn't have to dispense any punishment for failures to appear. Once they were out of earshot, Savantin instructed Ohric that they were to plan their excursion in his quarters, as the maps he frequented were on his table. They noted places he had been in his search, places of interest, places where he knew his contacts could meet with him. They walked silently but quickly, making haste to ensure that they were not stopped. He would have to go back to the castle when they were finished here, relaying his plans to the king before they embarked. He'd feed him some story that sounded pleasing. Hopefully without the presence of his advisor, who would only impede the event.

Once inside, Savantin uncovered his maps and placed a candlestick on one of the edges to secure it to the table. He looked over it, seeing large red hatch marks near Larient, Lord's Valley and Opskaven, which was conveniently located close to the eastern border of Septentria, only a day's travel to Enmira. It was a small town but was very close to the ruins situated near Wind's Hollow.

"Where do you suggest we begin?"

"Rierdan," Savantin said and made a mark on the map. The town wasn't very large, but it led toward Opskaven, where he thought the ruins could play an integral part in discovering where Sindara had gone. He doubted she'd return to her coven. "What will be easiest is if I chart a direct course for the magistrates to follow, which will leave us with the flexibility we need. Almour, Emiel, and Staiman. They're tenured, experienced. Almour is strict and proper. While I don't necessarily care for his methods,

I know men under his authority will be refined. Almour will tail us in order to secure the provinces we inspect. Emiel will travel directly west through the center of the kingdom, dipping into the south just to be present in a few provinces that do not interest me. Staiman is aggressive but smart. I'll have him handle the northern reach leading from Egelle to the border east. We'll handle most territories across the south that lead to Septentria. Am I missing anything?"

"I don't think so. But what about Alken to the southeast?" Ohric asked and pointed toward it. "It would be leading us away from the tundra, but surely you won't want to overlook it."

"Ozrach has forgotten Alken exists. I searched it years ago, when Teren was still among us. That is how he got the fever that killed him. His leg caught an old blade that was sticking out of the earth. It started to rot in a few days, there was nothing to do for him on the road, and the town's medic would not see him."

"They refused help to a soldier?" Ohric asked, surprise in his voice.

"Unknowingly. We did not go there in uniform," Savantin answered. "I'll have to bring this plan to Ozrach's attention. Almour and his men will ride with us to Rierdan, after which he will delegate who stays, and follow a day or so behind. Emiel will head toward Esperanus, Leids, Karsten, and Savoi. I'll send Staiman to Egelle, first hitting Sarghost and moving downward to Sathenne, which will push him east toward Braem and Valspire. This will give me freedom between Larient, Lord's Valley, Opskaven and whatever outlying territories I'll need. I'll have Terganus join with us at Lord's Valley so that we can search out closer to the outlying territories in that area."

"Outlying territories... of course."

"There is something about Sindara I did not bring to discussion as I did not think it important, until now. She is a Sardon."

"A Sardon?" Ohric gasped. "She'll be near impossible to find."

"I know," Savantin answered, his tone denoting annoyance. "I'll have to find a way to establish contact. I... did some things that I would not have had I—" he stopped, looking toward his coadjutant, who already knew what he had meant. Ohric pestered him about it often, the risks he was taking were very grave, but the exposition of himself would be even more so. "She'll be looking for me."

"You're certain."

"Yes. She's not telling me something. I have always been suspicious of her, but I have a feeling that her interest in this exceeds what she's let on."

"I suppose that remains to be seen."

"Indeed," Savantin answered. "I will present our plan to Ozrach and retire for the evening. I suggest you do the same." Ohric nodded, heading off in the direction that Savantin knew to be the temple. It was always his destination before he slept, and he supposed his visit there would be longer now that they were set to depart. He shifted his thoughts toward the freedom he would experience tomorrow, but at the cost of meeting with the king once more. He hoped it would be the last time. At times he wished he could send Ohric in his stead, but the man was too nervous, riddled with anxiety. The queen intimidated Ohric, and the king? He wished to avoid him altogether. His paranoia created a fallacy that Ozrach would discover what they were planning, and everything would fall apart. He made sure to cover his tracks well, so much so that there was no trace of his intent. He tried to reassure Ohric once, but it fell on deaf ears. He couldn't be irritated, it wasn't Ohric's fault that his mind worked against him.

He crossed the gate, looking briefly at the two soldiers stationed there. Alert. The shift must have just recently changed. As he continued inside, he noticed the castle guard patrolling the gardens. The soldiers stationed outside were highly trained, the guards inside becoming as ignorant of threats as the people they protected. Just inside the arch that served as entrance to the first of the three large gardens that surrounded the castle was Gideon, speaking to the patroness of Opskaven. She boldly moved forward, calling him over. He hesitated a moment, weighing the outcome of ignoring them completely before obliging. Opskaven would be an important hold to have if he was going to use the province as a resting ground for his men as he searched the area surrounding.

"We have not met formally," she answered. "I know you and Gideon have met. He was just sharing his story with me as you approached."

"Was he?" Savantin answered. Feigning amusement was becoming tiresome, and he hoped his mask wasn't cracking as his focus was shifted.

"Summer, three years past. Though he and I may have different accounts," Gideon began. Savantin hoped the man wasn't going to pause in order to prompt further discussion of the event. He honestly couldn't remember, though if he focused heavily enough, he was certain it would come to mind. As Gideon continued, he remained silent, awaiting discovery of why he was summoned.

"Interesting days, those," Gideon finished, and looked toward Savantin.

"It seems those are all we are living recently," the patroness stated. "I am Avelina. I've one question for you, should you be so kind as to answer. I know you are a man of deliberate words, and with so much to do."

"Speak," Savantin stated. He had hoped his tone didn't reveal his disinterest.

"Since I suspect the king will not help fund the construction of the walls around my province, which are in very early stages mind you, do you think that additional soldiers would be an irrational request?" she asked.

"It is not. I will send an attachment with the coteries that will be departing at dawn."

"A generosity."

"My responsibility as commander of the legion. If we are finished here." A statement rather than a question.

"One more thing. You said you would ensure my province is protected. That means I should be expecting you. Perhaps we will have the time to discuss matters outside present concerns. How long do you intend to stay?"

"That remains to be seen." He wasn't quite sure yet how long he would need to hold that position, though her interest in his company could make it difficult to proceed as intended.

"Yes, I suppose it shall."

He excused himself, something that had become very habitual. Surprisingly, he made it to the castle with no further delay. The throne room was empty, as well as the banquet hall. Given the time of day, although the circumstances should have provided different results, he suspected the king to be out on horseback with his few trusted guards while Neraea was at the temple. He supposed it was his duty as commander to await the king's return so that he could deliver the plans himself. The thought was displeasing. It would wait until morning, he decided, and turned back to where he could rest.

Rest was never truly an option for him. On the nights he slept, it wasn't for very long. He supposed it was because of his reluctance to please Norahn, though it could be a number of other things. His thoughts kept him awake. His past, his present. Anticipation. Lust. Need. Rest would be attempted, however, as he too was going to take the rest of the day withdrawn from the world. He opened the door to his quarters, abruptly and forcefully shutting it behind him. The disappointment in failing to reveal the location of his desire ran alongside losing the entirety of the Mask. The events prior to that morning frustrated him the more it came to mind...

◆ ◆ ◆

She placed her hand on the map, moving her fingers down the Frost's Kiss River and further south. "Here," she stated. "I've searched it. There is nothing that brings certainty to mind."

"So, you believe the man writing these letters to be deceiving us?" Savantin asked, reading the lines from the latest in his head. *Nightfall. Three days' time.*

"He has no reason to," she said and moved her hand from the parchment and to her face, obscured in a cowl. "It would be in his best interest not to."

"But they are hiding something." Savantin sat backward in his chair, slightly moving his head toward the wall. "The question is what." He looked toward the woman, mysterious and cunning. He had yet to discover her motives in all of this, though the one thing she mentioned was interesting enough for him to agree to her services. The box was in Cilevdan, and so was a sword. She offered to help him find the box, and in return, he would aid her. His resources, of course those that were easily obscured from the royal family, would be enough to aid her in some way. It was what he assured her when forming their alliance. His growing impatience reared its head at times, but she paid it no mind. It seemed she was just as determined as he was. He stood and placed his hand over the X he had drawn to symbolize the island. "He believes it to be there. Though I am skeptical, it does not completely lack potential. The place itself is lost to time."

"It's heavily fortified," she stated and placed her hands on her hips. "There are a lot of guards. Soldiers, even."

"Our acquaintance assured us that we needn't worry about them." Savantin looked down at his hand, removing it from the table as he noticed his veins became more prominent through his skin, darkening in color.

"Are you certain this is something worth investigating? I don't think it needs repeating that I've searched it as thoroughly as I could. Months, Savantin. I've been there for months."

"I wish to see it for myself. And, if we find his information to be lies, he'll see firsthand my abhorrence of anyone who wastes my time."

It was hard to read the woman, she seemed intimidated at times, but driven. He didn't ask her why she wanted the sword;

he hadn't even asked her why this sword specifically was worth seeking an alliance with him. He knew it was important to her, though, as she had briefly explained the lengths she went through to arrive here. He was very methodical in his search, as he even attested to the deaths of some of his men so that they could pursue his wishes outside of the walls. It was a simple exchange, their freedom for their unyielding loyalty. Only one had ever tried to flee. After not receiving correspondence from the man, Savantin sent others to investigate his disappearance with the order to kill him on sight if he was in no visible danger. It was reported that he was found inside of the brothel of Defaltor, seemingly acquainted with the women there. He was dragged outside of the city and killed in the fields that surrounded the walls, his corpse dumped in the river.

"Three days' time. When do you plan to leave?"

"Dawn."

◆ ◆ ◆

When he made it to his quarters, Savantin gazed toward his bed. Perhaps sleep would not elude him tonight, though his racing thoughts that kept reminding him of his recent failure stated otherwise. He felt the muscles in his forearm tighten, and looked down suddenly, seeing that the knuckles on his hand were slowly expanding. He made a fist, closed his eyes and took a breath into his lungs, now feeling the muscles throughout his torso mimic his arm. He watched it, attempting to breathe deeply to silence his thoughts as he knew that they would see him lose control. Suddenly, a voice behind him. His door closing quietly, locking. Keys falling to the floor.

"So. The rumors are true. I had to see it for myself."

"You have until I turn around to get out of here," Savantin answered. "I won't even ask where you've stolen those from."

"Why should I do that? I could scream for the guards at their posts, you would finally be removed."

"You are naïve, Haemad."

Haemad laughed. A laugh that frustrated Savantin further. "Oh, I don't think so. I will be revered highly by Ozrach when he finds out that I am the one who solidified the rumors that the commander of the legion is a monster."

"Any man can tell the difference between his own demise and the words of an exasperating louse. Yes. Destroy the reputation of the legion while so much is at stake," Savantin answered, taking a second to swallow. "Reveal to the king that a Seraphice was in Terrenveil's army for years before I set out to put down the people who are planning to dethrone him. Just the kind of idiocy I expect from you," the last few words faster, more forced than the rest. "How do you suspect you'll prove these rumors to him? I'll leave here, just like I always do, and return once again a man."

"I won't miss your sarcasm. Your arrogance. Your blatant disrespect for most everyone who inhabits the castle... actually, there's not anything to miss."

"Despite how we feel about one another, I'm trying to spare you," Savantin answered, this time struggle in his voice.

"Yes, that I definitely won't miss," Haemad said, and laughed. "Ever since the rumors began, I've studied your people. One child from every home. The priests. Your stars. Soon you won't be able to hide it. Isn't that right? Until the sun rises?"

"No," Savantin stated, his voice deepening. "So many of us do what we can to please the god, so we can feel the calm of the goddess. But I please no god."

"So, we needn't fear you at all."

"When you read." Another swallow. "Did it say what a Seraphice must do in order to survive their transformations?"

"I didn't find it necessary to continue. Your people are sick. Heretics. Not worth a second thought."

Savantin laughed softly, focusing his eyes on Haemad's chest. "A Seraphice must consume the organs of man, should they wish to ever again appear as one. Whichever one calls to them." His breaths were less labored now, but very audible upon exhalation.

He could see now that Haemad's eyes had widened, his demeanor opposite that of when he arrived. His confidence was gone. Not a trace of his derision left.

"I've always hungered after the one that is the loudest." Savantin took one final breath before smiling softly. "It's so clear now that I can hear your heart beating."

Haemad quickly dropped to the ground for the keys, Savantin grabbing his throat and forcing his body into the wall. It cracked behind his head, the bricks partially giving way to the pressure. Savantin placed one hand above Haemad's chest, now able to cover half of it. He moved to dig his fingers into his skin but stopped, and instead dropped him on top of the table. Haemad coughed blood, attempting to scream but could not call upon his voice. It splashed on his hand, warm, wet. The scent was potent, alluring, appetizing. Hunger. He looked toward his right arm suddenly, the prominent vein enlarged, running up through his neck and disappeared beneath his jaw. He held his head back for a moment, breathing in gasps of air. When he opened his eyes, Haemad began to struggle, tearing at Savantin's arm in an attempt to free himself. It was then he knew that he was dangerously close to something he would not be able to control. His eyes, no longer close to those of a human. The spots of blood in them had completely overtaken the whites, his pupils looking similar to a creature of the woods. Savantin held him there for a moment, closing his eyes, trying to gain control. Haemad grasped a penknife that was on the edge of the table, moving it to stab into Savantin's skin which had hardened, causing the blade to be mostly ineffective.

"This didn't have to happen," Savantin answered between breaths, his voice rough. He looked to the shelf that was at the edge of the table, grabbing the pitcher of wine that sat on it. He began to pour it down Haemad's throat. He then coughed loudly, discarding splashes of the liquid as he pushed it from his throat with his lungs. It splashed all over Savantin's hand and stained several documents on the table. Eventually, the amount became

too much for him to reject, and he became still, Savantin pouring
the rest of the wine down his slightly opened mouth.

Grabbing Haemad by his thick, curly brown hair, he pulled
him off the table, and forced him out of his window, tossing
the wine bottle out afterward. He heard Haemad's body hit the
ground, the glass shattering mere seconds later. He'd be found
in the morning, his death being reported to the royal family
who would mourn their loss, with the exception of Neraea,
he supposed. The thought of her made his pulse quicken. He
took a deep breath, his arm shaking noticeably. He hadn't been
like this in a very long time, having been able to last long days
without making sacrifice. It needed to happen tonight. He removed
anything that would immediately identify him, and went out
into the growing darkness, searching for the only thing to grant
him release.

◆ ◆ ◆

Ohric rushed down the halls, looking for the boy that had spoken
out during their introduction. He knew that Savantin held harsh
punishment for those who did not report, it was customary for a
commander, after all. These men were not reporting to a captain,
or a magistrate. Ohric took a chance with the boy, watching him
train in the courtyards. He was vicious on the offensive, yet with
a careful defense that Ohric had not seen in years. It would surely
take place of his inexperience. He hoped his commander saw it
that way as well. He was beginning to doubt the likelihood they
would see battle, not unless a province decided to rebel during
their search. The thought made him anxious. Though he and
Savantin sparred regularly, he hadn't seen battle in a very long
time. After searching the dormitory quarters, he headed south,
toward where the barracks met the wall.

This was beginning to become worrisome, and he desperately wished this entire ordeal to be over. He didn't know how
Savantin planned to juggle the war, the provinces, and his search

simultaneously. That didn't entirely concern him, he supposed. He knew that he would be told to handle certain accounts when Savantin was continuing his search, and that is what worried him most. A patron attempting to incite a riot, finding evidence of treason. Both were things he would want Savantin to directly oversee.

Ohric hurriedly approached the guards at the main gate, asking them if they saw a young soldier pass through recently. He almost went through the trouble of describing him when he saw him in the courtyard. He excused himself and approached the boy who spotted him.

"Why have you not yet reported in, soldier?" Ohric asked.

"I have, hours ago. I was restless. There was no meaning in what I was doing, lying without sleep, staring at the ceiling."

"Meaning or not, I will need you to report inside. We have important things to cover in a few hours, you'll need rest," Ohric answered, keeping his voice low. He looked at the passing guard, whose torch light barely illuminated the yard.

"I suppose I am just eager to leave Terrenveil."

"Ah. This is your first time away. I remember mine." Ohric turned his head toward Blacwin, his eyes hungering for the tale. "Alright. While we walk."

Blacwin nodded in response, his silence telling of his desire.

"It was close to eleven years ago, during the War of Red Tide. My coterie was set to march on G'vhas, but we were ambushed by the Jezhan. This was a war we lost. Before Savantin was commander of the legion. They were eventually eradicated by the Kingdom of Selos who were faced with the same threat."

"Your coterie, how many of you survived?"

"Me and two others. They set fire to their arrows and attacked from afar. They rode in on horses after the arrows stopped falling. They made quick work of us. Our captain fought well but was surrounded. Once most everyone was dead, a Jezhani threw his shield at me. I ducked, but I was knocked from my horse. She didn't make it, but she saved my life. I feigned death, so I could watch the direction in which they were headed. Five of them stayed behind to ensure there were no survivors. They started stabbing the corpses. One by one. The two who survived were going to run, I could see it, until they noticed I was alive. We were able to kill them. I was the only one who made it back to the Mountain."

"Were you afraid?"

"Terrified. The fear never really leaves."

"It's not fear that bothers me," Blacwin answered and looked up toward the sky, the hot and unforgiving sun. "It's the idea of not knowing. That should not bother me either."

"Not knowing what?" Ohric asked. The boy was... fascinating, but in a mysterious and gloomy way. Ominous, like the clouds that rolled in from the shores in Harbortow.

"Outcomes. Anything," he answered in short. Ohric could tell the thought continued to move through his brain, engulfing him, until they had reached the courtyard. Ohric didn't understand but didn't ask him to elaborate.

"There is time yet for the others to arrive. They were sleeping, last I checked. The only one that was missing was you." Ohric answered, looking down at his sword. He hoped Araele would reveal the right path to him. Unease. That was the feeling that gripped him currently.

"They say you are Araelian. Is that true?" Blacwin asked. It was as if the boy had read his mind. Impossible, though maybe not. For all he knew, the boy could have claimed to come from Valspire, instead arriving from Genisia.

"Yes. But Savantin gives no room for religion in his command. He and I have an understanding. I don't speak of Araele unless I find it necessary, and he does not berate my goddess before me."

"You've killed. Your sword, I'm sure has seen many men to their end. Yet you follow her. Hear her."

"I fight in her name. To rid the world of darkness. There is so much of it left. She thought that by purging the earth of the uncleansed, nonhumans, the darkness would recede. It was just replaced. Replaced by a lesser but invasive evil. I know I cannot cleanse this world alone, so I joined Savantin. He did not accept me at first. Thought me unfit...lost. But he soon discovered my loyalty, and then named me coadjutant."

"Do you often wonder where you'd be if you had never joined the legion? The world is vast, but unforgiving," Blacwin said. "If you believe your goddess has led you here, then it is not void of reason."

Their walk ended just outside the barracks, Ohric ensuring that the boy turned in to find at least a few hours rest. He too, would need it. He could not sleep either, something was amiss. Araele repeated it to him, over and over. He would head back toward his quarters, though, at the end of the wall nearest the barracks. He looked up toward the castle, perched upon the mountain watching over all. The walls were built to contain the rocks the castle depended upon for support. Savantin's quarters were up there, the highest of the walls. And as they descended the mountain, magistrates, captains. He could see torches from where he stood, knowing each room they inhabited. The grand balcony, each staircase. He wondered how much the castle guard was paid, wandering the halls for long hours of the night. There was an old story about a ghost traveling the halls of the castle, though Ohric did not believe it. Araele spoke of the lack of such things.

His quarters came into view, and he increased his pace. The chill in the air was growing with each night that passed. He wasn't ready for winter, he never was. The cold did not suit him. Suddenly the boy's question came to mind. If he hadn't joined the legion, perhaps he would have traveled to the southernmost reaches of Cilevdan to Ing Se Tah. The oldest of the temples was there, said to house the tablets etched by the goddess herself.

Upon opening the door, he noticed that he did not extinguish the candles near his desk. Foolish, but in part due to his weariness. As soon as he lay down to rest, a thought would come to him. Something new to think about time and time again. Outcomes, circumstances. He had always been told that drink would see an end to that, but in his religion, there was no room for it. He wouldn't dare go against Araele's wishes. He wouldn't know where to start. He'd have to rely upon trying to silence his ever-running mind himself, with the hope that he would drift off. Time would not stop; dawn would not cease. Tomorrow, they were leaving.

◆ ◆ ◆

The light came early, and Blacwin sleepily pulled himself out of bed. The men were rushing around the barracks, few of them he recognized from the gathering that took place yesterday. There was so much chaos, so much disarray. Shouting, madness. He watched as a captain entered the door, joining in with the rabble and making his voice as loud as he could. He grabbed what he could, a few blankets, rolled around some other belongings. There wasn't much he needed to take with him, he thought as he grabbed the hat that was sitting on his bed and placed it on his head, using it to move his blonde hair from his eyes.

He never really thought of home often, but this was a moment he did. His abusive father, drunk and abhorrent, never would suspect that his only son would belong to the legion. He thought back to his father instantly, cursing his name in his head. The various scars across his body belonged to alcohol and hate fueled blows. His mother was another victim, sadly, too afraid to leave or cry out. There was not much more he could do, so he left for Terrenveil, and didn't look back. He should ride to Valspire and sever his head from his body.

Blacwin's thoughts were suddenly interrupted by voices in the hallway outside, and he stood as straight as he possibly could, attempting to look eager and alert. He calmed only when there was no action pertaining to the words spoken by the captains and continued his walk to the stables. It couldn't be too early if the others were getting ready for the day, yet he saw neither Ohric nor Savantin anywhere. He suddenly heard laughing nearby. He shot a glance over instantly looking for whomever uttered the sound, wondering where the humor was in this dim morning light, but soon averted his attention elsewhere as his mind began to drift off again. This time, about the provinces they were going to travel to. He had never been anywhere besides Valspire, besides his travel to here from there and the roads in between. He arrived here three or four years ago, when he was sixteen, not knowing how to fit into a kingdom. He had never been so close to the castle in his life, watching as the soldiers marched up and down the roads. He would find where he was meant to be. Where his place was. He was no longer just a farm hand, caring for animals and then killing them for food.

When he joined, he heard rumors about his commander, and how the reputation of the legion was what Terrenveil held onto to survive. He heard about the languid king, and his overly religious queen. He also heard about their daughter, who recently had died in a skirmish on the roads while being drawn by carriage to meet a suitor for matrimony. There was no talk about a child since, and he assumed it was due to the heartbrokenness that ensued from the tragedy. He wondered then what it was like, to have a family that would miss him, but felt childish for thinking so, and moved on. Who would rule the kingdom next, once the king and queen passed on from the world if they had no successor to the throne? It would be a decision made by the king in his last hours, he was sure. How hungry then, were the members of the council to taste that seat of power? Corruption was never far from the throne. It was something his father would say before he turned to alcohol, but that was long ago. Blacwin could hardly remember those days, now.

Suddenly, Ohric came into view and looked over the men. They were mostly ready now, each of them rolling up their blankets into a pack for their horses. Blacwin wondered if there would be any resistance in the towns they visited, and if their horses would be spared the rebelling patrons. That must be why they were riding separately from the common troops, who would arrive in each province only a day after. He continually had more questions than answers but didn't bother to ask. There was no point in knowing. He was here, this is where life had led him. There was nothing changing that.

◆ ◆ ◆

Ohric looked over the men who they would be spending the next couple of months with. They seemed ordinary, standing in formation with their horses behind. He took a breath, and withdrew behind the stable doorway, not to be seen for several more minutes. He placed an envelope within his armor, covering it with the light riding jacket he was ordinarily not seen without. When he emerged, he spoke loudly, which warranted silence from the rest of the men who watched him.

"While our commander debriefs the captains, I am to discuss what is expected of you in the field. You will listen to either me or Savantin as we please to direct you. Remember that you have been chosen to play an important part in this campaign. There will be things that are asked of you that aren't customary. If you speak about them to anyone, there will be punishment."

"Punishment?" said a man from the back.

"Treason begets punishment." Ohric said, watching over the faces of his assembly. "You are to do as you are instructed. Without question, as that is what your oath upon the sword was when you joined the legion," Ohric said, a reminder. He hadn't really wanted to perform such a risky action, involving all these men to follow them when the routing was so intimate with Savantin's search. But they really had no choice. He knew most of these men shared the drive to do more, to stand out, which was his initial reason for approaching them, but how were they in loyalty and discretion? That he did not know. Savantin assured him not to give it mind, but it was impossible not to. Too much was at stake, too much could happen.

It was a few moments later that Savantin had come to his side, looking rather angered. He could tell what had happened last night wasn't planned, because there were still small spots of blood in his eyes. Ohric placed his arm in the way of Savantin's moving forward, looking at him. "A word," he managed as Savantin took a heavy exhale, nodding his head once toward the space behind the stable. "At ease," Ohric instructed the men before following. He watched his commander carefully, knowing that what he had just done would be seen as out of line. He hoped Savantin would see his intent, and not take a stance of aggravation.

"What happened last night?" Ohric asked. Savantin was typically volatile when this occurred, Ohric knew, his frustration and anger was usually what was first seen.

"I had an unexpected visitor."

"What have you done?"

"It is no concern of yours," Savantin said, harshly. Ohric persisted, "I only ask because I want to know what I can do to help."

"There is nothing, this time." Savantin sighed, taking a deep breath and closing his eyes for a moment. "It was Haemad. I nearly eviscerated him. But I didn't. I forced him from my window, if he's found before the animals devour his corpse it will be seen as an accident."

"Did he see..." Ohric didn't finish his question before Savantin nodded and opened his mouth to speak but stopped. "Have you been counting days?"

"As I have since I was brought to this. Why do you ask?"

"Because our business of late must have distracted you. Last night was the silver star."

"Noreda," Savantin said suddenly. He looked down at the chain around his neck and then back up, as if the thought was then erased. "No matter. We cannot delay plans any further. While we are free from Ozrach's gaze, we must investigate things we have lost track of."

"The woman," Ohric reminded.

"She will be dealt with. The location of the box is close, I can feel it," he answered, moving out to address the troops. Once he had, they straightened up instantly, most of their things packed away into a roll to attach to the backs of their saddles. He had forgotten how irritating it was being on the road during winter. The flesh could only take so much of the burden before the organs were affected, the heart, and the lungs. It wasn't unheard of that people froze to death in the smaller winter towns or closer west to Septentria. It was bitter, here on this mountain, the cold ice, the dark nights with howling wind that went through the body. He hardly felt it anymore; all the weather that winter brought them. He could hardly remember what it felt like. He watched the men carefully, looking at every motion of their hands, studying each weary sigh and readying stretch.

"As you are aware we are moving for Rierdan this morning. We will be investigating provinces of my choosing. Eventually we will fall into position with a coalition from the North Watch under Magistrate Almour for a short time. You are to regard him as usual, but you report directly to Coadjutant Ohric. If he asks what your business is, tell him that under the special session called by Ozrach, you are there to directly serve me," Savantin said, taking in a large breath. "As for Rierdan, it is small, so we won't be there for more than a night. While we are there, I will have Ohric speak to you about what comes next. Our mission will be very dynamic, and at times may have no protocol. Ohric is in full command of the provincial situation. I am there to advise him while we carry out investigations. Are we clear?" Savantin asked, looking toward the men gathered before him. They nodded silently, which was enough for him, and he left to handle the last matter at hand before they left Terrenveil for what could be months. Or so he hoped.

◆ ◆ ◆

Blacwin looked around at the other men to measure what the worth of each man was. Whether they were frightened, or anxious, or carried uncertainty on their face. They seemed able enough, and he presumed that he should get to know at least one of them. The difficult part. Common talk bored him. Tales of home, or women, or the weather. Most things that people did, in honesty. Life, its routines, its rituals. He wanted something more. Something to break the constant void that was presented to him. A purpose, a calling, an escape.

Thinking back to the present, Savantin just revealed that Ohric would be their reporting officer. Something he thought strange, but he was certain that Savantin would be busy keeping close contact with the head of each coalition and planning according to their reports. Out of all places to begin, they were heading to Rierdan. He had only heard of it briefly, and wondered what was so important about it. It was a small town indeed, only ever mentioned by traveling jewel artisans. There was a mine there, one that housed many different gemstones in frozen walls of rock. He wondered why the town was so small. It is said that they found the very gem in the amulet worn by Queen Neraea, a large dark sapphire within them. Though, the mines were picked to emptiness some odd years ago, or so the rumor projected. He heard a woman in town speak of it while he wandered the rich district just before dusk.

He let his thoughts drift from the mines to the matter at hand. They were leaving in several minutes to potentially discover enemies of the throne. The acts of rebellion became significantly more prominent over the past few months and Ozrach ignored it. But he wasn't interested in what the legion was sent to do. He was interested in what Savantin and Ohric chose him for, and why they were traveling separately from the majority.

"There is not much I can say now to prepare you for what's ahead. I can only say that as quickly as things may change, watch out for one another. We will be arriving a day before any of the battalions. It is Savantin's wish." Ohric answered.

"Yes, Coadjutant," the men stated, waiting for further instruction. Blacwin began to make observations of those surrounding him. He would need to get to know them well, after all, if he were to care enough to aid in survival. There were days he wondered what death would make of him. It would end the monotony. But what existed thereafter, if anything? To what lengths would he go if he remained? He often weighed each thought when he laid awake at night. He watched as Ohric spoke, moving his hands, characteristically. He was so lost in his own thoughts that he could not focus on what the man was saying. It didn't matter. He would again fall in line. The road awaited them. He had no idea what was expected of him. The only thing he knew was that they were riding off to deal with traitors. Something that was only interesting if he got to use his blade.

"Mount up, soldiers," Ohric demanded.

In silence, he made his way to the horses, gathered in a herd, some huffing and pawing at the ground. He chose a dappled gray mare and pulled her from the others, slinging his pack over the saddle, securing it with a leather rope. It was his father who gifted him the rope, said it was from when his grandfather served in the legion many years ago. Why he still carried it was a mystery to him. He had never known his grandfather, knew nothing about the man other than his occupation. It was a nice rope, and even though he didn't have reason to respect his father, he wasn't the kind of man to dishonor his family through the loss of a gift.

He could hear the soft voices of the men behind him, moving toward the horses as he had just moments ago. He looked to his left, seeing the gates to the mountain had already been opened, the common legion lining the road with their horses, waiting for the signal from their Magistrate. Blacwin mounted the horse he just readied, watching his coterie in order to discern who was speaking and who remained silent. It wasn't that it wasn't easy for him to approach others, it was that he didn't have the will to. There was nothing they could say that would interest him. So he would remain silent unless spoken to. Analyzing. Observing. That didn't last long however, as a man approached the horse beside him. He smirked, looking him directly in the eyes.

"Out of all of these horses you choose a small mare?" he asked, his Mordestan accent thick on each syllable.

"Mares are quick, smart. They withstand the pains of labor and must move on when their foals are taken from them whether it is by the hands of nature or the hands of a human. They have a fury that steeds don't share, a will to live that is greater than all others."

The man smiled, looking at the horse he chose. "A mare cannot hold as much as a steed can."

"I am not much to carry," Blacwin answered.

The man nodded, laughing. "Perhaps you and I should stick together then. You can be quick, where I can be strong."

"It's not a terrible idea."

"They call me Djeik."

"Blacwin."

"The North."

"Indeed," Blacwin answered, watching his horse paw at the ground, moving her head upward. He patted the side of her neck, stroking her mane.

"Do you know what's going on?" Djeik asked. "All of this seems so sudden."

"Only what Ohric has told me so far."

"I suppose all we can do is wait and see what our commander will tell us. He is not like I imagined him to be."

"No?" Blacwin asked. Something that interested him.

"He is angry. He carries it with him. But what goes along with anger is missing. Hate. I feel he may surprise us all."

Blacwin nodded in response, unsure how to answer. He could tell the man was angry, it was evident this morning. He spoke to them very briefly before abruptly leaving, and wondered if there was anything more to it. Why did he entrust this campaign to Ohric? He was lost in his thoughts and didn't hear the question Djeik had asked him, only to be disappointed by the subject.

"Do your people gain wisdom from a spirit above?" Djeik asked, his voice denoting curiosity.

"No. The people of Valspire have no spirits, other than those who have passed from this life and are still looking for the next."

"You hail from the haunted mists. I have heard stories."

"I can hardly remember home. I left it long ago," Blacwin answered, averting his eyes.

Djeik was silent for a few moments, watching the men at the gate. It wasn't long before he spoke again, "We are riding to Rierdan, and they say there are ghosts there, too."

Blacwin nodded at this statement, not knowing how to answer. Perhaps his grandfather was among them, walking along the roads of the battlefields trying to find home.

◆ ◆ ◆

The snow slowed considerably since their last time on the road, and Savantin wondered now when someone would find Haemad. It wouldn't be long; someone would realize his annoyances were silenced. Neraea would probably be first. She could not keep herself away from the constant blathering of his tongue despite voicing her revulsion. That would be something he would hear about upon return; he was sure of it. They'd first mention his disappearance before the matters of grave importance. The war, the provinces. However, if things were to happen as Savantin wished them to, he wouldn't hear the man's name ever again.

He heard the men behind him speaking softly, listening to the bells on the saddle of Magistrate Almour's horse. Ozrach thought it was customary to decorate his higher officials, giving adornments to what should be simple pieces of their craft. Savantin kept his saddle from when he was a simple soldier throughout every rank he had witnessed, not caring for the more lavish and decorative objects gifted with each rise in rank.

There was a considerable amount of speaking coming from behind him, older men telling tales of their adventures before coming to Terrenveil, young recruits listening in awe and wonder as they regaled them. He listened as a soldier several rows behind them told stories of the sea, fighting pirates and listening to the songs of the sirens from jagged rocks far off the coast. He spoke of ancient treasures, curses, wonder and beauty, but the only thing Savantin could think of was how much he hated the sea. It was cold and salty, tasting bitter as it sprayed up on the decks from large, aggressive waves.

He had only ever been on a ship twice, the longest being when the Emperor of Rustanzen and the other surrounding powers of the world called a peace conference in Asterbain, a miserable hot place over the seas past the Pointe of Ghosts. He was younger then, probably twenty-two, only recently being appointed as commander. As he suspected, Ozrach got on his knees and let the larger alliances to the emperor do their best not to recognize Terrenveil. It was a disappointing meeting on behalf of the kingdom, that was, until Savantin asserted himself, making known it was an equal power and was to be treated as such. It was now no secret that Terrenveil wasn't to be derided, and beyond that, threatened. He had been asked several times by the emperor to leave Ozrach's employ and join him, with promises of coin and anything he could ask for. But the box was the only thing Savantin wanted. The box was not in Rustanzen.

Two young recruits displayed their amusement by asking questions that were thought to be obvious. The older man laughed, deep and hearty and told them that his seafaring days were ones far gone, and he was probably their age the last time he sailed. There was another soldier talking and laughing amongst his friends over tales of a barmaid back on the Mountain. They made jests and spoke in a rather egregious way, making sexual sport of the young girl trying to make a living. They were all in high spirits, it seemed, which made it easier for him to carry on his work separate them. They would cross the river soon, underneath a dark and unforgiving sky.

It wasn't long before they arrived at the river, rushing and surging with the fury of the sea that it came from. Rierdan was only miles from where they were now, its citizens using the river to fish and hunt. It was what the town was now known for, what they contributed to the kingdom. In a few months, the river would be covered with ice, the people having to resort to the more primitive methods of the Septens to make their catches. He wondered what kind of life that would be. A quiet uninterrupted life. He almost had that once, now ten years ago.

They would have to travel south now, for at least another few hours. It was slowly becoming dark as the sun mocked him, taking its time to hide beneath the earth. He knew which moon would be above their heads tonight, and moved his hand to his neck, feeling for the chain in the darkness. He felt it, cool and flat in his hand, and moved his fingers down to where the ring was pulling it downward. He would avoid it again tonight, and the next. Ohric would not be happy with that decision, he never was, but with being this close to Almour's men there were things he could not risk. His needs happened to be one of them. Perhaps he would have time to slip away after speaking to the patron of Rierdan. His absence would not be questioned. He listened to the rushing water as his legion grew silent now, the only sound being made aside from the force of the water were the horses, who huffed and neighed as they trotted alongside it. It was then Almour approached him, stopping his horse so it was at the neck of Savantin's.

"Why do we move at such a slow pace now? The king will want to hear news of our first day."

"I will send word to him by bird as I always do. I am in no hurry to place myself among that province," Savantin answered, his focus turned toward the river. "You know very well that once we reach Rierdan, you and your men are to ride north for Lieds."

"Do you think you're being too hasty in this?"

"My orders are not subject to questioning," Savantin said sternly and turned his gaze toward him, hoping that there was nothing monstrous in his eyes due to the fast approaching and inevitable arrival of the star. "We will cover more ground if we travel like this. It is no concern to me the number of men that I am taking. I commanded that another battalion under Captain Verane follow only a day behind in order to fortify the province after we have left. If the provinces are rebelling, they'll send word to one another of our coming."

"Yes, certainly. But you are not thinking of the worst possible outcome, surely you see that?"

"What I see is your persistence becoming bothersome. Word will spread that the legion is coming. Once we leave these provinces, if they are involved with the impending rebellion, they'll continue as soon as we've left only for a battalion to arrive after."

"Thus catching them in the middle of their actions," Almour said and stroked his beard. "But you've only chosen a small few to do this with?"

"Yes. By continuously changing our courses, it will incite confusion and panic. Staiman, I have given a very unorthodox charting. A lot of unnecessary travel, yes, but it will be unpredictable when they arrive," Savantin answered.

"So, I am to ride with my men in a direct course through the center of Terrenveil."

"I'm pleased you remember," Savantin stated, his sarcasm biting. He hadn't had the time necessary to find patience, and it was evident in how he responded to others. Something he didn't particularly like, but it did limit most people from seeking out conversation with him. "I know your next question will be why that is. These provinces are closer together which means you'll reach each one faster than Staiman's battalion or my men. They will send word to the others. It also means you will have more time for your men to rest. And, since we are on this topic, I'll remind you. I do not want you to look for evidence, but more so be observant of the province while you spend time there. Once they realize you'll be there for more than just a few days, I would be surprised if they didn't attempt to continue their plotting somehow."

"I see. It will be done. Is there anything else you wish to discuss?"

"Not at this time. Return to your men."

Almour nodded at the order and circled his horse backward. He was growing tired of the incessant questioning he was receiving from all fronts. The council in Terrenveil, the patrons of the provinces, and even members of his own legion were full of vexing and menial questions. Perhaps he should carry out this campaign as he did all the others. At that thought he exhaled in weariness. Though fear was a tremendous motivator, it did not grasp all. He already assumed that religion existed for this reason, to scare people into being reformed. He often offered Neraea this thought, telling her that what she believed in didn't exist and that there was nothing for her after her life. She told him that he was a fool, that he was delusional. She spoke about the error of his ways and told him that he would burn in an underworld of darkness and misery, but he only told her that she had just proved his point.

She never understood his reproach of religion, never understood why he was so opposed to the teachings and followings of a higher power. He didn't believe in protective gods, goddesses, deities, for the things that he had seen and endured were enough to discount the notion. There would be no judgment for him in the end, only peace and darkness. She asked him why he was so bleak, so cynical but he gave one response. Experiences shape a person. Neraea showed her scorn, but he did not change his stance. These people thought that following the ways of a kindred spirit would grant them some kind of redemption at the end of their days. It was faith, as Ohric called it. Savantin shook his head. It was a coping mechanism. People fear death, the heartbreak that accompanies it, so they created a place where they could continue and again find their beloved.

Savantin took a moment to appreciate the silence. There wouldn't be much of it in the days ahead, not as he was interrogating patrons and listening to the concerns of his men. There would be concerns, he knew. There were always concerns. He was almost missing the company of his other men, the ones that died on the Isle. They were all depraved, and Savantin didn't particularly care for them, but they kept their concerns to themselves and remained silent until it was time to perform their duties. He hoped the men that Ohric chose would be fit for the tasks ahead, but he doubted it. It wasn't that he didn't believe in his Coadjutant, the little time involved in his getting to know them was where he harbored his doubts. If he again needed the Mask, he would have to take time assembling it. His plan was much different now.

Ohric came to him then, his voice quiet so that it could not be heard by others over the sound of the rushing water. He seemed nervous, his face matching his voice in lack of confidence.

"Rierdan is miles down the river, I know this. Even still, I cannot smell the fires from the city hearths."

"It is not quite nightfall; perhaps they have not yet been lit," Savantin answered, looking toward where Rierdan was located. There were large piles of wood on the top of each watchtower, kept lit at night to show the fisherman and hunters back inside after dark. However, the sun was still among them, if only scarcely, and the sky had not yet been painted over. It wouldn't bother him, the absence of light, yet he knew Ohric would not be satisfied until events were set properly.

Savantin rode ahead, his horse picking up pace as he tugged on the reins, looking toward the sky. That was where he would see the lanterns first, their brilliant orange glow across the darkening horizon. Above the sight was the scent, as the wood began to burn, the smoke was carried through the air in the wind. Sometimes so much so, that it could be recognized from the bank in between the rivers twin tributaries. They used the timber from the thick black mangled Spirewood trees that grew north of them in the furthest limit of the Glendoryn Forest. The forest itself was large, and stretched over almost half of Cilevdan, thinning out in areas. In these niches, where the trees did not grow, were where the innermost provinces of Terrenveil were built.

Most people would claim that the forest was haunted, the black gnarled trees being enough to scare off most of the common folk. Stranger still was the Lake of Knights, just outside of Terrenveil's border. It looked like a thick mirror of ebony, the surface so dark that no one ever visited it. Stories came of the lake, Savantin knew not where from, of people being spoken to by it, being enticed in by its mesmeric black glaze. He hadn't seen it of course, never having traveled south of Terrenveil until he visited the isle. He would have liked to see it, though, a body of water that manipulated a person's fears and led them in, where they drowned in slow dark misery. What would it show him, he wondered? Would it be anything at all?

The stories of the lake were only added to by the tales of the trees, knotted and ugly. The sap from them was a deep red color, and during the fall season was when the trees would secrete it, making it seem as if the entire forest was bleeding. That was when people were most fearful, and the tales became plenty in taverns and inns across Cilevdan. Sirens of the land, as they were called in myth, wandered in the trees and sang haunting songs appearing as if they were lost maidens. They were revenants, Savantin knew, as he insisted time and time again that not all creatures died in the purge.

The men quieted as they rode into the portion of the forest separating the Mountain of Terrenveil from the western winter provinces. He could tell how fearful they were, as the stories of what abided here became worse as they traveled west. People believed that ancient and malignant Septen shades roamed the western lands, seeking the living for use of their vessels. They drifted aimlessly through the trees, their haunting moans heard from all corners of the forest. Draped in the blackness of the shadows from where they came, their faces were covered until they came across a human, at which time they revealed their sunken red eyes and wrinkled faces trying to find a pathway to the soul. He wondered if they were hallucinations. The sap was known to obscure the mind if ingested, and he didn't doubt that people consumed it. Certain parts of the forest were so dark and dense that game was rare, and water was scarce. Perhaps that is where the tales came from. It didn't explain the murders, however, and the corpses found in the deeper portions of Glendoryn.

The legion had grown so quiet now that the smallest crunch of a hoof upon branch echoed around them. The men looked into the trees, unnerved and jumpy. A large bird dove off a branch, grazing its talons against the ground to capture what could only be its meal and soared off into the trees, making a man nearly fall off his horse from the proximity of its flight path to his head. The men around him chuckled, but returned to their previous silence as they continued along the bank of the river. A few of them stopped, filling their small metal flasks with the clear crisp water.

He turned his gaze to the path before him, listening to the wind through the trees. In time, they traveled down the river to where the trees began to thin out, the large monstrous walls of Rierdan coming into sight just as the sun went down. It was then they began to light the pyres, one of the men attending the watch taking notice to their approach. Savantin gave the order for Almour to ride North, taking his men toward the large wall.

"Open the gate!" the guard shouted down toward the ground, placing the torch back in its bracket on the wall. Within seconds they could hear chains rolling, and the large gate of Rierdan opened, retreating into the top of the watch. Savantin waited until the gate was halfway open before he made his way toward it, taking notice of the stable that was just outside of the province. Foolish. He supposed their line of thought was that the realms had been at peace for so long that the horses weren't in any danger. Horse thieves were easily dealt with, though at the cost of inconvenience, and beasts stalked the trees. He then wondered who built the city, who was responsible for its flawed design. They were met by a young man, tall and gaunt, his face covered in a thick dark beard. He saluted respectfully, and offered to take the reins of Savantin's horse, avoiding eye contact as he reached his hand outward.

"I will have our stable keep attend to your horses and make sure they are fed and watered," he answered as Savantin dismounted, placing the reins in the keep's outstretched hand.

Savantin had seen this man before, and focused for a moment, trying to remember. "You have my gratitude. I wish to speak to your patron directly, are you one that can lead me to him?"

"I am. There are places we can quarter your men…"

"That concern can be placed with my Coadjutant. Point him in the right direction, and take me to your patron," Savantin answered, taking an austere stance. The man stared at Savantin blankly until Ohric spoke up, grasping his attention. When the man returned to him, Savantin noticed he had a tick of nervousness, lowering of his eyes, rubbing his hands.

"Right this way," he answered, heading towards a large house in the middle of the square. Savantin nodded once, removing his helmet and following him silently as the night grew black and cold. He would do this to save face before he disappeared into the night. There were ruins south of here, an old town lost to the forest ages ago.

He began to follow the man through the row of houses that surrounded an old cobblestone street. He was told this was one of the richest provinces, and believed it upon sight, never having been here before himself. People looked out of their windows, a child on the porch of the house to his left. She began to wave, to which Savantin offered a smirk, returning one before her mother ushered her inside and closed the door.

"Our patron may be asleep at this hour, should I need to wake him, I will show you where is most pleasing to wait."

"Anywhere will be fine, your name?"

"My name?" the man asked in surprise. "It's Tirsing."

"After the fallen star. Septen bloodline."

"Centuries ago," Tirsing answered, forcing a smile. Either he didn't wish to speak of it, or he felt an impending judgment.

"This is his home?"

"Yes, follow me inside," Tirsing stated and opened the door. The patron of Rierdan was sitting by the fire, warming his bones. He was an old man, long white hair spilled over his shoulders. Tirsing strode forward, announcing Savantin's arrival. The man stood, and Savantin moved his hand forward to stop him, but realized he was blind.

"Commander. I am grateful to be in your audience," he stated. Savantin reached for his outstretched hand to shake it, and the patron dismissed Tirsing, who half bowed and left the house. "Tirsing told me about the events that have come to pass after he returned from the assembly called by the king. He rode through the night, just so he could make me aware. War. Most troubling."

"Yes. It may not come to that, but I am preparing each province and their outlying towns," Savantin stated. "You sent Tirsing in your stead?"

"Surely you see what has become of me?" The old man laughed. "My son is not interested in a life of politics, and instead has abandoned us to the road instead. Tirsing has taken to caring for me. He is a good man. I shall hope the rest of the kingdom sees it too, when I appoint him as my successor."

"You must trust him with your life," Savantin answered.

"My life and legacy. The legacy of my family. I only hope the boy accepts."

"You mean to say he doesn't know?"

"Not just yet. But the time will come. I have slowly begun to teach him how I keep Rierdan. He has a good heart. Tell me, Commander..."

"Savantin."

"You are a man young in age but rich in years, Savantin. Do you often wonder who will take your place when the time comes? Forgive me, I know you are here on duty, but entertain an old man for a few moments. I didn't think the time would come where I would ever get to meet you."

"You wanted to meet me?" Savantin asked.

"Is it as much of a shock as your voice suggests?" the old man chuckled. "Your reputation precedes you. You alone have forged a reputation for the entire kingdom. You would have my voice as your loyal subject, as I know you would make a great king, had you not the same notions as my son. You long for the road, don't you? To do what it is you're meant to do? I often wonder where I would be, if I hadn't been born to this family. Where my morality would be. Being in certain roles weighs heavily upon it but relies upon it as well."

"I suppose I do not give it much thought. As commander of the legion, I suppose my mortality isn't certain. The mortality of no soldier is certain. It may not be that I get to decide who replaces me. Not unless I survive as long as you have and am spared death on the battlefield," Savantin stated. He didn't plan on remaining in Terrenveil that long. Ohric would take his place, though he knew the man would neither want it, nor be able to handle it the way he did.

"Yes. The condition of man. So, you've come to tell me about the war?"

"Mauros is occupying borders, as I'm sure Tirsing has relayed. And, as I am sure he also relayed, there is a matter of rebellion."

"Madness. I can see why people are infuriated. But bloodshed is no means for change," the man stood, nearing the fire, using his hands as guide. "This may be a foreign concept to you, as warlord, but a plot to overthrow will only mean death. There is no way it can be done peacefully. Do you think both events are a conspiracy?"

A thought that had crossed Savantin's mind, once. He doubted it, though he could not leave it to chance. "I do not. If they somehow gained the backing of the Moroscan king, he would not take trade commissions in return for aid. He is a warlord. He will conquer and keep the throne for himself." Warlord. The patron used the term to describe him. The man believed him to be best suited for the throne. That was the foreign concept to him. King.

"I suspected as much, though I know you would not overlook the possibility. Rebellion is… difficult. I do believe it brave to put that much force behind their oppression. But slaughter will change nothing. Sure, as the killing continues, the rebellion could gain backing. But why not challenge the right to the throne instead? If enough people truly wish to see his rule end, it will work in their favor. Citizens keep their lives, and if a few provincials become casualty, so be it."

Savantin could see the reflection of the flames in the man's milky eyes. He was glaring into the fire, dwelling on his thoughts. "I must unfortunately relay that if anything is happening within Rierdan, I am ignorant of it. You may choose whether or not it is you believe me. I am an old man. I do not know when my time will be. I've lost my sight, my son. I will not be alive long enough to see anything change. But things slip by me. Slip by Tirsing. I wish I could be vigilant, but I am not able, and Tirsing spends most of his days tending to me."

"You needn't explain yourself to me." It was then he realized that he did not know his name. "I am here to assure you that your province will be strengthened in the event there are any enemy attacks, and my men will remain in Rierdan until some time after Mauros withdraws its soldiers from the wall."

"I know you are only doing as you must, but you have my thanks, as well as Rierdan's."

"I'll take my leave," Savantin stated and headed toward the door. Tirsing was the first man he saw, who folded his hands together and customarily lowered his head slightly. It was a symbol of respect in Terrenveil, his gestured hands a sign of his family's age and lineage. It meant *may our alliance long live.* The man's behavior was consistently surprising. Terrenveil could use a respectable and dignified leader.

There was only one way in, and one way out of Rierdan, the front gate was massive and loud. While every man that existed— aside from Almour, aggravatingly—knew better than to question his whereabouts, he still wished to operate inconspicuously. Not only to lessen the suspicions, but to appear serious about his oath as commander. He approached the gate in haste, instructing its keeper to raise it. As far as anyone could guess, he could be conducting business beyond the walls. Retrieving his horse from the stable, he began to ride through Glendoryn, following the map he had memorized. South, toward what remained of Astellan. It was no secret that Terrenveil's history was submersed in tragedy, the events spilling out into Cilevdan. Legends were plenty, as near every place had its own.

Savantin grasped the reins of his horse, heading toward the old town. Once he had made it there his horse nickered, and he dismounted by a tree several feet away from the entrance, tying her reins to a thin sycamore. They were abundant, the trees, foliage overgrown and overrunning the village. Some buildings had completely crumbled, stones lying on what were once pathways, now covered in dead grass. As he walked toward the old road he heard soft voices, whispers. No living person remained here. He passed a building when a rush of air moved from it, the door creaking in its wake. He turned then, pulling his sword and watching the empty streets carefully. The sounds stopped, the village becoming dead once more. Spinning quickly, he raised his sword to the throat of a young woman. "It's coated," Savantin stated. "Verithium."

The woman smiled and vanished, appearing on a low balcony next to him, sitting. "You know we are lost in the beyond."

"Not everyone is ignorant to the legend of Astellan."

"Legend," the woman laughed, her voice echoing. "Tragedy."

"In different words."

"Why did you come here? You will find nothing here but the dead, as we are all that remains."

"If the legend is true, the crusaders could not remove the chalice."

"So, you seek something?"

"Someone," Savantin answered. The chalice could only reveal things already seen. The book he found was old, dust covering each surface, the pages yellowed. It cost him a great amount to procure it from an archivist in Genisia, who was reluctant to part with it until gentle persuasion accompanied the generous sum he offered. He hoped that he wouldn't have to persuade this ghost differently.

"Why should I lead you?"

"You don't have to assist me, but you won't be fond of what I do to the remains of your village if I'm left to look for it on my own."

The woman looked at him without speech and vanished, appearing on the streets once more. "This way," she answered and began to lead him down the path toward a husk of a building, the materials from which it was made predating the others by years. The wood was rotting, sod eroding away, the stone crumbled. There was a small door on the ground, mostly covered in old grasses and weeds.

"Beneath. I cannot accompany you the rest of the way," the ghost answered, vanishing once more. Savantin crouched, placing one hand on the rusted handle and pulled upward, the door coming loose from its old, weak hinges. A rush of musty air came from within, whispers forming on either side of him. He looked within the darkness, making out an old wooden ladder, partially rotted. As much as he knew that he shouldn't attempt this in his human form, he detested the idea of giving into the star above. He decided to take the risk, climbing downward by scaling the rocks that had dislodged themselves from the wall. Jumping from the wall as a rock came loose, he touched the bottom, beginning along a path that led to an opening.

A golden chalice sat just beyond the opening, a spring just behind it. Nearing the spring, he took the flask from his pack and transferred water into the chalice, listening to it as it began to bubble and then immediately still. It was then he undressed, placing his clothing on the dry portion of the floor before entering the water, taking a deep breath of air into his lungs. He submerged, attempting to silence his mind. He called forth her scent, her voice, her face. The island. The inn. He closed his eyes tighter, as if it would make more efficient the effects of the magick of this place. He saw, clearly, standing in front of him. The scent of her hair. Her skin. She widened her eyes, and attempted to move away before he grasped her wrist, feeling something solid in the dark of the water. Ruins. An old pass. Snow. Sleep. Her refuge. A mountain path, far above Winds Hollow, must be.

He surfaced, taking a large amount of air into his lungs. She was still in Cilvedan. He recognized the mountain; only a day's ride from Opskaven. He would need to quarter his men there for a few days and set up a base so that it was assumed he was planning. They would leave Rierdan at dawn. Savantin collected his things, composing himself before he left Astellan, riding quickly toward the gates.

◆ ◆ ◆

Blacwin listened to the fire crackle in its stone refuge, giving off warmth in the dead of night. There was an occasional snore from one of the sleeping men; one would roll over, rustling in the blanket that was covering him. He sat up in his chair, looking deep into the fire's blaze and listening to the snaps and pops it made as it ravaged the wood it was consuming. He didn't know why he was so restless. It had been two nights now that he hadn't slept, ever since he was approached by Ohric in the canals behind the guard tower back in Terrenveil. Perhaps he would grow weary from being awake for so long, and finally be able to sleep. Blacwin drew his knees closer to his body, hoping to feel more of what the fire had to offer. It was more than the blanket that was lying on the bed in the room he had chosen for sleep. Sleep. Constantly evading him.

He hadn't seen Savantin or Ohric in hours, ever since they arrived here at sundown. Perhaps they were still interrogating the patron, whose name he didn't know. He wished they would have asked him to accompany them, to begin the work that he was so highly anticipating. Trust, he thought, something not yet established. Though, he was asked, and now was left wondering why. It didn't matter, he guessed, and shifted his thoughts to something more appealing. He was going to see Cilevdan. The other provinces. Maybe once he finished his years of service, he could travel. Find whatever it was that was out there for him. The world was vast. Something must exist to break the mundane routine he currently maintained.

As he continued to watch the glow of the fire, he felt a gust of cold air enter the room as the front door opened. He heard the hushed voice of a female followed by a man who ushered her to the front of the room where the innkeeper was standing silently. Blacwin listened as they passed behind him, and turned his head as they made it to the front desk, offering the weary innkeeper coin for a room. Just before he refused them, Blacwin stood, walking over to the desk.

"Let them have my room for the night. I obviously have not been using it, and it would save them from having to ride further in this cold," he said, watching the woman as she placed her hands inside her cloak, as if trying to warm them.

"Sir, I was under orders that this inn was only to be used tonight for the quartering of the soldiers," the innkeeper answered nervously.

At this, he felt a sense of anxiety sweep over the man that just entered as he took the coin off the counter and placed his arm in front of the woman who was assumed to be his wife. "If this inn is being used to shelter the king's soldiers for the night, then we should not trespass. We will see if we have better luck with one of the townsfolk."

"Why don't you stay for a few minutes, warm yourselves up by the fire before you go on your way," Blacwin answered.

"The warmth will only tease us. We have been in the cold for hours now. If we are used to the fire's gift then the cold will be even more painful for us," the man said.

"Don't be foolish. If you go back out into the night, you'll freeze to death." He watched their faces, the woman remaining silent, shy eyes toward the floor. The man did not remove his gaze, now very calm, yet insistent.

"Thank you for your offer, as it is very kind. But we will try someone in town."

"Apparently, I haven't made myself clear. This town is now under control of the legion. No one leaves without our consent."

"I assure you we are only trying to get home to Larient."

"That decision isn't up to me," Blacwin said and looked toward the door. "How many of you are outside?"

"No one, it is just us," the man said.

Blacwin placed his hand on his sword. "How many of you are outside?" he asked again, this time sternly.

"Five. There are five," the woman answered quickly. "But we are only trying to get home."

"You said that before. The decision is still not up to me," Blacwin answered.

"We didn't mean to cause trouble. This is the safest way," the woman said. The man next to her was now looking down, seemingly frustrated that she had opened her mouth.

"What is your destination?"

"I told you, Larient," the man said.

"Your eyes tell me a different story," Blacwin said.

"It's Eschilan," the woman answered quickly.

Blacwin smiled and drew his sword from his side, moving it swiftly to the man's throat. "No one likes a liar," he answered. The innkeeper quietly removed himself from the desk, walking down into the cellar.

"We feared that if we had said we were from Mauros then we would be executed."

"And why is that?" Blacwin asked. He wasn't aware that the potential invasion was common knowledge, but perhaps if he could retrieve information, it would please his superiors.

"There are rumors. From the walls," the woman answered. "Eschilan is a small city, I would be surprised if you heard of it. But word travels fast, as it is one of the only towns on an ancient route. Many pass through."

"Rumors." Blacwin laughed. "I don't think rumors are a cause for execution, do you?"

The woman stared at him blankly, and the man spoke in her stead. He was becoming a pest.

"We are simple farmers, trying to make a living in a land where we could know peace, but when we were denied lodging here, we did not know where to turn. This was the safest way to ensure we would make it somewhere else. The jungles are filled with hostile creatures, and we would freeze in Septentria. If we make it to Defaltor then we could hire a guide," the man answered, swallowing as he looked down at the point of Blacwin's sword, fixed like the fangs of a viper ready to dig into his throat.

"You've come at an interesting time. Even if your story is truth, you must speak to the soldier in command. I'd suggest not lying to him."

"Our king is not kind to those who leave," the woman said and swallowed. "Once the town soldiers discover we've gone missing it is only a matter of time before they attempt to track us down."

"That is not my problem. You have two choices. Be held here by us until you've permission to leave or try to run and be cut down on the road by my blade." Blacwin looked up as a soldier walked out into the room, watching him silently. "Make sure they don't leave your sight," he answered and turned to where he had been sitting by the fire, grabbing his coat. The soldier nodded and pulled his sword, walking over to them. Blacwin pushed the door open quickly, trading the warmth of the inn for the cold and howling night.

He looked around the streets, seeing several horses tied up outside the inn. He walked over to them, placing a hand on one of the saddles. Still warm, it had to be theirs, and the others couldn't be too far away. This confirmed his suspicions even more. By sending in two of their group, the others could escape if they hadn't returned outside to get them. He headed back to the inn, climbing the side of the building until he reached the roof. Hopefully higher ground would grant him the sights he wished.

Turning to the south, he waited patiently as he saw five shadows move into what looked like a small barn. He watched for a few moments, making sure they did not leave before he climbed down, returning to the inn to gather a few more soldiers. A few were awake already, Djeik among them, probably woken by the pleading from the man at the end of another legionnaire's sword. They looked to Blacwin as he walked in, one of them speaking.

"What in the hell is going on outside?"

"We've got a small problem on our hands. I'll need someone to come with me," he answered.

"Do I finally get to kill someone?" Djeik answered, moving his large dark hand over his sword.

"It may yet come." Blacwin grinned, moving his head toward the door in a motion that indicated to keep moving.

"No!" the woman screamed once, moving forward.

"Silence her!" Blacwin shouted, quickly turning to exit. Djeik and another soldier followed him, allowing the wind to close the door behind them.

"Damned wench. If they heard her then they are probably already on the move." Blacwin cursed, moving quickly through the cold winds.

"Who are they?" the soldier asked. Blacwin thought over what his name could be, but only remembered him occasionally being in the mess hall the same time as he.

"If my suspicions are correct, they are weapons runners from Mauros, trying to pass as deserters."

"Why would they bring a woman with them? She should not die for their mistakes," Djeik answered.

"She is just as guilty as they if she is hiding them. If they are what I suspect, they die tonight."

"Let us be quick," the Mordestan answered, looking down at his sword. He too, was dying to face battle since he joined, as Blacwin recalled him saying. He tried not to overthink what he would do next as they moved like shadows through the cold night air.

When they reached the door, Blacwin pressed his face up against it, as if listening inside. He nodded and Djeik kicked the doors in, moving inward. Inside were three men, and two younger ones, in the process of hiding rolls of burlap into the straw of the barn.

"Drop them, now," Blacwin answered.

The man listened instantly, dropping the roll he was holding to the floor. There was soft clanging, muffled due to the wrapping. Blacwin looked at the youngest of the boys who didn't appear any older than sixteen and spoke.

"Open it, nice and slow," he ordered.

"No. I will do it," one of the men beside them answered. Blacwin then took his sword and shoved it directly into where the man's neck met his shoulders. He ripped it out of the front of his chest and pushed him over into the straw.

"Open it!" he repeated, this time shouting.

The boy moved forward and placed his fingers on the ends of the burlap, carefully rolling it over. On the third turn of the burlap, several swords were revealed.

"Who are you supplying?" Blacwin asked, pointing his now bloodied sword at the package on the ground. Several moments passed, and no one spoke.

"Tell me who you are supplying, or you all die here, and I go beat it out of the man at the inn," Blacwin said. As silence held the room again, he grabbed the boy, pulling him over the piece of burlap lying before them.

"Do you think I'm playing around with you?!" he asked, taking the sword to the back of the boy's neck, pressing it into where his spine rested. Only when the boy screamed in fear did a man answer.

"We are traveling to Septentria."

"You wouldn't be heading south from Tarspun through our lands if you were headed to Septentria. The woman inside said you are moving toward Eschilan. Am I to kill her for so quickly lying to us? Who are you supplying?" After receiving no answer, Blacwin pulled the other young man forward, appearing in likeness of age to him. He punched him across the mouth, which caused the men to lurch forward, Djeik pulling the second sword from his side and moving it across his body.

"Tell me now, or I will continue to beat him until he can no longer speak," Blacwin stated. The boy threw a punch back, Blacwin dropping his sword to grab the boy's face. He landed another two punches before receiving another, pushing the boy into the wall and beating his head against it. He slumped down, and Blacwin grabbed his collar, pulling him upward. He beat him again, and finally gained an answer from one of the men.

"The woman, she is right. We are from Mauros. We traveled to Tarspun to get the weapons made by a very affordable blacksmith, much more affordable than our own, or your rebellious townsfolk. Please, don't kill my son. He has nothing to do with this; he is only doing as he is told."

"Then you decided his fate when you chose this task for him," Blacwin answered and jabbed his blade into the back of the child's neck. He tossed him aside and looked to Djeik. "Kill the others but leave the child alive. He will tell us who they are supplying. If not willingly, we will extract it." Blacwin wiped the blood from his mouth, spitting a large amount of it on the man before him.

"You monster! You think I will tell you anything now that you have killed my son?"

"I have ways of making people tell me exactly what I want to know," Blacwin said as Djeik moved toward the other men. He made quick work of two other men, leaving the one in the center in disbelief and anger, standing in front of the boy.

"Make this quick for me and tell him where the other packages are, and I promise I'll make your death quick."

"Rot in the depths," the man answered.

"Ahh. I was hoping you'd resist," Blacwin answered and looked on the wall next to him, two hooks used to hang meat from the ceiling coming into sight.

"Kill me like with honor."

"You turned down that offer when you decided to be brave to your cause. Now you will die like an animal," Blacwin answered and pulled the hooks off the wall, motioning for Djeik to throw the chains over top of the low-hanging rafters. Once they were over, the man suddenly grabbed a sword from beneath him, obtaining a defensive stance. From behind him, Djeik grabbed one of the hooks and pushed it through his shoulder, causing him to shiver in pain, but he kept hold of the sword. As Djeik pushed the other hook through his other shoulder, the man finally dropped it, breathing out, wounded.

"I think you know what happens now," Blacwin answered. "Now tell me, where are the rest of the packages?"

"They're in the straw... they're in the straw, just look for them they will be there."

"Who hired you?" Blacwin asked, looking at the red blade of his sword.

"I don't know. I swear, I don't. They promised us coin, and we were desperate. Or else my son wouldn't be here with me."

"That isn't good enough."

"I don't know his name, only Thecily knew that, if you haven't killed her already."

"Go make sure they haven't killed them," Blacwin said to Djeik, quietly. He turned his head back to the man standing lightly on his feet, now wincing due to the pain in his shoulders.

"Who did you buy these from?"

"A man in Tarspun."

"Again, not good enough. I need names. Or you are going to hang like swine ready for the butcher, and your boy will follow you."

The man spat in Blacwin's face, and he moved it to one side, waiting a moment before bashing him in the chest with the hilt of his sword. "Next time it will be my blade."

"His name is Dorian, he used a blacksmith in Tarspun so that if he was killed by anyone in your kingdom there would be death as punishment, he was hoping your king, if he found out, would take that bait. A man in Esperanus commissioned them."

"All of this..." Blacwin stated softly, continuing into a shout. "For my simple request!" his voice echoed through the empty barn, and he moved toward the gears on the wall.

"Wait! I told you everything. I even gave up Thecily. Let me down! Please. There is no one to look after my boy."

"I don't recall making the decision for your boy to keep his life," Blacwin said.

"Kill me now, or I'll scream."

"You have nothing to threaten me with. You're an enemy of the kingdom, and while you're here you'll be treated as such."

"Mauros will know I'm missing. They'll send people to look for me."

"I haven't overlooked that detail. But you didn't die here in a barn. Once I've killed you, the bodies of you and your men are going to be placed along one of the northern roads. You were killed by bandits and your weapons were stolen for their own hoards," Blacwin answered, looking down at the swords. He picked one up and moved his hand over the blade. "Your supplicant should have been wiser than to go with a blacksmith asking less than half of the others around. These blades would break after killing only two or three men. But I guess that was never your problem," Blacwin said and threw it at the man. It plunged into his chest and his head flung back with the force, taking his last breath simultaneously to the wound. Before Blacwin could wipe the blood from his blade on his cloak, he heard a rustling from behind him.

"Care to explain what it is you've done?"

Blacwin turned slowly to see Savantin standing in the door, with Ohric behind him, watching quietly from the street.

"I only do what is expected of me, Commander... the boy."

"Ohric will see to the boy. From what I understand there are others in the inn?"

"We will go, right away."

"I have unfinished business here," Savantin answered, stepping into the barn, directly into the puddle of blood left by the man first slain. It splashed up onto his steel boot, and as he moved forward it continued to flow backward onto the straw.

"You. What is your name?"

"It's Brogan, sir."

"Brogan, go with Ohric," Savantin stated, watching the fearful boy in the corner. "It's alright. Go."

The boy nodded, moving beneath the corpse of his father, and to Ohric's side.

"A mess we will have to deal with," Savantin said, turning to Ohric. "What should we do about this one?"

"I will ponder it." Ohric said, looking at the hanging man in disgust. He was certain Savantin wasn't happy about the boy acting so impetuously but gave it no further voice.

"What did you learn?"

"They're from Mauros."

Savantin turned his head toward Blacwin instantly, rage in his eyes. Blacwin continued, "I don't think this has anything to do with the war. The timing is strange, yes. The weapons were made by someone in Tarspun, but they were paid for by a man in Esperanus."

"Esperanus... I'll send Almour's men immediately."

"I'm sorry if I'm speaking out of turn... but why?"

"Our course is set for Opskaven. We must go without delay. There is something that needs my attention."

"I understand. Thank you, Commander."

"Let us deal with these corpses."

"I told him that we'd toss them along the roads. It would look like bandits killed them." Blacwin answered.

"Forgive yourself if you wished to uphold the honor of words spoken to a man who is now dead. There aren't enough hours left of darkness, nor men available to take them to the roads. I'll send someone to aid you upon my return to the inn. Drag them to the forest, just beyond the tree line. The wolves will take care of them," Savantin answered and looked at the display in the barn. The men were killed quickly, their blood still warm. He turned his gaze to the man against the wall, his face beaten inward, bleeding, eyes swollen. Blacwin had a few wounds to match, though the boy looked like he suffered his share of beatings in the past.

"Are there any loose ends to this matter?" Savantin asked. Blacwin swallowed the lump in his throat from the cold weather, taking a breath out. He watched the aura of white leave his lips before he spoke. "Only the woman in the inn. She was the one who told us they were from Mauros, while the man with her said they were headed home to Larient. Apparently, she was the only one who knew where they were going, so I sent Djeik to make sure no one killed her." He wanted to impress his commander, desperately. Success in the legion meant he never had to return home to his family, his abusive father.

"I will see to her myself," Savantin answered, looking down at the corpses upon the floor. Their blood had only recently stopped flowing from the incisions granted to them, their skin beginning to look pale around the wounds. "Drag them, now. I will send help," he said and turned from the barn, listening to Blacwin quietly behind him.

"What about the boy?"

Savantin let out a small laugh of amusement. "You need not worry about him."

Blacwin watched as Savantin left the barn, heading to the inn where he was just resting by the fire an hour ago. This could be the chance he was waiting for, the chance to prove himself among the ranks. He was eager and nervous at the same time.

◆ ◆ ◆

The wind blew ferociously as Savantin walked toward the inn. He could hear his men from inside. The night of the scarlet star was getting close, he could tell now. He ignored these signs and opened the large, thick wooden door, instantly feeling the heat of the fire against his skin as he took several steps inward. It was then he first looked upon the woman, who seemed untouched, though her distraught face said otherwise. He approached the few men who had gathered to the event inside and watched as one of them punched the man standing next to her for what looked like the tenth time. The man behind him stood him up, and he weakly slumped forward, unable to hold himself upright. Suddenly a few of the men saluted him, and he sent them to the barn, ordering them to assist Blacwin.

"Commander, this is the man who led them here, I have tried getting all that he knows out of him but figured you would want to question them yourself."

"You were correct. Leave for the barn," he answered.

The soldier nodded, and signaled to his comrade that had the task of holding the man upright. He pushed him onto a stool, following the other soldiers out of the lodge area. Savantin watched as Ohric's men made their exit. He took notice then that the innkeeper was nowhere to be found. That, he would have to investigate. He looked now at the woman, who held tears in her damp brown eyes. Her brown hair was pinned back and covered by a thick hood made of the hide of some hoofed animal. The man was bruised on his face, blood pooled on his left cheek. His eyes were swollen as well as his jaw, which showed clear marks of a fist.

"You are the commander? Perhaps you can speak to me about why we are being treated this way," the woman said softly.

"You are a suspected enemy of the kingdom, running weapons to help the start of a rebellion. And from Mauros of all places. I'm sure you've heard of the talk of war. Perhaps you can explain to me your innocence in this, and I will act accordingly," Savantin answered.

"Look at the man beside me! He is barely recognizable. I told your men no lies and yet they insist on harassing us for yet more information."

"Yes, but they haven't touched you, is that correct?"

"They have not. But he was only trying to protect me," the woman answered, looking in disgust at Savantin, then toward her counterpart once more.

"Tell me something," Savantin said, his question to regain her attention, her focus on him. "You do know about Mauros's standing army, do you not?"

"Yes, but what does this question have to do with..."

"You obviously are aware of the situation, since you are here running weapons. When there are rumors of rebellion added to the threat of war, as there is now, the King of Terrenveil issues his standing army to disperse the skirmishes before they escalate."

"I thought that by speaking the truth that we would be let go," the woman, called Thecily earlier, cried. "We are not a part of your rebellion, and we have no love for our king. He is cruel. Power hungry. A bloodthirsty warrior. He kills people who try to leave. He thinks it makes Mauros look weak. I will not raise my child there."

"You thought that by forfeiting your contraband you would be turned loose? I cannot take the risk of your further involvement in this. Undoubtedly you would warn whoever is accomplice. You will spend the night in a cell, transported to the Mountain when the opportunity arises."

"I should have known that here there would live a man who would torture a woman without care," Thecily said, her eyes glaring, fixed on Savantin. He laughed softly in turn.

"Torture? If one of those men issued torture, please, enlighten me. They know not to act against my wishes, especially not while I'm among them. They understand what will become of them if they do. Tell me what I need to know, and I will make sure your excursion to the Mountain is not perilous, at least not from those who are tasked with transporting you," he answered.

"Thecily…" the man beside her coughed, expelling a small stream of blood from his mouth. "Do as he asks." The woman looked at him for a moment, revulsion in her face, as if she was going to resist cooperation for what they had done, but upon looking back at Savantin she began to speak.

"You would not be able to reach our destination in time for the receivers of this bargain to still be there. Your efforts are for nothing more than exhaustion."

"Things will be easier for you if you speak," Savantin said. It was becoming stronger now, he felt it. The urges, the darkness. Even as he tried not to listen, he heard the woman's heart beating inside her chest, the expansion of her lungs as she took nervous breaths in. He inhaled and looked down at his hands, making a fist as if to control the movement of them. He didn't have much time now. He was no longer able to control it, and now, he was suffering his changes arbitrarily. He despised it. It was catching up to him, his months of avoiding Norahn. The old god was angry with him, manipulating him.

"We were headed to Garacen. But I'll tell you no more. I will not have more men die because of it."

"A name is more than enough for me to enact my interrogation. I will find whoever you are aiding. Mauros is not welcome in Terrenveil, and neither is rebellion."

"Your king is most abhorrent. He waits in his castle while people die on the borders by bandits and raids, remains warm in his chambers while his kingdom struggles in poverty. He is not fit to rule a kingdom. And you, to serve him, will follow him to the gates of the darkest underworld." It was something he agreed with, though he couldn't give it voice.

"I serve no man," Savantin answered.

It was then the man mustered enough strength to stand, running out of the inn. Blacwin came through the door, grasping the man at his shoulders.

"No, let him run." Savantin said. "He won't make it very far." He would become sacrificed, it wouldn't be difficult to track him, not while he was still bleeding.

Thecily looked on in outrage, turning to Savantin with fear in her eyes.

"Garacen and Esperanus. Were those your only destinations?"

"They were ours," Thecily answered, tears running down her face. "But there were more, headed toward Opskaven. The people of Opskaven don't know. The runners are headed toward Sarghost, and Savoi."

"Blacwin, inform the others of what transpired with the men you killed. But do not have them under the impression that we are going to march into Opskaven with swords drawn. I want you and three others to get ready to ride; you will go first, with the weapons we recovered from the dead."

"Of course, Commander... But won't they be suspicious of us if we arrive to them with more weapons?"

"As I have no doubt they will. We've recovered her name. Use it wisely."

"What do you want us to do once we've arrived there?"

"I want you to find out who they are, and once you've made the exchange, I want you to come back to our position on the roads just outside town."

"You want us to give them the weapons that we just secured?"

"Was there a tone of uncertainty in my voice? I don't want them killed. I want to decide for myself what is to happen to them," Savantin said. He was growing tired of the boy's questioning, just as he was tired of it from everyone else. He supposed it was in good faith though, he only wanted to assist. He ought to put the boy to the blade himself, things easily could have gotten out of hand while he was in Astellan. Instead, he would ask Ohric to keep more of an eye on him and be stern if he had to be. He didn't have the time or care to discipline him at the moment.

"Yes, Commander. But how will we know where to look for them? Do we know who they were looking for?"

"That is something that should have been asked in the begin-ning," Savantin answered.

"What will you do now?"

"I believe we are done here," Savantin said harshly, turning from the boy.

"Commander," Blacwin said, adding a bow to his head. Savantin took a deep breath, looking at the room around him. For now, he had to decide what to do with the woman. Despite what he told her, the prisons of the castle were no place for her. If the Maurosce sent spies to find their lost citizens, which he had no doubt they would do, finding her in the Mountain would be hazardous. She would have to remain here, in the small jail Rierdan kept. He would see her there himself.

"I won't place you in shackles, it is unnecessary. Come with me."

Thecily nodded in silence, her wet eyes blinking quickly as if holding back tears. "Please..."

"Say nothing else," Savantin answered and headed toward the prison house. He ran into Ohric on his way there, who was without the boy.

"What have you done with him?"

"He won't speak of it any longer. He was given Serethen, he will forget," Ohric answered. Savantin nodded, keeping his eyes from Thecily as she raised her hands to her mouth. "Take this one, too. The jail is the best place for her. The patron is kind, old. His successor is an honorable man. She won't be harmed there. They'll await orders from us on what to do with her after this campaign is over, unless of course, she wishes to have the elixir as well."

"Mauros?"

"She can't go back to Mauros," Savantin answered and walked out into the night. Sacrifice was crucial. He wasn't sure how far the man who fled made it, but he hoped it was at least to the forest. There were eyes and ears all over town, but it was less likely someone would witness. He couldn't worry about that now. Soon he would not be able to choose. He sighed, setting off into the night.

◆ ◆ ◆

Blacwin headed to the bar, where the others were waiting for him. He didn't expect to see so much action on their only night in Rierdan. The only thoughts on his mind presently were pleasing Ohric, but above all, Savantin. A man of immense power. The man was calculating, cunning, effective. The legion had a striking reputation because of him. He knew he overstepped bounds by asking so many questions in the inn. Hoping he wasn't a pest, he joined the others, who were quietly speaking amongst themselves.

"What happened here?" the man from the Baeld asked. "This... all of this. This is sick."

"They were supplicants to the rebellion," Blacwin stated. "Djeik and I dealt with them as we saw necessary. They had information we needed to know."

"We heard the screams. That is when I stopped listening," Harlan answered.

"Savantin has orders for us," Blacwin said, watching the eyes of his company carefully.

"Well haven't you become quite the captain," the man next to the Baeld stated and walked forward. "I'm taking a walk."

Blacwin turned to follow him when the Baeld grabbed his shoulder. "Let him go. He needs it. I'll go after him." He nodded, and watched the man go before turning toward the others. "He wants me and three others to head to Opskaven, to pose as those we captured tonight."

"I assume you've already worked out a plan of how we are to get away with it without a woman present."

"I am thinking about it as we speak. Further council will be needed before we leave, but I know we are to take the weapons we have just received and make an exchange."

"No doubt he wants us to find out who the traitors are. What does he want us to do with them?" Harlan, the eldest of them questioned.

"Nothing short of subduing them, he wants them for himself. I don't know what he wants of them yet, but we had better not tamper."

"What if they try to leave town once we've finished?" Djeik asked.

"I've thought of that. What if you take one other, who can immediately return to the rest of the troops when you go inside? That would eliminate any chance of them running before the others get there."

"Thren is right. If even one of them leaves then we would have a mess on our hands," Harlan said.

"Not a bad idea. So, four, then." Blacwin nodded. "Where are the others?"

"They went ahead, making sure villagers were in their homes and escorting them inside when needed. I let them know that we had this handled, and that we'd meet them back at the inn," Harlen stated. "The fewer who know of this, the better."

"And why is that?" Blacwin asked, trying to keep the offense from his voice.

"Dedication is challenged in times like this."

"That would mean imprisonment."

"Yes, and with our numbers as sparse as they are, it's best to avoid that. I think it best if a few of us carry out these tasks while the others do exactly as they are doing. I've yet to bring that up to Ohric, but I'm hoping he agrees."

"The man is right, Blacwin," Djeik stated. "We can't afford to weed anyone out."

"I don't think Savantin would approve of this."

"He isn't in charge of this directly, he said as much himself," Harlan stated. "You know I mean no disrespect, but I'm thinking in terms of our survival, our success."

"I guess," Blacwin answered. "Let us go back inside. The temperature is dropping even more still."

There were only seven others who hadn't joined them, split between a few rooms. Blacwin strode to a door, knocking on it and looking at three of the men, who were sleepily sitting up to the sound.

"Get the others; we're meeting in the large room across the hall," Blacwin said. Before he could move to the next room, he noticed that Harlan had already done the job of waking the others. He was very quick to act, an older man who had been in the legion for apparently as many years as Savantin. This made him think about how young their commander was. Only eleven years older than himself, Blacwin thought. Maybe following this path would grant him a brighter future than he had previously put to mind. He had just passed his nineteenth birthday and had already joined a force of great importance.

As the others gathered behind him, Blacwin took a deep breath as he opened the door to what was deemed Ohric's room, although throughout the night he hadn't reported to it. He wondered when they would sleep and for how long. He knew better than to embark right away to Opskaven, the people carrying the weapons would have slept normally and eaten before heading off.

Once the men were inside, Djeik took a quick look into the desolate lobby, closing the door behind him. The others remained silent, as they were just now waking from the sleep they somehow obtained through the scuffles that occurred this night.

"Our duties call upon us," Blacwin said, looking around the room. "While restless tonight, weapons runners from Mauros have been discovered. They are now dead, left in the wood to be disposed of naturally. Savantin has asked that I and three men go ahead of the rest of you and find out who is at the other end of this sword."

"Aye, and who will be going ahead?" the man from the Baeld answered from the back. He wasn't aware that the man returned. There were four towns that made up the Baeld, but he had traits of those from Harbortow. He was a tall, thick man with a red beard that could be mistaken to be from nowhere else. It was an identifier of their people. Blacwin was good at identifying where a man hailed from. His days as a guard in Valspire attested to that. He was amazed at how many men from parts of the world separate the kingdom were here in the legion of Terrenveil.

"I need one of you to accompany Djeik, Harlan, Thren and I to the town, so that when we meet with these traitors, we can alert Savantin and Ohric to their location. He doesn't want us riding in force. We may scare them off before he's had his chance to look them over."

"He doesn't want them executed? I wonder why that is."

"That is not ours to ask. But I am sure with more exposure we will discover what is to be asked of us," Blacwin said.

"I'll go," a light-skinned man from the back said, uncrossing his arms and pushing himself off the wall. "I am faster than any man I know, and quiet. I won't be seen."

"You're in. What do we call you?"

"Zareden."

"Zareden, we will go to the barn once we are done here to collect the weapons that we need."

"What shall we do while we are waiting?" another asked, standing right before him.

"Rest. If this goes the way I think it will then we will need your assistance."

"Thank the gods. I am tired of all this traveling without any action. I haven't had a decent glass of ale or a wench worth bedding in weeks."

"Quiet yourself Goring. We will have to wait out these rumors of war before we can do as we please."

"I know that Jurgen. I wasn't born yesterday. But I'm a free man and have my words until I am told otherwise," Goring defended.

Blacwin spoke quickly to avoid a fight. "I will await further instruction as to when we will be leaving. For now, I suppose rest is in order." He wished that sleep would call him into bed, warm by the fire. He left his blanket out there to be warmed and hadn't thought to move it when he left. He sighed, heading now to retrieve it. He didn't hear the words the others were saying, only opened the door and went straight over to the fire.

The fire had only died down partially, his blanket still neatly draped over the chair he had left it on a few hours ago. He picked it up; feeling the warmth it had collected as he drew it to himself. Maybe if he lay upon the bed set aside for him, wrapped in this cloak of heat, sleep would find his eyes. The amount of restiveness was building. He could not fail, not allow himself to. That is what he would strive for now, as he walked back toward the room he was stationed in. He blew out the candle that was sitting next to his bedside and rolled into the surprisingly comfortable cushioned bed. He closed his eyes, and after taking a few breaths, found himself off into a world of dreams.

◆ ◆ ◆

It had been a violent display, overtaking him without so much as a warning, other than his heightened senses. He was lucky to have found the man on the road, away from the eyes of all others. Above all things that troubled him, there could have been a witness to something no other person than Ohric had seen in years. He didn't want that, but his current condition was seemingly unpredictable. The last time this happened was after his own commander died in battle. It was only a year after that day that he had also been named commander of the king's legion. He remembered it vividly, his thoughts drawing upon it as he began to quickly decide which room he would take for the night...

The halls were silent the day he returned from the battlefield, covered in blood and dirt from the plain where the last man was struck down by his own hand. There weren't many at all who had returned, only he and another. He thought back to how it all began, in the light from the morning sun. Their horses became anxious as man after man gripped their reigns tighter from their own unease. Savantin watched from the front line, keeping his eyes fixated on the empty field before them. The star of Noreda would be with him tonight, being his savior for the time being. He could hear the quickly beating hearts of all who surrounded him, their eyes as one, staring into the fog rolling off the warm ground. He closed his eyes to take a breath, hearing his commander's horse pace in front of them.

"Keep alert. They were here last night," he said.

"Lieus, what if they are taking our pause as a chance to surround us?" his Coadjutant, a man by the name of Sarvius answered.

"I will not march my men into a trap. They could be waiting in the fog for us to move."

"We really don't have much of an advantage here," Sarvius stated.

"We have numbers; we almost have twice the men they do. It should not be hard to kill a band of raiders."

"We should never underestimate the enemy," Sarvius said—his last words. A spear slid out of the mist, lodging right between his ribs. He fell off his horse, dying in the mud. Lieus gave the order to raise shields yet wait like lambs for slaughter. He was convinced they would emerge from the fog eventually. Savantin didn't want to die like a lamb, even more than that; he didn't want to be pushed to the edge of inhumanity before every soul who had eyes to see.

Suddenly more spears were thrown, causing horses and men to fall all around him. He held his shield up, deflecting one that would have met him between the eyes. They were left now without horses, the ones in the back tossing their riders from them as they ran to the trees. It seemed not even numbers would matter in this fight, and as even more men fell to their fates, he thought that he would have to turn to Norahn after all. Suddenly the sun broke from the clouds, dispelling the fog from its hold on the earth. They stood, brandishing weapons, adorned in their furs and war paint. Their leader stood before them and shouted, running toward them. He hadn't even taken three steps as the rest of them followed, loud enough for their gods to hear them.

"Get into position. Do not let them break your defenses until the back lines are ready with their attack."

Savantin should have known Lieus would use this strategy. The most muscled men in front, to hold back the ravaging dogs while the lighter men in the back would spring forward once they were tired out. As they charged forward, the legionnaires waited to brace for the clash, using their shoulders to muster their strength behind the wall made with their shields. As if they anticipated their tactics, the leader of the raiders shouted, and a flurry of arrows flew from behind their lines. Only some of the men behind Savantin were quick enough to raise their shields above their heads to block the piercing rain. Lieus seemed intent on having them remain a wall, as he stood just behind them on his horse. Savantin didn't see what happened to him as the raiders bashed into them, using their own shields as a levy. It was only minutes before he threw his shield forward, bashing the man before him and using his sword to take the man's head.

Several more men filled in where the last man had fallen, swinging their weapons. Savantin moved his shield accordingly, using his sword to attack from his vulnerable side. He had taken down two of them when a large man assaulted, swinging his axe viciously to break through the shield. Savantin pushed it back, lodging his sword between the man's helmet and his chin, pulling it out and bashing him to the ground with his shield. The man's eyes went into a cold blank stare as he fell backward, thudding into the mud with such force that it splashed when he hit the ground. It was then that they heard the cry of Lieus, his sound a beacon over the sounds of the battlefield. He quickly cut down his next attacker, moving over to where the sound was uttered. The raiders seemed to be infinite in number, as the men around him were being swarmed and cut down. He hadn't looked to see how many were remaining, hadn't paid attention to anything other than his own sword. Lieus was on the ground, blood pouring from a gaping wound on his chest. He was coughing, looking at Savantin with horrified eyes. He mustered enough strength to point behind him, trying to form words.

Savantin turned instantly to see a man holding a battle axe above high above his head and cut him down at the knees. He pushed him back with his shield and dodged the attack of another who had picked up the swords of his fallen comrades. He threw his shield at his feet, letting it leave his grasp, and pulled his other sword from the strap on his chest as the man fell on his stomach. At that time, he suffered an incision on his back, slashed by a man behind him who was instantly cut down by one in his battalion. Ignoring this, he moved quickly to the fallen, swords ready for the bite into flesh. From behind, he felt a sword pierce his torso, right above his hip. It went through his flesh, cutting through his armor from the side. The sword ripped upward, the pain increasing. He fell to his knees, holding the wound as the sword was pulled from his body. His assailant moved on, rushing toward the remainder of the legionnaires.

Savantin looked up into the sky, as if searching for something and fell on the field next to so many dead. He thought he had joined them, lying amidst blood and soil, his eyesight fleeing his eyes. He still held on to his swords, gripping each of them in hand. Their leader turned him over to see the outcome of death, when he was cut down and pushed aside by another soldier. They fought off the last of the raiders, as he lay there, his heart rate rapidly decreasing. He lifted his hand from his side, looking at the blood that covered it. Even swallowing was hard to do, he felt as if he couldn't move, couldn't breathe.

The last of the soldiers, three in the Mask and one other. Quarrelling. The one, who had been reluctantly shoved into the legion's acting battalion from the small town of Arriksmad was quiet as the others spoke.

"Lieus is dead. The others are dead. Where are we to go? We can't assault their stronghold with three men," one said, ignoring the other soldier completely.

"He isn't the man I am worried about; I haven't seen the Captain."

"Don't tell me he's..."

"I found him," the last man answered, moving over to his position in the field. "It looks like someone's stabbed him right through his side."

"Take what you can off the dead."

"Loren... they probably don't have much of..."

"Take it and quiet yourself. What if we don't return at all? This is the perfect time; we have died here on the battlefield. We don't have to live this life anymore."

"I'll gather what I can find," one of them answered, jogging to the other side of the field.

"It's wrong. It should be buried with our brothers."

"Merreth, we're in the Mask of Death. We have no code. We take what we please. It's what we were ordered to do. Now that they're all dead, I for one am not going back. What, to listen to the king? He's an oaf. I'd rather nail myself to my own front door than listen to him ever again," Loren answered.

"You do what you must. As for me, I'm heading back. I can't afford to be found, not with my wife carrying child. You know what they do to deserters."

Loren instantly pulled his sword, pointing it at him. "You can't go back. You'd risk letting information about Horus and me loose."

"I wouldn't say a thing," Merreth answered.

"And you," Loren said, pointing to the man who had remained silent. "You can't return either."

"Loren, leave us out of this. If you run, so be it. I will not say a word other than telling him who's died here."

"And leave our names out of it?"

"I am no traitor. I will explain how you were dragged off with them. It's a believable tale. Ozrach never sends search parties. You know this."

"I cannot risk it," Loren said.

"Don't be foolish. If you kill me out here, then you will have only killed a friend and left a child without a father."

"We're all going to the fiery depths anyway," Loren answered, moving his sword forward in his hand.

The man named Horus stepped next to Merreth, looking closely at Savantin's body. "Loren, help me roll him over. He's got something on his finger. I can't get it from this angle."

This statement distracted Loren from the thought at hand, and he placed his sword in its scabbard, pushing past Merreth to the corpse.

"You shouldn't take things from the dead," the silent man finally answered.

"Oh, and why is that? Has Araele given you some divine interference? Fuckin' Araelians," Loren spat.

"I'm telling you. You shouldn't take things from the dead."

"And I'm telling you to recommit yourself to silence before I end your life," Loren yelled. He helped Horus push Savantin's body over with a struggle. Once the man was on his back, they saw that his wound was still bleeding. Horus bent down to his left hand, looking at his little finger. Around the second knuckle was a ring, polished pewter with two sets of purple gems in the shape of teardrops, pointing away from each other. Gray diamonds surrounded them, with two shining white in the center.

"How much do you think this will fetch in Defaltor?" he asked, grabbing the top of his large hand, using his other to attempt pulling the ring off his finger.

"It seems stuck."

"Cut it off," Loren said.

"No, I've got it... hold on," Horus said, the sound of great effort evident in his voice. Finally he pulled it off, watching now as the stones deepened in color. "This is beautiful," he said holding it up to the light of the sun. The fingers on Savantin's hand made a fist, and pulled Horus down to him, pushing his hand into his chest.

"Savantin, calm, it's me. Horus... we... we thought you were dead," he said fearfully.

"Your heart," he struggled to utter.

"Wh... what?" Horus asked.

Savantin ripped his skin back, pulling the heart from Horus's body. He then took a bite out of it, finishing the rest of it quickly before using his arm to wipe the blood from his chin. He stood, turning to Loren. His body began to change, veins present on his arms, his muscles slightly expanding. The irises of his eyes became the color of blood, blotches appearing around them making them perfect circles no longer.

"What in Deceferous's name..." Loren said, reaching back for his sword. Merreth moved from next to him, instantly becoming the next victim of his lack of control. He grabbed him by his throat, squeezing it as he lifted him inches off the ground. He began to cry out in pain, grabbing at Savantin's extended arm with both of his. He tore into Merreth's throat, ripping the organ from it before biting into the cavern it created, taking only several more before stopping. The color began to leave his body and he fell limp, the last breath of his life extracted with the last of his blood. Savantin threw him aside, looking now at Loren, his eyes darker now, filled with the blood he had stolen from Merreth.

"You were dead..." he answered, standing in shock to what he had just witnessed. "You were dead!" This time, shouting. He raised his sword and Savantin moved in front of him quickly. He grabbed his neck, slamming him to the ground, moving down with his body. He placed his palm over Loren's face, holes opening across it. Loren's blood traveled from them and into Savantin's skin as he held his palm there, pinning him down. Loren shouted, and began to struggle beneath Savantin's hold, pushing on his forearm with one hand and reaching for his sword with his other. Finally, he ceased movement as life left his body.

Savantin stood, looking to the last man standing on the battlefield. He walked to him, reaching for his throat when the man held the ring up to his face, in front of his body. Savantin took it, sliding it over the first knuckle of his little finger, trying to push it down further. He felt the release instantly, his eyes returning to their color of deep blue, the veins in his arms hid beneath skin. He could not push the ring any further than it was already fitting, on the first knuckle of his small finger.

"You. What is your name?" Savantin asked, regaining his voice.

"My name is Ohric, Captain."

"Ohric... to which coalition did you belong."

"I was moved to battle beneath Magistrate Bentore at the last moment."

"I see," Savantin said, looking at the ring. "Come. We have business in Terrenveil."

"Captain, what are we to do with the bodies of the dead?"

"I see no reason to make note of the dead when only two still live. We will leave them for the carrion birds."

Ohric nodded, picking up his shield. It was from there they made their long march back to the mountain, not saying a word to each other along the way...

"Savantin," Ohric said, his voice quieted from the cold of the night. They were outside the porch of the inn, standing around the large fire pit that had not yet died down.

"Leave us," Savantin said to the men who had been tasked with keeping the citizens indoors. They nodded and headed back toward the blacksmith's shop, where the smelter would give them ample heat.

"It has happened again, hasn't it?" Ohric asked. Savantin remained quiet to this, staring his coadjutant in the eyes. "The stars are changing now. You will need to sacrifice more often..."

"Do not tell me what it is I must do," Savantin answered angrily.

"I am telling you what you already know and choose to ignore," Ohric stated. "You cannot risk the men seeing this. Not at this stage of your planning."

"I know. This came on suddenly. I only felt the warnings as I began to change… It shouldn't be affecting me in such a way. Noreda's star is above us tonight," he answered, pulling at the chain around his neck. This silenced Ohric. His commander did not go through the phases of the three different stars of Norahn as the others did. He suffered them all at once and lived them out until the star of Noreda. There was no more order, this troubled him, but he dared not give it voice.

"Under her star I am supposed to remain the closest to human I'll ever be."

"But you can still control yourself beneath it… keep your mind."

"If I don't have the blood, the lives I need after it occurs, I fear I may lose even that," Savantin answered and sighed.

"That is why you must enact ritual sacrifice. If you cannot keep your transformations under control, all will be lost. You have two weeks until the next cycle of their stars."

"I am aware."

"Your kind was not supposed to be able to control this. Twice a month you become monsters, three days at a time. I've read the passages of Norahn."

"Your words are falling upon deaf ears. You are smart Ohric. You always have been. But I can still feel the presence in my veins. It hasn't gone yet."

"Then perhaps you are undergoing something more. You told me yourself about…"

"It shouldn't be happening. How am I supposed to get what I need from her if I cannot turn my taste—" Savantin stopped his sentence, as if caught in a deep thought.

"What is it?"

"I know where she's hiding."

Ohric looked at him suddenly, his eyebrows furrowed in confusion, yet amusement. Savantin let out a small laugh and briefly looked upward, shaking his head. "She didn't cover her tracks very well; she should have left Cilevdan after what happened on that island."

"You know where she's hiding? We haven't seen her since that night on the island… is she nearby?"

"No," Savantin answered wearily. "Siaden Pass. Are you familiar?"

"I am not. Though I presume it is near the border?"

"Yes. Opskaven will have us close enough, but we will have to quarter ourselves there for a few days. Come up with something to tell the men," Savantin stated. "I need to rest."

"You do," Ohric returned. "When do we leave?"

"I have ordered Blacwin and three others to leave tomorrow morning for Opskaven. The woman, she told us that more weapons were headed there."

"So we will follow?"

"Yes, but they are to go in first and make the exchange. We want to discover if the patron is responsible, or if the runners are staging an exchange there. They were smart enough to get them from outside of the kingdom so as not to leave a trail within the walls. I am taking one of the rooms above. I intend to move out two hours after sunrise," Savantin said and departed, sluggishly climbing the stairs. His body was weary, his mind as well.

Ohric nodded as he moved to sit in front of the fire, searching for a place where he too could rest for the night. The soldiers began to turn in for the evening, their voices echoing in the room. He stood and watched for just a moment, lifting his eyes from them and toward the innkeeper, who returned to his post. He was anxious. Sick. His stomach turned.

Somehow, Savantin found Sindara. The man was angry, frustrated, exhausted. Hatred toward being betrayed fueled the emotions that he was experiencing. Ohric feared for Sindara, knowing that while Savantin would hesitate to kill her, he was unstable. He had severely injured another Sardon who ambushed them several months ago, and while Sindara swore they were not together, the pieces seemed to fit, now. Ohric let out a heavy sigh, attempting to gain control of his racing heart, his breathing.

It would only be a matter of time, and his subservience would dearly pay off. As for now, at this moment, it was time to rest. Between now and tomorrow, only several hours waited. Hopefully in Opskaven he would be greeted with a decent night's sleep and warm meal. The cornmeal mush they had been fed here was good enough only for pigs, and the beds were nothing more than straw thrown on top of wooden frames. Despite this, he was sure it was the best they could muster up on such short notice for the king's men. The legion's arrival, Ohric now knew, was kept secret by the patron of the town at Savantin's behest. That fact was what was being paid mind to, not the poor excuse of residence, or the offering of partially burned cornbread. They should have taken an animal from their slaughterhouse, he thought, but at least they were being shown some kind of hospitality. Savantin hadn't paid attention to its worth.

The innkeeper was washing the counters with a rag, soaked in a bucket of hot water. He was carrying on, as they all do; about who was to clean up the blood and wash the scent of death away. He was adamant in saying that he had to bring in customers that were going to pay him, and that while he didn't mind his service to the legion, he needed coin to feed his family. Ohric knew that Savantin paid the man. If he did see anything, this would be enough to keep him quiet, at least for the time being.

The campaign had already become a disaster. The slaying of weapons runners inside the borders of town. And the boy, the boy was eerie, dark. As much as Ohric did not like him for this reason, his actions today proved he would be somewhat of an asset. He was eager, and while his methods were unfavorable, he would do whatever was asked of him. The Mask needed new flesh and blood. He hadn't thought about the Mask until now, not since Savantin relieved the old members of their service by whatever means he deemed necessary. In a way, Ohric was happy that they were rid of them. The men were sadists, and nothing was sacred to them. It was only because of Savantin's orders that they were not to touch Araelian temples.

After remaining by the fire for a few moments more, Ohric chose a room in which to sleep, closing the door behind him.

◆ ◆ ◆

Blacwin awoke, his eyes eager and searching the light for the start of his new day. The room he chose to retire to was surprisingly quiet, muffling the sounds of the men in the next room. The candle he lit hours ago had burned down to its end, the wick, black and crusted. He listened to the sounds of the outside world, hearing nothing but the quiet chirps of birds and a few horses voicing their discomfort in the cold of morning. He moved the thick gray curtains from the window, watching the sun just over top of the hill. It was deceiving how warm it looked, as it cast its reflection off windowpanes and the white stone walls of houses. He sat up, pulling the heavy, animal-skin blanket off him and pulling on a shirt. He sleepily grabbed his traveling gear off the wall where he had hung it with his coat. The leather felt cool against his skin as he tied it on, taking his coat from the same set of hooks. He turned, looking for where he had placed his sword and found it leaning against the wall near the small table across from the bed. When he picked it up, he noticed blood had discolored the blade. He had killed a man, last night. Several men, if he took the time to remember. Sliding it back into its scabbard, he pulled his boots on and grabbed the armor off the table so that he could pack it on his horse.

Opening the door to the lobby, he noticed that Djeik and Harlan were in their armor, speaking softly by the fire. Thren had just emerged from his room, rubbing his eyes before taking a seat next to Djeik.

"Has Zareden come yet? And Thren?" Blacwin asked, walking over to them. He set his armor down next to theirs, approaching the fire.

"I have not yet seen them, perhaps they had something to take care of before we left,"

"We should gather their weapons and leave for Opskaven. If they were planning on staying here last night, then perhaps they were planning on leaving before the sun even rose."

"That would make us late."

"That can be explained if they are still waiting for us. Let us leave now. If we ride fast enough, we can get there in just under two hours," Blacwin answered and withdrew his hands from having been tucked in his arms, moving toward the door. Djeik stood and grabbed his large mace, attaching it to the clip of his belt. He grabbed his armor and was the first to follow Blacwin to the stables. He confidently reached his horse, stroking its muzzle as he placed the armor in a large burlap pack, clipping it to the saddle. His thoughts then turned to the weapons. They should be clipped on as well, to avoid looking suspicious as they enter the gates.

Blacwin was about to mention their retrieval when Zareden emerged from behind one of the buildings, carrying two large sacks on his shoulders, dragging one behind him. He thought of it also, it seemed. He placed them down in front of him and looked up, his eyes scanning the stables.

"It's a shame we don't have more of these. They would be very useful in disguising the armor we have with us."

"Maybe we should just leave the armor behind," Djeik answered and looked at his own, taking up the entire back of his horse.

"He's right. What if it raises suspicion?" Harlan asked, climbing onto his horse as he fastened it on.

"I don't think it's something we should risk. What if we are caught in battle, an uprising breaks out within a city, not having our armor would eliminate our chances of survival," Blacwin answered, looking toward the gates to the city. The road was calling to him. Thren hurried out of the inn, his armor in a bag that he was dragging along the ground. He watched Zareden, who had begun to fasten the weapons to the horses and quietly approached, pulling on his horse's reins.

"You look as if you haven't slept a wink," Harlan said.

"I haven't. I can't wait to rest at one of the inns in Opskaven, I've heard good things," Thren said, letting out a convincing yawn.

"Let us go," Blacwin said and shouted, giving his horse a small jolt. He was off against the cold and solid ground, moving quickly through the air. It was cool in his lungs as he took a breath inward, feeling soothing if he held it in for just the right amount of time. He listened to the horse's hooves across the ground in a rhythm, touching down every few seconds in a speedy gallop. The others joined him, keeping at a close distance. He hoped he was right about the town being within reach in a few hours. He hadn't had a meal since the cornbread last night at the inn, and his stomach was becoming unsettled. The coin he was given would be spent on a hearty bowl of soup at the inn, or a leg of turkey. He wondered now if Opskaven would have the same seasoned roasts as home, with honeyed mead to go along with it. Not even Terrenveil had that to offer except for the few summer months when travelers from Valspire would bring it for sale. He was being too hopeful, and his stomach was thinking for him, something he wished to avoid. He stopped thinking of it as quickly as it came to mind, realizing that taunting himself with the memory would only add to his hunger.

Blacwin slowed as a notched sign came into view, several pieces of wood pointing off in the direction of where towns rested. Opskaven was in the middle, pointed southwest. He didn't realize how close it was to Septentria and pulled his coat closer around his torso. It was about to become colder, though he didn't want to believe it. The winds at home usually brought this chill, but the snow never lasted longer than a few months, not like the tundra where it remained most of the year. Before spending too long at one point, he pulled the reins tightly again and was off, heading in the desired direction. They passed some of the frozen fjords as they traveled the roads, the ice almost shimmering in hues of violet and blue as the sun beat down upon them. They were surrounded by ice, the mountaintops beginning to be covered in white. The cries of birds were starting to become different as they passed through the terrain, and upon coming upon the outskirts of Opskaven they almost ceased. It was a quiet little town, despite the sounds coming from the large logging houses that were set up on the river, which was also frozen over. He wondered if it was part of the Frost's Kiss but deemed that impossible as it ran north to south from just outside of Terrenveil's border. He heard it called the Unfreezing River in most parts of the land, and no matter how cold it got in Terrenveil from the winds blowing over the Tundra, the river did not freeze. He imagined it frozen at the source though, for the waters were always cold. He thought about going to see it one day, but realized since he was still so young, he wouldn't have the time to go and travel for leisure.

They rode close enough to town to stop their horses, being seen immediately by a man at the tree line who cautiously walked into one of the houses that bordered the trees and the rest of the houses. He had never seen a city in the Kingdom of Terrenveil that had no wall.

"That house... do you think it is where we must go?" Thren asked, his voice hushed. Blacwin looked at it, the smoke from the chimney slowing before it stopped. A man opened the door and began walking over, silent as he watched them.

"Perhaps we should speak so that we do not look as intimidating," Harlan said quietly, looking to Djeik.

"I think we should wait until he approaches us first. What if he is not the man we're looking for?" Thren asked.

"Did you have a woman with you?" the man asked, his breath heavy with the scent of smoke.

"We did. But she remained in the inn in Rierdan. She said she had something that needed tending to," Harlan said quickly, watching the man's hands.

"We are looking for a woman, with brown hair, brown eyes and a scar on her arm."

"We speak of the same woman," Blacwin added.

"I wasn't aware there would be a slave with you," the man said, looking at Zareden. He kept his green eyes low so as not to jump at the insult. He pulled his cloak over his reddish, bandaged hands and remained silent.

"He watches over our fleet while we do business, makes sure that no horse thief gets lucky. He's very good with his blades. We'd choose no other," Blacwin said, his horse pawing at the ground softly.

"I see. Follow me and tie your horses. I assure you there are no thieves around here," the man answered and turned, walking back toward the house. Blacwin was the first to dismount his horse. He held the reins lightly as he walked alongside her, leading her where she could be hitched. He heard Djeik touch ground, knowing he could not be silent even if he tried. Blacwin trusted they were all following his lead as they passed under a large stone arch that could have only been built to secure a wall. He wondered how a province so rich did not have the means to build one. Blacwin tied his horse to a tree, fashioning the rope so that the mare could easily break free if she needed.

Blacwin made note of the men waiting behind the arch as they came into his peripheral vision. It seemed as if they did not trust the land around here, and whether these men were waiting to defend their town from raiders or the legion, he did not know.

"In here," the man said and looked up to the chimney before opening the door a crack. Blacwin could smell the inside. Something had been cooking over a fire, and more of the same smoke on the man's breath was inside. When the man opened the door the rest of the way he saw few other men inside looking over maps on the table.

"Ay, the company we've been waiting for," he answered.

"It's about time; we were told you would be here early morning."

"We were held up in Rierdan. The legion is moving across the land as you've heard. They were in town last night. We waited until they slept to make our exit," Blacwin said, walking beneath the door frame.

"The legion is in Rierdan?!" the youngest of the men gasped. "They could be here within a few hours."

"Unfortunately, we were unable to risk getting close enough to listen to their plans. It would be best if we did this quickly," Thren stated. "That way we're out of here long before they arrive."

"Before we bring the weapons in, what am I to be paid?" Blacwin asked, holding a hand up at the door, signaling for Djeik to wait.

"Our agreement was to send the coin to your distributor, and you'd be paid by him."

"I'm changing the agreement," Blacwin answered, waiting for the silence to take hold.

"You dirty bastard," one man said and stood.

"That's far enough." Blacwin stated, Djeik moving forward. "Being paid only enough to make it back home interests me as much as it would you."

"We're not paying you a coin more. I've no care for what you get paid on your end. A deal is a deal," the man who had granted them entrance answered. "Give me the weapons or find yourself at the wrong end of my blade."

"Calm down Herahm. He has a point," a woman's voice from the corner. "They risked all traveling all the way here from Mauros."

"Your leader is wise," Blacwin answered and waved his men forward, hoping his display was convincing. It seemed to be.

"I cannot offer you coin for all you've done; I only have enough coin to pay your supplier. The only other payment I have is notes from Terrenveil, which I know are of no use to you," she answered, curiosity in her voice. Blacwin was young, inexperienced with women, their intuition, their cunning, but he was not inexperienced with suspicion. "We can discuss that further once we see the blades."

"I believe you will find a way to compensate us, a way that our supplier need not know about," Blacwin said. It was then that Djeik moved forward with the weapons, setting them down on the table before him.

"They say warriors like you come from Mordestai," the woman said, taking notice of his dark skin, her eyes flashing. "Do you live in Mauros, too?"

"The road is my home," Djeik answered and rolled open the burlap pack, the swords shining against the candlelight. The woman picked one up, looking it over and handing it to the man next to him. "Inspect them all." She shifted her gaze back to Blacwin, who watched on with eyes unmoved. "How old are you, boy?" she asked suddenly, her eyes turning to Blacwin like a hawk. She moved her deep black hair from her face, which displayed a large sparkling ring on one of her fingers. She had to be the patroness of this town, or from that family.

"I am young, but I have seen enough to make me as experienced as any of the men behind me."

"Are you the son of your supplier?" she asked.

"I am not."

"How did you get a job like this, being so young? You don't look any older than my youngest brother."

"I like to keep my past behind me," Blacwin answered.

"You will tell us now, or see his threat become truth."

"There is no need for that. If it concerns you so much, I will share," Blacwin said, one hand up toward her, the other at his side. "I was raised on a farm, no more than a butcher to provide meat to the surrounding lands. I was caught in an alcohol-induced fight when I was fourteen, killing the man I had dispute with. I did time for it and was released two years later. They couldn't prove I killed him. I couldn't go back home, not after that, who would hire on a child that was accused of murder? I've been with

BLOOD BENEATH THE VEIL

my supplier for three years now. He said he could use someone like me," Blacwin answered.

"Most interesting. I suppose this entire market is filled with murderers and thieves," the woman stated. She turned back to her men, one of them nodding at her and taking the weapons back to the rear of the house. She moved her hand along the side of her face, covered in a crimson cloak, her black and white bodice paired with tight black leggings standing out against it. Blacwin tried to get a glimpse of her face but could not. "Are you planning to stay in Opskaven?"

"I'm afraid not. We were caught up last night, we must return to our supplier, or else they will think that we've run on them. Even though the coin is sent directly, if we abandon, they will put bounties on our heads," Blacwin stated.

"Then I will spare you some coin of Terrenveil. If you stop at Defaltor they can make an exchange in currency for you," the woman said and delegated the task to the man who let Blacwin and his company into the room. She then disappeared behind the curtains. The man went to a chest that was sitting next to the hearth, using a key to open it up. He fiddled around with it for a few moments and finally got it open, handing Blacwin a velvet bag. He shook it in his hands, listening to the coins bounce inside of it. He wondered how they were supposed to fall back into their ranks now that the woman had seen their faces, that was, if she was the patroness. His question was solved, for Zareden entered hurriedly, closing the door.

"What is the meaning of this? Why aren't you out with the horses?" Blacwin asked, crossing his arms.

"Legionnaires, I can see them from the road, just over the hill," Zareden answered.

"Then we leave now, out the back before they find us here," Blacwin said.

"Out of the back?" One of the men laughed. He pushed his brown hair from his face and stood. "You'll do no such thing."

"We've made the exchange. I see no reason for us to stay," Blacwin answered.

"You'll stand and fight with us, won't you?"

"You're planning on fighting the legion?" Thren asked, his voice denoting shock.

"It's why we've asked for these," one of them answered and flipped open the burlap.

"You're insane. A group of rebels against the legion? I think you'd be better off waiting them out," Blacwin answered and looked to his men, pointing to the door. "I really don't think you'd want them to find us here among you. If we leave you might even have a chance at surviving if you're smart enough," Blacwin stated.

"Is that an insult, boy?" the man asked, picking up one of the weapons.

"It's an observation. The Reaper is surely with them; do you expect to survive with chances like that?" Blacwin asked. The man who had remained silent rose out of his seat and pushed his arm across his partner. "He's right. The best we could do is hide these weapons and hope they have no reason to search this house. Someone should warn the Lady."

"Show us a way out of here that doesn't require using the front door and I'll speak to her before we depart," Blacwin said quickly.

Zareden opened the door a sliver, peeking through it. "They are closing in," he said, overtop of the sound of horses.

"Go, through the curtain and out the back. She'll be in the house at the end of the street," the man answered. Blacwin nodded and the others followed him through the curtain. There was an old wooden door that led them out into the chilly air, where he could see the people of the town acting nervously yet continuing with their lives.

"Go around the back and meet up with everyone else. I'm going to speak to their patroness for a few moments," Blacwin said. It seemed his suspicions were correct.

"What if you are asked for?" Djeik asked.

"I won't be long, I promise," Blacwin answered and quickened his pace, searching for the house that was just spoken of. The woman made him uneasy, something unfelt since before he left Valspire. He heard the soldiers arriving at the arch and pulled his hood, knowing that he probably had eyes on him. He quickly walked to the door, and placed his hand on the knob, turning it slowly. He could smell the perfume when he entered, strong and smelling of flowers that he could not recognize.

"Hello?" he asked, looking around at the room. It was decorated in dusty purples, tapestries and pillows of matching material. Candles were lit in two of the matching alcoves holding windows, the ledges covered in black satin to catch the wax. He heard heels click on the floor and watched as the woman turned the corner, holding a goblet of wine in her hand crossing one arm over her body. She leaned against the door frame and looked him up and down.

"I assume one of my men told you where to find me?" she asked, her voice showcasing aggravation as she briefly rolled her eyes. "We have nothing left to discuss."

"I've only come to warn you. My men have left ahead of me, but it seems the legion just came into town. We escaped them in Rierdan this past night, thinking that we would have plenty of distance between us, but they travel fast," Blacwin answered.

"Was their commander with them?"

"I'm afraid I don't know; I've heard the rumors. I have never seen the legion up close, and that is something I'd like to continue."

"I see. I'll make it worth your while if you go to him and tell him that I've an open invitation to my long house, and that his men are welcome in our most lavish inn. But the other soldiers can stay in the quarter house. There will be enough ale there to keep them occupied."

"You want me to ride to him? What about your men?"

"Did I show hesitation?" she asked brazenly, bringing the goblet of wine to her lips. "My maidens are tending to the quarter house, and my advisor is... not in town. I don't feel like fetching anyone else, so you will do." She removed herself from the doorframe and over to the table where a satin drawstring bag sat. She picked it up and tossed it to him, expecting him to look inside. Blacwin opened it, his eyes coming across several sparkling gemstones of all colors. He sealed it, placing it in the interior of his coat, nodding.

"I will tell him for you; though I have the suspicion he may not let me keep my life."

"That makes two of us," she answered and set her glass down on a cream-colored cabinet, walking around the corner. Blacwin exhaled; his worries about rejoining his rank were over. At least now it would be alright if he was seen conversing with Savantin in the open. He wondered what plan there was for this town. Its patroness was brash, a woman that greatly surpassed him in years. Beautiful. He set his fantasies aside and left the house, heading straight for where the legion had gathered in front of the arch. He heard the men speaking behind him, women hurrying inside of their homes. He passed the small house that they had just made their exchange in, and ignored the laughing from the men who were sitting outside of it.

Savantin and Ohric stood, speaking to the few men who tended the opening to town, trying to get information. He could tell from Savantin's tone that it wasn't going smoothly and watched as Ohric pulled a scroll from his side. He was close enough to hear their voices now, and stopped awkwardly behind the men to whom they were speaking.

"Your patroness should have alerted you to our coming. She had attended the council called by Ozrach just a few days ago," Ohric said and handed the man the scroll.

"I will waste no more time speaking to those steeped in ignorance. Where is she?" Savantin interrupted, his question directed to the man who had just stepped in front. He scratched the back of his head, as if clueless and began to open his mouth when Blacwin stepped forward.

"I just spoke to the Lady. She told me that your men are to take refuge in the quarter house."

"Someone with a tongue approaches. Where is the patroness?" Savantin asked. The men he was questioning turned to Blacwin, looking at him curiously. He knew he had never seen him before and did not know where this information came from.

"She waits in her house at the end of the street. She told me that she has extended an invitation for you to meet her there so you can discuss her concerns."

"Make yourselves useful and stay out of the streets," Savantin ordered to the men he had just spoken to, two soldiers stepping forward to escort them to wherever they lived. Blacwin took notice to how Savantin was orchestrating his legion now, much different and more controlling than he had in Rierdan. He supposed there was a reason for it, he seemed angry, impatient. He waited for the men to leave their sight before speaking to them.

"Commander, is there anything else you ask of me?" Blacwin asked.

"Nothing. I want you to go to the quarter house with the others. Make sure they stay out of trouble, and make sure Ohric enjoys himself," Savantin answered, and began to walk away. Blacwin nodded and headed over to where he saw Djeik and the others waiting. Hoping that ahead of him was a day of rest.

◆ ◆ ◆

Ohric grabbed Savantin's arm, looking around him before speaking. "I am receiving sign from Araele. Something is amiss. The woman..." he said.

"I can tell this already from my previous meeting with her. I've a feeling she will try to mislead me."

"Araele says she is not to be trusted."

"Then do not follow. It's time you've deserved your own luxury. Go with them; make sure you take what you need, and properly feed yourself."

"Should I make use of myself while I am there?"

"I don't want anything to happen until after I've met with her. Take the money the men have been given from the patroness. It will be safe in your hands," he said and walked away from the men, heading down the cobblestone street. He didn't listen to the civilians who were speaking quietly from their porches, or to the shouts of those working over in the log house by the river. His men would escort them inside soon enough.

He had several ideas as to why the woman would invite him to her house immediately upon arrival. He remembered clearly that she showed interest before he quickly dismissed himself from conversation. He wondered if she still felt sorely about that, with the way she carried herself. She took pride in her appearance, ensuring that when each time she appeared, she looked desirable. She was attractive, only appearing to be ten or so years older than himself. He was a man that was not swayed by much, and only had one desire. She would try.

Savantin passed the inn, walking up to the house where Blacwin had emerged from just moments ago. He briefly wondered how Ohric's men fared in the weapons exchange but would inquire about that later. Ohric would handle it initially, which would buy him time. He didn't knock on the door when he arrived, assuming there was no need since she was expecting him. She was sitting in a lounge chair facing the door, her crossed legs exposed underneath her long coat. She was wearing heeled shoes and held a glass in her hand. She brought it up to her red lips and watched him with deep brown eyes. He was correct in that she was attempting to seduce him. Her long ebony-colored hair covered her breasts as she had it parted to sit over her shoulders. He set his sword down in the chair by the door and took his helmet off, sitting it right on top of his blade. She looked now into his dark blue eyes and brought the glass down from her mouth, setting it on an end table and sitting up, swinging one leg over top of the other.

"You requested my presence?" Savantin asked, his voice deep and warm.

The woman smiled and crossed her arms. "And what a presence it is. I haven't forgotten about your... demeanor when we last spoke. Though I do not blame you for being such a busy man. You must have been eager to begin your travels."

"You have my undivided attention in this moment, Avelina," he said. It was important to use her name. She seemed lusting, and he could not decide whether it was the alcohol she had ingested or something else entirely. He had no doubt she practiced something of a different nature. An occultist. Perhaps it was due to his recent transformation, or the rumors of his being a nonhuman.

"Oh," she let out softly, "a man who puts names to faces. And here I believed you to hold no love for the court."

"So much as to ignore names?" he laughed, and took a breath in. He could smell her now, beyond her perfume. "Perhaps I will surprise you yet."

"Perhaps you will. I am hoping for it, in fact," she answered playfully and pulled her coat closer to her skin.

"So, we discuss the matter of Opskaven. We'll begin with your priorities and finish with my expectations?" Savantin asked. He would bring the weapons runners into conversation afterward. He had a feeling she was involved, but he would have to interrogate her to discover the truth.

"My priority is our lack of walls. If Mauros invades, we will be overrun and destroyed within moments. I've no idea if they take prisoners, and do not know how they will treat them if so. I worry for my people. Secondly, the timber trade is important to Terrenveil. Unfortunately, so much is requested of us that we cannot build our walls until demand slows," she answered.

"A coalition will be here soon to offer protection until we can confirm that Mauros will not invade. It's the only relief I can offer for now."

"I will not express anything other than my gratitude. It is the most we've been offered in long years," she answered. "Come; let us speak over a glass," she said and picked up her goblet, walking down the hall. Savantin smirked, following her. She walked into a room with a bar that ran across half of the wall, leaning over it to grab another glass off the wall behind them. A bottle was already sitting out on top of it, and he smelled the strong grape scent from its mouth. She poured another glass for herself first, moving to pour the next when Savantin held his hand out to halt her. "Nothing for me."

Avelina smiled and put the bottle away. "Just like my husband, before he met his unfortunate end." She said," she said cruelly.

"And what happened to him?" Savantin asked, watching her move off the stool and walk over to him.

"A logging accident. There was a lot of blood. Working the mill is dangerous. I told him that there were more experienced men other than himself who could handle the job, but he would not listen," she said, offering a small laugh before taking another sip from her glass.

"Are you sure you want nothing?" she asked and returned to the bar for the bottle.

Savantin touched her arm, and she looked up at him, her eyes longing. "Nothing for me," he said and let go after several seconds. He heard her heartbeat quicken at the moment of his touch. Normally he would not have touched her without her consent, but with her demeanor, it seemed she sought it.

"I should have figured you wouldn't mix business with pleasure," she answered.

"Business is often pleasure. Between you and I..." Savantin began.

"Of course."

"Any time away from the Mountain is sought and cherished."

"It must be tiring, directly working with a king such as him. Not to show any distaste for the man, but it does not seem like it would be appealing to a man such as yourself. If it weren't for your profession and his... birthright, you two would not know one another at all. And if you did, I don't believe you'd speak."

"I did not come here to discuss my relationship with the king," Savantin answered. "I am here to air concerns and seek answers to them. And, of course, dispense any action I deem necessary."

"Yes, I forget myself," she answered and brushed her hair behind her back. "The walls. I don't know what aid you'll be able to secure. All previous requests were ignored. Bandits attempt to take Opskaven. The last raid we had was only three weeks ago. The town guard has been fending them off, but they've had to train citizens. So many of them live in fear, Savantin. They cannot sleep at night. They fear that they'll be killed."

"I'll voice concern. Though I cannot promise he will listen to me, either. Not right away. It is important, do not mistake my words. I am only presenting verity."

"Yes, well. We've lived without it for this long, we will make do until relief is reached," she answered.

"It is time now to voice my concerns, if you have no others," Savantin answered. He was trying to decide how to approach this. She was manipulative, deceiving. She would say whatever she needed to in order to see results that favored her.

"Of course," she stated and poured another glass of wine. The scent took the air as soon as it was forced from the bottle, filling the room with its presence.

"As you are aware..." Savantin was interrupted by a man bursting in, out of breath.

"Bandits!" he shouted. It was then Savantin pulled his sword, heading into the streets. The bandits were upon horseback, torches in their hands. Some had dismounted, his men filling the streets now, beginning to engage. Savantin pulled one down from his horse, stabbing him through the center. He moved forward as two bandits circled back, the hooves of their horses thundering. He moved quickly to avoid them, killing a bandit who was attempting to break down the door to a house next to that of the patroness.

Two bandits overpowered one of his men, killing him and tossing his body down. Ohric appeared at the door of the quarter house then, taking one of them instantly, as it was by surprise.

Savantin lunged his sword forward to meet that of a bandit's, his blows strong enough to send the man crumpling. He severed his hands from his body and laid one slash across his chest, tossing him aside.

"I want one of them alive!" Savantin shouted toward his men. A bandit jumped from behind a porch at that moment, cutting into Savantin's shoulder. He elbowed him in the chest, using the loss of balance to cut him down. Before he could assess his injury, another appeared from behind the manor house, leading several others into the streets. Ohric had given the order for his men to fall into position as the fighting continued. He would have to fight his way toward them.

Taking a deep breath inward he swung his sword in front of him, watching the three bandits that held hungered eyes to his frame. Two rushed forward and he parried attacks, ducking to avoid a blow to the head. He grabbed hold of the one closest to him and pushed him in front of his counterpart's attack, pulling the corpse toward him before the bandit could dislodge his weapon. He stabbed his sword through them both, pulling it and quickly dropping it into the street. The last bandit began to turn and run, not to surprise. Savantin grasped one of the fallen weapons in his hand and threw it, piercing the fled just below his neck. After he fell to the ground was when Savantin moved to join his men, who began to make quick work of their foes once they became discouraged.

The remaining brigands made a break for the hills, Savantin holding his hand up to cease the killing. "Stand down. I don't believe they'll be back."

"They've killed Morrly and Brehg!" one of the men, always seen beside the Baeld, shouted. "I'm going after them."

"I said stand down," Savantin answered, so sternly that his voice warranted silence. "I don't believe they'll be back, but we should not leave another attack from the realm of possibility."

"We will not divide our forces," Ohric stated.

"Yes, Coadjutant," the man answered and moved his eyes toward his commander. Savantin took a short breath and turned back toward the manor house. "Secure the rest of the area. Stay within borders. Use the houses as cover but scope the trees. More men will be arriving tomorrow."

"And if we find more of them?"

"Kill them by whatever means necessary."

Blacwin and Djeik regrouped with the men at that moment, pulling a bandit in by the shoulders of his coat. "We captured one. He didn't realize his clan was in retreat. One of the men who was running weapons," Blacwin stated, catching his breath.

"I should have killed you in that house when I had the chance, Valspirean dog," the bandit cursed.

Savantin offered a small smirk. "Ohric, interrogate him. Take the boy with you. I've unfinished business with the patroness," Savantin answered and walked through the cold streets against the rising wind.

◆ ◆ ◆

"Take him into the stable," Ohric said. "Djeik, I'll have you fall in with the others to work on securing the town." To this, Djeik offered a nod and made his departure.

"I won't tell you a thing," the bandit spat and rose to his feet.

"We shall see." It was Ohric's last statement until they reached the stable, Blacwin grabbing chains from the railing on the inside. Ohric shook his head, only saying *not yet*, and looked the bandit over.

"What are you doing?" the man asked. "If you don't think I can take you both you're making a mistake."

"Oh, it's not that I think you can't. It's that I think you won't," Ohric answered. "You see, I'm sure you're used to this town, used to the guard here, the people. But you didn't expect us to be here, did you?" The man took to silence, avoiding eyes. Ohric laughed softly and moved his head downward, shaking it twice. "Ah. So, you did."

"I told you I'm not saying anything."

"You don't need to," Ohric answered. "But it would be in your best interest if you did. Blacwin, chain him to the chair."

"Or you'll what? Torture me? Go ahead and kill me, you'll gain nothing. The gods never favored me. I was only in their company so I could survive," the man said and struggled against Blacwin, who dispensed a blow to the head. The man fell slightly forward before Blacwin jerked him backward into the chair, wrapping the chain around his chest.

"You were only in their company so you could survive," Ohric repeated, softly. "Let us see just how strong your will to survive is. Answer these questions for us and we won't have to resort to inhumane means."

"Inhumane?" The bandit laughed. "You should have never let them run. They'll come back for me and take the heads of your men with them."

"They'll come back for someone whose only reason for alliance was to survive? Either you're lying about your role, or you're trying to discourage us. Either way, it doesn't matter. You'll talk."

"We can stand here in a bloody stalemate until witches are done drinking the blood of babes and the sun peeks over the hills, I still won't speak."

"Very well then," Ohric answered. "Blacwin, take his fingers."

Blacwin smiled and pulled his sword when Ohric shook his head and held his hand between the two. "Use that."

"A hay knife?"

"Yes," Ohric answered.

"It's dull. Rusted."

"It'll give him enough time to decide how much he enjoys his hands intact."

Blacwin shrugged and pulled the knife from the table, placing the man's hand down upon it.

"Who paid you for this attack?"

"Rot," the bandit said and spat at Ohric's feet. He sighed and gave Blacwin the order, causing the boy to saw at the pointer finger of the bandit's left hand. The man began to yell, struggling against the chair, attempting to knock it over. Blacwin tightened his grip around the man's wrist, finally wrestling the pointer finger free. The man continued to jostle against his seat, in attempts to either free himself or hit the floor.

"Are you ready to answer my question now?" Ohric asked. The bandit put forth continued opposition, and Ohric released a heavy sigh. "Again." He looked away as Blacwin attempted to cut another finger from the man's hand. It was during every interrogation that Ohric wished they would just speak and forgo the torture. He didn't care for it, didn't wish to take part. It was necessary, he knew, so he would continue to choose men to perform it in his stead while he asked questions.

"This will stop when you provide me the answers I'm looking for. Do it quickly enough and there's a chance you'll outlive the infection your wounds will grow if not seen to."

"Fuck off, Araelian. Waste words on your hallowed whore."

"Take every finger from his hands. Don't stop until the last one is sitting on the table as totem of his disrespect," Ohric said. It was once Blacwin reached the man's seventh finger that he started to plead for mercy, falling deaf upon Ohric's ears. Blacwin dropped the tenth finger on top of the others, looking to Ohric for further order. The man's panting, paired with his sobs was the only sound in the night air to exist for a few moments.

"Who paid you for this attack?" Ohric repeated.

"Kill me, you dog!"

"Take his hands."

"Wait!" the man shouted. "The woman. The woman paid us. She paid us for the weapons and for the attack."

"The woman?" Blacwin asked.

"The patroness. Avelina. She told us that if we disrupted the town that she'd make sure we never went hungry again. That we wouldn't have to return to Garecen."

"Blacwin, unchain him," Ohric answered and exited the stable with haste. His commander had returned to a trap.

◆ ◆ ◆

Savantin stepped over several corpses as he continued back to the manor house, opening the door to Avelina, standing by the bar with a knife in her hand. "Are they gone?" she asked quickly, rushed breath, without a heartbeat to match. He moved for his sword when he felt one at the back of his neck.

"You're lucky I was not quicker," Savantin answered.

"Toss your weapons to the lady."

Savantin complied, tossing his swords at her feet. "What is your aim? Ransom? To start your rebellion? Whatever it is, this is unwise."

"The mighty Commander of Terrenveil rendered helpless in Opskaven. It'll give the provinces the confidence that's needed."

"So, you execute me in public. Make an example of me, is that it?" Savantin asked. "You'd have a better chance taking my head and displaying it."

"I didn't expect you to make jest when I'm in control of your life."

"You need me alive, or else you'd have killed me already."

"Avelina, chain him."

"Listen to your husband," Savantin answered.

"Perceptive," Avelina said and approached him with chains. "It'll no longer help you."

"I don't need it. I have you both where I want you," Savantin answered.

"Drop your weapon," Ohric answered from the doorway. "You are now wanted for treason against the kingdom."

"I could kill him before you stabbed me. It is you who should drop yours."

"This will not go as you anticipate," Savantin answered. "Trust me in that you want to listen to him. You don't want to witness what I'll do if you strike me."

"I'd rather take you down before dying at the hands of the legion!"

Ohric quickly pulled the man backward and stabbed him, moving him toward the floor as he began to choke on his own blood. Avelina gasped; her hands clasped to her lips.

"You will suffer the same fate as him if you do not comply," Ohric stated. "Place yourself in chains."

"You would have me trap myself?"

"I would not touch you," Ohric answered.

"I will take care of her. Speak to the captain of the guard. Tell them she is to remain imprisoned here until the coalition arrives. They can vote on whoever will take control of Opskaven. At this point I no longer care."

"Yes, Commander," Ohric answered.

Once he spoke to the guard, Ohric decided to turn in, his body weary from the day's ventures. His men had reported in as well, two stationed outside of the inn as he ordered. They would remain there for a couple of hours, two others to replace them. Fresh eyes. Ohric watched over the men, all enjoying the food and ale given to them by the many pretty barmaids. They were so fascinated over the women's lack of modesty, parlor blouses hardly covering their perky breasts. There was no purity here at all, Ohric thought to himself, drinking his tea quietly. He heard the laughter of his men after one of them had made a jest and was highly observant to the young girls handing them their food. He wanted nothing further to happen after what transpired during the meeting with the raven-haired woman, and he intended on keeping things under control until Savantin returned.

Even Blacwin seemed to be enjoying himself; the usually hesitant boy was sharing conversation with one of the barmaids over a meal. He supposed that maybe he too should be loosening up, as the last town they were in met them with less hospitality.

It was becoming troublesome, he thought. Here they were, sent out on a crusade to make sure that these provinces were behaving, and both involved the smuggling of weapons from an outside source. Perhaps Rierdan did not know about the weapons. That seemed to be the consensus, anyway. Maybe the next few would be subservient. Though he doubted it. They would on the surface appear so, but as soon as they left, keep to preparations. Hopefully soon there would be a solution in ending their preparations. That would perhaps slow, or even eliminate the possibility of rebellion, and he could go back to his life near the temples.

He sipped on the mug of tea again, thinking back to the warning Araele had given him. *Something wasn't right*, she had cautioned. But that something he couldn't figure out. Perhaps it was Savantin, and how he was caught among his urges despite the serene star overhead. Perhaps it was the woman, black haired and pale as death. He figured it didn't matter now, as she was heading to the town's prison.

The night went on, and after a few hours passed his men began to become tired and one by one turned in for the night. Blacwin and the large Mordestan were the last two out in the halls, laughing over something that he could not overhear. Once they withdrew for the evening, heading their separate ways to gain rest, Ohric relaxed, drinking quicker and turning back to his meal. Bones of the small game hen he had chosen lined the bowl along with the skins of various vegetables. It had been a while since he had something like this, and wondered what the cost of it was. Surely, he would have been able to afford it back in Terrenveil, his pay as coadjutant was never light, but it wasn't the coin he was worried about. He wondered why, upon entering town, they had been given so much welcome. This province was one of the ones Savantin and the king both suspected of rebellious deeds, and it had just been proven. Perhaps hospitality was a front, something to bring their guard down and make them vulnerable to the attack that happened this afternoon. It was over, and he thought of it no longer, enjoying the last of his gift.

It was shortly after he finished that Savantin walked in.

"Has she been seen to the prison?" Ohric asked, smelling the lightest bit of perfume as he neared.

"She will no longer be a problem."

"Did you..." Ohric asked.

"No. She rests in a cell. I trust you spoke to the captain of the guard in what his role will be moving forward?"

"Exactly as you ordered. What next?"

"I will go to the pass and find Sindara," Savantin answered.

"Are you certain she will be there?"

"We will not make progress if I do not go. The others will stay here until I return. See to it that they get rest."

"When do you leave?"

"I will set out upon sun's light," Savantin answered, and began to make his exit. Ohric nodded and picked the bowl up off the table, taking it over to the bar. One of the barmaids was taking to collecting the dishes, placing them in a large wooden crate.

"Thank you for your hospitality," he answered, turning.

"Wait," the girl said, her eyes watching him.

Ohric turned, greeting her with friendly eyes.

"Is it true what they say of you?" she asked. "That you are a follower of Lady Araele, you receive her visions?"

"Yes," Ohric answered, moving his sleeve up to show her the white, eight-pointed star, scarred on his forearm.

"You follow the legion, which brings about much death... How can she be your guide?"

"Sometimes the world needs death to birth new light," Ohric said, moving his sleeve back down over his skin. "Araele has enemies, some of whom do not stay from violence. I make sure they are no longer here to threaten her grace."

"You're her soldier?" the girl asked, moving her red hair from her face. Her freckles were highly visible on her smooth face. She had hazel-colored eyes, full of intrigue and youthful curiosity. He guessed her somewhere around twenty but could not tell for sure.

"Yes," Ohric nodded. "I am, ever since I was a young boy."

She had to be talking about his reticence, how he was quiet, and did not openly admire women as the other men did. He dared not forsake Araele's teachings. "That's a long time. I was hoping you'd say they were lying." the girl said and blushed a little, picking up the crate and carrying it to where her coat was. He did not look at her legs beneath her short skirt as she walked by and turned away, smiling as he bid her goodnight. Most knew of the celibacy that came with following Araele, though her soldiers typically never followed the true ways of the Lady. Blasphemers. He ought to punish them himself. He believed that if there were a woman that was supposed to be in his life, that the Lady would send her his way. A priestess of the temple perhaps, or a soldier all her own.

He went back into the room he was given, sitting on the bed for a moment. He decided to be bold, though it was against his teachings. He walked back outward toward the hearth, peering behind the bar. The girl had vanished already, no sign of her to be found. Sleep called him away from his sudden desires, and like his Lady, he didn't want to keep it waiting.

CHAPTER 6

A JOINING OF STONES

The Sun spoke in its different voices. It hadn't silenced since I put the armor on. I was beginning to learn each voice, the cadences in which they spoke. There was a woman, her voice a whisper behind the others, an echo. She seemed passive, and it was her words I held onto most. Another woman paired with a man, their voices loud and prominent. The woman, angry. The man, stern. There was another, who too, spoke out of alignment with the pair. They came in at random, speaking the phrases either long before or long after the others. They repeated the same line numerous times, not ceasing, as if the sole determination was to force me to listen to them. They seemed unaware that I did not know the language they were speaking, and persisted, as if I was ignoring them.

I felt shame in my inability to understand it. Knowing nothing about the magick that was fabled to rest within the blood of a Sardon. Their bond with stones. It was all a form of mysticism to me. A large one, called the Black Sun, rested beneath flesh, manipulating my movement as a muscle would. I felt it, an object foreign to my body, but so strangely natural. I peered down at the stone that nested within the niche of my vambrace, almost indistinguishable in the dark of night. The stars reflected in it as

I passed beneath the cover of porches and into the streets. Mine. A Sardon claiming to be my brother appearing before me with revelation, these things to follow. The Sun, the armor, this stone. Life as I knew it, altered in moments. Morrenvahl. It was the only path that would see these questions answered.

Morrenvahl was a place often unheard of in this part of the world, though it existed within it. A place shrouded in mystery and shadow. The silvery birch of the Glendoryn eventually stopped growing and was replaced by tall, thick blackwood trees. Beyond that was where Morrenvahl was rumored to be situated. Perhaps once this was over, I would see myself there. Find the one who claimed to be my brother and learn of what the Sun incessantly spoke. That is, unless the path I was currently taking would be my end.

I made it to the brothel, sitting atop the only slope in the entire city. An orange glow from weary torches illuminated its three front doors in the darkness of the city, only just beginning their shift for the night. The atmosphere it provided was warm and friendly, a testament to what we discovered here. A city we initially believed to be dangerous and inhospitable was welcoming and kind. I passed through the doors, quietly closing them behind me and headed toward the lounge to see if anyone was left awake. It was quiet, I could hear soft breaths falling in the rooms surrounding me, someone snoring from upstairs. I heard footsteps behind me and turned quickly only to see the Madame.

"It is me," I said and removed the hood of my armor, revealing my face. She sheathed her weapon, tucking it beneath the belt of her laced black dress.

"Apologies. I almost did not recognize you. The others arrived a little over an hour ago, they are in the hall, dining. I assume you'll be embarking at dawn?"

"Yes," I answered. "Did Eshkan mention that?"

"I have ears all over the city, Sardon."

"Cethin," I answered. I did not see the harm in revealing my name, though if her resourcefulness was as stated, she likely knew it already.

"The woman asked after you, I told her that I'd let her know when you arrived. But she is resting, she needs it."

"How does she fare?"

"She is fine," Karstentia smiled. "She speaks highly of you."

"And I of her."

"Ah, yes. Cherish it while it yet lives. Sometimes a bond can take many shapes, and wither where you wished it to be most fruitful."

"Meaning?"

"Perhaps I outspeak," she stated and looked aside. This woman had been hurt before, deeply. Before we could develop further conversation, she withdrew, her heels clicking against the floor. I thought of her for a moment longer, her scent lingering in the air. Berries, lotus flower, sandalwood. From the shores of Lycinea.

I returned to my room, placing the satchel I carried from the manor of the city's lord next to my pillow. I took the key from it, placing it in my armor and entered the hall, watching the lively morale of my counterparts. They laughed, sharing food and drink amid the women of the house, who showcased curious senses of humor and worldly knowledge. I sat in a chair nearest Dacian, who pushed a plate of meat and fruit toward me. "These berries come all the way from Lycinea, apparently from large, thorned trees. That one told me that they train monkeys to climb the branches and pick them. I believed that to be only a thing of show."

"It's true," the copper-haired girl laughed. "We asked Karstentia to bring us one, but she said the cost was better put toward food and drink, so no one went hungry. We tried to tell her that people would pay to see it, but she seemed disinterested with even that."

"There's no reason for it," Parsena quickly added. "She provides much for us already. Where in all Cilevdan would we be so aptly fed every night? Given shelter?"

"Her hospitality is greatly appreciated," I answered. This could very well be the last time we were met with the hospitality she provided. Eshkan took notice of me and smiled. "It seems as if Thurlowe had a gift for you indeed," he said. "It was good that we came here."

"I would have to agree with you," I answered.

"We need direction," Dacian said and sat back in his seat, motioning his hand to the table in front of them. "Perhaps we should meet after dinner in one of the rooms provided to us."

"Indeed," I answered, though I didn't know how much privacy we'd receive. Thurlowe's words of where Karstentia's loyalties lie were reassurance enough. "For now, enjoy it. I've something to attend to, I'll return."

Eshkan met me with a nod, and I withdrew, making my way to Cahya's room. A woman walked from the door, smiling at me girlishly. I attempted to return one and moved the curtains aside, walking inward. She sat upright in her bed, sipping hot liquid from a mug. "Cethin," she said, her eyes lighting up instantly. "Your armor... a gift from Thurlowe?"

"Yes. This stone, the one that was found in my room last night. It... somehow it belongs to me. I don't know how. I still don't know who left it."

"Do you think it was the Madame? Or one of her guests?"

"No. I think it was a nonhuman. So, perhaps it could have been one of her guests. Thurlowe not only gifted me this armor but gave me something very important to hold onto," I answered and removed the key, handing it to her. She turned it over in her hands, a small metal mechanism, hollowed with design in certain areas. Others were filled with bone, markings on each fragment. There was a keyhole in its center, and it appeared that seven points would unfold from its top like a flower.

"What is it?"

"A key. It's said to belong to the box."

"Two keys. Do you think…"

"I don't know. Thurlowe mentioned another, though he did not mention whether or not he knew its whereabouts. He told me to take it, so that if the commander returned here, he would not find it."

"What if he finds us?"

"As long as we keep our distance, I don't think he will know we exist."

"I pray for that to be true," she answered and set the mug down on the end table closest her. "Our lead in Sathenne, do we have a plan?"

"Not yet, but I hope to achieve one tonight after speaking with Dacian and Eshkan."

"That is wise," she stated. "When do we aim to do this?"

"Now, if you are ready. Have you eaten?"

"I have, though not much. I was given several things to take with us for the road ahead. The women here, they are so kind."

"It is nice to be met with such kindness after what happened, especially in a place you'd least expect it."

"Thurlowe did say we have a place here once everything is over," Cahya said and looked at me. I smiled. "An offer most gracious. He is… an interesting man. Do you feel rested enough to meet with the others?"

"I am. And I am eager," she answered and rose.

We departed from her room, heading toward the dining hall. When we made it to the lounge, Dacian and Eshkan walked toward us, laughing quietly to themselves. "Let us go to my room," Eshkan said. "It is upstairs. Mostly secluded."

I nodded and began to ascend the staircase, Cahya next to me. Eshkan pulled the curtains, revealing a room with a large balcony. It overlooked the river, the chill air of dusk greeting us.

"Karstentia allowed us use of one of her maps," he stated, unrolling it and placing it on a table. "Sathenne is a day's ride west. I suppose we will speak with the patron about their plans, mention Thurlowe's name. There is not much we can do for now."

"I don't think we should leave it to chance," Morard said, placing his hands on the map. "I think that once we get to Sathenne we should pick a place to wait for the legion he sends to enter. If the provinces are seriously upholding their resistance to the kingdom, then they will gladly help us in this action. Kill enough of his men and he will take notice."

"I don't think we should involve the people at all. I think what we should do is find out where he is planning to travel and find him on the roads. If we follow them, we can discover their methods and attack. It will give us a better advantage in dealing with the commander. If we wait until we are in a province much could go wrong," Dacian stated. "Involving the people will only harm them. He will take notice, yes, but a coalition disappearing in one of the provinces will only mean that more men will be sent, and the people at risk."

"We will exhaust energy in seeking him out. Don't you see that? If we devise a plan with one of the patrons of a province, then not only will we have resources, but we also won't have to look for him. He will come to us," Morard countered.

"What if he does not go to Sathenne at all? What if he sends a general?"

"He will have to pass through eventually," Morard stated. "I don't think he will take news of the dead lightly."

"But what if it's too late? And he finds what he's looking for before that time?" Dacian asked.

"Once we leave Sathenne, I am going to find my people in Morrenvahl. With their council I will discover the information that is needed to kill him. I will need complete control of the Sun if we are to survive him and his men. There are only five of us, now. We will not be able to survive his legion. Yes, there is a possibility of the provinces taking up arms after they hear about the killing in Sathenne, but if it is unsuccessful, they will not seek cause to follow."

"What will happen to us? Morrenvahl isn't a place known to be hospitable. Are you certain it is the only way?" Morard asked.

"I must find my people. If he finds the box, I may be the only chance at stopping him. We could rally as many rebels as we wanted, but if Zheki is right about this box, there is not a human force strong enough to end this."

"Heading separate ways is foolish. We should travel with you and find a place where we can await your return, Cethin," Eshkan stated.

"But what if he doesn't return?" Morard asked.

"You think he would abandon us when we are so close to vengeance?" Dacian asked, in outrage.

"He did not mean it that way," I answered, looking to him. "He wonders if I will be accepted by the coven or if I will be killed among them. Sardons are known to be protective of their kind, but also spurning. This is the only chance I have. I was called the Bloodheir of Zerian of late. If they do not believe this then I will have no choice but to show them the only thing I can about what I wield," I said, looking down to my arm. The Sun was still speaking, though it was easy to ignore now that I was speaking to others. "They will have to accept me, unless the other Bloodheir is among them, and challenges me to fight for what is also his birthright," I answered, thinking back to when my brother approached me in Ophidian. He had said that I would know where to find him, Morrenvahl. The others were silent for a while, looking at the map, or at me. It was Cahya who spoke next.

"I will follow you wherever you must go, Cethin," she said. "No matter the cost or the sacrifice."

"And I will follow my commander," Morard answered reluctantly. I knew there were risks he didn't want to take, and that he didn't want to commit the last of his life to something that could kill him. Eshkan and Dacian were silent, still looking at the map before them.

"It is settled then," Eshkan answered and stood back. "After we seek an alliance in Sathenne we will travel in search of the Coven of Tarporen," he said.

"That still doesn't solve our question of what strategy we should use to strike our enemy," Dacian answered.

"We can devise what is to happen once we leave Morrenvahl. I will be better equipped for our task, and whatever will follow," I stated.

"What do you think will happen once we kill him?"

"Once we kill him, if we kill him, I've no doubt the king will retaliate. We will be deemed enemies of Terrenveil and will have to make our way to Rustanzen, or some other far off land," I said.

"If we kill him? You are making this seem like an impossible feat," Morard said.

"The future is uncertain. If the rumors are correct, and he does find this box, how do you think we will fare? We cannot rule out the possibility of failure. It would be foolish of us. If we do kill him, we can make plans to escape south to Rustanzen, and if we are hunted there, then further still. Perhaps even Agado, Mauros. If we must cross the seas, we must be ready," I answered.

"Do you think they would follow us into Mauros? Even if we are able to escape there, it is a known enemy of Terrenveil. Any soldiers that follow us there will be killed and a war will start. That would most certainly involve the people. Their king is cruel, practically a dictator. We would be looking over our shoulders, living in secrecy. Is that the kind of life you want?" Morard replied.

"We have much to think about," I stated. "I implore you all to think, come up with solutions. We can share them on the road."

"I don't think they will send soldiers, but mercenaries surely. I am sure we are not the only assassins that exist in Cilevdan," Eshkan answered.

"We must make sure that when Savantin dies, whatever plan he has dies with him. We can't do that if soldiers or mercenaries hunt us. We will be questioned as to why they make chase." It was Dacian who spoke now.

"If we stay in Cilevdan, we will all be killed. There is no question about that. If we plan this out, we will kill whoever Savantin rides with and be able to escape Cilevdan without so much as a whisper of us being there. If we kill him while we are in town then those people will incur whatever wrath was meant for us. If we kill him on the roads, then there is no one to blame. Through interrogation they will discover that none of the provinces had a hand in it, and no innocents will die for our actions," I said.

"I suppose we will all listen to the words of the Sardon?" Morard asked, looking around the room. No one answered him and he sat back also, shaking his head. "Sieges on the road never end well. You would be better killing them off one by one in the cover of a town, where there are plenty of buildings and places to strike from. Cahya and I did not receive the training you have."

"You need not remind me," I answered. "Enough innocent blood has been shed. If we can do this while preserving more, I will not discuss another option."

Morard let his thoughts simmer for a moment before speaking. "I do not agree. We need a better strategy. We could likely die by whatever men he has with him. As you keep reminding us, we are only five in number," he said.

"Do not think I have not given it thought. Even I am hesitant in assailing him directly, but if we can stop him from finding what he wants then it is a risk I must take. I still stand by what I said when we left Ophidian. If I must die, I have made my peace," I answered and stood.

"When are we to leave?" Cahya asked, attempting to break the tension in the room.

"When we wake. It will be a long journey to Sathenne, and we've no time to waste."

"We should retire for the evening shortly," Eshkan answered.

"I will take my leave, then," Dacian stated.

I acted in kind, escorting Cahya to her room. She turned as she reached her bed, grasping my hand.

"Stay with me," she said suddenly, tugging my hand as a sign that she wanted me to come closer.

"You know I won't refuse," I answered and kissed her forehead. She quickly nestled into the bed, bunching the blankets up close to her but moving them so that I could climb in. Once I became comfortable, she rested her head on my chest and adopted the smile that I loved most. "Tell me about the time you went to Cenai."

"You have not tired of that one yet?" I asked and looked down at her.

"It's my favorite," she answered and opened her hand, revealing the small whale bone I had brought back for her, easily hidden in my armor when reporting to Vortain after a successful assassination, or so he thought.

"It was raining when I landed there, eager to remove myself from the boat that landed on the shores of Stirae. I wish I could have stayed longer; the continent holds so many lands filled with wonder and mystery. Genisia among them. The fragrant blooms were the first thing to reach me, and trees full of flowers lined the roads. It was a straightforward contract, the city of Cenai lying deep within the reaches of Aberanza. It took me a week to get there, staying mostly in barns or sleeping in forests along the roads. When I arrived in Cenai, it was nothing like I expected it to be. I didn't know why Stirae is called *the realm of magick*, and Cenai seemed to be like any town you'd find in Cilevdan. That was, until I began to discover its secrets while hunting my marks..."

It was the fourth day of rain. I still had my room at the inn, trying to remain in cover as a student of magick embarking on a journey to Redista. Eshkan told me that it was a common occurrence, and that if I remained careful, it would be easily believed. It was a busy inn, its keeper an elderly man, portly, with a kind face. A few girls worked the bar as the room became lively at night, travelers and residents alike partaking in ritual frivolity. I joined them one evening, listening to people talk among themselves. A few men dressed in colorful elegant clothing were quietly watching the women at the table adjacent theirs, dressed in kind. Across from me was a group of mercenaries, men and women dressed in leather armor.

A hunter entered from the world outside, his offerings wrapped neatly in leather so they would not get wet. Water dripped from his clothing and onto the floor, the animal pelts mimicking his state despite his careful attempt at protecting them. He took an offer for a reduced price in order to take shelter in a room for a few days, to wait out the rain. Shortly after he passed the people at the front of the room, one of the rich men said something of note.

"Brant mentioned that he does not care for her," a man in a blue doublet said, taking a swallow of his wine.

"He says one thing and means another. But she arrives in Cenai in two days' time. I'm hoping he has things planned. To be unprepared would mean disaster," a man dressed in dark green robes returned.

"How do we know that he will be successful? If he is, this will also spell disaster for anyone involved. With the oracles being as powerful as they are, what makes you think that they do not suspect this already? I told him time and time again that he needs to accept the course of things."

"He will not," the man in blue, again. "It is his only daughter."

"A thing most tragic. But she was chosen."

"When do you meet with him?"

"Tonight," the shortest of the three answered. "Though that is only if he will open his door. He is being driven mad over this. I fear that he will not be the same no matter what occurs."

"Perhaps a curse already," the man in green said. "I do not know what made him even conceive this plot."

"He was never the smartest. I must unfortunately take leave. There are things I must attend to before we meet."

"Be careful, Lorn. Do not think I have forgotten about the bet you lost."

"I have not forgotten it either."

I waited several moments after the man exited the inn, quickly glancing at the square before climbing the nearest roof in order to spot him. He was headed west, past large houses with brightly colored decorations on porches aglow. He entered a house at the end of the street, and I took refuge in the niches of a roof nearby, waiting at least an hour before he emerged again. He wore a cloak, now, to protect his frame from the ongoing rains. I tailed him, until he reached a house in the sector of town that was much quieter than the boisterous inn. He entered, and I quickly scaled rooftops to find an entrance, or, alternatively, a place to listen to their conversation. If I could not kill him this night, there was still time before the Genisian arrived.

"I told you not to arrive until after the inn quieted. Were you followed?"

"No. I looked everywhere. Rochi is concerned. He says the oracles may already foresee your plans. He thinks it will cause everyone great turmoil."

"Rochi is not involved. Do not let his opinion distract you from your role."

"You forget what he..."

"I do not forget, Lorn. I do not care. Her safety is more important than the world of magick."

"Safety. How safe do you think she will be in Stirae if people find out what she is and what you've done? You'll be killed, and she will be left without a family. At least there is a possibility to see her in Genisia."

"They do not allow people in the sanctum of the oracles, Lorn. I have weighed every possible situation and its consequences in mind. This is the only way. She and I will leave Stirae. Two days."

"Brant."

"Do you not care about Keoy? She should have the ability to choose."

"Is that your reason? Or is it that you cannot let go of her? You will be hunted for the rest of your days, both you, and your daughter."

"Do not try to dissuade me."

"I am not. I am only asking that you reconsider," Lorn answered. "I wish to help you. You are like a brother to me. But this... what you are proposing is madness."

"You did not seem to think that way in days past," Brant stated.

"That is because I did not. She was chosen, Brant."

"Impede my progress, and you will regret it."

"Let me take her tonight. We will go far away. Choose. Cilevdan. Rustanzen. I would even take her to Agado. You do not have to resort to murder."

"And what will you say? That she ran? If they have predicted this, they will know."

"So that means you must kill? Listen to yourself. Where is she?"

"No one will find her."

"Brant. I'm begging you."

"Leave at once. I now know our brotherhood means nothing."

"I will not stand in your way. But I will not help you," Lorn answered, and left abruptly, closing the door behind him and disappearing into the night. My chance. I climbed down from the roof, entering through the window on the balcony behind Brant. Quickly grasping his head, I pushed it down onto the table, knocking a dagger from his hands as he withdrew it.

"What is it you want?" Brant coughed. "You haven't killed me yet; you must want something. Money? Treasures?"

"I can't be bought."

"So, you are here to kill me. Why hesitate?" Brant asked.

"The oracle. Where is she?"

"I will never tell."

"There are worse fates than Genisia, Brant."

"Who is paying you? Rochi? Laeca?"

"I'll only ask once more."

"I'll take it with me to the grave," he answered and tried to pull his arm from my grasp. He reached for a penknife with his other, and I grasped his hair, pulling him up from the table in attempts to turn his arms from my reach. He sliced my upper arm in the struggle, grasping for another weapon when I removed the hood from my face, staring into his eyes. He dropped his weapons, focusing on them.

"Where is Keoy?" I asked.

"My daughter. Keoy."

"Yes. Where is she?"

"She. She's safe. It's a father's job to protect his daughter."

"You've done so. She's safe. Where is she?"

"She's... She's..." Brant's pulse began to elevate. Fear.

"I'll make sure no one hurts her, but you have to tell me where she is," I stated.

"Gorse Bravada," he stated. He struggled with the first syllable, repeating it a second time. He continued, his eyes turning milky in color. I withdrew vision immediately, pulling my hood over my head. I reached for my weapon when Brant walked past me, his vision fixated only on what was before him. He continued to speak; the name repeated several times.

"Genisia. They spoke of spring," he stated, moving to a chest that was at the end of his bed. He opened it, pulling out several pieces of paper. Maps. Letters. Drawings. "She spoke of spring. Spring is where she waits. Spring is when I will meet her. Spring."

Madness. His mind was fragile already. He was no longer a danger to the Gatherer. I looked down at the dagger strapped to my side and let my hand fall. I had very strict instructions. Kill Brant Socovoy, for he is planning to murder a Gatherer from Genisia. I stood, very still, watching him. He moved about the room, plastering the pictures on his walls. Pictures that his daughter likely drew for him, his late wife. He continued to speak of Spring, walking past me several times to reach different walls. He was now a man who could commit no murder.

I left his house in the same manner I entered, climbing onto the roof, his voice being drowned in the rain of the night. The threat to the Gatherer had been eliminated, but there was another matter entirely. Where was the Oracle? I was left with a name. I could not leave Stirae without finding her. Master would agree with me. I could already hear the criticisms of Jadoq, harsh on my decision to pursue her delivery to Genisia. He held no respect for the world of magick, and at times, I didn't even think he held belief. Gorse Bravada. I did not know what this name meant, nor the nature of it. It could draw attention to myself. It could place the girl in danger. I was faced with numerous problems and no visible solution. Lorn. I turned from my path to the inn, his house my new destination.

I arrived, rain the only sound, now. The city was asleep, the lanterns on the porches now dark. Candlelight in Lorn's window. I jumped into the nearby alley, looking around quickly for eyes. Once I was assured there were none, I walked to his porch, knocking on the door. I hoped this wasn't a mistake. It was a few moments before he opened the door, looking at me quizzically.

"Do you know what hour it is?"

"I've a message from Brant. I mean you no harm despite my appearance. May I enter?"

Lorn hesitated for a few moments but moved aside. "What is so important that he must send a courier? Who are you? How do you know him?"

"I am a student of magick. Redista. My current area of study is Genisia."

"Ah. I see. So what does he send you for?"

"He's had a change of heart. We both know he has no love for magick, but he's decided to listen to me this time."

"About time he listens to someone. I tried to convince him just a few moments ago that he was not thinking clearly."

"We must have missed one another. Perhaps you had hand in it," I answered. "Though I do need your help."

"What can I do?"

"Gorse Bravada. It is the only name I received from him. His daughter, Keoy. I do not know where he has taken her."

"Shhh." Lorn said. "Not here, follow me."

I nodded, watching as he placed his cloak on. "We must exit the city." I did not say anything in response, only followed him as we headed to the stables where Eshkan left a horse for me. I mounted, keeping pace with Lorn as we rode through the terrain, stopping at a large tree several miles from the city. The tree looked as if it was out of a fairytale, full of purple flowers, each adorned with a small blue glow. Cahya would be enamored. Its long trailing branches touched the ground, creating an umbrella from its canopy. Lorn moved them aside, showing me the way in. He followed, carefully moving the branches behind him. He spoke a few words, his eyes glowing a bright blue while signing something with his fingers.

"You're Magar."

"Yes. I've been living in Cenai for ages, under the cover of a statesman. Redista is a beautiful village, by the way."

"So, I've heard," I stated. "Why Cenai?"

"I suppose you would like to know that. But you do know that the Magar have no affiliation with Redista, so that is conflict of interest."

"I've no affiliation with Redista, either. Merely want to use its resources and learn from those who claim to have the knowledge I seek. Perhaps one day I will seek out the Order."

"I wish you luck. Induction is no easy task or process," Lorn said, still eyeing me.

"That, I do have knowledge of," I said, simply.

"There is a talk of a pheonix in Stirae, owned by a beautiful and deadly Afheina. That is my venture of late. Being a student, you know of the very prevalent and ever growing magick that Stirae imbues."

"That is why I travel to Redista and seek to make home in Stirae."

"Yes, it is where most respected students start. But let us continue with the matter at hand. You are aware of what this tree is, yes?"

"I am," A Caiaca tree was known for its silencing property, the guardian of secrets. "Gorse Bravada. Do you know who that is?" I asked, hoping our dialogue would be enough to lower suspicion, to form a trust.

"It is not a person, but a spell. There is a place, a place I showed him long ago. I told him that if he was ever desperate that he should go and speak it. But I did not think that he would do this," Lorn sighed. He closed his eyes for a moment, shaking his head three times before continuing to speak. "There is a price to pay for entrance. The spell opens the door, but it does not offer protection from what may be inside. It's a tomb of the Magar, created in essence of Agaehara itself."

"How far?"

"I can take us there. As I have been in Cenai for ages, I have been tasked to keep it."

"Let us waste no time."

"Before we go, I must ask," Lorn said, sternly.

"Anything."

"What do you intend?"

"Keoy must go to Genisia."

"Yes. She was chosen for the gift. To deny the Genisians this would create chaos. We are at an understanding. Do not stray. The stone is nearby," he said, and exited the tree, again mounting his horse. We rode on, stopping as we reached a large stone pillar. The Magar moved his arms out to his sides, his palms facing the stone.

"Gorse Bravada."

The symbols on the stone glowed a bright blue, splitting it down the center. As it moved apart, a portal of the same color occupied the gap. "You must enter before me. Once I am inside, I must seal it until we are ready to leave."

I nodded, taking a deep breath inward. I walked into the stone, and a sharp pain radiated through my body that dissipated within seconds. The air inside felt cold, silence surrounding me. I closed my eyes to isolate my senses and intently listened when Lorn arrived through the portal, whispering into his palm. With a breath, a shining white powder escaped it, causing the portal to fade. He spoke a spell, small orbs of light swirling in circles from his fingertips before encircling his eyes.

"You will need to remain still if this spell is to work."

"No need," I answered and removed my hood. "I will keep my eyes from yours."

"A Sardon?" he said, surprise in his voice.

"What I said remains true, I mean you no harm. Nor Keoy. We will see her safely to the Genisian."

"I shall trust you."

"You shall find it easy," I answered.

"The day becomes more interesting still."

"Let us hope it plateaus," I stated. "Where do you suggest we begin?"

"We must listen. In order to find her, she must want to be found."

"The silence is endless; how will she know we've even arrived?" I asked, turning my head towards Lorn, keeping my eyes lowered.

"I will have to share my last memory of her with you. The strongest. Hold your hand outward, you won't even realize you're gone."

"Gone?"

"The memory. It must be you."

I took a deep breath and raised my hand in front of me, my palm toward the ground. The Magar stretched out his fingers, the color of his light returning to his palm. I moved my head sideways as the light grew in intensity. As it surrounded us, I closed my eyes, only opening them as it began to die. I looked around, confusion soon dispersing as I realized that I was no longer in the tomb. Lorn's voice came from the silence, suddenly. Muddied, ghostly, but clear enough.

"I see you've made it intact."

I looked to my surroundings, an old house in the valley below, dim light from flames in the windows on the lower floor.

"This is the feeling of her memory. The night I saw her last."

"You've projected me into...your mind?" I asked, looking down at my hands and at the ground beyond them.

"The tether between mine and hers," Lorn answered. "And now you see why it cannot be me. I cannot guide you, for doing so would place too much of my influence on the tether. In order to draw her out, she must feel safe within the tether. Only then will she recognize it, me, and lead us to her corporeal form within the tomb."

I took a deep breath and headed toward the house in the valley. The only obvious visual obstacle. As I neared it, I could smell rot in the wood. The house seemed abandoned, forgotten. The lack of its tending created a hollow vessel that sought nourishment. I moved the door, barely pushing it with my fingers as it creaked inward, the floorboards on the porch beneath me following suit. I followed the long hallway, the shadows becoming darker as the light began to fade. I heard sobbing from the upper floor, and moved to the stairway, listening to the house groan and creak furthermore. As I continued along, the house was worse in condition. Pieces of the floor missing, dust covering frames of torn pictures on the walls. I stopped at the base of one of the portraits, worn in color but free from the weight of the dust that claimed the others. Dead flowers sat in the cracked glass vase that was beneath it, a burned and tired candle. It was a woman, dressed in a dark red gown, her light brown hair tied to the top of her head, black flowers pinned to it. She held a parasol in one hand, stones in her left. An arbor was in the background, flowers around it. I picked up the matches that sat beside the candle when the sobbing increased in intensity and sat them down to investigate.

In a bedroom not much further down the hall, a young woman sat in the middle of a bed, a stuffed bear at her feet. She looked up, then, tears falling from her sad brown eyes. She shared the hair of the woman in the picture, freckles across her nose and cheeks.

"Did you… did you know my mother?" she asked. "She said you would be coming."

"Me?"

"Yes. She said a man in dark clothing would come. That I would know when things would be alright. Can you take me to her?" she asked and wiped the tears from her face.

"Take you to her?"

"She said that is what you would do."

"Where is she?"

"She… she's gone. She said that if I trusted in the path, that everything would be okay."

"The path…. The oracles," I stated.

She looked at me and nodded twice, brushing her fingers against one cheek. "She knows about the oracles. Father didn't agree with her. He called her a witch. He said cruel things to her. He found her stones, her garden, and beat her," Keoy said, her face twisting in sadness. The creaking became louder, the unrest in the house. The hall behind me grew darker, the lights from the stairwell dimming. "She's escaped him. But has left me all alone. It's so dark without her."

"Speak of her memory," I answered. "Let us go to her." Keoy moved from the bed and grabbed my hand, following me into the hallway. I walked toward the picture, picking the matches up off the counter. I lit the candle, watching as her face lit up in conjunction with the flames. The candles in the house also took flame, the hallways bursting with color and life. Keoy suddenly disappeared, the house slowly returning to what seemed to be its former self.

"Amazing. It appears in this path of mind the house represents her heart. Now that she trusts you, we will find her," Lorn said. The world surrounding me began to become fuzzy, and off-kilter as it faded into the one I left behind. Lorn waved his hand, the blue light that had previously encircled it disappearing.

"How do you intend on finding her, exactly, that doesn't involve my being transmitted into a different plane?"

"Not a different plane, Cethin. But if you're truly planning on going to Redista…"

"Semantics," I stated. A word I had learned from Vortain. He and Jadoq argued so often that it was common I picked up fragments of their speech. I detested Jadoq, his condescending tone toward me, his mocking, though I could not deny how much he seemed to know. Lorn laughed at my retort, taking the first step toward the entrance of the ruins. Lorn reminded me of Vortain, in a way. Master taught me all that he could about language, stating that it was an art as useful as my training if in the right situation. It was why he sent Eshkan on the missions that he did, why he was trusted. We continued to turn corners, Lorn using his light to gather sight. I stopped, closing my eyes and taking a deep breath.

"How often do you tend this place?" I asked.

"Every few years, as it is called for. Much has been forgotten here, despite it being a land vested in magick."

"We have company," I stated and pulled my sword. Lorn readied spells in his hands, a moment before two Veracith bounded around the corner, saliva dripping from their jaws. Eaters of the dead. They were beasts, dark gray flesh, not biped. They had fingers that ended in points, sharp, to rip into the chest cavity of their prey. Feet shared similarity, although the claws on each toe were significantly shorter than their finger counterparts. Their jaws could extend much farther than anything humanly possible, two rows of sharp teeth lining them. Their eyes were hollow, noses without form, ears absent.

The smaller of the two jumped onto the wall, springing off it to attempt a tackle. I turned, slicing it across its stomach. Its corpse slid down the hallway behind me, Lorn burning the other attacker with bright blue flames. It screeched as the light emitted furthered its death. I looked toward Lorn in that moment, nodding back toward me. An unspoken understanding.

"But what?" Lorn said.

"They have to have gotten in somehow," I stated.

"I will trust your senses as you trust my magic. At sight of them, whatever else is here must be silenced."

"We follow them, we find the source." Lorn returned a nod, and we continued, traversing a hallway lined with abalone and golden colored wood. A mosaic, deer beneath a large tree. Death was a sacred thing to all humans, it seemed, though there was little evidence that suggested the Magar were human. The silence that filled the halls was strange, hollow. The aura was like that of the memory. It didn't last too much longer, however. The hallway ended in a large room with a pedestal at its center, several Veracith turning toward us. They hissed, crouching low and moving their shoulders backward.

I turned my sword defensively, listening to their steadily rising pulses. As they attacked, we made quick work of them. I focused on making each swing of my blade count in proper dispatchment. Lorn summoned light to his palms, their weakness. It seemed endless, as soon as we committed the creatures to death, hissing came from other parts of the ruins.

"Something isn't right," Lorn said, suddenly. "There hasn't been a Magaran death in quite some time. Even the youngest corpses are decades old."

"Something is manifesting them. We must destroy it," I said.

Lorn nodded, speaking a spell under his breath. "We will have to discover where they are strongest," he responded. The hissing continued and grew louder still until we reached an open room with an altar in its center. And then, silence. Lorn spoke for the light to intensify in his palms, and we were faced with hollow eyes. Tens of them. I crossed my sword in front of my body when they began to recede from the center of the room. Keoy was sitting in front of the altar, her head slumped to the floor, body in a curl. One hand rested on her knee, the other one touching the stair next to her opposite thigh.

"No," I said and sheathed Seligsara, watching them carefully as I neared her. The ones closest to her hissed as I approached, one of them snapping its jaws as I moved to touch her face.

"She can't be dead, or else they would be attacking," Lorn said, keeping his eyes to the creatures that surrounded us. One jumped down from the wall, pacing in front of the exit. I moved the backside of my pointer and middle finger down her cheek, stopping beneath her nose and mouth. "There is breath. But it's weak. Her heartbeat is weak too. So weak that I can barely hear it," I said and looked back at Lorn.

"Cethin, hold onto her, tight. Shield your eyes."

I moved an arm beneath her legs, rolling her frame into my arms. As I buried my face beside hers and into my shoulder, I heard Lorn speak loudly.

"Sah alinesh sperog spelane. Zi kesh na."

I opened my eyes to rainfall. The girl I held in my arms was still breathing weakly, and I could feel her frail pulse where her body rested against mine. Lorn stepped from the stone a moment after me, speaking a spell to seal it. "We must get her to my house. Hurry," he said. "She must ride with you."

I climbed up into the saddle on my horse, Lorn handing her up to me. I secured her and followed him back into the city. The rain fell hard, our horses' hooves digging into wet ground as they raced toward our destination. Cenai was quiet when we arrived, not one person wandered the streets. The clouds made dull the sun, the area surrounding us obtaining a gray tint in the persistence of rain. Lorn opened his home, water falling onto his floor from our clothing. He hurriedly lit several candles, and I placed her across the long table that separated the room in two. Her head was upward toward the ceiling, one hand up by her eyes, the other falling just short of her thigh and off to the side.

Lorn spoke, and I watched on, anticipating she would awaken. When she did not, I looked at him and he spoke softly, a somber tone to his voice. "Not a spell, but a prayer. There is nothing more I can do. She is in the hands of the Genisians now."

I said nothing in response and continued to watch her, candlelight dancing across her pale, graying frame.

"Keep her heart alive in your thoughts, and she will be told of you if she wakes. The oracles will know…"

◆ ◆ ◆

I awoke, looking down to see Cahya's head on my chest. I felt her breath upon it, soft and warming. I let her sleep a while longer, cherishing each minute that passed. It could be many moons before we again have this chance, very many moons. Perhaps it would not be; though hopeful, I continued to remind myself that we may not live to see tomorrow. In moments such as this, thinking such things robbed joy. I spoke to her, running my hand through her short hair. She stirred, stretching before looking up at me.

"Is it time to go already?" she asked, offering a small smile.

"It is. We should see ourselves fed and take to the road."

Cahya emitted a small sound during her stretch upward, gathering her clothing from the nightstand. The candles that were lit last night had burned down to their ends, cloaking the room in darkness. After she dressed herself, she grasped a match, igniting it and moving the flame to meet the wicks of the candles on the shelving against the wall.

"I had a dream last night," Cahya answered and pulled her boots on. "It was of a place I had never been to, but it felt like home. It almost looked like it could be here, in Defaltor. You and I were standing in a street in a market square, facing one another. You brought me flowers, but a horse that was walking past took a large bite out of the top. It started raining. You handed me the lonely white daisy that was left, and we took cover beneath the smith's roof, laughing," she laughed, looking downward quickly and back up again.

"What happened after?" I asked, watching her face. I was enamored with the way she lit up when she recalled happy events. There was a light that nothing could dim, a glow that even now, radiated through the darkness.

"Well after that you kissed me, and the blacksmith chased us off. We ran down the street to a house where there was a hearth, an older woman, children. But you woke me when we got to a balcony."

"I knew I should have let you sleep for a few more minutes," I said and sat up, pulling my own boots on. I grabbed a shirt and pulled it over my body when Parsena walked in, adopting a large bright smile on her face. "Your friends are waiting for you in the dining hall. Karstentia had something special prepared for your last meal here."

"She spares no expense in her accommodations, for which I will spare none in gratitude. Does she join us?"

"She does. She's asked after Cahya. How do you fare this morning?"

"Better, thank you."

"Splendid. Come, it is a tradition we all see our guests off together," Parsena said and opened the curtain. We gathered our things and entered the hall, sharing a sight similar to the night before. High spirits. Cahya sat next to Karstentia who signaled her over. Declan stood, walking toward me.

"Cethin, a word," he said and looked toward the hallway. I returned a nod and we exited, Declan looking back toward the gathering before looking at me.

"I just. I wanted to mention."

"You do not have to hesitate when speaking to me. What is it?"

"I wish to go to Aubergrun. Once we reach Sathenne, I will make my journey north."

"It is quite perilous."

"I know. Madame Karstentia gave me a map of Cilevdan. It marks old trade routes that are close to cities. Ones that should be protected and traveled."

"I wish you luck. You'll travel by horse?"

"Yes. The madame also gave me enough food to make it there. I said if my road allows it, I will return some day and see the kindness repaid. There is something I wanted to discuss. The key, when I helped you into the armory. I believe it to be the to the box."

"Show me," I said. Declan pulled it from his pocket, handing it to me. It was triangular in shape, a seven-pointed star on the bottom.

"And Vortain had this?" I asked and took it from his fingers, turning it over. "I think I have an answer for you," I said and reached into my armor, removing the key that Thurlowe entrusted to me. Placing the two together, I turned Declan's key, which caused mine to open, seven points flipping open from its center. The center was a blackness unlike any I had ever witnessed. A shadow so dark that I could not see through it. I quickly turned the first key to lock the second, handing the smaller one back to Declan. "Thurlowe told me about this. What they are, what they do. We should not keep them together."

"I will take it to Aubergrun."

"You're... you're sure about this?" I asked. "This object. It's dark. It was created by a nonhuman. The priests will not welcome it. They may shun you."

"They will not know I carry it with me. They may live in recluse, but they do not wish evil upon the world."

"Declan, the priests live in recluse because they do not want evil to find them," I stated. "This... if this is found. If it's discovered."

"Then perhaps it is best that I lose it on my travels there. At the bottom of a freezing lake, or deep within the caverns of Alkamet."

"Alkamet is a dangerous journey."

"It is not far from Aubergrun, Cethin. You, all of you, are doing all that you can to end whatever madness he's concocting. I will do my part in ensuring that this key is not found."

"I do not wish to lead you astray, but if you have the willingness to prolong your journey..."

"You've my attention."

"There is a Magar in Stirae."

"Are you certain you'd entrust something like that to a Magar?" Zheki asked, appearing from the light of the fire. I turned, surprise evident on my face. Declan watched her in captivation, an almost boyish look in his eyes. The eyes of a crush too shy to raise voice. "The order of Magaria is convoluted. They claim to belong to a structured and sacred order, yet it is filled with sorceresses, witches, warlocks, and druids who further their own powers in whatever occult practice they see fit. There are no borders between good and evil, and their boundaries are their own."

"The one I speak of; we have a past. I trust him," I answered. "I dare not suggest Enshrova."

"I do not blame you. But this does not sit well with me," she said and placed a hand to her mouth in thought.

"Can you take it?" Declan asked and moved it forward in his hand.

"I cannot," she answered. "They will find me. Sense it. But there must be a solution that does not involve this high amount of risk."

"It was entrusted to Declan. Where he goes with it, what he does with it is his decision," I said. "I cannot take it. The two parts will be together. If I am struck down..."

"I have my faith that you will not. But you are right. That would be damning."

"It will go with me," Declan answered softly. "I will tell no one where it will go. If either of you are involved with those who seek it, they will not get its location from you."

"Smart," Zheki stated. "However, I insisted that I aid you. While Thurlowe was not thrilled with the idea, he understood. Undai and I will accompany you to Aubergrun."

"Are you certain?" Declan asked. "He does not need you here?"

"He does. But he has others who are pledged to our cause in Defaltor. He knows how important this is to me, to the world,"

Zheki answered. "We will meet you just outside the gate in an hour. I'll return to them only to gather supplies for the journey."

"Thank you, Zheki," I said. She smiled as she vanished, light particles lingering before dissipating.

"An hour, then," Declan stated and turned toward the dining hall. I waited by the hearth for a moment, gathering my thoughts. At least Declan would have people to protect him on his journey. My mind immediately jumped to Thurlowe. He made it clear that he loved Zheki. I wondered how he felt about her leaving, though I knew it was only for a set amount of time. I returned to the others, sitting next to Cahya, across from both Eshkan and Dacian. Morard was quiet, listening to one of the women next to him in wonder. She was thick, fiery hair with bright blue eyes. Her voice was pleasing, rising and falling several octaves as she continued with her tale. She was a master storyteller. I almost felt bad for taking him from this place, although I continued to remind myself that he was on this journey of his own volition and could walk his own path at any moment. Despite this, I somewhat felt responsible for his accompaniment. I took my leave, stepping outside to the morning air.

Lost in thought, I did not realize how much time had passed until Karstentia joined me, lighting a long thin pipe, inhaling and releasing a short puff of blue smoke. She looked upward, smirking. "You're not the only one who uses magick here."

"Defaltor seems to be a place that doesn't accept it."

"It does not," she answered. "But people are smart enough not to come here on a witch hunt. I pay the city lord for protection although I need not to. It's more to show my appreciation for his vigilance."

"What brought you here?" I asked suddenly, surprised at my sudden action. I was beginning to find myself interested in other people's stories and experiences. I never gave it much thought before, on the Island.

"That is a conversation for another time," she answered. "Perhaps you will return to Defaltor once you have finished your endeavors?" I paused for a moment, unsure of how to answer her. I was under the assumption she knew what we were seeking to accomplish, though if she did not, I didn't want to possibly risk her life if our enemy returned.

"Yes, and I am sure Cahya will want to return as well."

"Take good care of her, Cethin. Treasure her with every passing moment."

"It is my intention."

"Make it your pledge," Karstentia said. "You bond will only grow stronger."

"That I am sure of. I only hope I can protect her in the days ahead."

"If you do all that you can, it is what will be remembered and cherished." She inhaled from the pipe another time, moving her head upward to release its aftermath. "The others are about finished; shall I tell them that you await them here?"

I nodded and watched the streets as she disappeared into the house. I stood in silence, for long, drawn out minutes before the others emerged, the smell of the kitchen wafting forward. The walk across town was quiet, Cahya and Morard speaking from behind. Declan strode forward anxiously looking at the large gate. Once we passed it, Undai stopped speaking to Zheki, who had her face covered by a tan colored cowl. She removed it, taking a breath inward. "We've charted course. I hope you do not mind."

"I am grateful," Declan answered.

"We will split ways after crossing over the Frost's Kiss. There is a direct trade route north that will take us most of the way there," Undai stated. "That will also put you halfway to Sathenne."

"I will lead the way," Eshkan stated and mounted his horse, trotting off toward the road. We followed; the venture silent for a few hours. Zheki and Undai spoke in Mordestan, and I glanced toward Cahya who listened intently. Eventually they included her, the exchange livening. I looked ahead, keeping pace with Eshkan for hours more before we stopped to make camp for the evening. Declan began to feed the horses, and Undai disappeared

into the wood with Zheki for quite some time before returning
with firewood. I took the first watch, customarily, and listened
to the sounds of the forest before being relieved. We were well
within provincial woods, threat mostly coming from the region's
carnivores. The night was easy, and upon dawn, camp was broken
down with haste. The great river could be seen in the distance
after traversing a small mountain, the valley below filled with a
lush forest. Eshkan accelerated his pace to a gallop, stopping as
he reached river's edge.

"I can smell the tundra in the water," he said as I reached
him, taking a deep breath into his lungs. I watched as the rapids
quickened, mist creating a rainbow against the glare of the sun
as water splashed down over top of several large rocks. "It's
calming, a scent I haven't smelled in a very long time."

As the others reached us, Undai lowered his flask to fill it,
drinking its contents and repeating the process. Zheki removed
her cowl to soak up the sun, before looking up and to the horizon.
We rested for a moment, enjoying the cool water before I led
my horse across. She neighed softly, hesitating at the force of
the rapids. I stroked her mane and gave the command to cross,
waiting for the others on the other side. Eshkan was next, suddenly
looking upward and inhaling. He placed his hand on my arm
and tightened his grip on his reigns.

"Do you smell that?" he asked, looking ahead.

I took a breath in, the smell of burning flesh and smoke
reaching me. "What do you make of it?" I asked.

"I'll scout ahead and access the risk," he answered.

"I'll wait here with the others, have Dacian go with you."

Eshkan nodded and signaled for Dacian to follow him. He
crossed the river, and they rode off, the sound of the hooves
disappearing in the thick forest.

"What is happening?" Morard asked.

"Something is burning. About a mile from here," I answered,
holding my hand out to keep them from speaking. I looked behind
me, moving my horse around to block the others. I quickly moved

my gaze to the trees and pulled Seligsara, the others arming themselves.

"Cethin..." Cahya whispered. I ignored her words for just a moment, my eyes searching the motionless forest. Several moments passed, and I still saw no movement, heard no noise. I closed my eyes, taking a deep breath in and listened closer to the silence around me, hoping to pick up a breath, a heartbeat. My search came up empty.

"Hmm," I said and sheathed Seligsara. "If there was someone watching us, they aren't anymore."

"I felt it, too," Zheki answered. "Hard to read."

"Dacian and Eshkan are still out there. Do you think we should assist them?" Cahya asked.

I ignored her question for a moment as the wind shifted, the smell stronger now. Morard coughed, covering his mouth with his hand as if to escape it. Cahya had made a face that determined she smelled it too, and climbed off her horse suddenly, walking over to a bush and becoming sick. I watched her, getting off my horse as well. She saw me approaching and held her hand back to me, a sign she was alright.

"You failed to mention it was people that were burning," Morard finally said, trying to keep himself from choking on the foul-smelling air.

"As I said before, it was worth investigating," I stated, looking into the trees.

A few moments later, Eshkan and Dacian rode back into the small clearing, Eshkan shaking his head. "Carn. Burned just as Ophidian was. The people were locked inside their homes. But there was something else, too. Among the dead.... they had the same symbols that were carved into the chests of our brothers on their wrists."

"You think they're here?" Cahya gasped.

"No. I think they may have stopped there on their way back to Terrenveil." Dacian took a breath, "But their commander was not among them."

"Do you think some of the villagers survived? Killed them?"

"Doubtful," Eshkan added. "They were likely killed by the men with the symbols, all in the same manner. Carn was known for textiles."

"Monsters," Cahya muttered.

"I'm going," Zheki said and rode off. Undai sighed and whipped his reigns, heading in her direction.

"I thought I sensed someone watching us from the trees, but when I focused on what was around me, they were already gone," I said.

"It's reassuring to see that they have enemies," Eshkan answered, shouting so his voice would carry over the sound of our combined horses.

"There's something about it that doesn't make sense," I shouted, joining his voice in octave. "I only have one thought, if those are the men who killed our brothers, perhaps deserted when they found we were killing their own, who killed them?"

"That I am not sure of. This will be painful news to bring Sathenne, if they don't know about it already. There are hardly any flames, most of them are smoldering," Eshkan said, skidding his horse to a halt. Zheki was crouched over one of the bodies, rubbing ash together in her fingers.

"Things just continue to worsen," Declan stated and moved as far forward as his horse would go.

"There is a great darkness here," Zheki said as we reached her. She closed her eyes and vanished into the sunlight. Undai walked toward one of the houses, holding his hand over the latch to ensure it cooled before opening it. He kicked it inward, opening the door only enough to see that it was barricaded with furniture.

"They locked themselves in," he said softly. "Monsters indeed."

I was beginning to become used to the smell, which severely cloaked the scent from the tree line. I examined the dead, rugged. Their eyes; dead, empty. Zheki returned, dropping a man on the ground before us. He was bleeding out through a wound in his gut that he had covered in dirt to try and stop it. He coughed;

the blood expelled so dark that it appeared black. "I can't get him to speak," she said. "Perhaps you could?"

"There's a chance it may not work. He's weak, brink of death," I said and removed my hood, crouching to become eye level. We locked eyes and his widened, appearing to become dizzy.

"Who did this to you?" I asked. "The wound?"

"Terrifying. A monster. Of the old world."

"Did they live here?"

"Here?"

"Yes. Did the monster live here?"

"Came out of nowhere. Unsuspected," he answered. "He... he..." the man began to mumble, staggering his speech until he collapsed. I shook my head and stood. "He wasn't strong enough. Fruitless."

"We know it was no man," Zheki said.

"The Araelians are slipping," Undai answered. "There was a time that this was unheard of. No offense of course," he said, looking at me.

"None taken."

"We should distance ourselves from the aftermath," Zheki said and returned to her horse. "This was no monster. A monster cannot set fire to its dead."

"The farther the better," Cahya stated.

"The waypoint is just ahead; we will split ways there."

I nodded, looking back over the pile of corpses. Things were becoming dark in Terrenveil, as if a shadow reached in and grasped it by the throat.

We re-entered the forest, birds chirping softly. I felt a presence again, this time within reach. I stopped my horse abruptly, everyone else following suit. Eshkan strode to my side, peering deeper into the forest. "Do you think it is whoever murdered those people?"

"No. Someone has been following us. I felt the same presence at the brothel. And here again, now. It's elusive, strong and then faint."

"Another nonhuman," Eshkan said and reached for his blade.

"Don't. It may only escalate things," I answered, listening to the sounds of the horses behind us.

"Cethin," Cahya whispered, her voice crisp against the silence. I looked toward an old tree to the left, watching as a bolt sailed in front of us, hitting the ground. I gained control of my horse, Zheki arming herself with light, her eyes glowing a bright golden. It was then a Sardon revealed herself on a long thick branch, two swords on her back, a loaded crossbow in her hands. I dismounted, nearing where she stood.

"That's far enough," she said.

"Leave the others alone, I've a feeling your quarrel is with me."

"Correct," she answered and lowered her weapon. "You have something of interest. You and the non-combatant."

"You'll die trying," Zheki said.

"Listen to him," the woman returned. "You needn't involve yourself. I'm not your enemy."

"I am protecting what you seek. You involved me," Zheki's voice a weapon.

"You mistake my intention. I do not seek the box."

"Neither do we," I said. "We are ensuring that the keys are never found."

"We have the same wants."

"They are in our possession; they are our responsibility. Turn back, or I will have to engage you."

The woman jumped down from the trees, pulling each sword from her back, swinging them. "I made an oath to my people. I must have them."

"Then you must face me as your enemy," I answered and grasped Seligsara, bracing for her attack. Zheki jumped from her horse, and I moved my hand to the side, fingers extended outward. "You must pursue if I fall."

The woman rushed me, laying several blows. The Sun began shouting, louder each time she attacked. I ducked and moved my blade upward, pushing her swords off it and kicking her in the stomach. She fell backward and used her upper back to propel herself back to her feet, twisting quickly and whirling her blades around her.

"The coven will be happy to see the sword return with the keys."

"They will see neither," I said and ran forward, using a tree to take three steps to flip over her head and bring my sword down with force. She fell into the pressure and elbowed me in the breastbone, speaking one word that caused her to make a wall of ice beneath my feet. It began to freeze them in place, and I jerked them forward to free myself. She repeated it, pulling her arm forward. The ice followed, grabbing hold of me again. She neared me, and I ducked, blocking an attack from her. As she moved to disarm me, I grabbed onto her forearms. She pulled them apart, coming at me again. I flipped Seligsara and propelled one of her blades into a tree. She traded hands and whispered words to command ice a third time. It began to climb to my knees, and she looked into my eyes, ceasing her attack.

"It can't be," she gasped.

I withdrew my sight and she retreated, doing several backflips to retrieve her swords and vanished again, several drops of blood on the ground where she once stood. The ice melted instantly, and I regained control of my movements.

"Perfect," Morard said. "Now we have your friends trying to kill us, too."

"She would not have killed," Zheki answered. "If that was her intention, she would have done so while we did not know she was in the shadows. Cethin, did you know her?"

"I have never seen her before this moment. But she saw something in my eyes. That is when she left."

"Whoever she was, I don't think that is the last we will see of her," Dacian stated. "Remain vigilant. Perhaps next time she will not attempt to ask."

"If she does not want the box, maybe she can help us," Declan said.

"There is no way to really discover her intentions," Eshkan answered. "She could have crafted that as a guise."

"I feel safer if the keys remain with you," Zheki took a long sigh before continuing. "In your possession, split so far apart they are less likely to be found."

"But not impossible," Declan returned. "I will take it, but if she follows to my destination there is not much I will be able to do."

"We do not know if that will happen, let us keep thought from mind," I stated. "Is this where we split paths?"

Zheki nodded. "This will be the most direct route to the hills. The sooner we reach it, the sooner Undai and I can return to Defaltor. I will prepare so I can meet you in Esperanus in four days' time."

"Esperanus? Is there reason?"

"An old contact of Thurlowe's. He owes him and will help us. If we are to do this, we will need to pool our resources. He has no love for the king. This commander must be stopped."

"It is there we shall meet," I said and nodded. Zheki directed her horse to the north, signaling for Undai and Declan to follow. As their horses disappeared from view, we were left in the silence of the woods again.

"We should stay off the roads," I stated. "If the legion is moving across the kingdom, we're at risk of being searched, questioned."

"I don't think I have to tell you what rests in the woods," Morard said, sternly. "Cilevdan is known for its misfortune, there is a reason people are advised to travel the roads." Cahya looked between us, her eyes shifting back and forth. "Surely you can't agree with this madness," Morard continued moving his arms to either side of him, raising them up.

"He's right," Eshkan said. Dacian nodding. Cahya took a deep breath, also nodding hers.

"Have you lost your minds?" he shouted. "We don't know what's out there, let alone how long it will take us to travel to

Sathenne through the forest. We could lose our horses; we could lose our lives!"

"If we are stopped by soldiers, we can only try to talk ourselves out of it. Surely, they will approach armored people on horses. We would have to craft a tale that we are mercenaries, and hope they do not further inspect," Cahya answered. "They will likely not listen to me, which will leave you and Eshkan in charge of persuading them to let us go. How well do you think they will listen when they see a Sardon among us?"

"That sounds a lot better than being ripped to shreds by an old-world creature lurking out there. How long will he be able to protect us?" Morard asked, pointing at me. "His own race attacked him. She's likely to return with others. None of us are prepared to fight an enemy that isn't human. We can escape soldiers."

"And remain wanted throughout the kingdom?" Cahya asked. "What if it's an entire battalion Morard? What then? How well do you think we'd fare at escaping?"

"We could be spending this time traveling to Sathenne," Morard stated. "But I suppose if I cannot reason with any of you then I must walk a path doomed."

"Take the roads," I answered. "If you feel it is right."

"Are you mocking my concerns?" he asked.

"Now you're making a fool of yourself."

"Insult me once more."

"Both of you," Cahya said, riding her horse between us. "This is not the time nor place. If you want to take the roads, you may reach Sathenne before us and can get a feel for the town. Inns, markets, how quartered it may be. It would be an advantage." Morard looked toward Cahya and sighed, shaking his head minutely, twice. I moved my eyes toward him, watching his mannerisms closely.

"If I'm stopped, it will be easier to evade suspicion. I will go ahead. I've not been to Sathenne, is there a plan?"

"I have," Eshkan stated. "There is a stable outside the walls, as well as a few farms. People in and out, constantly. Town guard, dogs. They'll be attentive at the gate but entering and exiting won't be a problem. There is a farm there, owned by a woman named Emeirzi. Once you scope the town, go to her. She will host you until we arrive."

"I will go with him," Dacian said and looked at me, signing something to Eshkan. He rode off, following Morard to the road in silence.

"He does not trust him," Eshkan said.

"Morard?" Cahya gasped. "He's stressed, frightened. We've been through so much. Now we're faced to end a plot most terrible."

"There is no way to ever know a man until he is faced with adversity and mortality," Eshkan answered. "Dacian will make sure."

"I don't like this," Cahya said and crossed her arms. "We are weaker divided."

"Go with them, if you'd like," I answered. "I cannot travel the roads; I'd be a risk to you all. I don't know how mercenaries or soldiers would react to you being alone."

"I can protect myself, Cethin," Cahya returned, whipping the reins of her horse, she rode off in the direction the others went, disappearing within a few moments.

Eshkan shook his head and offered a chuckle. "Fiery, that one."

"We should go," I stated quickly, and guided my horse to where the trees began to thicken. I have never seen her wield such ferocity. I would ask her about it later, if she gave me opportunity. I cleared it from mind, focusing again on the world around me. Seconds became minutes. Minutes, hours. We reached a small clearing, stopping at the tree line and scanning the area thoroughly. "No scent, no sound."

"Should we find another way?"

"We could walk around the edge to make it to the other side, but the roots of these trees have claimed the forest floor. Our horses could break their ankles," I said. "Neither option is ideal. Remain vigilant."

I looked toward the tops of the trees as I made it toward the middle of the clearing, quickly shifting my gaze downward. Eshkan reached for his bow, arming it slowly. We reached the tree line, and I stopped as I felt opposition against my horse's stride, a large net swinging across the tree, entangling me. I attempted to reach for my dagger as I was caught, but the harder I fought, the tighter it became. I looked toward Eshkan, who was being escorted over by two hooded figures, his arms bound.

"Take him to her," a woman said, jumping down from the dead tree to my left. "We will take this one after we've made sure he is no threat." I felt a blow to my head, and then, blackness.

◆ ◆ ◆

Balgolig seht am sher. Sorica, sorica, sorica. Stilet corscae. Sorica vehnt. Eereshe merbog sorich.

◆ ◆ ◆

I awoke. A sturdy wooden cage, ropes around my wrists. A thicker one was around my neck and chest, holding them to the wall. Seligsara, gone. My weapons. The key. My armor remained; my kidnappers must have been unable to remove it. Eshkan, where was he? I closed my eyes tightly, trying to fight off the grogginess sustained by my injury. Blood coming from the wound on my head. Deep breaths, trying to discover my surroundings. Moisture, cold. We were in a cave. I heard footsteps, approaching slowly. The time would be now to try and escape.

"It's awake," a man said and walked over.

"Don't get close. Draega will want to know that it's conscious. She's the one who will handle it."

"It's locked up and harmless."

"It eats people, children. It can paralyze you with its eyes and suck your soul out."

"That's mostly false," I said. "Where are my things?"

"And it speaks our language. Perfect, it'll have a good idea why she's going to execute it."

"She ain't going to execute it, Mag. Go get her."

"Why me?"

"Because if I go, you'll do something stupid."

Mag cursed, walking off to another part of the cave. The other stayed distant, looking over periodically. I looked around, the torches closest to me burning brightly. A new set of footsteps joined the familiar pair and a woman entered, dressed in tight leather, Seligsara attached to her hip.

"Leave us," she said.

"Are you sure that's so wise?"

"I said leave us!" she shouted. I laughed softly as the two left, which seemed to irritate her further.

"You haven't tried to wield her yet, have you?" I asked, trying to lift my head.

"No more questions from you," she said and held up the key, tossing it once in her hand. "Now, be a good boy and tell me what this is," she continued, holding it toward me. "How do I open it?"

"Try wielding my sword," I said. "If you can manage five minutes, I'll tell you."

The woman looked down at it and back up toward me, her bright green eyes dulling. "I'm not in the mood to entertain you."

"Return to me when you are. I'll tell you nothing," I said. The woman's eyes took a darker shade, and she looked to where she had just sent her men. "She said you'd be difficult. Even said we would have to do this the hard way. But that's fine by me. I'll come back tomorrow. Maybe a full day in the cage will free your tongue," she hissed and scratched the cage with her claws, leaving marks across them. Archegals. I closed my eyes, isolating my mind from the present. I would need to be of sound mind to determine how I was going to make my escape...

◆ ◆ ◆

I sat at the dock for hours after people had stopped coming, staring into the dark of the ocean. He returned to it. It was his wish. As he grew older, he would come for both sunrise and sunset, until he could no longer wake at dawn. I did what I could in caring for him, years and years of living with a human, being raised by a human saw me successful in that. I remained well until after the sun left me, the water reflecting a pale moon.

The torches around the docks were still lit brightly, the occasional guard passing by with one in hand. I returned to his house to gather my belongings. He sold it two days prior to his passing. He said that he would sell the house, and with the money, buy a new ship. We'd live there for a while, if I wanted to stay. *Where else would I go?* were my words. I lost my mentor and inherited a ship. But where else would I go?

I remained in town for a few days, but without the mariner to keep me busy, there was no reason for it. Eventually I decided that I had no use for a ship and tried to find someone who would buy it. I was making a round in the market one morning when a meek man in his forties approached me, garnering interest in it. I wasn't hard to find.

"Are you the twice orphaned son?" he asked, his eyes bright and energized. Almost too much for my liking. The twice orphaned son was what they called me in Harbortow, though prior to losing the mariner, it had only been once.

"I am."

"I heard that you're selling a ship," he replied looking toward the harbor. "Do you care to show me which one yours is?"

"Are you looking for one?" I asked. Another thing the old mariner taught me. If you're going to look a fool, it might as well be in words and not actions. There would be no point in walking the length of the harbor if the man was here for business other than what I had in mind.

"Yes, I'm looking to hire a vessel to take me to Rustanzen so that I may sell my prized furs from the Septens," he said. "With that money I would be able to not only pay the ship's owner and crew handsomely, but in turn purchase the ship."

Furs from the Septens. There were many species of animals that had fur. Foxes, wolves, rabbits, bears. But there were also the beasts that hunted every single one of those. Knowing what types of furs he carried would give me an understanding of what kind of man he is.

"Does it get cold enough in Rustanzen for fur?" I asked, my eyes moving toward the harbor again. "I suppose rabbit and fox pelts could be sought after for different purposes."

"Only in the empire's remote peaks. There are still people that inhabit those. The ones closest to the imperial city are said to seek exotics. However, those in the imperial city may also be interested. I was told to sell at that market first."

"Why go through the trouble of climbing the peaks if you can see them to new hands in one place," I said. "I've no crew. I've not yet hired one. The ship was my late father's." It was the first time I used the word. "He bought it two days before he passed. But he was a seafarer his entire life. He knew a good ship when he saw it."

"My condolences," the man said and placed three fingers over his heart, holding them outward. A custom I was unsure of in nature. "Has it ever been on a voyage like that before? Across an entire ocean?"

"We bought it from a woman who lived in Tovai. She came here on the ship. So, it's made a voyage at least once," I said.

"When do you plan on hiring a crew?" he asked. I looked at him and exhaled in short. "I only plan to sell the ship." Disappointment and something else became written on the man's face following the statement. Be it frustration, or hostility at being denied, I could not tell.

"I see," he decided. "I'll speak to my associates. Perhaps we will speak again someday," the man said, nodding his head once and disappearing into the crowd of the market. An excursion to Rustanzen would have taken me from the Baeld, where I had nothing left. Yet I had never captained a ship on my own, nor had the men to see it there. I turned in late that night, taking to the cliffs above the sea for a time. I stared into the sea until the sky darkened above it. It was then I looked at the stars. Where else would I go?

Someday had turned into the next, as the man who had garnered interest in my ship approached me a second time, accompanied by a merchant from the mainland. The man introduced himself with the name Hisai, the merchant Kresi. I did not give my name, saw no reason to. At first it annoyed me, their seeking me out, until the one called Kresi mentioned he would be willing to pay for the ship without first traveling to Rustanzen. Had he not said it sooner, I would have parted ways. It didn't take long for an agreement to be reached, and in parting I found myself walking toward the cliffs. It became a ritual at this point. Once a day, a few hours at least. I suppose it was because it was the last place that I sat with the mariner, listening to the cry of the sea, a happy memory. The next morning was different. A small boat pushed out into the waves; his body wrapped in thick cloth.

The day was ending, and the agreement was to meet before dusk at the end of the docks. I jumped down from the ledge I was standing on, landing on one a few feet beneath me. From there I climbed down to where there was a path on the side of the cliff, making it back to the village as the sun was starting to turn the sky different shades of orange and pink. I approached the pair, Hasai adopting a smile on his face, Kresi tapping his foot expectantly.

"You're late," he said, his tone one of disapproval.

"The climb down took longer than expected," I said, looking up toward the cliff face. Believable enough for him to dismiss his disdain. He shook it off, looking at the torches surrounding us. "Come. We must make it inside before the guard begin their patrol."

"Guard?" I asked. "I didn't realize we were doing something that warrants avoiding them."

"Not now," Kresi said and waved his hand around. I was beginning to dislike him. I obliged, however, following the men into a house that was a short distance from the last pier. It smelled like smoke inside, most villagers took to burning different plants to mask the scent of fish from the market during seasons when it was plentiful. It was well lit with candles on every surface. Once we had entered, an older man appeared from the back, sharp eyes embedded above a hooked nose.

"This won't do," he said. "This won't do at all."

"He's the one with the ship," Kresi said. "The one who's selling the ship."

"And I said it won't do." He shook his head and threw a pair of old leather gloves on the table in front of him. "How has he got a ship?"

"It was inherited," I said, which caused the old man to obtain a look of interest. It left him rather quickly, and he shook his head once more. "I told you that it needed to be inconspiteous."

"Inconspicuous," Kresi corrected, provoking an unamused glare from the old man.

"All of you get out of my sight. His hood likely alerted the guards already."

"My hood?" I asked. "I always wear it. It would be stranger if I was seen without. I'm just looking to sell my ship; I won't be kind for too much longer if my time is seen wasted."

"Easy lad, no need for threats," the old man said. "Are you well known in town? I ain't see ye before."

"Well enough to be given a name among its inhabitants," I answered. I was growing tired and hadn't yet put any thought into my hunt tomorrow. It had been a few days. The people in Harbortow didn't know there was a nonhuman living among them. The mariner was quick to tell people that the reason he kept my face and head covered in daylight was a deforming injury. It sufficed. The man looked to his counterparts, offering a hesitant glare before concluding.

"Take him to see Geil."

I let a heavy exhale from my lungs. My patience was dwindling. I followed the men away from the house, and toward a cottage positioned outside the city wall that separated Harbortow from Terrenveil. When we arrived, smoke was pouring from the windows and beneath the door. Hasai stopped in his tracks, moving his arms to his sides to stop us.

"Do you think he's inside?" Kresi asked, worry striking his eyes.

"I told him that he needed to move inside the walls," Hasai said. "It's dangerous out here."

The fire ravaged the inside of the home, flames now seen through the front windows. I pushed past Hasai, making it to the door when I felt a blade at my back...

◆ ◆ ◆

I took a deep breath inward, the memory leaving me despite focusing on it. I smelled earth. Sweat. Blood. The woman returned, this time with my things in a satchel. She dismissed her pawns and tossed the satchel in the corner. She smirked, her eyes aglow beneath the narrow of her brows. "Have you decided to talk yet, Sardon?"

"You were asking after the small gray cylinder?" I said, watching her face sustain distrust.

"What is it?" she asked. After a moment of silence, she smiled. "My sister told me what to do in the event you won't tell me. If you won't help willingly, I will bring out our prisoners. We'll cut off their skin, day by day until you become so starved that the animal within you is released. And then, when you're at the point at which you can no longer control yourself, we'll bring out your friend so you can eat him alive. And once you've returned to your consciousness, you'll tell us. Or we'll continue this cycle over and over until you forget who you are. I know it won't be long before your friends in Morrenvahl come searching for you, so we'll have to do this my way."

"Friends?" I laughed. "No one is coming for me. You're wasting your time."

"It's no secret that one Sardon doesn't come without another."

"I wouldn't know," I said, resting my head against the back of the cage.

She scoffed and paced, once more looking at me. "What... they exile you? They cast you out? And these are parting gifts? You expect me to listen to you?"

"If you didn't want to listen to me, you wouldn't be. Whether or not you'll take what I say and process it is another manner entirely. But no. I wasn't cast out. Or exiled. I've...never been there. So no, if you think you need to expedite my torture there's no need."

"Why are you telling me this? I'm your mortal enemy... we are enemies."

"No. Sardons and Archegals are enemies. Me? I'm just a rogue who's looking to save my friends. Human friends. Like the one you captured with me. I couldn't care less about whatever feud your first has with... Zerian? Because to tell you the truth, I'm nothing like him," I said.

"You're right. I am listening. But I won't process. I've read about it all. Your acts of deceiving. Your tricks. Your strength. And I won't let you use it against me," she said and paced the front of the cage again.

"If you've read it all then you know about what we can do with our eyes. The hypnosis. The deconstruction. And if I was going to use it against you, I would have by now."

"So why haven't you?" she asked. "Why haven't you attempted to escape?"

"Because we both want the same thing, Draega," I said, prompting a scoff from her.

She laughed for a moment, looking into my chest. "And what could I possibly want... that..."

"To live," I said. "And to protect those we care about. Our friends...or our kinds. If you starve me, I will get out of here. Except I will not be able to control it, not until I kill and take enough lives to sustain myself. It's been a very long time since I've been to that point. Years. I killed so many that day. Don't do this. Are a few trinkets really that important to you? Worth the lives of your people?"

Draega let a shallow exhale from her lungs. "Fine. I'll help you. But once I let you out, it's on you to disappear," she said and grabbed a dagger from her pants. She moved to the front of the cage, ripping the door from the hinges. She hesitated for a moment but then tore the bonds that tied me to the wall. I grabbed my things when I heard Draega wince from behind me. I turned, her arm bleeding from a large wound she had made with the dagger. "I'll give you a head start."

"Thank you," I said.

"Don't. Because if they catch you, you'll be left to whatever fate they decide," she said. I made haste from the room, quickly taking to the shadows of the cave walls. As I closed my eyes to focus on the sounds around me, I extinguished a torch that was overhead. Eshkan had to be close. I continued in my exploration of the cave's natural corridors, rendering every torch along the way useless. It wasn't long before I heard shouting from behind me. I didn't have much time now. I looked down a second corridor, extinguishing the torch that marked entry. I waited in the darkness for a few moments until I heard soft voices and followed them, kicking open an old wooden door. Eshkan was hanging by his wrists inside, two Archegals preparing a hot iron. I swung Seligsara, decapitating one, kicking the other one downward before stabbing him through the center at his spine. I rushed quickly to Eshkan, looking at the rope and cutting it, catching him on his way down.

"I was beginning to wonder when you'd get here," he coughed. "I've been counting the hours, can smell the air, see the light through the hole in the cover above us. It's been two days."

"Two?" I asked. "The others have likely made it to Sathenne by now. They're probably worried."

"What happened to you?" he asked, moving toward his shirt on the table in the corner. He had scars from where they had introduced the hot iron to his skin. "I feared the worst."

"I convinced one of them to let me escape," I said and looked toward the door. "We won't have very long though, can you stand?"

"I'm impressed," Eshkan laughed. "Yes. I need but a moment to gather my things."

"A quick moment. I convinced her to let me escape, I didn't convince her to aid us."

"I see," Eshkan said. He grabbed his sword and bow, pulling his leather armor over his chest. "They have to make it difficult," he groaned, pain seen in his face as the armor was introduced to his wounds. "It is also your assumption that this is the first place they'll come?"

"Yes. It is also why I've darkened the cave. Stay close to me until you can adjust your sight."

"So, they are looking for it too? Who are they?" he whispered, crouching down behind me, following in my footsteps.

"I don't think they were looking for it, merely took an interest in the key once it was found. They're Archegals. She told me as much."

"In Cilevdan?" Eshkan said, surprise in his voice. "I thought they were nearing extinction. They're being hunted in Stirae and Tovai. They have been eliminated in Agado and Rustanzen."

"I don't think their appearance here is coincidence, but I don't think it directly linked to this. We need to get you to a healer."

"I won't oppose, my friend," Eshkan said. "I've been listening to them in and out of here during my time as prisoner. What they've looted may be left if that interests you. I think we should at least see if there is any coin, it would be useful."

"Lead the way," I said and followed him through the cavern. What had just happened was as perplexing as it was frightening. What if Cahya had been with us? What if Dacian or Morard? We reached a door, torches to either side of it. Eshkan moved to extinguish them, and I grasped his wrist. "If we don't, they won't suspect we've entered."

"And if they do?"

"Do you remember Avilar?"

Eshkan picked the lock, and we entered. "How could I forget," he laughed. He closed the door slowly and carefully behind us so as not to make a sound. "These Archegals, they're bold."

"Desperate," I corrected. "To our advantage." I picked up a large pouch of coin, jewelry to the side of it.

"Do you think we could deliver these weapons to Sathenne upon horseback?" Eshkan asked, pointing to a mass of swords in the corner.

"How do you intend to sneak them past the remaining Archegals?" I asked. "Even if we could, if we arrive with weapons..."

"And the legion is already there, we could send them to their graves," Eshkan said and nodded. "To Sathenne, then."

We waited until the sounds outside slowed before we opened the door enough to see the cave.

"What's our plan then?" Eshkan asked.

"I sniff out the exit and we kill whoever tries to stop us," I said.

"Or" Eshkan said. "Or we wait until they sleep. They'll have a patrol, sure. But I doubt it will be more than a few men. They likely believe we've escaped already."

"I don't exactly have the luxury of time," I answered, keeping my eyes at the door.

Eshkan nodded, striding forward. "Understood. Like old times, then?" he asked. I placed my hand on the door in affirmation, pushing it outward slowly. Whispers from deeper within the cave, several loud voices on the other side of the wall. I followed Eshkan as we navigated the passage. As we continued, the air began to smell fresher, and the damp of the cave left my lungs. The light from the torches ahead of us cast shadows of two bodies. Shifting my gaze upward, I tapped Eshkan once, motioning for him to follow. We jumped upward, using the roof of the cave to position ourselves above them. *The places a serpent may hide are many. In shadow, underneath, overhead. From there they may strike or remain watchful for the desired opportunity to arise.* After they passed by us, we returned to the cave floor, making our way to the exit. Four bodies. I motioned for Eshkan to take the far wall toward the mouth of the cave, and I moved for a boulder that separated my position from a torch. I would wait for the one closest me to pass by and pull them into the shadow, giving Eshkan a chance to strike at his targets.

Just as the man's foot touched the ground, I stood, covering his mouth and pulling him into shadow. I stabbed him through the neck, coiling him behind the rock. Eshkan moved then, arrows hitting the two that stood sentry. I rose, sliding across the floor to cut the legs of the man who turned at the sound of his comrades' corpses hitting soil. An arrow hit the top of his head and I stood, patting the dirt off my pants. I sprinted towards the entrance, making it to the tree line to gain sight of our horses. Eshkan joined me moments later, his bow still in his hands.

"How many do you see?" he asked.

"Two are visible," I said and closed my eyes. "But there is one behind that old stone wall, watching them."

"Your plan?" Eshkan asked and readied an arrow.

"We'll follow the tree line until we're close enough for you to be in range. Once I disappear behind the wall, release your arrows."

"How far away do you think I have to be?" Eshkan asked, a smile on his face.

"I'm not doubting you. Once you've downed them, take our horses to the edge of the lake through those trees. I can smell it from here."

"What about you?"

"You don't want to come behind that wall. I won't be long," I said and quickly headed toward the wall, keeping low at the tree line. The two men in the front were preoccupied in speaking to one another, their voices heard above the crackle of the torches that lined the wall. I positioned myself in the trees behind, waiting for the perfect moment to strike. A few minutes passed before my target turned toward the men in the front, watching as they suddenly dropped to the ground, arrows through their hearts. It was then I moved from the shadows, rushing toward them and placing my hand over their mouth, wrestling them to the ground. They threw an elbow into my chest, and I fell victim to the force, regaining my balance quickly. I turned them over, pushing the hood from their face, seeing bright glowing green eyes staring up at me in hatred. I quickly snapped their neck, consuming what I needed and raced off toward the lake.

I crouched to the water's surface next to our horses, taking handfuls of it to my mouth to wash the blood from my face. I turned suddenly, pulling Seligsara to see Eshkan in a tree, bow drawn.

"Was only going to test you," he said and jumped down.

"I know. Your arrow would have gone straight past my ear and into the water," I answered, returning to my crouched state, taking more of the water into my hand.

"You really should try taking up archery," he said and walked toward the horses. "We the have time now."

"Not much," I said and looked at the distorted reflections on the lake's surface. I sheathed Seligsara and mounted my horse, following Eshkan out of the forest to the road.

"You know, it wasn't my choice, at first," he said. "Over time I became very good at it. Vortain eventually stopped offering me swords. I didn't even take them on reconnaissance. Just my bow, four arrows and a few knives. It's very easy to pass as a hunter."

"Four arrows?" I asked. The number was very specific.

Eshkan offered a smile and looked down to the quiver strapped to his horse's saddle. "Three in the event I need to get creative. When it comes to marks, I never need more than one. Luckily..." he said and pulled one of the arrows from it, holding it upward. "Luckily I was able to recover my stock from the cave. You see the arrows like this are what I use for killing," he said and turned it around in his fingers. "Lightweight, the head is serrated. It'll do more damage removing it than it will leaving it in. But these..." he said, replacing the arrow and pulling another. "These are heavier. They'll still kill, sure. But they take a lot more effort. I've shot these into a wall in Tovai so I could scale it. For countless other things too, but that was the most impressive."

"Wouldn't believe it if it wasn't coming from you. I'll indulge. What happened?"

"The reason I needed to make a quick escape wasn't due to the reason I was in Tovai. That was... well more of an extracurricular activity," he laughed. "My orders were to investigate the docks in the city of Chin Maesa. Long story short, the last remaining man belonging to a very old family died. The daughter... well we'll just say she inherited everything. Including a very old, very dangerous statuette. Of course, she didn't know I knew that."

I smirked, shaking my head. "The one Vortain locked in a chest and tossed in the bottom of the shallowing caves?"

"Ah, you knew about that?"

"I was there," I said. "Do you remember my first summer in Ophidian?"

"Not as well as you, obviously," Eshkan said. "Go on."

"I was... less agreeable than I am now."

"You mean attempted to kill Vortain twice, successfully killed some of his guards, and threatened to kill, skin, and consume Jadoq... three times?"

"It was more than three," I said. "The shallowing caves were my least favorite place. As I'm sure it was for many. But the day I found that statue was the day Vortain and I finally respected one another."

"Okay. The student surpasses the master," he laughed. "Now I'll indulge."

"Vortain was a torturer for a very long time. I could tell. I tried to outthink him and was unsuccessful. Most people, when faced with the instrument of torture, protest. They fight. I did, in the beginning. Before they learned that starving me only made it harder to contain me. I started to fight less against the methods of torture I hated most, and more against the ones that I could stand. I fooled the guards. Vortain too, until he caught on. So, he continued to send me to the caves. Horrible. Trying to hold your breath. Memorizing how long you'd be under when the tides shifted. When the waves came. Sometimes it was seconds... when the waves would push the water upward and fall back down again. But other times it would be minutes. It was never enough to kill you, if you were smart enough to survive it. Time things. Practice. At first, they'd release me before they fed me. But... when my defiance grew worse two guards would come when the tide was low to toss me meat. I learned that the water would rise and fall again before the guards returned, which was enough time to push whatever body part they offered me into the water to wash to sea. That was going to be how I escaped. I was going to break from the chains and make it through the marsh before the sun rose. But that's when I noticed the chest," I said. "It would have been hidden if not for the small bronze corner that either wasn't painted, or the paint had chipped off. The guards returned on the second day, and things weren't good. I was starting to fall victim to the failure of my own plan. If I satisfy myself fully, I don't need to eat for several days at a time, a week even. But if it's partial... small... incomplete... hours. The longer I'm without it, the worse I become. But it also makes me stronger," I said and sighed. "So, on the third day I broke from my restraints. I took the chest from the caves, and I took it to Vortain's tower. Guards had me surrounded with blades. I entered his study and dropped it on the floor. He told his guard to leave for the night, and we remained there for a while. It was an understanding. I could have gone anywhere with that chest. And, he could have done anything in retaliation to not only my escape but the removal of that artifact. We talked for hours. About the island, about the artifact and why he had you steal it from Chin Maesa."

"I didn't steal it. I... exchanged a favor for it. That took me longer than I thought it would but, in the end, she saw her end of the bargain, and I saw the statuette to Ophidian."

"So, you bent the rules too?"

"Famously." Eshkan laughed. "He wasn't very fond of it in the beginning. I was also sent to torture a few times. He was an angry man for a long time. I didn't really know why. Why he did this, how he came into possession of the island. He lost his wife to the plague. But even after she was gone, he was still angry. He once placed me in solitary for two days for missing a boat back from Rustanzen. Instead of me at the docks, they found my bird. He sent after me, you know. I don't know where he got them, but it was amusing watching them attempt to track me. I made sure to tell him that, but of course made it sound like I was thankful for the training he gave me. It was probably my mouth that landed me that stay. And perhaps the note."

"What was in the note?"

"I more or less said that I got tied up with Viona, and that I would make the next boat home. That was the name we gave the mission. I'm not sure if he did that with you or yours. Every single mission I went on, whether it be for reconnaissance, or retrieval, or murder would be given the name of a woman."

"Birds," I said and offered a smile. "It was always the name of birds."

"The man surprises me even in death," Eshkan said. "The mission we were preparing for... before the fires... did he tell you anything?"

"No. I was surprised that he wanted to involve me in planning it at all. But the way he spoke about it to me... he told me in the stands."

"In earshot of anyone listening?" Eshkan said and brought his hand to his chin.

"He just spoke of our next quest being extremely difficult. That he was gathering people he knew he could trust. After what happened in Arriksmad he believed Savantin to have resources as good as ours."

"Which means he suspected someone was whispering," Eshkan said and sighed.

"Arven said that he heard Jadoq speaking to a woman. But he didn't see her, only heard her voice."

"He didn't see her face?" Eshkan asked. "There weren't many on the isle that had access to his tower."

"Which leads me to believe that she was an outsider," I said.

"One would have to be very skilled in order to sneak into his tower like that... Unless Jadoq had hand in that, too," Eshkan answered. "There is no real way to know, now."

"Not unless you know a very powerful necromancer," I said. Eshkan enjoyed regaling, so I was surprised by his lack of response. Which meant to me that either the thought of such magick was disturbing to him, or he knew one and didn't wish to speak of it. We rode without stopping for the remainder of the journey, passing several wild groves of olive before we reached the short walls of the city. On it were several tall towers with worn peach and blue tapestries hanging from the windows. I could see guards moving within them, keeping watch over either the wilderness or the streets. The city gate was open, as the sun was burning bright above our heads. It would only remain there for another few hours, and the night would come upon us soon with its cold breath.

We halted before the gates when we were stopped by a short and haggard stable keep. He smelled of horses and pulled his locks of messy brown hair into an old, frayed hat, motioning us over to him with filthy hands. We decided that keeping our horses tied up outside the stables would subject them to being stolen in the night and paid the fee he asked. Eshkan gave him several coins, dropping them into his equally dirty palms. He counted them, flipping them over a few times and decided it was acceptable, leading our horses into the well-built stable.

"With any luck, they'll still be at the farm," Eshkan said and led me east. After some time, we reached our destination, Eshkan sighting his contact.

"There she is, now," he said. She was standing in a field with several others, children playing nearby. She looked up and shook her head, walking to the house that was in the center of it all. We reached the door when it was opened from the inside, a short Rustanzi woman standing with her hands on her hips. "Anxiously awaiting your explanation. The gods favor you for arriving at this moment, as I've had a few days to lessen my anger."

"I shall explain everything, Emierzi. Our friends? Where have they gone?"

Emierzi scoffed, crossing her arms. "The Mordestan woman went into town this morning. She said she was waiting for someone named Cethin."

"I am he," I answered. "Did she say where she was headed?"

"To seek audience with the Patron regarding the current state of Terrenveil. I wished her luck. As gaining an audience with Alaies is difficult these days."

"I'll take my leave. Where shall we meet you?" I asked, turning toward Eshkan.

"The inn?"

"Here," Emeirzi said. "You may return. Until this morning I'd have refused, so do not extend gratitude. It was the woman who changed my mind."

"She is remarkable," Eshkan agreed.

"She's gracious," she said brusquely, and turned back inside. Eshkan looked at me, expression only in his eyes, and followed her inside, gently closing the door behind her. I headed toward Sathenne, passing under the large arch that made its mouth. The city was large and brightly colored, with citizens to match. Despite their outward appearances, they paid no mind to my drastically different one. I had a lot of ground to cover before I could find the others and could only think of one place to start. They likely assumed that Eshkan and I were dead and formulated a plan of their own. Emierzi reported that Cahya entered town this morning, so perhaps she was in the patron's audience already.

The colors that adorned the markets stalls were remarkable. Deep blues and affluent purples bordered bright viridian and sultry crimsons on patterns that hung from the rafters like banners. Amidst these were the works of artisans, crafting sparkling jewelry or large canvases capturing countryside groves or the lands bordering the sea. I didn't know why I always focused on the markets of the places I visited, beyond it being the best place to find leads and answers to secrets, it mostly showcased creations crafted by human hands. Sadder still, the stalls were rarely visited by any of the passersby despite there being an abundance of people in the streets. The artisans put their passion into these objects, and waited to see if someone would take interest.

I wandered around until I found an apothecary and patiently watched while they finished crushing herbs together. A woman strode over, looking at the several cures that were sitting on the left side of the stall. She left as soon as she came, disappearing into a small crowd outside of the baker's stall. He hadn't noticed me standing there as he continued to grind up his mixture, now a paste in the small stone bowl. I moved my hand to pick up one of the bottles on display, setting it down as he looked up from his task.

"May I help you?" he asked, looking at me suspiciously. He had given off the indication that he did not trust me and squinted to see me better.

"I'm looking to learn about some of the herbs that grow around here. I'm a traveler. It has been said many times that the herbs that grow close to the river do well against the cold weather and have very unique properties," I answered, casting my eyes over to his collection.

"You are right in that," he answered and stopped grinding the herbs, reaching behind him and adding a spoonful of pale pink liquid to them. "Where do you hail from?" he asked.

"It's been a while since I've returned home. South, across the seas. Parents send their children off if they do not take up profession," I said picking up another one of his bottles, looking it over and placing it back down. "I've always been quite a scholar, just never took well to formal school."

"Ah. You are not so different from me. All I know I learned from my father, and he, his father before him. Medicine is best taught from a man, and not a book."

"My father was a mariner. Up until late in his life he spent it on the seas. I took care of him until he passed from the plague."

"So, I guess your mother was the one who sent you off?" he asked.

"I went off on my own, really. I was certain I wouldn't be missed," I answered.

"A free spirit too? Knowledge is always useful for that kind of disposition. I got into many fights while I was younger," the man said, standing from his seat and grabbing a jar of small yellowed seeds, adding them to his mixture. "This here is something that they order in bulk across the land, keeps the body from becoming sick during the colder months. Perhaps I should teach others how to make it. I wouldn't have to fill so many orders myself."

"Do you get that large of an order?" I asked.

"Ever since the queen found out about it, she ordered me give the recipe to her apothecaries up in the mountain. After that, the provinces discovered me. I ship most of my stock to the provinces closer to the Tundra, but of course there are other provinces that request it as well."

"Even all the way up in Valspire?"

"Rarely, but there is a case in which it happens. Most of the provinces order when winter is on its way, but I've been backed up lately with the large quantities wanted by the provinces to the west."

"The ones closest to Septentria?"

"Yes. It seems Neraea's alchemists don't really have the recipe quite right. I might have left out an ingredient for potency. But you didn't hear that."

"While we're on the subject of things we didn't hear," I said and grabbed a leather pouch from my side. I tossed it on top of his table, and he looked up at me, strangely. He took it into his hands after a few seconds and pulled the drawstrings apart, looking at the powder inside. He smelled it carefully and made a face indicating it was strong and closed it up.

"How in Araele's name did you come across this, traveler?" he asked.

"I found it around the water supply of the men I was staying with before I traveled here. I figured it was meant for me, too," I said, bending the truth slightly. The man shook his head and pushed it toward me, shaking his head. "I know nothing of it."

"Certainly you do, or you wouldn't have asked me how I had gotten my hands on it," I said.

"Listen, if someone put that in your water then..."

"They wanted me dead, as they killed everyone else around me. I have a knack for being in the wrong place at the wrong time," I said.

The man quieted his voice and leaned forward. "This here is a variation of Rythran. It's a rare one, created only in the coldest temperatures, underground. I know exactly where it came from, strangely enough. Where did you say you escaped your would-be killers?"

"I didn't. But it was here, in Cilevdan."

"Araele's blessing be upon you..." he gasped.

"Don't worry, you are safe. I lost them in the Glendoryn forest, near the Lake of Knights."

"Wise. Not many who travel there make it out alive, especially after dark. I'm afraid whoever tried to kill you is very resourceful. This particular powder comes from Vesiljan."

"Agado?"

"Yes, very hard to come by, very expensive. Not to mention the difficulty of finding someone who will sell it, that's another matter entirely."

I was silent, looking down at his hands on his instruments.

"I shouldn't have said that. You wish to search for it, don't you? So much for keeping my name out of your troubles," he said and turned, grabbing a small jar of tiny mushrooms. "Though, perhaps there is a chance you can handle it," he said and looked at my sword.

"You needn't worry about that. If I tell you more…"

"Go on," he said, his brown eyes fixed on his mixture.

"This killing was organized. One of the parties who had hand in it is dead, but we're not sure how he got his hands on this."

"It may be a very long and harrowing search," he stated. "Be wary, I would advise against pursuing it, though I feel it will fall upon deaf ears," he said and grabbed a clear jar from the table on the other side of him and tipped the bowl upright, allowing the mixture to take its time as it slid out. "Vesiljan is dangerous, traveler. It houses criminals, cutthroats."

"Similar to Defaltor?"

"Worse than Defaltor. Defaltor is controlled, there is a code that is honored. You would not be stabbed in the streets and robbed of your things. The King of Agado is blind to all that occurs across his land. If you do not have business in Vesiljan, do not go. It is a place people do not return from."

"I see, my gratitude for your admonition.

"Are you staying in Sathenne?" he asked.

"For a time, but not long. I'm afraid my travels take me elsewhere. To Redista, and beyond," I answered.

"Redista?" I felt the man's suspicion rise and he looked at me for a moment, speaking again. "I know better than to ask you who you really are, traveler. I only ask that you make sure no harm comes my way."

"I only aim to bring peace," I stated and turned away from his stand, looking wherever Cahya could be. I was certain that she would be looking for sustenance at some point and decided that checking one of the small taverns would be lucrative. I could smell the hearth as I approached the door, a fire crackling and offering shelter from the cold air. I saw two men enter a door across the street, looking around before disappearing into the shadows of the house. I moved through the crowd, following them.

As I pushed the door open, I heard voices and noticed the room was full of people talking among one another quietly, the sound a blur of seven different conversations. A man stood at a podium at the corner farthest right. He was an older man, perhaps in his fifties and had dark brown hair streaked with gray above his ears. He had a kind face, strong jaw, and bright attentive eyes that scanned the room as he spoke. He began to speak of laws the king recently issued that they would not follow, jumping to unnecessary taxation and the matter of the legion's travels. I continued to listen, very interested in the last topic. I was surprised that this meeting was taking place so publicly, and with no visible security. Terrenveil lost Sathenne, this confirmed it. Eshkan would have an easier task than he anticipated. I looked to my left, seeing that Cahya and Dacian were standing in the back and made my way over to them. The young woman in front of them turned around and tried to get a good look at my face before turning her attention back to the speaker.

"The king isn't going to deal with this problem himself. We've sent countless emissaries to ask him to change several of his greed-driven and ludicrous decrees, yet he sends them back with nothing. The only time he's called us into council is when he is changing something that will better him. And now, he sends the commander of the legion to deal with any of the actions he deems traitorous. Ozrach thinks that once this happens the unrest will end, but we all know what will happen once the Reaper leads his men into our towns. He will kill whoever he wants to kill for whatever reason." This came from a man in the crowd, his voice strong and confident.

"I doubt it will come to that," the speaker said. "Yes, the legion will come here. But there will be no hangings. No deaths. Savantin is not interested in the court, the provinces. I believe the legion's commander to be preoccupied with the war. Internal affairs are easily silenced, but a foreign attack, which brings forth the possibility of a conquest, would be a blow to Terrenveil that he will not see."

"You speak of the man as if you know him," said another man from the crowd.

"Merely thinking of what he has on his plate. Wouldn't rumors of rebellion seem less of a worry when the Kingdom of Mauros is occupying borders?"

"They're occupying borders?" A woman gasped. "Do you think they really plan to invade?"

"I can't say. But Savantin thinks they will. It is on the forefront of his mind."

"What are we going to do when they arrive?" another woman panicked. "I fear for my husband's farm. I heard what happened in Alken."

"Alken is a myth," the man next to me stated. "The citizens died from the plague, and the farms followed. They weren't searched and destroyed. I don't know where you hear these stories," he continued. "It's best if we just wait, see what comes of their occupation and ride this out. It would be foolish to continue to plan rebellion while they are so close to us."

"I agree," the man at the pedestal stated. "He may surprise us. I have done my part to ensure that Sathenne is free of suspicion. I implore you to remain calm in their presence. If Mauros does not invade, they will return to the mountain soon enough."

"We don't have very many options here," a woman said in agreeance. "A Mauroscan raid may weaken the defenses. If the legion is victorious, they may not be able to repel an assault from us."

"We do not have the proper arms!" a voice from the front of the room.

"These are not present concerns," the man at the podium again.

"We have a lot more pressing matters to worry about," the man next to me returned. "If Mauros is invading, how many of us do you think will be left. If anyone runs, we will be cut down. They are beasts. We will be forced into slavery. As much as we want to dethrone Ozrach we cannot afford to do so now."

"When we are so close?"

"Close? You dare say we're close when weapons runners have been cut down?"

The statement caused gasps from around, as the man next to me moved to the front of the room. He looked to the man leading, who nodded and crossed his arms, turning to watch him. "All of them. In Rierdan, Opskaven will be next. My scout has informed me. The legion moves in all different directions, sporadically, with no known plan. The Reaper and his men are moving toward Opskaven as we speak. He said that his coadjutant leads the operation in looking for treason. He's under the assumption that Savantin is handling Mauros on his own."

"If they've truly killed the runners in Rierdan, then the suppliers will not be happy."

"They've been killed. And not by the hand of the Reaper or his coadjutant. They have a very vicious boy with them. Sadistic, he's described. Pray to your gods that it isn't his coalition that arrives here, but another," he concluded and began to walk through the crowd to the back of the room.

"Where do you go?" a woman asked, crossing her arms.

"To gain message from my contact on where they plan to go next, if they haven't discovered him yet," he answered, and left the room, closing the door tightly behind him.

"Once we hear from him on what the legion's next move will be, we will adequately prepare. Until then, we are to go about life as usual," the man at the podium answered and exited through a door in the back, someone else taking his place.

"That was Alaies," Cahya said and looked up at me. "Geira said that she would be able to get us into contact with him in the next day or so."

"This is Geira," Dacian said and motioned toward the young woman who looked toward me before. "Emeirzi introduced us upon arrival."

"Alaies is a hard man to meet with these days. But, if Mierzi is right in what your plans are, the similar interest is something he will not neglect."

"As soon as you can, Geira. Appreciated," I answered. She nodded once and dismissed herself, the others in the room returning to their speech. "We should be going."

"Where were you?" Cahya asked, an intensity in her voice I hadn't heard in years.

"Eshkan and I were captured."

"Captured?!"

"Archegals."

"In Cilevdan?" Dacian asked.

"We were taken by surprise, too. Obviously. They almost made off with our weapons, and the key."

"You're lucky," Cahya answered. "Aren't they enemies of Sardons?"

"I keep forgetting you had free reign of his library," Dacian said.

"Apparently so," I said and sighed. "Where is Morard?"

"He was right outside when we entered. Maybe he went back to the farm. I'll go ahead," Dacian stated and picked up his pace, heading toward the gate.

As we watched him disappear in the crowd, Cahya tapped my arm twice, looking at me with strange eyes. "What happened?" she asked.

"It's best if I displace it from memory," I answered.

"I was worried sick," Cahya said and looked away from me. "It's almost like you think yourself invincible. Without care about those who care about you. You do realize that without you, all of this will fall apart, don't you?"

"I realize that, Cahya," I said, blowing a breath outward. "I should have listened to the guard and took the roads here. When we were captured, they took us to a cave system. I woke in a cage." I stopped for a moment, exhaling again. "They were planning to starve me until I couldn't distinguish friend from foe, and then drop Eshkan before me. There was an Archegal girl who was tasked with my torture. I was able to strike a deal with her."

"A deal?"

"Yes. Her life and the lives of her people for our freedom. She believed me. I wasn't lying to her, though, those Archegals...the manner they were proposing... No one would have made it out of that cave. Not even Eshkan."

"My god," Cahya whispered. "I'm sorry I..."

"We needn't talk about it anymore," I stated. She looked at me, moving closer and I kept my eyes low. "It's over. Done. Did you learn anything interesting while you were here?"

"Cethin."

"Cahya, please. I'm fine. What did you discover?"

Cahya hesitated a moment, letting a brusque exhale from her lungs. "The woman who owns the farm was angry at first when we mentioned Eshkan's name. But we told her what we were planning to do, and she conceded. That is when she introduced us to Geira."

"What is her role?"

"She's trusted by Alaies and his family. She will be able to grant us an audience with him. But it is a matter of time."

"Time we may not have."

"We don't have any other options," Cahya said and shrugged, her arms extended. "We can't just drop in uninvited, Cethin, he will not listen to us."

"I understand. Perhaps it is best you and Eshkan plan this."

"What should we do while we wait?"

"Care to walk town with me?" I asked. Cahya smiled and began to walk down the main street, looking back to ensure I was following.

"Eshkan and I managed to recover a large amount of coin from our captors before we made our exit. It will come in handy in the path ahead," I said.

"Perhaps the gods have not abandoned us yet."

"Eshkan seems to share that thought."

"Don't you? We survived the destruction of our home. We were given gracious hospitality and met people so willing to help us. Things could have been much, much worse for us."

"I was raised without them, so it never comes to mind. I suppose I could stand to be more gracious," I returned.

"Have a little faith," she said, looking at me with bright eyes.

"I suppose there is no harm in trying," I said as we came across one of the artisan's stalls. Jeweled turtle sculptures lined its surface, rocks and stones of many colors in bowls to their right.

"The turtle is a symbol of friendship," Cahya said and picked one up, turning it over and looking at the stones inside of it. "There is a story, of course," she let out a small laugh, placing the sculpture down.

"Ah, it's been a long time since I have heard someone reference Akisa," the artisan said, moving her wrinkled hands toward her tools. "The most fascinating stories out of Mordestai always featured animals."

"There is reason for that. We honor them as they honor us," Cahya smiled. "Have you been there?"

"It is wonderful. I go every year to trade for stones. From which village do you hail, Mordestan?"

"Kintosabe."

"One of the oldest, and smallest. I have not seen you before in my travels," the old woman said and covered her eyes to shield them from the sun overhead.

"I have been away from home for a long time, soon, I will find myself there again."

"I hope it is everything you want, traveler." The artisan smiled, grasping one of her tools from the hook on which it hung. Our journey led us to a large tree in the center of town, small bells and tassels hung on each branch. Cahya strode over to it, grasping one of the tassels in her hand. "There's a note here, but I can't make out what it says." Cahya pulled the tassel gently, trying to see if she could get a closer look without removing it from the tree. I reached her, looking at a small scroll that was nestled against a dark blue cloth. Some sort of symbol, something I never saw before. I looked up at other branches, many of them harboring tiny scrolls. "Do you think they worship the tree?"

"Perhaps, perhaps they worship the wind, and offer words to its strength."

"But wind destroys," I said. One summer a hurricane swept through Ophidian. It destroyed orchards and stables, anything that wasn't made of stone was dismantled. The structures were rebuilt sometime well into the following winter, exhaustion coupled with cold rendered most of us useless after a day of endless building.

"Sometimes things that destroy are worth worshipping. Fire. It's dangerous, but it offers many gifts. The same goes for water and for earth. Your people, the people of the Baeld, they pray to the sea, yes?"

"They do. They are devoted to it, rely on it. They follow old rituals and ancient ways. There was an Abregskan down shore from the marina, miles past where cliffs began to tower of the beach. Old worshipers would take their herbs there, bones of sea creatures, feathers of aquatic fowl, most importantly red chalk. They'd make offerings to the deities of the sea, chanting in their old tongue. Most of these altars were in hard-to-reach locations, and very secret. I never asked why that was, the people of the Baeld have no enemies of faith. A Baeldic legend says that luck befalls someone who finds their way to an Abregskan, but depending on what the deities see in them, it could be good or bad."

"And what did you think the deities saw in you?" Cahya asked.

"It's honestly hard to say. While what happened a few moons ago was tragic, and most would consider that foul luck, I wouldn't be here with you if it had not. We wouldn't be able to speak so freely, I wouldn't be able to hold your hand," I said, and reached for it, gently moving my fingers over the top before curling it in mine. I watched as a large smile took her face, causing her to look from the scroll to mine. "I do not know who to thank for the crossing of our paths, whether that be old gods, or spirits, or chance. I am thankful that even beneath a punishing and cold sky, I am allowed these moments with you."

"I cherish them too, Cethin."

"Almost every night I was on that isle I drifted to sleep over thoughts like this."

"Almost?"

"The other nights I thought of leaving. Days there were hard. Why do I defend him?" I asked, suddenly losing myself in thought.

"Defend him?"

"With words and honor. He taught me so much, I have become so much, but he did not hold back in torturing me for defying him. Beyond that, he used my weaknesses against me. He didn't just conceive the methods of torture, he enjoyed it."

"I can offer nothing that would answer that for you. But, if you wish to continue, know that you have my attention," Cahya said and squeezed my hand lightly.

"What happened doesn't grasp at me the way I think about him does. He was unkind to us all, in different ways. He's dead. Why does my mind still unbury him?"

"It may be something you must navigate, something that could bother you for years to come. You won't have to do it alone."

"I think the gods favored me, that day," I said and stood back from the tree, listening as the wind passed through it. Two red bells from the top of the tree began to sing, the rest joining in unison. "They'll be missing us."

We reached the farm, Emierzi cooking stew in a spit over the fire.

"We still do not know where Morard has gone," Dacian said, standing quickly.

"Where did he say he was going?"

"He did not."

"I'm going to find him," I answered quickly. "Stay here, I shall return." I left abruptly, heading toward the stable where his horse was hitched. Upon reaching it, I realized she wasn't there, and mounted my own. I could follow his scent, and her tracks. I now understood Dacian's distrust. I eventually found Morard's horse, tethered to a tree by a small cottage. The Sun began to speak, the voices overlapping as they conversed among themselves. I felt warmth in my arm, then, and it traveled through my muscles quickly.

I crouched, peering over the downed tree in front of me. It was covered in moss and mushrooms. My eyes came across a bear trap to my left. I turned suddenly, catching a blade on my forearm. I blocked the next attack from my assailant and parried his follow up blow, rendering him defenseless for a moment. He returned for me with intention to kill. There would be no reasoning with him. I forced his blade aside again and waved my sword across his throat, watching as he slumped down onto the ground. He set off a trap, catching his leg.

It was then I heard a voice, soft and light from behind me. It belonged to that of a young girl. She could be no older than sixteen. She was holding a blade in front of her, watching the wound on my arm from where the armor was torn from the blade. It began to close slowly, and as it sealed, I moved my head toward her, which caused her to raise her sword higher. I caught her by her arm, holding her still and looking directly into her eyes for a moment before seeing something I couldn't believe. I released her, shaking and murmuring, and backed away slowly, raising my hands up in front of me as she broke out of her paralysis still gripping the blade tightly in her hands.

"I should kill you," she answered, finding her voice. She turned the sword in her hand, using the other to push fiery hair from her eyes. Revealing her ambiguity, she looked to where my arm was bleeding. "What are you? What do you want with me?" she demanded.

"I'm a Sardon."

"A Sardon?" she asked; her voice not betraying her emotions.

"Yes, I…"

"I know what that is," she said and lowered her knife. "I thought Sardons stayed in Morrenvahl after the purge. What are you doing out here?"

"I would ask the same about you, princess, but I have already read the answers in your eyes," I said. She moved quickly, coming toward me with her sword holding it against my throat. I looked down, keeping my eyes from hers. I needed to gain her trust.

"I meant no threat in my words. I merely chose to reveal to you what was seen. Your friend's death was unfortunate. I had every intention to speak, but that is not what he wanted."

"I will not go back there. If you are planning on taking me then we will fight until one of us dies." She then turned the blade to her throat as her eyes widened. "I will take my own life."

"I am not here to take you to your father," I answered sternly.

"Then why are you here?"

"I'm looking for someone. I left Sathenne only hours ago. His horse is tethered back there," I said and pointed off in its direction. "So, I know he came this way."

"Friend of yours?" she asked.

"Not quite. Put the sword down, I am not going to hurt you."

"I don't trust you," she said, her fright returning to her. She pulled the sword closer, and I looked directly into her eyes, feeling them change as hers became void of all emotion. She became enthralled in them as I neared her, pulling the blade out of her hand. I took several steps backward and broke her gaze, looking down toward my arm.

"I am not going to hurt you. I have friends in Sathenne. Friends that are looking to meet with the patron. But we can't talk about it here," I answered.

The girl nodded; her pulse still significantly raised. "Go back to Sathenne," she answered, turning to her door. "I won't be here for very much longer."

"We might be able to help each other," I said quickly, exacting the response I wanted.

She turned around, crossing her arms in front of her torso. "How could I possibly help you? You're an assassin by the looks of you, dressed in the attire of your homeland. I doubt a human girl could help a Sardon in any way except one day become his meal."

"I can help you. I promise," I answered.

"Come inside. But quickly. I'll be having enough of a time clearing out his corpse before the sun rises," she answered, opening her door and disappearing in the shadows of her house. My eyes came across the man on the ground for a few seconds, his blood covering the ground beneath him. In leaving him, I followed her. Closing the door behind me, the heavy scent of burning herbs and spices invaded my senses, covering something dark but brooding. There was a small table where two bowls were placed, and benches on either side of it. The table was covered in candles, symbols drawn on it with the juice of a red berry. Hanging from the walls were animal skulls, a sigil drawn in between the eyes of each one. In the corner was a pillar made of bone and the ebony feathers of a crow. She moved toward her fireplace, poking the embers with a large stick that she was trying to burn.

"The man you were searching for. What is it you wanted with him?" she asked.

"We were forced out of our home, him, me, and a few others. When he didn't report back to where we were staying, I decided to seek him. The trail ends here."

"He's around the back of the house," she answered. "But I doubt you'll want to take him back with you. He's dead."

"You killed him. Do you greet all guests with a blade?"

"If they aren't our usual traders from Sathenne, yes. At first, we didn't know what to make of the situation. He was attacked by wolves, which was strange to both Leirend and I. His horse had no wounds, but he did. On his leg, his arm. Leirend couldn't refuse help to someone who needed it. We started to clean your friend's wounds when he mentioned that he had important information for someone in Terrenveil and that he needed to get there immediately. I think you can put together the rest."

"Terrenveil? Did he say why?"

"Oh, believe me, I got as much information as I could before we killed him. I needed to know if we would still be safe here. Leirend had just gotten through throwing him in the ditch when you arrived."

"My friends may be in danger," I answered and moved for the door.

"Wait," the girl said. "He had letters on him." She moved to the top of the mantle and pulled them from a box, handing them to me. Jadoq's letters to Savantin.

I took deep breaths to try and calm my rage. "The man who wrote these letters betrayed us. He must have taken them before we left the island. We intend to move for Terrenveil once we've rallied enough citizens to act on their plans for rebellion."

"Rebellion? You're going to kill my father?" she asked, her voice acquiring a different tone.

"No, your father has made many mistakes, but none worth the death that will follow me."

"What, then?"

"The legion is on the move. Your father has sent them from the Mountain to secure his lands. Alongside the rumors of rebellion that circle the castle, Mauros is occupying borders."

"They're on the move?"

"Yes, and it will only be a matter of time before they come here," I answered.

The girl stood, sighing and placing her hands on her head as she walked to her window. She turned, shaking her head and offering a short laugh. "They think I am dead. They have for years... all except...."

"What happened to you?" I asked.

She sighed, taking a deep breath. Unnerved. "I was on my way to meet a suitor, someone who would make a nice prince for the kingdom. A prince that one day I was supposed to inherit, be his queen. I had insisted that I ride on horseback with a few men, but my father said that no man would want to betroth a woman riding on a horse as if she was a peasant or knight. I was adamantly opposed to the idea, I hate carriages. I hated the dressing up, the feasts, living in that despicable castle. I am thankful to be alive, but I will never go back there."

"I understand the relief of leaving a life you didn't wish to live."

"Then you'll understand me. My carriage was being attacked by bandits. The man driving was killed, as were the men riding alongside me. The carriage stopped and I heard voices talking about me. I was knocked unconscious, and woke a few hours later, bound inside a small dark room. I could hardly see, but I could smell. Old wine. It was dirty, damp. I sat myself up, trying to remain calm. Whoever had captured me was smart; they had put something over my face, a burlap sack. I ended up getting the ropes around my hands wet enough to pull them apart." She pulled her sleeves from her wrists, revealing the scars around them. "It took hours for me to get out of them. That was when the door to the room opened, and I was truly afraid of what would happen next. I heard the footsteps nearing me, until they stopped, just feet from my body. I could only see shadows and watched as the person crouched down in front of me, moving his hand to my cheek. It was warm, warmer than anything I had touched before." She moved her hand to her face slowly, as if in a trance and closed her eyes, holding it there for a few seconds before starting again. "He moved his hand across my face, removing the sack from my vision. It was the commander of my father's legion. He told me what he did to ensure I wouldn't be found. He hired the bandits to attack the carriage and then killed them when they were through. His voice was soft, his demeanor gentle. As it always was when he was speaking to me. But there was something in his eyes that I didn't like. He looked like he was forcing something back, he wasn't himself. I used to sneak out of the castle while the soldiers were training. He'd train me when he could, even bought me that sword for my eighth birthday. I *know* him. That wasn't him."

"What else?" I asked, almost regretting I had spoken.

"He knew I didn't want to go back. Told me that he'd report my death to my family. I remember his voice, as if he was reading my mind. Reassured me that he knew I wouldn't take the throne, that I didn't want it. He told me that he didn't want it, either. But that's when his voice changed. He held his head toward the floor, taking deep breaths. When he looked up, his eyes weren't his own. I was afraid, I didn't think clearly, couldn't, so I pulled the small knife that was folded in my boots, cutting him up across his cheek to his temple. He looked at me, his eyes dark and bloody. I plunged the knife into his chest, but I couldn't push it in very far. He winced, moving to pull it out of him and I ran, making it to the door just as he had. I heard it fall to the floor before I made it out into the woods. That sound haunts my dreams. Maybe he was just showing me what happened to him, why he didn't feel at home in that place either," she said and looked away, her eyes watering. "I only thought about it later. I felt terrible. But I couldn't go back to apologize to him. I'd have received beatings by my parents and been locked away in my room. Forced into marrying some idiot prince who only cares about how rich the kingdom would make him. The fact that I hurt Savantin. That I hurt the only person that ever cared about me haunts me every day," she said; remorse weaved in the sound of her voice. "That was six years ago. You're the first person I've told this. That man outside, the man I loved. He didn't know what happened. He fled Terrenveil after me. We had plans to meet in Shinton. The things they say about Savantin, that he's evil, that he's cold. He's not. But the rumors... the rumors are true," she answered.

"I am sorry; I didn't mean to..." I responded.

"Maybe I've done this to myself. I was his daughter more than I was to the king and queen. And I hurt him, left him alone there," she stopped, turning toward the fire. "I cannot be found."

"Come with me to Sathenne. There are people that can help you. We can make sure you are never found," I said. I couldn't leave her here. Not after what I'd learned, not after what I'd done. I'd never hear the end of it from Cahya.

"If I am going anywhere, it is away from these damned shores and across the sea to Rustanzen," she said and looked down, letting her hair fall in front of her face. The remorse hadn't left her, not yet. She was defeated, hiding her eyes. "I know that if he were to see me, he wouldn't... we wouldn't speak about what happened, he wouldn't hold it against me, and every time I think about that, I cry," she said, tears falling across her cheeks. Their trails were brought to sight by the flames of the fire.

"Forgive me, I don't know what to say...I'm—"

"A Sardon. You don't know what human feelings feel like," she said, hastily.

"You're wrong. I wasn't raised by Sardons. I've been around humans my entire life."

"Now I'm the one asking forgiveness."

"You needn't. I had no idea that he was so close to you... I assumed..."

"That he's the monster everyone makes him out to be? Please. Savantin isn't simple. He's not the evil shadow that people say will purge Araele's light. He's not a bloodthirsty hound that everyone says seeks war and death. He's not after the throne like everyone surmises. He can't stand injustice; he detests the state of the kingdom. He's one man. He can't change everything. Else he would have by now."

"If he detests it so much then why are he and his legion enroute to find and bring to justice everyone who is planning on betraying the king and queen?"

"The only thing he detests more than the state of the kingdom is having to be present in the castle and court. He probably jumped at the chance of leaving and secured it by saying he'd see to it himself." She crossed her arms, looking at my face in lack of speech. "I disappoint you, is that it? Wanted me to validate the stories that he's some bloodlusting heretic out to feed upon entire villages and set them to plague?"

"You can't stay here," I said, simply. Disappointment? That could be the word.

"Do you think I want to stay here?" she asked.

"No but trying to stow away on a ship to Rustanzen is an idea that could get you killed, or worse. If anyone finds out who you are... you'd be putting yourself in a lot of danger. If you come with us, we can see you somewhere safely. Dark things have happened of late, realizations that have complicated things. The people we are working with are seeking to remove your father from the throne."

"He doesn't deserve it." She sighed. "Doesn't care about anyone other than himself. But you do realize that removing him won't be simple."

"We're aware. We're meeting in Sathenne to discuss it," I said. "But we aim to remove both the king and his commander."

"You're trying to kill Savantin?" the girl asked and looked at me venomously. "There has to be another way."

"There is no other way," I said. She was tense, anger and sadness laced her glassy eyes. I sighed and relaxed my posture. I wasn't the only one who lost something. "He's done something terrible... and..."

"Haven't we all? I abdicated, left Terrenveil and involved someone else in this... curse because of my name. I've stolen, killed. I've killed so many men. Leirend helped me, after the first I was near inconsolable but then it became easier. I got better at it. And you... you've probably done your share of the same. Who are you to decide who gets to live or die?" she asked, tears again were no longer held captive by her eyes. I looked at her, expressionless, speechless. The voices of the Sun replacing my lack of words. She took a deep breath, wiping her eyes. "I'm sorry. I guess I didn't realize just how badly I feel about so much. About everything."

"No, don't apologize. I didn't know you were so close to him; I wouldn't have…"

"What? Confessed you were going to kill him? I don't know which would have been worse," she said and buried her face in her palm. "Do you know how he became the commander of the legion?"

I shook my head, watching as the girl smirked and moved to the hearth, pouring herself a bowl of stew. She pulled out a second bowl, but then sighed and put it away. "After suffering crippling losses to the Jezhan, The King of Learthes, Leuroth, sought help in Ozrach. The two kingdoms became allies for a time, to remain until the Jezhan were put down. Savantin was a captain during this war and was stationed on the Learthan-Terrenveil border. They drove back the enemy, and Leuroth became interested in him, after hearing so many stories from the frontlines. Leuroth asked him to join his army and when Savantin declined, he was angry. Angry enough to hire an assassin. The man attempted to poison him but couldn't. Another soldier drank the remainder of the wine, dying nearly instantly. At first, they thought it to be the Jezhan, that was, until a man snuck into Savantin's tent at night and tried to stab him in his sleep. He got him, once in the ribs and once at the base of his throat. The other soldiers reported that the man was thrown out of the tent into the middle of the grounds with his heart missing from his chest. That is why they call him the Undying."

"I know that it will be difficult."

"You don't understand," the girl said. "After the man was unsuccessful, Savantin discovered that Leuroth was behind it. He abandoned his post, leaving another soldier in charge. He went to the castle, taking only the heart of his dead and the bond letter and threw them on the base of his throne. The bloodshed that ensued left Learthes in the hands of the king's only son, then a ten-year-old boy. The only reason any of us know about this is that when Savantin returned he told the soldier he left in charge. Someone overheard them speaking and from their camp sent a bird with the message. Ozrach was terrified of what happened. Terrified of Savantin. Terrified that Learthes would retaliate. It never happened. But the day he returned was the day Ozrach named him commander."

"I'm left with no other choice. He came to my home; his actions caused the death of close to a hundred innocent people. He was looking for something, something that he didn't find. If I knew the king had a spine I would ride there and ask to deal with him myself."

"He was... obsessed with something, though. Some kind of artifact, that was as far as he would let me in. I pressed him about it, but he said that if my mother found out he'd never hear the end of Araelian speech. But what you're saying he did... It doesn't sound like him at all. Are you positive it was him?"

"Yes. The letters you found on that man's body prove it. Right now, he is carrying out your father's wish of scouring the provinces and ridding of traitors. But I know that is not all he is up to. Whatever he's searching for must be of grave importance to him."

"Do you know what it is?"

"The Box of Barroqas. But we've no idea why."

"What are you planning, Savantin?" she asked, staring into the fire. "I should have known I would never be free of this madness. I won't help you kill him. The very thought of it..."

"You can tell me. If I wasn't going to listen to you, I'd have left an hour ago," I said, careful not to look directly into her eyes.

"It repulses me. Angers me. The sting of our last meeting, all the regrets, and woe, and sadness is called forward like a flood. He taught me to survive, to take care of myself, to be true to myself... and most importantly he taught me that you don't have to be what you were born into. He helped me leave it all behind, my fate, my royal blood. And he helped me leave him behind too, I know he didn't want that. But, like a father who only wants the best for his daughter and her heart, he did. If not for him, I would be destined to play dress up, play pawn in a game of marriages," she sighed, wiping her tears away with the back of a worn shirt sleeve. "I will go with you to Sathenne. Only if you promise me that you'll handle this another way. At least try," she answered.

"You have my word," I said.

"I will hold you to that," she said, simply.

"You also have my word that my friends and I will protect you as long as we breathe."

"I suppose I'll have to take your word for that, too." She then walked toward the small room at the back of the house. I heard her footsteps back and forth across the floor uncertain at first, and then calmer, heading back out to where I was waiting after several minutes. She carried a bag around her shoulder and changed her clothes to ones more suited for travel. Her hair was tied behind her head in a dark riding cap. It was then I noticed there was a scar on her collarbone, deep and pale. She walked to the hearth, grabbing something off it and placing it inside her bag, only looking at me once she was done. I rose slowly, paying careful attention to her anxiety.

"I will follow you," she said, giving her refuge another glance before feeling confident enough to leave it behind.

"We aim to speak with the patron. My hope is that upon our return we can. Take Morard's horse."

"The patron?" the girl asked suddenly, her anxiety surging.

"Do not worry. He is said to have a hand in planning the rebellion. If anyone recognizes you, I'm certain they wouldn't speak of it."

"I cannot shake the omen I have," she answered.

"No harm will come to you while you are with us. I am sure you haven't been using your name since you escaped."

"It's not my name I am worried about. Everyone knows the only daughter; the only child of Ozrach is pale skinned with fiery hair."

"Then we will cover it. Use your hood to cover your face as I do, they will not question. Once we get into town, we will be able to acquire what is needed to mask it."

"How foolish of me, to have not asked you what your name was. I suppose in the rush of things it slipped my mind," she said quickly, changing her pace to keep up with me.

"I too do not use my real name. They call me Cethin," I answered.

"Well, Cethin. Now that I know you aren't going to kill me, I will act formally. My name is Zerae, but I have been going by Cosette for years."

"Then that is what we will call you," I returned. Cosette nodded, and rubbed her fingers toward her shoulder, pulling the strap to her bag tighter across her body. She looked back to her house, blinking back a tear as her eyes grazed across the corpse of the man lying on the ground. She turned her head away quickly, eyes pointed toward the forest in front of us. I had a considerable amount of remorse weighing on me, for killing her only confidant. There was nothing I could do about it now, however, nothing shy of offering our camaraderie.

"I've never met a Sardon," she said, patting the head of the horse that now belonged to her. "My mother forbade me to look at books about the dark races. Nonhumans. But she was never present in raising me anyway. It was the oldest of the servants, Magelda who watched over me most. That is until I turned six and started sneaking away to the soldiers' grounds. At first Savantin insisted on returning me to Magelda but I protested. Said I didn't like it up there. He kind of laughed and said he didn't either, and let me stay. Have you lived in Cilevdan all your life?"

"I have. I lived in the Baeld for a long time."

"The fishing villages?" she asked. "What are they like? Savantin said that they were cold, and it's always raining. He brought me back a piece of a whale bone from there, said it was what every mariner sought. Did you see any whales?"

"Only once," I stated. "It was massive, larger than any living creature I've ever seen. I wasn't sure how the humans were able to bring it to shore. I've heard that whales are peaceful creatures, so in a sense I didn't like the sight. But I think that was the mariner rubbing off on me. He saw whales as sacred, agents of Taranost. It was him who raised me, I didn't know my parents."

"It's funny how blood can become nothing," she sighed. "My father was too concerned with his parties and feasts, and my mother I hardly ever saw. She didn't seem very happy. Some mornings she did, and it was always a night after she visited the temple."

"Temple of Araele?"

"Yes. Perhaps that's the reason she was so disapproving of me, other than the other reasons of course. I don't believe. Savantin doesn't either. But his coadjutant, Ohric, he's not much older than me, he's devout. When they'd pray together, I would sneak out to the training yard. Of course, my father was never around to see me out there and no one would dare tell. The only people that ever made me feel like Terrenveil was home were Leirend and Savantin."

"I don't think I'll be very well received by my people," I said.

"Why is that?"

"I wasn't raised among them; I have no idea how I came to be in the care of the mariner. I don't know their language. I only found out very recently that I have a brother, and that he and I belong to...I guess you can say the equivalent to a royal family."

"So, you're like me. In more ways than one."

"I guess we can say that."

"Tell me about your friends, what are they like?" she asked. "I'm assuming they aren't like you."

"Eshkan and Dacian were trained the same way I was. We were assassins."

"So, you'd be paid to kill people? Did you ever kill anyone in Terrenveil?"

"No, not exactly. We weren't paid at all. The ruler of the land would give us the names and we would act. These people we killed... they were planning things that would alter life for humanity by nefarious means. So, in turn, it didn't feel like we were serving him at all, instead doing things for a greater purpose. But he was cruel to us if we did not listen."

"He was like a king?" she asked, picking up pace so that her horse was next to mine.

"No. His tower was full of books, objects, secrets. But it wasn't lavish. He had no feasts, no parties. There was no court, no markets full of color. There was the tower, the labyrinth and the grounds. A farm, orchards. It was right by the sea. During spring you could smell the orange trees in the air. That was Cahya's favorite."

"Cahya?"

"She is traveling with us," I said. I could not keep her from mind.

"Who is she?" Cosette asked.

"She was a commander, head of the guard."

"That's what she did. Who is she?"

"She's very brave, very wise. She has a kindness that I've witnessed no other human possess. There is no other like her," I answered. "Her skin, her eyes, her smile. I would sit next to her for hours, just to watch the stars in silence. We risked a lot to see one another. We both knew the punishment but as time passed it was harder to stay from one another's arms. We were reunited in a sense. Very recently. I confide in her immensely. She makes me feel balanced in a world that lacks it."

"So, you love her."

"What?" I asked, only realizing how stupid I sounded after it escaped.

"You love her." Cosette laughed. "If just being around her makes you happier than anything else, if you don't need anything else, it means you love her. You haven't told her, have you?"

"I haven't," I stated.

"You should. You'll like the smile on her face when you tell her." Cosette adopted a smirk. "Don't want me telling her for you, do you?"

I looked toward her without knowing what to say, when she continued.

"I only jest. I wouldn't. Love is an important thing."

"I suppose it is," I answered.

"Are you so serious all the time? You shouldn't be. Not all the time," she said and looked around at the trees.

She was inquisitive. I didn't mind, the speech made our trip back to Sathenne seem shorter in nature. Questions I had never been asked. I only recently became close with people, close enough to speak this way. I was suddenly caught in a memory, as if it had happened only days ago.

◆ ◆ ◆

I was watching them. Eating soup out of stone bowls and speaking among one another in various languages. I could pick up upon a few, the mariner teaching me all that he could before he was carried away by illness. My silence was mistaken as fear among those who did not witness my first trial. I remained in the corner of the room, watching as they finished their meals, carrying on with one another. It was then two of them approached me in my peaceful silence, pushing my empty stone bowl off the table.

"Where is your ration, snake?" a large man had asked me, his dialect placing him from Esperanus. I chose to ignore his question and only raise my head toward him, my eyes covered from view.

"He asked you a question, it would be wise that you answer," the man next to him said.

"I was sitting in silence and there I will remain," I said, shifting my head toward him.

"Just because you passed judgment doesn't mean you are one of us. Let's see how a Sardon bleeds." The first said, grabbing the spoon off the table and driving it through the top of my hand.

I took a breath before pulling it out and driving it through the man's eye, pushing him backward. He let out a scream, disrupting the mood of the entire room. It became silent, for only a moment, numerous eyes focused on us. The other serpent came forward, and I grabbed his arm, breaking it quickly and pushing him aside to finish the dispute that began with the screaming man on the floor. He pulled the spoon out of his eye, tossing it across the floor in an angry wave of his arm. His blood was prominent on his face, and the smell was tempting me, the sight.

He spat a curse at me as he stood up, taking his large hand to his face to hold the liquids that bled from him inward. The wound was burning him, I knew, as he screamed at me, removing his hand to inspect it. Blood ran down his face once he removed pressure, and he made a fist.

"You'll die for that, you filthy worm," he said and spat blood on the floor, lunging toward me. He pushed me to the ground, my head bouncing off it from the force of my assailant. He began to taunt me, placing his large hands on my throat and rolling my head across the floor. As he moved to punch me, my head was freed from the hood of my armor, and I made eye contact instantly. He released his grip on me, and I pushed him onto the ground, quickly standing. He sat upright, shaking his head and looking at his hand a second time. He looked up and jumped at the sight of me, backing away toward his writhing friend.

Vortain's guards entered during this time. I surrendered, and they came behind me, securing my arms behind my back. I was taken to the cells, where I sat in conviction that I would be receiving another thrashing at the hands of the torturer. I was there for hours, feeling peace in the silence the prison had to offer me. I could hear nothing but the breaths of the person in the next cell. The wound in my hand had finally stopped coursing blood, the incision deep and raw. It was difficult to move my fingers; the pain from where a nerve had been struck was slowly climbing in severity. I heard the lock to the door of the prison unclasp, chains rattling as they slid off it. The sound of footsteps led to my cell as Vortain appeared in front of it, his eyes full of worry and bemusement.

"Release him," he said looking to Haldis.

"Are you certain that is a great idea with him suffering a wound?" Haldis asked, his accent thick and prominent.

"Cethin, are you able to compose yourself?" Vortain asked, looking at the top of my head. I rose slowly, as to make myself seem a lesser threat and spoke, bowing my head to him. "I will be alright as long as I feed soon."

Vortain nodded to Haldis who jammed the large key into the door, turning it several times before the lock snapped open. He placed his hand on one of the bars to the door, pulling it on it. It emitted a loud scraping sound as it grazed the floor and he stood back, waiting for me to exit.

"Master, my apologies for the assault, I..."

"There is no need to apologize, Cethin. One of your brothers told me what happened. You were assailed by one of the older men. They are foolish in their games, of which I have reminded them several times, that to treat a brother in that manner is forbidden. Gashol learned the lesson I had been intending to teach him through you, it seems. He will no longer be able to fight. Not with the injury you have given him."

"What is to happen to him?" I asked, genuinely concerned. To cripple a man from his labor was not an honorable deed.

"He will be given a place among the villagers. There isn't much else I can do for him, I am afraid. His brash decision to attack you struck him from my eyes as someone I can trust as a guard."

I nodded, unknowing of what response to give. I often asked Vortain to release me, but he would not entertain that request. He believed there was something in me that would benefit the whole of us, brothers, Serpents. I hadn't considered the others my kin, which was something that needed to be done. I merely pretended so that I would appease Master Vortain, and it seemed to have worked thus far.

"It seems Scarkhan has his own decision to make while he recuperates from the injury you granted him. I feel though, that he will share the same fate as Gashol. The breaking of bones is very debilitating."

"I did not mean to harm them so, master. When he drove it through my hand it awoke in me, my instincts. I almost killed him. I would have if your guards had not arrived."

"I am happy that they were perceptive of the situation. This question may seem unimportant to you, but it is one that I must ask. Why have you not spoken to your brothers? Every day you take the same position, unspeaking and unreceptive."

"It is easier to remain in silence than it is to make friends. They all know what I am, now," I answered.

"Friends are a matter of trust. They are not your friends, Cethin. They are your brothers. Brothers that share the same oath and are thus placed beneath a bond much stronger than trust. If they fear you it is because they do not understand. They will gain the trust they need to accept you as a friend, but they know that they must accept you as a brother if they wish to survive," Vortain answered, placing his hand on my shoulder.

"Fear is something I cannot yet trust myself with, Master. Though I have been given a different life, a different choice, there is something that dwells deep within that cannot yet be purged by a state of thought."

"You will learn to control it in due time. I don't believe another will mistake your lack of words for weakness, not so soon," Vortain answered light-heartedly. "You should speak to Dacian. He is the one who came to me, speaking of your innocence. He seemed unmoved by your display, only concerned that you were going to be punished for an event you did not start."

"Thank you," I answered.

"Do not thank me. It is Dacian who deserves those words. Had he not told me of what he witnessed you would probably have suffered an amount of repercussion, nowhere near as much as the others, to say the least," Vortain said.

I nodded and bowed my head. "Am I given permission to leave?"

"Naturally. But before you go, speak to Haldis. There are a few who are scheduled for execution this week, I am sure that one of them can meet their fate early. It doesn't matter whom." I nodded, graciously accepting his offer. It would spare me the energy of hunting, something that was hard to do morally. I found myself consumed by the thought of morals when feeding. I was lucky this time, Haldis could tell me what each person did, making the choice easier. Easier. They were my prey, or that's how I was supposed to feel. Vortain left the cell, and I followed close behind, my vision starting to distort...

◆ ◆ ◆

My memory ended as I felt Cosette's hand upon my arm. I looked toward her, and she stopped; her expression one of expectancy.

"Were you listening to me at all? Or should I repeat myself?" she asked, her tone sharp, one completely different than several minutes ago.

"My apologies, I was focused on something else," I answered.

"I took notice. Before we enter Sathenne I think there is something you should know," she answered.

"You have my attention," I said, stopping and turning to her.

"If there are people there that are loyal to my father, and they recognize me, I could be putting everyone in danger. Undoubtedly, if my father catches wind of this, he will task Savantin with bringing me back. He won't do that... but he will have to do something to save face."

"We will not let that happen; I promise you that."

"I hope I can soon place trust in your words," Cosette replied, looking at her hands anxiously.

"Are you ready? We are almost there," I said and pushed the branches back from a large thick tree bordering the forest from the fields surrounding Sathenne. She looked toward the town in solace, the walls appearing regal in the hopeful reflection of her eyes. We walked across the field in silence now, Cosette's mood lightening significantly.

We reached the farm and I knocked twice, Emeirzi appearing at the door. She quietly let us both in, looking at the girl up and down before closing the door.

"And who is this?" she asked. "I don't run an inn."

"I lived in the forest just outside Sathenne. My betrothed brought you mushrooms every fourteenth day."

"Ah, yes," Emierzi said. "He does not come?"

"He's dead. Along with their friend," Cosette answered. Cahya brought her hand to her mouth as soon as the statement left her tongue, standing.

"He had the letters on him," I answered and tossed them on the floor in front of the fire. "He was going to Terrenveil."

"A traitor?" Dacian asked angrily.

"Maybe he was taking them to the king to plead our case," Cahya said in defense. "It is what he suggested just days ago."

"Cahya is right," Eshkan answered. "He thought that the path we are taking is dangerous. Maybe he wanted to see if he could solve it without us risking our lives."

"It wouldn't have mattered," Cosette said. "Cethin filled me in on the way here. If you're pleading a case to Ozrach regarding Savantin it will be impossible to win."

Geira entered, then, in clothing that suggested a formal event. "Alaies has agreed to meet with you. I will lead the way."

"Our gratitude," Eshkan stated. "Will you all be coming?"

"Yes, I think it best," Cahya answered and stood.

"If he does not extend the invitation to stay in the manor house, you can come back," Emierzi said. "I'll have enough stew to feed you. The men can sleep in the barn," she finished and shot a fiery glance at Eshkan.

We headed to town, Cosette traveling alongside Cahya and me. She observed us, listening to Eshkan and Dacian talk to each other. She seemed to feel comfort as she walked along the barren streets, her eyes moving across the landscape before us, obscured by houses. From this I could tell it had been quite some time that she had been away from life, been inside of a city. Her eyes displayed captivation, and reminiscence. As we neared the poorer parts of the city, we watched as children, covered in dirt and in ragged clothes, quickly snatched bread from the hands of shopkeepers. Their clothes weren't much better, their old, worn stands slowly greeting death. Much of the province appeared this way, old, shoddy. A cat passed by with a mouse clasped in her teeth. She quickly darted into an alleyway, disappearing into a large crack on a building.

"The letters," Cahya said quietly. "Did he have all of them?"

"It appeared so. I was too quick to think he would betray us."

"These are strange times, Cethin, stressful. What befell Ophidian was tragic. After Jadoq, it was hard to trust anyone. Morard said that he wanted to see justice, he just didn't agree with your methods. What happened to him was because of the path he chose. While unfortunate, none of us can take ownership over his death." I said nothing in return, only offering a nod. He would still live if he had stayed at the farm.

We reached the house, only slightly larger than the rest, lanterns hanging from the roof. Geira spoke briefly to the guard posted at the front door before entering. The guard sleepily acknowledged her and allowed us entry. The house was scented with cloves, myrrh and burning teakwood. We reached a large room at the back of the house, A broad-shouldered man just a few inches shorter than I was speaking to an older man and a boy who looked to be no older than Cosette. They appeared to be looking over a map before their attention was turned to our arrival. The elder and boy were dismissed, and Alaies stood, calling us forward with two waves of his fingers.

"I'll admit, you weren't wrong when you said they looked like mercenaries," Alaies answered. "Will you be staying, Geira?"

"If you would like me to, I will," she answered.

"Yes, do stay. Perhaps you may catch things that need attention," he said. "Please, sit. If what Geira says is accurate, and I've no assumption it will not be, we will be here for a very long time. Thurlowe said he would send aid, but I didn't think it to be... so unconventional given my request. Who leads you?"

"We've no leader," Eshkan stated. "He was killed during the invasion."

"Geira briefly mentioned that you were looking to join our rebellion but did not say why. You are free from Terrenveil, yes? So why are you here?"

"Those two and I, we were assassins."

"Assassins?" Alaies laughed. "I never thought there would be a day that there'd be assassins within these walls. Continue."

"I collected information on our marks and once successfully put down many. I've traveled across land and over sea. Watching, planning, charting. We would erase people who were plotting evil deeds, mostly dealing in artifacts and hexes," Eshkan continued. "Our leader's advisor betrayed him. For reasons unknown to us, it led to the slaughter of our people, and the destruction of our home. We shall delve deeper in a moment, but we wish to aid you."

"Sathenne isn't much, a town self-sustained on the hard work of its citizens, completely reliant on travelers and passersby. We gain nothing from the kingdom, no resources that are sorely needed, no funding. It is worse down here near the edge of the border; we are an old unfed dog, lying so ignored that if we didn't hunt on our own, we would starve," Alaies began.

"Do not let the outward appearance of Sathenne fool you. She may look like a gem, but she is hurting inside. If it weren't for my confidants and me, she would be in shambles. We are lucky that the king does not venture down here, or else our income would be seen hauled away in wagons to his avaricious fingers, spent on nothing more than wine and expensive trinkets for his covetous queen. We need this rebellion. To survive we need to act. If we do not, then we will all drown. It will only be a matter of time before they reach us here. We have a palpable conflict amidst us, and we cannot delay our response," Alaies said, sighing. "What we are planning, it is very dangerous, but we cannot see our people mistreated any longer. What world can we give to our children if our oppressors are our own king and queen? We're rallying as many as we can, and we plan to take the Mountain."

"One of our friends thought that was the safest route as well. He now lies dead in a ditch, just miles from here," I answered.

"You question our strategy?" Alaies asked, surprise and irritation in his voice.

"Sending an army of rebels to dethrone a king is dangerous. Especially when Mauros is occupying borders. What if they invade while you sneak into Terrenveil? Now would be the best time to usurp the throne with the army as dispersed as it is, but how many men do you think are left behind to protect the city?" Eshkan asked.

"What is your proposal, then? We wait? Don't think we haven't thought about those details in our plans, we are not dense."

"You mistake his meaning," I answered. "There is one issue that I am sure you have not overlooked, but I surmise that you haven't exactly figured out how you are going to handle it."

Alaies sighed and looked toward Geira. "So, we are either stuck with the king until after Mauros invades, or we launch our attack in hopes that they do not," he said and began to move from the table.

"I think it best to replan and re-strategize, only so that everyone involved doesn't die," Eshkan said. "What point would that prove to the rest of the provinces? If you are cut down, it will make them hesitate in raising their voices."

"We were given an outline of where Savantin will be traveling by one of my spies, though I am almost certain that he will not follow it," he answered. "One of them hasn't reported back from Lord's Valley yet, which is alarming. If he has fallen into the hands of the legion, I hope he was able to take his own life before they began their torture."

"What if Mauros doesn't invade?" Eshkan asked. "What if in a few weeks, the armies start to clear out of the provinces? You could strike then; they would suspect it least."

"From the information my spy is giving me, they are leaving plenty in number."

"Strike while they sleep. Or better yet, poison them," Dacian stated. "Our brothers were given such courtesy."

"Rythran," I answered. "It is the same poison that was used to kill our kin."

"It's...low but it would ensure victory," Alaies answered. "It seems that this is the best course of action. I will have to notify the other provincials. Unfortunately, all I can do is propose the idea."

"Stress to them that it would be in their best interest to agree," Eshkan replied. "This is what we were born to do. Assassinate. It is the only outcome I can think of at present moment."

"What happened to you?"

"When our leader's advisor betrayed him, he sent a series of letters to two people notating the location of a sword and an artifact thought to have been housed on the island. These letters were written to someone still of mystery to us, and Savantin."

Alaies let a deep breath out and turned from the table walking toward the fire. He spun back around and placed his hands on the table, hanging his head for a moment before speaking. "What then? Did the traitor survive? Is that someone we need to worry about too?"

"No. Savantin killed him. Though the condition of his corpse suggested his death wasn't quick, he was lucky that he was killed before we reached the tower," Dacian said.

"It was torn down in conflagration, set by this monster's men. He was of the belief that we held something he was searching for but left empty handed. Nothing remains now, and those who we saved probably didn't survive their wounds. The villagers were sent to a citadel and locked in, where they watched the fire take the roof above them, screaming to get out of the building. Our brothers in arms were not spared from this also, their corpses left to rot in our quarters. As far as the eye could see the only sight was ash and smoke, and the only thing you could smell was the burning. The sick smell of people you knew, burning alive," Cahya answered. She suddenly got up, holding her stomach and heading toward the door. We could hear her getting sick in a room down the hall.

"You said he was looking for something?" Alaies asked, turning from where Cahya had exited to me.

"He was."

I did not take my eyes off the door and was about to go to her when Alaies spoke, this time slowly. "This island, it is in Cilevdan, yes?"

"Yes," Eshkan answered. "There was a mark left behind, one that caused us to initially seek out Thurlowe."

"A mark?"

"The Mask of Death," Dacian answered. "Carved into their chests. We are the last three assassins who remain."

"The Mask... I've always known it better than to call it a myth. I am surprised to discover Savantin has anything to do with it, though. But it would explain why whenever traces of them show up in their aftermath; it's completely erased from conversation," Alaies said. "There are only three of you left?"

Eshkan offered a nod. It was then Cahya returned inside, running her hand through her cropped hair to remove it from her face. She sat quietly and I looked at her, pushing my hood back slightly to show her my eyes. She nodded slowly, a sign to show me that she was alright. Alaies rubbed his hands together in front of the fire and looked over to me, shaking his head. It finally turned into a nod, leading into his next conjecture. "His coadjutant must be with the Mask. It's impossible he wouldn't be."

"This is of some importance?"

"Yes. Dire importance. If we can somehow prove that it would be...there would be no proving it. Erase it from thought."

"Who is he?"

"His coadjutant. Ohric is his name. As I said earlier, Savantin made it very clear that he has naught to do with religion. He allows his men to practice quietly but only if it does not affect their duty."

"He denies them practice when the monarchy is pledged to Araele?" Eshkan asked.

"Now you see why he is a dangerous man. In any kingdom whose monarchs are absolute and unshakable, the people would follow their religion devoutly. We've all seen it." Alaies sighed. "Whenever we're called to the mountain, patrons or their emissaries, we notice a pattern. If nothing concerns Savantin, which most of us hope for, he isn't present. The king conducts with the help of his advisor. A man I don't care for, but I digress, when Savantin is present he takes complete control of the room until he deems he is no longer needed, and leaves at will. What troubles me, deeply, is that his coadjutant is devoutly and zealously Araelian. If he is in any way involved with the Mask..."

"He poses as a holy man?" Cahya asked.

"No, that's just the thing. He doesn't pose. He believes that she grants him her words. That she graces him with her presence. He believes that he sees her. His mind is twisted, shaped by whatever misfortunes had passed through him as a child. He believes that he is her soldier and will do whatever is commanded of him."

"If Savantin has such an aversion to religion why have a holy man as his right hand?" Eshkan asked.

"Gods know," Alaies huffed. "It's obviously for a reason, unless he just likes the kid. Savantin isn't very social. None of us have seen him other than at the Mountain. When Ozrach needs the legion's help in the provinces Savantin arrives with men that he knows will do the job to his standards and disappears. I've only ever been able to speak to him once. He is very intimidating. His reputation, how he carries himself. But I didn't see the eyes of a monster. I saw torment. Something is tormenting him. I've seen the look before. On a man who was drowned by his demons. When we spoke, I asked him one question, to see what kind of man he was. But then I saw very different eyes. He is no man," Alaies said and looked at us, his glare deep and unmoving. The dread that lay behind them was thick and embedded. "Rumors circulate throughout the kingdom, but they are not tales. You would be foolish to think otherwise."

"Alaies, what are you talking about?" Cahya asked.

"Savantin is from Seraphician. That land is unlike ours. Here men walk among us, but he is no man. I'm sure you are familiar with your knowledge of artifacts and hexes."

"A Seraphice. Devourer of man. Halbane's curse," Dacian said suddenly.

"The provincials fear him and believe we must find a way to dispose of him, but I don't think death is the answer. Everyone is quick to kill these days. You," Alaies said and looked toward Cosette. "You have been quiet this entire time."

"I lived in Terrenveil once. I know your enemies. What they've proposed is your only chance."

"Remove your hood, I wish to get a better look at you," he said and stood.

"She doesn't want to show her face," I stated.

"You forget whose house it is you are guest of."

"It's okay," Cosette said. "I've heard enough, I think I'm safe here." She took a deep breath and removed her hood, her hair shining brightly from the flames of the hearth. Alaies' eyes widened. "Princess... everyone thought you to be dead."

"And that is how I wish it to stay," Cosette returned. "A long time ago, Savantin helped me escape the castle. But after seeing your people, the children, your buildings, it's time my silence is broken. I will aid you, but we mustn't let them know I still live. If they know, they will send for me. The only person they would send is Savantin. I already assured them that he wouldn't take me back there, but he would have to do something to prove that he tried. He will go to any length."

"There are many places we would be able to hide you... you can..."

"Let me explain this another way. The first time he told my parents that I was dead. Likely used the corpse of one of the bandits he killed, destroyed her face so they would not question it. This time wouldn't be that simple."

"But still, you are heir to the throne, do you understand what position this places us in?"

"I have still not decided whether or not I want that to be placed on my shoulders," Cosette said. "Birthright means nothing to me if I have no will."

"The provinces that are loyal to the monarchy will want to see you placed," Alaies stated. "If you are not, then it may escalate to a civil war."

"If I appoint someone, they will have no foundation on which to start one. Until several minutes ago, I did not want to make it known to any of you my identity, Cethin was the only one who knew. I will travel with them until I feel it is right to return. With the legion on the move, it may not be smart for me to remain here."

"Where will you go?"

"To Morrenvahl," I answered.

"Morrenvahl?" Alaies asked, unable to keep surprise from his voice. "First assassins, next a Sardon."

"I need to seek council with my people. And it is one place they would not look for her. I do not speak for everyone, but that is my destination."

"I follow you, Cethin," Cahya said.

"As do we," Dacian stated, looking to Eshkan who nodded. Alaies then looked at Cosette who crossed her arms. Alaies moved his hand to his jaw in thought. "So, I propose that we hold off on our attack until the legion begins to clear out of the provinces, and coordinate attacks to thin their numbers as much as possible. I'm sorry princess, I do not know how to address the matter of your appearance here to the one who is helping me plan our rebellion."

"You may tell him, but it is as I said. If word of my life gets out, he will come here with the authority to do whatever he needs to in order to take me back there. He won't, but if he is as determined in his current venture as they say, his patience will be worn thin. He will resort to anything to get back to the task at hand."

"I will send my son, so that it is not in writing," Alaies said. "Geira, please retrieve him."

"I will go instead," she said.

"What? You have never left Sathenne, never ridden on the roads."

"Assign to me guards, then. You needn't involve the life of your son."

"He knew what was at stake, Geira."

"If something happens to you, who will take your place?" she asked. "Send me with two of your most trusted. We will reach Lord's Valley in only a few days."

"And if the legion beats you there?"

"I will take some of Emierzi's spices with me to sell at the market. You know that it will be seen as routine. There are very few Rustanzi in Cilevdan, spices from our homeland are sought after."

"As much as I do not like it, I cannot argue that. Go, but please. Be careful."

"Once I have alerted him, I will return."

Alaies nodded, Geira making her exit. "You see how dedicated my people are to this. Geira may be young, but she is smart. She and her sister came here when they were younger still, their parents were arrested by Neraea's temple soldiers. They were killed for heresy."

"Gods above," Dacian said.

"People are murdered for different practices?" Cahya asked, shock in her voice.

"The queen is a devout Araelian. The soldiers that make their rounds here are to confiscate and correct anything or anyone that forsakes the goddess. It happens a lot less often than it used to, now that Savantin is commander of the legion. I'll give him that. Because of his aversion to religion, he spared no men to her crusade. Our only problem with Savantin is his role in the kingdom and the unpredictability of his wants."

"What do you mean?" Cahya asked. "Unpredictability?"

"We largely agreed the only issue we had with him was that he is commander of the king's legion. The idea was once tossed around that we could convince him to betray the king. It's a dangerous situation. But we do not know what he wants. Right now, it seems to be this current venture you speak of... but what comes after?"

Cosette spoke, suddenly, "Before I was supposed to be wed, we spoke of the throne. I told him that I didn't want the throne, I didn't want that life. He insisted that he didn't want it either and had something else planned. Neither of us felt loyalty to the king or queen," she said and looked at all of us quickly before continuing. "He doesn't want the throne... so I don't know why he's keeping his role, why he wouldn't just leave too. Unless... unless he's using the kingdom, his position in it so he can find whatever he's looking for."

"It would make sense," Alaies stated. "But either way, if he comes between us and overthrowing Ozrach, we must deal with him."

It was then that someone came through the door, a look of panic on his face. "Alaies... there's something... It's Siska," he said between heavy breaths. "She's not returned."

"The task wasn't exactly a simple one, she could be..."

"Her horse arrived at the gate just moments ago."

"I'm going after her," Alaies said and turned toward the chair beside the hearth, grabbing the sword that was sitting in it. He walked with a slight limp, though that didn't discourage him.

"I will aid you," Dacian stated and rose. I nodded, standing also.

"We sent her to the Alcades to see if she could chart any movement beyond the Glendoryn. From the vantage point there, you can see the Mountain through a spyglass."

"About a day's travel, then?" Eshkan asked. "If you take the route through the foothills and up the Sine."

"Probably the best route," Alaies agreed. "Spawning season is over which means that there will be no bears on the banks. We leave immediately."

"I wish you luck. I will remain here with the others," Eshkan said, to which I nodded.

I turned toward Cahya, handing her the key. "Guard this. If someone comes looking for it, do what you must to escape. And take the girl with you. She trusted me, she will trust you too."

"You have my word," Cahya said softly. "We won't go far."

"I will see you back here soon," I answered.

Alaies looked toward a woman that had just walked in, grabbing his coat from near the fire. "These are guests of the house, treat them as such." She nodded, and we made our exit, reaching the stables within moments.

"We sent her three days ago. For her horse to return here... I fear the worst. She will be hard to track up there, though it shouldn't have started snowing yet."

"We'll find her," Dacian assured. "This is what we were meant for."

Our horses were well rested, taking the path quickly as ordered. Within the hour, we could hear the river, and within a couple of more, we made distance up the bank. Alaies was a quiet man, which was preferable to me. I spoke more in the past couple of days than I had in months. Dacian kept silent as well, watching the surrounding area carefully. While spawning season was over, as Alaies pointed out, there could still be predators waiting in the trees. Food was about to become scarce, and animals that relied on the hunt bolder. Dawn came quickly, the sky lightening up before it became alive in reddish pinks and purples. As the sun rose over the base of the mountain, the river reflected it. Alaies slowed his horse, dismounting and leading it to the river's edge. I followed, Dacian stopping just behind me. My horse walked toward the edge and lowered her neck, drinking.

"We aren't far, now. There is an old path up the mountain that she would have taken to get to the lookout. The Sathenian guards found the path ages ago, there isn't much up there now aside from an old stone slab."

"Does the sun rise over it?" Dacian asked.

"Yes, it faces the sun."

"Basilin be praised," he sighed. "Most likely belonging to the old gods."

We crossed the river after a few miles, continuing up the peak to where it opened, the aforementioned slab sitting on the edge of the cliff. I dismounted, walking over to it. At the base there were marks in the soil where it looked like something was dragged down the mountain on the other side. I followed it, looking at the brush growing a few feet away. Glass, and blood. I walked past the charred sticks that were used to make a fire and crouched down to the ground.

"It's about a day old," I said and touched it, working the bloodied dirt off my fingers. "I can smell the iron, whoever it belongs to ingests a lot of meat. Who else knew she was coming up here?"

"Only Refaem. I sent him here a day after her, to take her some supplies."

"There is only sign of one struggle," I answered. "Did Refaem return? Was that not him who alerted you of her disappearance?"

"No. Whatever happened to Siska must have happened to him as well," Alaies stated.

"We shall soon find out. There is a trail that leads down the mountain. Blood, and something being dragged," I answered, climbing back onto my horse. "We shall follow it until it can no longer lead us."

Alaies nodded, following me, Dacian after him. The scent of another joined in, signs of a scuffle just below us. Embedded hoofprints and the large markings of a body, as if someone was rolling around. A piece of cloth was caught on a branch nearby, footprints, and scuff marks leading toward it. Dacian pulled the cloth from the branch, smelling it. "Mint, blood."

"Siska," Alaies said. "She used mint to keep the insects away from her."

"It looks like she put up a fight," Dacian answered.

"She doesn't give up. She knows I'd send after her, so there will be more clues left for us. She was taught that as a girl."

I stopped my horse suddenly, listening through the trees. Quickly, I held two fingers toward Dacian, signing for silence. I dismounted, pulling Seligsara from my side. I motioned for Dacian to follow, and I pressed my side against a tree, looking forward.

"Two, likely looking for firewood before dusk," I said and looked up toward the slowly darkening sky. "We need to find their camp."

"I'll follow one, you follow the other?" Dacian asked.

"Leave that one to me," I stated and gestured toward the one wearing blue.

Dacian responded in a nod, crouching and moving through the trees quickly. Alaies reached my side, whispering. "Who are they?"

"We're following them back to their camp. Remain out of sight but follow me," I answered and moved through the trees. I stopped suddenly, one of the men splitting off and heading in Dacian's direction. I stopped, watching as the man reached a tree several feet from me, tearing a low-hanging branch from its parent. Alaies made himself small, ducking by a boulder and a dead tree.

As the man passed, I continued alongside him, Alaies keeping distance. He collected a few more branches, looking into the thick of the trees and shouting, "Dunn!"

After receiving no reply, he grasped another branch, placing it on top of the others and turning around, causing us to follow. He exited the forest through a clearing, and we stopped as he approached a caravan. There were ten horses, a wagon and a steady fire. People surrounded it, a spit on top with the scent of rabbit pouring from the lid. Across from the wagon and closer to the outside of the circle was a man tied up, blood all over his wrists and chest.

"Rafaem," Alaies said and moved forward.

I placed an arm on his chest, pushing him back. "Not yet," I answered. "We wait for Dacian."

"What if he doesn't come? Rafaem is injured, that means Siska must be…"

"Patience," I answered. Several minutes passed, men laughing from around the fire. "There are far too many of them. You aren't armed."

"Where is Dunn?" one of them asked, standing. A feminine voice.

"Must be out there gathering," the man we tailed returned. A bowl was thrown at him, the conversation escalating.

"Why do you think I sent the both of you together? There are wolves out there, Bryn. Bears."

"I'll go find him and—"

"It's too late to find him now!" she snapped. "We'll have to wait until morning. Extra silver to the person who finds his corpse."

"Come now, Neterra, do you really think he's…"

"Something got him, 'else he'd be back by now," she said and stood, heading toward the wagon. She grabbed a crossbow from it, fitting it with an bolt. "I'll be sleeping with this tonight. I suggest you do the same."

"Neterra!" a man said from the opposite side of the clearing, walking into camp with another. "No sign of the girl."

"She won't make it very far. She's bleeding. She'll come back for her friend."

"Siska," Alaies whispered. I turned and looked behind us, Dacian appearing through two bushes slowly.

"Where's your mark?" I asked.

"Drifters," Dacian answered. "The one that killed my mark didn't see me, but he wasn't alone. Couldn't have been. We don't have much time before he comes this way." Alaies' pulse raised in panic.

"This doesn't leave us with many options," I said.

"Wait it out," Dacian suggested and let out a sigh. "Or attempt to befriend a side. It looks like they have enough weapons to be able to fend them off," he continued and gestured toward the wagon.

"Do we climb?" Alaies asked.

"I have a better idea," I answered and grabbed a rock from the ground before me. "If the Drifters can't follow scent, they can follow voice. While they're engaged, we rescue Refaem, and look for Siska."

"Our horses..." Alaies answered.

"If they still live, we'll return for those, too."

"I'll go and..."

"Stay here. I know you wish to help, but now is not the time," I answered and threw the rock as hard as I could toward the camp, hitting the wagon.

"What was that?" a man asked and stood, another startling out of sleep.

Neterra stood, aiming in the direction of the sound. "Dunn stop playing games," she answered. "You'll get yourself killed."

Dacian reached onto the ground and grasped something, tossing it toward the camp. It struck the wagon and one of the men walked over, picking the stones up from the ground. He held them up toward Neterra and she raised her crossbow.

"Reveal yourselves, or I'm sending after you," she stated. Within seconds of uttering those words, she motioned two men in our direction. I looked toward Dacian and nodded, readying my blade. As they came through the thicket and were out of sight, I pulled one of them in toward me, covering his mouth and stabbing him through the back of the neck. Dacian downed the other man and pulled his corpse into the bushes beside him.

"Ermin, Lark, what do you see?" she asked. After several moments of silence, she walked to the wagon and set her weapon down, grabbing a sword. "Something's out there."

"We've been here long enough, move," I said and quickly moved through the bushes and around the woods to lessen the distance between us and Rafaem.

"If there are drifters out there…"

"Then they'll know where the corpses are. I'm hoping this will lead them right into camp," I said. "And if they've left, we'll pick them off until there's no one left. Find a good place to hide."

Alaies nodded, searching the darkness quickly before finding a fallen tree.

"Stay close to the fire!" Neterra shouted. "If it's an animal, it won't come that close," she stopped, as the sounds of twigs snapping echoed in from the other side of the clearing, close to where we once were.

"Show yourself!" she shouted. "If you're looking to rob us, you won't leave here alive."

A man emerged from the other side of the thicket; his hands raised. "I aim to rob no one," he said.

"Who are you, what are you doing out here?" she asked, raising her sword.

"That's no way to greet someone that's unarmed."

"Something is out there killing my men. And as it stands, you're the only survivor. Who are you?" she asked.

"Who I am doesn't matter," he answered. "I have lost my friends as well. Perhaps we can find them together."

"Tragun, search him," she said. A man stood from the fire, nearing the stranger with a dagger in hand. The stranger raised his hands slightly higher, waiting as Tragun approached him. He began to search his coat pockets, shaking his head in Neterra's direction.

"He's got nothing on him," Tragun answered.

"Nothing at all?"

"No. No weapon, no belongings, nothing."

"What are you doing all the way out here?" Neterra asked.

"I got lost hunting. I was chased by wolves. Lost my bow. I'm trying to make my way back to Shinton. Perhaps you could point me in the right direction?"

"I look like a map to you? Keep moving."

"Surely you know a landmark, a path, something," the man continued.

"I said keep moving," she replied, raising her bow.

"You'll regret that," the man said and quickly grabbed Tragun, relinquishing his sword and using him as a shield.

Neterra laughed and shot Tragun in the heart, the man continuing to hold him upright. It was then the other two drifters came from the trees, attacking her men. I watched as they fought, looking at Dacian. "When do we plan on moving for the captive?"

"Perhaps now while they are engaged," he replied. I nodded, jerking my head once in a motion to where Rafaem was bound. I moved closer to where the fight ensued, the men quickly tearing through Neterra's forces. It was after she was silenced that I revealed myself, which gauged a surprised reaction from the men.

"State your purpose." The question was posed by the man who approached the bandits initially, his men watching me closely.

"We were only tracking our own," I said and pointed toward Rafaem. Dacian freed him, helping him to his feet. "These people took him."

"And you'd let us do all of the killing for you?" he said, laughing to himself after. "I don't blame you, though you look capable enough."

"Your affairs do not concern us," I answered.

"And you were only here for him then, that right?" he asked. I hesitated a moment, debating whether or not I'd reveal Siska. The man looked down and shook his head. "Must we kill you, too?"

"I fail to see why anyone else must die," I answered, looking at their hands. Weapons relinquished from their dead. Neterra's bow was still on the ground, kept by her corpse.

"No one else, so long as you aren't here for the reason we are. We're here for the wagon. Keep moving and no one else will die."

The man's words fell short as he looked at Rafaem, who had begun to speak. "Please... They have families."

I looked between the two, pulling Seligsara. "What's in the wagon?"

"I'm afraid now we must reconsider death," he said and held a sword up toward me. He charged, attacking, but withdrawing himself at the last moment as if anticipating me to strike. "Fight me you coward," he taunted. I listened to his heart, watched his feet. His left wasn't firmly planted on the ground. Prior injury. I lunged forward, turning to his left side. He had moved to parry, and I slid Seligsara through his thigh, stabbing him through the back and into his chest. After he fell to the ground absent breath, his men braced themselves, gauging me.

"Don't mistake my hesitation for weakness, I'm offering you a choice," I said suddenly, their images burned into my sight.

"Not a chance, Sardon," one of them spat.

"Have it your way," I said and spun Seligsara once. It was then an arrow sailed through the trees, hitting the man who taunted me in the back, piercing his chest. Alaies sprung for Neterra's crossbow and aimed it at the other. I smirked, nodding.

"On your knees," Alaies said. "Now." The man laughed and Alaies forced the bow forward. "Now!"

"Acting tough until your last breath, that it?" A girl walked from the trees then. She could be no older than nineteen, her reddish-brown hair braided and pulled back. She had a decorative cloth covering one eye, a scar peeking from under it. The girl reached the man's back, kicking his knees in, which caused him to fall forward. She grabbed onto his hair, pulling a dagger from the scabbard attached to his side.

"Where were you meeting them?" she asked.

"I knew I should have killed you on that hill," he said, causing her to slice his cheek.

"Siska!" Alaies said, retrieving no reaction from her.

"You won't get anything further from me!" the man said. "You're nothing but a child thinking she can change what's always been."

"I'm affecting you somewhat, else you wouldn't be hurling insults," she answered and revisited the cut she left on his cheek.

"Siska..."

"There are people in that wagon. People they're planning to sell," she said, looking at Alaies, then between me and Dacian. "It was these three that found Rafaem and I on the peak. The one you carved up over there came first, no weapons. Said he was tired and wanted to rest, asked if we had any food. We were distrusting at first, but he wasn't armed so we let him stay. Then these two came," she said and stuck the blade in his cheek again. He cried and she pulled his hair back, ordering him to silence. "We fought them. We descended the peak, running toward the woods when I was grabbed. I fought that one off and that's when we found this camp. We took our chances," she said and took a breath. "We were armed, tried to explain to their leader what was happening, but she didn't believe us. Tied Rafaem to that post. I managed to escape after one of her men grabbed me. I bit his throat and spat it on the ground. One of them called me a nonhuman and they chased me with fire. I made it down the hill and was able to hide. A few of them gave up and returned here, but I killed the last."

"What about the wagon?" I asked. She narrowed her eyes at me and looked to Alaies, shaking the look after a few seconds.

"I asked that one why before I killed him. He was smart and talked. He said they were planning to sell them to Archegals."

Dacian and I looked at each other then. The man on the ground moved to strike Siska and she plunged the dagger into his tricep, twisting it. "I know you were planning on taking the wagon for yourselves. Which means you know where they are."

"Ah Fuck!" he wailed, his breathing heavy, labored. "They choose when to meet us," he said finally. "We send word when we have their shipment and they come. They pay bandits to gather them, raid the villages. Half first and half after. Then they pay us to kill the bandits and give them the humans. We get to keep whatever we find and the gold they were paid, and they get the wagon."

"Filthy creatures," Alaies said.

"Where were you taking them?" Siska asked.

"To Shinton," he said. "But only because the road there is so long. By the time word reached them, they could have met us on the road." Siska's face twisted in anger, and she pulled the dagger from the man's arm, plunging it into his neck. She kicked his corpse over, taking several breaths before moving her hands over her mouth and nose, weeping.

Dacian freed Rafaem, who made haste to Siska's side, hugging her shoulders. "It's okay now," he said.

I looked at the wagon, signaling Dacian to follow me. He readied his weapon, and I pulled the cover off, seeing two women, a man, and three children bound and packed into the bottom. They started to make noise, and I reached in, pulling a small girl upward. Dacian cut her bounds and the tie around her mouth, brushing her hair from her face. "She's cold. We need to get them to safety."

"We can take them to Sathenne," Alaies said. "The inn will have warmth and food. Gods know how long they've been without it."

Once the children were out of the wagon, I helped the women outward, freeing them of their bonds. The first hugged me, burying her face in my chest, crying furiously. I made eyes to Dacian who shrugged, helping the man to his feet. The woman joined with the children, and as Dacian cut the tie from the man's mouth, he spoke. "Thank you. Thank you for freeing us."

"Where did they take you from?" Alaies asked.

"Kenstead," he answered. Alaies shook his head and looked toward the wood. "We're quite a ways from Kenstead."

"You mentioned Sathenne?"

"Yes. Sathenne is my city. We will go immediately, given that we're finished here," Alaies said, looking toward us.

"Shinton," Siska said suddenly. "It's not far from here."

"We don't know if they've made contact," I answered. "But I'm willing to investigate."

"Archegals..." Dacian said. "The same ones that ambushed you and Eshkan?"

"Must be. Unless there are more than we thought," I returned. The world outside Ophidian was a dark and cold one.

"We should get these people back to Sathenne first," Alaies said. "You can catch the road to Shinton from the west gate. I doubt they will leave without a wagon. Which means we need to take it."

"Alright. But I'm going with," Siska said, looking at me. I returned a nod, Alaies opening his mouth to speak, but took to a brief silence.

"You're right," he decided. "If these people were taken from Kenstead, it wouldn't stop bandits from taking our people if they travel outside walls. I'd trust no other with the task."

"Archegals mean bloodshed," I answered simply. "Eshkan and I were ambushed on our way to your city. They... they're vicious in their means of torture."

"They cannot be left to continue to hurt people," Siska said.

The woman who hugged me spoke; her eyes big against the fire's light. "What can we do to help?"

"Rest. For now," Alaies said. "When you return to Kenstead, educate your village. Let them know that it was bandits. Perhaps Sathenne can be of aid. Or Esperanus. It's closer. I'll send one of my men on horseback. Should only take a day and a half."

"They won't be needing their horses," Rafaem said and looked toward the lot of them. They had calmed, grazing.

"I will take one and gather our own," Dacian said. "I'll meet you back at Sathenne."

I returned a nod when the man from the wagon spoke, walking toward Dacian. "I'll help. I'm a herdsman in Kenstead. Known for its livestock."

"Be careful Alvis," the older of the women said, keeping the children close to her. Alvis kissed her on her forehead, following Dacian.

"I'll steer the wagon." Alaies said. "Rafaem, you help guide me. You won't be any good trying to steer a horse your own, with your hands like that."

I hadn't paid any attention to the man's hands before. The skin on the top of each was severely burned from rope, his wrists in kind. Alaies climbed up into the wagon, holding his hand against his left leg suddenly. "Will you make it to town?" Rafaem asked.

"Yes. I'll be fine," he said and looked toward me before looking at the crossbow he had placed at the wagons' front. "I'll keep this up here with me. Cethin if you don't mind posting yourself at the back of the wagon in case we run into any trouble."

I nodded in affirmation, taking the reins of a horse passed to me by Siska. She climbed on the horse next to it, taking one last look around the camp before riding to the wagon's back. It seemed I was going to have company. We continued through the forest, on what looked like a merchant's path back toward the main road. It would be too dangerous to take the wagon up the peak, Alaies decided. The man knew the land better than I, so I offered no protest. The journey back was quiet, mostly, with the children in the wagon chattering. The matron shushed them a few times, the oldest of the three mimicking her movements. The other woman clutched the pendant that was around her neck, speaking softly to herself. I took to watching the trees, focusing on the sound that came from them.

It was midday when we reached Sathenne, Alaies pulling the wagon through the gates. Several guards met him at the front of the wagon, first taking his order to show the people from Kenstead to the inn. The elder and the boy from before were present, Alaies signaling both Siska and I forward.

"Cethin, this is Kratch, and my son, Wren. I may as well introduce you now, seeing as you will be very involved in our plot."

"We've met with your friends. Master Eshkan, and Lady Cahya," Wren said. "At the manor house, they're awaiting your return."

"One could say we're impatient," Cahya said and walked forward, Eshkan behind her. "Were you successful? Who are these people?"

"Bandits on the road. They were hired to steal them," Siska said, fire in her voice.

"For what purpose?" Cahya asked. "Do we know if they worked alone, are they dead?"

"They're all very dead," Siska said. "Rafaem and I were chased down the peak to where the bandits were. They were going to take us, too. Rafaem got caught, told me to run but I wasn't going to leave him, wasn't going to leave any of them. And that's why we're going back."

"Oh?" Eshkan asked.

I looked at him and sighed. "Seems our trouble with Archegals isn't over yet. They hired the bandits but had a side scheme going. Their mercenaries kill the bandits and take the gold, the Archegals get the wagon."

"They're dealing in human lives?" Cahya said and shook her head. "I'm coming too. They'll sense you once they gain sight. It will be better if they only see us," she continued, looking at Siska, who nodded.

"I know you're not implying I stay here. That's out of the question," I said, near defensively.

"Of course, you aren't. You'll be covered in the wagon."

"We've already saved these people," Dacian said, "What more must we do?"

"There have to be more of them out there," Siska interjected. "I don't know where you've come from, or why, but right now we may be all these people have. The only ones that can protect them. The smaller outlying villages don't have walls. Maybe a guard or two."

"I'm with her," Cahya said. "It is just that we protect the innocent. You can't have forgotten our vocation already," she said, looking toward Dacian who slumped in posture, nodding.

"I forget myself. Forgive me. What shall I do?"

"Speak to Cosette. About the Mountain, see if you can learn something," I answered.

"Doing this will show the other provinces that we are able to take care of ourselves," Alaies said. "That may be the push we need to gather more of an alliance."

Eshkan nodded and offered a small shrug. "Garner hope and take out some slavers in the process. Something you should probably write your patrons about."

"Let us go inside and speak more. Siska, take whatever you need. Meet us at the house when you return."

"Got it," Siska answered, signaling Cahya and I to follow.

Cahya secured her ax to her side, fastening the leather gauntlets on her arms. Gifts from Thurlowe. "How far is Shinton?" she asked.

"It's quite a way from here. However, the only road in is not far, an hour or two," Siska said. "I assume that we'll be stopped before we reach it. What do you intend to tell them? They hired both the bandits and the drifters. They've seen their faces. They won't believe us if we say we killed them all."

"What exactly transpired?" Cahya asked.

"The drifters killed the bandits. We killed the drifters. Siska interrogated the last alive, that's how we learned of this," I answered.

"So, we're drifters too," Cahya decided. "We were going to rob the bandits while they were sleeping. Once they were killed, we finished the job."

"Sounds solid," Siska said. "Solid enough that they'll believe us."

"And if they don't, Cethin will know when to aid us if necessary," Cahya stated and headed toward the wagon. "Do you know how to steer one?"

"I do. I've been doing this since I was eight years old. Alaies is my uncle. My parents were killed by bandits when I was very young. Two, three. When I was old enough to realize, I asked him why I didn't look like his children, and he told me. He's never been the sort of man to lie. That's when I said I wanted to learn how to protect others. So that if the bandits ever returned, I could kill them. He didn't refuse, had the village guards train me when I was six. Alaies contacted someone from outside the city, a warrior who went by Bex. I trained under their methods for years. It was very hard. I'd almost given up once. But I didn't. I returned to Sathenne when I turned thirteen and I've been head of the guard ever since."

"A girl after my own heart," Cahya smiled. "I was also head of the guard where we come from. The ruler of our land trusted no other, thought no other capable. He once told me that I needed to act with my strength, but also compassion. He said anyone can have strength, but the strength of compassion is equally as important," she looked at me then. "It's a shame that someone so cruel was also so wise."

"Someone recently told me that we're all capable of terrible things, but if we can also act in kindness, if we mostly act in kindness, we're supposed to consider some sort of forgiveness. Almost sounded like something Vortain would say. Even in his death we're ever so reminded," I said, gaining an inquisitive look from Cahya. I looked in the back of the wagon, hay lining the bottom. "I'll be listening," I answered, and climbed in. Cahya looked at me, her eyes meeting mine briefly before she pulled the cover over the wagon. It reminded me of the night she first kissed me, many moons ago...

◆ ◆ ◆

The night was young, stars scattered across the sky with no pattern or reason. She said that when the night was upon us and the sky free of clouds that the Serpent could be seen above the tower. Constellations, master called them, were where the stars met in outline, creating shapes and pictures. It was hard for me to believe. Upon looking at the sky I saw only a network of chaos that glimmered against the striking dark. We continued to climb the stairs on the outside of the furthermost tower, free of guards due to her orders. It was a dangerous and foolish notion, to be out here alone with her by the off chance that someone's eyes wandered from their post, or worse, an attack occurred. But I cared little, if at all. Tonight, only she existed, only this moment.

She picked up on my hesitation and grabbed my hand, pulling me up toward the rooftops, assuring me that it would not be long now. I could only listen to her, her soft voice kept low. She had a smile on her face, carefree. She was happy, and if it ended tonight, she would have no regret about how she spent her day. We finally reached the old stone roof. She walked ahead of me, stopping near the other side and looking up into the sky with hopeful eyes. I stood behind her, feeling a sense of comfort and removed the old leather hood from my head. Sudden cold air against my skin. I felt a shiver at first, having not felt this sensation in close to three years. It was liberating and for the first time in a long time, I felt free.

She looked back to me, watching as I held my head skyward, looking into the array of stars above us. We did not know why they were there; why they held position against the dark, lonely and untouching. In their reticence they held secrets, knowledge that was unconquered by our kinds. Perhaps they were there to guide the night traveler in the dark. I did not doubt that far from here there were those making a journey across the forests, across the seas, audience to the very same sights as us. These thoughts led to hopes of one day being among them, being able to watch the stars from my own path.

"Do you see it?" she asked suddenly, pointing across the horizon of Ophidian, beyond rooftops and the courtyard. In between master's towers, there was a pattern in the stars, a wavy alignment with a forked tongue. I stared at it for quite some time, remembering the story master told us about Basilin and his sacrifice for his people. He gave himself to the sky, to make sure that we would always find our way in the dark. I didn't believe the tale until now, my upbringing telling me that there was a different entity that existed. Perhaps all of them did, only revealing their signs to us in ornate nature, or times of need.

"They're interesting, the stars. Vortain says they are only balls of light. What do you think holds them there?" she asked, crossing her arms. I continued to stare at the snake, unmoving and unchanging.

"I could not say. It is a mystery, even to me."

"Your eyes..." she said, walking toward me.

"Cahya, don't," I said, moving my hand toward my hood.

She reached me at this point, placing her hand against mine which stopped my actions. "Continue to look forward, I wish to see them," she said, staring into my face. After a few seconds she moved her hand toward my chest, brushing it downward and replacing it at her side. She was watching still, and I continued to look ahead, seeing her only minutely from my absence of gaze. It was becoming hard not to look at her, her eyes shimmering from the light of the stars above us. Her closeness was soothing, and her touch brought comfort.

"They are so different. The color of them is unlike anything I have ever seen in a person," she said, moving her hand to my face. I grabbed her wrist before she reached it, looking at her, just above her eyes. "That's because they are not human, they resemble an animal's," I answered.

"I think differently of you. People may say that you are nothing but an animal, a creature because of what your appearance tells, but I know the heart that rests within," she said and gently pulled her arm away, placing it against my face. "You can tell yourself that you are a creature just as the rest of them do, but mere words will not make that fallacy a truth."

It was then she kissed me, standing on the pads of her feet to reach my face. The feeling was met with a rush inside of me that I couldn't explain, didn't understand. So, we continued, underneath the dark sky with only the stars to witness our actions of flesh...

◆ ◆ ◆

The wagon slowed to a stop, Cahya and Siska's feet heard touching ground. I shifted my position to the opening Cahya made in the burlap cover, watching as they approached the person who stopped them.

"I see you've our wagon," he said. "But I've never seen you before. Tell me how it came to be in your possession. Your lives depend on it."

"First," Cahya said. "Where are your counterparts? Only a fool would travel alone, even more so in dealings like this." The Archegal smirked and raised his arm, waving his hand forward. Another came from the trees on the right side of the road, one from the ditch on the left.

"My question. Answer it."

"We're drifters," Siska said. "Came across your bandits and aimed to rob them, waited until they were asleep. Yours showed up and took care of them for us. They didn't know we were waiting for them."

"You two? Killed our men?" The Archegal laughed and Cahya quickly pulled her ax with her left hand, stopping at his throat. "They didn't see us coming. Check the forests, you'll find their corpses."

The others pulled their weapons, Siska following suit. The Archegal at Cahya's mercy waved his men back, laughing softly. "Forgive me for underestimating you. Assuming you interrogated one of them and found out about us, why not just raid the camp?"

Cahya slowly moved her blade downward, looking at the other two before letting it fall limp in her hands. "Like I mentioned," Siska said. "We're drifters. It seems we just proved yours weak and you're in need of new ones."

"You are right about that," the Archegal sighed.

"Sergen, you aren't seriously thinking about..."

"Silence. Elaria will not be happy that the humans we've hired are dead. Perhaps she will forgive us if we present her with new... more able ones," he responded.

"Is that the name of she who leads you?" Cahya asked.

"Of course," Sergen hissed. "We're based in a cave not far from here."

"And what about pay?" Siska asked. "The men we killed said you paid the bandits gold and let them keep whatever else they could find."

"The question I was waiting for, drifter," Sergen said and looked between the women. "As it stands, we're the only operation in our clan that deals in human slaves so you wouldn't have any competition if Elaria approves."

"I'm sure once she sees your shipment suffered no losses, she won't have much room to disagree," Cahya said.

"Careful now. The matter is not our choice. You two, the wagon, go."

The Archegals approached, weapons pulled. As the first grabbed hold of the cover and pulled it back, I stabbed him in the chest, swinging my sword to parry an attack from the other. I continued to do so, kicking his elbow upward, breaking it. He cried out and lost balance enough for me to lunge out of the wagon, continuing to fight him while he attempted to reset his arm by jerking it outward. I counter-attacked him quickly, spinning so that I was standing next to him, and severed his head from his shoulders. I rushed toward Cahya and Siska who were engaged in combat with Sergen, Cahya quickly disarming him of one of his blades. Siska jumped on his back, moving her blade to his throat when he grabbed her wrist, squeezing it so hard that he dislocated it. She cried out and dropped her sword, but forced herself backwards, taking Sergen to the ground with her. She had her arms around his throat at the base of his head when he elbowed her in the ribs, causing a grunt to escape her while she kept hold. He threw his blade up and attempted to catch it in such a way he could stab her when Cahya kicked it, the blade falling down the hill. Another Archegal appeared from the hill behind us, and Cahya threw her ax, lodging it in their face just between the eyes. I walked forward, sheathing Seligsara, and joined them.

"Sardon filth," Sergen said and spat in my direction. "And traveling with humans. Making your prey thralls now? I never expected Zerian's kind to mimic our methods. I thought it beneath you."

"They're no thralls. I accompanied them," I said and walked forward. "Only to ensure everything would go as planned."

"You expect me to believe that?" he said and began to try and wrestle Siska again, who tightened her grip. "Foolish to not believe it when all of your men lay dead before us," she taunted.

"So, you're a defender of humans, that it?"

"Defender of friends. But I'm not the one who planned this, nor am I the one with arm around neck and blade at throat. And I'm not the one who's going to kill you," I said.

"What, deciding who's going to do it? Or are you contemplating letting me live? Humans are so..."

The Archegal was cut off by Siska snapping his neck, pushing him from her with her legs. She rose, brushing herself off. "Do we think they were telling the truth? When they said they were the only ones capturing humans?"

"We can't know for sure. When Eshkan and I were captured, we found no other humans aside from their thralls. Why or for whom humans are being collected remains a mystery. Tread carefully as you investigate this," I said.

"Let us get back to town," Siska decided. "We can talk more on the way there," she said, climbing up onto the wagon. Cahya followed and gave me a smile, nodding her head toward the back.

"Alright, alright," I said and jumped into the back of it, sitting against the far wall.

"Was it Thurlowe who sent you?" she asked. "You come from a land far off, what cause do you have to aid us?"

"Our home was destroyed by the king's men. We sought justice, initially. But in our resolve, seeing the state of things here, we're trying to help in whatever way we can," I offered. Cahya raised an eyebrow, glancing back at me, but returning her gaze to Siska. "Where we come from there was no poverty, no greed, no starvation."

"You mean Mordestai?" Siska asked. "I've always wanted to see it. Alaies tells me that there are places like Mordestai where everyone lives as they did before the ages of kings and queens."

"Cethin and I lived in a place like Mordestai. No one went hungry, no one was richer or poorer than anyone else. We've no idea how the ruler managed this, but I have my guesses. After our home was destroyed, we initially sought revenge, but I guess in seeing what the world is like, what it's like to live in the shadow of a kingdom that ravages its people... The only thing I want is alleviation of the suffering... and I feel Cethin does, too."

I nodded, and she smiled, looking back to the road ahead. "I will do what I can to aid these people. I began our journey with a much different mindset. Things have a way of shaping, changing. I'm not certain that revenge is a quest I wish to pursue."

"Oh?" Cahya asked. "An interesting turn of events."

"Cosette. Something she said, things she's told me. I don't know why it weighs on me so, but she made me promise something. I won't go back on my word."

"Care to share with me?"

"I was going to do so when she and I returned to Sathenne, but a better opportunity has presented itself. When I mentioned to Cosette that we were going to confront Savantin, kill him, she met me with emotion I did not anticipate. She said that what I recalled did not sound like something he would do, that he was more like a father to her than the king ever was." I sighed. "I think what changed the way I viewed things is when she told me that she ran away from the Mountain. He devised a plot to help her escape. She struck him, a dagger. He didn't retaliate, didn't chase her. That is when she told me that every day it haunts her. That maybe he was just trying to show her the truth, so she could see that he trusted her. She blames herself for everything, for his obsession with the box, enough to hurt people for it, to do whatever he must. She asked me to promise her that I would try to do things another way. So, I told her I would."

"She cannot take ownership of… there is no way to know for sure. But if you've promised her then it means I will honor your promise. Even if I don't agree."

"At first, I was so… focused, so determined. He was plotting something evil, and I needed to be the end. One final assassination. But to see someone with such genuine, severe emotion touched me. It doesn't mean what happened is forgiven, or it's absent in my mind. I don't understand it, Cahya."

"Compassion," Cahya said. "We're a long way from home. Home we were used to. We were used to the same feelings and emotions. Day in and day out. We are free of that place, experiencing things we've never seen, never felt. I do not think you're wrong for feeling, Cethin. You cannot explain it, nor do you need to."

I felt comfort in her words, they calmed the sea in me.

"The princess is alive?" Siska asked.

"She is. She's been in hiding for years. Do tell no one, she doesn't wish it to be known. But seeing as you're a relative of Alaies' it's only right to reveal it to you. Knowing he will do so in time."

"Is she to stay in Sathenne?"

"She doesn't wish to put anyone in danger, so she will travel with us for as long as she wishes," I said. "We don't yet know whether or not she wants anything to do with the throne, seeing as she left it behind for a life in a forest as a reclusive herbalist."

"I remember when the news arrived of her passing," Siska said. "It was strange. No one from the Mountain talked about her when she was alive. Only after death. Sad is what it is. I'd have played dead too."

When we returned to Sathenne, Siska pulled the wagon to the gates, which opened slowly upon arrival. Once stopped, I jumped out of the back of the wagon and strode up front to where Cahya was seated. "It's been a long day, we should turn in," she said.

"Are you staying at the manor?" Siska asked.

"We haven't broached the subject with Alaies. Eshkan, with us, he has a friend at one of the farms outside the walls but there's... tension," I said, looking to Cahya, who laughed. "A lot of tension."

"Alaies won't refuse, not after all you've done to help us. I couldn't have done this without the both of you," Siska said. Her eye lit up and she moved to a small, cream-colored horse, placing her face on the horse's muzzle. She spoke to it, stroking its mane and then placing her hands on its cheeks. She grabbed an apple from the basket closest to the stable keep's door, feeding her horse before checking her saddlebags to check over a sword, a quiver, and a dagger among other things. She praised her horse another time and rejoined us.

"The guards who came to the manor to inform us about you and Rafaem said that your horse arrived at the gate," Cahya said.

"I told her to go. Didn't want those men to hurt her. It's a good thing I told her to come back here, I couldn't have killed them all myself, and I wasn't going to run. It didn't take long for me to teach her. A few months. She never lets me down. Alaies will want my report. We should hurry." Siska took a breath and relaxed her muscles as I opened the door to the manor house, letting her and Cahya pass under the doorway first. It wasn't long before we heard shouting, Voices belonging to Dacian and Cosette. We got to the door, Cosette's arms crossed and face red.

"Now it's time I make you understand something. You..."

Dacian stood up quickly, causing Cosette to turn as well. "Thank Basilin you've arrived, there's no reasoning with this one."

"Reasoning?" Cosette laughed. "You wouldn't have to *reason* with me if you'd just listen absent word."

"There is entirely too much yelling for reasoning of any sort, compose yourselves," Eshkan said and took a deep breath, rubbing his face with one hand. Alaies was sitting by the fire, falling in and out of sleep despite the noise.

"I only wished to learn what happened to those people," Cosette said. "I've been away for so long. Even when I lived at the Mountain there was no word of this. Or if there was, I was too young, too removed to have heard of it."

"And so, you went to the inn to speak to people about it. Without asking any of us to accompany you," Dacian said, his voice slightly raising.

"I don't need an escort, I found it very easily on my own," she returned.

"I don't care about how easily you found it; I care about what people might do if they see you. You said it yourself, there could be people that would tell your family that you're alive."

"The king and queen are not my family," she said and pulled her hood up. "I'm going for a walk." Once Cosette's footsteps were no longer heard, Dacian shook his head and started to set off after her. He muttered something as he passed through the arch of the hall, vanishing.

"Let's make this quick," Eshkan said, tapping Alaies' shoulder. He startled awake and looked up, moving to stand but winced, rubbing his leg.

"Help me up, will you?" he said quietly, looking up toward Eshkan. Once he was on his feet, he limped toward Siska who met him in a hug. "What did you learn?"

"We killed them. They said they were the only ones doing this, that they were trying to prove it a useful venture to their leader. We left them where they were slain. In case others come looking for them, they'll realize that it's not. We must warn the other provinces and the towns not protected by walls. I will leave at morning and…"

"Siska," Alaies said, simply. Her eyebrows wrinkled in an emotion that could have been frustration but felt like despair. "Help me pen the letter at midday. You'll have had time to process it, time to rest. Everyone should rest," he said and directed his attention to us. "Any of the rooms on the upper level are available for you to use, save the three at the end of the hall."

"We are grateful, thank you," Eshkan said and turned to leave but spun around quickly. "Tomorrow we will discuss Savoi and Egelle?"

"I know Egelle well, I used to pick up supplies there," I said. "My contacts will remember me, if they still live."

"Perfect," Alaies said. "We will meet here in the morning."

It was then fatigue started to set in. The adrenaline of the day had subsided. I let Cahya choose the room, the first on the left being where she set her things down. I closed the door behind us, waiting for her to get settled before I removed my blades, setting them on the dresser nearest us. Cahya strode forward and handed me the key before sitting on the bed, taking her boots off. "I've been thinking about what you said earlier. About Cosette. What happened?"

"I followed Morard's scent to the house, only to find myself at the end of a blade when I got there. A human, young, Cosette's lover. After I killed him, Cosette aimed to end my life for ending his. Instead, I convinced her to talk, just like I intended on doing when I arrived. She told me things I... didn't expect. She's scared, Cahya. She's upset, agonized. She's only ever had two people, I've already killed one of them."

"And by killing Savantin..."

"I promised her I would try to find another way," I repeated, sitting on top of the bed. "But that wouldn't avenge any of them. I don't understand how the will to avenge my brothers was so strong until it was put up against the testimony of a young girl."

"Maybe it's because you know that deep down, it was Jadoq that killed them. And because you killed one of the only people in Cosette's life, you feel you cannot kill the other."

"I thought you didn't agree with me," I said, immediately regretting the statement.

Cahya laughed softly and shook her head. "I don't, but that doesn't mean I'm not going to help you through what you're feeling. I think you should think about how you're going to tell Eshkan and Dacian. I feel they'll need time to dwell on the idea."

"They will. Eshkan will handle it a lot better than Dacian will."

"You think so?"

"Eshkan is wise, compassionate. He'll hear me out and consider my words truly and examine every element involved. Dacian is loyal, faithful, but he's also unbending. He wants justice for our brothers and already has it in his head that ending Savantin's life is how we'll do that. You're right, we can't only blame Savantin when it was Jadoq who caused all of this."

"We're all still holding onto that place, Cethin. We're free, we're finally free. We're used to always having a purpose, always working toward something. We don't know what living is like yet. Maybe I need to examine things differently, too."

"We're still missing something though. The other person in the letters. That must be how Jadoq and Savantin knew one another to exist. Without that link, they may not have known one another at all."

"And none of this would have ever happened," Cahya said. "How do we find them?"

"I... I don't know. I haven't a clue. We must be missing something."

"Let us shift conversation to something known. Egelle. Tell me about it."

"In a moment," I said and hugged her, holding her hair in my hand. "I want to resonate in feelings I am familiar with. In all that has happened, fortune favors me. I get to hold you in my arms."

THE
COVEN
OF
SHADOW

CHAPTER 1

BLOOD ΛND TWIN KEYS

Savantin reached the outskirts of Septentria, cold harsh winds and snow flurries greeting him. Soon he would be near the Siaden pass, a place man had forgotten. It was no wonder Sindara chose this place to hide. He'd have sought it out eventually, though it wasn't his immediate thought. The archaic ruins that remained there were from man's first attempt to cultivate the frozen land. Their crafters had all perished as a result of the land being inhabitable. Eventually some of the ice melted away, and tribes began to build outside of it. It shaped Terrenveil, other kingdoms, and free colonies of Cilevdan. Or at least that's what humans claimed when they wrote their books of ancient knowledge.

Savantin found history amusing in some respects, realizing that he himself was searching for an antiquated box fashioned centuries ago. In fact, he spent so much of his time looking for it that he learned much about the land. How it was riddled with remnants of ancient nonhumans, limited lore scattered in books. Human settlers pledged their lives to the religion of Araele to lessen their fears. Ideas and beliefs could not vanquish a visceral, tangible fear; at least that is how he felt. He had feared nothing for so long that he could scarcely remember what it felt like.

His destination was a few miles to the east, the town of Eivher, a place few traveled and even fewer inhabited. The pass was beyond it, watching over the town from the mountain it was situated under. It was in a direct path of the storms of Septentria, making it a cold shell of a town, the people equally as frigid. He wondered why people would stay, and not move somewhere warmer like the rest of Terrenveil had. Perhaps they were Septens, he thought, wanting to be somewhere close to home, yet experience a slight change in season.

It had been hours since he left Opskaven, the moon and stars now directly overhead. He could hear the whispers, the voice of Norahn steadily becoming louder, angrier at him. He looked up into the sky, feeling his eyes begin to create spots of blood across them. It seemed Norahn would have his sacrifice after all, Savantin thought, hoping that he could reach his destination before giving into the call of his denounced god. It was becoming stronger in each passing moment. He would have to time everything perfectly, as he knew there would not be many chances to face her again if he failed. He tried to stop thinking of factors that would make him frustrated, as it only hastened his impending lack of control.

He pulled the reins to his horse tightly and headed to town, focusing on the ground in front of him. It was becoming hard now, as time seemed to be slowing down around him and he could hear the heart of his horse beating rapidly. He knew next would be the smell of blood, and beyond that was the surrender. When he reached the outer portion of the ruins, he fastened his horse to a tree, knowing very well that Sindara would be able to catch its scent if he hitched it any closer. She was very perceptive, which made her dangerously hard to fool. He wasn't planning on fooling her, no. He only planned on getting answers. When he dismounted, he heard his feet crunch the snow beneath him, the sound loud in his ears. An owl flew from one of the treetops nearby, flapping its large wings as it changed its location for the night. The owl would patiently anticipate its prey elsewhere, watching it as it made its nocturnal voyage. Its prey would be unsuspecting of the demise that awaited it, and once in talons, it would be too late to escape. A stealthy predator wasted no time in thinking. It had to make a kill to carry on until the next time it had to take a life. It had no higher power to which to sacrifice life, Savantin thought. For a moment he envied the owl, for being so free in its movements, but then felt foolish for even thinking so. The owl was a bird, not capable of thought or speech or emotion. He only half believed that. A living creature smart enough to stalk its prey in the cover of the dark could not be so mindless. He supposed a part of that was instinct, wired into the creature by whatever forces created the earth. He didn't bother himself with theories of creation, as the scholars or thinkers did. He had one higher power to appease, and he would not even believe in that were it not for what he had become.

Three strokes past midnight, he estimated. Superstition ruled that the dead roamed the earth. The stories scared people into hiding, and like ghosts, they would not appear until the next day. Ghosts, he thought. He heard that a ghost was an emotion, twisted and torn; resulting from a death so violent that its vindictiveness would be manifested in the form of a haunting. If that were true, he wondered where all the ghosts were for the people he had killed, and if he would ever meet them.

As the stars shifted in the sky, he found his way to the largest of the ruins, paying close attention to the frame that created its mouth. It was cracked from years of exposure to the weather. He wondered how much longer it would hold, as it appeared to be waiting for eternal slumber. He took a deep breath inward before heading inside, making sure to feel for any differences in the world around him. There was only one way to track Sindara, he knew, and prepared now for its embrace. It would take much from him, the relinquishing of his sane mind to the other side of himself, but the risk was worth the sacrifice if he could discover the location of his desires. It always was.

He paid close mind to the frozen walls, smelling nothing but dirt and thousand-year-old bones. And suddenly, blood. It seemed this place had been vacant for quite some time before Sindara arrived, and his curiosity on whether or not anyone else had decided to take refuge inside it was sealed. He continued along the main passageway, coming across the corpses of bandits, frost encasing them. One was killed recently, his blood still warm. His mouth watered at the scent. He closed his eyes in focus and followed the old walls. He reached a point where the roof had collapsed, and climbed over the stones as quickly as possible, watching the veins in his hands send large amounts of blood toward his heart.

It felt completely empty now, save the bats that hung snugly in the ceiling ten feet above his head. He heard their breathing, listened to their heart beats, slow, indicative of sleep. It began to become louder. His head pounded with the sounds, and even when he closed his eyes, it was difficult to focus on the ground ahead of him. He was certain that once he was under cover of the heart of the ruin that the taunting would cease, and that he would control the temptations of the lurid world his condition created. Lurid, not with the sounds of wind or voices or snow, but instead with that of hearts and lungs and of course, the smell of blood.

He could not hear his own breathing, only the processes of any living creature that was within his presence. There were many creatures, he could tell now, yet the one he wished to find was absent. Sindara could not be felt anywhere, which at first frustrated him. He found himself slipping away and focused his thoughts on the fact that he now had the advantage. He came across a large room, one that ended with no other entrance besides the one he had just used. He thought of turning around, waiting for her in the narrow corridor so that he could keep her from running, but the pounding became louder, his breathing quickened to match it. And so, he stopped in the middle of the ruin, closing his eyes and thinking of something to keep him from slipping. He opened his eyes, the room seemingly moving around him in slight vibrations, the corridor he had just traversed was growing dark. The darkness bled into the room, making it suddenly impossible to see. He would have to keep his eyes closed, despite this, as he was already beginning to feel the calling.

It felt like hours had passed before he felt her presence, slowly entering. Her footsteps echoed against the empty walls, sounding as loud as his did when he first embraced the snow-covered ground. He dared not move, though the anticipation of finally finding her was overwhelming. Once she became closer, he heard her breathing. Calm, close, such focus. At this point anything could send him to the other side, and as she entered the room with a gasp, his wait was suddenly over.

"Do not run. It will not end well for you." Savantin took a breath, his eyes still closed. His voice was gentle, despite trying very hard to contain what lay just beneath his flesh. He felt a sudden wave of fear seep through Sindara like a river and smiled, its softness matching that of his voice. "You're tense, Sindara. Have I frightened you?" he asked, keeping his eyes from opening. He wanted nothing more than to look upon her, to see.

"I will retreat to the shadow, as I've done before," she answered sternly.

"Would you rather speak or fight? You will not leave here if you try to run," Savantin said, keeping his fists from shaking.

"You can never have it. It was not meant to be opened."

"You're wrong," he answered, his voice still calm. "It was created to be opened, or else it would have no key. You know where the keys are, don't you?"

"I will tell you nothing."

"Then you have left me with no choice," Savantin answered and opened his eyes to her. "You've made a mistake in crossing me, Sindara, and now you will see what comes of it."

"I know your intentions and I cannot allow it," she answered, the words forced from her. He could feel how badly she wanted to run. Instead, she stood, preparing herself for whatever was about to happen. He could almost hear her thoughts, then. He disliked how she knew so much about him; how she knew what he was when they first met.

"Savantin, think about what you are doing. If you open the box, the entire world will suffer. An entire world of people. Why are you seeking it Savantin?"

"Why would I tell you? After all you've done?"

"Is it revenge? Power? Surely your plight could not warrant something so grave."

"Plight?" Savantin said, anger in his voice. "Awfully careless in choosing words for events you are ignorant of. Events you wouldn't have wanted to survive. You always thought you were step ahead, and I'll admit, you were for a while. But there's something you don't understand, Sindara. You underestimated my will to obtain the one thing I want more than anything else. You don't get to ask me why I would go so far to end my plight," Savantin answered, his hands now orchestrating his words. It was pain in his voice, now. She never knew he was capable.

"Do you honestly care about the world, about these humans, Sindara?"

"There is no way to contain it. They are our prey, Savantin. We could not survive without them. It would be genocide."

Savantin's face turned to one of intrigue, and he took a shallow breath as he closed his eyes briefly. "You do know where they are," he said and took a gasp of air into his lungs, looking up at her. His eyes. He knew they were consumed, now.

"I will protect their location with my life. If we must fight, so be it."

"Do you think that is wise? You know what drawing my blood will do," he said.

Sindara swallowed, taking a quick breath to reaffirm herself. "I know exactly what I am doing."

"I trusted you," Savantin said, turning to anger. "You were trying to find it so that I could not," he laughed and looked upward, bringing his eyes back toward her. "You hid your intentions well."

"Don't," Sindara said calmly, making her palms flat and slowly moving her blade behind her, putting it away.

"Tell me where they are."

"I will tell you nothing."

"Tell me Sindara," he demanded, his voice loud. It echoed through the ruin.

"I will not do this. Savantin. Listen to me," she said, taking a step backward. "There is another way to do this."

"There is no other way."

"Forget about this madness, forget about the box, and I will aid you."

"You have the audacity to make an offer such as that? The time to bargain is over, Sindara. Tell me where the keys are. I am losing my patience. I continually give you chances, yet soon I will tire of it. It is becoming harder to hold myself here. If you unleash this then you will not leave here with your life."

He heard a blade sliding against its sheath, a sound he knew as her opposition to his request. She disappeared into the dark, yet he heard her speak, her breath a whisper, a word in Sardon he did not know. He became quiet, listening to the sudden deafening sounds of her breathing mixed with the quick beating of her heart. The sounds became his sight as they illuminated the room, revealing her location to him. As she took a breath he saw her silhouette, her heartbeat creating a reddish aura surrounding her and softly dissipating into the dark. He moved toward her quietly, watching her look in every direction before taking a step. She was being cautious, he thought, but felt her fear as he neared her, watching her reaction to feeling the sudden warmth of his body. She slashed at him with her blade, but he dodged it, grabbing her wrist and knocking her blade across the frozen ground. With his other hand, he brushed her hair away from her neck, pulling her in close to him. He moved his face to her neck, taking a breath in as he lowered his head toward her collarbone. "It doesn't have to end this way. Where are they?"

"I will tell you nothing," she said, her words forced.

"Don't make me do this."

"I will die protecting them, Savantin. Do what you must, but I will tell you nothing."

"You will," he said, brushing her hair softly. He then squeezed her wrists tighter, listening to her heartbeat quicken. "Is your oath so strong that you must die to attempt secrets?" he asked.

"You and I have both read the tomes. That is something that should be lost to time, forgotten."

"It will end with me."

"Do you expect me to believe that? What is written has always been. You will lose yourself."

"No," Savantin said and placed two fingers under her chin, lifting her head. "It will bend to me."

"That is your plan? It could devour you, leave you with no mind, it could..."

"There's something I didn't tell you. Though if I had, your betrayal would have been almost understandable."

"What aren't you telling me?" she asked.

"You don't get to ask," Savantin said, his words slowed, breath heavy. "Where are the keys, Sindara?" She had stopped speaking, either that, or he could no longer hear her. "Your heart is so loud," he said, moving one arm across her throat. "So loud that I need to make it stop."

"Savantin... wait. Please."

Sindara's eyes widened as he became unresponsive to her speech, and for the first time in a long time, Savantin did not resist.

◆ ◆ ◆

Ohric knew what traveling like this meant for them. The harsh winds made him feel as if he was unclothed, fighting against the cold in his bare skin. He thought he would be used to it now. Ohric lived in Cilevdan his entire life, even spent a winter on the western border to protect Araelian soldiers from brigand attacks and worse. Even though most claimed the snow beasts of Septentria were a myth, he knew that bandits alone were not responsible for all the missing livestock and beyond, missing people.

The wind continued to bite and sting; it howled over the frozen ground as if searching it for something lost. His horse was even showing discomfort despite wearing a blanket, grunting every so often. He watched his breath spew from him as he exhaled in a short puff, feeling how dry his lips were. He should have worn a scarf of fur, he thought, knowing that Glacier Ridge was entirely encased in ice for ten of the twelve months. That was how it gained its name, he was sure. Savantin returned only an hour ago, and Ohric could tell that something substantial happened. His commander hadn't said much to him since he returned to Opskaven, only asked for his assistance. They set off into the night, to a destination unbeknownst to him. He hoped Savantin would tell him more about finding Sindara and whether or not she still lived. He would have to ask, regretfully, and would have to work up the courage to do so.

As it became dark, their path began to look the same for miles, snow-covered trees lining the Carvelian Road. With each gust of wind, some of the snow would fall off the dense branches, all lined with needle-like leaves. He could smell them as the wind blew, sweet sticky sap running from the soft bark that was hidden beneath the greens. Looking up toward the darkening sky he saw just how tall the trees were as they towered over him, seemingly touching the stars with their pointed tops. The temperature would suffer another drop soon. This circled back to his previous concern of remaining warm, and he pulled his coat tighter at his throat, looking ahead of him. Savantin said nothing for the entirety of their journey. He could see his commander's breath coming from him as he began to get closer but ultimately chose to remain behind. His horse began to grunt loudly now, rearing slightly as Ohric pushed his heels into its legs, making it move forward.

"The animals seem not to like the snow very much," he muttered, not caring if he was unheard. It had been hours since he last heard anything besides the sounds of the horse's feet, or the wind, and wanted to make sure his voice was not frozen along with his body. He could scarcely feel his fingers inside his riding gloves; the fur lining them was also cold, as the wind pushed its way through the opening around his wrist. He wiggled his toes in his boots for a moment, relieved that he could feel them. Frostbite was a common ailment here in the wild, and losing his toes would be detrimental to his service. He doubted he would be able to leave Terrenveil if that were to happen. Though, maybe he could live in Arriksmad or one of the larger provinces devoted to the Lady of Light.

"It isn't the snow. There are creatures in the trees, hunting," Savantin answered suddenly. It was unexpected.

"I do not see them." Ohric looked into the dense dark forest. He tried to look for anything he could, teeth, eyes, movement in the dark. He then realized how foolish he sounded, and remained silent for a few moments, watching with his eyes.

"You won't," Savantin stated taking a deep breath in.

"Where are they?" Ohric asked, shivering slightly. It was making him unsettled.

"Just beyond the tree line. Hesitant." Savantin drew another breath. "Animals have a way of sensing things they'd rather not encounter," he said.

"Are they making a mark on us?" Ohric looked from his horse into the trees. He had heard stories of the wolves here, larger and more fearsome. The bears here were the same, with jaws large enough to tear the legs from their horses. He didn't want to think about running the rest of the way to Glacier Ridge. He knew Savantin would not allow for them to be seen as fools by its citizens. He wondered then, what would happen if the creatures of the night ambushed them from the trees. He gripped at his sword, trying to feel its hilt with his half-frozen fingers.

"It would be wise of them not to," Savantin answered, his voice unusually dark.

Ohric nodded, though he knew the gesture wouldn't be seen. There was an understanding of silence with Savantin. He often did not wish to speak, and kept his thoughts concealed when traveling. Ohric was used to speaking little, as he was not a man of many words himself. He only began to speak freely when he was named coadjutant, before only being a soldier with no name, no rank. How things have shifted. A lot of the time he was too anxious to give his thoughts voice and worked better when not having to speak at all.

The trees moved now, with the power of the wind behind them, creating a sound of rushing chaos to go along with the howling. It could be the wind, Ohric thought, or maybe it was the animals, hunting them. The road was lonely, long and dark. He knew that if anything were to happen, it would be days before they were found. He tried to stray from that thought and focused on where he was guiding his horse, suddenly wishing he hadn't been chosen for this specific assignment. Who else, though? There was no one else. He wondered how his men were faring alone, without him. It was a position he didn't want to leave them in.

The patron had been jailed, and the city secured, but he didn't feel safe leaving it in the hands of even the eldest of his men. Harlan, as he was called. Savantin assured him that there would be nothing to worry about, and he supposed that should have been good enough for him, but he could not remove his mind from it. His thoughts jumped back to the recently removed patroness. He knew never to underestimate a woman, especially one who had an aura about her that Araele cautioned against. Though, he wasn't certain that she was even alive at this point. They were at a delicate stage in their planning now and if anything went awry, then answers would have to be provided for why they were not with their men. Ohric hoped that traveling to Glacier Ridge would be beneficial. He wanted nothing more than to return home, to pray to his Goddess, and if this accelerated that, he supposed he couldn't complain.

The sky grew darker still as they continued along the road, the trees seeming thicker as they rode closer to the small town. It was another hour before they reached it, and upon arriving, they tied their horses in the stable just outside of the quiet tavern. He was almost certain he was frozen now, his face feeling numb as he tried to close his eyes. He could feel how tight his muscles were, and longed to find a fire to warm himself. Savantin seemed as if he had been riding in a different environment, climbing off his horse quickly and pulling his gloves off. He wore a riding jacket made of thick leather, to cover his chest and torso. Ohric hadn't worn armor either and used multiple coats and fur to keep himself as warm as possible. As he climbed off his horse, he took a few moments to feel for his limbs as he walked slowly, making sure he did not stumble. His legs felt like ice, and he thought that they may even shatter if hit. The cold was unbearable. Hopefully they would return to Opskaven during the day, where the temperature was at least above twenty degrees.

The door to the tavern had a thin sheet of ice on it, and as Ohric hurried to open it he noticed that it had frozen shut. He hadn't taken his gloves off yet; he didn't dare to. With another tug on it, his hand slipped off and he stumbled backward slightly, trying to make it seem as if he only backed away, deciding to give up. Savantin looked at him for a moment and smirked, placing his large hand on the handle and pulling it, the door prying from its frame. Those inside were surprised at the sudden sound, watching the two as they made their way inside. They turned their heads away after a few moments, their behavior unchanged. There was an advantage to dressing as civilians, it seemed. No one recognized them. Savantin looked around the room for a moment, taking note of the people sitting around the various tables, obtaining a small hot meal, or a drink. It wasn't uncommon at this time of night for people to be here in this part of Cilevdan. Often their own houses would be too cold to sleep in, which made the business of the taverns and inns plentiful during the frozen months.

"Warm up at the bar," Savantin said and put his hand on Ohric's shoulder as he moved past him, walking toward the back of the room. Ohric sighed in relief, walking opposite him. A man not much older than him was sitting behind the counter, a book in his pale hands. It was a moment or two before he glanced upward, the fire crackling in the reflection of his hazel-colored eyes. He glanced at the board behind him where the choice of meal was scribbled, mead being the only choice in drink. He asked for hot water instead, unveiling the small purse of coin he brought with him before they left the mountain. The stew would also warm him, and he settled for a small bowl.

◆ ◆ ◆

Savantin approached a table where a man was sitting, his legs on top of it, leaning back in his seat. As he reached it, the man slowly sat upright. He lifted his hat upward, looking at Savantin curiously. He was dressed in dark leather armor, his face in shadows beneath his hat.

"Ah. The Seraphice," he said. "I presume there is a good reason you've made contact."

"There is," Savantin said. He knew to tread carefully. He pulled a pouch from the pocket of his jacket. Once he dropped it on the table it made a loud clinking sound.

The man moved forward to touch the pouch, and just as his fingers grazed it, he smirked, sitting back. "Sit."

Savantin reluctantly obliged, watching the man's movements. The man knew his secret, but Savantin also knew his. The man closed his eyes and looked upward, exhaling deeply before returning his gaze. "This is about the Sardon? So, you've found her."

"Kindly refrain from doing that again," Savantin said, trying to keep his voice neutral.

"Come now, I had to make certain you weren't deceiving me. Go on, then."

He hated having the disadvantage.

"I did find Sindara." The first time he used her name. "But I also discovered who has the keys." There was no point in withholding any information. He likely knew already, and if he didn't, he could effortlessly find out. The man chuckled and looked to the floor before looking up again. "Why not just join the Viscera? A lot more lucrative than spending your life searching for a box that may not even be in Cilevdan."

"Because that worked out so well for you. I'm not paying you for advice."

"Very well then," the man said, gravely. "Who do you need me to find?"

"There is another Sardon, traveling with a group of humans. She found them in the woods closest to Defaltor, she's been tracking them. The other Sardon has a key."

"Where there is one Sardon, there are more. The location of Morrenvahl isn't exactly a secret, you know. They could be taking it there."

"She's brash, not stupid. I don't believe the Sardons are after it."

"How are you so sure?" the Viscera asked, his Galistoni accent thickening.

"It's not an artifact of Zerian."

"Ah, yes, Zerian," he answered and took a breath, picking up the mug on the table and taking a swig. "They'd dare not disobey their god. A foreign concept to you," he laughed, setting the mug down, the smell of blood escaping his mouth. "From what I hear he's a very vengeful creature. Ruled his entire race by fear until Decepherous claimed him. Be careful you don't meet the same fate."

"I appreciate your concern," Savantin answered flatly.

"It can happen to anyone who interferes too closely. Though, digressing, there are two keys, and you mentioned your Sardon only had one."

"There is another. He's just recently left them, embarking on a journey to Aubergrun."

"Monks." The Viscera said, his eyes flashing.

"Find them, and I will double this. You already know how to find me," Savantin stated and stood.

"That I do, Savantin. That I do," he answered and raised his mug again, staring him in the eyes. Savantin turned and began walking to the front of the room where Ohric awaited him. As much as he wanted to limit his correspondence with the man, Savantin knew that by hiring him, failure was impossible.

They would be meeting with Almour's men soon, and that would limit the time of his search. He still had no leads on where the box itself was, but with knowing the location of both keys, it had to be in Cilevdan. The cults that worshipped Baroqqas lived here, which meant that the creator of the box did also. He'd continue his search until he found new leads, finding every historian, leader, and affiliate human he could find. Someone somewhere had the information he sought.

Ohric was finishing a broth, watching the men from the tavern. He hadn't said much to the barkeep, or anyone for that matter, and took the last few sips from the mug next to him before Savantin spoke.

"Did your contact not come?" Ohric asked, looking around the room. "You didn't wait very long at the table for him."

A trick. A very lethal one. "Once we return in Opskaven, Almour's men should just be reaching it." Savantin answered, changing the subject. If the Viscera only revealed his appearance to him, it would be unwise to speak of it.

Ohric nodded and placed his mug down on the counter, looking toward the back of the tavern. "Will they be staying there?"

"He will decide who he wants to leave behind. I don't doubt he will choose wisely. While I wished to leave this task to you, I will also have him approach the leaders of outside colonies to warn them about Mauros. Mordestai especially."

"Mordestai? Armies have never approached Mordestai before."

"The Chief is no fool. He knows that no one is mindless enough to attack. Almour is under strict order not to raise hand nor weapon while there. Warning them of Mauros is a favor I do intend on seeing returned."

"What if he's seen as a threat, and attacked?"

"Then he had better hope he dies with dignity at my behest. Because if he disobeys me, I will make him into a reminder of why acting in opposition is unwise."

"Is that why you killed them all?"

"Before I climbed the tower to confront that traitor and the ruler of the island, I told them to scout the village and return to you with what they found," he said and took a breath. "I can only imagine how anxious you were that they acted in opposition. The burning must have been Hirek's idea, he was restless, openly expressed his wishes to raid when we had left Sigth Fall untouched. He harbored resentment. He had the notion that the Mask meant they could mindlessly kill and destroy, to have no rules, no laws. There are laws for everything in life. And he forgot what mine were."

"I went looking for them, that's when I came across all those dead men. They'd been poisoned, but they carved the symbol into them."

"Foolishly and needlessly," Savantin said, fire to his voice. "I gave them a head start. I told them if they could outrun me, they might have a chance at surviving."

"When you told me to investigate the island further..."

"Hirek decided to influence the others in raiding a small village in a town on the road from Defaltor back into Terrenveil. I rendered him helpless while I killed the others. Moved their corpses into a pile and lit them on fire before dropping him on top of it. The world is better robbed of him. Of them all."

"Let us hope that Almour is as obedient as he seems," Ohric said, quietly.

"I've reprimanded him once; he shouldn't need reminder. That, and it was one of his ensigns who made himself an example to his entire sector."

Ohric remembered the day well. After Savantin killed King of Learthes, the Learthean soldiers who were stationed along with their men began to fight for their fallen king once the Jezhan were eradicated. Savantin made clear to Almour and his ensigns that he wanted no civilian casualties. The ensign of topic disobeyed orders to wait for the Learthean insurgents to clear out of Sahtun before mounting an attack. Although successful, after the civilian death toll climbed, he was told that Almour wasn't the person he was going to be answering to regarding it. The ensign was found unresponsive with note in hand two days before he was to return to the Mountain with report of the attack.

"And, just like everything else, Ozrach needn't know about Mordestai. We will move for Larient once he arrives," Savantin finished, taking another drink.

"Larient isn't of defiance. Everything will be in order," Ohric answered.

"We will have to be resourceful, then. I'm sure you will find a reason to take your time there. A temple was just built upon the cliffs between the two mountains. I'm sure you want to see."

For the first time in a long time, Ohric was delighted. He could offer the Lady of Light his prayer and worship while there, and the men could do nothing but wait for him. Neraea would see it as an appropriate practice, and Ozrach could only allow it. A wise move on Savantin's part, and it had been a while since Ohric had time to worship Araele in a proper temple. His last consultation with her was in Terrenveil, in the large temple built on one of the smaller mountains that border it. It was a blessing, to be able to return to her while on an assignment. Savantin believed in nothing other than the stars, and Ohric was often not able to practice his own beliefs while traveling. "I'll take my time to worship my Goddess, while putting a proper face to the time spent there. Neraea will ask the priests if the question arises in council, and I know exactly where to be, and when."

"Perfect," Savantin stated and took a more relaxed position at the bar. "I found her."

"Where was she?" Ohric asked quickly, keeping his voice low. The anticipation was that of a child, receiving gifts.

"She was hiding in ruins. Ruins thought lost to time. We spoke, but only for a few moments. I'll have the keys soon enough."

"Is she…"

Savantin shook his head twice. "I've no doubt she will return to Morrenvahl, though. She will need to."

"Is that where you're going?"

"You needn't follow me where I'm going. Sindara played her part. I've no use for her anymore. She knows that, now. And she also knows that if we cross paths again, I will kill her."

Ohric looked down at his drink, taking another few swallows. An indication that he did not know how to reply. There wasn't a need for one.

"In the morning we will return, they will be looking for us," Savantin continued and signaled the barkeep toward them. "It was foolish of us to travel here when we did, it would be even more foolish for us to return now. I'm turning in." He placed six coins on the bar, taking two keys from the barkeep and handed one to Ohric. He headed toward one of the rooms on the leftmost side of the tavern without saying a word more.

The sound of a door closing drew Ohric out of his mind long enough to take a breath. He could calm himself some. Soon, he would be within the walls of the house of his Goddess.

◆ ◆ ◆

Blacwin opened his eyes, feeling restive in his bed. It was warm enough, the heavy wool blanket feeling soft against his skin. Yet for a reason he couldn't explain he did not feel comfortable. He rose, moving to where he kept his belongings, wrapped in a blanket on top of the dresser. He picked up a small, green leather-bound book and opened it, his eyes searching the pages. It was something he had picked up on his travels, a place where he kept all his meanderings and thoughts. He found that when he did this, he was able to find solace with his life on the road.

He came across his first entry, something he hadn't read in quite some time. It was the day that he had left his home in Valspire, threatened by his father for killing a sheep. He remembered the event in his vivid detail, recalling how soft the wool was as he read about stroking its back, the sound of it bleating as he pulled its wool back tightly before taking a knife to its neck. His father had come in during the middle of this, throwing a ceramic pot at his head. Blacwin then raised his hand and touched his face, feeling the small scars across his cheek where it had once shattered and drew blood. There was a sharp pain that came from it, the shards cutting deeply, and the blow giving him a large bruise.

His father had cursed at him, coming after him next with whatever tool was hanging closest to him on the wall. He couldn't see very well now, the blood covering his eyes from a gash just above his hairline, matting his light-colored hair. His father had thought he was being ritualistic, calling nonhumans and things of a darker nature. In truth, he hadn't done anything besides experiment with his urges to kill. He thought that the sheep would not have been missed but should have taken one of the slaughter animals. At least then he could have salted the meat to preserve it until it was needed or taken it to the market to sell for a high price. But then the kill would have been justified, consumed, even. This felt different, as there was no reason for the sheep to meet its end. He hadn't done his job in several days, his hands hadn't met his tools, and he hadn't visited the old shed where the smell of cow's blood was as strong as the perfume on a brothel girl. He wanted to explain to his father that he needed to work, to stop this feeling, but knew with how he was being beaten there was no use in him trying to speak. The blood was in his mouth now, traveling down his throat, the metallic taste making him feel sick.

The night ended in him taking his things and leaving without saying goodbye to either of his parents, headed on his horse to only the gods knew where. It was a few days after that he found himself on the road to Terrenveil, buying this book from one of the small towns on the way there, so insignificant that it wasn't even marked on any map. He thought of staying there for a while, honestly, where an old woman most claimed to be a witch lived in a shoddy looking house, and the citizens were quiet and hard working. He might have even fit in, he thought, letting the book rest against the bed in his fingers. Yet there was no need for a butcher in a town with no livestock, and no need for a boy who had no coin with which to buy residence. He let out a long sigh, closing his eyes and leaning back slightly.

Djeik busted through his door, his hand on its frame as he looked inside. This did not startle Blacwin, and instead he looked toward the man with half closed eyes.

"There is something that needs our attention," he said then, looking back out into the lobby.

"What is it?" Blacwin asked, placing the book back inside his blanket. There was no need for anyone else to see his thoughts on paper, for most scoffed at the idea, thinking it something only a scholar would do.

"There are a few men who plan on leaving."

"Deserters?" he asked.

"Yes. They are packing their things. When I came across them, they said they were going to tend to the horses, but I told them I knew better. I assured them I wanted to leave also, and so did you."

"What is your plan?"

"We follow them," Djeik said.

"Shouldn't we alert Ohric of this?"

"Harlan said he saw them leave late last night. It will be up to us. I do not want to anger Savantin. If we do not act, he will place his vengeance upon us. You know once he hunts them down, they will speak my name."

Blacwin nodded, grabbing his things. "We will follow them outside of Opskaven and kill them once we've hit the trees."

Djeik nodded and turned his head out the door where the others were waiting, watching him with suspicions unknown. "Quickly, now. I don't like the eyes they are giving me."

"Do the others know what is happening?"

"No one else is awake, save us."

Blacwin rose from the bed and pulled a shirt over his chest, grabbing his coat and sliding it on. He left his blanket and walked out of the door, Djeik closing it behind him. Blacwin was remembering now how it felt to take the life of the lamb, looking at who would be next. One of the men from the Eastern Baeld was standing in front of them, his reddish hair showing prominently beneath his riding cap. Blacwin was surprised that Goring hadn't joined him but didn't remember the two speaking to each other while they were in Rierdan. He hadn't remembered him speaking at all. The other man who stood next to him was quiet also. He could only guess him from one of the smaller inward towns of Terrenveil. He looked not very different from Thren, with pale brown hair and greenish-hazel eyes. He wasn't much bigger than Blacwin, and looked nervous or awkward as he held his things. Once they joined the men, Blacwin noticed that they had no weapons on them at all, or at least none that were visible.

"Where are your blades?" he asked.

"We aren't bringing them," the man from the Baeld answered. "If we are found then the weapons would identify us. If we don't have them then we will only be seen as travelers."

"I didn't think of that," Blacwin answered, looking down at his side where a dagger was strapped. He did not make any movements that would give away its position, and looked up slowly as if he was just holding wandering eyes. He looked toward Djeik next, hoping the Mordestan would say something to mask their suspicions.

"I will lose mine once I'm sure we are clear of any threats. I don't want to be on the road and be found without a blade.

Perhaps we should go somewhere that is rebelling and sell off our things," Djeik stated.

"Ah, good thinking. Quick, let us hurry before the others wake," the other man said, his voice hurried and hushed. He looked around the room before turning toward the door, paranoid in even his smallest steps. As the man opened the door the cold leaked in, the night still dark.

"Should we take our horses? They will find them missing," Blacwin suggested, hoping to at least grasp their thoughts for a moment. He had hoped that by getting them to think that they would not leave at all, and instead turn back to the warmth of their rooms for the night. It was growing colder by the minute, the temperature dropping as the hour grew later. At least it was not snowing, Blacwin thought, and took a warm breath in to ready himself for the cold.

"Do you think they will exhaust their energy looking for our horses once they've realized we've gone?" the other asked, his paranoia manifesting in his breaths.

"The only thing he will do is look for us. We had better stop guessing about this and get going," the Baeld answered, quickly as if to cut him down. Blacwin could see his frustration raising, quite evidently with every word the other spoke.

"If they see that our horses are still here it could be a while before they find we're gone. What if when they wake, they don't have plans to leave right away?" Blacwin asked.

"You mean to say that they have unfinished business here?" the man from the Baeld asked him, turning to face.

"Yes. I overheard them speaking last night. If they see our horses missing, then they will immediately draw their attention away from the task at hand to find us. If we go now, without them, then it could be hours before they realize we've left at all. That would give us more than enough time to make it elsewhere and sell off all our things for a horse."

"We might freeze on the roads. A horse will see us to our destination faster."

"Then what do you propose? We steal some from the lady's stable?" Blacwin asked, rhetorically. He almost wished he hadn't asked that as he saw the keen look in the other man's eye.

"No. Theft is something else. That will be noticed before anything. We will walk. Larient is not far from here. It will only take us a few days."

"What if that is where they are headed?" Djeik asked.

"Then we will have time ahead of them. It is not hard to notice a legion on the move. The forest will provide us with cover. They will not stray from the roads. Why would they have to?"

"We do not need to be seen standing in the streets. There is nothing that we could say that would justify why we are awake at this hour with all our possessions in hand. Someone might see us out here and alert high command."

"Even if the town is rebelling?" Djeik asked.

"There will be no rebellion. He's made that clear. He is something no man has ever crossed and still lives."

"Is that why you run?" he asked.

"There are more reasons than this to leave. But this, this is among the greatest. When Ohric came to me, asking me if I wanted to truly serve the people of Terrenveil, I thought he was offering me a way into his life, to the voice of Araele. But this... this is madness. I believe that murder is needed, but not of the innocent," the man answered.

The Baeld then scratched his beardless chin, looking at him. "You knew it was of darker tidings, Belddin. Ohric said once we'd joined there was no way back until the job was done."

"Then forgive me for being foolish," he said and pulled his pack over his shoulder, walking toward the stables. The city remained unguarded. Blacwin wondered why, especially since the patron claimed that bandits raided them often, stealing wares and killing livestock. It was as if she was inviting them inside, giving her a reason to rebel against the king instead of just following the common opinion. He focused on the men in front of him, as they passed beneath the large stone arch. They were silent now, not speaking to one another. Blacwin looked at Djeik, who was keeping on their heels. He realized he was falling behind, watching the distance between them grow. The ground was hard, the soil most likely frozen already. He strived to see in front of the men but could not. There was no moon above them this night, and hardly any stars. They would have an advantage if they entered the forest first, using the dark to escape them. He picked up his pace, trying to silently reduce the distance between them, so that they did not become suspicious. They stopped once they reached the trees, looking up into their dark canopies.

"Why have we stopped?" Djeik asked.

"A mere superstition, we should continue," the Baeld answered, pushing on Belddin's shoulder, being the first to enter the trees. Djeik was the second, Blacwin stopping before he reached them.

"Do you fear what lies within the dark? Or do you fear the life you will lead if you turn from it?" Blacwin asked the man, watching his face. He was staring into the forest, and sighed, moving his hand to his chest. He moved his fingers, signing what Blacwin assumed to be the sigil of Araele.

"There is nothing to fear with her guiding light," he answered, for what could only be for his own reassurance, and stepped into the darkness. Blacwin followed, immediately searching for Djeik and the other. They had taken several steps, making it to the base of a very large tree when Belddin stopped. The silence was discordant, almost unbearable as they stood, peering up into the tree before them. It had monstrous thick arms that twisted in every direction, knotted and thick. The tree was so black that it could be easily seen in the darkness, appearing as if it was a spectre, or something from the tales of nightmares.

"Where have they gone?" Blacwin asked. "I thought when he said we were leaving that we would all go together."

"I am not sure... I do not hear them. They've already been swallowed in the dark," Belddin answered, looking back toward the town.

"We can't go back, not now," Blacwin said, grabbing his shoulder.

"There will be other chances to run." He panicked, looking behind him, past the tree.

"You are letting your fears delude you. Calm down," Blacwin answered.

"We have to go back..." he said, looking around. "We have to."

Belddin began to run, Blacwin immediately following him. "Belddin! Come back here!" he shouted, grabbing for him through the dark. He grabbed hold of his coat and used the entirety of his strength to pull him backward.

"Get off of me!" he shouted, thrashing him. Blacwin pulled his blade, sliding it through Belddin's back. He set him upon a large tree root, and moved his hands from him, feeling a wet, warm substance upon them. He turned suddenly, feeling a breath and deflecting a blade, focusing his eyes through the thick blackness to see the Baeld, swinging his sword once.

"I should have known there would be reason you wanted to leave with us so desperately. You're just as bad as they are. Trying constantly to gain favor by acting in the same vile ways as they," The Baeld said.

"You know the penalty for desertion," Blacwin said, looking toward the shape in the darkness.

"And so, you'd gain further favor by killing those who wished to escape? I thought of it myself, killing Belddin before he had the chance to run."

"Then why did you decide against it?"

"Because he was right. There is no honor in what we do. This kingdom looks down upon us like we're covered in boils, plagued. Why fight for it? At least if we leave here we have a chance of peace."

"Do you really believe that walking away from this will bring you peace? Blacwin asked.

"I belong to the sea, and to her I return," he answered and lashed forward, cutting Blacwin's arm. He winced, moving his sword upward to deflect another attack. He continued to parry. They were both at a disadvantage from the dark, but for some reason, Blacwin could hardly make out shapes. He ducked another swing and backed away, wishing now that he had been born of Septen blood. He heard the man's blade swing through the air, and jumped backward to dodge it, moving forward and meeting his steel with his own. He felt his arm becoming numb and switched his blade to his other hand. His sword began to feel heavy, his arm shaking.

"Come and let me kill you!" the Baeld shouted, swinging his sword relentlessly. Blacwin caught the end of the blade in his chest and ducked, moving sideways, trying to obscure the man's sight and avoid another injury. Within seconds he felt Belddin's warm corpse, blood leaking onto his leg. He stumbled backward over the tree root, landing on the flat of his back. He tried not to make a sound, knowing that his body had done enough. After seconds of laying in silence, he heard the man's footsteps nearing him, and then cutting off as he heard something large swing through the air. The Baeld let out a scream and two faint thuds followed; something had fallen to the ground.

"Blacwin?" Djeik's voice through the cold air.

"I'm down here," Blacwin answered, trying to get up from where he had fallen. He moved his arm from the ground, trying to move the other along with it, but to no avail, it was now completely numb, a feeling that was growing in his chest. They were slowly beginning to feel hot, increasing in intensity as time passed.

"The Baeld was sneaky; he climbed a tree to escape me, when he yelled for you, I found my way back here."

"He's struck me," Blacwin answered, trying to look at his hands through the dark. "I'm losing blood, and I can't see from where."

He suddenly felt two hands pull his arm up, lifting him from the ground, and after staring into the darkness, he closed his eyes.

BLOOD AND TWIN KEYS

Their night proved successful, Savantin thought as they made it through the trees, watching the sun climb upward in the sky. He moved his hand toward his forehead for a moment, as if trying to shelter his eyes from the sudden sight, and removed it, his face one of concern. Ohric looked at him but did not speak. It was often this way.

"I smell blood," Savantin answered, looking toward the stables of Opskaven. He rode forward, his horse slowing as it reached them. He didn't know where the scent was coming from; let alone who it belonged to. The scent was heavy, but hard to trace. He dismounted, handing the reins to the stable boy who shyly accepted, leading the horse away as he walked toward the large inn where Ohric's men were bid to stay. He hadn't paid attention to where Ohric was, and only assumed that he was following him as he opened the door, seeing several of his men sitting by the fire. The large Mordestan stood, bowing his head to him, saluting. Savantin nodded once, looking around the quiet room. There were no bards, for which he was grateful, and no barmaids. It was a different atmosphere than it was when he left last night.

"Where are the others?" he asked abruptly, looking at the two men who had also made their salutes.

"They still rest. There is a matter that would be best Djeik explains to you. He was there when it happened," the older man, Harlan answered. Savantin nodded, deeply inhaling as he closed his eyes for a moment. He could only fathom what he was about to hear. Ohric then joined them, showing his disdain for the cold as he moved toward the fire. He still wore his riding coat, pulling his gloves off and sitting them upon the table before it, sticking his legs as close to the fire as he could without catching flame. He was vigorous in his attempts to get warm, rubbing his arms quickly.

Djeik looked at his commander nervously, looking back at one of the rooms against the west side of the building.

"What is it?" Savantin asked.

"Last night, after you and the Coadjutant left Opskaven, I awoke to the sound of clinking outside of my door. I rose, opening it to see two of ours, packing their things and taking what they could from the food stores. It seemed strange to me, so I asked them what they were doing. They said they were going out to feed the horses, but I knew that wasn't it. I told them I was going with them and took Blacwin with me as well."

"So, they were trying to abandon?" Savantin asked curiously. It was the first time he had been seen without his armor on, and as he crossed his arms Djeik watched his deep blue eyes, set on him with fiery focus.

"They were. Which is why I thought following them would be best. Blacwin agreed to it, and we set out, planning to kill them both when we hit the trees."

"And my speculation is that you were successful..." Savantin continued.

"For the most part we were," Djeik stated.

"For the most part... I expected a straight-forward answer."

"My apologies, Commander. I entered the trees first, with one of the men from the Baeld. He was quick. It was so dark that I hadn't seen him climb a tree to escape me. He was onto us."

"Most likely by your decision to take Blacwin with you, though I suppose going alone was the less wise of the two choices."

"Yes. I lost the Baeld, looking for him around in the dark for several minutes when I heard shouting. That's when I found them, in a clearing near where we entered. While he was attacking, I swung my axe, cutting him down. Blacwin called out to me where he was laying on the ground, close to where he set Belddin's corpse. He had been hurt, and I carried him back here. I assisted Mortan in cauterizing his wounds, and he was given medicine to keep infection away."

"Where is he now?"

"He's sleeping, in the room across the hall. He hasn't stirred since I brought him back here. Mortan doesn't know what's wrong with him."

"They are both dead, then?" Savantin asked. Djeik offered a large nod in reply, looking toward the room that Blacwin rested in. He supposed he ought to see what his status was, and if Mortan had any predictions on his development.

"Find the blade that struck him," he said, and walked past Djeik toward the door that held the soldier's attention, listening for any sounds that might be indicative of Blacwin's condition. When he entered, Mortan looked up at him, using a cloth to wipe blood from his hands.

"Commander…" he said, trying to place his things in one hand to salute. Savantin moved his hand forward, excusing him from the motion and looked to the room, stepping forward.

"He has still not woken. He's taken an incision to the chest and the upper arm on his left side. The one on his chest was deep. The one on his arm was longer, but luckily only caught him across his flesh. The boy's so thin I'm surprised it didn't do more. He may be able to fight again," Mortan answered, finally finishing cleaning his hands. He took the soiled rag and stuffed it in his pocket, brushing his hands together as if ridding of something. "That is, if he makes it through the night."

"You don't think he will survive?"

"I'm not sure. At this point anything is possible. I've given him a vial of maerkelt, to keep infection out of the wounds, but he's lost a lot of blood. Djeik had it all over him when he returned, carrying him here. If he does survive it might be a while before he is able to pick up sword. His chest didn't look well when he brought him here. I had no other choice but to burn it together. There was no time to sew it and let it heal on its own. Another ten minutes and the boy would have been dead," Mortan said.

"And he hasn't woken? Not at all?"

"No. He was brought to me unconscious. He didn't even stir when we placed the hot steel to his flesh. I thought he was dead, but he still had a pulse, though weak, and his lungs still took air."

"Will you be able to transport him if he does not wake?" Savantin asked, watching as the doctor turned his head back toward him quickly.

"Transport him? I suppose we can use one of the supply wagons."

"I want it ready by midday. I will make sure that it will be under your control."

"Almour's wagon? What if he cannot spare it?"

"He will do as I say. They will not need it where they are going," Savantin answered and walked into the room, his eyes coming across Blacwin, still and pale. He stayed only another moment before leaving, his eyes only minutely searching the room as he left. He entered back into the cold, snow beginning to fall in flurries. It melted upon landing on his skin, leaving small traces of their being before that too, disappeared. The flurries had no wind to carry them, a sign that the day ahead would not be as cold as previous ones.

He had a lot on his mind. Sindara, the keys, the boy. Fate was fate, however cruel or unjust. He wouldn't stop now, though, no matter the cost. He was beginning to care less about the men gaining suspicions of where he was going, though, he supposed he should have put his armor on before walking to the ale house where Almour and his men were stationed. It was already too late for that, as the Magistrate had seen him upon entry, and rose to greet him suddenly.

"Commander," Almour said and bowed his head. "I heard about the incident last night from one of my men. Is the boy doing alright?"

"As of now it is not known whether or not he will live. Which brings me to another concern."

"Speak, with hopes that I can fill it," Almour answered.

"Do you best to make your next remark acceptable," Savantin said angrily, his voice enough to reduce Almour to nervousness, raised pulse. "Apologies, Commander. What is it that you need?"

"If you ever so much as breathe in my direction with that arrogance again, you will be permanently relieved by my doing. Is that clear?"

"Yes, Commander."

Savantin took a moment before posing his demands, trying to find the mind not to remove him immediately and give his position to the young captain standing behind him, who tried to hide a smirk at Almour's reprimanding. He would take the rank with pride.

"I will need one of your supply wagons. As you are aware, one of my men was injured and will need to be transported."

"Transported?" he asked, his eyebrows moving in interest. His forehead wrinkled slightly as his face was fixed in thought.

"Must I make it simpler for you? Terms you understand?" Savantin asked and deeply exhaled. "I need you and two men to travel to Mordestai, send the rest of your coalition to Esperanus."

"Why would you want us to travel there? It is not a part of the provinces..."

"I do not need a history lesson," Savantin answered quickly.

"Mordestai is not of any importance to Ozrach. I do not understand why you need us to travel there," Almour stated.

"I don't need you to understand; I need you to follow orders. I don't want you to act, I don't want you to engage. I want you to seek an audience with the Chief and inform him of the impending invasion."

"What if they are aiding the rebellion? What if they attack?"

"Your orders remain the same. Do not act, do not engage. If they attack, you are at their mercy. If I find that you disobeyed me, I will handle punishment myself. Is that something you are capable of?" Savantin asked, watching as the men who accompanied them slinked away at the raising of his voice.

"We are very capable, I'm certain if you thought otherwise, we would not be the ones supplementing you."

"I could do without your insolence as well. You are not to question my orders; you are to give them to your men under my instruction. Do not make the mistake of thinking you are indispensable, Almour. I assigned you. If you can't seem to find the respect that you misplaced, I will give your title to one of your ensigns. I don't think I need to explain where that would leave you," Savantin said, his voice unbending. Almour withdrew his gaze and nodded.

"Forgive me. I only wish to know Ozrach's meaning in all of this. You know he places a lot of trust in us to complete those tasks."

"As do you. But it is not your place to question what he asks of me, nor is it appropriate of me to ask why he does," Savantin countered, waiting for Almour's response. When he offered none, he continued. "Leave your men in Esperanus, you are only to go with two others."

"It will be done, Commander."

"Make sure your presence is not unsettling. Ask permission to enter their villages. You are only to seek an audience with the Chief. Nothing more."

"Yes, Commander. We will move out immediately, and make sure to leave you with one of the wagons," Almour answered.

Savantin stopped paying attention to his words, instead looking to the men who were sitting at the table across the room, their helmets off and weapons lazily leaning against its wooden legs. His concentration was being broken easily of late, his focus on his own hunger. It only slightly irritated him, the task at hand doing the most.

"Commander?" Almour asked. Savantin moved his eyes from the men to the Magistrate, causing him to withdraw his again. "The wagon will be left by the stable; I will make sure that my men leave the supplies," Almour said, preparing to salute until Savantin stopped him with speech.

"Have them clear a place for the boy to lie. I'm taking him with us to Larient," Savantin answered. Almour looked up, then, his slightly wrinkled face was alert and receptive. "You're taking him with you? When it's not likely he will make it?"

"Why do you think I've asked for the wagon?" Savantin asked sharply.

"For supplies, honestly, Commander."

"This is not a place for a burial. These lands are harsh and cold. At least in Larient there are summers. Word can be sent to his kin from there if he's written of them."

"How considerate," Almour said, a sarcastic undertone to him.

"You are intent on trying my patience today. Neraea will want to know her people are being taken care of. There is a temple in Larient."

"Then why cover your intent?" Almour asked.

"I did not come here to have you question my words and why I've said them," Savantin said, he could feel his eyes shifting. There was no hiding it now. His heart was beating rapidly now, hunger. Almour looked downward quickly, and his pulse climbed.

"Have your men readied and leave for Mordestai. If you return, and I am satisfied then I will give you your next assignment," Savantin settled on.

"An arrangement, I see. I will handle it," Almour answered.

"Remain there until you've heard from me. Someone will be sent for you."

"Sent for me? Pardon if I don't feel comfortable in the way you've phrased that."

"You'd better hope it isn't me," Savantin answered, taking his leave.

Humans were funny, in that way. Interpretation. Overthinking words and their meaning. It worked to his advantage here. While he would have liked to dispense proper retaliation to Almour, it would have lowered morale to do so in front of his men. He hoped that he wasn't making a mistake not doing so, however.

Savantin refocused, taking a moment to collect his thoughts, reduce his aggravation. He was debating whether or not he would leave for Larient immediately. His next destination lay just outside of it. A cave, an altar, shrines. He returned to the inn, now intent.

Ohric was staring into the fire, his coat sitting next to him in the otherwise empty chair. He seemed pensive, holding the amulet in his hand and speaking what he knew to be verses, praising his goddess. He let Ohric sit, moving straight to the room behind them where Blacwin was resting. The boy was still not moving much. His chest rose and fell partially, his shirt crumpled and, on the floor, covered in blood. There were bandages on top of it, and Savantin could now see the large cauterization upon the boy's flesh, right on top of his sternum.

It was a scar not unlike his own, the cauterization, and he thought about the wounds on several of his own muscles. They appeared to be fused together by something caustic. He looked to his own bicep now; the small hole on the inner portion of it was jagged and slightly raised. It had shrunk considerably in size since the day he received it, remembering now when he pulled the tendrils from his body, they spewed something onto his flesh that sealed them shut. He moved his attention from his own perils and remained in the door frame, watching Blacwin for only a few more minutes before Ohric noticed he was there, joining him.

"Savantin, what do we plan to do?"

"Almour's men are headed to Mordestai presently," Savantin answered, not moving his eyes from Blacwin. He wouldn't have noticed his coadjutant if not for his speaking.

"So now we move for Larient?"

"Yes," Savantin said and moved from the doorway, his massive frame previously blocking the sight from Ohric.

He looked into the room with a shamed look on his face and made the sigil of Araele over his chest, speaking a small blessing under his breath. When he had finished, he looked at his commander with an alarmed look on his face. "You're taking him with us?"

Savantin let out a heavy breath, becoming irritated by the question. He knew Ohric meant no harm in it, as he was not prying as Almour was.

"I want someone to scout ahead."

"For?"

"Let us talk by the fire."

Ohric nodded and they walked slowly toward it, Savantin not straying his eyes from the blaze. He was attempting to prioritize his thoughts presently, Larient being his number one concern. He knew Ohric was anxious about his men, something that Savantin knew he had to give voice to, or else his coadjutant would be worrying himself sick over it. Ohric had wasted no time in resting before the fire, sitting at the edge of the chair.

"Their actions were no fault of yours, Ohric," Savantin said, noticing his tense posture. "There was no way we could have known they were planning to abandon."

"I..." he started, looking into the fire as if trying to find the strength to continue. "I could have been more vigilant in recognizing signs. I could have."

"There was nothing you could have done. Where some of your men were treasonous, the others showed loyalty that exceedingly measures worth. Take that away from this," Savantin replied, taking a piece of kindling from the hearth and placing it in the fire.

"You're not angry?"

"Angry is not the word, Ohric. I am tired, I'm frustrated. Aggravated. Irascible, of late. Impatient. It's coming out in how I speak to them, how I react. Almour is beginning to imitate Haemad in level of irritation. But I do have leads. I intend to see to them once we are in Larient." Savantin sighed heavily, a bit of his voice escaping with it. "Ozrach wants the patron of Larient to be carefully guided back into subservience if committing sedition."

"That's... that's. I have no words."

"It's reprehensible, is what it is. The king is a weak, pathetic pest." Savantin grasped another piece of kindling, repeating the same action as before. "As for what happened with your men, no,

I am not angry. I asked you to accompany me. It's tragic what happened to him, but it was no fault of yours."

"I suppose you're right," Ohric stated. Savantin knew that thoughts on the topic wouldn't cease for some time. Ohric would be focused on it all day. Seeking out a thousand different possibilities, events in his head. He let him remain with them, knowing that his words would make no difference. Ohric often needed constant reassurance, something Savantin would only give once.

"I've told Almour to be wary while he's in Mordestai."

"You know he will be. He longs to please you."

"He longs for a promotion. That won't happen as long as I'm alive. He almost met the end of my fist a few moments ago."

"Sounds to me he's gotten worse."

"That was the last time I'll remind him to watch his tongue," Savantin said.

"You'll kill him in front of his men?"

"I won't kill him," he said and scratched his head with two long strokes. "Probably. I haven't yet decided how I'll handle his demotion but if he is as petulant in speaking as he was today then I just might strike him. If I have to resort to the methods I used when I first became commander then I very well will."

"I'm surprised you haven't, yet. You're surprising the men."

"I am growing tired of this campaign and it's increasingly evident," Savantin stated, not paying mind to his volume. Ohric looked around suddenly, making sure no one was there to hear it and Savantin shook his head, looking toward him. "The present situation offers no ears, but now you see my impatience is growing. We will leave for Larient soon enough. While you console your peace, I must take care of something. I want someone to scout ahead to see if there are any surprises awaiting us."

"You've another lead?" Ohric asked.

"I'm not certain. But it's all I have right now. The box *is* in Cilevdan, Ohric. That much I know. Someone will know where it's hiding. The first key will be ours shortly, and we needn't rush for the second. It will be at rest when it reaches its destination," Savantin said, taking a deep breath and looking toward the fire. It gave off much comfort to humans, something else he had learned. There were many nights in Terrenveil where when he was a soldier, his commander would spend an evening by it just sitting in silence. The man would stare, for hours peering into it for solace or direction.

Savantin stood back, pulling the chair out to the side. He turned away from the fire, hearing Ohric only after a few steps.

"Where do you go?"

"To rest. We will leave at dawn. Tell me if the boy's condition changes. And tell the men to ready themselves," Savantin said and exited.

Ohric looked toward the door for a few moments, the wind blowing in one last gust of snowy air until it was closed heavily. He didn't know what to think of those last words, or what to expect of what his commander was planning. He would do his job of alerting the men, however, without hesitation. He'd delay it only presently, sitting by the fire for warmth. He knew that they would have to look after Blacwin before they went anywhere, something that only Djeik seemed worried about. He wondered if the story was truth, though the two men who were claimed dead were not here in the inn. He saw no reason for the Mordestan to lie and put his straying mind to rest as he stood, pushing the chair close to the fire as he grabbed his coat. The men were staying in individual rooms, he knew, which would take time to gather his audience. He wondered how responsive they would even be, thinking back to the story Djeik told Savantin. If the two men really were trying to desert them, what was their reason? Was it because of the rebellion? Mauros? Or was it because of the pressure of this inescapable life?

The first door he reached belonged to Zareden who was sharpening his blades with a black board from where he sat on the bed. He saluted, partially, and continued his work, lifting his blade to look at the sharpness it had acquired. It shone a brilliant blue against the candlelight, a blade from his homeland.

"We are planning to move for Larient," Ohric said.

"Larient? A holy city?"

"Yes. It was marked. There is something there we must take care of before it ends in rebellion. It very well may."

"You think we are that close? The people are afraid. They may not show it in the meetings, but they know what war would mean."

"What does that have to do with the decision?" Ohric asked.

"Nothing, other than the fact that they may try to avert their plans to avoid it. I saw the faces of the people in the towns we've visited. None were of someone who wished for a stalemate."

"We will see where this road takes us. Will you be ready if it comes to it?" Ohric asked.

"My words are erroneous of my true intentions. If war is the outcome, I will readily accept whatever it is that is asked of me," Zareden answered, continuing to sharpen his blades.

"I must ask something else of you."

Zareden looked up at his coadjutant, placing his sharpening block down on the small wooden table next to the bed.

"Blacwin, as I'm sure you know has taken severe injury. I am making sure Djeik stays alongside the wagon we are transporting him in, but I will need someone to ride ahead to Larient and find the priests in the temple. They will need to make accommodation for him to rest. They follow the king, but do not wear your armor. Instead, put it in the supply wagon."

"It will be done. Shall I leave my weapons?"

"No. Take them," he said, and found himself staring at the blade's remarkable blue color. "They will not identify you of the legion."

"Yes, Coadjutant," Zareden answered and picked up his things, sheathing both of his swords. Ohric had left, heading toward another one of the rooms. He would gather them all together in the lobby before making his own preparations to leave, looking forward to visitation with his goddess.

◆ ◆ ◆

It was a distant shore that he dreamed of, one where the mussels and clams were plenty upon the low tides brought to them by the moons above. The sand felt rough against his feet as he walked in closeness to the water, feeling the cool licks of the excess that the waves brought in. He had run away again, another fight at home now had him hours away from the farm, listening to the sounds of the ocean. He listened for sirens, or mermaids, calling out to fishermen in the tumultuous waves. They had beautiful voices, he heard, and hoped that maybe they would call him away as well. He was partially confident in his ability to swim, never having done so before. How hard could it be? He wondered, as he took one step into the cold surging waters.

The water receded quickly, rushing back out to the body before him as if a diminished army retreating to its strength. He closed his eyes and breathed in the salty air, listening. There was not much to be heard, besides the crashing and scraping and rushing. He continued down the shore, his feet still covered in ocean water. He hadn't realized what time it was, as he looked out over the endless miles of thick blue until the point where his vision ended. There, an array of darkness painted where the horizon would be, and where the sun would in a few hours rise. He was disappointed in what he did not hear as he continued along the shoreline, wondering how long he could linger out here before he was sent for. How would they have known where he had gone? They never followed him, never looked for his horse. He could spend an eternity out here, listening to the sounds of the sea.

Finally, he had grown tired of the coldness on his feet, despite the summer air, and walked up from the beach, climbing the small cliff up to the mainland. When he had thrown his hand over the edge, pulling himself over it, he noticed that there was another horse tied up with his. He was curious now, who had come out here during the night and why. Perhaps it was for the same reason as he, though he doubted it. As he walked over to the tree, he took the reins of his horse and stroked its nose, looking at the other one paw at the ground gently. He thought of staying to find this other night traveler, wondering if they could share conversation but ended up riding away from the shore, heading back toward the barn.

There were several towns around Valspire, smaller ones that haven't even been marked on maps. They were just assumed a part of the province, their duties to the kingdom being collected when the debtors visited the manor house in Valspire. Perhaps he could stay at one of those for the night. Perhaps, he could stay at one of those forever. He had no interest in going back home, racing his horse through the green plains that led toward the towns. It wasn't far enough away, and word could travel to his home of where he was taking residence. He was the butcher, and though his name wasn't known, he had a fateful likeness of his parents. His mother he didn't mind, her soft face and kind eyes were complemented by bright hair, which he acquired. He took the look of his father, however, with dark eyes and a strong jaw. Though not unfortunate looking, he wasn't as handsome as the other men in town, and his sand-colored hair gave him away almost immediately. He had no money, nothing to pay people to remain quiet about his appearance in town, which was something else that could not be avoided. In the smaller parts of the world people enjoyed talking. Almost too much, he thought.

He only had his skills as a butcher, to kill and cut and sever. There was no use for this without a farm, without animals to deliver. Maybe when he was old enough, he would leave and find a place where his skills were more useful. But he was only fifteen, and most guilds or armies did not employ boys until they had seen their eighteenth year. He had quite a while before he could do so, and decided to head his horse back home and endure whatever other punishment he would receive for running off. His chest and arms had finally stopped bleeding, yet he could still feel the bludgeoning he got from the shovel found hanging on the barn door. The handle had broken halfway through the skirmish, his father using the pointed end instead to assail him. He wondered how horribly bruised he would be when he woke the next day, and how his mother fared her beating when trying to stop it. He had become angry after seeing the blow dealt to her but could not act as he was lying in the corner, a bleeding pained mass of skin, muscle and bone. He could not lift his arms without them hurting, and despite this, left just a few minutes after his father had finally stopped.

He took a deep breath in, feeling the pain on his chest....

Blacwin opened his eyes, looking around at the dark room illuminated by candles in the corners. He was in a stone bed, softened by many blankets of animal pelts, sheep and wolves' skin. He looked at his arms, expecting them to appear bruised, but realized that he was no longer sleeping, and this was no longer a dream. He went to move, feeling an intense pain on his right arm, where a wound ran between his bicep and forearm. Taking a breath was painful, as his chest felt tight and sore around his expanding lungs. He let out a small cry, staring into the ceiling made of beveled glass. It was an astonishing sight; the rainbows of the pearly structure being made alive by the flickering of the candles around him. He wondered if he was in a chamber being prepared for burial, with its serenity and the calm, muted scent of a light and airy flower. He smelled strong incense from the hallway and felt a churning in his stomach. He sat up quickly despite the pain he was in, and expelled vomit into an urn that sat next to him, filled halfway with water. He watched reluctantly as the two mixed, feeling his heart rate climb dangerously. The tightness in his chest was permanent now, and he continued to feel it as he tried to pull air into his lungs. He found himself panicking after long, and a woman walked in, covered in light colored linens with pearl-like beads in her blonde hair. She moved to him quickly, gently guiding him down onto the bed, being careful as he winced and cried out. She took a rag from the table next to her and wiped his mouth, placing it down and snapping two leaves from a small tree in the corner.

Blacwin tried to reject the offering at first, turning his head and closing his eyes but the woman persisted, and he heard her soft voice for the first time.

"It will take away the foul taste, so you will not be left with it once I go."

"Where are you going?" he asked slowly, working hard to have his voice escape his chest.

"I am going to get some herbs for your wounds. They could easily become infected. Your friend came before you and said to take care of you as best we could until then. He promised an offering for our services."

"My friend?"

"Yes. He was tall, thin. He did not look like he was from around here and had two deep-blue blades hanging from his belt. He had said you were attacked by animals, and the only thing he could do for you was burn your wounds together. They're still raw and need tending to."

"Animals," Blacwin repeated, trying to think. He didn't know why he couldn't remember. "Where am I?"

"You are in Larient, in a temple dedicated to Araele," the woman answered, moving the urn beneath them aside. She knelt on the ground, her bare feet crossing behind her. "My name is Alayvia."

"Blacwin," he said. Why did he have these wounds all over him, and what he had done to receive them?

"You were sick when you came here. A fever held you even though you did not wake. I am happy to see that you have. The fever comes and goes, some nights it is worse than others."

"This is the first time I've woken?" Blacwin asked, still trying to make out the room around him. His sight was failing him, yet his sense of smell was unusually heightened, the incense and scents of various flowers making him feel calm despite the intense pain he was feeling. He had thought about asking her for something to relieve it, but found his voice trapped behind his tongue.

"Yes. And you are speaking. It is good to hear your voice. Usually those gripped in such fever do not regain it," Alayvia answered, reaching up to his face. He welcomed her touch and wished that he could see her face better. He was sure that she was beautiful, if her face at all matched her voice. His vision was still blurred, and he continued to stare at the ceiling, trying to make all the shapes he saw focus into one.

There was a voice from the doorway, commanding and strict. The girl rose suddenly, bowing and leaving the room. Blacwin tried to move his head sideways, feeling the pain in his chest return.

"He's awake." Another, different voice. Perhaps he hadn't been left behind after all.

"I will speak to him."

"Who is there?" Blacwin asked, squinting to try and focus his eyes.

"It seems as if he's still gripped in fever, Ohric."

"Ohric," Blacwin said, a certain light in his voice.

"He recognizes me," Ohric answered and pulled a chair toward the bed. He sat in it, his arms crossed over the backing.

"Speak to him." The other voice.

Blacwin groaned slightly, trying to move. He wished to look upon his visitors, hoping then he would remember what had come to pass. He could not do so, and struggled back into his current position, letting out a small cry of pain.

"Remain on your back. Do not use your remaining strength for an action that is not needed."

"I am sorry," Blacwin uttered, coughing slightly.

"Sorry? For what?" the strict voice.

"I did not mean to slaughter the lamb," Blacwin said, his voice weak.

"What is he talking about?" Ohric asked. It was the only voice he could place name to.

"The lamb, I know it was not necessary to kill it. I haven't worked in days. I needed to take its life; don't you see? If I didn't take the lamb, then I am afraid it would have been something else. I have tried to explain it to you, time and time again."

"He is still gripped in fever; he's not speaking of the present." The strict voice again.

"Do you think he has suffered loss of memory?"

"It seems to sound that way. Unfortunate, I thought that upon waking he would remember who it was that assailed him."

"Blacwin, do you remember what happened a few nights ago?" Ohric asked him.

"I killed the lamb."

"The other night Djeik saved you. But you were stabbed with a blade coated in poison. How do you feel?" a question from the other voice, sounding less harsh.

"D...Djeik? Why are we in Larient? The girl told me we were in Larient," he asked. "A...Alayvia. Her name was."

"We're looking for information. The only thing you need to do now is rest," Ohric answered.

"I need one question answered. The man who stabbed you, did he say anything?"

"Stabbed?"

The man sighed heavily, a sign of disappointment. Blacwin did not know what for. Why was he here? Why was he covered in burns and incisions? It was not the first time he was beaten like this, but they said he had been stabbed. Could his father have stabbed him for killing the lamb?

"Send word to Ozrach. Get this man's records. I want to know where he came from and who he was," the other voice said angrily, leaving the room as evidenced by large and loud footsteps.

"You did your best; do not worry about what your fate will be. While you rest in Araele's sanctuary you are to remain at peace. Find comfort in her warmth," Ohric said.

"Am I to die?" Blacwin asked.

"I will ask Araele to spare your life, and whatever happens is in her grace. If you pass, accept her hands. Alayvia will be here to care for you in your pain."

"What happens when you are ready to move on from here?"

"You will remain here with the Lady of Light until you've been healed. You do not want to continue this path if you are in pain. The medic said that you would be able to fight again if you survived this. Do not rush into it, or you may not live," Ohric answered.

"I am useless if I stay here. I can still finish my work. I need to finish my work."

"It is not up for debate. We are trying to save your life. If you endanger it by traveling, I cannot help you. If you remain here with my people, I will do everything I can," Ohric answered.

"When will I be healed?" Blacwin asked.

"I do not know. Honestly, with the poison used on the blade you weren't supposed to survive the night. The fever was supposed to kill you. I feel Araele is already working toward your future. Place your trust in her," Ohric said and stood.

"How can you trust in someone you cannot see? A voice you hear when no one is speaking? A touch you feel when you are unconscious?" Blacwin asked.

Ohric received the question and was silent for a few moments, searching his mind for the correct words to form an answer. "Faith, Blacwin, is something that is not easy to achieve. It comes to us when we expect the darkest possible outcome and a light shines through, or when you ask for peace, forgiveness, solace, and it is given. Araele does many things for me, shows me the way when I see none, speaks to me when the world greets me in silence. It could be the same for you if you accept her light."

"But you kill."

"Death is something that no one can escape. It is inevitable. But a painful death is something you can avoid," Ohric answered, watching the boy. He did not move his eyes from the ceiling, and his chest rose and fell in a slow, steady pattern.

"When is it you are leaving?"

"That, I am not sure. It could be days. Depending on what we find here. But I will be alerted to your condition, and once you have healed, I will send you the location we are currently occupying."

Blacwin did his best to nod, his head only moving partially from its spot upon a pillow. "Are... are the injured usually cared for in temples?"

"No. Injured soldiers are usually slain on the battlefield. You have been spared that."

"Why?" Blacwin asked.

"Only the Lady of Light knows. Faith, Blacwin. Never forget it," Ohric answered and turned away, heading through the doorway. The inner sanctum was his destination, where a statue of Araele would grace the walls before several pillars. The pillars would each have a remnant of her undying light upon them, housed inside thick glass spheres. She cast her light here when she fought the battle to save their earth from the swallowing darkness and split that light among the surviving humans to see it never return. It was said that the small glass spheres were built by the first of her followers, making certain the light could never be touched or tainted by those meaning to do it harm. He found the sanctum, his eyes coming across several short, cream-colored pillars, gold rope wrapped around them and ending on the flat of their pedestal tops. A circular groove cut into them made it so a sphere could rest upon each one gently. He looked into the room in wonder, a feeling of happiness blooming inside him. He heard that the temple was one of the most beautiful in all of Cilevdan and was worked on for days at a time by skilled artisans, all with unquestioned devotion to the Lady of Light. The feeling was one he hadn't harbored in a long time, a feeling of peace, serenity. There was no comfort the world could offer him that would come close to what Araele gave him.

Araele gave him something else that day, a chance to spare a life. The young boy was not going to live through the night, not with the dose of Rythran he had been given at the point of a blade. He wondered if Djeik had ever found the sword used to cut Blacwin, but that was another thought entirely. The story was that the boy was alive, though fevered and in an amnesiac state. Perhaps now, even if he could not return to battle, he would be spared further from his oath to the legion.

Ohric was baffled however, on how the boy could remember his face, his name. The only thing that seemed to be on his mind was a lamb, from his past, he was sure. It showed promise to him that the legion was struck from his mind, but remembering the name of his coadjutant was not encouraging news. Time would tell if he could remember what happened to him, about the war, about the killings in Rierdan. If that happened, and the boy was unable to return to service then he would undoubtedly have to continue his service in the castle. It was still strange to him that Savantin would go to these lengths to aid him in recovering. He always, however, had meaning for things that he did not give voice. He liked few people, Savantin; though Ohric wasn't sure he actually liked Blacwin. Perhaps he would secure a prayer in hoping that the boy did not gain his memory back, only so that he would be spared a fate that was inescapable. Death was inevitable, he told him, but a painful death was something he could avoid. Ohric sighed and walked into the sanctum, breathing in the incense that burned on a pedestal in each corner of the room.

He knelt before one of the pillars, the light inside the sphere becoming brighter as his face became level with it. He let the light feel calm upon him, listening as Araele offered him council. He hadn't given her prayer in quite some time, not in the proper manner at least. He felt gracious now, inside her refuge, grateful for the time he was allowed to have here. Just as he was about to speak to her, he was interrupted, the voice of a human coming from where he thought Araele's would be.

"Are you in need of anything?" a priest asked, quietly speaking to him as if not to interrupt others praying to Araele in closeness to her statue.

"Only a quiet word with my goddess," Ohric answered.

"I am sorry to interrupt you. I am required to meet all the needs of those who travel here."

"I know my mission, and only seek to hear Araele's guiding voice. There is no way you can assist me."

"You are a soldier?" the priest asked in surprise.

"Yes."

"How can you call yourself an Araelian if you have spilled blood?"

"Was it not Araele herself who spilled the blood of the shadows that threatened to swallow our land and enslave us?" Ohric asked, his voice stern.

"It was, but she did what was necessary to banish the dark so that we would never have to shed blood."

"You clearly do not understand the sacrifices I am making," Ohric said and stood, closing his eyes as he turned from the pillar and toward the priest. "What is your name?"

"Jarum."

"Jarum, there are enemies of Araele so vile that the only way to destroy them is to end their lives. They seek to destroy the light that she's given us and see the dark return. Not everything was destroyed in the purge; you know this to be true. So, she picks those who she thinks are strong enough to commit their lives to her service. My judgment will come from her, and no one else," Ohric answered.

"You think that she wants violence answered with violence?" Jarum asked, trying hard now to keep his voice at a whisper.

"She tells me that even though the killing is distasteful that it is necessary, that in her kingdom only the light should remain, and we should vanquish the dark. Men drown one another in famine, greed, lust. Instead of showering love and offering their assistance they meet their own kind with selfishness. They do not understand what they've been given by Araele and do not deserve to have it. So, I will take up sword and let her hands guide my own."

"She speaks to you... that cannot be so. She would not lead you on a path that brings about blood," Jarum stated.

"She only asks me to stop those who shame and dishonor her light. She did not die so that we could feed the dark. Brother turns on brother, and nothing was done to stop it."

"You are fooling yourself," Jarum said.

"Me? Fooling myself? Who are you fooling, priest? She knows what you do when you are *absent service* as you call it. When you're not here in these walls. You haven't been so chaste, have you? I can smell the girls from the brothel you visit on your breath. Araele can overlook your fall if you return to her light."

The priest said nothing and looked down at the sword hanging from Ohric's side, the Wolf of Terrenveil engraved clearly on its hilt.

"Is there reason you stare?" Ohric asked, harshly.

"I know who you are, now."

"Does it make a difference who I am? I only live to serve her. I have heard her voice, guiding me for nineteen years. I trust in her path and whatever she asks of me."

Jarum offered a sly laugh as he looked into Ohric's eyes. "Yet she has not asked you to sever the head of darkness itself? She has not told you to end the cruelty of the man you serve directly under?"

"She is at an understanding. I make no mistake in my loyalties. If she had asked me to do so then I would have," Ohric answered, turning away from the priest.

"Your words are folly."

Ohric turned abruptly, looking the priest up and down, staring into his sneering face. He waited a moment before speaking, watching as the priest's glare failed to diminish. "Do not try to understand what I speak of. Abide by her teachings and leave my assignment to me. I am who she speaks to."

The priest said nothing as Ohric turned from the pedestal and headed toward the back of the room, looking up into the eyes of the statue of Araele. She held a dove in one hand above her head, a sword in the other. Her hair was strung with flowers, white valley flowers, incense smelling of them, honey and spice.

Her cheeks were facing upward, toward the skies as her eyes were, and the dress she had worn on the day of her commitment to the world was carved in tremendous detail, each fold and wrinkle accounted for as it fell from her shoulders, down to her knees. Ohric placed his sword before her, and knelt, closing his eyes and holding his arms out to either side of him.

"Araele, please cleanse the blade that has ended your enemies, for their blood taints its majesty and homage to you," he said, breathing in the smell of the flowers. They calmed him, entering his lungs and cleansing him of all the blood he had spilled for her. She smiled at him, surely. He did what was necessary to spare the rest of her followers from bloodying their hands, yet none would understand his sacrifice for them. They were unworthy, all of them, of what she did to save them. They didn't realize how much pain she endured to spare them from living in the infinite dark. Perhaps he should allow them to see what they had been saved from, and then in her name end them for their sins. There would be fewer priests like Jarum, who preached her words during the daylight but at night took to the streets, encouraging the lack of purity in the coins he spent. There would be less of the hatred toward fellow man, the ravaging greed that had civilians in a chokehold. It made him angry, how his motives would be questioned by the ones responsible for the foul deeds that desecrated her.

He stood from his kneeling position and picked up his sword, bowing to her before leaving the temple. Into the streets he went, still feeling a considerable amount of rage. These blatant offenders of her ways knew not what it was like to watch people tear each other apart, watching as others suffered in places where they were supposed to feel safe. He walked past his men, all waiting for Savantin to return from wherever it was he went. It was beginning to get dark, and he doubted his commander was still questioning the patron, someone else who was responsible for the poverty seen just outside of his province. He had hoped Savantin put an end to him, but then wished to recant the thought, only so that he could do so himself.

"Ohric!" a voice called out his name from behind him. He turned, hearing Araele call his name also. He waited for her next statement, but it never came, and as Djeik approached him, he wished he hadn't stopped at all.

"We were told to wait for you. Savantin went outside of the walls. He said there was something he needed to attend to."

"Did he find anything while questioning the patron?" Ohric asked, feeling foolish for letting the question leave his lips. Savantin would not tell his men what he had uncovered, and if he had found anything at all would have first come to his coadjutant.

"That's just it. He asked you to speak to him. He thought you may find something that he did not. But he told us to be ready for our next assignment. He seemed rushed in his speaking to us, only telling me that he wanted to speak to you upon his return."

"Thank you." Ohric answered.

"What do you want us to do until then?"

"Make sure no one leaves the city. They know who we are, there's no fooling them. If anyone leaves, bring them back as prisoners of the monarchy," Ohric said and turned away, headed toward anywhere he could clear his head. He had a considerable amount of stress and anxiety on his mind lately and found himself growing impatient as well. This campaign of Ozrach's was growing tiresome, and the source of greed and selfishness sat tucked away in his castle, comfortable and languid. He was not a man deserving of a kingdom, not in anyone's eyes. If the goddess herself wanted him to see the light and fix the mistakes in his ways and he resisted, then he was not worthy of the crown. Neraea was another matter altogether. His queen was a harlot, only pretending to be faithful for reasons unknown. Be it power, or riches, or vanity, all three were a condemnable source. Ohric knew that she spent nights with Savantin, who had her begging him for his touch, to enter her and invade that which she had pledged to her king.

They would be better dethroned and placed on display in front of Cilevdan as examples of corruption. Ohric walked slower now, his eyes scanning the streets. Perhaps he would find a woman he could guide to Araele's comfort, or a man doing something that was punishable. It had been a while since he cut down someone for their ignominious actions, and he was feeling as if it was something he should have done as they started their journey. If the patroness of Opskaven was still alive, he could have put her to punishment at the tip of his own blade, marked her for the things she had done. She would never be revered the same way again, not a powerful leader, but a murderer, a traitor. Heresy.

He thought back to Terrenveil, back to the people of the court. There were tens of them that needed the same reminder the patroness did. They lived like animals, husks of themselves feeding off the sinful entities around them. Like parasites, sucking and feeding and draining. They would all meet the ends of their overly sumptuous and avaricious existence. Their way of life would only place them in the dark.

People feared the dark before the purge occurred, the purge that had thousands of men killed on battlefields by dark and twisted creatures. Sacred grounds were covered in blood and yellow entrails. It was said to have been a horrible sight, by the only survivor, the last soldier of Araele. Ohric remembered the book well. The one where every fight was accounted for in such vivid detail that he almost believed to have been there himself. So many casualties were had, on both sides, and though it was recalled as a victory, he knew better than to believe that all the evils had really been vanquished. The dark and unnatural forces seemed everlasting, yet now instead of laying at the mercy of a hoard of daemons, humans were subjugated to the oppression of their own kind by their own kind.

Wandering along the road he was stopped by a voice behind him, turning to watch as children were ushered into a house that sat away from the others by a heavyset woman, her face kind and matronly. The house was lonely; its old, washed stone surface had stood many years in the spot it was now, with a tangled weedy yard coming from directly behind it. There was an old dog lying near a couple of bowls, polished and shining gently under the light of the stars. He scarcely moved, curled up on a bed of straw, pungent and sweet smelling. His thick gray hair was enough to keep him warm in the world outside, and Ohric watched as his body rose and fell with each breath he took.

A small child opened the back door and the dog's head perked up instantly, his tail gently beating against the ground as his eyes came across her. She untied the rope that was around the dog's neck, quietly leading him inside. A few other children behind her giggled softly, the tail on the old boy moving quicker at the sound. He moved forward and gave the girl a large kiss. She petted his head and called him a good boy, closing the door behind them. Ohric looked up toward the sky, watching as white smoke climbed from the chimney.

The innocence and care of a child was beautiful to him. The dog would sleep in front of the fire tonight instead of in the winter, against the words of the house's matron. But what punishment would she offer a child who sweetly led a friend to warmth? He hoped the answer was nothing. Eventually children grew, and their hearts changed along with their years. Whose fault was it that the world was like this? That children forgot their altruisms, that men lay their hands upon their wives, their sisters, their daughters. Was it the kings? The gods? Only one path mattered now, the one that would bring order to a world that had fallen in shadow and forgot what it was to respect, to empathize.

He shifted his direction to the patron's house in agitation, knowing it was something he should do best not to show. The king instructed Savantin not to be harsh when reminding the patron of where his loyalty should rest. Ohric detested the fact and knew Savantin could not be bothered with it. Perhaps the task was best left to him, at least then he knew that the patron would be spared whatever castigation Savantin would dispense. His commander was becoming restless, careless in his pursuit.

They must be close. Either that, or dangerously far. He doubted that Savantin would be able to accept another wall. Both keys were found, so that must mean the box is in Cilevdan. It must be. Ohric would hope it was. Almour misplaced his respect, and Ohric misplaced his fear. It was creeping back in now, fueled by the thoughts of what could happen when he returned to town. *He wanted to speak to you upon his return* is what the Mordestan said. It was usual, frequent, expected. Still, there was no shaking the racing of his heart. Where had he gone?

Ohric made it to the house where it was reported the patron lived. It was large but unassuming. A brick building among all the other brick buildings. He walked up to the door and listened to the sound of silence. No crackling of a fire, no footsteps, or the settling of wood. Nothing. He moved to knock on the door and noticed then that it was partially opened. No good would come of investigating this alone. Or should he? He really wished Savantin hadn't left town, he would have been brave enough to go inside. Brave? That wasn't the word. Confident. Without worry. After a few fateful moments, he headed back to the inn, claiming Zareden from his room. He ordered Harlan to watch the inn with Djeik and Mortan.

By the time they approached the patron's house, Ohric had already explained the mission to Zareden who nodded quietly in acceptance. He did not speak if he didn't have to. This was just his very educated speculation, however. Zareden's homeland wasn't vast, and it bred killers. He was told about it, and how it was the birthplace of many creeds in service of shadow gods, and worse.

Ohric took a deep breath before pushing the door inward, Zareden's hand above one of his blades. The room was dark, unlit. It smelled only partially of food, a sign that someone had enjoyed a meal here quite recently. The smoky smell of ashes followed as the two walked slowly inward. The light from the torches outside revealed to them a lone candle. Zareden picked it up, and touched the top of it, the wax still soft. He turned away, cupping the candle before returning it to the center of the room, setting it down in its metal cage. Ohric took it into his hands, then, and moved to light the small white candles that called home a large candelabra, coming up from the floor. Zareden pulled his blade as they heard shuffling from upstairs, Ohric waving two of his fingers downward. He peeked up at the stairwell, the sound intensifying before it abruptly stopped. Zareden continued the silent pull of his blade against orders. Ohric dismissed it, and the two walked toward the second floor, candle in tow. The hallway was empty, so quiet a man could hear his thoughts before they formed words. Zareden was ordered to the left and the pair walked down slowly, opening every door on the way to the hallway's end. Zareden stopped three doors in and patted Ohric's shoulder. A man lay dead on the floor, trauma to his head. There was a small club lying at the base of the window, which was open. A small breeze drifted through, causing the light in the candle to dance quickly before it regained its strength at the wick.

"The patron?" Zareden asked, finally, putting his swords away.

"It must be," Ohric said, moving to the corpse. "It's still warm. With the hour it is, and this reportedly being his residence, it must be him."

"What now?" Zareden asked. Ohric hesitated a moment, trying to form a response in his head. "Go, make sure no one is trying to leave. In the morning I will inform the town that it is under monarchical investigation. Tell no one, and we will instruct the others to mind the gates and watch the city."

"And Savantin?" he asked.

"He will be notified when he returns. I fear his investigation will be cut short as well," Ohric said, hoping that Zareden wouldn't further question. Ohric hoped he would be back before dawn so that he could seek direction. He was certain the patron had many enemies, both in the monarchy and those against it. But to be murdered in the middle of the night? Ohric moved the candle over the patron's body, blood coming from the wound on his forehead.

"He knew his attacker. Must have, he's not been struck from behind," Zareden said and took the candle, manipulating the flame through his fingers quickly. "He's bleeding from his nose too, looks broken."

Ohric looked on silently for a moment. "Either that, or he didn't know they were coming."

"Killer would not strike a man who didn't know they were coming anywhere but from behind. Behind means there is no chance of detection, no chance that the target may shout. This man knew his attacker, sure of it."

"So, we narrow it down to the people he interacted with most. I'll check and see if he has any family and speak to his advisor," Ohric said. Zareden nodded, silently making his way down the stairs and out of the house. Ohric decided it was best he left in the cover of darkness, too, or else someone may see him leaving and think it was him who did it. Would someone believe that? Anything was possible at this point, the proof of that lying on the floor before him. Before heading back for his men, he stood in the street for a moment, agonizing over whether or not he should knock on the advisor's door and ask about his family, or if he should wait until morning. Should he tell him at all? What if he was the one that did it? Ultimately, he decided on the latter of the two choices. One way they could prove the advisor's innocence is if they went to the house together in the morning and discovered the tragedy at the same time. Depending upon his reaction to the patron's corpse, of course.

When he got back to the inn, Harlan was waiting by the fire, a blanket around his shoulders. "Evening, Coadjutant," he said in a salute. Ohric nodded toward him and sat in the chair across from him, staring into the fire with unmoving eyes, rubbing his fingers together. He started to pick at his left thumbnail with his right one, taking a deep breath before looking around the room.

He moved his head downward, speaking in a hushed voice. "I went to the patron's house, to speak to him."

"And?" Harlan asked, moving forward.

"He's dead," Ohric said, simply. He hadn't looked up to see Harlan's reaction. He looked around the room once more to make sure that no one else had entered, though.

"Did he threaten you?"

"No. He was dead when I got there."

Harlan took a deep breath and sat back in his chair, moving the blanket off his shoulders. "What are we to do?"

"I'm going back in the morning with his advisor. No one knows save you, me, and Zareden."

"You're not taking anyone with you?"

"No. For this to look believable I must go alone. Zareden is watching the gate. I'll need the rest of you to keep an eye on the village. You're overseeing. Report to me as necessary. We must find out who's done this before they attempt to leave. Or worse."

"Worse?"

"Someone else dies, or Savantin returns, and we've found nothing," Ohric said and shivered. "Attempt sleep. As far as we know no one else knows he's dead." Attempt was the operative word. He would probably get one, maybe two solid hours in. His thoughts and troubles would keep him awake most of the night, feeling nauseous and ill beyond that. He had all night to decide what he was going to do, he supposed. It would be early when he knocked on the advisor's door, so that no one had time to go to the manor house.

Dawn arrived at a sluggard's pace, Ohric tossing and turning agonizingly. He sat up, feeling jittery, his heart racing. Zareden had not returned, though he didn't really expect the Tovian to. Tovian was a guess, but nothing else made sense. He watched the man control fire but chose to say nothing. Years ago, it would have intimidated him, but that was before he became Savantin's most trusted. He was thinking about their pact a lot lately, out of terror. He knew better than to be so cautious when he returned, but he didn't know how much longer he'd be able to suppress it.

Ohric put fist to door, knocking three times before a lanky man answered it, his face brightening.

"Ah, I knew we would meet before long," he said and extended his hand. Ohric shook it weakly, looking around at the inside of his house before returning a gaze. "Proper introduction is in order. I am Arai Sento. I involved myself in the building of the temple. How can I help you this morning?"

"I am to speak with the patron, I thought it was best you accompany me. I wished to speak to you about the temple on our walk."

"Of course. Your worship is known throughout Terrenveil, I was pleased to know that you'd come to see it."

"It's beautiful," Ohric said. "I've not seen anything like it, not even at the Mountain. The temple there is antiquated, comfort in its age."

"I wished to model it on the temple at the Mountain but have not been there myself to see it."

"The priest that makes it his home…"

"I know which one you speak of. Recently pledged his life, though I see old habits die hard. Unfortunately, I am not allowed removal."

"Though you've been given the title of Arai?"

"Merely because most of my wealth was spent in constructing it. The higher order will deal with him, as I've sent word."

"My respect," Ohric said. Sento returned the gesture in a bow of his head, saying nothing until they reached the door to the patron's house, slightly opened.

"Was he expecting us?" Ohric asked, trying to hide the shaken feeling behind his voice. His stomach bubbled.

"Something is amiss," Sento said quietly. Ohric placed his hand on his sword, nodding toward Sento, who pushed the door inward. The house was in the same condition they'd left it in, the candles in the brazier almost down to their ends. "Alarde?"

Sento said, looking up the stairwell. "Are you here?" Silence was the return, and Sento turned toward Ohric, concern embedded in his face. They reached the top floor in a matter of moments, shadows dancing across the floor from the sun peeking inward. Ohric's pulse climbed as they searched the rooms, knowing that very soon they would make discovery.

Sento moved his hands to his mouth, his eyes wide as the patron's corpse came into sight, a small gasp denoting his shock. "A murderer walks the streets of Larient."

Ohric strode forward, looking into Sento's eyes which had become glassy. "Forgive me, I must weep," he said as his face twisted with sadness.

"He's cold," Ohric said, trying to hide his disgust at touching the corpse a second time. "This happened hours ago."

"We must alert the guard," Sento said, hurriedly.

"Not yet," Ohric said, panicked. He regained control after two deep breaths. "We must speak and plan a course of action. Did he have any enemies, anyone who could have done this?"

"Alarde had plenty of people that disliked him. The man lived impulsively and had little consequence from the monarchy. But I didn't think any of them capable of, or willing to murder."

"I will need your help in locating them, speaking to them. We will not leave until the town is secure. Do you think this will be the end?"

"Hard to say. I know I will not sleep with ease," Sento said and deeply exhaled. "How many men accompany you?"

"Four. We suffered casualties in Opskaven. There was a raid, bandits."

"My condolences."

"I have tasked one to watch the gates. It's protocol, though help will be needed. Can we trust the town guard for aid?"

"We should speak with the captain, Haeden, first. She will know who to assign," Sento stated. "Shall we go?"

"Yes. But first, you mentioned people disliked him?"

"There are a few. Hensing, Alarde's brother-in-law. He is a potential heir to patronship, which would be a motive. Though, I don't believe he was necessarily after it. It was likely a feud spawned from marriage to his sister. There is Saraen, also a town noble. Her distaste lay in his frivolity and the oversight of his crimes, as she called them. Genat, a Rustanzi who settled here. He is a fletcher. Alarde was known to be prejudiced during times of intoxication and on several occasions entered his shop and threatened to remove him from town. The only other person I can think of is Remi, widow to one of the guards here. He was rather egregious at the funeral. Do you intend on speaking to them all?"

Prejudice. Disgusting. Ohric thought. "I'm unsure," he said. He didn't know if he could let others handle this and felt a complete responsibility for the task.

"If I may suggest, speaking to Haeden first would be wise. She can assign men to watch the denizens, they know everyone and will notice if someone is acting strange. She will insist her men help your own. Shall we alert them first?"

"No, they are taking their own patrol. For now, it will be best not to distract them," Ohric said. He didn't know if the nausea would ever cease. He hoped it would at the very least dissipate as they made progress. Sento nodded, looking once more at the floor. "What shall we do with him? I don't believe his wife and son will take it well to see him like this. But I do not know how we'll move him to the crypts without the citizens taking notice."

"A cart with a cover," Ohric said. "Why are his wife and child not in Larient? The monarchy tasked everyone to stay, the punishment is not forgiving," he continued. Ozrach would impose none, he was too far removed from the situation. Though he didn't think Savantin at this point cared, he still needed to keep the illusion strong.

"They left weeks ago, before the orders from the Mountain came into effect. His son is ill, fraught with night terrors so bad that he wakes neighbors. She was certain she knew the remedy to help him, but Alarde wasn't to go with them. It was obvious he needed to stay here, but she was adamant about going alone."

Strange. Could she have known that he was going to be murdered? Or was she honest in her intentions. He came up with several scenarios in his head and hadn't realized Sento continued his speech.

"Coadjutant?"

"Apologies, I was taking a closer look at his wounds," he said. "We should see Haeden about aid and a wagon."

"The only person I know with a wagon is the crypt keeper. But it would be too obvious I fear."

"We cannot leave him here."

"Unless we ask one of the merchants. The potter has one. I could offer him coin to borrow it. He won't ask questions if he's paid."

"Splendid," Ohric managed. He wanted to get to the guard as fast as possible. He was beginning to feel the emptiness of his stomach in addition to its anxious protest. They embarked silently to where Sento said Haeden and her men were stationed. Once arriving, Sento offered words to the one guard outside of the door. He nodded, pushing the door inward. They passed through a small and unassuming hallway, which opened into a large room where weapons hung across the walls. There was a shield on each wall in the center, one bearing the wolf of Terrenveil, and the other he did not recognize. One man occupied the room, Sento immediately asking after the whereabouts of their target.

"She's speaking to two men that were found outside the walls. Went down there about an hour ago, maybe some less," he offered, scent of smoke coming from his breath. "She only took Vraen with her, didn't think it was necessary to take anyone else. Shall I inform her once she returns?"

"I will seek her out," Ohric said.

"I am with you," Sento replied.

"I must insist you stay; we don't know if there are hostiles," the guard, quickly.

"She's been gone near an hour and you're questioning whether or not the men were hostiles?" Ohric asked. "Which gate has she left from?"

"Down the hill, to the left. It's a small door inside the wall."

Ohric said nothing in reply and made haste to the hill, Sento quietly in tow. Ohric stopped only to allow him to catch up and looked toward him. "Are you certain you wish to accompany me outside of the walls?"

"I've my own weapon," Sento said and lifted his coat, revealing a small thin blade. "Can't be too careful anymore, the growing presence of bandits in the outer territories is making all of us nervous."

"Understandably," Ohric said simply. The guard at the door lazily opened it, Ohric placing his hands over his eyes briefly to adjust to the strengthening of the sun. To the right of the city was the wood, quiet and ominous. Due left was the road north, two people in armor standing at road's edge.

"That's her," Sento said and set pace. Ohric followed, attempting to listen to their conversation before they ended it. It was unsuccessful, though, Haeden turning to them as they approached.

"Advisor Sento, a surprise this morning."

"Good morning to you as well, this is Ohric of the Light, legionnaire Coadjutant."

It had been a while since he was introduced to anyone formally, he couldn't even remember the last time. He often didn't need an introduction and respected the Arai for taking his time in doing so.

"Greetings. I am Haeden, captain of the guard here in Larient. How may I be of service?"

"Walk with us?" Ohric said and moved his arm outward toward the door in the city wall.

"Stay here, I will send another to your position," Haeden said quickly to the guard at the road. She crossed to their side, looking back at the road once more. "Two men, citizens of a smaller outlying town close to here, Wivran. They said they heard terrifying sounds from the mountain wall, one of them thought they saw a revenant."

"A revenant? Here?"

"He had this look in his eye, a fear I've not even seen in men I've killed," Haeden replied. "He's seen something. I told them to make haste back to Wivran and we'd send guards to check it out."

A revenant. Savantin likely was investigating the very thing they ran into. He knew better than to give away position, though. "I'm afraid you'll have to push that off for now, we have a serious matter to discuss," Ohric said. "Alarde is dead."

"Dead?" Haeden gasped. "What do we know?"

"Not much yet," Ohric said. "Sento assured me that you could have your men watch town, bring anything to my attention that can help us apprehend his killer. Right now, one of my men is watching the gate but I'll need him during my investigation. Do you have anyone that can handle that task? I trust I needn't stress to you the importance that they do not fail."

"You needn't. She will not," Haeden said and turned toward town. "I will go alert my men of their new tasks. If you need me for anything further, please, if I am not in the barrack find Neveng."

"I'm afraid I'll need to know where you are at all times," Ohric said. "If someone out there is killing officials, I don't want to assume your safety."

"I can handle myself. I will not rest while the killer is on the loose. I too know the importance of not failing," Haeden stated. "I will return to the barracks only after I reassign my men and meet with yours at the gate."

It made Ohric nervous. He knew that Zareden wouldn't talk, he hardly spoke to begin with. Despite this, his heart began to pound.

"Shall we speak to Hensing first?" Sento asked. "With Alarde's wife and child out of town, that makes him next of kin."

"Yes," Ohric said, snapping himself from his thoughts. "We should see him immediately."

"Let's waste no time then, he lives in the center of town," Sento replied, leading the way. "The town is split into four quadrants. At first it meant nothing but a means to find your way around. Now it's... got a separation that no one wants to speak about. Alarde has abandoned a lot of things. I'm trying to help ease it a bit, with the temple. My efforts will only go so far. The sick will get medicine, the poor food, but that's only because Neraea demands the temples be taken care of. Sad, isn't it?" Sento sighed.

"Sounds like he's not well-liked by most," Ohric admitted. The man sounded insufferable, in all honesty, but he dared not say. He didn't want to be painted as a suspect himself. He'd even go as far as saying he'd liked to have been the one who did it.

It was a short journey to Hensing's house, an unassuming cottage toward the front of town near the gates. Sento offered three knocks on the door, fumbling heard inside shortly after. A man opened the door, hair unkempt, the house inside smelling of fresh bread and juniper.

"Ah and the legion is here. Wonderful," he said. "How may I help you both?" the man finished, his sarcasm both loud and unappreciated.

"We're wondering if you've seen Alarde in the past day. It could be that he's locked himself in his home again, but I've not seen him. Ohric here is due to speak with him while they are in town, and..."

"We cannot move on until I've spoken to him," Ohric said, quickly. Perhaps if he mentioned their departure, he would be more helpful.

"No, I've not seen the man. As much as under this circumstance I wish I had, I haven't. As you've said, he's likely locked himself in his home again. Goddess knows he doesn't leave it for anything other than parties or feasts. I wish you both luck in your endeavors. Now if you'll excuse me," Hensing said and shut the door abruptly.

Sento sighed and motioned for us to walk further. "He's always been a kind soul."

"That doesn't prove his innocence."

"Yes, although I believe him when he says he hasn't seen him. Let us move onto the next suspect."

"Which is?"

"I believe Saraen may be the best, there is a meeting scheduled tonight that Alarde shouldn't miss, being patron. I've not yet figured that out, but with his wife being so far away and Hensing being so removed we are left with no choice but to end this investigation swiftly."

"Did you not think that something worth mention?" Ohric asked harshly. He could feel his pace sink to his bowels.

"Apologies. Though I do suppose I can have Haeden postpone it. She has the ability."

"Let us question the noble first," Ohric said, the breath that followed giving him the strength to contain himself. "After we can regroup at the post, and then question the fletcher and that widow."

"As you wish, follow me."

Ohric obliged, following the Arai closely. He still was not yet sure if he could be trusted, though thus far he seemed genuinely helpful. He'd keep a close eye despite that fact. Before long they arrived at a large white and blue house, gold banners outside of the doors.

"This is house Laren, Saraen is lady of the house. The most charitable town nobles are revered by Queen Neraea and given these banners to hang outside their homes."

"Where does her wealth come from?" Ohric asked, inspecting the house up and down before they reached the front door.

"Her family was one of the first to colonize Larient, they control the mines to the east, where the large rock walls are," Sento stated. "Recently things have been a bit of a mess for the mines, I anticipate her to bring it to light at the meeting. Shall we?"

Ohric nodded, walking forward enough to stand next to the Arai while he knocked on the door, two knocks. It was a few moments before Saraen opened the door, soft wrinkles by her chestnut brown eyes. Her blonde hair was wrapped in a bun, red beads dangling from a clip that sat on top of her head.

"A surprise at this hour," she said and crossed her arms, amusement sweeping her face. When either man said nothing, she let out a soft hum, standing aside. "I see this must be about something to be discussed at length. Do come in gentlemen, I've just made tea."

"Very kind, Lady Laren," the Arai said and nodded his head once. She smiled, looking toward Ohric, taking a very large breath into her lungs. "So, I see the legion is here, to what do I owe the pleasure of the Coadjutant in my house?" she asked.

"We've just arrived this morning, Lady Laren, but there is something we must discuss about the meeting this evening," Ohric said, trying to keep his breathing steady.

"Yes, it seems that Alarde has—"

"Gone missing," Ohric quickly interjected. "He's gone missing."

"We've checked his home, had guards dispatched to his summer home. They returned with no answers either. Did he come here?" Sento asked.

"Missing?" she asked. Shock in her eyes. "He most certainly did not come here. Do you believe he will turn up in time for tonight's meeting?" Saraen took a breath, and with a defeated look on her face, set teacups down on her counter. "Of course, there's no way of telling."

"I'm sorry, but with his disappearance, we may need to ask Haeden to postpone tonight's meeting," Sento said.

"Yes, and she would need word from two town nobles," she sighed.

"What do you think?" Sento asked.

"What I think is that he's just run off from his responsibility yet again," Saraen said, rage in her voice. "But I suppose I can continue to place my trust in the city guard for another few weeks. These attacks on my mines are a high priority, I need support from the legion. I cannot get that unless he expresses its importance to the royal family."

"I can assist with that, if you are willing to speak to Commander Vescain upon his return."

"You mean directly?" Saraen asked.

"If we cannot find Alarde in time for tonight's meeting, Savantin may have time to personally assist," Ohric said, knowing it couldn't be farther from the truth. Savantin was consumed.

"Hm yes. May have time," she said and nodded. "Allow me to assist in locating Alarde in the meantime then. What can I do?"

"Nothing as of yet," Ohric said. "Do not leave your home. If this was an abduction, we do not know whether or not there is a threat to the other nobles. My men are at the gates, and Haeden's are watching the city."

"Is that an order?" she asked.

"No, not an order, just a friendly warning," Ohric stated. "We'll be on our way, we've other nobles to warn."

"Perhaps I can assist with that. Sento and I know them best, we could…"

"I will send one of my men to your home, should you wish to warn other nobles, he will accompany you. You will recognize him by his blades," Ohric said and turned abruptly, walking toward the door. He had his doubts about her, but Zareden would deter anything from occurring that was out of his control. Sento followed, and quickly. If Saraen was the killer, Sento was not working with her, else surely, he would have stayed. When they had made it to the street, Ohric called two guards to send for Zareden. No time to waste.

"So… the fletcher or the widow?" Sento asked, stopping in the street. "They reside in different districts. These are going to be tricky; they have no affiliation with him in everyday life. It will come off that we are questioning them."

THE COVEN OF SHADOW

"So, we arrive at his shop, he overhears us speaking about it. Depending upon his reaction, we can get a sense of whether or not he had a hand in it. Not the most solid plan, but better than directly speaking to him about it," Ohric said and looked down at his feet. So heavy it was hard to move them. There was no way he'd be able to pull this off.

"I see. What are we to do about the widow, then?" Sento asked. He was only trying to be helpful.

"I'm unsure. She's removed from every possible situation there is. She won't be involved with the meeting that these nobles are clutching onto, so we cannot make that the reason for our visit. Her husband is deceased, so we cannot use his status as guard."

Sento pointed off into space twice, clearing his throat. "I could...I could bring to her that since the temple is open, we could have a ceremony for him if she so wishes. He had a small military funeral, and the sole priestess in the city had died days prior to his own passing."

"You would do this?" Ohric asked.

"I would," Sento said. "She mentioned taking his ashes by cart to the mountain but has never passed through those gates."

"Excellent," Ohric said. "Perhaps you make off right now to meet with her, and I will see about the fletcher."

"You think splitting up is wise?" Sento asked, a hand through his hair. That was just it, he didn't think splitting up was wise, but they were pressed for time. Severely. Certainly, Savantin would return at any moment now, and they still had nothing to report. Sento noticed his hesitation and spoke.

"It is something I am quite capable of, and if you don't take offense to me asking, how exactly are you going to interrogate the fletcher?"

Haeden approached them then, a look of concern on her iron face. "Alarde's wife has returned," she said. "Unannounced. She waits outside of the manor house. My soldiers are trying to stall her as much as they can, but she is insistent upon entering her home."

"So, no one's told her what happened?" Ohric asked. "No one is giving her a reason why she's not allowed entry?"

"We thought it best coming from one of you." A sigh left her mouth. "Unfortunately, this isn't the only time he's kept her out of her home," Haeden scoffed.

"Let us go, then," Ohric said and motioned for Haeden to lead the way.

◆ ◆ ◆

He didn't expect to find the box when he entered this place the first time, that would have been too easy. But he did expect that perhaps he'd missed something. He'd be more thorough now. Either that, or his impatience and frustration on beginning to feel lost had him needing to connect to the place, become one with its secrets. A mysterious cult that one day vanished. He had no doubt that the purge had hand in some of it, and perhaps while dwindling in number, they hid themselves away. It was acceptable to him. He had no intention of reviving it, and rather they didn't rise to meet him. He kept vigilant, knowing that if they were still here that it would be a fight. Risky, if they had no heartbeat, no pulse as written in the writings he secured from a tomeskeeper in Stirae.

The entrance to the shrine was a fissure in the black rock wall that cut into the forest six miles north of Larient. Presumably the reason a large temple was built just outside of the city. He entered, letting darkness take him. His curse gifted him sight if nothing else, and he breathed deeply while retracing his steps. There had to be some evidence left of when it was taken from here, although he knew he was becoming desperate in his search. Restless. Frustrated. Irascible.

There wasn't much left inside, remnants of the creatures that lived here. Old tables, broken bowls scattered on the floors beneath them. He continued along, following the dark winding halls with anticipation. His destination was only a short distance ahead, an altar, rows of pews lining the pathway toward it. The altar was empty, an antiquated pedestal adorned the middle of it. He reached it quickly, square in shape and made from sleek black obsidian. He ran his fingers across it, feeling his way from the front toward the back. Nothing. Rage enveloped him. How could he have gotten so close just to be taken so far? His pulse began to stagger, quickly and then slow. The fluctuation could drive him to madness.

He grasped a pew and pulled it aside angrily, drastically moving its position in the room. It was here. Perhaps ages ago, perhaps a decade ago, or less. He stopped his lashing out before it began, looking at the base of one of the pews closest to the altar. Beads on the ground. How could he have missed this before? He picked them up, inspecting them closely. Glass, gold and red colored. Each one had a symbol on them, glyphs, something that indicated status or culture. Someone would know something about them. A jeweler, or an occultist. Perhaps he'd take them back to Defaltor, or to the jewel smith back at the Mountain. How would he get to either of those places while he was on his campaign was the question.

There was a Thaumaturgist inside of Marestith, well known now that the town survived the religious inquisition spawned by Neraea and her priests. He could take them there, and with any shred of hope find out something about them. He would probably be better off taking them to occultists in Tovai, or anywhere at all in Stirae. That would delay him several months, years, even, if Mauros did indeed decide to invade. Time he did not have, and would not sacrifice. Another lead that could end in nothing. He would take them, though. He put them in the pocket of his jacket, retracing his steps to the outside world. His horse was waiting where he had left her, and the two made haste to Larient. He would develop a plan for Marestith, one that granted him time to slip away. Marestith was a dark place, but unlike many of the dark places in Terrenveil, the town captured Neraea's forces, bargaining their freedom from Terrenveil for their safe return.

Ozrach of course tried to send troops to retrieve them, but the stalemate eventually ended in their sovereignty.

Upon his return to town, Savantin found Ohric immediately, drinking anxiously in a tavern. His hands shook as the mug reached his lips, not looking away from the counter. Savantin didn't mention where he'd been or what he'd done when he joined Ohric at the bar, he almost didn't mention the town at all until the bartender did, saying something about the excitement dying down.

"Excitement?" Savantin asked, setting two coins down in front of him. He turned to Ohric, silently, expectantly.

"Meant to speak to you about it," Ohric said and took another sip from his mug. It was like this many nights. Lonely, dark taverns, struggling to get tea without sideways glances from bartenders and innkeeps.

"Well?"

"The patron was murdered. We have the killer in custody, currently being picked apart by the town guard."

"I'm impressed," Savantin said, something Ohric was not expecting. "So, the state of Larient?"

"The late patron's sister was to assume control of the town, in compliance with her husband's wishes. However, it seemed the guard chose his advisor because of his assistance in solving the mystery. Sento is going to send word to Ozrach about taking responsibility."

"I see. I suppose I will have to speak to him regarding his report of the incident?"

"Already taken care of," Ohric responded. He hoped he had done enough appeasing to grant him a good night's sleep. "He aided me in searching for the killer. Without his help we'd have not found her."

"Her?"

"Yes. The patron's wife did it. She was thought to be away, so that no one would suspect her. It wasn't until we were notified that she arrived that we discovered it was her. He abused their child."

"Despicable," Savantin said. "It's a shame she hadn't done it sooner," he continued, sitting down next to Ohric.

"I am sure their child will rest easy now that he's gone."

"Murder seems justifiable, perhaps they will grant her freedom. I would see to it, had I the power," Savantin said and sighed. "I have plans. We're moving out once we're sure the state of Larient will be stabilized."

"Stabilized?"

"With the late patron's advisor taking control of Larient we must ensure there is no cause to create chaos. Political aspects aside, we can't have chaos in the streets. Which means I must speak to the town guard and the new patron," he sighed again heavily.

"So, you've found a lead, I take it?"

"Not here. Finish your tea and walk with me," Savantin said and stood, making for the front door. Ohric shivered. He wanted nothing more than to sleep.

Savantin watched the streets darken as dusk set upon them. People eyed him, quietly hurrying back to their homes. It was the same everywhere he went, people's minds ensnared by superstition, tales. He couldn't tell whether or not he was beginning to enjoy the overall quietness of the streets, or if he so desperately hated the Mountain that the quietness seemed enjoyable. The latter was probably it. He was always told by travelers that missing home was how they spent most of their time. As much as he wished he could relate to them, he couldn't. Home to him was where he had the nicest bed, but it surrounded him with displeasure and contempt. He missed only the forge, the smell, the heat, the sound. That feeling was easily replaced by another, and by a place far from the castle.

Ohric emerged from the tavern, his eyes wrought with worry and heavy from exhaustion. He sleepily walked over, looking up toward the lanterns on his way.

"I'm heading to Marestith."

"Marestith? That place is..."

"I know. I won't be there for long. There's a Thaumaturgist that lives just inside the gates, I aim to have a discussion with them regarding my lead."

"What did you find?" Ohric asked.

"Beads. From some sort of amulet. Foolish sounding, I know. But I missed them the first time I entered that place."

"Not foolish, thorough," Ohric said.

"I know this makes you uneasy."

"Uneasy isn't the word," he continued, a breath outward.

"Don't go with me," Savantin said, taking a step off the porch and motioning for him to follow. "Stay in Seresten with the others. It won't be a challenge; the patroness is Araelian. There's a small temple inside of the walls, to counter the energy Marestith exudes."

"Energy? Surely you don't believe that."

"No, but you do. And so does Brezena," Savantin answered. "We'll stay here for another day or two. After the patron addresses the town and we are certain that the guard has everything under control we will move out for Seresten."

"Perfect," Ohric said and took a breath in, looking up at the lanterns a second time. Normally he'd have scurried off to find a suitable place to sleep, taking the last of Savantin's plans as an exit, but there was too much on his mind. Savantin took notice of this, making mention of the present hour.

"It's just... what should we do about Blacwin?" Ohric asked.

"Leave him. He will have time to heal here among your people. You've already made the arrangement to receive word once he betters?"

Ohric had nodded, still expectant of an answer.

"That is when we will disclose our location," Savantin answered and placed a commending hand on Ohric's shoulder before moving to gain shelter for the night. He had taken a few steps when Ohric spoke, nervousness in his voice.

"Savantin, there is one other thing." He hoped that his words would not be wasted. Savantin stopped, turning his head for a moment. When Ohric did not speak, he turned around completely, rejoining Ohric and taking a seat next to him.

"Blacwin, he seems to not remember anything at all. He continues to make remarks about the lamb, whatever is meant by it. I did not bring anything to his attention about his service, because it seems he does not have it in mind. What if he never comes out of this state? Will there be cause to kill him?"

Savantin's face was one of intrigue, as if the thought had never crossed his mind. His commander was a man consumed, sure. Yet, Ohric had almost expected him to at least mull this event over in his mind once or twice.

"I am surprised you would not want to put him to blade yourself, Ohric. He's killed children. Do you think Araele would want you to spare his life just because he cannot remember the horrible things he's done?" Savantin said, watching Ohric's eyes for a moment. After no response from him he let out a small laugh, continuing his thought. "I will leave that decision up to you. You know I care not for religion. I am sure there is a way that he can be forgiven if he accepts her light, some kind of new beginning he can have. I can almost hear your thoughts now, that she's touched him, given him the chance to start over," Savantin said, taking a breath in casually.

"And is there something wrong with that thought?" Ohric asked.

"I will only say that the decision will be left to you on the matter, again, I am surprised you want to save him. Do not mistake my words, they are only meant to derive thought from you."

"One more thing. Do you think sending Almour's men to Mordestai is necessary, and why him?" Ohric asked, almost wishing he hadn't. While it was questioning Savantin's orders, it was more so to place his own mind at ease. Something he seemed to need more and more as of late.

"As much as I loathe the man, yes. Warning the tribe is a favor I do intend on seeing returned. If I must go there, if they know anything, I will be welcomed."

"Do you think they know anything?" Ohric asked.

"That I am unsure of. They worship their own gods, have their own magick. It's possible, but my search has not yet led me there. But to the matter at hand, I want you to pay close attention to the men as we make our way to Lord's Valley and Seresten. There could be more of them looking to defect. I haven't yet addressed the men on the matter, but Djeik has made shining examples of what comes of defying the legion. Blacwin, too, I suppose. I will make that inherently clear before we reach Seresten."

"There aren't many of them left," Ohric said, simply.

"Less men to keep track of," Savantin replied. "Get some sleep. Tomorrow, I aim to meet with the patron and the guard, collectively. I want you to arrange it."

"It will be done," Ohric said and offered a nod of affirmation. It had been a long, agonizing day, and he finally felt that he could sleep through the night.

◆ ◆ ◆

Savantin could almost say he didn't care about the state of Larient. He would, if he were there to witness the apprehension of the murderer himself, make a statement about how her motive was justified. He supposed he still could, but, for now, his lead was the only thing that mattered. Of course, Ohric did a good job while he was away, but now he needed to come up with a description of where he had been and what he was doing, if anyone was bold enough to ask.

The new patron was silent, listening to the captain of the guard with a very grave, very serious face. Haeden ended the discussion about reinforcing patrols around Larient, turning towards Ohric, directing several questions. Ohric stammered, finally finishing his initial response before turning to Savantin to intervene. He was hoping it wouldn't come to this, in all honesty.

"Do you suspect there to be any cause for violence over his induction as patron?" Savantin asked. "This is the reason we remain in Larient."

"We do not, Commander. We suspect there to be initial unrest among the nobles, but they're easily calmed."

"I can only begin to fathom it," Savantin answered, contempt in his voice.

"Perhaps I should speak to them before it's acknowledged by the monarchy," Sento said. "I should have a more direct face with them."

"You do not need their approval," Savantin said. As much as he hated politics, loathed them, he always found himself involved in one way or another.

"As I am also sure I do not, but perhaps that will solve things. They know me as Alarde's advisor, and an Araelian but nothing more," Sento responded. "They could contest it, and very likely will."

"Do what you must. This brings me back to my previous concern; do you suspect any reason our involvement in Larient should be sustained?"

"No, Commander," Haeden responded.

"We will move out by day's end," Savantin answered, abruptly leaving the room. It was as much as he could stand.

Ohric waited for Savantin to exit before he made his own, quickly motioning signs of respect toward Sento, and a half salute toward Haeden. He wanted to get to the temple before they left for Seresten to secure a few blessings, and to see how Blacwin fared. Upon arrival he could smell wounds, blood old and new. This was customary now that temples were used as places of healing. He thought it seemed unclean, almost sacrilege, but knew the pureness of the action was a part of Araelian culture.

"You again." Jarum's voice. The contempt for one another brought unnecessary addressing, it seemed.

"My appearance here is obvious, I come to look after my wounded. I've nothing else to say," Ohric stated. He walked past him, begrudgingly, and entered the room where Blacwin lay. He was still. Either sleeping, or so weak that he could not do much else. A priestess entered the room, almost surprised to see him.

"We've done all we can for him, I'm afraid. He clings on to life, but he is very diminished."

It was what Ohric feared. He would be left here, in solitude, with nothing but his life to wake up to.

◆ ◆ ◆

Daybreak. The ride through the night to Seresten had been arduous. Savantin was relieved to see the town, and surprisingly, rest was his priority. Like many towns outside of the major trading posts or resource production hubs, Seresten was tired. Before he could find the closest inn, Brezena found him, near cornering him as she approached. She wore a deep plum dress, matching that of her lipstick and the beads in her thick, chocolate-colored hair. Her skin was dark and flawless, and seeing it reminded him of his nights in Seresten amid the renewing of contracts five years past. He had been selected for Seresten, as the rumors of rebellion had started there. In opposition to Ozrach's behest, he found himself a guest of Brezena's house for the entirety of his stay, and much more, Brezena's bed. It made things complicated, needless to say, telling in the manner in which she approached him. She waited a moment, looking briefly toward Ohric and his men before crossing her arms, looking to Savantin expectantly.

"Dismissed," he said simply, looking toward them with empty eyes. As they moved out, Brezena laughed to herself softly.

"Are we going to pretend that..."

"Whatever is simpler," he interrupted, looking down into her eyes.

"Simpler?"

"I'm here for a reason."

"You were here for that reason five years ago."

"And I'm here now, for the same reason, because he's sent me across the territories. I didn't have to come here," Savantin answered.

"You didn't?" she asked. "You mean to tell me that you chose to come here on your own volition, and not because he's sent you here again?"

"Correct, though would it really matter?"

"Believe it or not, there are conditions to wanting to see you," Brezena answered.

"You're safe. He suspects nothing."

"Not here," she said and looked around the streets.

"Where do you suggest?"

"The gardens. The sound of the water will drown out our voices. This way," she said.

As much as he wanted to sleep, he obliged, and they stopped at a small fountain, sitting on the bench beneath it. The sound would have been calming, if he didn't want to be elsewhere so badly.

"You're sure he suspects nothing?" she asked.

"He suspects the rumors are more than such but has his full trust in me and my men. He doesn't have an army without my word."

"Well then let us pray on your word," she said and sighed.

"Don't sound so delighted."

"I know you have other sentiments."

"More like yours than you'd think," Savantin said. "He needs to be removed."

"Yes, but you don't care beyond that. The plight of the people…"

"I didn't come here to debate this with you."

"Then why are you here?" she asked, throwing one leg over the other and smoothing her dress down. "Amuse me."

"Marestith. What do you know about it?"

"Goddess above. Do not go to that place," she said and assumed a straightened position.

"Am I amusing you yet?"

"The light left that place long ago, it was forced out."

"The light or lack of it is not what I'm interested in," Savantin answered.

"They kill people there, Savantin. You can't just go in expecting they won't try it. No one goes there from the outside."

"Until now. I'm only going to talk."

"And you think they would so willingly talk to you?"

"It's not a matter of will. Someone lives there that possesses the means to obtain the knowledge I desire. I will not let the past and the fears of other people stop me."

"What is so important to you that you must go there?"

Savantin said nothing and stood, glancing up briefly. "There was a time I would have told you."

"That's not fair," Brezena gasped.

"You left me stranded."

"They couldn't have caught us together. You know that."

"The point remains the same," Savantin responded. "I'm left with no other option."

"I'll pray for you, although you detest the sentiment."

"I'm sure Ohric already has, I'm certain he's found the temple."

"Ah, yes. Your coadjutant. Assuming he won't be any trouble while you're away?"

"You won't even know he's here."

"So, he's not like you," Brezena said and stood.

"Meaning?"

"Impulsive, aggressive..." she said, and stood, moving toward him. "Brazen," she finalized, her face in his.

Savantin stared into her eyes until she looked away, slightly shivering.

"Don't like what you see?" he asked. After a brief pause, "He's young, anxious, and devout. But he's reliable and loyal. You should have no trouble in trusting him until I return."

"What if you don't return?" Brezena asked. "What then?"

"Don't act so concerned. I will be back before nightfall," Savantin answered.

He left her in the garden, headed to where his horse awaited him. Perhaps he wasn't going to rest after all.

Marestith was an evil place. At least that's what the religionists said. As far as he knew, it was all humans that lived there. They cast themselves into black magic and occult rituals, winning their sovereignty by way of human sacrifice. Another move of cowardice by Ozrach. The answer should have been to storm the town no matter the casualties and bring all inside to surrender. However, Neraea's begging to save her priests caused Ozrach to honor all their demands just so the killings would be brought to an end.

They kept to themselves, somehow sustaining their town on the small amount of land they secured from Ozrach's treaty and declaration. He supposed he *was* interested in seeing it. As much as he condemned the event, despised the result and how it exploited Terrenveil's weakness prior to his days as commander, he felt as if it was a place he could belong to had he not set himself on his current path.

Marestith had a gate, but it was said to never be closed. Each day the denizens would paint the ground outside of it with symbols made in blood. He hadn't a clue what they meant, just knew that it would deter anyone from entering. Anyone except him, that was.

He smelled it as he approached, the metallic taste hitting the back of his throat as he inhaled. He couldn't be here for very long. Not unless he intended on endangering the populace and putting himself on display. He dismounted, walking toward the gate slowly with reins in hand. Pushing the hood of his riding jacket off, he noticed the empty eyes of Marestith's denizens staring at him as he entered. There was a stable, no more than three horses occupied it. Upon reaching the small girl at the stable, he offered a piece of amber larger than her fist. She accepted, taking the reins and leading his mare alongside another.

"Thaumaturgist lives in the house made of black wood, far left corner of the settlement," a man said, lowering his hood over his brows, shying away from the sunlight that came from Savantin's turning toward him. "Hopefully you've another offering like that for her."

To Savantin's silence, the man laughed, but offered nothing else in the way of conversation. He charted his course immediately, setting off toward the house made of black wood. Every resident he passed stared at him in silence yet awe, as if they knew his secrets.

The house was gaunt and old, several crows perched at the top of it. Or were they ravens? From his position on the ground, he could not tell. Taking a deep breath, he approached the door, laying three knocks upon it. It was a moment before he heard rustling from inside, footsteps, and another moment before the door was opened. In its frame stood a young woman, not much taller than five foot three. She had ash brown hair that ended just beneath her breasts, loosely curled at the ends. Her bluish gray eyes were accentuated by the lightest of freckles scrawled out beneath them.

"Come in," she said simply, moving to the side of the door frame. Once Savantin entered, she lit a lantern outside of her porch, securing the door closed. He made note of the walls, unusually bare save the taxidermy in the large room in which he had stopped walking. He heard her footsteps behind him, and her muttering. He tried to focus on her words but could not.

"What is it you've brought for me?"

"Straight to the point. I need to locate something. This is the only lead I have," Savantin responded, pulling the beads from his jacket.

"I may need some time with them," she said and carefully took them from his hands. "Beautifully crafted... you said you're looking for someone?"

"No, something. I believe the owner of these beads to be long dead, but they're telling of my object's whereabouts."

"I see," she said and pulled a tray from a large desk, placing them beneath a spyglass. "Now, where have you come from?"

"I prefer we don't speak of it," Savantin said. "Though I will disclose that I've ridden from Terrenveil."

"Brazen. You do know what these people, the people of Marestith did?"

"I have no love for Araele or her religion."

"So, being a resident of Terrenveil, you're fine with the slaughter of priests and zealots?"

"Less of them means less indoctrination, less hatred, and fewer lies."

She fluttered her eyes twice before offering a nod. "You really do have no love for her religion."

"Would you like my synopsis before you continue or are you just curious?" Savantin asked, hoping the question didn't sound as harsh as he thought it did the moment it strayed from his tongue.

"Unfortunately, few are brave enough to enter, and as of late my clients are dreadfully boring. I must act interested while I perform solutions to pregnant mistresses, sick children, or revenge quests," she stated. "And yes, more than half of these people belong to the church. The others pretend in order to avoid public flogging."

"Ah, the age old. Ruthlessly murder anyone that is suspected of heresy rather than attempt to convince them to join the church. All while explicitly stating that murder is punishable by afterlife in darkness."

"So, you're one of them? Pretending in order to avoid public flogging?"

"I pretend nothing. My revulsion is well known."

"My name is Salowe," she said and looked down into the glass another time.

"Savantin."

"Your beads. They're of Traksi origin, very, very far from here. What exactly do you hope to find from them, Savantin?"

"Their owner entered a place forbidden, took something from it, and then vanished."

"And you want to find out where she took it," Salowe answered and turned to a bookshelf on the wall behind her. "The wayward children of the Traksi are branded, and it is practice that they fashion bracelets from beads to turn their outcast into something sightlier. Code was that the men wore gold and black, while the women wore red. Eventually the wayward were driven out of their communities, cruelly, usually fatally," Salowe continued. "It makes me wonder how she ended up here, in Cilevdan."

Savantin said nothing and watched her retrieve a book and jar from the shelf, moving back over to the table. Salowe reached into the jar, sprinkling blue powder over the beads. She spun around quickly, grabbing another jar from the shelf. From the second jar, she applied oil, causing the powder to fizz and smoke. "Svi alloch shenar," she said, waving her hand over the event. Her eyes began to glow, and she inhaled deeply holding her hands outward. "They've been to so many places and have seen so much blood... so much blood. She took the box and was attacked on her way out of the cave."

Savantin tensed at the mention of it.

"The trail ends there. There is a faint touch, orange oil. There aren't many places to get that in Cilevdan," she said, snapping her fingers once. The smoke cleared, the beads shimmering from the light of the candles around them. "Do your best to find a trader, perhaps in one of the larger, richer cities. The apothecary back on the Mountain, even. Both would be able to tell you where you can find it."

"Your payment," Savantin said and moved his jacket aside, reaching into a pocket. Salowe shook her head, waving her finger twice. "I decide how I'm compensated, and coin will not do."

"I can get you anything you ask for."

"Oh, I'm sure of it," Salowe answered and reached for an empty jar, removing the lid. "Though, I'm not sure how happy you'll be about my request."

"Try me."

"The blood of a Seraphice."

"Dangerous."

"Very. It's why I'm asking before the light of the sun leaves us," she said, sitting the jar on the table.

"I should warn you that it's not the sun that keeps me, and the cycles of the stars grant no solace," Savantin answered. It was the most he had ever given away about himself to anyone other than Ohric.

"A curse... and you aren't here to try and lift it. Peculiar."

"Do people often come to you in order to lift curses?"

"When the church cannot help them, they seek other methods. The fortunate find me."

"And the unfortunate?"

"The Viscera. The Magar. Those who would turn them over to Neraea's soldiers."

"Why do you need my blood?" Savantin asked. He wasn't welcome to the idea, though her boldness interested him. Her pulse rose after he asked, a sign that she wasn't completely fearless.

"Not need, want," she said softly.

"What gave it away?"

"The blood in your eyes. You do realize that is why no one here has met you with hostility?"

It must have been the blood at the gate that drew it out of him. He would need to hunt before he returned to Seresten. He wanted to deny her request, tell her that it would be safer for both her and the residents of Marestith, but knew initially that her services came at a price.

"Just a little will do," Salowe said and placed a blade on top of the jar.

"You don't want to be here when I do it," Savantin said and picked the blade up. "I can already hear your heart and how quick it's becoming. Use something to mask your scent and hope it's enough to keep me from you."

"The beads," she said suddenly. "I'll keep the beads."

Savantin nodded and set the blade down on the table. "Wise."

"Farewell, Savantin."

Savantin nodded a second time, turning from the house and walking back out into the street. The number of people staring and moving quickly from his path was telling of how close he was to being consumed. He could hear every single one of their hearts now, faint, echoing, calling. Would this place be his end? Or would he be the end of this place? As he found the stables, his vision began to become as red as his only release.

◆ ◆ ◆

Ohric spoke his last prayer as the patroness approached, kneeling beside him. He moved to stand, and she placed her hand on his forearm, pushing him downward.

"Pray with me, Coadjutant."

"I will not deny you that," he said quietly, looking up at the statue of his goddess. Pure, beautiful, exhilarating.

"Savantin told me that you would be spending most of your time here."

"He is correct. Being on the road there aren't many chances to worship at a proper temple, only at the way shrines along the roads. I've been blessed thus far in our journey to visit most of the temples to secure my prayers."

"Do you know where he's gone?" Brezena asked suddenly.

"I'm sorry?" Ohric asked.

"Savantin. Do you know where he's gone?"

"Marestith, place of pure evil. I cautioned him against it, but he's determined. Something exists there that he needs."

"I cautioned him against it as well," Brezena said, looking toward him. He found himself lost in her eyes for a moment, withdrawing his own. She was beautiful. She sighed, looking up toward the statue of Araele. "He was always determined, always driven. Even when he was here so long ago, looking for something. I hope he finds it."

"He will, eventually."

"Do you know what it is he seeks?"

"I'm not at liberty to say."

"Secret intelligence for the king?"

"We'll say that," Ohric said simply. Brezena stood, pushing her dress down over her legs. She was through, he thought. He didn't reveal the information she sought, which is what he believed the reason for her visit to be.

"My gratitude for sharing a prayer," she said.

"The pleasure was mine," Ohric responded, bowing his head. He would have to keep an eye on her. He yawned, rising. Rest was in order.

He made his way into the street, making observation of the world around him. Every town, city, and village seemed to be the same. He was interrupted on his walk about midway through, as he had been called to by a voice familiar. He looked ahead of him from where it came, seeing that Savantin had returned. Ohric offered a weary half salute before Savantin stopped him, looking around the streets as if to make sure no one would be listening to them.

"My meeting with the Thaumaturgist proved useful after all."

"Have you hunted?" Ohric asked suddenly, ignoring the words he had previously spoken.

"If you must know, yes. The beads revealed a lead to me, something tangible this time. We will go to Lord's Valley, just as soon as I settle some unfinished business here."

"Lord's Valley? There is nothing there but tens of dairy farms."

"Lord's Valley is also home to a large market, a renowned apothecary."

"An apothecary? What will you need from them?"

"Information. As I've said, the beads revealed a lead. They had a remnant, a trace of the past. Orange oil. We find the locations where they acquire it, we find out where the box was taken. It may still be there, or we may find another lead."

Ohric sighed in relief. It could be almost over. "When shall we go?" he asked.

"Tomorrow, as the sun rises over the skies."

Ohric nodded and let out a slow yawn. He hadn't meant to do so in Savantin's presence, not while they were speaking of matters such as this, but the hour was late, and it had been a long few days for him. He desperately wanted to go into an inn and sleep, or back to the temple and take one of the pilgrim's beds. Perhaps that is where he would lay his head tonight, amid the sweet smells of incense and soft, cloth-covered mats.

"Take rest. I am afraid once we make it to Lord's Valley there won't be much time for that," Savantin answered.

"Do you leave for the house?"

"I intend to do that now," Savantin said and watched as his breath took the form of a white cloud when he pushed it from his lungs. Ohric nodded and sleepily rubbed his eyes for a moment before clearing his throat, trying to return the conversation to a more dutiful standpoint so that he could rest his head, but words escaped him. His weariness was all that was left at the present moment, clawing at him.

"I will wake with the sun. If I don't, send for me. I want to begin our departure as soon as possible."

Ohric gave a lethargic nod and headed back toward the temple, deciding that is where he wanted to rest for the night. In peace, beneath the sanctuary of his goddess, his only love. There was a bittersweet feeling to this, seeing their plan to its end. He was thankful that they were upon it. He thought of it as a ravaging of the shadow. The world would be changed, he was sure of it. The greed and corruption of Terrenveil could finally meet its end.

◆ ◆ ◆

Lord's Valley was a town that was surrounded by the forest, its gates only seen through all of the thick black trees that inhabited the soil. That was also claimed to be evil, for having sprouted such monstrosities across the land, nourishing the horrific expressions of nature. It was all superstition, Savantin thought. It was yet another confirmation of how people would believe anything they were told when occurrences bore no easily reached logical answers. He didn't bother himself with why things happened, or what caused them to be. Things just were, and he would deal with them as they happened. His life proved to have become much simpler once he adopted this mindset, and for that he was thankful.

His men seemed nervous about the drastic changes in direction, something he ignored. With the sudden loss of Blacwin and the departure of Almour's men to Mordestai, the others seemed to be treading carefully in what was asked of them. They could tell their commander was becoming impatient, something even Savantin himself wasn't too keen on admitting. Ohric hadn't spoken much since they had left Seresten, his demeanor also in dire opposition from when they had arrived there. Perhaps it was just the journey weighing down on them all. Not being able to sleep or eat regularly was most likely causing unease in his men, along with the tedious work of travel with no visual progress. Maybe it would be best he shared with them what was about to happen, but then, he thought to himself that if they knew there would be more propensity for something to go awry. If that happened, he would rightly lose his mind.

The horses seemed to be grateful for the slow pace they adopted once moving toward the province, after being ridden for hours without stopping. He could feel the amount of relief in his horse as soon as he had given the order to slow up, looking at the wilderness surrounding them. It was quiet, save the sound of a bird in the trees above them. Savantin raised his fist, causing the men to stop behind him as he took a deep breath in and then out, trying to listen to his environment over the cry of the moon. It was beginning to wear down on him, and he could feel the longing surge beneath his willpower. He was playing a dangerous game, but the things on his mind made him pay no mind to his instincts. He almost envied man in that way, how they could ignore things they needed in order to achieve their wants. The longer he ignored his needs for his desires, the stronger the calling would become, and the more dangerous the result. Ohric approached his side at this time, looking hesitantly through the trees.

They were received in the usual manner; a guard striding out of town quickly to greet them and offer to take their horses. Savantin almost told him to save the formality and show him directly where he could find the market, though he suspected that would showcase insanity. Insanity may not be the word, he thought, riding inward. Instead, he let a small smile take him as he looked toward the manor house, his eyes darting back toward the fearful guard in front of him, a boy probably no older than Blacwin.

"Take the horses, make sure they are watered and fed," Savantin instructed. "Go with him, and keep watch," he said to whoever happened to be standing behind him. It was Zareden's lucky day. Everything was so repetitive now, something that frustrated him.

He nodded quietly and dismounted, leading his horse down toward the stable, only turning when the rest of the men followed suit. Another guard was posted against a support beam to a nearby building, sleepily looking over the encounter in his unmoving gaze. It wasn't long before others saw them at the gates, and a well-dressed man appeared out of a house across the street. He began moving toward them in a scurry. He reached them, out of breath, and placed his hands on his knees briefly. He took a large swallow of air into his lungs, gasping as he straightened.

"Commander, I did not know you were going to arrive at such a late hour, my apologies for the lack of custom upon greeting. My name is Fahming, advisor to Thaldivir and his family," he said, speaking quickly.

"There is no need for the customs of the court. It seems Ozrach wants us back at the mountain sooner than expected," Savantin answered, his voice cold. He allowed himself to show a slight exhaustion, trying to keep the tone of the advisor jovial.

"Allow me to provide to you and your men board for the night, so that way you are well rested for when you speak to Thaldivir in the morning," Fahming answered, smoothing his hands over his dark purple attire.

"Yes, do have something prepared for my men," Savantin said looking back toward them. Fahming formed a smile that contorted his face and waved off several guards to fit the order. "I will speak to the patron in the morning. Despite Ozrach's impatience I can only return once I have spoken to every patron of his provinces," Savantin said, a tone of boredom taking his voice.

He pushed the reins of his horse toward the young guard and looked up toward the manor house, and then to Ohric. He was becoming tired of the routine each area gave to him. Stabling, quartering, sleep, and sustenance. They were all needed, yet frustrating. He was certain his men were tired of it too. Zareden tired of it most, he could tell without even speaking to him. The man was born and bred for battle, for killing. Ohric was eying the advisor in contempt, likely due to the clothes he was wearing and the many gems on his fingers. Djeik had said nothing in days, and the other men were quiet as well. The journey was wearing on all of them. It will be over soon, though. Once he found the box, nothing else mattered. Everything would end, the monotony, the redundancy.

The late hours came and went, Savantin waking from his slumber as the sun rose overhead. The city began to wake, sounds of voices obscured through the thin walls. He would be preoccupied in speaking with the patron of Lord's Valley soon, so he wasted no time in making his way to the apothecary's stall in the market. It was small, unassuming. He expected it to be much larger, in likeness to the place that surrounded them. He was the first there, unsurprisingly, and waited for the woman to stop searching a bag before he made his presence known. She had wrinkles at the corner of each eye, telling of her time spent gifted with life. Her flaxen hair was tied up and hidden under a hat, color matching that of her clothes. She set the bag aside, long fingernails with different colored powders beneath them.

"Good morning, you're rather early," she said and covered her eyes from the rising sun in order to get a good look at him.

"I've a question for you; you might be able to help me," Savantin said and stretched his shoulders. The bed he had slept in last night was not at all comfortable, and this came from someone who had slept on roads in years past. It had been a very long time since he slept on the ground, though.

"I'm in no position to decline," she said, looking at his armor, his swords.

"Do you often decline questions from potential customers?"

"Depends on the question," she smiled.

"Orange oil. Do you know where to find it?"

"I have some, yes. Though it is hard to come across now. I used to get a steady supply from a contact in the south, but they've stopped sending couriers. I'm now forced to get it from Rustanzis. Rare anymore that anyone from Cilevdan carries it. There are a few traveling traders known to have it, so I make sure to clear them out whenever they're in town. But beyond that, I'm not of much help I'm afraid."

"Savantin!" It was Ohric, from the other side of the market.

"You've helped abundantly, thank you," Savantin said and turned toward his coadjutant, who had rushed over.

"People fled in the middle of the night." Ohric mustered, catching his breath. "Djeik discovered a near-empty stable by the farms."

"I don't doubt we will be met with adversity when we speak with the patron. We will have to do this carefully."

"What do you suggest?"

"If we take the men, we could exacerbate things," Savantin stated. "But if we don't, and things don't go as I foresee, attempt to take us as hostages could be made. For that, there would be bloodshed."

"So, we leave them at the doors, they'll be outside in the event that we need them," Ohric suggested. "Though that could be seen as a threat as well."

"Let us go, just you and I," Savantin said. "They'll be tense to begin with, we don't need to give them any reason to suspect we're onto them."

"Onto them?"

"Fleeing in the middle of the night is not the action of an innocent. They have something planned for us," Savantin said, sighing. "No need to delay things any further."

"Must we consult with that loathsome advisor?" Ohric asked.

"He's likely already at the house, furthering their plot for the morning."

"I feared as much," Ohric sighed. "His greed is abhorrent."

"That it is," Savantin settled.

"I let the men know where we were going. They're waiting for Terganus and his men."

"Who should be arriving soon."

"Should we wait for them to arrive before we go?" Ohric asked. Savantin knew his anxiety to be rising, now.

"No, I trust you've told Zareden to alert us when they arrive?"

"Of course."

"That will be enough," Savantin said. "If in the event they are not planning anything, this will not be perceived as a threat."

"And if they are? We'd be walking right into a trap."

"Trust in me, Ohric," he said simply.

The two reached the manor house, a large behemoth of a thing. It was two stories tall, something very unheard of in Terrenveil. He could feel Ohric cringing at the boast. They were greeted by two guards, both of which saluted as they approached. Ohric saluted back, as customary for him. Savantin ignored the event, given his title it made sense, but Ohric knew it was because of his current condition. Exhausted, driven, consumed.

Fahming was in the doorway, a smile taking his face. "Ah, perfect timing. The servants just got finished with breakfast, would you care for anything?"

"Servants?" Ohric said under his breath.

"No, thank you. As I've expressed to you yesterday, Ozrach is anxious for our return and needs me back immediately."

"Yes, I shall fetch Thaldivir," Fahming said and exited. Savantin looked around, making note of how many guards were in the halls. Surprisingly not very many. It was moments later that Thaldivir appeared from the stairs, following Fahming slowly.

"Commander, it is nice to finally meet like this. In all these years we've only but heard one another speak at the castle," he said and extended his arm. Savantin firmly gripped it in a shake, quickly withdrawing.

"A more intimate discussion is finally in order. As I've told your advisor, Ozrach is calling me back to the Mountain as soon as I am finished speaking with you here. It seems things with Mauros have escalated."

"That must have been troublesome for you to hear, Commander. Where would you like to have our discussion?" Thaldivir asked, looking toward the room to the left.

"It does not matter. If you've a place where you're more comfortable take us there."

"The great hearth," Thaldivir suggested. "It is quiet there, and there will be none to bother us."

"As you wish, lead on," Savantin answered.

The three began to walk inward, Ohric watching everyone with careful eyes.

"Things with Mauros, you said? Unless you are not at liberty to discuss..."

"I am not; however, the people have a right to know what is happening," Savantin sighed. "It seems they are occupying more borders than we initially thought. This is why I've been quartering soldiers across the territories. Most provinces have no walls strong enough to withstand an attack, and the guards won't be enough to defeat their soldiers."

"A service we are all grateful for. Is it true what they say? That they take no prisoners?"

"They destroy and kill everyone they raid. The reports from my spies in the north are with accuracy, I can assure you."

"This is harrowing news. When will your men be arriving?"

"Shortly," Savantin said. "They will make sure your people are protected should Mauros invade. You know, I've had this discussion countless times with countless patrons," he continued. "Each time is more painstaking than the last. I'm being called back before I can finish my campaign. I cannot personally assure anyone else that they will be taken care of. I'm restless, Thaldivir. Perhaps you can empathize with me."

"I am unsure that I can, Commander. Your service knows greater sacrifice than anything I've ever done, anything any of us have ever done."

"So, you know what position this places me in."

"I can imagine. The people have been restless as well, awaiting your arrival."

"I'm certain," Savantin said. "Though, I wonder why that is."

"Commander?" Thaldivir stumbled in his speech.

"Most would be relieved, secured. Especially when such a vicious enemy faces us. You see, I am very strict with my men. All of them. They do not act egregiously. They know the punishment that comes of it, so mind me in not understanding why you chose the word *restless*."

"I suppose in trying to empathize I chose incorrectly."

"Incorrectly, or hoping I would not catch it?"

"Both," Thaldivir said and pulled a blade from his clothing, pointing it at Savantin's throat. Ohric pulled his sword, only for three guards to pull theirs.

"Bold, but unwise," Savantin said and turned toward the hearth. "You need me alive, don't you?"

"Or else I'd have stuck this straight into your gut," Thaldivir answered.

"Such hostility for one who has little to do with your problem with the king. Surely you realize now that I've no involvement with politics."

"It's something we can't leave unanswered."

"Who is set to replace him? At least answer me that before you attempt to imprison me and my coadjutant."

"They've named me," Thaldivir smiled.

"Pathetic," Ohric spat. "One greed-ridden lout for another."

"That's enough out of you."

Fahming walked in from the door and near jumped at the sight, withdrawing quickly.

"Where do you intend on holding us, Thaldivir?" Savantin asked, looking down at his knuckles. "I trust it will be somewhere well guarded, fortified. You'll want to be sure of that."

"We will succeed where Avelina failed."

"Ah, yes. Opskaven. I do hope you have a better plan than her. Though it seems as if you're lacking the numbers."

"You're one to talk. Your reinforcements haven't yet arrived, and we have a surprise for them once they make it to the gates, the walls."

"Forgive me if I don't believe you've subdued the Tovian. Just like you will never subdue me."

"Those rumors, all the mystery. It means nothing to me. You don't frighten me, Savantin."

"I should," he laughed, pulling his own sword. "Let us settle this in honor."

Four more guards marched in, one of which wielded a halberd.

"You're not at liberty to choose," Thaldivir taunted.

"I will get my fair fight," Savantin said, and dragged his sword across his forearm, inhaling deeply. "A man with so much to live for has much to lose, Thaldivir. I learned that the hard way. And in that, I learned the ways of the ones who took my life from me. If you long for something enough, you will do unspeakable things to see your wishes attained. I have done things that the person I was would never conceive of doing."

"You are insane," Thaldivir said; his eyes widened in panic.

"I have been called many things, but I have never been called insane," Savantin said and tensed, his senses beginning to change. He looked down to his knuckles again, watching them expand at a quickened pace. "Ohric," Savantin managed before he succumbed to what seemed to be a pain in his head.

Ohric quickly disarmed a guard closest to him, running out into the streets. The sight was abominable, villagers fighting the soldiers that had seemingly just arrived. Parts of buildings were on fire, merchants hiding in their stalls. Zareden and Djeik joined him then, their backs pressed against his sides.

"We came as quickly as we could," Djeik said and deflected a sword, stabbing a man through his chest.

"Where is Savantin?" Zareden asked.

"Inside. It is best we do not enter."

"Is he..."

"Alive. We needn't assist, but we should make our way from here. Find as many guards as you can and kill them," Ohric answered. Moving past the market he felt the sweltering heat of the fires, the smoke subtly obscuring his view.

"Understood. We spoke to Terganus upon his arrival, he wishes to speak to Savantin on his findings."

"I will have to do, I do not know when we will be seeing him, and what kind of condition he will be in," Ohric said.

"I implore you to allow me to assist," Djeik said and looked back toward the manor house. Screams were heard above the chaos of the streets.

"He's done it, hasn't he?" Zareden asked. "Revealed himself."

"Find Fahming. I want him alive," Ohric said. Zareden nodded and set off for the task, Djeik silently staring off toward his house.

"Our mission now is to find Terganus."

"He was last seen in the center of town, many soldiers died at the gate, they were waiting with fire and arrows."

"Then we've no time to waste," Ohric said and took off past the markets. Djeik was in tow, the two coming upon three guards who were standing over the corpses of legionnaires, riddled with arrows.

"Give in," one of them laughed. "You're outnumbered," he shifted his eyes behind the two, quickly looking into their eyes. Ohric allowed himself a small smile before he ripped his sword through the air behind him, feeling a familiar heaviness to it, paired with the cry of a man. He then replaced it in front of him, turning quickly to deflect a blade to his left, stabbing one of the guards through his torso. "We are no longer."

"Soon there will be more of us, we wait in buildings until your men believe the fighting to be over," one of the remaining guards sneered.

"They too will perish," Djeik said.

"What's this?" one of the men suddenly asked. "The lieutenant without his commander."

"You'd rather be facing me right now," Ohric said. "And even still, it will be the end of your life." He could feel the sweat accumulating on his brow, and the heat radiating from his blade. Though he was becoming uneasy, he watched the men carefully, not allowing the present condition of the atmosphere to showcase weakness. "Surrender or join them in the afterlife."

"Surrender was never an option. We would either fight or die."

"Then you have chosen death," Ohric said and moved toward him, allowing his blade to deflect the angry blows coming from his opponent. He was fighting with fury, something that was causing each attack to be overdrawn and hasty. Ohric continued to block, moving his blade as easily as fingers through water. The ripples that were being created against him were now becoming desperate.

Ohric pushed his blade back against the man, causing him to turn his wrist in just a slight enough manner for him to be vulnerable. He whipped his blade inward, cutting the man across the chest and entered in for a deadly strike between his eyes. No one was to remain. Not one of these blinded fools who would switch one avaricious monarchy for another. Djeik finished fighting with the other guard, dropping him to the ground.

The two continued along until they found Terganus fighting alongside several of his soldiers, attempting to avoid becoming surrounded by the mixture of guards and citizens who had taken up arms. Ohric and Djeik began to kill the outer ranks, stabbing as many as they could from behind before they became aware of their presences. Once the rebel's attentions were divided, the legionnaires were able to overcome them swiftly.

"Coadjutant."

"Captain. We were told there were more of them waiting inside houses," Ohric said.

"What do you propose?"

"We burn them down," Ohric said. "All of them." All of them, with affinity to the avarice these people boasted.

"All of them?"

"Nothing left." Their heresy would be a reminder to the rest of the kingdom. He was sickened. Everywhere he looked there was sacrilege and greed.

"Burn them!" Terganus ordered, waving his hand forward toward the buildings to their left.

"Leave the manor house standing and leave us a path out of here," Ohric said. "Make sure anyone who defies becomes absent breath. Anyone who surrenders is to be chained to the wagons and taken back to the Mountain for judgment."

"Ohric!" It was Harlan, limping over with an arrow in his leg.

"Get him a medic immediately."

Terganus nodded at the request, sending off one of the soldiers to his side. Harlan had reached them, out of breath. "The others didn't make it. They tried to climb the towers to stop the archers but there were too many rebels in the streets."

"They will be made to pay for this," Terganus muttered. "Where do they rest?"

"Nearest the inn. People fled through the back of the city; they're riding to warn Savoi."

"Ride now and cut them down immediately," Terganus barked at the horsed men next to him.

"Djeik, ride with them. Return to the Mountain once they no longer breathe," Ohric commanded. He nodded, climbing up onto a horse, reins shoved in his direction. They hadn't saved many horses from the stables it seemed. Ohric would send men to scout for however many escaped, and secure one for Savantin and himself.

"Your men helped me escape, though I'm not sure how many are left. I cut down as many as I could on my way here," Harlan said and moved his hand from his side. Blood began to leak through his armor. Ohric closed his eyes for a moment but nodded. The only way out now, was death. When Harlan hit the ground, he coughed blood up onto it, clumping against the dark colored dirt.

"Do you believe what happened here will happen in Savoi?" Terganus asked.

"I am uncertain," Ohric said. "Though once word of their failure here reaches them, they will be hesitant to try."

"You truly think so?"

"This is the second time a patron has attempted to have us captured, Terganus. How many more do you think will try after learning this?"

"I pray our men reach Savoi first, so that they may warn our own," he said, looking toward the buildings that were beginning to catch flame.

Zareden appeared out of the smoke from the side of the market, pointing to a section west. "I tracked him back to his house; he was packing his things."

"I trust you will see this place reduced to ash," Ohric said and followed Zareden.

The town began to smell of smoke, fire and death, now, the shouts from its heart dying down. There were not many guards left, Ohric thought, knowing that his men would make quick work of those in defiance. He wondered now what would be said to Ozrach about the slaughter, as clearly it had started just an hour ago in the streets of Lord's Valley. A letter would be sent by bird, he was sure, as Savantin did not trust the human temptation to speak when given a task of silence. He had a severe mistrust of humankind, something Ohric had wondered about at first, but only grew to respect as he had carried out Araele's wishes during his campaign. They did not deserve to be trusted, not with the lies they cast so willingly among one another. Devils, he thought, with forked tongues and devious eyes. Deceit escaped their mouths as easily as smoke billows from hellfire, and not one felt remorse.

He only made it a few paces down the street leading west when Zareden approached one of the houses, waving him inside of it. Once he made it close enough, Zareden spoke. "The man you want is inside."

"Is he alive?" Ohric asked suddenly, a rage inside of him.

"Of course, Coadjutant," Zareden answered, offering a partial salute.

The warrior from Tovai, Ohric thought. He turned out to be one of his best soldiers. Zareden stepped aside, making the entrance accessible. Ohric took no time in his entering; looking around at the home he had just stepped into. The walls gave away much about who lived here, and his suspicions were correct. Not only did the man decorate himself in such a boasting fashion, but his home was in likeness, the walls adorned with expensive paintings and intricate sculptures. Ohric wondered where the man received the money to build his estate, coming upon the conclusion that it had to have been directly from Terrenveil. When Ozrach decided to pay his many patrons they received the amount in a heap, as he was too lazy to send carriages regularly. The coin was to be used to pay the patron and his associates, but also to the temples of Araele to help ease the poverty that existed in nearly every town, now.

Ohric angrily pushed a sculpture from a pedestal, ripping its stand out of his path as he headed toward the back door of the room. There was no temple in immediate sight of the town, which meant that this louse funneled the rest of the payment into his need for extravagance. He tore a curtain that was hanging from an opened corridor, looking as Fahming was knelt on a stone floor, bound with a piece of his clothing tied around his eyes.

"You blinded him?"

"Yes. It is tradition for us to blindfold, whether or not you needed it done, I did not know. But if you wish to remain anonymous in your butchering of him you may," Zareden answered.

"Thank you. I will need you to help the others secure the town. Have you made sure no one will come looking for him?" Ohric asked, listening to Fahming's utterances of fear.

"Everyone is dead," Zareden answered.

"Take want you want from his home as a reward. He will no longer need items that belong to this world."

Fahming began to shout, calling out for whoever could hear him. Zareden smirked and walked back out into the world, leaving the two men alone. Ohric listened to Fahming's shouting and smiled, his joy eventually turning into a laugh with every pleading scream.

"Scream. Scream louder. No one is coming to help you. Your guards are dead, you see, and your errant ways have delivered you to me."

"Let me go, I've done nothing!"

"Nothing? No... I am here for quite the opposite," Ohric answered.

"Please... you have no reason to kill me. I was not a part of Thaldivir's rebellion!"

"I know this," Ohric said softly, watching as Fahming's face took an expression of confusion. "You wouldn't get involved because you are loyal to whoever will grant you gold. If the king was taken from his throne, then you might suffer a loss in your wages, does that sound about right?"

"I am not a man for rebellion... I thought that if I kept out of it that I would be safe," Fahming said quickly.

"I am not here to kill you because of your involvement; I am here to kill you for the way you live. It is vile, disgusting," Ohric answered looking around the room in which they shared. It was covered with trinkets of value, silk curtains and paintings as well as jeweled statuettes. Ohric knew of their worth, seeing similar ones in the castle on the great mountain.

"The way I live?"

"Your greed adds to the famine that plagues this earth, the poverty-stricken slums where people must scavenge for scraps left over by the likes of you. Children wear rags, their bodies skin and bone, as you sit idly in your palace with your expensive worthless adornments. You are repulsive, and my contempt for you rises with every miserable breath you take into those unworthy lungs. The world will thrive without you."

"Please... I will change my ways."

"There is nothing that will save you from this justice. If I let you go you will continue to live this way. I have heard hundreds of lies from the likes of you. You would never give up your comforts."

"I will do anything you ask. I will serve in the temples... I will give away my things to help the people... I will..."

"Stay your tongue. I have no more wish to hear you speak. You are a coward and would be molded into a lifestyle by fear. You would not believe what you do is right, you would only merely do so to avoid death," Ohric stated and pulled his sword slowly, listening to the sound the blade emitted as it scraped against the scabbard.

"Besides this I am innocent... I have killed no one. I have hurt no one. You will really kill me because of the way I live?"

"Most certainly," Ohric said, holding back his anger behind his sword. He gripped the hilt tighter, his hand trembling.

"And what does that say of you, hmm, Coadjutant? That you would kill a man who has never killed? What would Araele think of you then? Blood on your sword, blood of a man who can be led to the correct path by his past transgressions, someone who can still be saved," Fahming answered, bravery coming to him in that moment. It meant nothing, Ohric thought, he knew as soon as he left the man would go back to his voracity.

"Araele guides my hand, Fahming. She has guided me to you. I don't expect you to take your punishment with courage, your cowardice is too strong. I have told you why you must die, and why you will die. You would never change your ways, no matter how much you pleaded, no matter how much you begged."

"They were right about you. You claim you are a prophet; you fight Araele's fight. You do nothing of the sort. You claim to be avenging her, but you kill anyone *you* think is unworthy to live."

Ohric flung his sword forward suddenly, lodging it into Fahming's chest. "I claim nothing," he said and pulled it out, cutting him across his throat in anger. When he pulled it from him, blood spewed from the wound, pouring down the front of his chest creating a sanguine fountain. It stained the purple clothing he was wearing and began to cover the ground. Ohric then took a breath, hearing the world silence around him. He stood there for several minutes, watching until the blood finally slowed. The wound was more visible now, an incision that swept across his neck, revealing the organ which carried voice. Ohric seemed satisfied with this, and left the room, walking through the house. His eyes came back across its adornments, and in becoming sickened again he took his sword and cut down a vase on a pedestal, smashing it against the ground. Fahming prevented many from living the life that they deserved, Ohric thought, and in his death the world would no longer know his greed.

◆ ◆ ◆

His eyes were swollen and stung, a feeling that he knew well now. He always felt like this after being beaten, the miserable aching that he was left with. His body was usually weak and covered in bruises that accompanied raw wounds. He tried to move, feeling the pain in his chest escalate. Letting out a cry, his body fell backward, back into the straw that had become his bed for the evening. He took a breath in, trying to determine if the blood he had smelled belonged to him or one of the animals he had killed last night. He felt defeated, as he often did, wondering how he hadn't bled to death. He swore one of these nights would be his demise. Bleeding, and left to die in the barn where the animals were killed. A vicious irony, he thought, being killed where he slaughtered livestock. He was often mauled so terribly that he fell unconscious each time, and each time became worse than the last. Blacwin supposed that was what happened to him last night, not being able to remember anything besides his work.

He just finished with the goat, making sure the organs were separated from the meat. There was a bucket beside him where he placed them all, keeping them together so that when he was finished, he could dispose of them in the river. He thought it strange, placing the entrails in a place where they would travel downstream. He was always told that the fish or other animals would be able to eat them, but the only thing he could think of was the water supply. Most of Valspire collected water from the rains, placing buckets and troughs, but when the rain never came, they went to the rivers. The very same rivers where Blacwin was instructed to rid of the organs of his dead.

Brushing that thought aside he looked at his hands, bloody and covered in chunks of meat. He would wash them off when he went to the river, he supposed, and laid out the strips of meat he had procured. Salting them would be his next endeavor, but ridding of the bones had always been more important to him. The bones of dead animals were often used by nonhumans for their rituals, as well as witches. He often thought of selling them, taking his multiple horned skulls into the darker mists of Valspire to showcase his offerings. The one time he had, he was almost taken captive until he was able to talk his way out of it, using his wit to impress the mind of an old witch.

Staring at the bones of the goat, he felt a certain woe drift through him. It was as if he had been audience to one of the rituals, watching an old woman crack the skull open while calling forth a dreadful spirit, drinking the blood of a virgin girl. He heard terrible stories from the innkeepers in different parts of the land, each one becoming darker as he approached the haunted mists. The dead would remain there, and so the living had no place. At least that was what the old innkeepers would say as they focused on cleaning the tables near the kitchens. He was happiest whenever he was told to deliver meat to the inns, taking in stories and warily searching the roads for any of the creatures from them. He was a butcher, which made him somewhat frightening to the people of the separate towns. They knew also of the power of bones and knew that humans often did unspeakable things to create an alliance with the nonhumans that survived the purge. In truth, Blacwin only once sought them out, which he swore he would never do again, having only escaped by the skin of his teeth.

That was the last thought he remembered before his memory failed him, realizing that he must have been hit hard on the head to not recall the maiming. His father must have come in behind him while he was cutting away the last of the bones; the sound of the knife scraping against them was oft times loud as he made sure no splintered shards would remain inside the meat. He slowly raised his arm to the back of his head, feeling a piece of matted hair with his fingers. He moved them in front of his face, trying to fix his eyes on his skin, seeing only a small bit of blood. His fingers ran together, and he could scarcely tell them apart, the blood only working to taint the image.

Looking away from his fingers, he began to search the room with his stinging eyes, trying to make out shapes and objects. The world around him was a blur, a symptom he never before encountered. What was it that he was beaten with last night, he wondered, taking a swallow of saliva down his throat. He hadn't had a drink of water in what felt like days, only now partially gripping consciousness. He could smell water nearby but could not move, and instead surrendered to the straw in the most pain he believed he ever felt. He found himself wishing that he knew what comfort felt like, but then realized it was better he did not. It could never tease him, a soothing touch, for he had no recollection of its embrace.

His vision did not become any better, as he searched the rafters in an attempt to solidify shapes, perhaps find the tool that maimed him. Usually his father would toss it into the trough, where water was kept to wash with after a day of butchering. It became soiled quickly, blood mixing with it to create a sanguine bath. Blacwin looked to the corner of the room, where a metal bucket sat. He was so weak that he felt sickness in his stomach and leaned over, moisture being created in his throat. He opened his mouth, letting it escape and suddenly vomited, ridding yesterday's meal into the straw beside him. It was not much, and he continued to dry heave, his stomach feeling sicker and sicker with each cough. It was minutes before he stopped, and held his stomach as he curled up, hoping that at least his own arms would take some of the pain away.

He was too tired, too sore to become angry, and instead reached for the shovel that lay against the wall next to him, hoping to use it for support. His own arms prevented him from moving, and it was then he gave up for good, almost wishing that he had passed in his sleep. It would never be that easy, he thought. He would always be alive to submit to the rigorous torture of his father, his vicious alcoholism that caused him to smile while he beat his own creation. Oft nights he would scream and shout at him that he should have killed him when he was born, crying and still attached to the cord.

Taking a deep breath in, Blacwin realized how difficult it felt. Had his lungs been bruised also? He wondered if it was even possible, the bruising of what lay beneath flesh. He took another breath, each one with more difficulty than the last, his mind still traveling back to what had been used to beat him. Perhaps he would never find out, and here he would sit for hours, for days, until he was feeling strong enough to move. He had been out here for days once; his mother coming to check on him while his father went to town, doing what he could only guess was purchase the poison that caused their suffering. She offered a kind touch, cleaning his wounds and helping him eat what food she had brought for him. She had been there for hours, helping comfort her son until her husband returned, creating a scene in front of the barn until she came out.

Blacwin had pleaded for her not to go, not to leave his sight but she had only kissed him on the forehead gently, telling him that one day he would understand. He held her arm as she pulled away from him, telling her that he would only hurt her, but she pulled away, a tear falling down her cheek as she turned from him and left into the night. He had heard the first strike, becoming filled with anger. Next was the sound of his father's voice, a mocking and reviling tone, laughing at him for not being able to protect her, for being so weak that he was unable to move. He screamed that night, mustering what was left of his voice to curse his father, shouting at him that one day his miserable life would end just as it was lived. He did not know why he was spared the punishment for speaking out, but he was thankful, and sat where he sat now, breathing softly against the fluid-stained straw. He slept there for another three days, feeling so malnourished when he woke that he resorted to looking for whatever meat was spared from his last slaughter. He soon realized that it was taken. From his short coma he had woken, ashamed and depressed. Why did he continue to wake into a world where he was continuously mutilated by words and blades?

Figuring that there was a reason he must have survived, he collected himself, feeling dizzy as soon as he tried to stand, falling to the floor. Upon hitting it he opened his eyes, the blurred vision returning to him. He took a few deep breaths in, trying to focus his eyesight on the object directly in front of him. The smells of organs and vomit had left him, being replaced by a light smoky aura of cinnamon and cloves. Comfort, he decided. This must be what it is like to feel comfort. He moved his arms, still sore, yet blanketed by a soft throw made of animal skin. His wounded skin felt enrobed in warmth, and he almost shivered from it. Had he died after all, and found his way into the afterlife with some benevolent spirit?

The many objects in his vision had finally solidified, and he found himself staring at the ceiling of a room that he did not recognize. Incense burned from a long stick, emitting a slinky line of smoke across the air. That is where the smell came from, he decided, and sat up in the bed, looking around him. He was dressed in garb he had never seen before, a light-colored cloth tunic over brown pants of the same material. They were not his clothes, as he never wore light colors when doing his work. It was then he wondered what killed him, whether it was his fall to the floor, or if it was before that. For now, he would stare at the room, taking in the sweet smell that the incense provided him. He heard light footsteps across the floor outside and remained quiet, his heart seeming to be still.

A girl not much older than him stopped in the doorway, setting a small pile of clothing down on the bench that was inside the room. She gave a sigh of relief and a small smile when approaching.

"You are awake, and well I see. A lot better than you were a few days ago."

"Awake?" Blacwin asked, watching the girl. Her long hair was pinned back onto her head; two curled strands hanging down to slightly cover her left eye. She smelled as the incense did, with a soft undertone of vanilla. The warm scents were comfortable to him, and he took another breath in as if to savor them.

"Yes, the fever came back after the first day. You were out for a few days, comatose. I didn't think you were going to make it."

"So, I am alive?"

"You are."

Blacwin looked around for a moment, trying to remember how it was he got here. This was obviously a temple of some kind, but temples like this were nowhere in Valspire. "Where are we?"

"We are in Larient. It seems you don't remember what happened any more than you had the first time you woke."

"How did I get here?" he asked, confusion replacing his ability to think. Was he truly the victim of amnesia? He couldn't be alive, not here. He knew that the dead did not dream, but nothing explained this in his mind.

"One of your friends brought you. You were beaten badly when they gave you to me. Someone even said that you had been poisoned."

Blacwin let the answer rattle around in his mind for a few moments, trying to process the parts of it. Being beaten was explained, as that was what his life consisted of, but he did not consider anyone to be his friend save his horse.

"Poisoned..." he answered, more a statement than a question.

"Yes, I believe it with the fever you were in. There were no infections to cause it," the girl answered, turning and tending to the incense. Blacwin watched her carefully, his eyes not leaving her as she blew gently against the smoke, sitting on the floor. "Where are you from?"

"Valspire," Blacwin answered, keeping his responses short. He decided that he did not trust her, this woman that was in his dream, or in his afterlife. He continued to look around the room, wondering why death sent him here.

"Valspire? That is quite a way from here. I have heard there are no temples, is this true?"

"There are no temples because of the mists. People fear them more than they love their gods, and don't want to incur the wrath of whatever waits in them by erecting holy monuments."

"That sounds... terrible," the woman answered, a small hint of sadness in her voice. She sat on the floor with her legs crossed beneath her, moving her hand to her face to move the curls of hair from her cheek. She looked at Blacwin with intrigue now, as if she wanted him to finish an incomplete thought.

"I was surprised too, to wake up here in this temple. I have never seen one, being in Valspire for so long... I have become used to the stories told of why no one embraces religion. Why do you think it is, that the monarchy who so adamantly believe in its need, don't build the temples anyway?" Blacwin asked.

"In truth, I believe it is fear."

"Fear will do a lot to a man. It will make him bend, contesting his mind and body until there is nothing left of him but a shell of what he used to be. But it is a method of control. I may be beaten so often that I'm close to embracing death, but I do not fear the hand that afflicts me. I despise it."

"Hate is worse than fear. Fear is a struggle; fear is a battle that can be won. But hate, hate consumes. Hate destroys," the woman answered, now watching him with eyes of concern.

"Fear keeps people from their beliefs, robs them of the life they were promised. With a trapped mind and forced ideals, who is free to live? Fear imprisons, hate merely destroys," Blacwin answered, now looking to the woman's eyes. She was fascinated by him, though he could catch a glimmer of fear in her amber eyes as the light from the flickering candle glinted off them. "When one is afraid, they will not voice what they believe if the source of their fear believes different. When one fears for their life, they will change anything in order to avoid that fear. Hate destroys what fear created, and so hate will destroy that control."

"We are taught fear so that we can be brave, but we are not taught hate so that we can love. We are taught that love is what heals. Is that not why you were brought here before us?" the woman said.

"The fact remains the same," Blacwin answered, watching her. He felt some of his strength returning to him, something he hadn't expected.

"Did you not ever think that love can do the same as hate?" the woman asked, watching his face turn to one of intrigue, now. He leaned forward a bit, watching a smile take her face.

"Love can vanquish fear, if strong enough. Love can turn fear into understanding; Love can conquer just as easily as hate can," she continued.

Blacwin smirked, offering a laugh. The woman's face turned to one of hurt and he immediately corrected the action, speaking softly to her. "Love may give you strength against the pain, but it will not stop it. Do you think the person that does this to me could ever love?" he asked, looking back up at the ceiling. He still wasn't sure what to think of this place, this temple. Dead, in a trial of judgment. He took a breath, crossing his fingers in his lap and looking down. If this was a test of judgment, he was certain he failed. The woman stared at him, not uncrossing her legs or showing any sign of wanting to move despite the views he had just given. Perhaps she was interested by him, someone so different than she. He wondered what her initial thoughts were, a young man appearing at her temple, bruised and comatose, now waking to spew his hatred. He wondered if she had any thoughts at all, if she was just a priestess for the deity granting him this test.

"Your friend had told me that you were injured on the roads… not that someone had done this to you," the woman answered softly.

"I guess that is almost believable, with the creatures that inhabit the forests around here. I was on no road, priestess. These wounds come from my father, who enjoys beating me whenever he returns from the taverns. He is a sadist; I can almost feel the pleasure he gets from striking me as if he was spending the night beneath a harlot. He does not love either me or my mother."

The woman paused for a moment, searching her mind for words. When she had finally found them, she looked into his eyes, the amber-colored spheres becoming focused. "He is lost."

"Lost?" Blacwin asked out of outrage, trying to muster enough strength to sit forward. "There is not a night I am spared affliction by his hands, and you tell me he is lost? He does not deserve the life he lives. Every breath of air he takes to his lungs is one too many; I would rather him be dead than lost. There is no path to show him, no higher power could ever change him. Even if he became an invalid, and lived among swine it would be too good for him. He deserves nothing but meeting his end."

"Killing him will solve nothing, Blacwin."

"Killing him? Even that is too good for him. He deserves the torture he has given my mother for the past nineteen years of his life," he said and sighed, feeling a sudden sense of exhaustion. Raising his voice had him out of breath, and he could now feel pain in his chest. He moved his hand toward it, feeling a large, raised mass of skin beneath the thin cloth shirt he had been given. This wound was new, yet it had already been sealed shut. He felt it, pushing his fingers onto the skin of his chest. Never had his wounds been closed for him, as he had always been left to die out in the barn, his father hoping for it. He never knew why it was this way, he never asked but he knew that whatever the reason it was not worth the pain he endured night after night.

"You have so much hate within you, yet you are young. If you learn to let go of these feelings you will lead a much better life. If you hate a man, you are giving him control of your emotion, just as you do with fear. Forget and forgive the transgressions caused to you, only then will you truly be free of the ones who cause you harm."

Blacwin watched the girl, who continued to at him from her spot on the floor with no intentions of moving. He had so many questions he wanted to ask of her, but probably never would. He thought that maybe the words she continuously spoke to him would be useful to his attestation when he came face to face with whatever deity would send him to his afterlife. He sat back down on the bed, suddenly feeling weak and tired, the same as he did after every night he suffered the rage from his father's fists. He then became dizzy and laid back, watching the ceiling again with eyelids that were becoming too heavy to keep open. He would sleep, he decided, and gather his strength. He would need it when he returned to the haunted mists, to search for his father so that he could bring an end to the misery he created.

CHAPTER 2

SPOKEN FROM THIS BLACKENED EARTH

Alaies set his hands down on the table, taking a deep breath into his lungs. Siska had already left for Savoi with some men, leaving us with the task of Egelle. It wasn't far from Mordestai, which delighted Cahya. She didn't think she would ever see it again.

"Both Egelle and Savoi are important to our cause, but they're very unprotected. Considering these abductions and the Archegals, my thoughts shift to warning them immediately against any potential attack," Alaies said. "You must travel to Egelle and warn them."

"We will see it done," Eshkan said. "Are there any other messages you would have us deliver?"

"Yes. The patroness is hesitant. She sees the flaws of the monarchy but sees security in the legion."

"And without her backing, you'll be one city less," Eshkan said and placed a hand to his chin. "What do you suggest?"

"I will continue to try and rally her support. They live near an area rich in iron and supply the Mountain with it."

"So, what is this message?" Dacian asked.

"Cethin is the message," Alaies said. "She will not move without realizing we have the power behind our words."

"And you think a nonhuman appearing in her city is the best option?" I asked. "Most people want to set me to flame. Pardon me if I say I am not comfortable."

"I'll speak to her," Cosette said suddenly. "So much for not being involved," she muttered.

"You will?" Alaies asked, surprise in his voice.

"Yes. I don't know how much good it will do, but I will," she said and fastened her hood up around her hair. She sighed, pulling her blade from the chair nearest her.

"She will be expecting me, but I can't rightly leave now," he said, the sound of irritation following.

"We will send your regards," I said. "We should move for Egelle now."

"Farewell, Alaies," Eshkan said as he turned away.

"Safe travels."

◆ ◆ ◆

Egelle was gripped in moonlight when we arrived, against my wishes. I suggested we find a place to sleep at an inn on the roads, or sleep in the forest in shifts. No news ever came delicately in the middle of the night. Although the only thing Alaies wanted was for us to speak to the patroness of Egelle, I was hesitant to accept. It was Cahya who came to my side upon entering town, looking around carefully at the surroundings.

"This is where the legion gets its iron and steel?" she asked.

"According to Alaies, yes," I said and watched as a man tied his horse to a post and entered a house. Candlelight was seen in the window a few moments after, light flickering and dancing above its host. The town was quiet. I could hear crickets in the fields behind us.

"Shall we seek out the patroness in the morning?" Cahya asked.

"We have no choice," Eshkan said. "Unless you're willing to wake a woman from her slumber to pester her about things she may not even want to discuss."

"Should I take the lead?" Cosette asked. "When speaking to her?"

"Only if you wish it so," Cahya replied. "If you are not comfortable, I will."

"Perhaps you first, then. If she is not convinced, I will step in."

"Perfect."

"Let's make our time here short," I said and looked around before leading my horse to the post outside what could only be the inn. "There's something I don't trust."

I entered, passing coin enough for four rooms to the tired innkeep. Had it been hours ago, he probably would have asked us questions about our travels and offered us sustenance. With the hour, however, all he did was turn over keys. I happily accepted, wanting to keep conversation with anyone in town from my tongue. We each took rooms, Cahya slipping into mine once Eshkan and Dacian had turned in. I moved to hug her when we heard the door to the inn bursting open, the innkeep addressing guards.

"Where did they go?" one of them asked, haughtily.

"Those rooms, there," he responded, fright in his voice.

"Stay hidden," Cahya said to me, and peeked out the door through the keyhole. "Do not leave unless it's through that window."

"Cahya."

"Not up for discussion, and we don't have time. Let me handle this."

"They likely know about me already."

"Stay here. And if you do slip out, do not follow us."

"I can't..."

"Cethin, please."

I nodded and slid back into the shadows, turning to the nightstand and extinguishing a lone candle. A man opened the door quickly, looking around as Cahya stepped forward. "May I ask what the meaning of this is?" she asked, placing a hand on her hip.

"The patroness wishes to speak to you and your friends."

"At this hour?"

"Enough questions, you will speak to her at once."

"I will follow. Where are we to speak with her?"

"The gardens, immediately," the second guard interjected, motioning his hand outward for Cahya to exit. She complied, closing the door behind her before looking in my direction. I would have to apologize to her later for finding a vantage point to view the gardens. I slipped out the window, climbing up the roof quickly. No guards took watch on the rooftops, which made following them incredibly easy. Dacian and Eshkan had swords to their backs, their weapons relinquished. Cosette and Cahya were in front, unshackled, likely due to their lack of weapons. I ducked lower as I climbed along, until the gardens came into view. It was there a woman was standing outside of a shed, wearing riding pants and a jacket that ended at her waist, a hood covering her face. She stood next to a man of similar height, her advisor, must be.

Eshkan and Dacian were led into the shed, the two guards entering after them. I knew Cahya could handle herself, Cosette as well, but I'd need to help them escape. I climbed down and stuck to the shadow, passing by the gate of the garden once the patroness and her advisor had eyes fixated on Cahya. I moved around the back of the shed, pressing my ear to the shuttered window.

"So, you're mercenaries, that it?" one of the guards asked. I peeked through the crack in the shutters, watching as they shackled them to chains in the walls. A simple gardening shed it was not. The shorter guard's torch came close to the window, and I ducked a moment, adjusting my eyes before standing again.

"Yes. We rode here from Sathenne after their citizens were being abducted by Archegals," Dacian said. "We have no reason to lie."

"Why come here?"

"We are on our way to Esperanus," Eshkan stated. "Meeting with a friend."

"Even so, she will have to decide what to do with you," the other responded. They opened the front door, closing it behind them. It was then I opened the window, looking inward at them.

"Cethin! How did you evade being captured?" Dacian whispered.

"A story for another time. How tightly are you bound?"

"Not very," Eshkan answered. "Ropes."

I made a face, shaking my head. "It'll be easy for me to untie you," I said and climbed through the window swiftly, pulling my sword. I quickly cut Dacian's binds, moving to Eshkan next. "Act as though you are still bound."

"What?" Dacian asked. "Are you crazy?"

"Much less than your hostess."

"No, he's right," Eshkan said. "We do not want to offend her if she comes to her senses, but we are free in the event they try to kill us."

"I do not want to leave it to chance."

"And what?" I asked. "Storm them in the garden while she and her advisor are unarmed? Cahya seems to think she can speak to her. Follow her lead."

"Where do you go?" Eshkan asked.

"Back to the inn. I promised Cahya I'd remain there."

"I... I see," Eshkan said. "Shall we return for you once we've... made progress here?"

"Yes. I would much like to be a part of it," I returned, and climbed through the window. It was then the front doors opened, the patroness and her advisor walking inside, Cahya and Cosette beside them.

"Cethin," she called. I sighed, and walked back toward the window, looking inside of it. "I thought I told you that I could handle it."

"And you did," Eshkan said and stood. "He simply didn't believe that we could."

I shrugged in response, Dacian standing up as well.

"I apologize for our cautiousness. We've endured so much, and have lost so many," Cahya said and turned toward the patroness. "This is Eshkan and Dacian, and that is Cethin."

"Pleased to make your acquaintance. I apologize for my cautiousness as well. Cahya tells me that Alaies has sent you."

"Yes, though I did not lie to your men. We are on our way to Esperanus."

"Though we are making a stop in Mordestai, to see my people," Cahya said. "Moving to the matters at hand, can we count on your support?"

"You can count on my silence. I am in a difficult position, Cahya. We supply the legion with its iron and steel. If we were to turn against them now, our livelihood and the lives of my people could be squandered. However, if the tide changes, and a new leadership is formed, my allegiance will belong to it."

"It is understandable," Cahya said. "We will move on with our journey and play our part in uniting those who wish it against this menace."

"Wait," Dacian said. "There is still the matter of the Archegals."

"Archegals?!"

"Yes. While we were in Sathenne we intercepted a group of hostages. They are alive and well in Cilevdan it seems," Cahya said.

"How on earth did you save them?"

"We had help. We did not face them alone," Cahya said and looked toward me. "They are tracking wagons on the road, and taking whoever they belong to."

"I will make my men aware at once. Are they attacking cities?"

"As far as we know, no," Eshkan answered. "Though you should exercise caution."

"We shall send our messages by bird."

"They may think twice about taking your people," I said from the window. "Once they discover your ties to the legion, I'm sure they will turn tail."

"Yes, they may. I doubt they want an entire battalion hunting them down and eradicating them."

"It's what they deserve," her advisor said. He had been quiet until now.

"I thank you and your men for your warning, Cahya. You are welcome to stay in Egelle for as long as you need. But be warned, the legion is coming to visit in five days' time."

"We will stay the night. We have already paid for rooms in your inn and shall return to them. After that, we continue on our path."

"I wish you luck in that, Cahya," she said and smiled. She and her guards retreated then, her advisor nodding in our direction before he followed them.

"Mordestai next?" Eshkan said and rubbed his left wrist with his hand.

"Yes," Cahya smiled. "At the first light of day."

We didn't say much on our way back to the inn, until I gripped Cahya's arm in my hand before we reached the doors. Eshkan, Dacian, and Cosette walked ahead, entering without caution.

"Too late for a stroll don't you think?" she asked, looking up at the moon. It was full tonight. The patroness was brave to interrogate newcomers under a full moon in Cilevdan.

"More so thinking we could get a better view than this," I said and walked to the side of the building, ivy strongly rooted within an iron lattice. "This should hold. You first."

Cahya smiled and placed her hands on the lattice, pulling on it twice before climbing upward and onto the roof. I followed her, watching the sky. Stars lay scattered across it, twinkling in bright delicate contrast. One of them burned out, falling toward earth before disappearing into the darkness.

"That's the fourth one I've counted since we've left," she said and laid back against the roof, taking a deep breath. "Fallen stars are warriors, being sent here by the gods in times of true darkness."

"Are the gods speaking to you now?" I asked, keeping my eyes on the small auras of light.

"To me? No," she said and laughed softly. "They don't speak in voices. They speak in actions, usually small. The stars, I have not seen this many fall in such a short time."

"Do you think we will find them, your warriors?" I asked, sitting next to her. She was calm, relaxed.

"It remains to be seen. We shouldn't stay long, I feel uneasy."

"We will leave at dawn's first light, before the village wakes," I assured her. "Come. We should rest."

◆ ◆ ◆

Day was almost upon its end, Meshari thought with happiness. It wasn't that she minded the role she had been given in the village, it was the work that came with it she detested. The backbreaking work, the beads of sweat that pooled on her coffee-colored forehead she did not mind, nor did she mind the way the sun beat down on her skin for hours as she harvested the wheat fields. It was the task itself that troubled her. Most of the women in the village were hunters, who alongside their men, tracked game in the plains and forests. She wondered why she was chosen for this, as she picked up her large basket and slipped it onto her back with its tough arm straps. Her thoughts moved to how someone else in the village spent their days tanning leather. She supposed tending the grain fields wasn't so terrible, as she stripped the last plant in the row of its contents and funneled the morsels into her basket.

She thought about other towns, the ones that shared the same earth as her, and how they mocked them for neglecting their forges, their taverns, their gods. They did not need them, their chief said, and it was how they had avoided war and famine for so long. Coin, he had said, was an evil concept. Why would you limit your own people to how they could live with something as small as a stone? A person's life was not meant to be limited, especially not by the person who is supposed to unite them. Their leaders are supposed to lift them up, high on the wings of the spirits, and make sure that each and every one of them has prayers answered and homes abundant. So, despite many requests from the king of outside nations to peacefully join his kingdom, their chief refused each time, noting that it would be the end of their livelihoods.

Their chief had done justly, Meshari thought, knowing that there was no famine, and no death here. They kept the evil, gold they called it, out of their lands, and because of it their 'primitive' lifestyle endured. *Primitive*, the merchants from beyond the plains called it, trying to buy their stone weapons, handmade pottery and furs from them. The chief had kindly refused their coin as well, before turning them away. Only traders were welcome here, as they had something practical to offer in return for their hard work. He told the merchants that their coin was even less useful than the manure of their cow herd, for at least that could be used to enrich their fields. She laughed at that, although it was not meant to be an insult, but something for them to consider. All people were welcome under the stars of Kaishani, their spirit of the night.

People from the outside nations went to their chief for freedom from their poverty; and in becoming initiated into their lands, worshiped the spirits and began to live a life of reward, prosperity. They received the same food as everyone else and enjoyed a roof over their heads. No longer did they need to steal to feed their children. There were quite a few people that left the cities and laws of Terrenveil to join them. Although tidings came with those people that there was a storm cloud darkening, threatening to swallow the land in shadow. She listened to their chief that night, telling his people that they would continue to play ignorant of the greed of the outside kingdom until the day came where they would have to drive them away from their lands through blood and fire.

The others had already gathered their day's harvest and left home to their families after reporting to the chief's compound with their grains. It would be made into breads and sweet rolls by those who were proficient in baking. Every day they would do this, until the Days of the Spirits were upon them. Midweek, she thought, was closer than it was far, and for two whole days she could spend her time doing what she wanted to do, which was exploring beyond Mordestai's edge. It was forbidden to go there, under no real consequence aside from risking her and her family's safety and grace beneath the spirits. It was heresy, her father called it, while spitting at her offerings a few weeks ago as he jarred them from her hands and into the fire. Heresy that she ventured to places not protected by their spirits of worship. There was a reason Mordestai had the borders it did, her mother had said as if to console her, though she scarcely needed consolation. They described the lands beyond their own as dark, with evil behind every tree. She thought of their tales as folly, a manipulative tale of fear to keep her from the border's edge. She wouldn't listen to their admonitions, however. While she did believe in the Spirits, she did not believe that her gentle exploration would enrage them, so long as she killed no animals that were sacred.

Maybe that was why the lands beyond the border were deemed forbidden to traverse. The lands beyond their own could be sacred, she thought, but suddenly rejected that. Other people lived on the same lands as they, and likely did not worship the Spirits. She often ignored her father's seething, his distrust of those who were different. They spoke an entirely different language than they did, worshiped entirely different gods. She often wondered why distrust circled his mind, the people who joined them were as kind as those born here. He did go on to say that it wasn't distrust of those who joined them, but distrust of those who continued to approach with things they had no interest in. Coin, offers to join the outside nations.

She wondered why they were so important, such small shining disks. People worked to earn those to survive, not to help their land flourish and survive. The king and his court, she heard from some of those close to the chief, were full of greed, and did not care about the people that served them. They did not exist as normal honest people did, and it was because they did not have the guidance of the Spirits. A statement also spurned by her father when she told him that she wanted to explore the land. After hearing all of these things, she was thankful to belong to such a place, even if it did mean she would be harvesting grain until the age when she was old enough to give birth, if she so decided. Some women did not want to be mothers, and instead joined those who would hunt. That, Meshari thought, was what she wanted to do with her life. She wanted to join the thrill of the warriors, the excitement of the hunt. She would gain a skill that would help her anywhere, if she did leave Mordestai against the wishes of her father. She was free to do whatever she wanted, her only bonds to this place being her duties if she stayed. Her mother would understand, although she would not enjoy the decision, but her father would never forgive her. He often sneered at her having no hobbies that would indicate being a "respectable young woman". He hoped she would seek union with one of the chief's sons when old enough but often told her that she would have a better chance at courting one of his daughters with the way she carried herself. She did not mind that, she thought the body of a woman was just as pleasing as that of a man.

She made it to the edge of the grain field, toward the southernmost border of the land, when her eyes came across what her father spoke of. Just as she had emerged from the hearty stalks of grain there were soldiers, three in all. She felt her heart beating quickly inside of her, pounding against her chest as if it were a prisoner trying to escape her flesh. She froze, knowing that she was spotted. She spilled her grain as the first approached, the offering to her great land and protector wasted as it spread outward like a sea toward the feet of those moving toward her. They began to speak to her in a tongue she did not recognize, shouting with a sense of angered urgency. It was then, Meshari realized, that although their freedoms exceeded those of any other colony that existed, it did not keep them safe from greed.

◆ ◆ ◆

The road was long, showing the vast forest that circled most of Terrenveil. The many nights toward Mordestai had been spent with limited sleep, Eshkan and Dacian offering to watch over the others when I left to hunt. I knew there would not be many opportunities to succeed, being so far into the forest and so far from civilization. However, it made them feel better that I left to do so. I would do my best to put them at ease, even if that meant taking a menial walk through the woods a few paces from where we stopped for the evening. Cahya herself was worried, though did not share the same concerns as the others. She was worried about her homeland, lands normally at peace. She was with the others now, sleeping upon the blankets she packed.

The nights had grown colder, which made it difficult to keep warm on the roads closer to the mountain. I looked around the forest, its dark silence casting an aura that granted feelings of unease. Despite this, Dacian and Eshkan worked to build a fire, thinking that we were too deep in the bowels of the forest to be seen on any road. They did not worry about the other inhabitants of the forest, such as the nightwolves who preyed among those asleep, drawn out by the smell of blood. I supposed our only options were to become preyed upon by things alive or freeze until death.

I wasn't long on my search when I decided to turn back, knowing that no man ventured beyond this point of the forest. It was Dacian's idea to travel close to the southern border when heading to Mordestai, attesting that it would be safer for us if we did. He was sure that there would be less possibility of being approached this way, the forest dense and uninhabited. We had superstition to thank for that, the people of this land believing there to be evil in the dark trees. I looked upon them while continuing back where the others were sleeping, staring into the tangled mass of branches, thorns clustered in large points across them. They were bare this time of year, the flowers they bore during the summer were supplicants of nectar to vibrant colored birds. It was strange how the tree gave birth to small tokens of beauty, yet they were surrounded by crowns of venomous thorns.

I smelled the horses through the trees as I came across our encampment watching as Eshkan sat close to the sleeping women, tending the fire by adding pieces of the black branches above us. Dacian was also asleep, between the horses as we had been ordered to do many a night on Ophidian. I made it to Eshkan's back and sat upon one of the large logs they had procured as a place to rest. He jumped suddenly as the fire revealed me, each strand of flame seen against my armor. He had grabbed a sword until I moved my hands before me, pulling down the mask that was attached to the chest piece of my armor, my face becoming visible to the human eye.

"Damn it Cethin... that was enough to scare the bones from my body."

"My apologies. I did not mean to frighten you."

"I didn't see you at all, not until you stepped toward the fire. I keep forgetting your talents, Sardon," he answered.

I nodded, looking over the others, who were peacefully resting beneath a large and knotted tree. "I am thinking of waking Dacian soon, I am in need of rest."

"I am not able to sleep. The forest has me feeling very nervous."

"I can assure you there is nothing nearby; I felt nothing while on my hunt."

"Forgive me if I do not sound relieved. There is something about this forest that makes me feel victim...as if something will descend upon me at any moment wanting to take my life."

"The trees give off that feeling, inside them is substance the color of blood, strongest when the weather is changing. They will soon become dormant, and the last of the life inside them is trying to escape. If there was something preying us, I would have found it already."

"Even so I will remain awake a little longer. Dacian just fell asleep; I am sure he needs more rest before he is called to watch again. That night in Egelle was too short," he said, sighing. "What I wouldn't give for a hot meal and a warm bed."

"Once we find Cahya's people, I am sure they will accommodate us," I answered, moving forward to feel the heat of the fire on the skin of my face. My armor was surprisingly protective, the thin material keeping my body isolated from the elements.

"Do you think we will be safe when we cross into Morrenvahl? I understand while you may be, we are prey," Eshkan asked quickly, staring at me from over the smoke of the fire, its crackles becoming louder now as silence took us. I could not think of a response to the question, realizing that I did not know the answer myself. I did not want to admit that to him, knowing that the response would set him on a train of thought not easily broken. I sighed and stood, wearily looking toward the horses.

"I have something of dire importance to them; they will have no choice but to accept me, and I will make it clear that you are not to be harmed. But if they do not, we must be prepared to fight," I answered. To that, Eshkan gave a nod. Whether it was acknowledgment of my statement, or a response to display his lack of an answer, I did not know. When he offered no more words I walked to the horses, crouching down to shake Dacian's forearm. He woke suddenly, his eyes coming across me in the darkness.

"I need your eyes. Eshkan will not sleep and tends the fire. The wood worries him."

"I will keep watch over the others," Dacian answered sleepily and rose from his position on the ground. He stroked his horse on the nose as he stood before her and made sure the reins were still secure around the tree she was tied to. He gave me a small nod before heading toward the fire, speaking to Eshkan quietly as he approached. I sighed, looking over to where Cahya was sleeping beneath the large black tree. She was curled against herself, shivering slightly beneath the blanket she was using. I moved to her, carefully pulling the blanket away enough to lie beside her. I could feel her soft breaths leaving her lips and moved close to her to stop her from shivering. She opened her eyes slowly, looking upon me as I took the hood off my head, removing the cowl from my shoulders.

She said nothing and smiled, moving closer to me and resting her head upon my shoulder, expelling air from her lungs in relief. After a few moments she stopped shivering, nudging me softly a few times with the side of her face. Laying here with her, every breath I took felt soothing, as if each before this moment were taken merely to survive. The euphoria of feeling her heartbeat and inhaling every calmed breath she exhaled warmed the heart within the shadows of my being.

I lay awake for another hour, watching the sky above me. It was obscured by the thick mangled branches of the trees, making it hard to see almost any of the vast deep blue that painted the night. I wished there was a small opening of branches, so that I could gaze upon the stars. It was she who had first shown me their beauty, unafraid as I removed my eyes from cover to see. I thought about this memory often, one I cherished. I finally took a deep breath out, closing my eyes to prepare for rest.

I was shaken violently as the sun rose; it was Dacian, who was looking around himself in a panic. I did not know the meaning of his demeanor until he quieted me, continuing to look around us. Cahya stretched lethargically and looked at him, surprise in her face.

"Dacian... what are you doing?!" she asked and pulled the blanket up over her body.

"Quiet Siress...there is something in the trees," Dacian answered and took a slow step backward, reaching for Basilin's sword.

"I do not hear anything. Cethin said this was a safe place to set up for the night," Cahya answered, her voice in a whisper. I could feel her looking at me from the corner of my eye.

"It was, and it remains to be. Whatever was preying on us has left here," I answered, suddenly catching a scent in the air. "No... you're right," I said and quickly stood from the blanket, taking Seligsara in grasp. "I smell something in the wind. Something foul."

"Death," Dacian replied, continuing to look around him carefully. I looked around quickly, not seeing Cosette or Eshkan anywhere.

"Did you see where they have gone?"

"Eshkan... he was caught in some kind of delusion... he had said that there were things... crawling out of the wood of the trees. I couldn't stop him from running off. Cosette woke from his screams and helped me try to track him down, but the fog became thick. She was lost to me, and I used the scent of the fire to make my way back here."

I began to walk off suddenly, hearing Cahya's voice as I reached the line of trees that surrounded us.

"Let us accompany you. There is no sense in wasting time. If we work together, we will find them with haste," she urged.

I nodded quietly and looked at Dacian. "If I suddenly split off from you it is because I have found something, but I want the two of you to stick together. It will be easier to become united again if we stick to that plan."

I stopped, looking to where Dacian stood. "Did he come in contact with the blood of the trees?" I asked.

"None of the trees bear injury, Cethin."

"Something is wrong," I answered and headed off into the growing fog. I could hear the horses stir behind me, Dacian keeping them together. I could smell death, thick and creeping through the fog as if it was closing in around me. I kept my eyes sharp and unmoving as I stood, waiting for the others to approach.

"The last I saw of them, they went this way, through the forest. I saw old stone ruins as we continued to run, losing them behind pillars. I called for them, but my voice was caught as the fog grew thicker," Dacian answered, looking at the treetops. "If we keep going this way, we will find them. I paid attention to the patterns of the stars through the trees, but when the sun rose, I lost trail," he answered.

"The constellations..." Cahya answered. "Once the stars join us tonight, we can use them to find our way to Mordestai. If we follow the sign of the hunter, then we will make it there quickly."

Dacian offered a nod and looked toward me, pointing ahead in a northern direction. "The fog is thickest this way, it is where I lost them," he answered.

I took a deep breath in, the stench of death becoming more apparent. "They don't have much time," I answered and began to move quickly, hoping that the others would keep pace. I did not wish to separate from them, only to hasten my arrival at the location of the ruins. The fog was menacing, thick and obscuring.

I finally stopped moving when it felt as if it became sparse, the lack of trees making it scatter across the ground and between old buildings. The silence here was heavier than it was before. I was standing in what felt like timeless moments, the fog obstructing my sight. Suddenly a screech came to my ears, and I moved quickly, flipping the handle of Seligsara in my hand and sweeping the blade to the origin of the sound, catching contact with something. The screeching ceased as I felt something heavy slide across my blade, and slump onto the ground, yet as I pulled it back to me there was no blood that ran to my flesh. Most of the fog diminished, the ruins that Dacian described coming into sight.

I looked to the forest floor seeing a man sinking into it, appearing cold from years of death. A revenant, from the looks of him. It could be nothing else. I should have perceived this from the heavy fog.

"Damn these creatures. How do we know that Eshkan still breathes?" Dacian cursed, peering into the stone ruins.

"We can't take a chance. If he still lives, then it will not be for long if we do not come to his aid. A revenant makes a terrible death," I answered. A screech was heard the moment the words rolled off my tongue, and the fog began to return.

"There is another!" Cahya said, brandishing her hand ax in front of her.

Dacian readied himself suddenly and looked to the ruins, squinting as if to gain sight. "I see her. She is haunting the ruins, searching for our blood. She can smell us, but she has not found us yet."

It was then we saw Cosette, sitting upon one of the tallest structures. She stood once the shrieking stopped, looking around her, watching the woods while looking for the best way to climb down.

"I will try to make my way to you," she said suddenly, her voice carrying over the silence.

"Were you injured?" I asked.

"When I was running my foot got caught on a large root. It pained me to continue, but I made it up here. I laid on the frost covering the ruins to lower my temperature. Revenants. Magelda used to tell me tales of them, despite my parent's wishes."

"Will you be able to walk?"

"Not very quickly... I will try to make my way back to camp. The horses won't be targeted. Perhaps if I lay with them, I will be overlooked should there be any more," she answered.

I nodded and looked at the path behind us, feeling at ease about it now that the fog had cleared.

"We will return to you as soon as we find Eshkan," I said.

"You have not yet found him?" Cosette asked. "Watch out!" she shouted and strung her bow quickly. She shot an arrow behind us, and it hit a revenant directly between the eyes, causing it to fall toward the ground.

Dacian turned and sliced another one several times with his sword. Another had come from the trees behind us, and Cahya swung her ax beneath its chin, the blade stopping beneath the creature's ears. She pulled it out, feeling remorse for the dead young boy. He too, was swallowed by the frozen earth.

"We will have to find the source of them. Once we destroy it, the rest should follow," Cosette answered, re-stringing her bow.

"They must have been killed here," Cahya said. "It is said they only roam close to where they perished. I wonder what keeps them tied to our world."

"We may never find out. I don't plan on keeping one alive long enough to speak to it. These creatures know no empathy. They live to kill, to steal the heat from living souls so that they might once live again. You are right, it is said people who have died the most terrible of deaths become them. Those who were betrayed or have seen great tragedy. The emotion carried with them when they died was strong enough to keep them alive in this state, a haggard, sadistic creature looking to kill whoever had wronged them. Everyone they cross can become casualty if not careful," Cosette shivered.

"I have never heard of them in numbers like this. What does this mean?"

A scream from just past the ruins took our ears, one not of pain but of fright. "He still lives," Dacian answered and began to run, which had me immediately following him. We continued through the brush until we saw him, cornered near a tree with his sword gripped loosely in his shaking hand. There was a woman, speaking to him from just a few feet away, enticing him toward her with her long pale fingers. Though we could see her for what she was, I was certain that Eshkan was under her spell, seeing a young maiden where we saw a beast. Cosette placed an arrow in her bow, pulling it back as she held it up toward her eye. She took only a moment to steady it and released her fingers, the arrow making hardly a sound at all as it sailed through the air and landed in the woman's temple, cutting through the other side of her skull. She had let out a horrific shriek then as she fell to the ground and slowly sank back into it, her cold dead arm being the last to disappear beneath the ground.

Eshkan suddenly came to as his hypnotist returned to the grave, the color returning to his eyes. He had one large handprint on his bicep as evidence of his struggle, and claw marks on his back. They had ripped through a layer of his armor, his cloth shirt showing beneath it. He was lucky to have not had his blood drawn, and beyond that, was lucky to still be alive. We

THE COVEN OF SHADOW

approached him slowly, my eyes searching the wood for any other creatures that could be waiting.

"They were at the camp, watching us from the trees. Thank Basilin you found me when you did. I was trying to resist her gaze, yet it was becoming harder as the fog grew. I would have been killed," Eshkan said and placed his hand against Cosette's arm, nodding to her in thanks. He took several deep breaths and sat on the ground, closing his eyes.

"I know you are exhausted," Dacian stated. "When we reach camp, we will spare whatever food we have left from Egelle. You should eat, for strength."

Eshkan nodded and took another long, deep breath, gathering his wits. Revenants were draining creatures, and those who survived them often suffered deep exhaustion from their leeching. He was lethargic, I could tell with every minute movement of his limbs, and even the way he was breathing.

"We should get moving," Cahya suggested, looking around. "There may yet be more."

"Cosette, how do you fare?"

"I am alright," she answered.

Eshkan breathed a sigh of relief and nodded, being slow to stand. "I would much like to return to camp. The sooner we get to Mordestai, the sooner we will be able to gain the hospitality of Cahya's family."

"We will be well received. My father runs a farm toward the south of the province. He will have plenty of resources for us to use. He also is very close with the chief of our people. When his son was born, he offered them livestock as a gift. That is a sign of respect in our lands. If we need anything, we will acquire it."

"Do you think they would help us fight for our cause?" Eshkan asked.

"They have always held opposition to the king and his ways. Often, the queen's emissaries come to 'reform' them. It is seen as an insult, and while they know they are just doing what their religion calls for they will not abandon their ways. If the legion is as threatening as we have discovered it to be, then my people will not want to leave their customs at risk. Our gods have kept us safe for all these years. We will not abandon them, as they have never abandoned us," Cahya answered.

"I hope that it does not escalate to a full insurgency," Dacian said, looking up toward the sky.

The air was clearer than it was, however, there was still a bit of fog surrounding us. I picked up a familiar scent as it returned in abundance and suddenly spun, pointing the tip of my blade at the throat of a revenant. He had no eyes, as most of them did not, the sockets dark and vexing. There was a deep darkness around them, as if they were holes for peering into the cores of their victims. His skin was pale with a tinge of gray to it, as death crept across his body.

"Ahh... a Sardon. I should have known better than to try sneaking up on you," he answered, his voice hollow and dull.

"We have no words worth speaking," I said and gripped the handle of Seligsara, about to strike.

"But we do, Sardon, we do," he said, withdrawing slightly. "You have found our home, where we used to live out here in the forest. All of us, the ones you have sent back to our graves, used to trade here, fish here, use the resources, and bear children. Until one day our lives changed forever."

"State your purpose, before I send you to your end," I stated, being unusually harsh. It was known that a revenant spoke to their victims to hypnotize them, appearing as they did when they were alive once under spell. I knew their sorcery wouldn't work on me; for they could not look into my eyes the same way they could a human, yet his closeness to the others made me uncomfortable. They had powers over the mind that one could not explain.

"He was here... the one you look for. A black box, one that is antique and holds within it terrible things. It is unknown whether or not he turned my people. The Seraphice are a mystery to us, as they are to most. We told him that we did not have it, but because we worship He who created the box, he thought otherwise. Our people have not had the box in thousands of years."

"You were... Velgrothan," I said, looking at the mark on his hand.

"He came to us in daylight, so that we could not fight back with our strengths, yet his strength also comes from the night sky. It seems that we are not the only ones who have perished by this daemon."

"You know what he is looking for?" I asked, watching him closely.

"I do, though it will be something difficult to find. It belongs to us; it is something that must never be opened. You underestimate this creation; it endangers the entire world. It is a very old story, one that has been lost to the purge and only known by those who survived it."

"What do you know of it?" I asked suddenly.

"Yes. The box. A black box. It holds terrible things within it," the wraith repeated. "The box of Barroqas was hidden by a Velgrothan named Salka. She destroyed the one sharing the name of the box, one who had the power to turn the sun into eternal darkness upon the world. Most of the nonhumans implored him to do so yet Salka knew that if Barroqas did, then they would all suffer. Humanity would weaken as a result of the lack of sunlight, and their food supply would eventually die. She destroyed Barroqas and took his power, sealing it in a box for the rest of time to come," he answered, turning his gaze toward the others.

"The mariner spoke of a box similar to this, one that was fought over by people of the earth long ago. No one could open it because it was never in the same place for a long enough time. The sea faring people tried to find it, to put it to sea, but they never prevailed."

"The box. It holds within it terrible things," the revenant repeated. The creature had lost his mind, floating within the world on a thread so fragile that it could be broken upon a breath.

"This is the box that Savantin is looking for?" Cahya asked, her voice frail.

"If what he speaks is truth, it is," I answered, ignoring his constant rambling.

"Mercy of the gods. If he gets his hands on it then all hope will truly be lost," Eshkan said.

"How long ago did he do this to you?" Cahya asked.

The revenant continued to ramble, walking into the forest as he spoke. We watched him go until he was no longer audible, cursed to walk the earth until their murderer was brought to justice.

"We should gather all the resources we can from Mordestai," I answered.

"Mordestai is leagues from Morrenvahl, Cethin. You said yourself that if you hope to defeat him you will need to learn the words of your people so that you can control the Sun."

The words Dacian spoke were true, and the Sun manipulated his words, playing them over and over again in its several voices until it began to speak in Sardon.

"He has an army with him, one that will not cease to do whatever they must in order to please him. Sure, the entire legion might not be willing to wield their swords for him once they find out what he is planning. Who knows how many diligently serve him now. Beyond that, the king is still hiding in his castle, afraid, ignoring everything that comes to pass. We are going to need allies if we are going to stop this, and maybe we can save the rest of these people too. Have you already forgotten about Sathenne?" I asked, gathering silence. "They are counting on us. Once we dissolve the rule of the king, things will become easier for them. If we do not unite as many provinces as we can in the meantime, the cause will be lost. Alaies told us of their plans."

"What if he finds the box? What if the entire world is drowned in darkness? What then?"

"Then I will make sure that it finds its way back to the light," I answered and turned away, headed back to camp. I knew that humans were moldable, and that fear distracted them from their goal oftentimes creating a change in them. Dacian seemed to meet my thoughts with question, something I had not entirely expected. I was about to showcase my frustration in words until Cahya came to my side, gripping onto my arm with her soft hand.

"Do not be angry at him, he only wishes to help," she answered.

"He only thinks of the large break in the well, not the tens of small ones that can rupture it further."

"You have more empathy for life than any human I have met; I admire that about you Cethin. I must thank you for how much you wish to protect these people, but Dacian is worried, he's anxious. What if we truly cannot stop Savantin?"

"I will do everything in my power to stop him from his quest. And I will do everything in my power to liberate these people," I stated.

"What if you cannot do both?"

"To do one without the other is only delaying the misery that will come to pass. This king is doing nothing to help his people. They will starve and die. But if the box is found... a warlord becomes a god. How do you expect me to choose?"

"I do not. I will not. But I will follow you."

I smiled at her kindness, not knowing the words to say to her. She saw my smile, must have, as I noticed her eyes watching my face from the sides of my vision. She began to smile too, a smile of radiance. I wish I could find words that would justify the way I felt about her, just so that she could hear me say them, yet I could find none. I often brought her back trinkets from my travels, including a pendant made of blue goldstone. I haven't seen it in a long time, and I didn't know why it was suddenly brought forth to memory. I purchased it in Mosveca, a small commune of nomads who made residence southwest of her home of Mordestai. I hoped that those would speak for me, and in offering her small gifts that both of us would have been punished for, she offered me words.

"Wherever the path takes us, I am with you."

I smiled at her; the gesture being understood. I sighed, looking through the forest.

"What is it?" she asked.

"The girl," I answered.

"What about her?"

"I feel responsible for dragging her into this."

"She seems to be making herself at home among us." Cahya smiled. "She seems to really enjoy Dacian's company."

The two were laughing, Dacian inspecting Cosette's bow.

"I think she will be alright, Cethin," Cahya said and moved to join them.

Eshkan strode to my side, giving a shallow exhale. "I didn't have a chance to thank you back there."

"Not necessary, but appreciated," I responded.

"Necessary. Had you all not found me, I would be dead," Eshkan said and offered a small laugh. "Cosette, she's brave."

"Very."

"We are lucky to have her with us," Eshkan said and looked upward. "So, Mordestai?"

"Yes," I answered. "Cahya will want to commune with her people."

"Anywhere with a warm bed sounds fine to me," Eshkan said. We joined the others, a chill wind approaching. Once we made it back to camp, I looked across the horizon to plan our journey to Mordestai.

The sparse plains of Sarcanat along with Cahya's homeland were built upon an old volcano that had come from the sea, according to the stories told to me by the Mariner. While those lands bore witness to temperatures of heat, Septentria was the portion of the sea that had frozen over. There was no logical explanation for the Eastern Baeld, however, and while it did experience its winters, snow rarely fell upon the communities, who fished during every season in the seas north of them.

"If we travel when the sun reaches the cover of the mountains then we should make it during the dark of the morning. That will work to our advantage if the dogs of Terrenveil have already made it upon them," Cahya said, turning to look at the mountains.

"Before we go... it seems as if this little stream is bountiful," Cosette answered. "Perhaps we should fish it before leaving here." She looked around the trees and pulled a large branch from beneath them, using her knife to sharpen an end of it. Dacian took to aiding her, Eshkan sitting at the base of a large tree, expelling a deep sigh. He held his head upward, closing his eyes.

I looked at Cahya who nodded, gently pushing me off in his direction. "Go make sure he's alright. I'll help the others."

I sat down next to him, being quiet for a time, until he opened his eyes. "I'm starting to feel stronger," he said suddenly. "It was... horrible. I can't explain how it began. All I remember is that I was tending to the horses when I noticed something in the woods. I went to inspect and that's when it happened. She looked like just a young woman. She had silver-blonde hair and dark green eyes, reaching toward me with her skin that appeared pale yet warm. She was the opposite, and somehow, I knew it although I could not see. She ripped at me with her fingers when I would not follow her, and once they grazed my flesh I felt immense pain, perhaps the pain she felt when she died. I felt sadness, such deep sadness that I thought I would never again feel the joys of living. It was when I ran toward the ruins that her true being was revealed to me. Black hollow sockets where her eyes had once been, grayish pale skin. She had long fingers with sharp claws and let out this horrid shriek. Even in all that we've seen, I didn't realize Cilevdan held such horrors."

"I'm still lingering on what was said to us. They worshiped the box, held it sacred. If they didn't have it, and didn't know its whereabouts, then who does?" I said and joined Eshkan in looking at the sky.

"I know someone who may be able to help us," Eshkan revealed. "She's hiding her identity, however. I was told only to go to her if the stars were falling out of the sky, intent to set the earth on fire."

"I'd say we're close. Shall we go?"

"Not yet," Eshkan said. "I know what you're thinking, but I don't think she'd be happy to see me based on what she'd deem a fool's chase and no cause for alarm."

"No cause for alarm?"

"He doesn't know where it rests either."

"But every day he could become closer. How could she help us?"

"She's Magar."

"Ah," I said, simply. "I have worked with two before."

"Of course you have," Eshkan laughed. "I should have known. So, you know that she's capable of finding something for us to follow, a lead. I doubt she'd accompany us, but..."

"I always thought they hoarded artifacts. Took them away from the hands of humanity, just as we did, but they have proved me wrong."

"Therein lies the difference. Most seek power for their own means. We hid it away." Eshkan sighed. "It bothers me, greatly, that there is now no one protecting those artifacts."

"Vortain hid them well. After retrieving them, I never saw them again."

"I almost want to go back there, to ensure bandits don't get their hands on anything they should not. But I still trust in his decisions."

"As do I," I said.

Moments later we smelled fish, cooking over an open flame. Cahya and Cosette ate first, Dacian handing a plate to Eshkan before making one for himself.

"Cosette packed a lot of things," he said. "I'd have never thought to bring this."

"She is resourceful," Eshkan said. "We should eat and push ahead. I don't want to spend another night in this place. And there's no telling what might be attracted by the scent of our meal."

Another worry. Bears roamed this region, as well as wolves. The bears I wasn't too worried about, they usually shied away from people. Wolves however, especially if starved, would get close.

I mulled my thoughts over and over. Velgrothans. Why was Savantin after something sacred to their kind? I continued to think on it, not concluding an answer as we stopped our horses just outside of Mordestai.

Cahya pulled ahead, stopping her horse at the large field of grain that stood between us and the villages. She took a deep breath, letting it out slowly as she dismounted, affixing her horse's reins to a large tree. I realized how much this meant to her, returning to a land she hadn't seen since she was a little girl. We followed in kind, standing next to her as she stared into the ocean of endless grain.

"Something isn't right," she said suddenly, urging silence.

As soon as she uttered it, we heard a voice from the tree, its leaves coming downward from branches, falling like water from rock.

Cahya answered in her tongue, a whisper, one word. Within a few moments, a girl emerged from the canopy of the tree, climbing down the sturdier-looking branches. The girl rushed forward to Cahya, embracing her in a hug. She spoke to her in a comforting tone, rubbing the back of her head softly.

She spoke to the girl then, a few exchanges before she looked up toward us. "Three of them."

"Only three?" Dacian asked, looking toward us with furrowed brows.

"They saw her, but she ran, climbing this tree. She hasn't seen them since then."

"When was this?" I asked.

"Minutes ago."

"Was he with them?"

Cahya looked back to the girl and spoke to her hurriedly. The girl shook her head and uttered a few words.

"So, he doesn't think it's in Mordestai," Cosette said. "But what is he doing?"

"If he isn't here, then that could mean anything. Deserters, perhaps," Cosette answered.

"How do you know that?" Dacian asked.

"He's not known to send his soldiers off; he doesn't trust most of them. I cannot venture any further until I know this place is clear of them. I cannot risk being seen. They report to Savantin above my father, they would have to tell him first or they risk death for breaking the chain of command. While that would work in my favor, I wish to spare him whatever feelings would arise from discovering I'm alive," Cosette said.

"What do you suggest we do?" Eshkan asked.

"Stay with her, and use the cover of the Spirit tree," Cahya said, looking up toward it. "No one will find you, and so you will be safe."

Meshari looked toward Cosette and took her hand, pointing up to the top of the tree. She then looked to Cahya and said one last sentence before she led Cosette to the base of the sacred plant.

"She told us to use the grain as cover. I know where it leads," Cahya said and looked toward it in urgency.

"It is now me who is with you," I said. She smiled in response.

Eshkan nodded and moved toward the grain, holding it aside for the rest of us to enter. "I will take a position behind. I will hear if anyone is coming behind us. The sound of the wind through the grain can be misleading."

As we made it through the field toward the villages, we began to smell a sweet smoke. "Herbs," Cahya answered. "Burning as a sacrifice to our gods. My people do not feel threatened."

"How can you gather this without being near them? Without having seen them in years?" Dacian asked, his face full of curiosity.

"There are things I will never forget."

"Do you think the soldiers made it to the villages?"

"It would be a very different substance they would be burning if they were going to wage war. The root from the plant our ancestors used in battle to heal wounds also has a harsh property when burned. The smoke gives the gods a sign that we are calling upon them for their aid. The different scents not only alert them, but it spreads throughout the villages," Cahya said.

"Smart. That is sure to elude intruders as a warning system."

"It is much more than that Dacian. But you are correct. It has worked for thousands of years," she said with a smile on her face. Though the circumstance was less than one of blissful nostalgia, I could tell she was looking forward to entering the village.

We made it to the edge of the grain field, peeking through stalks as we moved them aside. We could see the soldiers, speaking to very few who knew the common tongue of the world. Suddenly, a man dressed in distinguishing attire moved from one of the houses, being led to the others by one of Ozrach's men, hand on sword. Cahya lurched forward but I grabbed her, shaking my head. We watched for a few more moments when Cahya began to take off her armor, beneath it, an outfit of dark green, black and gold. She was given new clothing of her homeland from Vortain every year on the day that marked her birth. Though, I did not know she wore it beneath her armor each day.

"I will emerge, as if I was worshiping and on pilgrimage. I will find out what is happening here. If I look toward the fields and raise my hands to the sky, that means I need you."

"I do not like that plan. There are too many things that could happen."

"It is the only chance we have. If I can convince them to leave, I will. If I must kill them, I will."

"Why go alone?" I asked.

"Because the rest of you will give us away. Trust in me," she answered and pulled the thin hood over her hair. She then took a deep breath and walked out of the grain, one of Almour's men pointing to her. One of them approached her abruptly and she held her hands up, speaking. I was tense, and Eshkan could feel it.

"She will be fine. She needs you to trust her. She is strong, fierce."

The leader of these men looked at her now, speaking to her. Her voice was calm, though it was beginning to be hard for me to hear what they were saying. After a few moments of calm, the leader of the men took a step back and raised his voice, which caused Cahya to hold her hands to her sides.

"He asked her where she came from, said that he did not see her when he saw the girl," Eshkan said, his eyes closed. I was too nervous to do the same. My eyes would not leave her frame.

"She said that she was worshiping the tree, and it is something she does regularly."

I was becoming uneasy by the hostility seen in the leader of the soldiers. He was not collected and was under a lot of pressure. I could feel how nervous he was, and almost smell the scent of sweat on his palms. What depended on his success here?

"He is asking her of the provinces. Asking her if she's come from Esperanus."

I became increasingly tense, wondering what her next move would be. I wished that I was there to shield her from his sudden aggression. When could we intervene? Could she convince them to leave the villages? So many questions raced through my mind, and I continued to wonder how long we would be waiting among the grain. I wouldn't take my eyes off her as long as she was with those men, my mind would not allow it.

Trying to convince myself that she would be unharmed was becoming easier as the conversation played out, though I could not hear it. It reminded me of times when she would speak to Vortain after so recently having met with me, feeling as if the deeds of flesh were written upon her for the world to see. Vortain was not a dull man, and oftentimes I wondered if he knew.

"She told them she hasn't been outside their lands, but it seems he doesn't believe her." I stood, tensing, the Sun enjoying every minute of my despair.

Eshkan placed a hand on my shoulder, urging me to hold back. "If you make yourself known now, they might see it as a threat and slaughter her."

"I won't remain idle and do nothing."

Suddenly the man raised his voice, pulling his sword from its scabbard. I stood, Dacian's hands around my arms.

"He's threatening her," I answered. "Unhand me. I can't promise what will happen if he touches her, and you still have your hands upon my flesh."

"You and she…" Dacian said suddenly, backing away.

"Now you see," I answered.

"Any sudden movements from us could have her killed, Cethin. They are unpredictable. If you love her, you will not risk that. Think. He is threatening her now, but if you approach, he might act rashly. Cahya is a smart woman, brave. You know this."

"She is brave. She is intelligent. She is the peace that this broken world needs. The light. The warmth. I would protect her with my dying breath, Eshkan."

"And our brother's wish is also our own," Dacian said.

I nodded once, to show my gratitude.

"They are not in the proper position for us to mount an attack," Eshkan answered. He then held his hand out to us, looking toward the fires. "Quick. They are going to the tree."

Eshkan took a breath, watching as the captain sheathed his sword, his two guards following. He pointed past the field, shouting. My eyes did not leave her as they approached, walking past us as they moved toward the tree. Her eyes caught mine as she was being followed closely by two of Ozrach's men.

"The horses," Dacian said quickly. "What is she doing?"

They reached them, Cahya grabbing her ax from her saddlebag. "Leave. Now," she said, looking toward the field.

"What is this?" the captain asked. "A priestess turned warrior? You should not have threatened me. Now your spirits will have to protect you from death."

"Ne'aoko shaki teitza," Cahya said and swung her ax once in her hand. "They are with me now."

I stood, Eshkan and Dacian standing with me. "Not yet. Look, the other two men aren't armed."

I broke from my brothers' grasps, emerging from the thick wheat field and toward the captain, whose face turned to one of amusement.

The captain laughed and looked up into the sky, then back to Cahya. "Is this your spirit? Is this who you've conjured to combat me?"

"I will not interfere unless I have to," I answered.

"You do not look Mordestan, spirit," he said suddenly, trying to look at me from the light of the closest fire. "I will kill you once I'm finished with her."

I pulled the hood off my head, reaching toward Seligsara.

"A Sardon? You are far from Morrenvahl. What interest does a Sardon have in Mordestai?"

"To protect it. From you, and those that think like you. You're one of his captains, to do his bidding."

"Of course I am. But don't think I enjoy that. There is something wrong with this world, Sardon. Something terribly wrong. The purge didn't kill all of you, and it should have. This world doesn't belong to you, dark and twisted creatures. I despise all of you, and most of all him."

"Then why do you serve him?"

"One does not resist him, Sardon. Not unless you want to end up like the rest of his dead. Oh, I loathe him, but I also fear him. Do not make the mistake of believing any different."

"Now you must make the decision of what you fear more," I answered, my hand shaking, weighted down with the anger of the Sun.

"Nothing is more frightening than what will happen if we fail him," the captain answered.

"We do not kill those who lay down their arms," I stated, trying to hold back my rage. He had threatened her, more than once.

"You have mercy; it is something that he does not."

"Aid us in ending this, and I will spare your life," I said.

"I do not bargain with creatures."

"You do, it is why you are standing here, why you haven't acted yet."

"Are you here to kill me, Sardon?"

"Not unless you wish it so."

"Answer me this. What is he looking for?" he asked, lowering his sword.

"I will not speak of it," I said.

"You will, or I will kill her, and I will kill you."

"You will not get close enough to do either."

"Just as I don't believe in her spirits, I do not believe in your devices. I cannot believe I am wasting my time standing here speaking to any of you. He sent me here for a reason, one I thought to be banal and insulting, but now it seems I have a chance to do more," he said and raised his sword again.

"Lower your weapon."

"I don't think you understand that you are outnumbered," the captain stated.

"Do not sacrifice your men in your place. I have no interest in them. They blindly follow you because they must. They do what they must to feed their families. You do it because you're afraid. They would only harm someone if they were ordered to, because if they didn't, they knew that their children would starve, and yet they would likely hesitate before doing so."

"You assume much about them."

"I can hear it in the way their hearts are beating right now, quickened, nervous. They were moving at a normal pace just before you suggested they would be your aid in silencing me."

"Doesn't every warrior become nervous before a fight?"

"Not if his heart is in the right place."

The captain snickered, wiping his brow. "I am taking advice on the heart from a creature that hasn't one."

"Your hatred blinds you," Cahya said.

The captain looked toward her, keeping his weapon steady. "You two know each other. I can hear it in your voice, see it in his eyes," the captain answered and stopped for a moment, laughing at us in disdain. "You give yourself to this monster willingly, making you just as vile as it is," he said and raised his sword toward her.

"Now, it is you who is outnumbered," Cosette answered, stepping from the tree, her bow in hand. Dacian and Eshkan came from the darkness of the wheat, walking to my side.

"Princess," he said quickly. "Risen from the dead. The company you keep is enough to send you back there."

"You're in no position to make threats," she said and pulled the string of her bow tighter.

"If harm comes to anyone here, then war will be cast upon this peaceful land, which is why we must come to an agreement if you wish to leave here. I know you do not care about those people, but I do. I do know one thing you do care about," Cahya answered.

"And what is that?" the captain sneered.

"Your life," Cahya said.

"You speak of mercy and then threaten me?"

"I only have mercy for those who deserve it. If you will not change, then all I can offer is death."

"So be it," the captain said and swung his sword toward her. She blocked it with her ax, pushing him backward and kicking him in the stomach. He bent to the blow, looking up at her angrily. He let out a shout, running at her with malicious eyes. The two continued to fight, and I watched, my hand on my weapon. The Sun continued to chant louder and louder until I could not hear their weapons clashing. He spun his sword forward in his hand, Cahya jumping backward. She ducked at another swing, the blade cutting across her arm. She tackled him, dropping her ax on the ground, and began to lay punches to his face. He reached for his sword, and she kicked it aside, continuing to assault him with heavy blows. He blocked her most recent swing with his forearm, pushing her backward and onto the ground, grasping his blade. Cahya quickly rolled and grabbed onto her ax, lifting it upward to block a swing from the captain's sword. He kicked dirt in her face, and she stood, unable to see. He slashed forward, and the blade swung upward from her stomach to her chest. She stumbled backward, dropping her ax and holding onto her chest.

I was instantly engulfed in rage, moving toward the captain with speed. He swung his sword at me, and I quickly jerked my arm forward, the blade becoming lodged into my tricep. I used my hand to grab his throat, moving my other arm forward, disarming the captain whose expression was now one of disbelief. I punched him in the mouth, placing all the anger I held behind the blow, listening as he began to choke on his teeth, blood welling from where they had once been held to his gums. I stood back from where he had fallen, rushing over to Cahya. She sat up against the tree, holding her wound to prevent blood from leaving her. Eshkan and Dacian moved from her at that moment, allowing me to become close to her.

"Don't let the light leave your eyes."

"I can't feel my fingers, Cethin," she said, holding one bloodied hand to her face, her fingers shaking.

"Keep your eyes on the light," I said, wiping the tears that were slowly falling from her eyes.

"I see it, in the stars and in you. You're the only light I've ever needed," she answered weakly, touching my face. She then looked down at the wound, moving her hand slightly to look upon it. I moved my hand to hers, placing them both against where the blood was rushing from her body. "It's too deep, Cethin. We will never make it to my people in time."

"I will take you to them. I will find what it takes to heal you," I answered and moved my other arm behind her, trying to lift her forward.

"Cethin, I'm sorry," she said suddenly, and coughed, a small amount of blood coming from her mouth.

"Cahya," I said sternly, not moving my eyes from hers.

"If you move me now, the blood will flow faster. Here I can last moments longer."

"Cahya, you..."

"I want you to hold me, as you did that night in the compound when we knew our lives would be entwined forever," she said softly. She coughed; this time weaker than before. "Where we did not worry about the darkness of the world, and not even our binds to that place could keep us apart."

I nodded and moved toward her, sitting behind her and wrapping my arms around her torso, nestling my head against the side of her face. She removed her hands from the wound, placing one on the back of my head, and the other on top of mine. I quickly placed my hands on the incision, feeling the blood pour out of it without relent.

"My love for you will never cease, even as my body is taken to the spirits. Death's touch will not stop the fires that, for you, burn within my heart," she said.

"Don't let the light leave your eyes," I repeated, holding her tightly now.

"I must tell you now, before they call my name," she whispered. "I..."

"Shh... there are only minutes left for me. Joy has been ripped from your hands, a much undeserved fate for the defender of mankind. Your light will serve as a beacon for all those left in the dark. Shadows of greed, avarice, malice, hatred...will be vanquished by your kind and sympathetic heart. Your compassion is what will bring this world to peace, Cethin. You will bring this world peace. I have no doubts that you would have been the same as a father, compassionate, and loving. And although our last words will be those which I lament to speak, I am the only one that can make it known. I regret to tell you that neither of us will now meet your child. The blade has pierced that which rests within, and now I must take them with me," she said and moved my hand over her stomach. "I love you," she said slowly, struggling to complete words.

"Cahya," I said, breathing heavily, my face still next to hers. No answer came to my words. "Cahya," I said, this time louder. After a moment of silence, I moved my face, shifting her gently in my arms. She was still, her eyes looking upward toward the tree. Her chest rose and fell no more, and her hands were cupped beneath her wound, blood still slowly pouring into them. I looked down and closed my eyes, taking a deep breath as I felt moisture well between the lids.

I stood suddenly, resting her gently against the base of the tree, and looked toward the captain, who was now standing at the mercy of Cosette and Meshari. I moved Cosette gently, grasping the captain by his throat. I quickly grasped his collarbone, pulling it from his chest and using it as if one would use a knife, tearing his flesh toward the opposite side where the bone in symmetry rested. He screamed and I listened as the Sun silenced while my rage escalated. I continued to beat him, his neck, his skull, his chest. He had finally stopped moving, the twitching in his hands now very minutely. I moved from him, staring at his lifeless corpse. I was surprised at my aggression, somewhat ashamed, but could not stop it as it flowed from me. He took her from me, tore her from my life.

Meshari covered her eyes, Cosette holding onto her shoulders. Dacian and Eshkan stood near his men, holding them at the mercy of their blades.

I slowly reached down to pick up his sword, the blade that sent her to her spirits. I removed her blood from the tip of it with my hand, rubbing it across where my heart was within my chest. I pulled the necklace from his corpse and looked it over, seeing the mark of Terrenveil upon it. I clenched my fist angrily, throwing it on top of his body and walked to his men, who immediately held their hands upward in surrender.

"We were under orders to come and warn the chief and his people about Mauros, we were explicitly told not to attack, even if they perceived us as a threat," one of the men said, looking downward.

"He speaks truth," the other said. "We have no weapons. We were not to bring any with us. Almour, our general, he's the one who defied. Brought a dagger. We didn't know he had it or else we wouldn't have come."

"And we're supposed to believe you?" Dacian asked. He would be my tongue.

SPOKEN FROM THIS BLACKENED EARTH

"I'd die before facing him. He detests defiance. Makes every single person who is stupid enough to do so into an example of why no one should test him. We've all seen it. This was supposed to be Almour's chance to redeem himself. We all thought he was going to be killed in Opskaven."

"He is right," Cosette said. "I know it isn't what you want to hear, especially now."

Eshkan and Dacian looked at her, then back to me.

"Where are the rest of you?" Eshkan asked.

"Esperanus. They were told not to come, if we returned or not."

"The orders were to move on with or without you?" Dacian asked.

"We aren't lying. Swear on it. If you go, you will see."

"We are to meet Zheki there," Eshkan said. "This poses a problem."

"If you allow us to return, we will make sure they don't know of you. We'll say we killed him. Found he was concealing a weapon. Dragen will believe us; they'll move out within the day."

"How do we know we can trust you?"

"There's no way, other than believing in the fact we don't want Savantin to know he's been crossed. He'll believe in our innocence. But if he finds that we did nothing we will be punished as well. Even worse if he's found out we ran."

"How would he find out if you run?"

"Don't want to risk it. Not with what they speak of him," one simply stated. "We're at your mercy now."

I took a deep breath, knowing everyone's eyes were on me. "Let them go," I said, attempting to withhold the pain in my voice. "She would want the same."

"Cethin..."

"They've done nothing wrong. They don't have weapons. She would not want us to slay two men who have done nothing. Let them go," I said. I turned to look at her, resting at the base of the tree.

She sat a portrait against a still horizon, beautiful and unmoving. Animosity was building beneath me, as I felt it in every twitch that overcame my muscles, the very fibers of my mind fraying. I pushed my fingers over her eyelids, and gently took her into my arms, saying a word to no one as I walked toward the village. A few of the villagers had gathered, watching us as we approached. I heard them whisper as I held her, looking into her face, one that had before been filled with so much love for the world was now void of expression, her eyes still beneath their lids.

A man wearing decorative garb moved toward us and held his head downward in sadness. The villagers led me to a small alcove, surrounded by plants and flowers. In its center was a bed covered in vines. I laid her upon it and looked down at her face, wishing that her spirits would grant her one last breath so that I could tell her that I loved her before bidding her farewell.

I kissed her lips, and then her forehead as I gently set her down upon the bed, grasping her hand tightly. Two villagers moved forward, burning herbs and chanting softly. I hadn't even looked to see if the others had followed me, hadn't seen a man approach my side. I moved toward her, not shying away as they lit the vines aflame.

As the flames surrounded her, they resisted the touch of her body at first, and then slowly covered her. I continued to hold her hand as they ravaged her corpse, her beauty unfading. I could almost feel her pulse in her palm as I squeezed her hand tightly, not wanting the feeling to dissipate as the flames began to consume her. Wishful thinking, a trick my mind played on me. Her head fell to its side; her mouth opened slightly, her eyes still beneath their wet eyelids. I watched as the fires began to turn her frame into ashes. Releasing her hand into the blaze, I slowly dragged my fingers down each of her own, gently rubbing her fingertips. I knelt then, at the base of her hand, realizing that it was all that was left of her, now slowly being swallowed by the flames of her people. I hung my head, staring into the grass. I caught sight of something shining against the inferno that engulfed the enchanting vessel which had once housed her soul, turning it into the ashes that now passed through my lungs. A ring fell from her hand, the one that I had brought her from Stirae. The light that would never leave her eyes.

I picked it up from the ground, closing it in my fist, wishing that I could once again feel her pulse against my flesh. I continued to squeeze it shut, as if the tighter I held it, the feeling would arise. There was nothing, no warm embrace, no voice as sweet as the blossoms during summer. All that existed was the small circle of metal, cooling against my flesh. I looked upwards now, watching as the fires carried her ashes toward the sky, to join her with the spirits that watched the land. I felt as if the very stars had burned out with her, leaving the world in impenetrable darkness. The emptiness that formed within me was becoming filled with the enmity of my rage, the Sun's voices returning.

I felt a man sit beside me, watching as the fires burned on, her bones now beginning to catch with them. He remained silent for some time, taking soft breaths inward. His vision shared the same path as mine, and he softly began to sing a song. I could remember her singing it to me while we laid beneath the starlight at the Tower of Silence, a place where Serpents were burned after death, an offering to Basilin.

"The night grows dark, and time still passes although she is gone. Yet, time will never pass the same for us. She will no longer grace our minutes, share our hours. I saw a face that I thought I would never see again, but if I knew that her appearance here meant her death, I would have wished her a long life."

I watched the flames lick at one another, the sound of wood crackling as her bones were continuously devoured.

"You loved her."

"I still do," I answered softly, my chest starting to feel as if a stone was lodged inside of it.

"I regret having to meet you like this, warrior."

I nodded. "She spoke many good words about you."

"I wish I deserved them," he said suddenly, his eyes still on the flames. "Did Cahya ever tell you why she left home?"

"She only told me that she was saved by Vortain while exploring the forest."

"Her mother died when she was very young, warrior. After suffering a loss like that, I sheltered her, trying to keep her safe from mostly everything a child must experience in order to learn, to grow. I promised her mother that she would never feel pain, but that meant I had to keep her from life's most important lessons. She wanted to be strong and courageous like her mother was and told me that she would never learn those virtues if I did not let her go." Her father broke into tears, wiping at his face with a cloth of blood-orange tint. "Forgive my tears, warrior."

"If there was only one lesson I could grasp from my time in the Eastern Baeld long ago, it would be that tears do not make a man soft, and love is the greatest motivator of them all."

"The sea folk are kind and wise," her father answered, swallowing once before attempting to dry his face. The tears continued to roll from his weary eyes, and he shook his head, recognizing his efforts to cease the product of his emotion were useless.

"There is an old tale, one that has been shared among the lips of my people for years. I am sure you are aware of the gem Queen Neraea wears around her neck? It was a gift from our people to the royal family, and the only way to keep our lands from slipping into their fingers. Well, there is a sister gem, one that is green and red and orange when you turn its facets upon the sunlight. In the beginning of our time, we had both gems here, natural beauties, granted to us by our spirits. The brilliant deep blue and purple one that Neraea wears, one that resembles shadow, and the other, full of light," he said, watching the fire. I had not taken my eyes off it, staring deep within its coils of heat seeing that not even her bones remained.

"The gems were given by the spirits to the first clan of our people, which included several Septens who had joined to escape the frigid cold. We were told to guard them, as they embodied the power of our spirits," her father said and took a moment to take a deep breath before he continued, bringing the cloth to his eyes again.

"When Cahya heard this story, she set off to find the gem so that the spirits would again smile upon us. I cautioned her against it, for she was only nine years old. I could not change her mind. She left one night, after the village had gone to sleep, sneaking out past the grain field and beneath the big tree. That is the last time I saw her."

"I suppose you want to know how she and I came to know one another."

"I would enjoy hearing stories of how my daughter grew up," the man said softly.

"I met her ten years ago, when I too was taken to an isle called Ophidian. It is hidden well from those who do not belong to its ranks. Or was, rather. I was brought in a scared hungry creature, fending for himself due to the death of his caretaker. After my first fight, I was inducted into training, and it was then I met her. She was commander of his guard."

"You were a soldier?"

"No. I was an assassin. Forbidden to speak to anyone in his guard, or among the townspeople. Being what I am, I was placed under the strictest of watch, and was given courses of training more rigorous and taxing than that of my brothers. When I gained his trust, I was given the task of watch on the border one night and was told to inspect the cemetery. She was there, flashing lanterns to mimic a legend that frightened some of the guards. She had no fear of me and had asked me to show her the one thing she feared most of all. After that night we met on several occasions, even if it was just to spend time together beneath the stars where they wouldn't look for us," I answered. "She was kind but brandished a strong hand when she needed to. Not many defied her orders. We both had a feeling that Vortain knew of our relationship but did not give it voice. I have had my share of weeks within his prison cells. We shared stories on how we both ended up crossing paths. Cahya was being chased by a horde of bandits, she was lashed twice by them before she escaped, and was hiding in the marsh that bordered his Ophidian. One of the bandits pulled her from the plants, holding her by her leg and was about to chop it off when an arrow sailed from the trees nearby, striking him down. Several followed, killing the others, and my brother Eshkan, as well as Vortain himself appeared and took her in."

"Her life was saved by him, so she pledged hers in return."

I nodded.

"Did he save your life as well?" the chief asked, glancing over at me for a moment, but returning his eyes to the fire.

"In a way. My relationship with him was a bit more complicated than that. I killed men of his while roaming the land, a victim to my own hunger. The others tried to kill me, but in realizing what I was, captured me instead, tying me to one of their horses. I had to follow on foot until we made it there. I was too tired to attack or to try to free myself. They intended to use me as bait in his arena, where he chose members for his guard and for assassinations. We can see where my fate has led me without having to say more," I answered.

"And so, you remained?"

"I had no other choice."

"Why not run?"

"The others would follow."

"And you had nowhere else to turn?"

"Afraid not. My parents disappeared when I was young, and I was found by a seafaring man who died of a fever. Morrenvahl was not on my list of places to see," I sighed.

"A man who was given no place to call home faces many trials until he finds it. It seems as if in staying with this man who you call Vortain, you found a place that you felt you belonged to."

"Or so I thought, I still do not know where to call home, or if that place ever felt like it."

"The world is a dark place, warrior. Home is not where you are born, but where you are surrounded by those who make your life whole and give it meaning. I am sure she felt enamored by the love you showed her. Love is the most powerful motivator of them all, warrior. Remember that," her father said and rose from the ground, watching the fire for another moment or two before seeking shelter inside one of the houses behind. The others had gone inside as well, Cosette sitting by my side for several moments. I said nothing and did not take my eyes off the fires until she, too, disappeared inside the warmth of the houses behind us.

I remained until dawn, when the fires stopped burning, and only ashes among charred frail sticks were left. It was there I had fallen into sleep, my head touching among the soft, sweet-scented grass.

I opened my eyes sleepily to a pink and fading night sky, my vision coming across what had once been a pyre. I moved; the wound of her absence pained deeply, as if my muscles ached from the lacerations of war. The world surrounding me was silent, as if every sound from a scream to a whisper faded into nonexistence.

I stood; the scent of ashes mixed with her decay hitting me in a wave with a force enough to reduce me to my knees. My eyes could not look upon anything other than the structure before me. I approached it, looking down into the grass for anything that might remain. Placing my hand down upon her cold ashes, I gently gathered them into my fist, holding them tightly. I held out my forearm, sprinkling her ashes upon where the Sun laid inside of it. "I promise you. I will carry out my life in your honor, the way you would have wanted me to," I whispered, the sound of my own voice making me weak.

The warm wind blew gently, the leaves of the trees mustering their voices as they were touched by this force of gravitation. Cosette strode to my side, looking out toward the plains. "The world is cold, Cethin," she said, keeping her eyes from mine. "It seems as if we become closer to ending this, the more we lose."

"I will not stay from seeing this to its end," I answered.

"Loss can consume a man," Cosette said.

"Don't worry about that," I said, looking toward her.

She held her head toward the field, watching it as the sun rose over the plateaus. It illuminated her eyes, showing off their light-emerald color. She took one long breath out and bowed her head in respect to Cahya. "Don't let it consume you."

"I'm going to Morrenvahl," I said, causing her now to look at me. "It is up to you if you wish to follow, but that is where I intend to go."

"I understand," she said. "But I cannot go there."

I nodded and rose. "Where will you go?"

"I will stay here, if the Chief will accept me. If his people will accept me. If this all ends, if they are removed, send word to me."

"You wish to take their places?"

"I feel it is the right course of action. If the people are successful in removing them, if Savantin is not successful in finding the box."

"I wish you had more faith in me," I said and started toward the chief's house.

"It isn't that I do not have faith in you, Cethin," she said. I turned, looking toward her, sharing one moment with eyes locked. "It is that I have too much faith in him."

I moved my head downward before Cosette and I traveled together to a house in the center of the village. I opened the door slowly, noticing upon entry that Eshkan and Dacian were both awaiting me. They sat on benches made of wood, fashioned in the shape of lions. They had jaws in snarls, looking as if they were fixated on prey.

"Cethin," Dacian said softly, trying to grasp my attention.

I looked up toward him, not using my voice.

"What now?" he asked.

"I'm going to Morrenvahl."

Eshkan nodded, looking toward the face of his brother. He then looked back at me, standing. "And what of Esperanus? What of Cosette?"

"We will go to Esperanus, we will find Zheki. But after that, I will go to Morrenvahl," I answered, looking toward the door. The sun spilled beneath it, illuminating the old wooden floor. "If you wish to turn from me, I will not see it as abandonment. You know what Morrenvahl is."

"We would follow you to the end," Dacian said and stood, grabbing his sword from the bench. "Our oath to Vortain might have died with him, but that does not mean we are no longer brothers," he answered.

"You follow me to death," I answered and removed my hood from my eyes. "I cannot promise you that they will welcome me, and if they do not then they will certainly take no care in sparing your lives."

"So be it," Dacian answered and attached his sword to his armor, fastening the buckle in the front. He then walked out of the house, heading toward the field.

I sighed and hung my head, looking down at Seligsara.

"He seems convinced that it is the only way," Eshkan stated and felt the string of his bow. He placed it on his back, attaching it to his quiver. "And I too see no other answer."

"You know very well what danger awaits us."

"It has never been a cause for desertion, Cethin. We have faced danger before; we survived the siege of the isle," Eshkan answered.

"Then we leave within the hour," I stated and gave him a nod, walking to where daylight broke over the cliffs surrounding the village. I placed my hood back over my eyes, feeling the sting from the light of the giant sun. Once my vision was relinquished from its gaze I was met by warriors, who watched me with careful eyes.

The chief walked among them, moving two of them apart to reach me. He smiled as he approached, looking toward me. "Warrior," he said, placing a hand on my shoulder. "There are words we must have before you depart," he stated, looking toward his army.

"Of course," I said.

"We removed that man from our fields. But he will not be buried. He will not be burned. He will not be given passage to his afterlife."

I nodded, my tongue a victim of my wordlessness. The captain would be left to rot beneath an unforgiving sky. His corpse would begin to decompose beneath the heat, becoming unappealing to even the most emaciated of carrion birds. I imagined the man who struck down Cahya, the heat boiling his entrails. The insects would take him next, slowly consuming what was left of him until they took most of his flesh, leaving only bones to be unrecognized by those who found him.

"This may mean that he will come for us next, the king. He will not be happy that we took his men from him," the chief answered and walked toward his home. "But we will not give into him. Whether he comes with sword and fire, or with words, we will be ready."

"He may not," I answered. "The men who came with the captain spoke of his treason. They said that they will report to their detachment and tell them that they killed him for killing one of yours. They do not wish to face the wrath of he who leads them."

"And you believe them?" he asked.

"They spoke to me with slow hearts. Not the heart of someone who would lie. But if they do return with men…"

"If they do, we will be ready," the chief repeated, looking off toward the horizon. "I will not lay helpless and accept the death they will promise me."

I nodded. The both of us watched over the horizon, the sun bright. Despite its illumination of the earth, it was weakening. The cold drew from its heat, thus numbing its power. I looked to the east, to where we had left our horses. I hoped they remained at the tree.

The Chief and I shared no more words. When I turned from the field, from the ashes of the pyre, he placed one hand on my shoulder.

"Do not let your hatred for what he's done consume your mind. I know he has taken from you, from all of us. But hatred is hatred. It consumes, it poisons. Hatred changes, distorts. Be careful you do not become different than the man she saw in you."

"You will know when things end," I answered.

"Remember, my son. When the time comes to cast the hand of death upon those you feel responsible, do not cloak it in hatred. Let death speak."

I bid the Chief farewell, turning toward where my brothers awaited me. They would be preparing for travel, leaving behind what would be wearing them down. I could not leave out that my heart was weary, and that I wished for release from these feelings. This was what the mariner called mourning. He lost his family at a young age, just as I had. I would often hear him weeping from his bedroom on cold nights. He said that the pain of loss never truly leaves you, rather, you learn to suppress it for a time. He cursed the gods, in what he thought was a voice low enough to keep me from hearing. I don't know what he expected, whether it was to keep from me his sadness, as all parents did for the sake of their children, or to keep him from looking weak, troubled.

I found his journal one night when he was on an expedition, bringing deep sea fish into the ports, and read the words inked upon the old, faded pages. He said that there were no gods, and that the cold sting of loss was only numbed by the mentioning of their existence. There was no afterlife, and that once someone was plucked from the world it would be your last embrace. Part of me, though foolishly so, wanted to believe the old man had penned it while in his lowest point of grief. Grief is immeasurable, deep, wounding. The heavy heart that staggered to beat within my chest, swollen from the pain of emptiness so desperately hoped that I would be granted the solace of looking into her eyes once more.

I heard the warriors begin to sing behind me, something I perceived as words to honor the souls of their fallen and grant them safe passage to their spirits. Humanity was a disgusting race, yet a beautiful one. Compassion and love struggled to fight in the shadow of deceit and selfishness. How could a man as avaricious as that captain belong to the same race as a woman as kind, endearing and loving as Cahya was? A question that would remained unanswered for all of time.

Morrenvahl. I hoped that my kin would be accepting and would not slay my company on sight. It was the first time that I anticipated something yet felt such dread within my heart. I would never forgive myself if they followed me to their deaths, something I knew was a possibility. I supposed that only time would tell what would become of us, and if they were assailed, I would die with a sword in my hand defending their lives.

◆ ◆ ◆

Eshkan and Dacian stood outside of the hut, their dark green clothing visible against the house's structure, shining vehemently in the sun. I reached them, looking around quickly before addressing them.

"Esperanus, what do you know about it?" I asked, Eshkan taking a breath. "It's heavily fortified by guards as called for by the patron. There are rumors circulating that he's very loyal. I don't know how trustworthy Thurlowe's contact is. I hope we aren't stumbling into a trap."

"Well, after what we witnessed in Egelle, I don't think things can get much worse," Dacian said, shaking his head. "That woman was riddled with paranoia."

"We are lucky Cahya knew how to reason with her," I responded, closing my eyes and swallowing at the mention of her name.

"Do we wait for the cover of night to sneak into town?" Dacian asked.

"It's probably best, especially if soldiers are still quartered there."

"Then that is what we will do," I stated, my statement being the last spoken as we took to our journey once more. "I have one more thing to do before I leave here. Wait for me."

I headed toward the tree, seeing Cosette sitting beneath it with Meshari. Meshari noticed me, smiling before standing and heading back to the village. Cosette too offered a smile, sadness in her face. Tears suddenly fell from her eyes, and she instantly wiped them from her face with the back of her sleeve, shaking her head.

"Forgive me," she said.

"No need," I answered and sat next to her.

"Are you leaving now?" she asked, directing her gaze to the grain.

"We are," I said and let a breath from my lungs. "I wanted to thank you. For aiding us, for trusting me."

"I am happy I followed. I meant what I said, when I asked for you to contact me once they are removed from their thrones. Will you send word?"

"One of us will, you can trust in that," I said and stood, Cosette following. She hugged me, and I returned the gesture, placing my hand behind her head until she released me.

"Remember what I said, Cethin. Until we meet again."

I bowed my head, turning from the tree and made my way back into the village to join the others. Silence followed me. Pain, close behind.

In moments, we reached the grain fields. The wind passed through the grain as we passed by, causing the stalks to move as the sea moved. The sound was a peaceful rushing, though I could not feel it on my skin through my armor. Cahya would say that after a night of killing, the souls that are left behind are trapped in the wind, moving with it as they try to find their place, neither seen nor heard. Was she within it? I expelled breath upon its passing, as we wandered toward the forest to find our horses, my eyes welling with tears at the thought.

The world seemed a darker place, each sound foreign, sights the same. It was as if nothing had changed, yet everything felt different. I could no longer think of what I held, or deserved to hold, as it was all ripped from my hands within an instant. I still had her blood on my forearms, the last organic physical proof that she once existed, that she chose to share with me her heart.

We found the horses grazing in the field just past where we hitched them, assuming that the smoke from the fires caused them to relocate. The horse belonging to Cosette still grazed, unmoving as we took ours from its side.

We were on the path before midday, the landscape changing color as the sun went through stages of height in the sky. I was silent, listening to the hooves of my horse beat gently across the ground, replacing the sound of my own heart. It was a while before my voice was brave enough to leave my body, as we crossed the old dirt path leading from the wilds toward Esperanus. I could hear both Eshkan and Dacian breathing, exchanging words with one another quietly. The horses huffed, trying to keep the cold wind from entering their throats. I was trapped with my own thoughts, and when trying to break them if only just to speak, was led to another.

We reached a point on the path where Eshkan rode ahead, leading us into the forest. "Our horses should remain safe here, we are close enough to the walls that if something were to prey upon them, the predator could be slaughtered by the town guard."

"We may hope," I said and hopped off my horse, tying her reigns into a loop and spiking them into the ground.

Two lone torches were hung outside of the gates. A guard stood on either side, each with a smaller torch in hand. "Heavily fortified?" I said and moved closer.

"It is what my contacts have always said," Eshkan responded. "Perhaps they are slack because most of the guards must attend an audience with the legion."

"Perhaps, but this will make our entry simpler," Dacian said. "Where should we attempt?"

"I'll scout the walls and report back," I answered. "There has to be a place to climb, or a sewer to breach."

"There," Eshkan said and pointed to where the city wall met the face of a cliff. "If we go around the other side, not only will we gain a vantage point, but we may be able to descend into the city as the sun descends."

"That will be shortly, we should get moving," I said and watched as the guards turned and started to enter the city.

"Change of watch. Now's our chance," Dacian said and sprinted across the plains. I followed, Eshkan in tow.

"We can climb up this way," I answered and placed my hand on a shelf just above my head. "It will hold." Eshkan nodded, Dacian being the first to follow me.

Once I finished scaling the cliff, a gust of golden glitter swirled before me, Zheki coming into view. "Seems the legion has cleared out," she said.

Dacian and Eshkan strode over, passing us and looking down into the city. "It appears as if the remaining soldiers are stationed by that temple. I spot five guards for the entire city save whatever may lie behind that building," Eshkan said and pointed toward the tower, a lone torch up top.

"Where is this contact of yours located?"

"There," Zheki said and pointed to a building close to the market. Torches lined the streets, their fires crackling in the otherwise quiet night. "A word of caution before we meet him. Do not let his demeanor fool you. He is smart, analytical, and knows many people."

"I'll let you do the talking," I responded.

It was then Zheki neared the cliff's edge, taking a quick scan of the city, looking to where the torches were, footsteps of guards. She turned to us and pointed to the left of us, an old dead tree. "We can use that to descend, but it gives poor cover. We can wait until the shift changes again, or we can scout the outside walls behind the city and assess if there are possible entry points. The only problem is that I'll be mostly blind unless there is something creating sound on the other side of the wall."

"We will be your sight," Dacian said.

It took mere moments to reach the torch, evading the sight of a few tired guards. We made it into an alleyway when Zheki returned to sight, placing her sparkling hand on a door frame. "Here. I will enter first."

I nodded, waiting until she was covered by the darkness of the structure. Once inside, we walked past several people sleeping along the walls. One of them looked up and gave us a glance, quickly returning to slumber.

"Who are these people?" Dacian asked.

"Those who escaped Neraea's priests. Worshipers of the Mordestan pantheon, witches, wards. Our contact ensures their safety. There are figures in every major city who form alliance to give these people safety until they can escape the reach of Terrenveil."

"Why don't the worshipers of the Mordestan gods just go to them?"

"They are being hunted and don't want to risk the people there. A pilgrimage to Rustanzen is being planned. I will probably be involved in planning it after this night, that remains to be seen," she said and pulled a blanket from its place in the door before us, entering slowly.

"Merek, I must have words."

"Zheki... I didn't think I'd see you so soon," a man said and stood, his eyes flashing blue once they came across me and my brothers. His dark hair was short against his head, his face free of wrinkles or scars. "Interesting, I assume these are no new recruits of Thurlowe's?"

"A Tovian?" Eshkan said, quietly.

The potential for danger surged. I would do my best not to reveal anything about the box.

"They're with me... Thurlowe doesn't know we're here."

"You've further piqued my interest. How may I assist?"

"There's talk of rebellion. I'm certain you've heard it," Zheki stated.

"You're here for the talk of rebellion," Merek said and looked at Eshkan, slowly moving his eyes between us. "What of it?"

"Who should my friends here talk to when they find themselves in Terrenveil?"

He laughed for a moment, stopping once he read the seriousness in Zheki's face. "Pardon me for not immediately divulging that information. How do I know they can be trusted?"

"They seek to aid in dethroning the king."

"Do they now?" the Tovian asked and stood from his chair.

"From there, please," Eshkan stated, resulting in Merek's laughter.

"Observant. Zheki, what have you told them?" he said, a tone of irritation indicated.

"Nothing," Zheki said. "You of all people should realize there are humans who bear the gift. They can be trusted. They ran work for Thurlowe, inside work."

"I can't argue with that," Merek said and pulled a book out of his desk. "But I'm still not comfortable. You? I trust you won't repeat a word of what I tell you, because it comes at a price. If your friends wish to help, tell them to destroy the caravan of soldiers that are resting in the Colanth forest outside of Eledes and to forget they ever came here," he said and vanished, the mirror behind him breaking.

"We don't have much time," Eshkan said and headed for the door. Dacian and I exchanged a glance and Zheki held her hand toward the exit. "You may want to follow him lest you'll discover what it's like to fight a Tovian Demon," she said. The world inside the mirror shards began to change and I swiftly returned to the outside world, the four of us taking refuge behind a building.

"That seemed to go poorly," Dacian said.

"It gives you a new target," Zheki stated. "Use it to distract the legion. News spreading about a piece of the legion being found slaughtered on the roads will sow chaos on the Mountain."

"That or it will hasten the deaths of nearby civilians."

"You're assassins. Enter their camp as they sleep and slaughter them. It should become obvious to Savantin that it is not the work of farmers or townsfolk."

"It will be done," I said. "From there, Morrenvahl."

"The Colanth borders Morrenvahl, dispose of them and continue west, you will find the coven. To give you some peace, the corpses may never be found. Strange things are reported from the forest, likely the work of your kin. West, you won't miss it," she said and disappeared into the night, the sparkles of her form vanishing once she was far enough away from the light of the torch.

"Cethin, a word," Dacian said. "This seems a hasty decision."

"A necessary one. We are not privy to the information the Tovian holds, but assured this would assist."

"Dacian, why do you caution so?" Eshkan asked.

"It is nothing. Let us continue," he said and made haste to his horse. We followed him, riding until we could smell the smoke of a fire. Dacian motioned his pointer and middle finger twice toward us, and once toward the northwest. We dismounted, cresting the hill and laying against the ground for cover.

"I will approach from those trees on the left," Dacian said. "It seems as though there is a weakness in their lines behind them, bushes."

"I will enter there," I stated.

Eshkan grasped his bow, placing an arrow against the string. "Once they sleep, their patrol will be eliminated by my hand."

"Giving us the cover we need," I said. "I will move into position now. Once their patrol falls, I will strike."

Dacian nodded and began to creep down the hill, which caused me to move toward my position, watching their fires carefully. I heard laughter, watching as they consumed the meat from a native animal. About an hour had passed, the stars becoming visible against the night sky, taken by darkness. Two arrows sailed through the trees, making quick work of the guards chosen for watch. I emerged from my cover, moving through the camp and taking the lives of as many soldiers as possible. Dacian entered from his post between two trees, causing bloodshed in likeness to mine. Once all were silenced, Eshkan joined us, putting out their campfire.

"West," I said and took a breath. Dacian nodded and sheathed his sword. Dawn. We traveled in silence, the trees becoming thicker in width, their closeness to one another creating a canopy of immense darkness. It was as if the sun held no power here, its rays ending on the ground, where large dark shadows of tree limbs boasted their resolve in banishing it. They were showcased in black patterns against illuminated deep-green grass, creating a pattern that not even the most skilled artisan could imitate on tapestry.

"Even the forest changes," Dacian said, looking into the trees.

"Be on your guard," I said and hushed my horse, rubbing the side of her neck. The steed carrying Eshkan reared, making sounds showcasing his anxiety. He tried to quiet the beast, yet to no avail.

"We will have to go on foot from here," I answered. "They do not like what they feel from it."

"Going on foot can be dangerous," Dacian said and looked back at me. "We will not be able to move quickly if we are ambushed."

"We do not want to give off the feeling that we are adversaries," I stated. "They likely know we are here already."

"Then why do we hesitate?" Eshkan asked and climbed off his mount. "We are finally upon it. You say that the answer lies within the halls of the coven, yet you wait upon your horse as if intimidation stays your hand."

"This is the closest I have been to my kind, yet the farthest I have ever felt from belonging," I answered. "As sentimental as it seems, I will not pretend that it has not haunted me viciously upon our traveling here."

"Do you lack compassion?" Dacian asked Eshkan. "You know what traumas we have recently endured."

"I lack nothing," Eshkan stated and took the daggers from the pack upon his horse, placing them in the quiver across his chest. "I merely wish to make haste. We have given Savantin enough time already. It has been long since we've left the island. How do we know he hasn't found his desire already?"

"I did not mean it to insult, brother," Dacian answered.

"As I meant nothing by it. If what everyone says about the king holds true, then Savantin has no opposition. Do you believe his men know what he is planning? You are right in saying time is short," Eshkan continued. "I say as soon as we are finished here, we go straight to Terrenveil to seek an audience with the man pretending to be king. Perhaps Morard was right after all."

"What if he does not listen?" Dacian asked. "What if he does his best to avoid our words?"

"Then we find people who will not," Eshkan said. "We have allies already that would see his head from his shoulders."

I hesitated, unknowing how to discuss my internal struggle, but it seemed now was the best time. "Cosette mentioned things to me about him," I said, "things I at first didn't believe."

"Something that will help us?"

"The opposite, actually," I said, looking up.

"What say you?" Dacian asked.

"Cosette said that he was like a father to her, while her true parents ignored her, used her as a pawn, forced her to live a life that she did not want to live."

"If she speaks truth, then why aren't they sharing that relationship now."

"She told me that he helped her leave her old life behind and wanted her to live the life she wanted. Even if it meant leaving him behind too."

"Cethin... I know you don't—" Eshkan said, causing me to immediately interrupt.

"It was Jadoq who concocted every plan to destroy us. Poisoned the water. Locked the villagers in the mill. Savantin was not innocent, and we must stop him, but she asked me to try a method other than killing him."

"But if he does not listen?" Dacian asked.

"Then we kill him," I responded.

A look of anger was seen on Eshkan's face, as he took a deep breath. "You don't mean that."

"I do. Cosette was right. Who are we to decide who lives or dies, unless presented with a perilous fate? We must stop him, but I will not let the past stand in the way of sparing him should we turn him from his obsession. If we cannot stop him, he will see death by our hands."

"Vortain's death meant nothing to you?"

"He died honorably." There was no point in stating how I truly felt about him, not at this time. Eshkan would not hear it.

"Honorably," Eshkan laughed. "Cethin, he shouldn't have died."

"We could not have prevented Jadoq's treachery. The only reason we aimed to kill Savantin is because Jadoq was already dead. Come, Eshkan. You know it to be true," I said.

Eshkan stopped, looking toward the ground. "I guess I feel guilt for not being there to protect him."

"You could have risked dying yourself," Dacian answered.

"A life for a life," Eshkan answered. "I suppose that wouldn't have made things right."

"Once the king and queen are removed, Cosette will see herself back there. Would you rob her of the man who has been more of a father to her than her own? Because he played a part in a plot that was created by a man who is now dead?"

"I ask one thing," Eshkan said, quietly. "If we must kill him, we do so swiftly. I have no doubt he will not turn easily from his obsession and may use cunning against us."

I nodded, Dacian looking between us both as if trying to break tension. "Shall we continue?"

I dismounted, petting the soft black mare down her nose. I reached for the weapons in my pack, sheathing Seligsara in the hilt that was crafted on the back of the armor I was wearing. "I am ready."

"Then into the darkness we go."

We delved deeper into the forest, our surroundings changing drastically. Upon turning to watch the field we had left; I saw rays of sun twinkling as they struggled to reach inside and penetrate the shadow. Moss and lichen covered the ground, as they were the only flora to strive without the sun. Surprisingly, there were bushes of a deep reddish black color, their leaves in the shape of spearheads. The silence that surrounded us was heavy, bearing down on our senses so that it made us feel like we were drowning. There were no birds, no animals heard as we progressed, not even the sound of our footsteps did not reach our ears.

Suddenly, we heard a sound, manifested in a voice behind us.

"You do not disappoint me, brother."

I turned, as well as my company as I looked upon the Sardon who had claimed before to be my blood.

"Why do you still wear the cowl upon your head? You are safe now. You are where you do not have to worry about the light," he stated.

I bowed my head reluctantly, and pushed my hood off, revealing my face. "I suppose we are lucky that you are the first to have found us," I answered.

"Lord Sahrkorin knew you were coming. He could hear the Sun as it approached," Vihren stated.

"Then I suppose an audience with him is where we stand," I said.

Vihren bowed his head slightly. "I will take you to Tarporen. But I must speak with you first."

"What words do you wish to share?"

"I must apologize for my rash actions upon our last meeting. It was not very brotherly of me, I must admit."

"That it was not. But I hold nothing against your name."

"I am pleased to hear this," Vihren said and nodded. "It is time you learn why you were not raised here."

"I have made peace with my past. It no longer bothers me."

"Yes, but you were placed among mortals for a reason. We are the last of the bloodheirs, brother. It is both a blessing and a curse. Those with that name have, as I'm sure you know, fought for the title of Zerian's most honored for thousands of years. Our uncle was driven mad with the thought of pleasing him. He tried to kill us both, you as a newborn. When I took you from our parents, I was but a ten-year-old child. I was told to run. I did not know where. I made it all the way to Harbortow when I was found by the man who raised you. I ran, leaving you behind. He would have surely known what I was and killed me."

"You ran all the way from here to the Baeld?" I asked. "To protect me?"

"That I did. I returned to Sahrkorin, who had reported to me that our father and mother did not return from taking the sword to the island."

"And what of our uncle?"

"Vanquished by Archegals."

"Why take Seligsara to Ophidian?" I asked quickly.

"So that it would never fall into our uncle's hands. It is the only thing that can kill a Bloodheir. The Sun cannot."

"I see," I nodded. "And so, they hid it with Vortain, hoping that he would never use it against us."

"Yes. It must be fate that you were placed there. Why you now hold it in your hands."

"If we are made to fight, then why not kill me?"

"I have failed Zerian and lost my chances at gaining his favor long ago. I lost you nearly twenty years ago. To do so again would leave me truly alone."

"This is why you found me before? To make me take it. To make me accept it."

"Now you see," he answered. "I have done something that Zerian will never forgive, and the only hope I have at pleasing him is to make sure you do not follow in my footsteps."

"You would do this for someone you hardly know, someone you have not seen in twenty years?" I asked.

"The world has taken your trust. I understand. I hope that one day you will have the capacity to call me brother," Vihren answered.

"I have no attachment to this, to Zerian."

"You must learn to find it within you. You hold both relics from the time of his rule over our race. Is that not proof that he did not abandon you? That he has not abandoned us?"

"Proof is not what I need," I answered. "I seek knowledge."

Vihren nodded and took a breath. "Whatever your wishes, I will see them met. Lord Sahrkorin anticipates your meeting with him."

"And what of them?" I asked, motioning toward Dacian and Eshkan. "Will we see them unharmed when we enter the coven?"

"As I said, whatever your wishes, I will see them met," Vihren repeated.

I became less tense, nodding at his offering. "I will speak to Sahrkorin, but when we enter the coven, they are not to be harmed," I repeated.

"No harm will come to them while they remain here. Tarporen is this way," Vihren said and moved his arm toward a darkened path, surrounded by dead trees.

"It seems that not much lives beyond the trees," Dacian said quietly, our voices still very prominent against the silence.

"The sun, although our natural enemy, is necessary for life to thrive. Here, everything is dead. There is no life beyond the trees. Even we must venture when hunting for sustenance," Vihren answered.

"Then why live here? Would it not make sense to live where food was bountiful?" Dacian asked.

"It is a lot different when your food source detests you," Vihren stated, and looked back at him briefly. "A Sardon encampment outside the homes of man means only one thing to them. A threat."

Dacian nodded. He knew this but seemed to be asking him questions to grasp his character. He did the same with me upon our first meeting. It was often people thought his constant questioning was bothersome, but he had his reasons. He would rather they think him bothersome than inquisitive. In this land, a mind as sharp as a sword was as deadly as one.

As we continued down the path, small fires began to light at the bases of old crumbling statues. Their limbs were on the ground beneath them, slowly eroding upon moss, the absence of someone tending them sealed their fate. Their faces had been eaten away by years, and craters marked where soft cheeks once were. The eyes were all that remained intact, for lips, noses and chins had been claimed victim by time. Guardians of a road untraveled, watching as the silence would see them to their demise. Upon their end, we found ourselves standing before a stone structure. It appeared in likeness to its watchers, delicate architecture withered. We came to a large metal door, seemingly impenetrable. Vihren lifted it upward in one motion, holding it so that we could pass beneath.

"I will take you to where he holds council, and report to him that you've arrived," Vihren said as we entered, closing the door behind him. It clasped shut, and as it did, the walls were illuminated by the light of small flames that enveloped the sconces. "The land is responsive, now that the Sun has returned," Vihren stated, looking at them in awe. "This land has been dead without it, ever since it was taken to Valkurdi by Sahrkorin's spy. But it was the best option to keep it safe."

"Valkurdi," I stated. "He had stayed concealed for a long time, hidden in an Araelian house of the dead."

"What has become of him?" Vihren asked as we made it to a stairwell, descending beneath ground. The temperature cooled significantly.

"I helped him escape with the help of a handmaiden. The king's men stormed his abode."

"You were attacked? It is a good thing you have come to us, brother. Sahrkorin's spy will have much to speak to you about."

"Who is this spy?"

"You will not know her, nor will you have seen her. She has been working a long time to try to hide both artifacts from those who would misuse them."

"And so, they came to me," I answered. We finally reached the bottom of the staircase, the air cold, yet dry. As we walked with Vihren to meet with Sahrkorin, there were others, moving about the chambers freely, speaking to one another in dialogue barely audible. As the light reached the sconces upon the pillars, they all turned head, and began to comment, their eyes coming across me. Just as Vihren had known, they all knew. The Sun had returned.

Sahrkorin's chamber was impressive. It was illuminated by fires spiraling up each one of the six pillars that surrounded it. As they reached the top of the room, the flames circled each pillar, creating a bright light in the spherical ceiling which faded as it reached where we stood. The floor created in the circle of the pillars was indented, covered with cushions of black velvet filled with the down of assorted nocturnal fowl. The scent of the room was engulfed by an alluring incense of spices, a poisonous berry that grew to the south, and an undertone of patchouli.

"Please, be seated. Lord Sahrkorin will be here shortly," he said, heading toward the back of the room. Reddish black curtains hung from where the ceiling leveled off and touched the floor.

"This places me in unease," Eshkan stated, looking around. "Do you trust him?" he asked, looking toward me.

"It is too early to tell. But we have no other choice," I said. "I must learn how to use the Sun in the event Savantin does not listen to us."

Eshkan nodded. Dacian began to look around, his eyes focusing on the ceiling of the room, specifically the half sphere that vaulted above us, catching the light from the fires. "It is truly amazing that the environment reacts to the Sun," he said.

"It is impressive," Eshkan responded. "Which makes me fear it. Septentria may have its secrets, its beasts. I have never seen the power that this stone wields."

"It is not just a stone, Septen." A voice from the curtains. Sahrkorin. He was dressed in dark armor, a stone shining visibly on his left wrist. Upon his neck was a dark reddish scarf made from a thick fabric, coiled. He wore nothing upon his head, which had no hair, but patterns in likeness to mine. A sword hung from his waist; his hands patterned as his head was. His eyes were also similar, except that one of them was darker in color. "Sardons have an affinity to the afterlife, and so we have also an affinity to necromancy, as well as the soul," Sahrkorin said.

He walked toward us and sat upon the cushion nearest him, crossing his long legs. He placed his hands in front of him, so that the stone in his wrist was facing upward. "The mortal idea of a soul is what we wanted to achieve, an entity that stores the basis of power. Our creator, the creator of all Citharen did not see it necessary, because upon our deaths we would return to a much different place," he continued. "Zerian, before his induction had devised a way to create our own afterlife, and through necromancy and vesselism, was able to create it. You will notice upon each one of us that you meet, we carry stone within our flesh. There are some of us who have learned from Zerian's studies how to will our power into the stones, so that when we die, they can be offered in our temple and transferred through the void into our own afterlife."

"That is its origin?" I asked.

"Indeed." Sahrkorin nodded. "The Sun was what Zerian chose to will his own power within, and when he was inducted, he left it here, taking only half of it with him."

"This is only half?" I asked, looking at my forearm.

Sahrkorin nodded. "It is pleasing to have it back here, if only for a brief amount of time. I trust you are not here to stay?"

"There are matters I must attend to," I answered.

"Forgive me. I do not wish to intrude," he said and took a breath. "So, you are here to learn how to command it, then. I see that you are indeed Bloodheir, as it would not be responding to you in such a nature were you not. That eliminates my need to test you. I have agreed to take you on as my pupil, so that you may learn what it is to hold the power of a Sardon. You know of the six elements with which we create power, yes?"

"I know only of fire," I stated.

"The others, light, shadow, earth, blood, and time are equally as important. As I'm sure you have discovered, the Sun is still very connected to Zerian, and will often act on its own accord because you do not know the words to command it."

"This I have noticed."

"We will change this in the only way we can. It is his power that you are borrowing, can borrow, as you are his direct descendent," Sahrkorin said.

I nodded again, waiting for him to continue. It was then a woman entered. She bowed to Sahrkorin, who nodded in response. She looked up, and then toward me rushing inward and speaking.

"If the moment presents itself, I must have word with the Bloodheir and his company."

"We are presently discussing his immersion and the Sun," Sahrkorin stated. "But, if the matter is as desperate as your voice tells it to be, you may speak, Sindara."

She nodded quickly, looking toward me. "You are the one who wishes to stop Savantin?" she asked.

I nodded. "And you are the one who attacked us on the road."

"There is much we must discuss. I am sure you are aware of why your homeland was burned and your people slaughtered," she said.

I provided silence in response, unable to read her.

"We must speak," she said and looked to Sahrkorin, who nodded.

"I will reveal to you now that I was there the night he slaughtered your master."

Eshkan and Dacian stood suddenly, hands on their weapons when I moved my own outward, looking upward to them.

"You would not have known he was dead had you not seen it with your own eyes. Tell me why I should not see you as adversary?" Eshkan asked.

"To do so would be a mistake," she answered.

"Explain yourself," Dacian said, watching her closely.

"I am spy to Lord Sahrkorin, sworn to protect the artifacts of Zerian with my life, as well as artifacts that involve the fate of the mortal race. The Sun was hidden for seventy years, so you could imagine my interest when it was mentioned to Savantin by the advisor to your master," Sindara stated.

"Jadoq. I hope his body still rots," Eshkan said and sheathed his dagger.

"I contacted Savantin in hopes that he would believe a Sardon wished to aid him. He did, for a moment. When I discovered his plot to find the box of Barroqas, using the Sun as a distraction for the king, I knew I had to act."

"How did he find out about the Sun if it was so well hidden?" Dacian asked, less tense at this moment.

"The advisor told him all. He was interested in the island after that and asked for the inventory of things taken there."

"Everything? Was it revealed to him?"

"Yes, he has an affinity to artifacts of a dark nature," Sindara said. "One would not take him for a scholar, I know. But his study of things that intrigue him have made his knowledge vast and insurmountable."

"A distraction. This is where our fates aligned."

"Yes," Sindara nodded. "The king believes he still seeks it in order to help him quell the uprising rebellions."

"We know this much," Eshkan answered.

"What you don't know is that whoever still lives that belonged to Ophidian is in grave danger," she said and removed the scarf from her neck, revealing several small holes in the front of her throat, bruises in the shape of a hand visible around it. "I am afraid I can protect the keys no longer."

"He's stricken you," I answered, feeling my anger rise.

She held out a hand to me, urging me in silence to control my rage. "It was my own fault. I should have realized it was a trap," she stated, wincing as she began to unravel the scarf the rest of the way. "I am not of concern, Cethin. Whoever else was at Ophidian when it was destroyed, that is whom you should harbor concern for."

"Declan," I said quickly and stood, looking at the door.

"One of you lives but is not present?" Sindara asked.

"There is another, a guard," Dacian said.

"Declan would be an easy target. He is with the monks in Aubergrun," I answered.

"There is not a weapon on the compound," Sindara said and looked down, shaking her head. "It is of utmost importance that we reach their temple."

"His life is now at risk?"

Sindara took a deep breath. "The fault is now my burden. The information Savantin was seeking has been uncovered. He knows where the keys are but does not know the location of the box."

"Basilin save us," Eshkan said and blew a deep breath out. "Anskirre forgive."

"Do you know how they came in contact with one another?" I asked, my arms shaking.

"Ophidian had remained hidden from the eye of Terrenveil until they first spoke. The burden of fault lies on the advisor," Sindara said.

"Curse that louse, even in the afterlife," Eshkan said. "I'd mutilate his corpse were it at my feet."

"He got what was coming to him. I only hope that his death was slow," Dacian answered.

"Calm," Sahrkorin said and stood. "You must go to your ally, but do not forget that we have business to attend to. I know your heart is steeped in the pain of loss. I can feel it tearing you apart, and for that I am truly sympathetic."

I looked toward him, words that I did not expect, from a creature I did not expect them from.

"Yet you are the Bloodheir of Zerian. Your destiny is tied to the Sun, as it is tied to the fates of each one of us. You will complete the immersion."

"Lord Sahrkorin," Sindara said, her voice low with the promise of subservience.

"I am bound to decide between protecting our sustenance from a plot that is beyond difficult to reverse and completing the immersion of the last able Bloodheir to rescue our true Lord from the void. You cannot expect me to volunteer his absence yet again, not yet."

"I will complete the immersion," I answered. "But I must rescue Declan. This man has never taken the life of another, nor will he."

"Sindara," Sahrkorin said suddenly, looking toward her. "Go with them. Assist Cethin in whatever he needs."

"It is not necessary to risk her life a second time," I answered.

"She is to protect the Sun with her life, and now that it rests with you, you decide her fate," Sahrkorin stated and began to walk toward the curtains. "Survive this trial and you will have more than proven yourself worthy of our respect. Carrying the Sun is not an easy task, and many before you have failed. I have two words for you," Sahrkorin said, his voice stern.

I bowed my head toward him, the rage welling behind my eyes.

"Valgolig, to heal," he said and moved his hand outward, his palm facing us. "And Meiratan. Light," he said as a bright sphere of white light was seen in his palm. "Remember them both when engaging the Seraphice. There is more I can teach you, but until I know that you can handle its power, I will only provide you with the words you cannot carry on without."

I bowed my head deeper this time, looking up at him from its lowered position. "I extend my gratitude."

"As I extend my knowledge. Forgive me. It has been years since we have been without the Sun, or a promise that we will free our Lord from that dreaded place. I hope for your safe return, and that you make peace with the pain that binds you," he said and turned, disappearing through the thick curtains.

"We've no time to waste," Sindara said anxiously, touching the swords secured around her hips.

"Come. We will use the horses at the stable nearest the road to Aubergrun. I am afraid the monks have blessed their lands against anything we might do to reach them faster."

We began to follow her from the chamber, onward to a place where I knew we would not be welcomed.

ACT III

SAVANTIN'S CURSE

CHAPTER 1

THE PURE OF HEART

We rode quickly through the night, leaving the coven after the sun fell behind the mountain, onward, to its next destination. He now knew how to get to the keys. I rode faster, until my horse's neck was at pace with that of Sindara's.

"A word," I said and looked over to her briefly, looking ahead.

"Of course," she answered.

"You said that he knows how to get the keys. Do you know where the box rests?" I asked.

"It must be in Cilevdan," she answered.

"In all of my time here I did not know such a thing existed," I answered, keeping my gaze before me. "You think it is here?"

"At first, I thought so, but now I'm not sure. My research points to it. But there are inconsistencies in reports. In all the raids that occurred over this land, all the documents destroyed, the trail ends. Vortain was brave. He died protecting it, but we still do not know where it is. I was on my way to council with Vortain when Jadoq suggested Savantin meet with him. Except when Savantin discovered that Jadoq was planning on telling Ozrach about his plans, he was enraged. This is why the tragedy befell your people."

"For the greed of others," I answered. "It is sickening."

"I must trouble you a second time. Jadoq planned the siege, told Savantin that the island was heavily fortified. Savantin thought he could convince Vortain to tell of the box's hiding place, but Jadoq insisted the only way to do so was to arrive with soldiers."

"I knew he was repulsive, but I did not know that he had the capacity to devise a plot that apathetic," I stated.

"He was yet another person who sees what comes of dealing with Savantin," Sindara said and pulled the scarf around her neck, shivering. I knew it was not from the cold northern winds.

"Jadoq was pathetic. A concept that man invented caused him to betray one who loved him as a brother and saved his life. It is just that he no longer breathes."

"It is," Sindara said. "I wish I could have been quicker, but Savantin is determined."

"What drives him?" I asked.

"It is hard to say," Sindara answered. "But it must be something dangerous. It is not for riches, not for a title. His intentions are clear, but as for his reason..." Sindara stopped speaking and shook her head. Eshkan and Dacian were riding behind us, for a reason unknown to me. We made it to the edge of Morrenvahl when Sindara next spoke to me, urging caution as we approached the road.

She looked out of the wood, listening in the silence for approaching horses or carts. Once she was certain no one was near, we breached the dark forest, becoming travelers once more.

"We must be careful here. There are those who take the purge seriously and will not hesitate to attack us."

I nodded. "Does this road lead to Aubergrun?"

"Yes. It is on the edge of Septentria, up in the hills where the ice does not touch."

"The springs of Santaiei," Eshkan said from behind us. "The monks are wise."

"Indeed, they are. I doubt they will willingly allow us entry. Cethin and I, for obvious reasons. You two are a little too armed and your scars belong to warriors. I anticipate trouble gaining an audience with your friend," Sindara stated.

"I am sure convincing them will not be a problem," I said, touching my temple.

"You mean hypnosis?" Sindara answered with a smile.

"If no other option presents itself, I will be left with no choice. They will not listen to our admonitions. We must protect them."

"I do not think they will take very kindly to our intrusion, whether or not you persuade the monks," Dacian said.

"I will take the risk of their disdain," I answered, knowing the method was rather cruel to utilize on men of peace. I wondered how Declan was doing among them, how he had acclimated to the life of enlightenment. They worshiped no gods, yet some believed in sentient beings that held the keys to knowledge. Though devout to peace, council with them would be intimidating. I wondered what they believed happened to them after death, if they made peace with nothingness then they held no fear. Power they would use against no one.

"We will make it there by tomorrow. Unfortunately, while this route will avoid most of the patrols, it is also slightly longer than using the king's roads," Sindara stated. Taking a risk of being spotted would be unnecessary, as well as careless. I had no doubt we could dispose of a patrol and hide them in the dark of the wood, yet if we were outnumbered, we could be killed. That was if we could not convince them that we were mere travelers. Our weapons betrayed that, and we could not part with them. I would die before Seligsara was wrought from my hands, and I knew Dacian felt the same of Basilin's blade.

We continued to follow the path, my horse keeping pace with Sindara's. It was now that I had the chance to examine her, as we climbed the mountain road that would in time lead us above Winds Hollow and cross toward the small compound hidden within one of the largest mountains in Septentria. She was short, her height could not be more than five feet and a couple inches. Her skin was tan, although I did not know what her bands of markings looked like, or if they differed from mine. She had the same eyes we all shared, yellow, her irises thin oval strips surrounded by reddish pupils. Her hair was the color of death and fastened atop her head in a pattern of buns. She moved the cowl above her head and over her face when the winds began to pick up, the smell of snow within their harsh choruses as they ripped past our ears with vicious force. There was a legend for the winds of Septentria. There was a legend for everything.

Sindara stopped as we saw three people atop horses, their torches seen boldly against the dark, bright vermillion spheres becoming enveloped by the night.

"What now?" I asked, stopping my horse just inches from hers.

"They will find it suspicious if we do not continue, that is, if they have not already found it odd that we carry no torches to light our way."

"I doubt they are soldiers. There would be plenty more of them were that the case," I answered. "Though I don't know why anyone else would be traveling at this time."

"It might be people seeking entry to Defaltor so that they may buy protection for a voyage to Rustanzen. The thieves own a ship so that they can sell their haul to fences in the empire. They would not hesitate to see citizens of the Veil across for a fee or for valuables."

"It would be foolish of us to assume this. How do we know they aren't deserters?" I asked her, as we started to move our horses forward. Dacian and Eshkan had made it over the small incline behind us, slowing their mounts as well.

"They of all people have reason to go to Rustanzen," Sindara said. "Come. We should continue to Aubergrun but be aware that they might follow."

"You think they will pursue?"

"We are close to Septentria. We will have to be mindful of brigands."

I nodded. We continued, slowly approaching those with fire. I could smell the torches, a sweet undertone to them. They were witches, from where I knew not, burning herbs to keep trouble from descending upon them. The practice had too, been made heresy by Queen Neraea, stating that any ritual not conducted in one of the Temples of Light was guided by Deceferous' tongue. I paid mind not to look at them as we passed by, yet it was difficult as I heard one of them utter a charm, moving her heavily marked hands.

"It is a charm for protection from evil. They know what you carry," Sindara answered once they had passed us by, traveling slowly down the road in the cover of darkness.

"Or perhaps they know what is coming," I answered and looked up toward the trees, listening to the sound of the crows.

"We cannot be sure. They must live out here in the wood. Neraea has been thorough with her crusade. She is not innocent either, Cethin. Many people have died at the blade of her 'priests,'" she answered. "This land breeds filth. These people harm no one. They burn their herbs and give flame to candle as an offering to the elements and are slaughtered because she believes her choice is more valid than others."

"Such is the way of man," I answered. "But they are worth saving, Sindara, whatever your reason for stopping Savantin."

"How can you say this? You have lived among them for years, watching their corruption day in and day out. I enjoyed when I was blind to it but my service to Lord Sahrkorin, Lord Zerian, and the Sun, changed all of that. What they do to one another is shameful. They are dangers to themselves."

"I am also witness to their kindness," I said. "Behind every divine ruler there are those who are slaves to the religion, their minds so caged by a set of guidelines based on control that they are afraid to speak out against their king. Behind every avaricious merchant is a family stricken with poverty, sharing old bread that they've had to steal in order to stay alive. Behind every war is a child, homeless and cold, hoping that someone will extend their hand. Yet despite all the selfishness, behind all the apathy there are those who have hearts. I was found by a seafarer when I was a child. He is the one who cared for me, knowing very well that I was not human. He kept me warm, gave me a home. He treated me like his son. I will not abandon his kindness and leave these people to die. After I stop Savantin, I am going to help Cosette return to Terrenveil and take the throne."

Sindara nodded, moving her face downward as a gust of wind passed through us.

"She will not stand for the corruption that festers at their touch. It is Araele they fear now," I answered.

"Araele," Sindara laughed. "The only thing she brings to this earth is prejudice."

"Is it true that Savantin openly opposes religion?"

"He was once tried for heresy," Sindara answered. "Each one of the accusers refused to speak when the day of the trial arrived. It is the heretic who controls the divine, now."

"Once we confront Savantin, we must make sure that Cosette takes the throne."

"You have much faith in this mortal," Sindara said.

"She is courageous, yet smart. She knows if she returns that her life is in danger. She knows that her parents have no care for anything besides their life in the castle. She has lived in the woods for years, hunting to scrape by, relying on strangers that use trade to survive. Her house was filled with things her mother would see her burned for. She is not like them, if that is your concern."

"I have no concern for them, Cethin. They are my prey. I must protect the world from darkness because without it they would not be able to thrive, and it would make it more difficult for us. With the sun's demise we would lose a major weakness but gain a new one."

"So, you do have concern for them, in a way," I answered. "You said you must protect the Sun, and that is why you are here, but I believe there to be something else. You know him somehow, Sindara."

Sindara said nothing, her voice lost against the growing winds. At last, she said, *it is best I do not discuss it*, and continued on, tending to the road with a watchful eye. While she was wounded, so was her pride. I supposed she did not want to elaborate on the subject, knowing that the sting of failure was running deep beneath her thoughts. It was whatever occurred between them that had her here now, along with the order from Sahrkorin to remain by the Sun, and with the order to bring it back to Tarporen should anything happen to me. She kept her secrets closer than her command, which was lethal. Though I did not believe her to want to cause harm to us, I did not entirely trust that she held no prior acquaintance with Savantin other than what she described. Feelings, perhaps. I did not yet know if it would become a problem.

As we climbed the base of the mountain, leading us from Terrenveil to the tundra, we were met by a drastic change of temperature, the fading warmth traded now with harsh cold winds. The trees became less colorful as we passed through a barrage of nature painted with the colors of a decaying autumn. Warm pinks, reds and oranges speckled with yellows of various hues. The trees appeared as if they themselves were torches, burning vibrantly in autumnal passion. Though not anymore. We had left that land behind, their memory a ghost, lightly tracing the mind with their images as if promising a warm return among passing. The trees were now bare, exoskeletons of a death promised to them each year by the ice and snow. The horses worked harder to climb the slope. Their muscles, though minutely, affected by the cold that now surrounded us.

Within minutes of travel, we made it into a thick copse of evergreen trees, lining the road on either side with thick hearty trunks, grown strong from withstanding years of winter storms that howled through their needles like a spectre. My thoughts moved to what lurked inside of it, and how we were now vulnerable to whatever that may be. Eshkan strode ahead, stopping his horse next to mine. "I will take lead. I may have been taken from these lands as a boy, but I vividly remember them. They are unforgiving, and we do not have the capacity to make error," he stated.

"Yes, you take the lead. That will give our mounts a rest, for a short while," Sindara agreed, reaching to touch the mane of hers as if a catalyst to the relief.

"We should continue to ride in pairs. There are beasts here stronger than those we are used to. They will feast on not only our horses, but us as well, given chance."

"What wards them off?" Sindara asked, looking toward him, her first time speaking to him as an ally.

"Fire, but we cannot use it without running the risk of being seen by brigands. They too prey on those upon the road."

"Brigands we can slay without penalty," I answered. "Do they travel this far south?"

"Most disperse from the heart of Septentria, traveling south, west toward the Baeld. The lakes will freeze over, the animals will take to dens, or travel to the plains. Most of the plants die except for the berries and gourds that can be salvaged from a winter harvest. Even then, it is not enough to feed the whole of the land. Only the old Septen farmers know the secrets and pass them on to reluctant children who wish to migrate to warmer lands. Anskirre's people are abandoning her, and it is the fault of that vile family. They first scourged the land with disease and war that caused them to divide from her grace. She waits for us at the river's origin. I am sure of it."

"And so, the brigands take no heed to his warnings of what will happen if they trespass, for the king's family is who trespasses among them," I stated.

"Indeed. I am surprised they do not raise sword against him to reclaim their land. The only thing that binds his name to this land is blood. No one offered it to him, no one sold it. The Septens had no king. It was the strategy of conquest, to leave them with only the snowy portion of their land so that they would give into his system of taxes. When they did not, they were left with the land that only they knew how to use."

"This land was once ours too," Sindara added, "Before the purge swept through and millions were killed. All in the name of the Goddess of Light. She breeds deceit. Kill those which prey upon you and in vengeance reign. She is not so different from the old gods of blood and battle. They think they are so civilized, believing in one entity opposed to what came before. They are just as delusional as the rest."

"Do you not have an entity from which you seek strength?" Dacian asked, out of honest curiosity.

"Only our Lord Zerian, who is one of us. Time will tell us where he has gone. Lord Sahrkorin swears he was trapped by the father of all nonhumans, like the rest of them believe. The only afterlife we claim is the one we've made ourselves, the one Zerian made. It is why we must rescue him." Sindara stopped, listening to a sound from a tree that we had recently passed by. It had slowly drowned into silence, the trees creaking with each small gust of wind that brushed past them.

"How far are the temples?" Dacian asked Sindara, his eyes searching the horizon. "I hoped not to spend the night on the road, with the number of things looking to kill us."

"We will reach the temples by morning, I am afraid, and that is if we continue through the night. We will arrive at the corridor soon, leading from this mountain to the next, over top Winds Hollow. We will see the fires from their inns as we pass," Sindara answered. "We must ride through the night, or we will leave too many hours open for Savantin to reach your friend before we do. The only problem is, I do not know how much he has seen. We could be endangering him by this journey, as Savantin might not have known he was there at all."

"You were in Defaltor," I answered. "You were the one who placed this stone on my person. You knew that he was going to Aubergrun, so Savantin knows this as well," I said. I surprised her with the remark, her silence the only indication. "Why not tell me this before?"

"Forgive my dishonesty. In poor judgment, I thought that if I revealed this, you would harbor resentment."

"It is no fault of yours. You were only trying to further point me in the direction of Morrenvahl."

"Further?" Sindara asked.

"Vihren. He came to me on Ophidian and spoke to me."

"He has always missed you. If Sahrkorin knew what he meant by exploring the marsh for rumors, he would have forbidden it."

"So, he truly wanted me to seek him on my own accord," I said. "Interesting of him."

"The bloodheir must accept his destiny, and not the other way around. It is how it has always been, or has been written to have been," Sindara said.

"It seems we walk the same path, and for me that requires your honesty. I will not be made fool by traveling with you for the same end if you are going to mislead us," I said. "We have come too far. If you know anything else about what he is planning, now would be the time to share it."

Sindara was silent for a moment, her voice heard in her heavy sigh. "There are some things I cannot share, Cethin, for it may skew you from the path that you must walk beyond this one. But for the present, he knows what I know. He knows that your friend is with the monks. Declan may not be spared. Were Savantin himself, he would not kill Declan, but his present state has him breaching the edge of Seraphician insanity. I am surprised that I live, and because of this I must make sure that I conceal that box."

I continued to urge my horse, listening as the hooves hit the slowly freezing ground harder upon each landing until the sound was thunder. The wind was loud as it raced past my ears, shrieking with the intent of disheartening all that bore witness to its orchestra. I could barely hear my company behind me, their horses almost in unison as the sound of their hooves upon ground was only half a second apart. Sindara indicated that we would reach the temples at dawn, a time still hours off.

My thoughts moved to Cahya, and how she would tell me that time cannot be changed. The statement resonated. Jadoq's treason was a catalyst to the events that had brought nothing but sorrow. Our brothers slain; the people burned. When we returned, we would place Vortain in the fires of silence, so that in ashes he would be accepted by his gods into an afterlife. It would be two that I have offered to the flames because of greed. Time cannot be changed.

An hour passed before I instructed my horse to stop, watching the figure in the middle of the road. They stood completely cloaked in black, a lone torch held out by a small steady hand. I approached slowly, stopping still several feet from them, seeing only their lips beneath the thick hood that adorned their head. They were pale pink, chapped rivets in them from the harsh winds. My horse pawed the ground, his breath a sheet against the thick cold air. The girl did not speak, did not move, even as my company rode up behind me, also coming to a halt. Sindara moved her horse to match mine, speaking.

"She's human. I can smell it."

"There are more of them in the trees," I answered.

"Do you think they will let us pass?"

"They have arrows on our horses. I smell steel as well as blood."

Sindara nodded, moving the reins lightly in her hands. "Then who is it that will make the first move?" she asked.

"A well-trained archer can strike a moving target from a distance away. Eshkan will tell you as much."

"Do we wait until they approach?"

"I do not think their intention is to kill us outright, but we must be ready."

Sindara nodded and looked back at Eshkan and Dacian to signal to them forward. She turned her head back toward the girl however, when she realized that she shifted her eyes to the trees. It was then a man in similar garb stepped out of the forest and stood next to the girl. It was then she lowered the torch, keeping it close to her. He looked toward us, shapes barely visible amid the dark. He took a few steps forward, stopping now to use his voice.

"In what name do you travel these roads?" he called, keeping his hands at his sides. After a moment of silence, Sindara spoke, causing me to turn my head to her.

"These roads are old and belong to the earth, children of Anskirre. We do not trespass upon it."

"You come from the direction of the king's road, yet you do not come from it. You are not from Terrenveil?"

"No," she stated. "But from a land within its reach."

The man stopped for a moment, moving his cloak aside and grabbing a sword. "Then it is not the soldiers who would miss you."

"We travel to seal the safety of humankind. To raise weapon against us is to make a mistake," I answered quickly.

"Off your horses," he demanded. "'Less you want them to be pierced from beneath you."

"You refer to your archers," I answered. "I could smell them before you stepped from the shadow."

"Your words do not warrant the response I seek. Off your horses, or they will be prey," he stated.

"There is not much to do but listen. Not until we can see his eyes," Sindara stated. She was right. Subjecting him to hypnosis would avoid casualties. I nodded and dismounted, Eshkan and Dacian following my lead. It was then six more of them appeared from the trees, approaching us and beginning to look through our packs.

"There's nothin' but weapons here, Gurin. Daggers mostly," one of them answered. He then placed his hand on a vial within Sindara's bag and pulled it, seeing a powder with a grayish purple hue. He pulled out a flask, opening it to smell it. Coughing violently, he dropped it on the ground, blood spilling upon it.

"Devils," he said and grabbed for his sword. Sindara took the moment to grab her dagger, raising it to his throat. The others grabbed their weapons, and I heard several bowstrings being drawn.

"Wait," the man in the road stated.

THE PURE OF HEART

"Blood, Gurin. The beasts carry blood in vials," his associate answered, holding both of his hands up in fright.

"It seems now I need to refill it," Sindara answered, malice in her voice.

"Kill them but save their horses. We can use them."

I slowly pulled Seligsara from its place on my back. I could tell it thirsted for blood, as I heard the voices of the Sun speak in unison as I held it. "You will not leave this forest," I answered.

"It may be wise not to pressure him," Dacian whispered. "They may kill our horses if they see there is no way to defeat us."

"Cowards," Sindara stated.

"What is it you want from us? If it is riches, we carry none," I answered.

"Then you are of no use to us alive. At least if we have killed you, we can take your horses and the weapons you carry."

"Try to take our horses and we will fight. Try to take our weapons and you will die," Sindara answered.

"Let us fight for them, then," Eshkan answered. "Whoever survives claims ownership to the mounts."

"Ah. A challenge then," Gurin answered, amusement in his voice. "My ancestors bid me to uphold honor. It is settled. He who lives will take ownership."

"Then in honor, will you call off your archers?" Eshkan asked, gripping a sword tightly.

"Of course," Gurin said and lifted two fingers, signaling them to cease.

It was then they were upon us, our horses stirring, trying to move from the fight. The two men beside me were thrashing relentlessly, trying to kill without any technique or form. I ducked, avoiding a strike to the face when the other moved for my legs. I parried, moving Seligsara quickly to block him. He lunged forward and I turned to my side, thrusting the sword along it with my opposing hand to pierce him between the lungs. He cried out, and I flipped the blade forward trying to impale the other in his throat. He quickly moved his sword in an attempt to evade it, but did not place enough strength behind the blow, causing my blade to pierce his shoulder. He tossed his sword to his other hand, attempting to incise, and I grabbed his wrist, allowing Seligsara to drain his blood until he fell weakly to his knees. I began to crush his wrist, until he fell under the pressure and cried out. I ripped my blade from his shoulder, using it to stab right between his collarbones, breaking the sternum. I then turned, seeing that Sindara and Eshkan had vanquished their enemies, Dacian delivering a final blow to the man who had cowardly killed his horse before attacking him.

Bowstrings being drawn were audible as Eshkan returned his sword to its sheath, two loud thuds heard as bodies slumped out of the trees and onto the ground beneath them. Sindara held a crossbow, aiming it for the trees on the opposite side. After firing a bolt, she moved aside as an arrow sailed past her face and hit the tree behind her. Eshkan quickly strung his bow and sent an arrow toward the tree, stringing it a second time and aiming it toward Gurin. Sindara had reloaded by this time, pointing it toward the girl with the torch.

"You can thank me later," Eshkan said and held his bow steady, Sindara only inches from him, her aim focused. She smirked, closing one eye to return to the situation.

"I did not anticipate your victory," Gurin answered.

"You owe us a horse," Eshkan stated. "The victor kept the horses, yet one has been slain."

"I've not one to offer."

"Then your life will suffice," Sindara said and moved her crossbow toward him. The young girl reached into her robes and Sindara muttered one word, and shot quickly at the dagger she revealed, causing it to fall to the ground.

"And I thought this road was far from Morrenvahl," Gurin stated.

"Not far enough," Sindara said, her aim fixed on the girl. "Tell your daughter to stand down or she will be next. I fire only one warning shot."

Gurin whispered to the girl who nodded, moving both hands to hold the torch in front of her. "I can see now," he said, approaching with both hands visible in front of him as to display his surrender. "Why you proved victorious among a number eight more than your own. If I would have known this, I would not have called off my archers."

"You speak of honor, but display cowardice," Eshkan answered.

"I no longer mean harm," Gurin said. "I only meant to compliment you for overcoming the odds. A Sardon among you. Interesting."

"Two," I answered, watching the girl's hands. "Joined by two of the best-trained assassins in all of Cilevdan."

Gurin said nothing and stopped, his hands returning to his sides. "Seeing as I cannot offer you a horse, perhaps I can offer something that might interest you."

"The only interest we have is time, and you've consumed enough of that already," I answered.

"To our deaths, then," Gurin answered and held his arms outward, his head down.

"No," I answered. I could feel their eyes upon me, weapons still drawn. "Only you will die. She will be free to return to whatever life she wanted before you forced her upon the roads."

"You would leave her without her father?"

"She bravely moved to protect you the second she thought your life was threatened, and you offered her life without trying to secure it. I would not call that the action of a father who loves. Perhaps she reminds you too much of your failures, the woman who left you behind. Those are no faults of hers. She deserves to live the life of a child, a life you took away from her."

"You know nothing about my family," Gurin said, anger beneath his voice.

"How you deliver your words says enough."

"And you spare her to what? To tear her flesh apart to sate your hunger? I would rather her heart be pierced by arrows, her corpse still, awaiting the falling winter snows to become her grave. Both would be less painful than loneliness."

"Go," I answered, his words resonating in my mind. I heard Sindara's sound of disdain from behind me. Gurin looked at me and nodded, quickly turning to grasp his daughter's hand and leave the road. Once they were removed from sight, Sindara turned me toward her, in outrage.

"We should have slayed them both to rot among the others. They killed one of our horses."

"Killing him and leaving a girl without her father is your solution to that?" I answered, staring into her eyes. She removed her arm from me and returned the gaze for several seconds before she looked away. "Your empathy prevents you from thinking clearly. Every minute we waste is a minute Savantin uses to his advantage. Your friend is in danger, yet you converse with a stranger upon the road debating whether or not to spare his life."

"Every life matters, Sindara. Not just those that are involved in ours. Some are deserving and others are not, but that does not mean that I am to pass judgment."

"Yet he would have taken your life had he the capacity within seconds, regardless of your character."

"That does not give me reason to behave similarly," I stated.

"Place your differences aside," Dacian said suddenly, coming between us. "There is no cause to argue. One of us will have to share a horse."

"No. There is another way. The animal would be slowed significantly due to the weight it must carry," Sindara stated and walked briskly to the fallen mount, quickly lowering to her knees. She pressed her head against its side and took a breath in. "The snow has slowed the decay. This should not prove difficult."

Eshkan scratched his head, and then shook it, keeping his eyes on the road. Dacian looked at me, placing his sword in its sheath against his side.

"Cethin," Sindara said and looked up from the horse. I looked at her, offering no words.

"We are about to discover my proficiency at teaching," she said and moved her hands quickly to the small pouch to her side, checking through it very quickly before returning her attention to me. "Familiarize yourself with these words," she said and looked up to me. "Illgoth surentha gog alzeneth valinthor murate. Mir halvolt sai curanthes vait."

As soon as the last word rolled from her tongue, the Sun picked up on it, each one of the voices repeating the words.

"And the last part, Rothin tar santherin mergal jacorum belethes," she said, producing the same result from the Sun. "Hear my voice from beyond the dark, surrender to my power. Hear my voice and obey. To the vessel of this beast the soul returns."

"You aim to reanimate it?" Dacian asked.

"Unless you plan to arrive at separate times, it is the only way. As I said before, two bodies upon one mount will impede its ability to keep up with the others. Cethin, please," she said, this time with some urgency. I took a breath and knelt beside her next to the steed. His rich reddish color was distinguished, even amid the dark.

"Place your hands upon him. Feel the vessel that once housed a soul," Sindara said, removing her own.

I placed my hands upon the fallen beast, feeling his coarse hair against the palms of my flesh. I felt the emptiness Sindara had described, the creature, void of life beneath my touch. The Sun continued the phrases until I laid hands upon the fallen steed, tapering off as I closed my eyes. "Illgoth surentha gog alzeneth valinthor murate. Mir halvolt sai curanthes vait, Rothin tar santherin mergal jacorum belethes," I said slowly. I felt a surge beneath the animal's flesh, and the Sun began to whisper yet again.

"Place your power behind it," Sindara said, her voice an order. I took a breath and repeated the phrase again, this time with strength behind my voice. I felt a small portion of my own strength leave my hands, and flow through the animal, causing its eye to flutter, yet to no avail.

"It was an idea I knew we were not prepared to enact," Sindara said and stood. "You could endanger yourself by trying something such as this. We always practice with sacrifice nearby."

"You and I should ride ahead," Dacian stated. "They will not be so far behind."

I ignored his words and closed my eyes, focusing on the Sun's voice. I took one deep breath inward and moved my hands farther apart, pressing them into the flesh of the horse. I repeated the spell again, my voice bold and militant. The horse's eyes opened quickly as it let out a cry, starting to kick its legs. I held contact, listening as the Sun repeated the phrase once, then trading it for something different, shouting at me, beseeching me. I began to feel lightheaded, shivering noticeably as I continued to make contact, ending in darkness.

◆ ◆ ◆

The compound was dark, the scent of the sea strongest in the heat of the summer. The scent was joined by that of nightflowers timely coming to blossom beneath a lonely pale moon. I left my quarters, in seclusion, watching as two weary guards made their way to the lower compound, their superstition causing them to avoid the paths near my domain. Looking east at Vortain's tower, my eyes came across the torch lit on his balcony, one that burned throughout the night as homage to his gods, to Basilin. He would have retired for the evening by now, and the blooming of flowers marked my time to see her. She would wait for me at the Tower of Silence, cloaked to cover her pale green eyes. It was where no one ventured, unless it was one of my own that had met their death.

She, in all her mystery awaited me. Her beauty untouched by any, her voice a song that quelled darkness, her radiance, light. Her bravery was that which I had seen before in none, yet she did not deceive her feelings with a mask of courage. It was her loneliness that gave her courage, it was her sorrow that gave her strength, but it was the love she held for herself that kept life in her heart. This, she now shared with me.

I walked into the opening of the tower, the nightflowers growing upon the rusting iron gate, their vines creeping toward the top of the structure. Years had seen them slowly forming a canopy across where a roof had not been built, slowly obscuring our view of the stars. Though properly maintained inside, the outside appeared as if the structure was forgotten. She sat upon the altar, her head raised toward the sky, moon and shadow playing across the front of her face, revealing to me only her lips. The ones, warm, that would soon be upon mine...

◆ ◆ ◆

Blood spilled across my lips, lukewarm from loss of temperature. It was from one of the dead, cooling with each minute that passed. I regained my sight, noticing now that I had consumed the flesh from his arm, and had stopped where his shoulder met the neck. I took a breath inward, closing my eyes to take another. I stood from the man, looking into his expressionless face as I tried to balance. The others were standing near the mounts, Dacian's hand on the hilt of his sword. I raised my own hand upward, signaling to him that I was again aware, and he placed his hand at his side.

Another few hours had passed of our racing through the woods, the sky several shades lighter than it had been when we first started our journey. We arrived in Aubergrun before the sun rose, the sky a brilliant teal. The sight was taken from us suddenly as we approached, smelling fire and smoke. As we reached the wooden pillars marking the entry to the temples, we could see the fires on the horizon. I hurried inside without so much as a word to my brothers, quickly dismounting from my horse. I pulled Seligsara and flipped it once, cutting a brigand down at his knees, stabbing it downward into his chest as he fell.

Sindara aimed her crossbow at the door of the closest monastery, releasing a bolt into the back of one of the brigands, catching the attention of several others. Dacian joined me, breathing heavily. "Of all things, bandits. We must find Declan," Dacian said, urgency in his voice.

I nodded and took off toward the monastery, engaging the ones who had collected in front of it. I parried the attack from the one closest to me, grabbing him by the hair and tossing him down the short flight of stairs to dodge the attack of another. I turned, jumping slightly backward and swung my sword forward in short bursts, adding strength behind each one. I broke his block, pulling my blade upward across his chest. I kicked him forward and stabbed behind me, delivering a fatal wound to the man I had earlier tossed. I ducked, quickly avoiding the axes of a brigand who had just joined, turning and using the stairs to gain an advantage. Once I was low enough, I slashed his ankles, breaking his weakened block through the middle and stabbed him in the stomach, ripping my blade forward to toss his bleeding body toward the road.

Dacian caught up to me, dispatching one of the men who had sighted our battle from across the courtyard and was closing in. Sindara took to those who remained, moving quickly, her darkened silhouette seen against the glow of a fire that was tearing through wood. I turned my head to the north, to where the mountain steepened, the large temple seemingly untouched. Banners flew slowly in the breeze as I felt it hit my face, tearing me away from the reality of the siege for a moment. He was there. I spun my sword quickly to avoid being hit in the chest by the angry swing of a battle axe, jumping toward the banister of the small temple I stood in just moments ago. I sprung off it, landing behind him only to take his head from his shoulders.

Before it hit the ground before him, I was off toward the mountain, the road becoming an incline. It was when I reached the second set of stone monoliths along the trail that I realized fires were being set above me. I continued to run, adding whatever strength I had left to push myself. I looked up, watching as snow fell from the mountain above, melting into the atmosphere before it reached me. The springs were nearby.

Just as I climbed the last set of stairs, I noticed two bandits standing outside of the main door, trying their hardest to carry a chest with them. Upon seeing me, they dropped it, gold spilling from its heavy lid as it crashed onto the ground. The pieces began to twinkle as the sun appeared, creating an array of rose and vermillion as the world lightened. They readied themselves for battle, brandishing an old, worn sword and what appeared to be a mace made of iron, rusted in portions from years of service. I wasted no time in waiting for their first move, approaching them quickly and parrying the attack from the first, ducking to avoid a swing from the rusted mace. I kicked backwards, landing a blow into his stomach. As he coiled from the pain, I turned, jabbing the hilt of Seligsara into his face, which caused him stumble backward, holding it and dropping his weapon. I turned my sword in my hand quickly to engage the other brigand and caught the edge of his blade across my cheek toward my eye. I deflected his next attack, ducking beneath his angered blows and searched for his weakness. As he began to tire, I began to more aggressively assail him, grasping his forearm as he turned in foolishness to try and strike. I pushed his elbow inward, breaking it. When I raised Seligsara to his throat, he pulled the fur cowl from his face with the arm that was still intact, revealing that he could be no older than fifteen. He breathed heavily as he tried to fight the pain, staring into the surface of my blackened blade.

"Why do you attack these people?" I asked angrily. "Do you know who you are murdering?"

Without response I kicked his blade upward and caught it in my hand, rendering him defenseless.

"Do you?" I asked, this time louder. I heard my voice surround me, echoing off the rock walls that formed the sides of the temple. "I know you did not remove your cowl without cause to speak."

"I have no words that would interest you, assassin," the boy stated. "My father told me that when it was my turn to fall, that I must show my face."

"Then I send you home," I answered and swung my blade quickly, drawing a large gash across his throat. He coughed once, raising his hand to it before he fell down the old stone steps, his corpse sliding downward. I turned now to the man holding his nose, who began to look around for something to use as a weapon. He reached for the sconce that was bolted onto the temple when I grabbed his hair, slamming his head into the wall. He cried out in pain as his nose began to bleed a second time. I then turned him, stabbing him through the center of his chest, waiting a moment to let his blood run through my blade. I heard shouting from inside and dropped the man instantly, rushing to the source of the sound. Smoke began to travel down long elaborate staircases, obscuring the gold-painted masks that lined the walls.

"Declan!" I shouted. I repeated myself, as I heard nothing in response. Upon shouting a third time I heard my name, screamed in a panic. I climbed the set of stairs closest to me, fatally stabbing a woman clothed in fur as she rushed my position, trying to escape the growing flames. I ran down the hallway, taking a second set of stairs to the third floor, reaching the corridor that led to a balcony. I could see the steam from the springs, and smell the sweet waters as I neared it, shouting Declan's name a fourth time. I heard nothing and quickened my pace, turning the corner to see him. He was sitting near one of the springs, holding onto his torso beneath his stomach. Blood was seen on his tunic and on his hand. He also had a considerably large incision on his chest and had stopped pulling himself toward the water when he saw me. He coughed, a small portion of his lifeforce escaping his throat. There were gashes on his arms, one on his leg, and blood was covering the knife he held in his opposing hand.

"I had to do it, Cethin," he said and sighed, coughing a second time. "I had to kill them. What does this make me?"

"There is a difference between sacrifice and murder," I answered. "You had to protect yourself. Just as Vortain thought he was protecting—" I stopped, hoping I did not give cause for question.

"They were after the key, Cethin. They have it," Declan said and coughed another time. "That was the key, wasn't it? The key to the box," he said and sat against the pillar closest him. "I couldn't protect it. There were too many of them."

"Where have they gone?" I asked and knelt to him, placing my hand over his large wound. "Valgolig," I whispered, feeling the Sun respond.

"A man took the key; he entered the temple and as he approached me I could no longer move. I didn't have control of my muscles. When he was leaving was when the others showed. They were in a frenzy, Cethin. I have never seen so many driven mad. They taunted me, telling me how they killed the others, and left them to rot in the courtyard. I was able to kill two of them before the last, a woman, fled."

"Did he speak?"

"He said nothing. He dropped me when he saw it hanging from the post. I was about to meditate in the heat of the spring when they entered. It made me realize that it was all that he was here for. I could but see his eyes. He was Viscera, Cethin." Declan sat upright, shaking his head. "We are too late."

"Viscera? You're certain?"

"Yes. They were under his spell. It cannot be coincidence that this happened."

"It is a terrifying thought that he went as far as enlisting the help of a Viscera," I sighed. "I will die before that box is opened," I answered and stood.

"And I will stand, burying them until I know that the light of the sun has prevailed," Declan stated and stood, weakly. He took a breath, holding the wound on his chest. I held my hand out toward him, my palm facing his body. *Valgolig.*

As it was in thought, the Sun worked to fill my demand, causing the wounds to stop bleeding. "They didn't fight back when the brigands began to maim them. They stood, letting them beat and stab and slaughter. They did not let their voices escape them, nor did they close their eyes. Cethin, they did not even try to run," Declan answered and dropped his knife upon the ground. "What would cause one to devalue their life so?"

"I do not believe that they did not value their lives, Declan. I believe their devotion to how they lived was stronger than their will to break it," I answered.

"Their devotion," he said and looked at my eyes. "Resulted only in their deaths."

I nodded, releasing a breath. "Perhaps they realized that they could not answer violence with violence."

"Yet you believe you can," Declan stated.

"I do not believe that this madness can be stopped without silencing it."

"And them," Declan said and pointed toward the courtyard. "Did they believe the same? Did they believe that the killing would stop if they did not raise hand against them?"

"No," I answered. "They knew that they would die. But, if they had raised their hands to stop them, they would have become no different."

"What do I have left?" Declan asked, holding his arms out to his sides.

"There is something, or else you would have died as they did," I stated and turned, looking at Seligsara in my hand before I began to leave.

"I would have, had you not come back for me."

"I swore to protect those who have taken this path," I answered, and stopped, turning toward him.

"Yet I strayed. I abandoned you."

"You did not abandon me. You merely found cause for your life elsewhere."

"What of the others?" Declan asked. "Do they still live?'

I looked to the floor, the pain of my loss coming over me once again. "Our numbers have dwindled. As the soul inside of me weeps."

"Do you know what they've taken from you?"

"Hollow is the heart that carries this burden. I'm trapped in ambiguity. Do I end his life in vengeance for her? Or do I show him the mercy that she represented?" I asked, mostly to give the words form.

"Mercy? Look at what surrounds us, does he deserve mercy? Do you think she would want you to give mercy after seeing this?"

The words stung, lying deep within my wounds and pushing fresh blood forth from them. "I do not know," I answered.

"There comes a time when things can only be settled in blood," Declan answered, taking a small, shallow breath. "You live for her memory. Make certain that she is remembered. It does not make you a bad man for ceasing death by creating it."

I was left with those words when Sindara joined me, acquiring silence at the sight beheld. There were three monks on the floor, resting in their own fluids, their tan tunics stained in the nectar that once granted them consciousness. She shifted her eyes upon the carnage one last time before addressing me.

"What of the key?"

"Lost to us," Declan answered.

"There is still time," Sindara said quickly and looked toward the door.

"He has it," I said suddenly, looking out over the balcony. The steam from the springs rose toward the roof.

"You are certain?" Sindara asked in a sudden panic.

"If not now, then soon," Declan said and took a step forward, clutching his leg. His face was twisted in pain.

"We must protect the second key," Sindara said. "Take it somewhere it will never be found."

"He may not know the path that leads through Septentria," Eshkan said from the door, working the strings on his bow. "We can take it to Winds Hollow. I know where it will be safe."

"We cannot go through Septentria, what awaits us is far more dangerous than encounters with the king's men," Sindara answered.

"Fear has no voice until you give it purpose," Eshkan said. "We will be fine. It will lead us past Mordestai, on the western side of the marsh where the tundra still borders. The area is covered by trees, no one will be able to see us coming in that direction, which is why I was surprised that Vortain saw me."

Sindara looked at me and then at Dacian who had entered only a moment ago. She nodded and looked down at the floor, taking a breath. "I suppose we will trek through the winter, then."

"The mines," I said.

"The dredging mines?" Eshkan said and closed his eyes, exhaling. "They have been abandoned for tens of years. We may face our end. The roads will be safer."

"The roads boast harm, the inns are full of thieves and mercenaries. Things that belong to us fetch a price in Defaltor. Our teeth. Our skin. Their need for currency to obtain supplies for the months ahead makes them desperate," Sindara said.

"I have not come this far, nor have I watched those close to me die to hesitate on which route to take. It is the most direct. If we do not take time to rest, our weariness will serve as only another advantage he has over us."

"There is one inn I would frequent when doing reconnaissance, that is where we should rest," Eshkan answered.

"How far from here?" Dacian asked.

"The road will see us there in days. The mines, hours," Eshkan returned.

"We take the mines and depart immediately," I answered. Turning to Declan, I bowed my head one time, acknowledging him. "I will not say farewell, for I hope to see you again."

"My only wish is that you prevail with your life," Declan answered.

"I make no promises, but I can assure you that I will fight until my last breath. My we meet again, my friend," I said, and began walking from the monastery to avoid another protest from Sindara. I looked forward to the rest we would gain in a few short hours but knew we would have to fight to get there. The mines would be crawling with those forgotten.

◆ ◆ ◆

I arrived at the old door to the mineshaft first, rotting from its hinges, one side barely hanging in its frame from rusted iron tacks. I dismounted my horse, stroking her mane as the wind howled behind me. I took a few steps closer to the mine, a chasm of darkness beyond its entry. Sticking my head inward, I listened as the nothingness crept inside me. Silence, darkness. The only scent was that of mildew, alerting me that something synthetic awaited within. Old tools, as forgotten as the hands they once filled lined the path inward. Lanterns, with candles half burned, wax yellowing from ages of rot. The mines seemed empty, desolate, void of life. That did not mean we would be without hazard, however.

The others caught up to me, leading their horses toward mine. "What are we to do with them?" Eshkan asked. "It will be too dangerous to lead them through the mine. For them, and for us. I doubt that we will be able to get new mounts once we've reached Winds Hollow. We have nothing left to barter, and horse traders do not travel this far north."

"I can get them to Winds Hollow," Sindara answered.

"No, we will need you with us in the caverns," I stated. "If there are Veracith, it will be easier for us to dispatch them in the darkness."

"You are right, they may be lurking," Sindara asked. She narrowed her eyes, as if searching in sight and sound.

"It is a strong possibility. Dark. Abandoned."

"Usually, their hives are built upon a food source..." Dacian suggested.

"Yes. But we should still use caution," I answered.

"So we are at an impasse," Sindara said.

"I will take them," Eshkan said. "I will ride as fast as I can."

"Are you certain?"

"We have no choice. It will not matter if we've made it to Winds Hollow if we have no means of travel," Eshkan stated. "You know how I am with the mounts. I will make it there."

"Fine. Eshkan, take the horses," I answered. "Your contact in the inn? Who are they?"

"Her name is Suthira. She has long dark hair and reddish eyes that match her skin. Easily recognized. She is the only Rustanzi to have ever lived there," Eshkan answered. "I'll meet you in town. When you get there, tell her that I've sent you. She's very knowledgeable, she may be able to help us," he smirked and shook his head softly, tying the reins of the horses together. "If I take the old hunting path, I'll avoid horse thieves."

I nodded my head toward him, and he returned the gesture. As he rode off, I looked toward the mouth of the mine, hesitating only for a moment. It would be untruthful for me to say that I did not worry about him, riding the roads alone. I stepped inside the dark, feeling the emptiness surrounding me as if it was cognizant of my presence. It tore at me, grazing my skin in silence as it searched for weakness. Once it had realized I had no humanness off which to feed, it left me, searching for its next victim. I looked to my left, recognizing a torch on the wall and looked back to Dacian, seeing that he was beginning to struggle in sight as we progressed. Sindara picked up on this too, grasping a torch from the wall and placing her hand over top of it, whispering to give it flame. She then handed it to him, speaking.

"It will blind them. Fire, light are their enemies."

"What creates them?"

"No one knows. Some say it was the Viscera," Sindara answered. "But of course, that is just what men speak. The tomes of the Viscera are esoteric. Only their circle has read them, and a few of the cognizant nonhumans."

"It would not surprise me," Dacian said, using his torch to break the shadows surrounding us. "Have you ever fought one?"

"I have not."

"Cethin?"

"No," I answered, using discretion in my steps. I could see the rotting wood beams on the walls, nearly calcified into them. Limestone. It was known to me now why I could not smell decay.

"I wonder how far these caverns lead," Dacian said, being careful to illuminate his path. He was looking toward the ground. Inadvertently relying on us to be his eyes.

"There doesn't seem to be many paths we can follow, so as long as this one remains consistent we should find the exit with ease," Sindara answered. Dacian nodded softly, keeping his torch steady in his hand. We walked in silence through the first tunnel, the scent of lime becoming more and more prominent the further we traveled. I heard shuffling in the dark, equating it to small rodents, or other creatures. I began to feel a sense of uncertainty, knowing that something else existed here with us. If the lime was enough to obscure my sense of smell, perhaps it was also enough to obscure theirs. Though assumption of this could be fatal.

The tunnels of the caverns began to become damp, water dripping in from the earth. It became less of a mine and more of a cave, as the tools and structures became scarce until they disappeared altogether. Sindara stopped in the center of our path, looking around. "Strange to me," she stated and turned to look at the last workbench we had passed. In likeness to the door guarding entry, old, swollen from the water moisture that seeped through the cave walls. "How the trails of human progress would just end abruptly like this."

"Moreso a sign that something happened to them," I said. "Though it would have had to have been years ago. There are no signs of struggle, death. We can only speculate."

"I wonder what story keeps people from entering this place," Sindara touched the dagger on her side. "Human curiosity is at most times more powerful than legends or fables."

"Not this time," I answered and moved toward the wall, touching a large crack through it with my fingers. "Dacian, your light," I said. In reaching me, the flame illuminated what looked to be claw marks in the wall, coupled with an incision from the tip of a blade.

"These marks... not Veracith..." Sindara said.

"Viscera."

"You think..." Dacian stopped, reaching for his sword.

"Do you see that mark on the wall, above the scratches?" I said and moved toward it. Dacian raised his flame. "These are sigils."

"I've... never seen this sigil before," Sindara said and neared it. "Only the crowns have a sigil, and their sigils encompass their covens." She looked at us quickly. "This means that whoever this belongs to isn't playing by Deventer's rules."

Someone with wisdom knew not to cross the Viscera, knew how cautious to be when engaging. We continued along, only stopping a second time when Dacian picked something up off the ground, turning it over a few times in his palm. The black stone produced a red and gold shimmer on one side of it, and he tossed it to me for inspection. "I find it hard to believe this survived years of abandon."

"Summoning stone," I answered upon catching it, handing it to Sindara.

"We are not safe here," she said and grasped her crossbow, affixing two bolts.

"If we are found...." I started.

"Then we will broach that when the time comes, but now we should focus on finding a way out," she answered and continued, taking more care to look at the walls. It was true that any staining from spilled blood would have been washed away by Earth water, any scent masked by the lime. It was as if the caverns wished to purify themselves despite whatever events took place here. I did not doubt it was an old sanctum of the Viscera, that we'd find altars, things trapped by countermeasures, the stone had proven that. But something beyond stories must have happened here that made certain humans avoid entry. My curiosity only grew the longer we wandered on yet was near sated when we came across an altar. Bones were strewn upon a dark-colored stone, a small tray made of amber stained in blood resting on top of it. Red candles were burned to their bases, ashes of a flower beneath them.

"Small organs," Sindara said, kneeling to inspect the amber tray. She rotated it to get a better look and backed away quickly. "This offering was given just days ago," she looked up at me in urgency, standing. "The exit, now."

"The air is different here," Dacian said. "There must be an aperture ahead."

Sindara nodded in response and moved ahead. Despite the silence in response, he did not repeat himself. We crept along the passage quietly, until we reached Sindara where the mine cliffed and dropped into a small valley below. Sindara was at the edge of the cliff, watching as two Veracith were feasting on the corpse of a young girl, her leg broken. The way they tore at her was savage, demonstrating their desperation as they sucked the marrow from her bones. The larger one snapped at its guest, snatching a bone from it as it was about to feed.

I turned Seligsara in my hand and Sindara moved her hand outward, reaching for her crossbow. She loaded two bolts, raising to her eye to take careful aim at our enemies below. She released the first one, and it lodged into the forehead of her target, killing it instantly. The second one turned in alarm and she released the second bolt. It sailed through the air and caught it in his temple. It reached for the bolt, but sank down to the ground, becoming lifeless. She held her hand up, waiting a few moments before continuing.

"Stay close to me, Dacian," she whispered as he flanked alongside her. "I will lead you through the dark."

"Wait," I said and stopped, peering across the valley. "Something festers as the tunnel begins again."

"More of them?"

"That, I am unsure of. But as it gets closer, it feels as if it is something else," I said and climbed down to the next level, squinting my eyes as if to enhance my ability to see. "It grows darker just past the frame of the tunnel. We should not go without flame," I answered.

Sindara looked around her, grasping the torch from the wall just past the door we had entered. "This will attract attention," she stated.

"But it will keep them away, so long as the torches do not go out," I answered and looked down to where the Sun was beneath my flesh. "Marakesh," I said loudly, watching as flames began to burn from beneath my skin. I winced slightly, acclimating to the heat.

"Using your skin as a conductor. Are you mad?" Sindara asked and looked at her torch, igniting it. She held her hand out toward Dacian, repeating the process.

"They will be less tempted to try," I answered.

"You are more like Zerian than you want to admit," Sindara answered. I ignored her words, listening as cries were heard within the bowels of the mineshaft ahead of us.

"They've already picked up on the fire. We need to keep moving."

"You need to take a proper conductor. If you continue to use your flesh, you will be consumed by your need to feed," Sindara said. "You put us all in danger, mostly Dacian."

"We do not have time for that now," I answered as the cries began to become louder. "If we don't move now, we will become outnumbered."

"I fear we are running straight into a trap," Sindara said. "I can sense how dark that tunnel is. That is where they are strongest."

"Then we will have to create light to combat them."

"Cethin, that will weaken us."

"There is no other way," I said and moved my eyes to hers, showing my sincerity.

"The old tunnel," Dacian stated. "We can use the old tunnel to flood them from this one. We might have a better chance at fighting them there."

"We do not want to become surrounded," Sindara answered. As the cries became louder, I looked down at Seligsara, watching the blade gleam against the fire on my arm.

"We do not have many options. It is either wait them out here or use the tunnel."

Sindara shook her head and waved us on, heading back toward the entrance to the mines. I looked toward the opening at the end of the valley, hearing snarling from wet jaws.

"Go with her!" I shouted to Dacian, breaking him from his stare. I watched for a few seconds more before following them. I was unsure of Dacian's suggestion to retreat, but I placed my trust in his strategy. As I reached them, I took notice of their readied weapons.

"How many do you think there are?" Dacian asked, a shred of nervousness in his voice.

"It is hard to say."

"Have you fought them before?" Dacian asked.

"I have," Sindara said quietly, holding her crossbow at an angle so that a bolt would sail just past my frame. "Do not let them strike first."

She did not elaborate on the statement as we waited, the sounds of the creatures coming from the dark. They slowly became louder, shrieks enough to drive a man mad with anxiety. Dacian pulled his sword, gripping the hilt gently in his hand. Sindara looked at me suddenly with a sense of urgency I had never before seen in the eyes of sister in arms.

"Make sure you do not become consumed," she answered and turned toward the door, casting a bolt through the cheek of an angry Veracith. She landed another, and pulled her sword, targeting the one directly behind it.

"Watch our backs. I'll need you to take care of them if they should appear," I answered. Sindara fought another off before a larger one crashed through the opening, targeting me with angry, burning eyes. Despite the flame that was deterring the others, it charged, hunger distorting its judgments. I stabbed forward first, twisting my sword from its chest and to its head. When it crashed down upon me, I grasped its arm with my own, setting it aflame. It shrieked, turning toward the distraction and I removed its head with one motion, kicking his corpse from me in order to throw another to the ground.

"Cethin, this is the last of them!" Sindara shouted and slashed one by the throat, turning to disarm another. His corpse fell to the ground, returning the cavern to its eerie silence.

More Veracith crept through the tunnel, hissing as they reached us. Sindara readied her crossbow and nearly fired as they began to back away, retreating into the walls from whence they came. It was then a man dressed in dark armor came into view; his eyes covered in blood.

"You've something I want," he said, looking at me. Sindara's eyes widened, and she lowered her crossbow, Dacian quickly reaching for his sword. She placed her hand against his wrist, pushing his arm downward.

"Wise," he said and redirected his gaze toward me. "The key. Hand it to me and I will spare you."

"I will not just willingly hand it over."

"These monuments, these structures. They are all to worship me," the Viscera said and stretched his hand outward. I became dizzy, struggling to reach for my weapon. "It would do nothing."

"You...you created madness in those bandits, caused them to attack the monks," Dacian said and moved forward, Sindara holding him back.

"Don't," she said.

"Do you want to experience the madness I can inflict? I will play with your mind and rewrite it; you would never see the outside world again."

"Cethin... hand it to him," Sindara cautioned. "He still does not know where the box is, we can take solace in that."

I took a breath and reluctantly reached into my armor, my hand suddenly freezing as I touched it. I no longer had control of it. My arm tensed, slowly moving outward toward the Viscera. The key floated from my palm, turning over twice before it vanished, our foe holding it upward toward his face. "Until we meet again," he said. He, too, disappeared.

The cries of the Veracith were heard again, and Sindara grabbed my arm, pulling me toward where Dacian had run.

He pushed his body against the old door with force, and despite doing so, it barely moved in its antiquated frame. Sindara joined him, the door breaking from its hinges. We breached the morning light; eyes being seen in the shadow of the doorway. Hissing, snarling.

"We didn't even try to fight him," Dacian said and turned, pointing a finger at Sindara. "How do we know you aren't working with him?"

"Dacian, she was sparing our lives," I said and exhaled. "I did not wish to part with it, but there were only two outcomes, both of which he gained possession of the key."

"Surely the three of us could have…"

"That is no normal Viscera," Sindara said and shivered. "He holds a power I have not before seen. I don't know what his involvement in this is, but I hope that is the last we will see of him."

"I still think we should not have given up so easily."

"Our corpses would be ravaged by Veracith in those mines," Sindara said. "Allow me time to think. We must be missing something."

"We should regroup with Eshkan," I responded. It was going to be a long journey. My thoughts raced, where could it be?

The wind was colder here, a light snow upon the ground. The wind kicked swirls of it upward, dancing until they could be carried no longer. Physical allusions to Septentria. It wasn't far from here, perhaps another hour by horseback. We arrived at the town of Winds Hollow; a lot larger than I imagined it to be. There was a wall built on the left toward the land of the Septens, people stationed on top with crossbows. Beneath it, the inn.

"Dacian and I will take a table. Find her," I said and walked ahead. I was feeling weary, the shortness of my answers displaying that fact. I hadn't fed in some time, and the energy used in the mines tired me further. After sleeping, I would have to hunt.

Sindara went ahead, opening the heavy inn doors. Light spilled from within them and illuminated the ground. Its brightness was unlike anything I had ever seen before, the closest sight being sunlight upon the stones of the courtyard in Ophidian. Once she disappeared inward, we followed and headed toward one of the tables. Dacian sat and stretched his arms. "At least it's warm in here."

"Perhaps you'd like to sit closer to the fire?" I asked.

"Here is fine. We have a good view of Sindara in case something happens," Dacian answered. I did not dispute him. Instead, I watched her sit at the end of the bar, waiting until the eyes of the humans surrounding us were taken off her. Whispers. Sardons from their coven. Suthira turned to stand directly in front of Sindara, smiling. They began to speak, Sindara quietly mentioning something that made her eyes light. She brought up Eshkan, she must have. Suthira looked toward us and spoke to the other barkeep who entered the kitchen. I watched the doors carefully, though it was only a moment before the man re-entered the room, carrying a small crock of soup with bread. The two had one more exchange before Sindara nodded and joined us, sitting next to me.

"She said that once Dacian is finished, we are to meet her upstairs. She'll leave someone to tend the inn."

"What can you read from her?" I asked.

"Well, she's genuine. She and Eshkan..."

"I saw her eyes," I answered and smirked.

"I suppose we are waiting for me, then," Dacian said and picked up the spoon nearest him.

"Eat. It is necessary. You and I should soon hunt," I said and looked toward Sindara.

"Where do you suppose we go?"

"We will worry about that when the time comes," I answered and watched as Suthira moved toward one of the tables in the back and picked up two empty flagons, carrying them back with her to the bar. Her clothing was distinct from Rustanzen. Dacian finished and stood, taking the bowl toward the front. He thanked the cook who nodded with a smile, Suthira taking notice. She began to walk toward the stairs, Sindara grasping my arm.

"What do you think we will gain by this?"

"I do not know, but we should not leave it to chance. Eshkan said she is knowledgeable," I stated.

Sindara replied with only a nod, and we entered the room, my eyes immediately coming across colored candles in its corners.

"So, you are the Serpents that Eshkan has told me so much about," Suthira smiled. "I am happy to see that some of you survived the fires. I sent my raven, but she returned with this. I assumed it was too late," she answered and presented us with a piece of burned cloth, once pink in color. "Your friend tells me that Eshkan still lives."

"Yes. He is traveling here now, with our horses. We had to make our way here through the old mines."

Suthira shivered slightly at the mention of it. "You survived Vorswoth. Fortune smiles upon you."

"Not so much fortune as will," I answered. "We had to get to you as soon as possible."

"I figured this wasn't a social call," Suthira said and offered a small laugh. "Shall we wait for Eshkan to arrive?"

"No, we can fill him in later. Sindara and I must hunt once we are finished here, given you do not mind if we stay here for the night."

"That goes without saying. It has been too long since last Eshkan and I saw one another," Suthira stated. "So, we begin. What is it that you wish to find?"

"The box of Barroqas," I said, evoking a bewildered glance from her.

"The box of eternal night, lost to time. The order has been searching for it for ages." Two Magar in Cilevdan. It was here.

"A Seraphice seeks to find it, we must make sure that does not happen," I added. "We had both keys, but they were lost to us. So much blood has been spilled."

"All for a box that cannot be found," Suthira said and took a deep breath. "Very well, what can you give me that will assist in my scrying?"

"My memories," I said and exhaled deeply. I didn't wish to become a potential victim to a Magar's control, but times were dire. She did not seem malicious, I don't believe Eshkan would confide in her were she that.

"Allow me to make preparations," Suthira stated and moved toward each pillar of candles, lighting them one by one. She moved a small bowl to the center of the room, a scented powder within it. She moved her flame toward it, watching as it caught fire. She sat before it and closed her eyes, breathing the fumes in deeply. It was when she opened her eyes that she motioned for me to sit in front of her. They glowed golden, shifting to a whitish blue. I complied, and she placed a hand on each of my temples, a surge of energy felt through my head. My eyes became golden as well, and I continued to breathe deeply to not resist.

"I see death. So much death," she said, her voice now doubled, two as one. "An island, surrounded by water, wind, rain. Orchards, villages. A tower, protected by ghosts. A tomb, scratches on the walls, a bracelet. A woman, shrieking. A death prison, designed to keep her contained. She had become something else. At the center... a box."

I fell backward, Suthira extinguishing the flames. "You must retrieve it. Bring it to me. We will hide it where it will not be found."

"You mean give it to the order," I said and rubbed my head. "Forgive me, I do not feel comfortable with that."

"You mistake my meaning," Suthira said and offered me a hand. I reluctantly took it, rising off the floor. Lightheaded, the room slowly spinning. "Eshkan will find a place to hide it, he has vast knowledge of Cilevdan. I will erase his memory of it, his memory of the journey to it."

"How will that eliminate your knowledge of it?" I asked.

"I am Suthira Aabndkojar, Magaria Loremaster. The world's secrets are entrusted to us, as we have mastered the channels of the mind. Each one of us is given shreds of a memory so that we alone cannot reveal its secret. Once I return to the order with the memory, the Grandmaster will dissect it, and distribute a piece of it to each of us. Only someone as masterful as Grandmaster Kaitaga would be able to reassemble them, and she cannot as her power is pledged to keeping them in pieces. There are those who would abuse power, but the Loremasters are sworn to keep arcane knowledge a secret."

It was then Eshkan entered, out of breath. "I could have sworn that I would beat you here."

"The box is on the island," I said.

"What are we waiting for?!" Eshkan said and looked toward Suthira. "Bittersweet this moment, I am off again."

"You're to return to me with the box. We will ensure its location to secrecy."

"A delightful journey that will be."

"We will have to hunt on the road," Sindara said and turned to leave. She hesitated a moment, looking back into the room. "Thank you, Suthira."

We were quickly upon horse, Sindara only speaking once we made it back into the warmer region of Cilevdan.

"That star," Sindara said and pointed to it. "He will change in two days' time."

"Have you seen it?" Dacian asked.

"Yes," she stopped for a moment. "He nearly consumed me, but he stopped, asking me what a Sardon was doing so far from Morrenvahl. I was scouting the area after being given a lead. It was then I began to feign an alliance with him. I was after Zerian's sword, his stone, when Savantin revealed he was looking for it."

"Do you think he has them? The keys?"

"It's hard to say. But either he does, or the Viscera does," I said. "I hope it's the former."

"A Viscera has the keys?" Eshkan asked in horror. "How did this come to pass?"

"The mines. We must have been tracked there," Sindara said.

"Was the Viscera alone?"

"He was," Sindara answered. "There was no way of stopping him. In my brief time dealing with the Viscera, I have never been that apt to lie down arms and give in. That encounter should not be forgotten easily."

"Nor will it be," I said. "Suthira said it was in the tomb and mentioned the bracelet. How could we have missed it before?"

"It must be hidden well if in plain sight," Eshkan stated. "The ghosts of Serpents past are all that stand between the box and the hands of another."

"We will be there in a few days," I responded. "Whether or not we are the first to discover it remains to be seen." The words marked a long, heavy silence. We were almost at the end.

THE DARK OF STARS

Days had passed since the burning of Lord's Valley. Ohric hoped that it was acceptable, and thought that if they destroyed the city, that others would be hesitant in raising arms against them. They made it to the small town of Savoi within hours of ensuring Lord's Valley was no longer, and Ohric anxiously awaited his commander. It wasn't until the third morning that Savantin arrived, his armor burned but he seemed none the worse for wear. It was likely far from the truth, knowing what happened in the manor house was an exhausting battle, also knowing that Savantin would not speak of it. Ohric had already dispersed Terganus' men to surrounding populaces, deeming Savoi was safe enough to stay in with his few men.

At first Savantin disapproved of Terganus' men leaving them so quickly, but the feeling left him as the day fled. The fourth day was when things became interesting, as a man dressed in black and darkened leather armor walked into the inn. Savantin tensed as he approached, Ohric becoming unnerved at the sight. He reached their table, pulling a chair out from underneath it and sat across from them, leaning back and crossing his arms.

"I'm surprised you thought this place fitting," Savantin said and loosened posture enough to gesture. "I'll need to retrieve your payment."

"I see," the man said. "Do so and return."

"Ohric," Savantin said. "Go to my quarters and return with the small chest. It'll be by the bed."

Ohric nodded and made himself scarce quickly. Savantin watched the Viscera closely as he manifested a goblet from the wooden spoons on the table. Savantin smelled blood shortly after and wondered who it belonged to. Was it someone he previously killed, or someone he left his mark on that suddenly dropped dead?

"It wasn't hard to find them," he said suddenly and took a drink, inhaling deeply. "A monk had one, and your Sardons the other just as you said. You didn't tell me the first knew the latter."

"I didn't know," Savantin said. "Did it matter?"

"Of course it did," the Viscera said, his accent thick, adopting a tone of irritation. Savantin nodded slowly. He knew better than to say otherwise. This was a powerful creature, and he didn't want to provoke him.

"I stopped the Sardons in the old dredging mines southeast of Winds Hollow."

"Isn't that where…"

The Viscera nodded. "Had they resisted, that place would have become their grave."

"They still live?"

"You didn't pay me for their deaths."

"I'm merely curious," Savantin responded. "Aubergrun. I didn't think we could step inside their ground, it's…"

"Blessed. Consecrated. Holy. I took care of that by…influencing some brigands to raid it. Once blood was spilled, there was no more barrier," the Viscera answered. He looked at Savantin once before smirking. "You should have been more specific when you made this contract, Seraphice. I would have spared them."

It was then Ohric returned, carrying a small chest in his right arm. He sat at the table and placed it in its center, handing the key to Savantin.

"I will give you this key for the others."

The Viscera nodded and set the goblet down, reaching inside of his jacket. He pulled two metal objects from it, opening one and placing the second one inside. They intertwined, and he set them down next to the chest.

Savantin's eyes widened at his prize. He finally had them. So close, yet so far. All that was left was finding that which he desired most. He reached across the table and slowly picked them up, staring at how small they looked in his large hand.

"I'll leave you to it," the Viscera said and closed the chest, standing. "Do reach out again once you've found it, I've always enjoyed doing business with you."

"You'll know," Savantin said simply, not taking his eyes from the keys. Within moments, the Viscera was with them no longer, three wooden spoons sitting on the table across from them. He didn't hear Ohric addressing him at first, lost in the aura of the objects he was just given.

"Commander?"

"We're so close now," Savantin said. "The box has to be in Cilevdan."

"Who was that?" Ohric asked. "Araele cautions."

"For good reason."

Ohric nodded, looking again at the keys. "Where will you put them?"

"They will stay with me. Always. If I am struck down, you must take them."

"Take them where?"

"To a place no one will ever find them," Savantin said and stood, walking into the cold. He moved the keys in his hand, feeling the intricate carvings of the larger one. His only lead now was from the woman in Marestith. Orange oil. Savantin placed the keys in his armor and pushed the door violently, walking back over to Ohric.

"It rests at the island."

"The island the mask burned? The one with the old man and his snake of an advisor?"

"Yes, Ohric. That island."

"We had men search there, high and low. Are you certain?"

"Something the Thaumaturgist told me."

"So, it's a guess based on black magick and chance," Ohric said, immediately wishing he hadn't upon Savantin's fiery gaze.

"What she revealed to me was crucial. Those beads I found in the old cultist cave were covered in some sort of orange oil. The apothecary in Lord's Valley said she had a source in the South that she could no longer reach."

"Likely due to the death that struck the island…"

"Yes, yes now you see. It's there, Ohric. All of this time, I could have had it in my possession." Savantin waited in silence a moment before he slammed his fist down on the table, creating a large crack in its surface. He turned abruptly when Ohric stood, calling out to him. "Where do you go?"

"I am going back there. If I must remove the buildings stone by stone, so be it. I should not have neglected this before," he said hastily and walked to where he had secured his mount. He'd reach the island in no less than three days now, if he traveled the inroads that had been carved through the mountains. Ohric would warn him of the dangers, but nothing else mattered to him now. Bandits, rebels, creatures. Nothing. He climbed his horse, the winds picking up now, carrying gusts of snow down from the peaks of Septentria. Howling in his ears with unspecified anger, an emotion he felt within himself. He had more than enough time to compose himself, on this ride through the wilderness, his coadjutant trailing behind. He hadn't ordered him to come, hadn't asked him. Yet he was there, until the end it seemed.

Had his mind not been so focused on anger, he might have even thought about the way the seasons seemed to change between where he was and his destination, though only a short distance apart. The strength of the Septen mountains was enough to have an impact on half of the region, and the Rustanzen empire carried its heat from across the ocean. It reminded him of a time so long ago, when his presence was required on distant shores...

◆ ◆ ◆

The ship had been tossing all night upon angry waves that tirelessly tried to sacrifice it to the depths. He waited, eyes closed within his quarters, listening to war between the elements unfold around him. Anxious cries of ship hands above partnered with the howling of wind upon sea created a cacophony of chaos. It had been quite some time since anything was louder than his own breathing. He was called upon by Ozrach, customarily without much notice before departure, to accompany him to the empire of Rustanzen. Why the Rustanzi Emperor wanted a meeting with Ozrach was unknown to him. He could guess.

The sea continued to churn until the early hours of morning, when he heard a cry from above. The man's voice was exaggerated, out of breath. The harbor to the empirical city of Sarcosos was in sight. Savantin stood then, putting on his armor in contempt. He wished to wear the sets that were usual for him, but it was insisted that he wear a royal set. This set was more elaborate, blue stone in the shoulders and spaulders, a pattern on the chest inlaid with anemone. He wanted to be decorated as much as the queen's handmaidens wanted to return to their peasant lives at their families' farms. He had no choice in the matter, never did, and picked up the helmet that was sitting on the chair adjacent to him. This one was blank, shining, new. It did not show his prowess in battle, the challenges he had overcome.

He thought that wearing his customary armor would show the emperor that Terrenveil's forces were not weak. There were many cracks from blades upon the spaulders, and accompanying scars across his arms to match them. The form-fitting piece for his torso had also seen damage, smashed directly by the head of a mace. Several indentations were created that day, as well as a large dark bruise beneath it that did not relent until he had sacrificed. Yet Ozrach thought it better to show off adornment rather than strength, and he had no choice but to comply.

He emerged from the darkness of the cabin, a light rain hitting him from above. It joined the water on the deck creating small ripples as it made contact. A mist was rising off the water surrounding the docks. Foreboding, he thought for a moment before his mind crossed over to thoughts of cold rains meeting warm waters. Ozrach joined him on deck, much softer than he had been in his own days of battle. Lazy. Weak, Savantin thought as he was directed to climb the ladder downward to be sure there was not a threat waiting for them at the bottom. Once his boots hit the wood of the dock he turned, staring into the faces of two Rustanzi guards. He assumed them to be from the palace, though from what he heard the garb of all guards was elaborate and colorful.

The men began to speak to one another in their native tongue, Savantin watching them with careful eyes. Ozrach reached him, speaking.

"Savantin, I ordered Ohric to remain on the ship. Should anything happen I know he will ensure its safety until the end of our discussion."

Savantin took the remark, breathing deeply before saying something that would make his king look a fool in the company of the imperial guard. He didn't want to assume their language wouldn't be understood and become the fool himself. If Ozrach had listened to him and filled the crew with more soldiers, a raid would be unlikely. It was then the guards turned, waving to follow. Ozrach looked on anxiously, and Savantin's own eyes stalked hungrily back and forth between the sights of the city.

Two large stone walls separated the docks from Sarcosos within, banners hanging on either side. Once they entered, there was a large barracks staffed with a garrison, watching as they walked toward the market. Thirty-two men, endless arms inside. Some watched, others continued to play a game atop an old mahogany table. Coin spent on the comfort of his men. The sight had him thinking of the mess halls at their own barracks, old tables that had seen their days in the palace lined the walls. They were only given to the soldiers because they were replaced with more expensive wonders.

They walked through markets, the spices and tapestries alive with scents he had never breathed in, colors he had never seen. Ohric would appreciate this, he thought, immediately returning to why he should be accompanying them. The stalls seemed endless, a boast to Terrenveil's own markets that were smaller in nature, and inherently less busy. Coin flowed in the city itself yet trickled in the outer colonies.

The palace was finally in sight, and in looking upon it he realized how impressive the visage was. Elaborately decorated in unison with the rest of the city, pillars seemingly made of gold. He imagined that when the sun was brightest, hottest, it illuminated the palace at such an intensity that it became an ever-present beacon in the lives of his people. Red stones lined the stairs, patterns swirled with smaller blue stones in the center. There were tapestries as they passed the large porch toward the doors and palm trees at each pillar that held the roof above them.

"I have never seen such majesty," Ozrach whispered, his eyes in wonder at the gems, the stones. Savantin did not answer, his mind focused on the contents within the palace and its many doors. He'd make note of the exit and watch the corridors and hallways inside. The guards from the docks opened large, dark doors and bowed their heads, moving their hands inward. A sign to continue without them. He allowed himself to relax a little, then.

The room was large, hollow except for pillars similar to the ones they'd seen just beyond the doors. At the end of the room was a large golden throne, the emperor of Rustanzen sitting upon it, having a conversation with a man in a dark blue robe, hood and sleeves outlined with a gold arabesque pattern. He bowed in obeisance toward the emperor, making his way toward a door left of the throne. It was then the emperor stood, his height in likeness to Savantin's and walked toward the two, the guards on the sides of the rooms moving their weapons upward. A woman walked out from behind the throne, dressed in a black and gold armor to fit her figure. She had two golden rings in her cheek, green eyes watching him like a viper. Her mouth was covered with a black cloth, a gold pattern on it that matched that of the hooded man. Her hand was lightly touching the scabbard of her sword, also gold in color.

"Aspesh, aspesh Aadeera," the emperor said softly. The woman returned her hand to her side. Savantin raised an eyebrow. His eyes met hers in a different nature now. The woman was seasoned. He could see the scars below her neck, her arms. He found himself fascinated, wanting to ask her about her journey to become the personal guard of the emperor of Rustanzen. It would be an interesting story, an inspiring one. Ozrach's generally sexist nature resulted in few women in his ranks, a mistake. There was a fire that burned within them, and they could be as passionate about battle as they were passionate about all things. This woman had a strong shell of focus, the willingness to protect and to fight until life left her eyes. Determination.

"Come," the emperor said, his accent heavily distorting the word. "I wish to speak somewhere more relaxing."

Ozrach nodded and walked side by side with the man, leaving Savantin and Aadeera to watch one another carefully before Savantin lowered his head slightly and extended his hand outward. The vipress paused a moment before following them, Savantin making sure he was not a step behind, or one ahead. He could hear Ozrach's muffled voice, speaking of the beauty of his city. But what was more interesting to him was the sound of Aadeera's heart. The pulse was not quick, it was steady, the sign of a perfect warrior in battle. Though not a lady of the palace, he could smell black currant and vanilla on her skin, a sign that she was passionate about her overall appearance. The thick dark liner that surrounded her eyes had also given that away to him. He imagined many men lusted for the woman yet feared even glancing in her direction. Her aura was pleasing.

They reached a room that held a large golden table, a small garden on the other side of it with a brook running through the center. There was a small open circle in the ceiling above them, sunlight shooting downward onto an exotic tree with reddish flowers on the branches. Nothing went without decoration here.

"This is better, yes?" the emperor asked and first sat at the table, inviting Ozrach to do so. "Aadeera, spath set arashna."

In response to his statement, she nodded and stood behind him, causing him to point toward the chair beside him.

"Karath sayma," she answered, which caused the emperor to sigh, a small smile on his face. She defied an order, just then.

"There is a reason I called you all of the way here to have audience with me rather than sending a bird," the emperor answered and held his hand outward, the hooded man returning and placing a roll of parchment into his hand. He thanked him, and the man nodded, backing into the darkness between two pillars to wait until he was called on again.

"This message from the Kingdom of Mauros made its way to me recently. One of my spies sent a bird, yet never returned," he said and furnished it to Ozrach. "The language will make as little sense to you as it did to me at first. My mage had to translate it for me."

Ozrach set the paper down, calling Savantin to his side. He scanned the page, the wording, the language he had seen before, but he could not remember where.

"If you would like, I can have him do so again, now. I know what the message states, but perhaps you'd like to see it relayed to you as it was to me."

"Yes... yes please," Ozrach said and nodded his head quickly. He was quick to show his awe, his eagerness. For being a man of politics, he was too easily trapped by the words of others. It was then the man in blue moved forward again, his hairless chin and lower nose seen beneath his large, thick hood. The man silently mumbled words to himself, moving his hands outward one another, and circled back toward. He ended the motion with the fingers of his right hand touching the palm of the left, a bright blue aura glowing from each word on the paper. Once the glowing had ceased, the words were readable in their own tongue. Ozrach read the page quickly, alight with joy at the fact that he could not believe what he had just seen. The emperor took notice and his eyes briefly rose toward Savantin's, who met him in a cold, digging glare.

"The Kingdom of Mauros seeks to lay siege on both Sarcocos and Terrenveil? Have they even the army?"

"That I do not know. Mauros is much bigger than Rustanzen, and as I'm sure you know, it is the largest kingdom in Cilevdan. It seems as if you will be first target, and if successful they will make their way here, by sea."

"I see," Ozrach answered. "You said your spy didn't return?"

"It is not something for you to worry about, I can assure you. I heard rumors about something in Mauros that belonged to my family and was in our possession quite some time ago. My spy was to find out where it was. When this was sent back, I realized that they were looking for more than just my heirlooms."

"When did this reach you?"

"Thirteen days ago. Its content is the reason I sent a bird to you, rather than messengers upon a ship. I thought that maybe the manner it reached you was not as important as the reason why it was sent."

"You are correct in that." Ozrach stated. "It seems we are facing a plot most dangerous."

"I believe that if ignored, a war will break out."

"If it comes to war, then we do not have the numbers to fight them," Ozrach answered. Savantin breathed heavily and closed his eyes. A statement of weakness. The emperor had already brought the size of Mauros in comparison to speech. A seed he planted in Ozrach's head to make further mention of it.

"I could send some of my soldiers to Terrenveil to help you protect your outlying colonies," the emperor answered and watched as his mage took his place again. "Perhaps you'd think about them remaining there until this threat is nullified by whatever means necessary, perhaps even after."

"That is an unreasonable request," Savantin said and moved forward, tired of watching his king being led into a trap. Aadeera placed her hand upon sword again, the emperor moving his hand toward her without moving his face from Savantin's. The expression he had was one of amusement. It was then Savantin removed his helmet so that his own expressions would be seen. "You first mention that their message threatens trade, an ally, and your people. These are all beneficial to you, important, and would be sole causes to extend the help of your armies. Are these things truly what has your concern considering this discovery?" Savantin asked.

"They are."

"Then why is it that you extend help by way of your forces in the form of a bribe?"

"Not a bribe, a suggestion. A topic of thought. If Mauros is brash enough to attack, who is to say that they would not at any time? Would you be ready to fight if it comes to a head after negotiations? Every warlord knows that a standing army in time of peace means preparation for war. If they see that you are prepared, they may not land their attack."

"And every warlord knows that an offer of soldiers from another empire in time of peace means that its emperor wishes to do more than just help an ally protect trade," Savantin answered.

It was the emperor who conceded, then. "Let us just say that my forces could help yours."

"I've no doubt they can, you needn't repeat to convince. The question I raise is for how long would we have our armies merged

SAVANTIN'S CURSE

within Terrenveil? How willing would you be to pull your forces back once this threat from Mauros has passed?"

"I see," the emperor said and placed his hand to his chin, removing it quickly as if ripped from thought. "You worry about our lasting presence in time of peace."

"There is never peace. Someone somewhere is always plotting conquest," Savantin stated and set his helmet upon the table. "We are your ally, trade between our lands is important. But does the mighty emperor of Rustanzen have his eye upon Terrenveil for a different reason?"

"Savantin I really..." Ozrach began, flustered yet timid. He was always timid when speaking to him.

"You have a very cunning Lord of War. A leader would be cautious, but a commander would question. Aadeera would have asked the same."

"I've no doubt she would have," Savantin said and lowered his head. Contrary to his reputation, he knew where to show respect. Ordinarily the remark would have had him sent to his death upon return home. Not only did he speak in place of his king, he challenged an offer from Terrenveil's most essential ally, a very powerful man. However, ordinarily, a king was not a coward and would not bend to whoever intimidated him.

"I can assure you that my intentions are pure. The threat from Mauros threatens us all. While we could easily crush them, we do not want their steel reaching our lands. The damage that war causes... irreparable. Lives taken, homes destroyed, families torn apart. I do not want this end. I do not want this end for your people. My offer still stands."

"We accept," Ozrach answered within seconds of silence. Savantin took a deep breath and closed his eyes, trying hardest not to shake his head. It would have shown strength to send agreement by bird, however he supposed it showed trust to accept his offer face to face. The two men spent time drawing up terms, Savantin's eyes glancing up at Aadeera's periodically. It wasn't that she was uninterested in the terms of the agreement, for she, as the emperor's warlord, would have to know it well. Savantin could not see in them the reason for her fixation. Perhaps she did not trust him, or perhaps the recent exchange intrigued her. He'd have liked to find out. Instead, the two continued to watch one another from across the room...

◆ ◆ ◆

The Island exuded the scent of death. Most of the buildings had been destroyed, leaving only remnants of what they once were, clad in the black of incineration. He pulled the reins to his horse and climbed down hastily, his eyes searching the once bountiful landscape. He spent no time waiting as Ohric's horse skidded to a stop behind his own. His feet hit the ground and hurried forward, the sound of his armor moving against itself was loud in his ears.

"Do you have any idea where you'll first search?"

"I'll begin there," Savantin said and shifted his gaze to the tower. It had somehow mostly survived the blaze; he had assumed because of its distance from other buildings. "There must have been something we missed."

"Even with the key being here as well?"

"It's the perfect trick Ohric," he answered and walked toward the door. It looked different from when he was here last, symbols lining the archway. He was sure each glyph meant something in the language native to their religion, perhaps a chant for protection, or an incantation to summon spirits to them. The halls were hollow, their footsteps echoing as they progressed. He didn't hear Ohric speak to him as they passed into the room at the top of the stairs. The corpses remained. Monuments to the event that occurred here. The old man's blood had dried beneath him, copper in color. His body was slumped over top of it, on his knees, head down as if he had died during a ritual. The other was in the corner, his corpse a black figure overtaken by shadow. Savantin placed his hands back upon the desk closest the window and moved his hands along the papers there, covered in the same blood that once ran through Vortain.

After finding nothing he placed his hands on the side of one of the tables, throwing it across the room in anger. Ohric was standing in the doorway, his eyes wide at the sudden outburst. Savantin moved toward the window, grabbing the corner of the desk and throwing it behind him, slamming the side of his fist against the wall in defeat.

"We'll be here for days, Ohric. Weeks."

"I will aid you in search until we find it," he said. "Let us think. Who did the beads belong to?"

"A woman. But I doubt anyone from the village. It would have had to have been someone he trusted; someone he entrusted the task to."

"So, we forego the village and look in the other buildings."

"The other buildings hardly stand," Savantin said and left the room, descending the tower stairs. "Except for that one…"

The building was small, ash surrounded its doors and collected on the ledges of the windowsills. He pushed the door open, the creak it let out was near deafening. His blood was boiling. His focus was sharp. He almost hadn't noticed the dark star of Norahn overhead, only glancing upon it when the wind blew ashes in his direction.

Inside the building was dark, and no shadows existed until Ohric came close, a torch in his hands.

"Savantin. The star," he said, cautiously looking on. The fact that his commander could now see in complete darkness caused him alarm. He was close, dangerously close to a line that when crossed would take him a long time to return from.

"I know," Savantin answered, his eyes scanning the walls quickly. Another dead end. That was, until his eye caught something in one of the stones on the floor. A golden eye, with a snake surrounding it. The rug had been disheveled enough to reveal it, probably when whoever was inside this building tried to make their escape. He grasped the spade closest to the hearth and jammed it into the floor between the marked stone and the stone next to it, applying as much pressure as he could until it popped out of the floor.

He reached down into the earth and pulled a burlap sack from it, unraveling it quickly. After revealing an old book, he searched the pages hungrily.

"Tespet. Merren. Aeyesh. Gerut. Sce. Syamet. Yeshten. Names. Each with something next to them," Savantin said, mostly to himself. "Each with something next to them. Drawings. Names. Artifacts."

"What have you found?" Ohric asked, moving the torch closer to him. Savantin winced at the sudden intensity of light. It was taking longer to become adjusted to things. He didn't have long. The fight at Lord's Valley was still clawing at him. Eating away his humanness.

"Every one of these names has something associated with it... every one of them except for Syamet."

"How do we find her?"

"She's dead," Savantin said and looked up at the tower. "But I am certain there is more about that up there." He grasped the book firmly in his hand and pushed past his coadjutant, taking a deep breath before he entered the tower for the third time. Once he had, he made his way into the larger room on the left side of the curve of the tower, standing before an opening in the floor. They were here first. He pulled his sword, entering the darkness of the stairwell, Ohric's light in tow.

There were tombs lining the walls, members of the Mask curled in death.

"So, some of them did make an attempt," Ohric said quietly as he lit one of the torches on the wall. This caused the others to take flame, and the silence that followed was monumental. It was then several spectres appeared, taking up arms.

"You are trespassing in this place," one of them hissed.

"One of your dead has something that belongs to me," Savantin said and tightened the grip of his sword.

"Nothing in this tomb is to reach the hand of any mortal, man, or beast," another said.

"Very well then," Savantin said and drew his sword, stretching his shoulders.

"You wish to fight?"

"I will not leave here without it. If that is the only way, I will do what I must."

"How do you intend to fight the dead?" Ohric asked.

"Undead. They may not be able to bleed but they can be eradicated."

"We do not fear that which lies beyond our service here."

"Then I reunite you with your god," Savantin said and moved forward with his sword, shifting sideways to avoid the strike of the Serpent he chose to fight first. He pushed his sword flat beneath his opponent's, pushing it upward with all the strength he possessed, and swiped his sword vertically through the Serpent's throat. The sword fell to the ground in a pool of ectoplasm, and another Serpent stepped forward, swinging her sword in her hand twice before charging him. Their skirmish lasted for a time, and when he ended her, three more took her place, one choosing Ohric as his target.

"I don't know how long I can hold him!" Ohric called out, parrying several attacks between breaths. Savantin looked his way briefly while fighting his attackers, using the smaller one as a shield while catching her blade on his forearm. The other continued to stab into her, trying to get to Savantin when he flipped her over his sword before she could turn into nothingness. As his sword swung upward, he disarmed the last, cutting him across the chest and turning toward Ohric and the remaining ghost.

Savantin threw his sword through the head of the last, the force pinning him to the wall. His body turned, dripping down the wall into a pool on the floor.

"Sorcery and black magick is all that is left here. We shouldn't stay long," Ohric said and took a breath. Savantin ignored the remark, pulling his sword from the wall. "Once we find her resting place, there will be no need to stay."

"Are they still here?" Ohric asked, picking up his torch. Savantin closed his eyes and listened, sighing after a moment. "No. The only heart beating in this place is yours."

Ohric made no sound, not even the sound of a breath. The two continued along the chamber until they stopped in front of an open door, Ohric's torch illuminating it. Upon entry, Ohric shivered at the sight, piles of bones lined the walls, an unspeakable horror tore them from their skins. Araele's voice was loud now, as she continued to tell him to flee.

"Savantin," Ohric said quietly. Savantin ignored this as he walked to the center of the room, picking up a bangle and dropping it onto the floor. He placed his hands on either side of the black pillar that once held it, pulling upward and removing a black cube made of the same stone. He stared at it for several moments, his heart palpitating in his chest. He raised the box upward, staring at the ornate patterns and sigils that ran along the lid, an indentation in the center for the keys to reveal its contents. Closing his eyes, he took a breath of solace, a breath of satisfaction. Soon.

Starting toward the door, he didn't hear Ohric call for him. It wasn't until Ohric repeated his name, this time louder, that he turned chillingly, and looked his coadjutant in the eyes. They had widened partially, a sign that his own looked something dark in nature.

"What is it," he said, more a statement than a question.

"It's just that..."

"I have little patience for hesitation. Either you'll tell me what it is that's on your mind or you will leave it unsaid."

"Araele cautions against opening that box. There are people who deserve it, but there are people who do not... Hope..."

"There is no hope left. Humans commit atrocities among one another, steal, lie, cheat, kill. The king bleeds his kingdom of resources and currency, leaving his subjects famished and poor in the provinces he's supposed to protect. He allows so much to happen under his indolent, dense gaze that his entire kingdom wants to dethrone him. Once I have destroyed them, I will make things right."

"Our plan called for his dethroning, but not for the absence of light. You are using these things against me, these things that you know Araele despises," Ohric said defensively.

"And what would you have me do, Ohric? Hand over the kingdom to Rustanzen? You saw how different life was there, how it was just for the people. But then, you wouldn't be able to worship your precious Araele. You would also be without the light."

"So, this is what it is for you? You open the box, destroy the sun… or you invite destruction to the kingdom and its customs?"

"Now… now you are concerned. These people aren't going to change Ohric. There isn't one left that would. Everywhere we went. Lies. People only out to empower themselves. Every patron of every town, city, and village lived in riches while others suffered in squalor. Do you think they will turn from their lifestyles to help their own people? They do nothing but poorly manage villages and take every bit of coin for themselves. They bleed them of life," Savantin answered, his voice stern, raising.

"And since when do you care about people's lives, Savantin?" Ohric replied, his eyes narrowing whilst saying his name.

Savantin looked down toward the floor, laughing softly and returning his eyes to his coadjutant, rage underlying his voice. "When have I ever lied to you, Ohric," he answered, taking a step toward him. "When have I ever had cause for it? You insult me. And that… I don't take lightly," he said and opened his hand, showing that they were beginning to change.

"You know I cannot let you do this."

"I need to bury the sun!" he shouted, his voice, his anger heard as a haunting echo.

Ohric was silent for a moment, speaking softly as he created a response. "It is what is needed for these people. The life in the trees, the animals. The world will suffer if you open that box and call its power. The world will die."

"So be it."

"I will not let you do this. You only aim to empower yourself. You are delusional. If you banish the sun from this world, you know what will become of you!"

"It was always my plan Ohric. I will find them and kill them for what they've done. But I cannot do so if the sun still rises."

"You never wanted to end Ozrach's rule... you only wanted revenge on those responsible for what happened to you."

"This will be the last time you insult me. Ozrach's rule needs to end. But so do those who created me. They will end now," Savantin answered and pulled the sword from his side. Large, fierce. Ohric answered in reply, hesitating only a moment as Savantin walked forward, lunging his sword toward him. Ohric quickly blocked, bending to the force of Savantin's swing. Ohric attacked, Savantin moving his sword aside so that his coadjutant's blade would slice his arm. Ohric stopped for a moment, looking into the eyes of a man he had traveled alongside for years, raising his sword in sorrow as he blocked another powerful attack. He stumbled backward a little, and in hesitating, blocked another that nearly sent him toward the floor. He pushed forward, sending his blade in that direction. Savantin had again moved his sword downward, this time taking a hit across the shoulder.

"Do not hesitate when you fight me!" Savantin shouted angrily, his voice of no humanness he had ever heard. He quickly unclasped the armor that surrounded his chest, letting it fall to the ground as he moved forward again, swinging twice, each blow becoming more and more powerful. Ohric moved his sword upward again to deflect, Savantin quickly hitting him in the chest, the blow casting his flesh toward the ground.

He stood, slowly, feeling the blood well within his chest. He took a deep breath, sending his thoughts to his goddess. He rushed forward, attacking with haste and anger. Savantin smirked, blocking each one until he threw his sword on the ground, catching him across his torso up toward his throat. The end of Ohric's blade sliced the chain around his neck causing the small ring to fall toward the ground. Savantin grasped the top of the blade in hand, a few seconds passing before blood began to drip down it. He squeezed his fist, the blood running faster as he closed his eyes, raising his head toward the sky.

"Savantin, don't do this," Ohric said, his voice shaking. "Please. You don't have to do this."

"I am a man who is not afraid to die."

"You are no man…"

"Not anymore," he said and moved his head downward, his eyes a color that Ohric had never seen before in a creature. It was then he knew that he must fight until the end.

◆ ◆ ◆

Ozrach paced the throne room nervously planning his next move. The threat of Mauros was still on the horizon, his provinces were on the brink of rebellion, and his commander had not reported to him in days. His disapproving wife sat on the throne, where next to it his lay empty. She watched him with venomous eyes. She crossed her arms as she watched his pacing, opening her mouth to say something when he spoke aloud. "I know what I'll do," he said and started walking toward the door to the right. "I know what I'll do."

"And what is that, Ozrach?" Neraea asked loudly, stopping him in his path. "You know well what lays in wait."

"Neraea, don't you think I know that?" Ozrach said and shot a glance back toward her. "Anything could have happened. There could have been an uprising. There could have…"

"Listen to you! You don't even know. You've lost sight of your active armies; you don't know what the provinces are planning… you've only recently discovered that Mauros is moving their armies west, yet you haven't alerted Savantin nor the emperor who has so graciously offered to lend his armies to you."

"Neraea these are delicate matters!"

"Ones that you are handling in opposite!"

"And what do you suggest I do? I have already sent message to Rustanzen."

"You sent message to Rustanzen without first alerting Savantin? I'm shocked," Neraea said and sat down.

"Time is running short, as you've said. Savantin's last message to me was that he had to execute a head of a province. For conspiracy of murder."

"He... he executed someone?" Neraea looked toward the floor and back toward her husband, a rage in her eyes. "No court, no trial, nothing except for his word?"

"His men have seen it, Neraea. Ohric has seen it."

"Yes. *His* men."

"If he says that it had to be done then it had to be. Why can't you just let this go and we can worry about the threat here."

"The threat?! Ozrach there are three threats present. Mauros, the provinces, and your commander."

"You'd better explain yourself well, Neraea," Ozrach answered, a sincerity in his voice, in his face that she had not seen for years.

"I didn't think I had to."

"Now is not the time for your obstinance. Savantin. What about him?"

"If you have to ask then you are either stupid or blind!" Neraea shouted, her husband's face of shock fueling her current state. "He leads your men, makes your decisions. He speaks above you in conference, and you just... you just let him!"

"Sometimes you need to learn when things are for the best. He has a reputation Neraea, and because of that so does Terrenveil. I do not need to be the frightening face of this kingdom."

"Ozrach, he's killed someone. He's killed a leader of a province. Did you even think about how bad this looks? This is even more of a reason for them to rebel."

"Goddess help me," Ozrach muttered and moved closer to his wife. "He was a conspirator. Someone who planned to kill us both. A message must be sent. Or would you have people like this free? We execute people for far less!"

"The provinces want to overthrow you! You've just given them another reason to do so! You're lazy, you've become less a king and more someone who hides behind the sword of your master."

Ozrach's eyes filled with anger, his voice becoming stern. "What did you just say?"

"You know it to be true! You've given him Terrenveil. The legion will not listen to a man as pathetic as you. I should have left here long ago."

"Enough of your insults! I will have you hanged!"

Neraea gasped in shock, anger taking her face. "Go ahead, give them another reason to kill you in the same way you threatened me. Haemad is lucky he's dead."

"I don't want to tell you to watch your tongue once more."

Neraea laughed. "You don't frighten me. If you kill me, you'll only free me from the misery of your company, this castle. You didn't even investigate Haemad's murder."

"Murder?!"

"It's astounding how much truly slips by you. He didn't drink himself to death. He was drowned in it. Castanian wine. The same wine Savantin keeps."

"You've been in his quarters?!"

"Not only has this man taken your kingdom from you, but he's taken me, too," Neraea taunted, her words a blade. Ozrach slapped Neraea across her face and she fell to the floor, rising to pull the dagger from her dress.

"It seems I've interrupted a moment most touching." A familiar voice from the back of the room. Opposite of its usual nature, calm, enthralled. They didn't know what to expect, a mix of emotions ran between them like rivers. They turned, watching as Savantin walked inward. His armor was missing from his body, large wounds across his chest and arms. The scent of blood was strong in the room, for it covering his wounds, his hands, spattered across his face. There were spatters in his eyes, the color of them unusually dark. The two were speechless, for very different reasons, and the only sound heard in the room was his heavy breathing.

He looked between the Ozrach and Neraea quickly, his eyes wet with the blood he knew was in them. They stared at him, their inability to give voice to thought written on their faces. "Are you displeased with my service, Neraea?" he asked and walked forward, stopping only as Ozrach stood in front of her. He smirked, laughing quietly to himself. "You've finally found courage, and so late in your life. Shameful."

"No, the only thing that's shameful here is your willingness to act upon your own regard and constantly disobey your king," Ozrach said and narrowed his eyes, looking up into Savantin's which had darkened.

"I follow the laws of no man, no god. All of you pledge your lives to a goddess who has a set of laws you constantly break yet go to her temple begging forgiveness. You think that if you confess the terrible things you've done you will be absolved. You are godless heathens like the rest of us, trying desperately to identify yourselves with a religion you constantly forsake. She says to give alms to the poor, yet you sit in this castle and look down on them while they die in poverty. She says to remain faithful to the one you are wed to, restrain from intoxicating drink, yet you hold parties and go home with whoever looks in your direction. She says that vanity is but attempting to elevate yourselves above other humans..." Savantin laughed and moved his arms slightly to his sides. "Look at what surrounds us. Hypocrisy at its finest. This needs to end."

"So. You and Ohric are on your own crusade. That is why you are here instead of where you belong, heeding my orders," Ozrach said and crossed his arms.

"You poor, simple fool," Savantin said and closed his eyes for a moment, heavily breathing outward as if wounded. "You know nothing of the reason I am here. You know nothing at all."

"What I do know is that we are going to think of a suitable punishment for this. Right after I have you removed and thrown into Terrenveil's prisons."

"And what are my crimes, Ozrach? I've done what you asked. I traveled to each province to make certain they were preparing for war against Mauros and not against you. I've stationed entire battalions there. I acted within my power as your commander and executed someone for treason. Someone who the rebelling provinces chose as the man to replace you... but you've no knowledge of what it is I've been doing for the past few years. I thought about making that known to you now. But there really is no need for it. Ohric knew. He knew all along, yet in the last few moments of his life he decided it was something he couldn't live with. I will miss that man."

"You... you killed him?!" Neraea said in outrage, face twisted in rage.

"He fought well. Honorably. We bled one another. But in the end, he called upon his goddess as the light left his eyes and life left his body."

"Why Savantin... why did you kill him?! Tell me!" Neraea cried, anger quickly leaving her.

"There is one thing that matters to me above all else. One. Your son knew this and chose his fate."

"What?" Ozrach asked and turned to Neraea. "Your son!?"

"She didn't tell you? And you thought your year in Cistane was frivolous."

"How could you have known that... this was twenty years ago... This was."

"A well-kept secret. You should know better than to ask me that question," Savantin answered and winced a second time, opening his eyes to them. Their own filled with fear as they peered into the black spheres that watched them hungrily.

"What have you done?" Ozrach asked and started backing toward his wife.

"I've found that which I had been searching for... but at a price. It's trying to find a place to nest within me. Attempting to destroy me to see if I am worthy of its power. But it's finding that I am... I can feel it."

"Have you lost your mind..." Neraea whispered in fright. Savantin began to laugh softly but cried out another time, moving his head upward as something moved beneath his flesh from his throat and into his chest. Ozrach screamed for his guards, Savantin hanging his head downward, his breath heavy. "They... they won't hear you," he said and folded as he felt something sharp within his chest. "I've already dismissed them from duty."

Ozrach turned to run toward the door when Savantin moved his hand back toward it, causing it to slam shut. "No one leaves this room until it's done," he answered, his voice regaining strength.

"Savantin... please... we can talk about this..."

"There is nothing left to say. There is nothing I want that you could give me. This place has little relevance to me now."

"Then why are you here... why are you doing this?"

"Because if for some reason I fail, these people deserve another chance. Just like she did," Savantin answered. It was only a moment after his words rolled from his tongue that Ozrach plunged a dagger into his shoulder, pulling it downward. Neraea screamed, Savantin grabbing hold of Ozrach's forearm, squeezing it and slowly pulling it outward, removing the blade from his flesh. No blood came from the wound, the blade was not stained with it. The three looked at it for a moment, Savantin allowing his voice to be heard in one exhale. "It's mine, now," he said and looked at Ozrach, grasping his throat and tearing it from his neck, shifting his eyes toward Neraea as his corpse fell to the floor.

"Savantin..." she said and placed her hands out in front of her. "This isn't you. Look at what you are doing... you've gone out into the world and contracted something that's poisoning your mind," she continued and took several steps backward until she felt the wall on her shoulders. Savantin stood inches from her now, looking down into her face. He could feel her heart fast beating and wanted to tear it from her.

"It isn't your fault. We can fix this," she stated and reached out toward his cheek. He turned his head to look at her hand, causing her to withdraw it slightly before reaching outward and touching his skin. "Look at your eyes... not yours... something else lives here now."

He felt her heartbeat quicken still as he touched her hand, removing it from his face and holding it by her chest. "He's dead, but we can cover that... you can take his place... we can..."

"Neraea," Savantin said, breathing out. She felt it upon her face, the scent of blood mixed with cinnamon and cloves. "We aren't going to live here anymore."

Her eyes filled with tears, her body slightly shaking. He took his hand and placed it behind her head, holding her hair. "This is how it ends." After those words she began to weep, convulsing until he took her and placed her head against his chest. "It'll only hurt but a moment."

She nodded, her breathing mirroring the tears she was attempting to hold back as he gently untied the very front of her dress. A sound of sorrow escaped her mouth, and he moved his finger toward her cheek to catch her tears. "Shh. This is how it ends, Neraea," he said and pressed his hand into her chest, pulling her heart from it.

CHAPTER 3

TRIALS OF THE SERPENT

The island was a corpse of its former self. The winds now carried ash with them along the ground where once petals moved in an intricate dance. Their scent was replaced by one of death, the fires having consumed nearly everything that once stood here. There was a heavy feeling that surrounded us as we stood in silence. Eshkan walked forward toward the compound. Desolation. Pain sifted through him as he stopped to look on.

"The place we used to call home," he said, watching the air carry ashes toward the remnants of the tower. "And we left it to burn. Nothing remains."

"It won't be in vain," I answered and strode past him, offering a quick search of the area before moving toward the shallowing caves.

"Your master was cunning to have been able to hide such an artifact for so long," Sindara said and moved her eyes across the landscape. The orange trees, still in their charred decay.

"He was anything but. That box spelled destruction for the entire island. Innocents, dead," I answered. "If it were elsewhere…"

"If it were elsewhere, you would not have known it existed. We would not have been able to stop him. I cannot do this alone."

"We may be too late already," I answered, looking toward the entrance of the cave. I pulled my sword, causing Sindara to arm herself. The river was high at this moment, covering the stones where the defiant were once shackled. The blood-tinged water foretold the deaths that happened here. Had he brought men to the tomb, discovered the box and in trying to preserve the secret, killed them? I looked to Sindara, motioning her at my side as we disappeared into the tomb, Eshkan and Dacian's footsteps farther behind.

Sindara looked downward as her eyes beheld the sight, her only motion was to place her dagger at her side. I followed in kind, approaching the corpse. She walked forward, slowly, whispering something as she moved to her knees, closing his eyes. There were no wounds caused by blade, only a hole in his chest where his heart had been torn from it. I crouched down, reaching for his arm when Sindara moved hers outward, stopping me from making contact.

"No. Let me."

"Are you sure you want..."

"Yes. I need to know what happened here. I need to know what he's done."

I nodded, taking to silence as Sindara reached into his chest, pulling what had been left upward, and severing it with her blade. Upon placing it in her mouth, she sat backward, placing her hand over her face.

"What did you see?" I asked. The lack of response caused me to repeat the question, Sindara placing her hand at her side.

"They fought here. Once he said he couldn't let him leave the tomb, Savantin demanded him to. Pushed him to continue. The blood, on the floor, in the cave. It's Savantin's."

"You mean to say..."

"He devoured his heart as the last carnal sacrifice. If he is not dead from his wounds, it means he's already opened the box."

"Isn't a Seraphice supposed to regenerate?"

"Only if they've been feeding. He's known to refuse. He could have died here. Ohric's emotions played part in his failure. He didn't want to do it, but he knew he had to try."

The light of a torch signaled the arrival of my brothers, Sindara slowly wiping the blood from her lips.

"He's found it. Now we must find him," she answered.

"It won't be difficult," I stated, my eyes fixed at the wall above the coffin. Eshkan lifted the torch, a message in blood revealed.

The end lies in wait where the moon has been captured for centuries.

"The bastion," Sindara answered. "Where the moon has been captured."

"Karech bastion. It sits atop the peak of Mount Alstende," Eshkan stated.

"You know of..."

"Yes. As children we were cautioned against the mountain. Children of Anskirre would leave her offerings under the moon, but that place... it was built by no worshiper of the old gods. The pilgrims never returned."

"We go immediately," I answered and stood.

"I can lead you there," Eshkan said.

"You know the danger firsthand."

"Cethin. I did not come this far to abandon you now. I have made my peace. If I perish there, it will be an honorable death."

"We've no time to waste. The blood, this only occurred hours ago, he's likely close."

"Take into account his wounds," Dacian stated. "We may reach him before he enters."

"We may have a chance. Even if he's done it, he will be disoriented. He may remain that way, or he may gain control. He's done his research well. In all the things I've seen..."

"I do not care what condition he is in when we find him. Speaking strategy matters not," I answered. "Eshkan. Let us go."

◆ ◆ ◆

I listened to her voice soft but passionate about the stars in the sky. We had been speaking about the old gods, how they cast manifestations of themselves across the dark. Her people said that they lit pathways across the earth, closing them only as the sun began to rise.

"There are still hours of night left, Cethin. We could find one of those pathways and be free of this place forever."

"Would they allow such a creature to inhabit them?" I asked, looking at one in particular. Haratha.

"Whosoever seeks their wisdom and gives respectful audience may enter. But no one has gotten them to listen in hundreds of years," Cahya answered and looked up toward me, deep green eyes twinkling. "I wish it were that easy to leave here. Know what it's like to live outside of these binds. Do you think about it too?"

"I do. Returning to the outside world would be... exhilarating yet strange. There is no place for me out there, no place aside from the coven of my people. I'd be trading servitude for servitude in a sense. I'm afraid that my time by the sea was the most freedom I'll ever know."

"You're wrong," Cahya said and sat up, moving from my arms to look at my face. "You'd be welcomed in Mordestai."

"Your people would..."

"My people do not care what you are. They care who you are. About your kindness, how you love. Maybe one day we'll be among them."

"Cahya," I said and placed my hands on hers. "You know that is the first place he would look."

A look of sorrow took her face as she looked away from me and released a small exhale. She nodded, looking back toward the sky. "There has to be somewhere we could go."

"And we will," I answered. "But we need to leave at the right time, so that there is a great distance he must search when he finally discovers we've gone."

"On your word, love," she said and rested back in my arms, her soft skin against my chest. It was almost sunrise when we retreated, the risk of waiting that long was foolish, but the risk did not matter now. We'd either die together here, or somewhere out there. The sole thing that mattered to me at this moment was what time I could spend with her, until we could be together for the rest of time.

◆ ◆ ◆

Wind, howling. The old stones that formed the front of the bastion were large, towering over us as we approached. The entrance kept an eerie silence, heavy upon the ears, reaching inward and pulling.

"He's inside. He must be," Sindara said and knelt toward a black pile of ash. "Braegans. We now know what's been killing your ancestors. One of the eldest. Before the races started taking to shadow."

"Was this place built by them?" Dacian asked and looked above, his eyes scanning the ceilings.

"It's very hard to say. It may have been built by something that doesn't exist at all, anymore. Or rather, something that is so ancient that it has discovered how to avoid detection."

I listened to them continue as I moved forward, looking at the piles of ashes on the floor, some of them thrown against the pillars and walls. The hallway opened into an inner sanctum, the box sitting in an indentation on the floor. Savantin was sitting in front of it, eyes closed. A smile took his lips as I entered the room, and he looked up, speaking.

"You've come."

"You didn't anticipate differently, or else you'd have not left that message. You know why I'm here."

"But do you know why I'm here?" Savantin asked. He opened his eyes and disappeared briefly in a black cloud of smoke, appearing again by the pillar closest his previous position. "From dens beneath the earth we hide and into darkness creep. To the hearts of men unburdened and watch them as they sleep. For against the terror of the sun their lives remain unobscured, so into our throats and vessels to sate us their rivers of blood will pour. It's all so trivial now," he said and moved forward. Sindara drew her crossbow when Savantin laughed and looked upward.

"Symbolism, dear Sardon. I've made my bargain. The world will not be swallowed," he stated and turned over the lid. "I have seen the beginning. Creatures created by Sekarth to shadow Ilhinia's agents of light. Balance. The Braegans that lived here. They did nothing to keep it."

"You want me to believe you are taking up crusade in the name of the nonhumans?"

"Is it so hard to believe? It would be noble of a creature created by Sekarth to strike vengeance upon humankind. They did not add another facet to the balance. They interfered."

"You do not seek nobility."

"That I do not," he answered and looked again toward the opening in the roof.

"Enough. What is it that you seek?" I asked, watching him carefully.

"I've found it. The question is, what will you do now that I have?"

"I made a promise, one I cannot keep. You have caused so much death, so much pain, only so that you could empower yourself."

"Then it seems you do not know me very well at all, Sardon. Forgive me for denying you that time," Savantin answered, his eyes still searching above. I moved forward to attack him, using the floor to spring toward his position when he vanished again, this time appearing on the balcony above.

"We will fight, this is what you want. But first I must make something very clear," he answered, a dark sincerity to his voice. "It may very well be that we both die here, just as it may well be that only one of us leaves this place with our lives. You will not indulge me, but I want you to think about this. Why, truly, are you here?"

"Enough of your words," I said and pulled Seligsara.

"Zerian's blade," Savantin nodded in acknowledgment. "You will try," he answered and vanished from the balcony, appearing just before me, his blade hitting mine. Sindara raised her crossbow, catalyzing Savantin's response in manifesting a telekinetic force, disarming her and my brothers. He vanished again toward the box, his voice in the form of a haunting shout.

"I will see to you once I'm finished with him."

"Fight me with dignity!" my own voice, raw emotion.

"Come now, Sardon. There is no need for insults when I am sparing your friends," Savantin answered and charged for me, knocking me backward with his blows. I turned to catch him off guard when he moved his arm aside, blocking my blade with his own.

"Why them? You didn't give your own a chance."

Savantin laughed, blocking another one of my attacks. "You wish to see how Ohric met his end?" he answered and feigned blocking, moving his sword away at the last moment, catching my sword across his chest. I tried to push harder, knowing my blade was sharp enough to sever flesh from bone when he looked up at me, his eyes a deeper black than anything I had ever witnessed. "It was much like this."

He knocked me backward, the wound on his chest closing slowly as I felt his blood travel through my veins, causing a minor disorientation.

"The blood of two creatures overwhelms you. Shall we continue to fight with dignity?"

The word for fire in my head caused my hand to ignite. I turned it, watching it take shape and watched the blaze's reflection in his eyes. He smiled, vanishing, the smoke resonating for a few seconds until he appeared to my left, attacking me with his blade. I blocked, sending my arm forward and grazing his own. It caught flame for a moment, the flames climbing up his arm before he moved it toward the door. It slammed closed, the wind rushing toward us and extinguishing both his arm and mine. He laughed as I spoke the word again, this time with more intensity.

"You'll need more than that, Cethin," he answered and moved his sword aside, deflecting a bolt from Sindara's crossbow. He took to smoke, standing directly under the opening in the roof where the moon was now seen above.

"This is the moment I break Norahn's hold over me. Never again will I have to sacrifice a life to him."

"So, you're trading the control of one for the control of another? You'll never be free of this," I answered, waiting for the perfect moment to strike.

"You're wrong. But I'll spare you the details. It ends now," Savantin answered and moved his arms aside, dropping his sword on the floor. He made a fist on the hand of which arm I burned, the charring beginning to heal, seemingly entranced. I moved forward then, my sword in front of me. I slashed forward, Savantin vanishing quickly, appearing only a few steps away. He grabbed my throat, throwing me into a pillar only to appear before me, his hand around my throat a second time. I grabbed his arm, attempting to release his hold on me with the flames of the Sun when he stretched his neck, the sound of cracks from his bones loud in my ears. He bit into my chest, my collar bone cracking from the force of his jaws. I cried out, listening to the voices of the Sun repeat themselves in my head. *Soliscant.*

"Soliscant!"

The word created a cataclysm of light, using my body as a conductor, growing in strength by feeding on my essence as I became weaker. I could not see for seconds as I hit the ground, holding my broken bone as the pain became more intense. I was still bleeding, my ability to heal had left me. Through blurred vision, I saw his form, only feet from me on the ground, immobile. I reached for Seligsara, wincing as the bone in my chest moved upwards in my flesh. I retracted my arm, trying to slide my body forward so that the blade was in reach. Moving through the pain, I sat up, losing all feeling in my arm. It was a few more moments before he stirred, standing but staggering. His body was charred, blood vessels exposed on his arms.

"The light has rendered you without ability to heal. You will die here."

"We will both die here," I said and closed my eyes, forming the strength to repeat the word aloud. I spoke fire instead, grabbing his arm as he reached for my neck. I winced as it consumed my flesh, watching as his body caught flame, ravaging his vessels. Mustering what was left of me, I sliced his forearm, and it fell, releasing his hold. Anger took his eyes as he raked his hand across his flesh, dousing the flames. He moved for me again and I knocked my palm into his flesh, the flames entering the caverns that the light had made. He fell to his knees, looking toward me. Taking a forced breath, he reached for his chest to extinguish it. He hit it and winced as his chest crushed inward from his strength, the flames slowly dying. As he opened his eyes, blood began to drip from the inexorable darkness.

"Well met, Sardon," he coughed, blood coming from his throat. "I shall mourn the loss of not being able to stop those who wronged me, but I will not mourn the path that has led me here."

"Your quest for revenge has brought you to your death. I don't know how much time you have left, but my hopes are that it is enough time to determine if your resolve was worth all of this."

Savantin laughed, continuing to cough. "I lost my life long ago. My happiness, my serenity. It died with her. Was it not the death of your beloved that strengthened your resolve? I know you thought about running, leaving all of this behind, leaving Terrenveil behind. You held no love for the man I killed on the island, you've pretended for long enough." He took a breath and gave up his stance, succumbing to the pain. "I cannot hate you. You have granted me audience to see her again."

"I have no words to say that will accept you."

"Then why have you not yet killed me?" he answered, the power in his voice weakening.

"You do not deserve a quick death. You will be left with nothing but your failure," I said.

"You are wrong."

I looked toward his face, my own twisted in confusion. The man was hard to detest despite the things he had done, the events he shaped and contributed to. The feeling brought concern to the forefront of my reason, though it was impossible to discern why.

"I'll save you my story, for your opinion of me will not change, yet there is something my commander told me a very long time ago. He said that the end speaks more about one's character than the beginning," he coughed in his hand, moving it toward his sight. He took a breath and closed his eyes, taking a moment to himself before again speaking. "I may have forgotten who I was while seeking vengeance, but I did not forget that innocence is to be avenged. There is only one way to drown corruption, Cethin. Blood. At what length would you go to destroy the ones who killed Cahya, had you not done so already?" he answered and reached inside of the box, grasping a small ring upon a chain.

He placed his hand on top of the box's lid, closing it. As he withdrew, his large handprint painted in blood stained the cover. The moon vanished as the sun began to rise overhead. He closed his eyes and made a fist, squeezing the ring in his hand. He took a deep breath as the sun began to burn the rest of his flesh and spoke one last sentence. "My promise remains broken, love, yet I am coming home." I sat up, watching as the sun began to reduce his skin to ashes. He moved his hands to his chest holding the ring in both fists, folding over slightly. In the blood on the ground beneath him a few of his tears splashed as the sun continued to carry him to his death. Moments passed, and the convulsing in his flesh had stopped. I huffed a short breath out, holding my head upward for a moment. Sindara ran toward me, placing her hands gently on my arm, assessing my injuries.

"We need to get you back to the coven."

"Just a moment longer," I answered, watching as pieces of ash floated toward the sky in gentle motions, being carried by the frozen winds from his corpse. I continued to try and breathe, my chest tightening.

"All of this time... and that was his reason," she said softly, sitting next to me. "Love."

We sat in silence, my eyesight slowly leaving me as I fell backward.

ACT IV

CHAPTER 1

The scent of the coven was the first thing I recognized upon waking. I took a deep swallow of air into my lungs and rose, feeling not pain but stiffness. My chest had healed, all that was remaining was a scar. I stared at the walls for a while, my emotions catching up with me. There was nothing left. No task that needed tending to. No mission that would have me on the road for days at a time, avoiding human contact. No orders coming from the mouth of someone who needed my service. Nothing. It was what it meant to be free, yet without her it meant nothing. The pain of not knowing what could have been was what I was left with now.

Sindara entered the room then, quickly approaching me and kneeling by my bedside. "You're awake." Her voice was soft, with a sense of delight.

I nodded slowly, placing my head back against the wall.

"Lord Sahrkorin will be happy to know. He wishes to speak to you before you depart."

"He already knows I'm leaving?"

"He trusts you will return one day, but he assumes you'll want to see your brothers, the other serpents. They were here, Cethin. Cosette told Dacian where to find her, if you prevailed. He thought it important to seek her out. She told him she'd return to Terrenveil, speak with Alaies. He wanted me to tell you that if you wished to join them, to meet them at Defaltor."

"That is where I will go. These people could still use my help," I answered, searching the room for my armor.

"Before you go, Eshkan also told me where you could find him."

"Did he return to Septentria?"

Sindara laughed softly and shook her head. "Winds Hollow. After he took the box, he remained there."

"I should have figured. He's a weakness for women. Always has." I looked toward the washing table in the corner of the room, Seligsara placed atop the large stone bowl. Sahrkorin had left it to me. Trust, respect.

"I am coming with you," Sindara answered and stood quickly.

"This is your wish?" I asked. "It is for the humans that I do this."

"Yes. Lord Sahrkorin does not understand, but he shows no opposition."

"Then we will depart. I will return in six days."

"Six days?"

"There is something I must do," I answered and rose from the bed, grasping my armor. My breathing still seemed shallow. The light had injured me to a point I did not anticipate. I was not sure how they had healed me to this state and unless I could not remember, I did not feed. Questions for another time. I took Seligsara from the table and nodded to Sindara once, setting off again into the world I had so very recently nearly left behind.

◆ ◆ ◆

Dusk. I closed my eyes and took breath into my lungs, trying my hardest to remember the orange blossoms that once took the air here. Silence covered every surface that was left, and in walking, ash moved from the path at the touch of my footsteps. The tower of the dead was the only construct that survived, the old iron gate still adorned in its crowns of flora. There were no stars tonight. The clouds covered them. They denied the world their splendor, knowing that at any moment they could burn out forever and no longer exist in the realm of man. I sat upon the stone, taking one pained breath before softly singing the same song that she did many nights before dawn arrived to take us from one another. At its end, I spoke her name for the last time, and let silence live on.

K MANSFIELD

Self-proclaimed nerd K has spent the better part of a decade writing and rewriting *Trials of the Serpent*, the first installment of a series rich with lore, and characters you'll love, love to hate, and hate to love. When K is not writing, she's gaming, being a menace at the local game store (you must block her with two creatures,) vibing out to atmospheric black metal, or organizing ghost hunts. K's main mission as an author is to craft deep, enthralling lore, and complex characters to embody it.

Milton Keynes UK
Ingram Content Group UK Ltd.
UKHW011037020624
443412UK00011B/102/J

9 798989 473120